The DCI Isaac Cook Thriller Series: Books 1-3

Murder is a Tricky Business

Murder House

Murder is Only a Number

Phillip Strang

Copyright Page

Copyright © 2017 Phillip Strang

Cover Design by Phillip Strang

All rights reserved. No part of this book may be reproduced, stored in a retrieval system, or transmitted in any form or by any means (electronic, mechanical, photocopying, recording or otherwise) without the prior written permission of the publisher, except by a reviewer who may quote brief passages in a review to be printed by a newspaper, magazine, or journal.

All characters appearing in this work are fictitious. Any resemblance to actual events, locales, or persons, living or dead, is coincidental.

All Rights Reserved.

This work is registered with the UK Copyright Service
ISBN: 9781549561337

The DCI Isaac Cook Thriller Series: Books 1 - 3

Murder is a Tricky Business

Chapter 1

'Murder is a tricky business when you don't have a body, a suspect or a motive,' Detective Chief Inspector Isaac Cook mulled out loud in the confines of the office. He may as well have called it home – he had spent so many hours there of late.

'What do you mean, "no motive"? The woman was a bitch,' Detective Inspector Farhan Ahmed replied. He was a dedicated cop, destined as was his senior officer, Isaac Cook, for great success in the police force: London's Metropolitan Police, politically correct and aiming to fast-track anyone of superior ability with a non-Anglo-Saxon background, a display of embracing all cultures, all religions, and all colours.

It was the ideal place for two ambitious men. Cook, the first-generation English-born child of Jamaican parents and

Ahmed, ten years in the United Kingdom, initially for training, and with no intention of going back to Pakistan. It irked some of the older police officers – Anglo-Saxon and white – now being overlooked for the late arrivals. The occasional disparaging comment in the corridors of Challis Street Police Station, discreetly aimed in their direction, was shrugged off, although it sometimes upset the young Pakistan-born DI.

'Who told us she was a bitch?' DCI Cook asked as he looked out of the window.

'Admittedly, those she worked with.'

'Being a bitch is not much of a motive. And we're still assuming she's been murdered,' DCI Cook said.

'We'll find the body. You know that. It's just a case of knowing where to look.'

'Do you?'

'Not yet, but we haven't rummaged in the dirt yet. If we dig enough, we'll find her, or what's left of her.'

'So where do we start?' Isaac asked.

'Her fellow actors on that damn-awful soap opera.' It was an unexpected outburst by the detective inspector.

'I've not heard you speak in that manner before.' Isaac felt the need to comment.

'It's my wife. She's obsessed with the programme.'

***

The death of Billy Blythe did not come as a surprise, forecast as it had been for several weeks. The final week before his death the magazines were awash with front page speculation. Eight million, five hundred and sixty thousand viewers, a new record the night he was bashed to death in the local playground by three youths.

The executives at the television station were delighted: record advertising revenue, premium rates. The only one assumed not to be delighted was the actor who played his fictional sister: she had gone missing. They had spliced in some earlier footage of her for the episode to conceal the truth from the viewing public.

The programme was pure fiction, but for millions across the country, compulsory viewing. Whether they recognised the soap opera for what it was, or whether it was an escape from their mundane lives, was for psychologists to analyse, advertising executives to take advantage of, and television stations to profit from.

The melodrama had been on the air for twelve years. The lives of an apparently benign group of individuals in a small provincial town had kept a nation enthralled. There had been murders, rapes, thuggish behaviour, even incest, but the characters still played out their parts in the innocence of a community where nothing ever changed. One week, it was a murder, the next, a wedding, and Billy Blythe, the local villain, had had his fair share of weddings: at least one every eighteen months to two years and none had lasted.

The country, or, at least, the less discerning – according to Charles Sutherland, the actor who had portrayed the erstwhile Billy Blythe – had been enthralled by his nuptials, but he had become fat and unpleasant, due to a more than adequate salary and an inappropriate fondness for alcohol and junk food.

Marjorie Frobisher portrayed his elder sister, Edith Blythe, in the series – her character matronly and demure, ashamed of her brother, hoping he would reform.

Isaac Cook considered the situation. He was a smart man, not given to extravagance and not inclined to speak without some forethought.

'So why does everyone assume it's murder? She's only been missing for three weeks. She could have just gone incognito, decided it was time for a break.'

Farhan saw the situation differently. 'The newspapers continue to put forward the idea that she's probably dead, even if it's not murder.'

'And we base our evidence on what the papers say?' Isaac Cook had not achieved the rank of detective chief inspector on the basis of 'someone said something' or 'what the newspapers are reporting'. He needed evidence, and so far, there was none, only innuendo.

'Of course not,' Farhan replied.

'We deal in facts, not what the press and the gossip magazines print.'

Farhan continued. 'Marjorie Frobisher is at the height of her profession. She had just been given another three-year

3

contract, at a monthly salary five times what you and I receive in a year, and there is her record of service.'

'What do you mean by record of service?'

'In the twelve years since the programme first went on air, she has only missed five episodes, and that was because she had no part to play.'

'Where do you get this information?' Isaac had asked the production company for some updates when they had first been pulled in to investigate, and he knew less than his colleague.

'From my wife, where else?'

Isaac sarcastically asked, 'Does your wife know what happened to the body?'

'According to my wife, there was a similar situation in another series about six years ago. One of the characters went missing for no apparent reason. Ted Entwhistle, the local butcher on the programme, just disappeared. You must remember, headline news for a couple of weeks.'

'So what happened to him?'

'They dragged it out, milked it for all it was worth. They thought they were dealing with a fictional disappearance, not a real-life murder. It appears that the actor portraying Ted Entwhistle had been messing around with an actress in the series, on-screen and off. Her off-screen husband got wind of it, strung him up on a meat hook in an old derelict barn. Poetic justice, the husband said when they caught him. Anyway, that's what my wife is saying.'

'A copy-cat killing inspired by a soap opera. Are you suggesting we seriously consider it?'

'Why not? Marjorie Frobisher's missing, and according to Detective Superintendent Goddard, she's probably been murdered.'

'Is that what's happened here?' Isaac had heard it all in his time as a policeman. The idea that a murder could be committed based on what a scriptwriter at the lower skill end of his craft could make up seemed implausible.

'Ted Entwhistle was real enough. Fiction often overlaps with reality on the television these days.'

'But you said you don't watch it.'

'That's true, but it's always on at my house.'

'If your Ted Entwhistle could be found strung up on a meat hook, what would Marjorie Frobisher's fate have been?'

'According to my wife...'

'Facts, please.'

'What I was going to say was that Marjorie Frobisher's character, Edith Blythe, had been the headmistress at the local school. In retirement, she took over from the church organist,' Farhan said, a little annoyed by Isaac's oblique criticism of his wife.

'Let's go out on a limb. What's does your wife believe happened?' Isaac felt there was no need for an apology.

'I know it sounds crazy, but she believes she's in a church.'

***

Charles Sutherland, a classically trained actor, or he felt he was, was not classical enough or not trained well enough, or the casting agents were defective in their recognition of genuine talent. He believed it was the latter. Early in his career had been a few walk-ons at some of the best theatres in the country in some of the most prestigious dramas. But they did not last long. It soon became apparent that he was deficient in two critical areas: his ability with accents and his attitude to fellow cast members.

Isolated and penniless, he had over the years been relegated to soap operas: the one area where he had achieved success. Billy Blythe had been his latest reincarnation after other long-running shows of a similar vein. He had been an undertaker, a shopkeeper, a philanderer, even a man of the cloth, but Billy Blythe had been his pièce de résistance.

They had killed his character; it was as if they had killed him. He knew it was the pinnacle of a disappointing career, and that he would neither forget nor forgive.

It had been assumed that his fictional sister would take on the mantle of bereavement, with the small, tight-knit community rushing to her side. The only problem was that she wasn't there. The executive producer was the first to react to his leading actress's disappearance with alarm.

'What are we going to do?' he had screamed at a meeting of his production staff two weeks earlier. The programme was always recorded one week in advance, so there was time to work round an integral character. 'Marjorie's gone and done a disappearing act on us. Has anyone any idea where she is?' Richard

Williams had been in the business almost for ever. He had reluctantly entered the world of soap operas as a script writer on a now defunct episodic programme. A plausible plot about an inner-city school full of delinquents and idealistic teachers in the north of England, it had somehow failed to capture the viewing public's approval.

He had left the University of Sussex over forty years earlier with a BA in Journalism, and a desire to be a war correspondent, travelling the world, helmet and bulletproof vest, ducking the bullets and bombs, 'bringing you the news from the front line'. The farthest he got was a protest outside the Iranian Embassy in South Kensington, when the police had come in with tear gas, and he had received a severe dose and a rock to the head for his troubles.

He was soft-spoken yet authoritative. He had guided this soap opera through its early years to where it stood now, predominant in the United Kingdom and sold to twenty more countries around the world. Nowadays, he mostly left it to others to deal with the daily episodes. It was rare for him to leave his elegant office with its sweeping views of London and to venture to the production facilities, a prefabricated town of frontages, held up by plywood and paint, located in what had once been an old industrial wasteland. He had reached his sixty-third year. He was not an attractive man, a little short, yet slim. His hair, once black and thick, now came courtesy of a bottle and an expensive hair.

'Marjorie is nowhere to be seen, hasn't been seen for a few days.' The script producer, Ray Saddler, had been with the soap opera for the last six years, and he had moulded a formidable team of script writers.

'Has anyone looked for her?' Williams asked.

'Of course, we have,' the series producer, Jessica O'Neill, said. She had joined the production team six months earlier. There had been dissension in the ranks on her appointment. Her demanding manner and excessive attempts at perfection, resulting in numerous retakes, sometimes late into the night, irritated some of the older hands in the business.

'Milady,' an antiquated term of respect for a female member of the British aristocracy, was often used in derision behind her back. Charles Sutherland had said it to her face once, but he had been drunk.

The meeting had not been going long before Richard Williams made a pronouncement, as he was apt to do when presented with an imponderable. 'Write her out, and if the woman turns up, we'll deal with it then.'

***

Isaac Cook had one uncertainty which concerned him greatly. Why, as a senior investigating officer, had he been pulled out of the homicide incident room to search for a missing woman? He needed to ask his superior officer. Detective Superintendent Goddard was a decent man, a man that DCI Cook respected enormously – their relationship based on mutual respect and friendship.

Challis Street Police Station, an impressive building, at least on the third floor where the detective superintendent had an office with a good view. Goddard sat behind an impressive wooden table with a laptop and a monitor to the right-hand side. In the centre, there was a notepad. A bookcase stood against one wall, full of legal books. A hat stand stood in one corner, where the detective superintendent's jacket and cap hung.

It was the office of an efficient man: a man who had an admirable habit of not going home at night to his wife unless the desk was clear and all the work for the day had been concluded and filed away. Some days that meant staying late into the night, but that was how he worked, and no amount of cajoling from his wife or his colleagues would change the habit of a lifetime.

He rose and walked around the table as Isaac entered. A firm handshake and both men sat down on comfortable black leather chairs placed to one side in the office.

'Sir, why are we chasing after a missing person?' Isaac asked.

'Do you know who she is?'

'She's just an actor in a mundane television drama.' The detective chief inspector, the only child of Jamaican immigrants, had been a diligent student at school, in part due to his parent's decision not to have a television in the house. His appreciation of the missing woman and her fame was limited.

'Marjorie Frobisher is hardly just an actor in a mundane drama; she's one of the major celebrities in this country.' Detective Superintendent Goddard understood the reluctance of his best detective to become involved.

'So why are we looking? There's no body, no motive and certainly no reason for us to be involved. It should be registered with missing persons.'

'Agreed, but you don't understand the situation.'

'What don't I understand?'

'Influential friends…'

'Is that a reason?' Isaac asked, although he had heard it before. Someone with influence using it to get preferential treatment.

The detective superintendent had hoped to avoid this conversation, and that Isaac would have continued with the case and got on with it. He realised now that it would have been best to have told him upfront. 'What do you know about Marjorie Frobisher? Apart from the fact that she's an actor of little note in your estimation.'

'I've no idea whether she is good enough for an Oscar or a bit part in the local drama society's production of *The Importance of Being Earnest*.'

'Are you telling me to keep looking for this woman?' The respect between the two men separated by nearly twenty years and rank allowed a little impertinence.

'This is highly confidential. It must never come into your discussions with anyone. Don't tell anyone in your office.'

'Okay, give it to me straight.'

'There is a very senior member of the government applying pressure to find this woman.'

'Any names?'

None that I've been told, but it's clear that this woman either knows something about someone, or she's important to someone influential for reasons unknown.'

'Is that the best I'm going to get?' Isaac asked.

'That's all I've got.'

'I'll ask no more questions,' Isaac said.

'It could be that she doesn't want to be found,' Richard Goddard said. Isaac thought his senior's statement a little obscure.

Chapter 2

Isaac's next visit was to the reclaimed plot of land that housed the fictional town of Bletherington. There were questions to be asked, the mood on the streets of the plywood town to be evaluated. He had been told that the series producer was the best person to talk to.

'Edith Blythe, what can I say? Brilliant characterisation, excellent delivery, great timing – undoubtedly the star of the show.' A well-dressed, prim and proper woman in her mid-thirties, Jessica O'Neill had come to the position of series producer through a torturous route. She had started some years earlier as a continuity editor on a period drama set in seventeenth century England. It had not been well-received in that the script writing lacked tension, and the intensity of the novel from which it had been adapted had been lost. It lasted one season before the production company pulled the plug.

Jessica, attractive, slim, and articulate, had found herself very quickly out of work after such a promising start. The one highlight of the programme according to Alexander Lewis, one of the directors of the production company, had been the quality of the continuity.

Jeremy Lewis, Alexander's eldest son, was only two years older than her. They had dated for a while, became lovers, moved in together only for her to move out two months later. No reason other than they both felt they were too young, and they still wanted to play the field. The one result of the coupling was that she acquired a close friend, and he had guided her career since then.

He ensured that her career progressed in a succession of increasingly important jobs, including a stint working with a news unit covering an outbreak of insurrection in the Middle East. She had been enamoured of the job when it was first offered – soon became disillusioned after she had become separated from her team during a demonstration.

She had found herself surrounded by a group of men who forgot what they were protesting about and turned their attention to her. It took a few soldiers and a lot of shots to get her away from them and to the nearest hospital. She decided after the wounds had healed and the trauma had subsided that she was better off back in England.

The series producer's job had come about as a result of the previous incumbent having a blazing row with one of the directors over editorial content, and storming off the set.

She had been brought in at short notice on the recommendation of her ex-lover, and most, at least the senior production team, agreed that the end result was good, but her dictatorial style was hard to take. She had taken control of the Billy Blythe episode where he met his fate and had done it well – even dealt with Charles Sutherland when he called her an arrogant little bitch. It was clear to her and senior management that she was going to stay, and a two-week stand-in had extended to six months and looked to be continuing for the foreseeable future.

Isaac Cook's previous question had generated a glowing reference. His next question would be more telling. 'Miss O'Neill, the actor who portrays Edith Blythe?' he asked.

'Call me Jess.'

'Jess, of course. Marjorie Frobisher, the person, not the actor.'

'Unless she's confirmed dead, I have to be careful what I say.' Her manner had changed. Isaac noticed that she had subtly pulled back from him. Before his earlier question, she had been close, personable. Now, she was professional and distant. The change interested him. He determined to persevere.

'Jess, you're right, of course. At the present moment, we're not dealing with a murder, only a missing person.'

'But you're here from the Serious Crime Division. I can't see why they would send a detective chief inspector purely to find a missing person. It seems incongruous to send someone as smart as you to look for her unless there's something you're not telling me.'

'Orders from on high or I wouldn't be here. I've got enough bodies out there looking for a culprit. Here is the last place I want to be at the present moment.'

'DCI, I'll give it to you straight, in confidence.'

'Sure, in confidence. This is not an official enquiry yet, so what you tell me doesn't have to be reported. Of course, if it does become official, then what you say may become relevant and on the record.'

'Marjorie Frobisher was not a nice person. In fact, she was not popular at all with anybody here. Always pushing her weight around, causing trouble, debating her lines, the camera angle, her profile. She saw herself as a prima donna, an A-List movie star, but what was she? Just an actor.'

'But you said she was brilliant.'

'Brilliant, of course, but this is hardly *Gone with the Wind* or *Casablanca*.'

'What do you mean?'

'She was at the pinnacle of her career. I know she believed she was destined for greatness in a major movie in America, but that was never going to happen.'

'Why do you say that?' Isaac struggled with the answer. Jess had once again relaxed and moved closer to him, disarmingly close. It was always an occupational hazard. Start interviewing a female witness and they were invariably charmed by his good manners and his black complexion.

He was not a vain man who regarded himself as automatically attractive to the opposite sex, but he was not impervious to reality. He remained single, not out of any great desire for bachelorhood but because a succession of attractive women was constantly heading in his direction and his bed. He did not want Jess O'Neill to be one of them, especially if a body was found and the missing person's case became a murder investigation.

Conflict of interest would have been an issue if one of the witnesses, possibly one of the suspects, possibly the murderer, was sharing his bed as well.

Jess continued. 'She was ideal for a television drama. For a woman in her fifties she was certainly attractive, but not attractive enough for a major movie, or, at least, not as one of the leading ladies.'

'That's a broad statement.'

'I worked on a major movie here in England. Just one of the script writers, but I interfaced with some big names in the business, Oscar winners.'

'And?'

'There's something about them. They had a presence, magnetism, a "je ne sais quoi". Marjorie Frobisher didn't have it.'

'Is that because they are major movie stars?'

'In part I would agree, but that definable quality is, I believe, with the person regardless of their star status.'

'Are you saying that Marjorie Frobisher was at the peak of her career, and it was downhill from here?'

'Yes, that is what I am saying.'

'Does she know this?'

'In the strictest confidence, yes. Please don't use it and certainly don't let the gossip magazines hear of it.'

'I'll agree, but if it becomes a murder enquiry.'

'She's becoming older, maybe too old for the programme. There's a decision to reinvigorate the programme. Bring in some younger characters; get rid of some of the older ones.'

'I thought you had record ratings.'

'Record ratings, but they drop and very quickly if you don't give them something new.'

'Older characters. Is Edith Blythe one of them?'

'She's out in three to six months at the most. They'll honour her contract, but she's going. We killed off Billy Blythe, her brother, now it's time for her. Mind you, Billy Blythe's death generated record ratings and substantial revenue. What do you think will happen when we kill her off?'

'This is your game. You tell me.'

'We had over eight million viewers in England alone for his death. She should generate somewhere close to nine if it's promoted correctly.'

'No doubt it will be.' It was odd that he had barely heard of the programme. He had watched a recent episode on the internet, three hours earlier. It did not impress him.

'Don't worry, they'll get the numbers. The increased revenue will cover the cost of paying out her contract.'

Isaac prepared to leave. The conversation had ranged from stand-offish to amenable, then to professional, and eventually back to very amenable. He was feeling a little uncomfortable with the situation, and a little concerned that he found Jess O' Neill an attractive woman. Any other time, he would not have hesitated to make a play.

He stood up to leave, sooner than he would have preferred. 'Just one question.'

'Yes, what is it?' She had made a point of shaking his hand and moved forward as if she was going to give him a hug.

'Did Marjorie Frobisher know that she was going to be written out of the series?'

'I told her in confidence.'

'How did she take it?'

'She hit the roof, gave me a diatribe about how she was the programme, and that once she left the ratings would plummet through the floor, and we'd all be out on the street looking for a job.'

'How did you react?'

'I stood my ground and told her the facts.'

'So when did she go missing?'

'She never came in the next day.'

'Do you believe it was you telling her that prompted her to leave?'

'I'm not sure. She may have been angry, but for all her faults, she was a professional. I can't see that it was the reason, although it may have been.'

'Just one more question, maybe two: was it your responsibility to tell her and whose idea was it to write her out of the script?'

'I told her on a directive from the executive producer. My timing was not great; I should have waited until we finished shooting Billy Blythe's death, but she had asked me a direct question about script development. Not really for me to answer, but it was a question, and I told her the truth. It seemed the only professional approach that I could take.'

'And the second question. Whose idea was it to write Marjorie Frobisher out?'

'I had put forward the idea some weeks earlier at a production meeting, and there was unanimous support. It was only a suggestion during a brain-storming session, but it appeared to hit

13

a nerve, and from then on it was accepted. The date when she leaves is not clear. There may still be a change, even at this late date.'

'Does she know the suggestion came from you?'

'After she stormed out of here, she drove out to Richard Williams' office, the executive producer, and confronted him. Apparently, he acknowledged the fact that I had been the catalyst, and she left soon after.'

'Any idea what was said?'

'You'll need to ask him. I only know what I was told. I'm told the conversation was acrimonious, lots of shouting, some bad language.'

'Who told you this?'

'The fact that she had confronted him? The executive producer's personal assistant. She'll corroborate my statement, but don't let on that I told you.'

'Marjorie Frobisher would see you as being responsible for her removal.'

'Clearly, and I don't think she's a person who forgives easily,' Jess O'Neill said.

***

Isaac Cook's dependable colleague Farhan Ahmed focussed on trying to find the missing woman: the standard approach, visit the nearest relative. Robert Avers, Marjorie Frobisher's husband, was an avuncular man who warmed to the young policeman immediately.

'Come in, please.' The house, in one of the better part of Belgravia, was obviously expensive and exquisitely decorated. Farhan was ushered into the main reception room. A maid went off to make tea: no milk for the policeman, milk and two sugars for his host.

'We've been asked to assist in finding your wife.' Farhan wasn't sure if his questioning would be appreciated. Typically, it would be the nearest relative who opened a missing file case, not somebody of 'influence'.

The reply allayed his fears. 'Detective Inspector, I don't know what the fuss is about. She's become a pain in the arse recently with her celebrity status. She sees herself as better than the likes of me.'

'Does that indicate any marital issues? Would that explain her disappearance?'

'Not at all. I just ignore her. She gets over it soon enough. Give her a few weeks, and she'll reappear.'

The maid entered, poured the tea and left some chocolate biscuits on a plate. The conversation temporarily halted while she was present. Farhan took one of the biscuits.

'Has she done this before?'

'When we've had a blazing row, she puts on this "you never appreciated me. I'm going to find someone who will" attitude, and then two days later she's back.'

'The marriage was strained?'

Robert Avers laughed out loud, a raucous bellow. 'Not at all, although this is longer than usual. Mind you, it's not aimed at me, is it?'

'I wouldn't know.'

'They're going to dump her from that soap opera she holds up as a beacon of art.'

'Does she hold it up?'

'In public, but she doesn't believe it, though. It's an inane insult to the intelligence.'

Farhan, increasingly comfortable with the man, said, 'My wife is addicted to it.'

Robert Avers adopted a serious tone. 'Apologies if I offended.'

'Apologies not needed.'

'Mind you, it paid for all this.' Robert Avers waved his arms around the room, indicating the house in general.

'Then it seems that you've both done well out of it.'

'Sure have. Let's be honest, Marjorie can be a bitch, especially with the people she works with, and then if we walk out the door, it's the photographers and the drooling fans. It's bound to make anyone a bit difficult.'

'Difficult for you?'

'Not really. I just let her have her tantrums, and then it's fine.'

'So where is she now?'

'She sends me the occasional SMS.'

'We're anxious to talk to her, check she's okay.'

'I don't follow up on her, although I suppose you could check the location from her phone.'

'It may not be so easy: rules and regulations, protection of privacy, that sort of thing.'

'I'll leave it up to you. Just let me know Marjorie is okay, but I don't need to know where she is or when she's coming back.'

'Why's that?'

'She's an affectionate woman. There'll be plenty of making up when she gets back.' Marjorie Frobisher's husband let out another raucous bellow. 'You know what I mean.'

***

Isaac and Farhan met later that day to compare notes, plan strategy. Detective Superintendent Goddard stuck his head briefly around the door for an update. He was off, apparently to another of the conferences which seemed to occupy a lot of his time. He was a man destined for greatness – or that was how he saw it. Any opportunity to press the flesh with the shakers and the movers, government or otherwise, and he was bound to be there.

'It's irritating, sir,' Isaac said when asked for an update. He had just made himself a coffee and was seated at his desk, Farhan on the other side, a cup of tea in hand.

'What's irritating?' The detective superintendent realised where the conversation was heading.

'We've got a murder of a ten-year girl, a grisly death down by the docks, and here we are traipsing around the countryside to try and find a corpse, or if she's not dead, a vain and silly woman with air and graces.'

'Understood, but this woman is important. I don't know why, but I'm bound to be grilled by a couple of people tonight, and some of them are very influential. And besides, we have a Murder Investigation Team dealing with those cases.'

'I'm the senior investigating officer. I should be leading them.'

'That's fully understood, but for now, you and DI Ahmed are to focus on the missing woman.'

Isaac, realising that any further debate was pointless, focussed back on the woman. 'Names, do you have any of these so-called influential names?' Isaac persisted, mildly irritating his boss, who was in a hurry to get any information he could pass on, in case he was waylaid by pertinent questions later. Apparently, the prime minister was to make the keynote speech.

'Official Secrets Act at the present moment. If it becomes necessary, then I may be able to get you a special dispensation. We've deputised your position on the Murder Investigation Team. You stick with what you've got. I don't know much more than you do. Just keep digging. Any updates, make sure to let me know.'

Farhan was the first to reply. 'The husband believes she's got the huff and taken off for a while.'

'Huff, not a police term that I am familiar with.'

Farhan realised that he had overstepped boundary of familiarity with the senior officer.

'Sorry, sir. Occasionally, when they've had an argument, she takes off for a few days – maintains contact by SMS. He's a little worried, but he assumes the news from the soap opera she stars in is giving her concern, and she's taken off until she cools down.'

'What news is this?'

'She's being dropped from the series,' Isaac said. 'Took it badly by all accounts. If that gets out, it may make my best contact hostile.'

'Don't worry, Isaac. I'll keep it under wraps. If they ask me tonight, I'll say that she has had an argument with the husband and is hiding out for a few days. She's done it before, and until we receive further updates to the contrary, that's our official comment.'

'Thank you, sir.' One significant doubt remained in Isaac's mind after the detective superintendent had left the room. *Why is she so damn important to someone in a position of influence?* he thought.

With the detective superintendent dealt with, Isaac and Farhan sat down to evaluate the situation. The office they occupied was not large, but it was freshly painted, with a good desk for Isaac, a smaller one for Farhan, as befitted his lower rank. To the right on entering the office were three comfortable chairs and a coffee table. More private conversations could be held down the corridor in a sound-proofed room. Isaac had all his accreditations framed, and up on the wall. Farhan was not so concerned and had none, just a calendar and a picture of his children.

'Farhan, getting back to the situation before our unexpected visitor poked his head around the door,' Isaac said, 'what did you find out from the husband?'

'Made me very welcome.'

'But what did you find out?'

'Her husband believes she's just annoyed and has taken off to cool down. She's done it in the past when they've had an argument. I suspect they have arguments quite frequently. Not my idea of an ideal marriage, but he seems devoted to her. Whether it's reciprocated, I don't know.'

Isaac attempted an evaluation of the facts so far. 'What do we have? Firstly, there is an assumption by persons unknown and influential that her disappearance is suspicious. Do these persons, whoever they are, concern themselves with her safety, or is that a minor consideration?'

'Why is she so important?' Farhan asked.

'You can focus on that,' Isaac said. 'Secondly, what was the blazing row between Marjorie Frobisher and the executive producer? What was said in anger? Was it just her sounding off at him for dumping her, or was there more to it?'

'Everyone has skeletons in the cupboard. We just need to find theirs.'

Isaac appreciated his colleague's style of thinking. Farhan had been born in Pakistan and had, like many thousands of others, made the trip to England and its cold and damp climate. A Muslim, his faith was private and pragmatic, and he blended into the department and society well. He was not averse to a half pint of beer on a Friday night – team building he would say – but his mother would have been shocked and his wife disappointed. There had been a murder six months previously in a pig abattoir, and he had even conducted the investigation. Pork was 'Haram', forbidden, but he was a serving police officer, and he carried out his duty without complaint. He never told Isaac about the three showers with a scrubbing brush when he arrived home that night, trying to remove the stench from his body.

'Thirdly,' Isaac continued, 'Does someone know something that we don't?'

He laid out a plan. In the absence of a body, it was just the two of them. Confidentiality required that no one else could be brought on board. 'Farhan, this is what we do. We'll follow your suggestion and try and find out what Marjorie Frobisher's importance is, and why someone influential is interested. I'll head back out to the production site and keep quizzing the people there. I'll also speak to the executive producer. See if he'll tell me all that happened between him and his star, or soon-to-be-ex star.'

'You'll need corroboration from his personal assistant,' Farhan said.

'You're right. I'll ask her confidentially, see if it aligns with what he says. I've also got another source that may or may not give me some further insights.'

'Jessica O'Neill?' Farhan quizzed. Isaac had already told him that she was giving the right signals, and he knew his superior's reputation.

'Don't look at me like that. If it turns out there's been a murder, she could well be a suspect.'

'I realise that. Until the mysterious lady deems to make a grand entrance, then we treat everyone with suspicion.'

It had been a long day. There was a slight drizzle as they left the office, and both knew that they were in for a slow drive to their respective homes. Farhan had managed to buy a small terraced house in Wimbledon, not far from the railway station. Isaac had secured a loan on a two-bedroom apartment in Willesden. It cost him more than his salary could bear, but he was an ambitious man. He felt he could stand the financial strain until his next promotion.

Chapter 3

The next day Farhan met up with Robert Avers at the Churchill Arms in Kensington. Farhan felt a neutral location may be preferable. It was evident that Avers appreciated good food. The Thai restaurant at the back of the public house served a good meal, and with a couple of pints down him, Farhan thought the man would be even more open than at their previous meeting.

His estimation proved to be correct. They had managed to secure a table inside, and there was no fear of being overheard. It was crowded as usual, and the noise from the increasingly inebriated patrons would ensure that no one could hear what they said.

'I'll be straight with you,' Avers said. He had just consumed his meal voraciously, almost shoved it down. His approach to a pint of beer was similar, down in two gulps. 'We had what is quaintly called an "open marriage". Hope I don't shock you there.'

Farhan, a conservative Muslim in an arranged marriage understood what he meant, not sure if he approved. 'Shocked? Not at all. It seems incongruous in today's permissive society,' he said.

'You're right of course. The young people of today certainly would not understand the concept. They no longer see the need for marriage, and having multiple partners without the sanctification of a priest is accepted nowadays. Marjorie and I come from a different generation, and we both came to the marriage bed, if not entirely chaste, at least relatively naïve. We've been married a long time, and for the first ten we were faithful, but then her career blossomed, and my business took me away from home for lengthy periods at a time.'

'So it was a mutual agreement?' It was not a subject Farhan felt entirely comfortable discussing, but he felt a direct answer from Avers could well prove to be significant. The well-fed and well-drunk husband continued to down the pints. Farhan stayed a distant second with two half pints of beer.

'I suppose so,' Avers replied. 'I don't know who was first to stray, and initially there were some incredible rows at home and over the phone, but then we came to an agreement. It's held us firmly together for the last fifteen years. I've shocked you, haven't I?' He repeated his previous statement.

Farhan was indeed shocked by the frankness of the man, but it did not seem wise to offer his opinion. 'I've heard worse.'

'Just one thing. When she takes off, there's never been another man.'

'Are you certain?'

'Totally. We're open if there is any dalliance by either party.'

'So, where is she?'

His fifth pint consumed, Avers willingly conceded, 'I haven't a clue, and honestly, this is much longer than the previous occasions. In the past, it's been a few days, a week at most, but now we're looking at over two and a half weeks.'

'It's imperative we find her as soon as possible,' Farhan said.

'You have access to her phone number. Did you trace the messages she sent me?' Avers asked.

'Inconclusive. Mainly from the north of the country.'

'Not like her to be secretive.'

'We're aware that her disappearance has raised concerns in influential circles. Anyone you can think of?' Farhan broached the question that concerned him the most, the primary reason for being in a noisy pub; the reason he had downed another half pint. The reason he was feeling decidedly unwell.

'Not really. Her history before our marriage is vague. Since then, no one I can think of.'

'You don't know any names?'

'She'd tell me if I asked, but I'm not sure I want to know. The openness of the marriage is more on her side than mine, and we've always been discreet. At least, I hope we have.'

With no more questions and thankfully no more beers for Farhan, they left the public house. Avers took a cab; Farhan walked unsteadily to his car and vomited in the gutter, stale beer and the Thai meal. He then took fifteen minutes to drink some water and compose himself. He felt ashamed that he had sinned; he would offer additional prayers by way of compensation. Before arriving back at his house, he sucked on some mints to remove the smell from his breath. His God may well forgive him, his wife would not.

***

Richard Williams, the executive producer of the soap opera, proved to be an elusive man. Isaac had come out early to his office in the city, not on the draughty and wet production lot. Williams' personal assistant, Sally Jenkins, a vivacious woman in her mid-twenties with a tight top, her cleavage showing, and wearing a skirt that could only be described as no more than a bandage, was most agreeable. She was steadily plying the detective chief inspector with cups of coffee and biscuits. He knew what she was, a prick-teaser. He had come across her type before, making out they were available, taking every opportunity to show the goods on offer, and then when a man got up close and cosy, they would go coy and tell him they were not that kind of girl. Of course, if the man came with a Ferrari or a Porsche, they would be available. She did not interest him.

After Isaac had waited forty minutes, Richard Williams came out of his office, apologising effusively. 'Busy day, production schedules delayed, temperamental actors, and the weather is not helping with the outdoor scenes. What can I do for you? My apologies, by the way, unavoidable.' His statement by way of an introduction, Isaac felt, was disingenuous, hurried.

He chose not to comment and responded in a cordial manner. 'That's fine. Sally's kept me occupied, looked after me well.'

'Sally, I don't know what I would do without her.' The executive producer looked over at her as he spoke. She acted embarrassed, yet smiled a knowing smile back at him. Isaac had seen the look before. He knew something was going on between the two. It seemed unlikely that she would give him much assistance about the fracas between her boss and Marjorie Frobisher.

In his office, Williams beckoned Isaac to sit on a comfy chair to one side of the room. Isaac declined, and sat instead on a chair on the far side of the large desk at the end of the room. A window, the entire rear wall, gave a panoramic view over the city.

Richard Williams, unable to maintain the upper hand in the meeting, acquiesced and sat facing Isaac in a high-backed leather chair on his side of the desk.

'Detective Chief Inspector, what can I do for you?'

'Marjorie Frobisher.'

'It's not the first time she's disappeared,' the executive producer said. Isaac noticed the slower pace of his speech. Before, it had appeared rehearsed, now it seemed measured. He realised that the man was used to manipulating conversations.

'We're aware this is not the first time.'

'Why the interest of the police? It seems melodramatic to me. The sort of thing we may well put in a script, but hardly real life.'

'I thought that is what you are producing, a representation of reality.' Isaac realised he was baiting the man to see how he would react.

'Have you ever watched the programme?' Williams asked. He had taken a defensive posture, his arms folded, leaning back in his chair.

'Once,' Isaac admitted.

'And what did you think?'

'It's not my kind of programme.'

Richard Williams weighed up the situation. He realised he was not dealing with a member of the viewing public, but a seasoned and astute policeman. His answer was honest. 'Fodder for the masses, but it draws the viewers in, makes everyone plenty of money.'

'Don't you feel some guilt that you are spoon-feeding it to millions of people?' Isaac needed to break Williams' guard.

'Are you one of those do-gooders, those holier-than-thou types who feel that we should be uplifting the people, educating them?'

Isaac knew that he had annoyed the man, his intention. 'Not totally.'

'This is a commercial world, dedicated to the pursuit of money. If a few million wish to watch the programme and pay us plenty of money, then so be it.'

'A few million? I'm told it's between seven and eight million.'

'Okay, okay, you've made your point,' Williams said angrily. 'I'm a busy man. If you haven't any more to discuss, we should end here. Any more questions or can I get on with what I do best?'

'There are some more questions. What did you and Marjorie Frobisher argue about the day before her disappearance, and what is your relationship with her?'

'There was no argument, just a heated discussion. Who told you this?'

'I am aware that there was an argument.' Isaac was circumspect. He did not want to reveal what Jess O'Neill had told him.

'You're right. She was going to be dumped. Good for ratings and the future of the programme, not so good for her. I can't blame her for being angry.'

'Were you angry as well?'

'In the end, I was. Marjorie's a professional, been in the business for many years. She knows how it works, and it's not as if we're putting her out on the street. There was every intention of paying out her contract.'

'But her career was coming to an end?'

'She's not immortal. It was going to happen at some time, and then there are all the chat shows and the newspaper interviews to keep her occupied. Maybe do a few adverts. She'd be fine.'

'Is that enough for someone like her?' Isaac asked.

'For Marjorie, never. She wanted the continuing adulation. She's welcome to it, but I'm no longer going to supply it.'

'How long have you known her?'

Isaac noticed a change in Williams' manner. He leant forward, rested his arms on the desk and said, 'I've known her for over forty years, ever since she had a one-line walk-on in a dreary period piece. We've always been friends.'

Isaac could see no more to be gained by prolonging the meeting.

He would talk to Sally Jenkins about the argument at a later date.

***

Charles Sutherland had accepted the death of Billy Blythe graciously. At least, that was how it had been publicly portrayed. The appearances on the chat shows kept him occupied for a few weeks, the bottle for a few weeks more. His agent had put out the feelers for some more work, but he was typical of many who had enjoyed the comfort of a long-running soap opera – he was typecast. The only parts were for villains, for another 'Billy Blythe', and he had had enough of him. He saw himself as a Shakespearean actor, a classicist involved in a major production at one of the major theatres in the country, not playing an overweight, aged hooligan. The tough-talking, the bad language if they could get it past the censors, the pointless fistfights – they always used a stand-in when his back was to the camera – failed to impress him. He saw himself on stage reciting Hamlet's soliloquy to an enraptured audience. *To be, or not to be: that is the question…*Maybe even, *Hamlet* Act 5 Scene 1: *Alas, poor Yorick!*

He had earned good money, and if it had been invested wisely, he would have had sufficient not to work again. However, an extravagant lifestyle meant that he continued to rent, although, in Mayfair, it was hardly a slum. Not like the place where he had grown up in the west of the country. His parents, good people, had struggled all their life. A son that always complained had not helped. The only motorised transport was a tractor that rarely started and an old Land Rover that did start but rattled atrociously. The food was wholesome. The animals: never more than twenty or thirty cows and a bull to keep them serviced, several dozen sheep, a few pigs and chickens. The 4 a.m. starts in winter to look after the animals and collect the eggs, before he walked the three miles to school over frozen fields, still brought back unpleasant memories. He had been an inherently lazy child, a trait that continued to adulthood, but laziness was not allowed by a stern father who was capable of removing the leather belt from his work trousers and giving the young Sutherland a good thrashing across his bare backside.

Charles Sutherland never considered that the principal acting parts eluded him because of his inability to resolve his West Country accent. He had made significant improvements, and for Billy Blythe, a country accent was just right, but the classics required an eloquent tone. To reach the heights he desired needed more than he could give. It needed discipline and perseverance, and he possessed neither. He was a sloppy man, both in his hygiene and his movements. His car, an ageing Volvo, was full of discarded crisp packets and sweet wrappers, the ashtray full of ash from unpleasant smelling cigarettes. He presented poorly, but he did not blame himself – he blamed others, and the person he blamed most was Marjorie Frobisher. He knew it was her who had him killed off, Jess O'Neill had told him, and he didn't have much time for her either. If he was to suffer, then others would as well. That was how he saw it.

***

Sam Avers, the son of Marjorie Frobisher and Robert Avers, was a major disappointment to his parents. Their income had given him the best of opportunities, the best of schooling, but he had a weakness for alcohol and an ever-increasing dependence on recreational drugs. His father was a heavy drinker, but he came from a generation where people drank heavily, got drunk and stopped. The son came from a generation where people drank until silliness and then started hitting the shots of tequila or vodka: his favourite, Slippery Nipple, a mix of Bacardi rum and Wild Turkey bourbon. He had grown up in the better parts of London, Chelsea mainly, and the clubs and the pubs were awash with binge drinkers. He had been flush with money; his father was successfully running an import/export business, his mother was an increasingly affluent and famous celebrity.

He had little time for either, and by the age of seventeen, his relationship with them was irreparably severed. The family home was big enough for him to enter and leave it without having to do more than briefly acknowledge them. The only time he granted them a conversation, short even then, was when he needed money or to top up his credit card. They gave in with little resistance. Their lives were full and busy. A delinquent child who had neither the innate charm nor the good looks of his parents left them with a feeling of apathy towards him. Marjorie Frobisher and Robert Avers could not love him as parents should, and the son realised this. The more alcohol in his system, the more he disliked them, the more vengeful he became.

There had been a period in his early twenties when a good and decent girl had attempted to love and change him. They had moved in together, enjoyed a loving relationship, mainly sober for three years before he had fallen off the waggon and hit the booze again. The relationship passed the honeymoon stage, although they had never officially married, and domesticity caused him some troubles. She moved out, and the intervening years had been of casual relationships, mainly one-night stands, and days spent in a drunken and drug-filled haze. He had attempted a career while sober, managed to find a job as a junior auctioneer at one of the most prestigious auction houses in the city. He wasn't sure how it had come about, but he figured maybe his mother was screwing one of the directors. Yes, he knew about her shenanigans and his father's. That was what men did, but his mother? He could never forgive her, them, for their lifestyle, their affairs, their wealth, when he had been forced to play second fiddle, even third, in their affections.

He hated them both with a passion – his mother, the most. *If they were only dead*, he increasingly thought. *Then I'd only need to share their money with that bitch sister of mine. There would be plenty enough then, enough for me at least.*

Chapter 4

Detective Superintendent Goddard continued to be reticent as to who was pushing the search for Marjorie Frobisher. So far, all the probing from Isaac had failed to elicit a clue.

It was now close to four weeks since Marjorie Frobisher had been seen. Her credit cards occasionally used in one location; the next time, a hundred miles away. Her mobile phone, switched on long enough for an SMS to her husband, – 'Home soon, love you' – and then turned off, barely gave time to triangulate its position.

'Sir, this is going nowhere.' Isaac Cook tried one final time to get an answer from his superior at a hastily scheduled meeting at Isaac's insistence. They met in the detective superintendent's office, an office that Isaac aspired to within the next two to three years. He regarded policing as a vocation; the detective superintendent's office the next major goal to aim for. A goal now being hampered by the forlorn search for a missing person.

He was determined to hammer out the situation with his boss. 'I'm suggesting we pull out until the woman is found, alive or dead. This is just a waste of time.'

Richard Goddard understood the frustration of the man sitting in front of him, but there was nothing he could do. The investigation had to continue. 'Isaac, you've got to stay with it. It's either the woman or the body. The pressure on me for a result is intense. I can't take you and DI Ahmed off the case.'

'But we're wasting our time. The woman was not popular with the people she worked with, but she's not short of money. And she messages her husband every few days. What's the point of all this?'

'Are you sure about the SMSs? Is she sending them and using the credit cards? Is there a signature?'

'The credit cards only need a pin number. We can't be sure about that either, but why? People go missing all the time. Normally, there's a cursory investigation, and then life goes on. Sometimes they turn up somewhere down the track, or they don't. It doesn't mean they've all been bumped off, weighted down and thrown to the fishes or fed to the pigs.'

'Isaac, I understand your frustration, but it's out of my hands.'

Isaac admitted defeat and left. He did not like leaving on such a sour note. His boss was still answerable to others and forced to follow orders, no matter how illogical.

Frustrated with the conversation, Isaac met up with Farhan, and they went out for a meal at an Indian restaurant not far from the office. It had been a long day, and neither had achieved much. Isaac had managed to speak to the executive producer's personal assistant, Sally Jenkins, but that had revealed nothing. He had even met up with Jess O'Neill, and she was still giving him hints that some further investigation, outside of office hours, was acceptable. He was tempted, but the timing was wrong. If Marjorie Frobisher did turn up alive, the first thing he was going to do was to ask the series producer out, even conduct some serious probing of a personal and intimate nature, which looked a strong possibility after his last meeting with her.

'Sally Jenkins, what did you expect?' Jess O'Neill had said. 'Did you pick up on the signals?'

'Her and Richard Williams,' Isaac proffered an answer.

'Yes, of course. He must be nearly forty years older than her, but he's a pants' man. Sorry for my crudity, but he hits on everyone if they're female and attractive.'

'Has he hit on you?' Isaac asked.

'Sure has, but I told him to shove it. I don't need a sugar daddy, no matter how much money he's got or what car he drives.'

'Out of interest, what sort of car?'

'Ferrari. Why?'

'I recognised the signals in the office with Sally Jenkins, surmised it was either a Ferrari or a Porsche.'

'I don't need a man with a fancy car. I'm more than capable of getting my own if I want one.'

'I've got a blue one, flashing light with a siren as an optional extra.' Isaac regretted the comment immediately.

'Blue car, flashing light, sounds fine to me.' Isaac no longer regretted his previous comment, but had felt embarrassed that he had transgressed from professional to personal.

Farhan continued to enjoy his meal while Isaac updated him. He omitted the intimate exchange with the series producer.

Farhan was more interested in finding out who the influential person was. Both were frustrated about where this was heading, or what more they could do. Isaac would continue to interview Marjorie Frobisher's fellow actors, the production staff, the script writers, but he couldn't see anything new happening there. It was evident she was full of her own importance, but he had spent time perusing the magazines in his local newsagent and it was obvious she was immensely popular with the public – the indiscriminating public, as he saw it.

The plan for the following day: the same as the current day, and those previously – keep probing, maybe turn up a needle in a haystack.

Chapter 5

Angus MacTavish of the Clan MacTavish was a proud Scotsman who spent most of his time across the border in England. This stance sometimes put him out of kilter with his clan brethren, advocating for separation from the United Kingdom. Elected ten years earlier to the British Parliament in Westminster, he saw no reason to moderate his views on independence or any other subject. A safe seat in the Scottish Highlands ensured him the opportunity to further his political and personal aims.

A man used to command, the position of Government Chief Whip suited him admirably. His primary function, to organise his party's contribution to the business of Parliament. If that meant twisting arms to ensure the maximum number of party members' votes at divisions in Parliament, so be it.

He was also expected to know of all the party members' peccadilloes and indiscretions. Sometimes to help them; sometimes to ensure they fell on their swords.

Detective Superintendent Goddard arrived early for his meeting with MacTavish. He presented himself at the security gates that closed off Downing Street to the general public. The necessary accreditation and his police identification, coupled with his name on the typed list of scheduled visitors, ensured entry. The office where they met, first floor, Number 9, was one house down from the prime minister's.

MacTavish wielded substantial unseen power, and when he spoke it was with the full authority of the Prime Ministerial Cabinet. The detective superintendent knew this; he also knew him to be a taciturn man who said little but implied a lot.

The man barely raised himself from his chair when Richard Goddard entered, other than to grab the policeman by the hand and shake it vigorously. A firm handshake – an indication of power.

'Detective Superintendent, my instructions were clear in this matter.' A gruff manner, deep-voiced, with a strong Scottish brogue, MacTavish intimidated many, scared most. Tall, with red hair, his forefathers had fought against the British at Culloden – killed more than their fair share. Even today at Highland gatherings over a few drams of whisky, Scotland's finest gift to the world in Angus MacTavish's view, those who had fought and died were remembered.

MacTavish was a pragmatist. Time had moved on. Nearly three hundred years separated the past from the future, and it was the future that he saw as important. He professed no great allegiance to the British Monarchy, but he kept his views guarded, and besides, he would not be averse to a seat in the House of Lords at the appropriate time.

'Sir, I realise that I was meant to keep my people from asking too many questions about why they were looking for this woman.'

'And you phone up asking me for this information.'

'My apologies, but this investigation is going nowhere. My people are charging up blind alleys, hitting dead-ends, and just wasting time. We know she was subject to bitchiness, and there seem to be some unusual arrangements around the marital bed, but they hardly seem sufficient to believe she is dead.'

'Detective Superintendent, you don't understand. Dead is not the problem. It's if she is alive that causes concern.'

Taken aback by the statement, Richard Goddard had to ponder the situation. His people were looking the woman, and indications were that she may still be alive. Why was she so important? He had the ear of the Chief Whip, now was the time to pressure for more.

'In confidence, I'll give it to you straight,' MacTavish said. 'I know about the so-called open marriage, her promiscuity when she was younger, and the banal programme on the television. What is of concern is who the woman has slept with. What dirt she has on them. What scandal she could cause if she spoke out of turn.'

'Is she likely to do that?'

'Yes. She's a vengeful woman, even threatened to commit such an act.'

The senior policeman saw it all too clearly. It was an election year; the government was likely to hold on, but only by the slimmest of margins. The last thing they wanted was a scandal, especially if the scandal was related to a senior member of the government aiming to hold on to his seat in a marginal electorate. 'But would she?' he asked.

'Detective Superintendent, she's soon to be out of this programme, and will be paid to dish the dirt on one or another chat show, and then there will be a biography of a life well led, or in her case well laid.'

'Can't you put a restraining order on its publication, Official Secrets Act?'

'If it's published in this country, yes, but if it's scurrilous enough, the publisher's lawyers will call our bluff, ask us for a reason for halting its release. Once the gutter press gets involved, well, you know the consequences.'

'Yes, of course.'

MacTavish relieved that he had given his reasons, phoned for some tea. Five minutes later, a pleasant middle-aged woman entered and placed the pot and two cups on the desk, with some small cakes on a plate to one side.

'Mrs Gregory makes them for me. Wouldn't know what I would do without her fussing over me.'

'Please sir, you'll make me blush.' With that, she left the office unobtrusively.

Cups of tea in hand, and cake consumed by both men, the conversation continued. 'Detective Superintendent, here's the deal. We know she will talk, and there's every sign that she is becoming irrational. We've had some experts assess her behaviour, and there are the early signs of premature senility. She may well say something inadvisable, even when she intends not to. We can't take the risk. If she's dead, then that's fine. Harsh to say, of course, but there it is. If she's alive, we've got to stop any publications and her talking out of turn.'

'But how can you do that?'

'That's the hard part. We're a democratic country, with free speech, so we can't restrict her or the media. I wouldn't agree to that anyway. It's a dilemma, and I'm pleased to say that's not my responsibility.'

'What does she know?' The detective superintendent wasn't sure he would get a response.

'You're putting me on the spot. It's privileged information, on a need-to-know basis, and frankly you don't need to know.'

'Sir, I can understand the dilemma, but is it that serious?'

'Political dynamite! Hits at the highest levels of the government. It could cause a major electoral defeat.'

'Who she's been screwing recently, or in the past, that sort of thing?'

'In the past, and yes, there's plenty of what you just intimated, plus some more.'

'We'll keep looking. I'll tell my people that it's important. They'll just have to trust me on this one.'

'Will they?' MacTavish asked.

'If I give my word, they'll accept it. It won't stop them fishing around.'

'If they get too close, let me know.'

***

On the face of it, Fiona Avers had all the right ingredients: celebrity mother, acting ability. There were, however, two elements apparently vital in the acting profession that the daughter of Marjorie Frobisher did not have, the most obvious being that she was not attractive. In fact, the less generous would have said she was plain, verging on ugly. The less obvious of her two main failings was a violent temper, coupled with an incredibly short fuse. Unattractive women have reached the pinnacle of acting success, but invariably they came with a winning personality, a willingness to understand their shortcomings – in fact, to embrace them.

Fiona Avers was a tall woman with what could only be described as masculine features. Her arms were bulbous and appeared a little short for her height: substantially taller than her mother, a good head and shoulders above her father. Her legs were also on the fat side, her calf muscles tending to bulge. Attempts at rectification through exercises – her parents had paid plenty to help – had come to nought.

Her face, some would say, showed character, but they were generous in their comments, and the only one who said it with any conviction was her friend, literally her only friend, Molly Waters. They had met at school, experimented with lesbianism, even when at their most precocious, most promiscuous, and most willing to screw any male they could lay their hands on. Unfortunately for both, there was a surfeit of young and attractive females, also at their most precocious, most promiscuous, and invariably both Fiona and Molly were left with each other to satisfy their carnal lusts. Molly did not find the experience unpleasant, Fiona did, although she endured and eventually embraced the experience.

Molly was fat at school, although she had a pleasant face and a personality to match. The fatness of youth had carried over into adulthood, and now she was severely in need of a healthy diet and a good makeover. The pleasant personality remained, and it served her well in life. She had tried men for a while, even found a man who treated her well, moved in with him for a few months, but realised from her early intimate encounters that it was women that satisfied her sexually, especially a woman by the name of Fiona Avers.

Fiona Avers, however, felt no such allure for the female body except for hers when a man was labouring on top of her, and that was rare. The world, the society that she moved in, was awash with attractive women, and she was invariably left the wallflower at any social gathering. 'The girl least likely to get laid' had become a catchphrase among those she regarded as friends, although they were fair-weather friends lured by her spending and her tenuous connection with celebrity.

Her face – only Molly Waters saw it as beautiful – was large with a pronounced forehead. Her eyes were sullen with overhanging eyelids. Her ears were small with a distinctive lobe which she concealed by growing her hair long, which did not help as her hair was curly and harsh. Her nose had also given concern. Cosmetic surgery had dealt with that problem, although it had done little to help with her overall appearance.

Her mother had elegantly balanced features and could only be described as beautiful; her father had a rugged look about him with strong masculine characteristics. Not handsome, but interesting – women felt comfortable in his presence.

Everyone in her close family, uncles and aunts mainly, always said that she reminded them of Great Granny Maud, but the only photo that Fiona had seen of the family stalwart was old and grainy – she could see no resemblance.

Her father had shown her great love, made her feel special; her mother had ridiculed her, kept her out of the limelight, and had belittled her too often. How often had she seen her mother telling her friends that her daughter's looks came from Robert's side of the family? How many times, when there was a function to attend or an event where the cameras would be clicking, had she been denied the chance to participate? She remembered her brother Sam attending, but then her mother had always said, 'He's much older than you. You're too young to attend such events. People get drunk, make fools of themselves. At your impressionable age, I want to protect you from such influences until you're older.'

Fiona remembered well enough. As the years rolled by through her childhood and formative teenage years, the non-attendance continued, although the reasons given varied.

Her father ensured that her mother's rejection was countered by his love and generosity. As a child, she looked for a mother's love. As a teenager experiencing her first period and then her first playground crush on a boy, rejected with scathing insults, she looked for a mother's support, a shoulder to cry on. As an adult, she no longer needed her mother, only her hatred for her.

Her father she adored. She knew full well her mother's promiscuous behaviour caused him great concern, although he never admitted it, at least to her. He always said that was the way she was, and they should accept her for her flaws. She could see the hurt in her father's eyes, and the look on his face when he thought no one was looking.

Her temper had been an inconvenience as a child, just a tantrum, but as an adult it had become an embarrassment, even to her. A failure to obtain an acting part, an inattentive shop assistant, a hairdresser who had failed to achieve a satisfactory result – not difficult given the substandard material that he had to work with – and she would see red, and blow off steam in an uncontrolled manner.

There had been a production at a theatre in the centre of London, and she had managed to obtain a decent part. Mainly because it required a name to pull in the paying public, and the daughter of Marjorie Frobisher was better than no name, but only just. Secondly, and less important, was that the part of an embittered unattractive woman matched Fiona Avers. The casting agent saw that little makeup would be required.

There had been a lesser reason, although to Fiona it had been significant. The director of the play, one of the Russian classics, had a perversion for unattractive women, which he made clear the first night of rehearsals, in his office at the back of the theatre. Everyone had gone home; she had stayed for some additional coaching at his insistence and encouragement. He had plied her with alcohol, vodka mainly, which had little effect, as she had a substantial capacity for drink, having regularly drunk too much since her teens. There, sitting close in his office, the touching, the compliments, and it was not long before they were both naked on the floor. The carpet was old and dirty, although both were beyond caring and it was her that was underneath, her breasts feeling the heaviness of his body and the scratching of his chest hair. It was soon over. Once he had expended his lust, she had quickly been hustled out of the office.

The next day he was cool, maybe from guilt, perhaps to show a neutral approach to the cast in his praise and criticism of them all. At least, she wanted to believe that, until she saw him approaching Mary O'Donnell, the lead actress, and his request for her to stay back for some extra coaching. Fiona knew that yet again a man had used her for his base needs and had left her high and dry, emotionally and sexually.

The weeks passed by, she kept her emotions in check, until he had criticised her once too often, and the cow Mary O'Donnell had offered some choice comment about Fiona's acting, and that she was an easy lay. It was clear that the director had told Mary about his night-time encounter with her and the office floor.

Unrestrained, Fiona slapped the woman hard across the face with such force that she fell back and banged her head against a box in the corner of the stage. They took her off to hospital and evicted Fiona from the theatre.

Since then the parts had been few, and she saw her career was at an end. She blamed her mother for her life, but the few times they had met in the last few years her mother had been unapologetic. 'It was my career, darling. I had to do what was right, what was necessary to look after the family, and you always had the best.'

Fiona knew she had had the best that money could buy, but not what she longed for, the love of a mother for a daughter. She hated her mother, the one emotion that was not subject to scathing comments from talentless actresses, critical seducing directors, and playground arbiters on her lack of good looks. That one emotion, hatred for a person that she should love, could only hate, remained constant.

Chapter 6

With Isaac out looking for Marjorie Frobisher, Farhan had taken on the responsibility of finding out why she was so important. So far, he had only come up with blanks, but he and Isaac had decided it was integral to the case to know, although they had been told to focus on finding her.

Their boss, Detective Superintendent Goddard, should have known better than to ask a detective to look in one place, avoid another. A good detective looks everywhere, no matter how insignificant and supposedly irrelevant. A jigsaw puzzle is meaningless without all the pieces, even if it's the smallest piece in the blandest area of white cloud or blue sky. A criminal investigation follows the same principle. Set out all the facts on a whiteboard, put all the names and the faces and the motives and the reasons there. Just one question mark and it's impossible to bring the investigation to a conclusion.

It had been Isaac who had suggested Rosemary Fairweather, Marjorie Frobisher's agent, the previous night. They had been going through the case. The fact that it was a disappearance, not a murder, annoyed them. The best they could do was to get on with it, find the damn woman and then get back to some serious policing.

Farhan noticed framed photos of some recognisable faces on the wall in Rosemary Fairweather's reception area as he waited to be invited into the inner sanctum – Barbara Reid's words, not his.

Barbara Reid, Rosemary Fairweather's personal assistant, was a talkative woman, smartly dressed, designer clothes. She was in her late forties, tending to middle-aged plumpness, but her face maintained the look of youth, or, at least, expensive cosmetics.

'I've been Rosemary's right-hand person for the last eighteen years,' she said.

'Good boss, then,' Farhan replied. He found her remarkably agreeable, with a mellow, soothing voice. His wife was a decent woman, but she was always covered as befitted a conservative Muslim woman. He could feel loyalty to her as his faith and his family required, but certainly not love, and rarely lust. She had given him two healthy children, a boy and a girl, with another on the way. His attraction to other women was not unknown to him, but his religion and his beliefs were important, and he would not stray from the marital bed. Farhan hoped that Rosemary Fairweather would not summon him into the inner sanctum too soon.

'The best,' Barbara Reid continued. 'When I came here there was only one client, Marjorie Frobisher, but now–'

'The photos on the wall.' Farhan interrupted the personal assistant mid-sentence.

'Yes, they've all been in here, plus there are more that Rosemary rejected, some big names even.'

'She's very selective?' He was enjoying his conversation. It was not often that he chatted with an attractive woman in a pleasant environment. It was certainly more agreeable than where he and Isaac worked. There it was clean and functional with everything in its place. Here it was bright, the walls in the reception area painted pale blue. The chairs where he sat were leather and comfortable. The coffee table was glass-topped, obviously expensive, and on the top rested some magazines, recent and related to the acting profession. Barbara Reid sat at a functional table, not overly large, with a laptop in the centre. A computer mouse was to the right, an additional monitor at the far right of the table. Apart from that, her desk was totally clear. From the outside the building, no more than two hundred yards from the Strand in Central London, was Victorian in construction and style, although inside the interior had been gutted and rebuilt in the very best modern style. It was a large building. Rosemary Fairweather's office occupied the third floor.

Farhan was on his second cup of coffee. The PA had been insistent that he try the freshly brewed coffee, and unable to resist such a pleasant invitation, he had agreed. To him, it was too strong, but he could only say, 'It's great, thanks very much.'

The inner sanctum summoned him, all too soon for Farhan. He carried the coffee in with him.

'What can I do for you?' Rosemary Fairweather asked. The reception area was tastefully decorated, the office more so. The carpet on the floor, fitted and plush, the walls adorned with original artworks. The desk, unlike the PA's, was cluttered with files and photos.

'Apologies for the mess. There's a major film going into production in three months' time. I'm trying to get some of my people onto the set.'

'You have many?'

'Too many. The photos on the walls are the primary clients. I suppose you recognised some of them.'

'Most, especially Marjorie Frobisher.'

'Marjorie, dear Marjorie.' Farhan could not be sure if Rosemary Fairweather's response was a sign of affection or sarcasm.

'I'm told that she was your first client.'

Expensively dressed, hair immaculate, and with an absolute assuredness of her own importance, Rosemary Fairweather sat in a leather chair behind a glass-topped table, her knees and legs clearly visible. In her fifties, but with few lines on her face, she sought to lower her age by a combination of clothes that were too tight and too short, and makeup which would have suited a younger person.

'My first client, my best client financially,' she replied.

'I saw some more famous faces out there. Some major movie stars.' Farhan had particularly noticed one face, an actor successful in America.

'Marjorie has been around longer than most, always employed in one programme or another. My commission adds up. The big star you saw outside; he's only come onto the scene in the last year or so. He's bringing in plenty of money now, but for how long, who knows?'

'Tough business?' Farhan said, realising that he needed to bring the interview back to the questions he wanted to ask.

'It's tough for the actors, harder for the agents, the poor suckers who have to keep them occupied, deal with their neuroses, their doubts, and then still try to find work for them.'

'Marjorie Frobisher?'

'She's fine. She can be a bitch, but I've not had any trouble with her. Mind you, I am as well. You have to be in this business.'

'Any idea where she's gone?'

'You know about her lifestyle?'

'Her sleeping arrangements?' It seemed the subtlest way for Farhan to mention the subject without giving too much detail.

'Discreetly put,' she replied.

'Is it relevant to her current disappearance?'

'Unlikely, and I don't know of anyone recently.'

'Has there been someone in particular in the past?'

'It's none of my business, but sometimes she feels like talking.'

'Anyone she could be with now?'

'She's taken off in the past, but there's never been a man. I don't believe she would be with anyone. She was always open with her husband when something was going on, poor man.'

'Why do you say poor man?'

'Robert, he's a good person. He went along with the agreement, but I don't believe he often strayed; no more than any normal heterosexual male, but Marjorie…'

'She was more likely to stray?'

'She was rampant in her younger years, but now…'

'Now?'

'She's in her fifties, menopausal. The fire doesn't burn as strong. It's part of the ageing process, unfortunately.'

'Are you saying she doesn't stray anymore?'

'Not too often, but there are tales I could tell you, who and where.'

'Such as?'

'I've said too much. Client confidentiality.'

'It's important that we know,' Farhan insisted, a little more forcefully than maybe he should have.

'I'm not at liberty to say more. She's only gone missing. It's not the first time, you know.' Her reply was curt.

'That may be the case, but we're treating it as suspicious.'

'Until it becomes an official investigation, I don't believe I can help you anymore.' With those closing words, he was quickly hustled out of the room with a flimsy excuse. He regarded her change in attitude as suspicious. Not about her, but the people that Marjorie Frobisher knew: her paramours, past and present.

***

Isaac had been out at the production lot. He had decided to keep clear of Jess O'Neill, not because the situation was becoming complicated, but because there were other people he needed to talk to. The production office, set at the rear of the car park, consisted of some portable offices arranged into a compound. They were functional and warm, which was as well as the rain was spasmodic and a gusting wind was blowing through the area.

Ian Stanley, the producer of the series, was not hard to find, a small man with a big voice. That wasn't how the person outside the office constructing a plywood-fronted house to add to the fictitious town referred to him: 'Loud-mouthed prick,' was his estimation, 'always pushing us around.' There were a few expletives which Isaac chose to ignore.

It was evident to Isaac on entering the first office building that he had indeed found Ian Stanley. A little gnome-like man, with accentuated features, pointy ears, an ungainly gait, and the top of his head barely reaching the shoulders of those around him, was holding court. *Napoleon complex,* Isaac thought.

'Yes, what do you want?' His initial response to Isaac as he stood patiently at the door, waiting for him to be free, was indicative of the man.

'Detective Chief Inspector Isaac Cook. I'd like to ask you a few questions.'

'Apologies,' Stanley's manner changed. 'I assumed you were here to sell me something.'

He may have had a Napoleon complex, but his office did not reflect his self-perceived *Big Man* status. It was relatively small, cluttered with papers, and had a distinct smell of cheap cigars. Isaac found out later that Ian Stanley was the least politically correct person at the production lot. He was not averse to insulting his actors, production team, scriptwriters – in fact, anyone who was subservient to him. He also found out that he was a sycophant who sucked up to those who would keep him in his position.

'Apology accepted,' Isaac magnanimously replied. He instinctively did not like the man. *Racist, crude, and a bore,* he thought.

'What can I do for you, although I suppose it's related to Marjorie?'

'We're trying to find her.' Isaac took a seat.

'I don't know why.'

'Her disappearance is regarded as serious.'

'It's playing havoc with the series, but apart from that, she's not been missed much, especially by me.'

'Why do you say that?' Isaac asked. Ian Stanley seemed to be a person who had no problem speaking his mind.

'Look, she's a pain in the arse, but for me…'

'Would you care to elaborate?'

'Yes, why not? It's a bloody hard job bringing this together on a day-to-day basis. We're here six days a week, most days fifteen hours at least, and that only gives us five days' worth of thirty minute daily episodes. It has to be run with military precision. We've no time for prima donnas past their prime.'

'Is she a prima donna?' Isaac had heard it before. In fact, it seemed to be the general view of Marjorie Frobisher.

'She's the only one I can't control out there, and the only one who holds up the production, apart from that stuck-up bitch Jess O'Neill. She's only here because she's screwing Richard Williams.'

Isaac was perturbed to hear the reference to Jess. He decided to continue with the interview and to come back later to that particularly disturbing piece of news.

'I was told she is brilliant,' Isaac said.

'Of course she is. Made the others look as if they were straight out of a school production of Macbeth. She knew how to act, I'll grant her that.'

'So why the pain in the arse reference?'

'As I told you, we need to run this with military precision. This is not the Royal Shakespeare Company. This is just entertainment for the masses.'

'Are you saying she was too good for the production?'

'That's what I mean. She could have achieved something in the theatre.'

'Any idea why she didn't?'

'Fame and glory.'

'I don't understand,' Isaac replied.

'It's a simple equation. Here, she is paid a handsome salary, King's ransom, or in her case a Queen's ransom. Out there in theatreland, she'd have her name up in lights being paid a regular actor's wages. She wanted the fame, the adoring fans, and the money. She couldn't have it all.'

'Was she bitter as a result?'

'Maybe, probably explains why she screwed around so much.'

'Did she?' Isaac asked.

'Not as much lately.'

'How would you know that?'

'She'd tell me.'

'Why would she do that?'

'You don't get it, do you? I'm a bastard, she's a bitch. With me, she could be honest. I wouldn't repeat what she told me in confidence, would I?'

'I don't know. You said she was a bitch, screwed around.'

'Everyone knows about her screwing around. And as for the "bitch", she'd admit to that.'

'Her current disappearance, what do you reckon?'

'Unusual. She's done a vanishing trick before but still managed to show up for her scenes. This time, it's out of character. Look, I've got a show to run here. If there are no more questions, I need to get out there and start shouting at people.'

'Just one more question Jess O'Neill and Richard Williams?'

'Richard, I've known him for years. He can't keep his hands off the women, including Marjorie in the distant past. As soon as Jess turned up, he was on to her.'

'And she succumbed to the charm and the Ferrari?'

'They all do, but most wise up soon enough. He screwed Jess O'Neill a couple of times, that's all I know. The personal assistant, you've met her?'

'Sally Jenkins.'

'She's the standby. Just a bit of fluff, not very competent. A screw at the end of the day, that's how Richard sees it.' With that, the series producer rushed out of the door shouting at whoever. Isaac also noticed that his language had changed, and a great deal of bad language spewed from his mouth.

Chapter 7

With little more to achieve that day, Isaac and Farhan met back at Challis Street. Neither was in a good mood: Isaac, because of the revelation about Jess O'Neill; Farhan, because spending time with Barbara Reid and then Rosemary Fairweather had made him realise how dull his home life and his wife were.

'Farhan, what are we doing here? We used to spend our time on worthwhile murders, and here we are, just messing around, making nuisances of ourselves, asking dumb questions.'

'And the woman is likely to walk in the door at any time soon.'

'Is that likely?' Isaac asked.

'What do you mean?'

Isaac was sitting on his side of the office, the window behind him. Both men had loosened their ties. Unless the situation changed, they would leave early, which in their cases meant before 8 p.m.

Neither was anxious to leave, mainly because where they were heading was less agreeable than where they were now. Farhan had a dreary house in a dreary street with a dreary wife and a dreary television blasting out all day and virtually all night. The children gave him comfort, but they would be in bed, fast asleep by the time he arrived home. His wife, heavily pregnant, would not be receptive to his amorous advances, and after spending time with two not young but very attractive women, he was in need of an outlet. There was no outlet, he knew that. The best he could do was to keep working until exhausted and then go home to sleep.

'I believe Marjorie Frobisher to be dead,' Isaac said.

'Why do you come up with that conclusion?' Farhan could see them remaining in the office for a few more hours. He recognised he had the traits of a workaholic, but he could never be sure if his diagnosis was correct, or whether it was a result of an unsatisfactory home life. It caused him great conflict. He had attempted a discussion with the Imam at the local Mosque that he tried to visit every Friday for Jummah, the most significant prayer time in the Muslim calendar. He rarely made it, and would on most occasions make his prayers in a quiet part of the office, or out at a crime scene.

The Imam, although excessively conservative, could offer no tangible advice other than 'Allah will guide you. It is for you to trust in his wisdom.'

'Let's look at the facts,' Isaac said. He was on his third cup of coffee, and hunger had set in. A potential world-class runner in his day, sub-ten seconds for the one hundred metre dash, but he was not as dedicated as he should have been, and academia had been where his parents wanted him to focus. He reflected on that fact as he ordered the pizza, the third that week, and noticed his slight paunch, a clear indication of too much fast food and lack of exercise.

'I realise we don't have a corpse,' Isaac said as he consumed the last slice of pizza.'

'You may well be right. Detail your analysis,' Farhan said.

'One, she's disappeared before, but never for so long, two, she's never missed her work obligations, and three, there's the interest of the so-called influential persons.'

'There are a lot of uncertainties in there. It wouldn't hold up in a court of law.'

'Farhan, we're not a court of law. We are just speculating.'

'Okay, then let's analyse what we know.'

Isaac stood up, moved over to the whiteboard and started to write. The whiteboard marker was dry. He chose another. It worked. 'Firstly, it is now over four weeks,' he said, 'almost five since she was last sighted. The most she has disappeared before has been a week to ten days.'

'What about the SMSs?'

'If it's not her, then someone else is sending them.'

'But why?'

'What if someone doesn't want us to know she's dead?'

'Is that possible?' Farhan asked.

'What else can it be?'

'Can we prove this?'

'I don't see how we can. We know the general location of the SMSs, but they are only triangulated off the nearest communication towers. They will be accurate to within ten, twenty yards at most, maybe more if it's a remote area.'

Farhan moved to the whiteboard. 'If one of the SMSs came from a remote location in the countryside it might be possible to pinpoint it. If the area is sparsely populated, then maybe it's possible.'

'And then one of us goes there and starts sniffing around.'

'It's a long shot, but what have we got to lose?'

'Okay, let's do that.' Isaac continued his analysis; Farhan resumed his seat after idly drawing a circle on the whiteboard and then rubbing it off.

'Secondly, she has never missed a work commitment before. That validates my opinion that she is dead. From what we know of the woman, she would not have missed her opportunity to play the grieving sister when her on-screen brother died. It would have been irresistible for her.'

Farhan could only agree. He didn't mention that his wife had put forward that conclusion. *A housewife and she comes up with a better result,* Farhan thought.

'These so-called influential persons, any luck there?' Isaac asked. He had resumed his seat. A cursory glance at the clock revealed that it was after ten. Outside, it was dark, and the rain had started. He sent a text message. He did not want to conclude the day with a hot drink and a cold bed.

'Not really. The most I've found out is that there have been a few previous lovers of significance, but they're not recent.'

'Her agent, what did she have to say?'

'She had plenty to say, but then she started clamming up.'

'Why?'

'She was very agreeable, as was her PA, but once I started to dig deeper, she hurried me out of the room. She knows the dirt, or at least some of it.'

'And she was not going to dish it out to you?' Isaac said, aware that Farhan's easy and pleasant manner of drawing out information, especially from women, was exceptional.

'If we have a body, she will give names.'

'That doesn't help us much, does it?'

'We're at a dead end,' Farhan said.

Isaac, before he could respond, was momentarily distracted by an SMS on his phone, *'see you in one hour'*. At least his bed would be warm tonight. 'Farhan, let's wrap it for this evening, meet tomorrow early and discuss our strategy. Interviewing people will not get us anywhere. We need to go and find this woman, or what remains of her.'

Farhan agreed. He had heard the beep on Isaac's phone, seen his smirking smile. He wished that it had been him going home to a willing and liberated woman. He had little to look forward to except the sullen expression on his wife's face, and a complaint about the late hour.

Chapter 8

Sophie White was a decent person. Isaac knew that well enough. They had met three years earlier, during an investigation he had conducted into the murder of a hooligan in an alley in Brixton. It had appeared to be a case of rival gangs indulging in a tit-for-tat: 'you kill one of ours, we'll kill one of yours'.

That was how they wanted to record it down at the police station. It was just too much paperwork, and one less hooligan only served society well. The police realised that catching the guilty gang members was the ideal, but invariably there were extenuating circumstances: still a minor, self-defence, deprived childhood, mentally unstable. There were just too many opportunities for the guilty party to get off: slap on the back of the hand, community service, or time in an air-conditioned reform home.

That was how Isaac's boss saw it. A gnarled, old-school policeman, he remembered a time when a kick up the arse and a good beating were perfectly acceptable forms of crime deterrent. He didn't hold with the modern style of policing: too politically correct, too cosmetic, too soft on the criminals. He believed that a villain respects authority and strength and that the police handbook did little to help.

Isaac, then a detective sergeant, fresh out of uniform, understood his plight, but he had been university educated, his boss had not. Thirty years previously, a different style of policing was suitable. Those were the days before heavy drugs, Islamic terrorism, and a population explosion. Isaac had studied the period. His boss had been prepared to write off the hooligan's death as death by misadventure, person or persons unknown.

Sophie White had changed all that. She lived in Twickenham, worked in Brixton as a social worker. As Isaac was wrapping up the case at his boss's insistence, she had come forward with new information. She had seen a person running away from the alley, his arm covered in blood.

The inevitable questions had come up when she walked into the police station: Why had she waited so long to come forward? Why did she believe it was not gang-related? Did she recognise the person?

She had answered them all with aplomb. One, she had just finished work and was heading to the airport. Her sister in Canada was getting married, she was the maid of honour – it was checked out, found to be true. Two, the person she saw did not dress like a gang member. There was no hooded jacket, no trainers, no surly look about the individual – in fact, he was dressed well in a suit. Three, no, she did not recognise the person, although it was not an area where you saw men wearing suits too often.

With the case reopened and his boss none too happy, it was left to Isaac to do the legwork, to further interview Sophie White and to wrap up the case, *tout de suite*. His boss had just bought a renovator's delight in France as a retirement project and was continually trying out his basic French. Isaac, who had studied French at school and spoke with a reasonable fluency, ended up the

49

recipient of some very crude French with a pronounced cockney undertone. It grated on Isaac's nerves, but he said little, only offered encouragement.

Sophie White proved to be a good witness with a remarkable skill. She had a photographic memory and was able to give an accurate description of what she had seen. She was able to remember the detail in the clothes of the assailant, the scuff mark on his shoes, his hair, which side it was parted, what colour and so on. It had been half-light, dusk when the attack had taken place. She had not seen the attack although she had seen the blood. As she explained, it happened all too often in the neighbourhood. Normally, she would not have stopped at the shop across the road from the alley, but she was feeling at ease, and her sister had asked for some favourite chocolates, not the sort they sold out at the airport.

The hooligan's name was Michael O'Leary. He had been born in the area, ran with a gang of ne'er-do-wells down by the water's edge. Nineteen and barely literate, apart from a few run-ins with the police he had not been in much trouble. He was of a lost generation with no hope of redemption. He had been cocky in his early teenage years, bragging about why he didn't need an education and how he had wagged school. 'What do those cock-sucking teachers know? It's out on the street that matters,' he would say.

Those he bragged to had ended up on the street as he had, indulging in gang-related warfare, partaking in petty theft when they could, and major theft if they had the brain power for such an activity, which most did not.

It transpired that he had got a casual job as a runner for an illegal gambling syndicate. They would organise the dogs for fighting in an old warehouse close to the docks. He would collect the money, transport it as required, and receive a commission for his efforts. He thought he was smart in creaming off another one per cent. It was an easy scam, virtually undetectable. An intelligent person could have made an easy one hundred pounds every few days, but O'Leary was not smart; he had got the percentages wrong. He had taken ten percent, due to his inability to listen to the 'cock-sucking teachers' that he had been so critical of.

The syndicate knew immediately. They sent in one of their people to teach him a lesson: a severe beating, a few broken bones and don't do it again. The story once they had picked up the killer – a standover merchant from up north – was that he had been brought down by the syndicate. And that O'Leary was not willing to take his punishment and had drawn a knife. The killer stated it was self-defence; he received ten years for manslaughter.

Sophie and Isaac became an item, and she had moved in with him for a while. A brutal childhood, a violent marriage in the past – domesticity did not suit her. She felt love for Isaac, he felt a fondness for her, but she could not commit and had decided that she needed a man and sex, but on her terms.

She and Isaac had formed a deep bond, and a phone call from either would often result in a coupling of bodies, no commitment. It suited Isaac, although he found sex without love intimidating. For Sophie, it proved an ideal arrangement.

She had sent the *'see you in one hour'* SMS.

***

The next day Farhan met Robert Avers, the now apparently long-suffering husband of the missing woman. This time, Avers had agreed to meet at his house in Belgravia. The detective inspector was more relaxed than in his previous encounters with the husband, and certainly more sober than their time at the Churchill Arms in Kensington. He did not want to repeat that experience.

Avers, accommodating as usual, welcomed him into the house. 'Detective Inspector Ahmed. Pleased to see you.' Still polite, still friendly, but the previous bon vivant was missing. The man, dressed in a suit, had a dejected appearance.

'Detective Inspector,' he confided, 'I'm worried. It's just been too long.'

'But you said she has done this in the past.'

'Not for this length of time,' Avers replied. Farhan could see the man was visibly distressed.

'There have been more than a few men over the years,' Farhan said.

'That's right…'

'And ideally, you would have preferred none?'

'It's how she's wired. She needed the men, the thrill, the sexual encounters.'

'You didn't approve?'

'I always assumed the need would pass eventually and then all would be fine.'

'Has that time arrived?'

'I believe so, but why this disappearance? I just don't understand it.'

'Sorry, I need to ask.'

'There had been some lovers in the past; some before we met who are now influential men in this country.' Avers wanted to talk; Farhan willing to let him continue. Avers was tense, sitting upright on a hard chair in the sitting room; Farhan sat back on the comfortable sofa. His posture looked relaxed; he was not. He switched off his phone. The worst distraction was it ringing at the moment of confession or revelation.

Chapter 9

'What did you gain from Robert Avers?' Isaac asked Farhan in the office, their end of day meeting. He was still in a good mood, a leftover from the night before and Sophie.

Farhan had had no such romantic encounter, only a lecture from his wife on why he did not spend more time with the children, how he loved his work more than her, and what time of the night did he think that was to come home?

'Robert Avers is a broken man, seriously worried,' Farhan said, although he was distracted. He realised his welcome home of the previous night would only be repeated, once he left the office. He sighed to himself. It was true, he did love his work more than his wife, but then work was exciting, whereas she was not, and as for his children, he did have some regrets, although he tried to keep Sundays free for them. Not always successfully, though.

'Let's state that the woman is dead,' Isaac said.

'I thought we agreed on that yesterday.'

'You're right, but we still maintained a glimmer of hope. Let's throw that out of the window and go for broke. No longer do we regard this as a missing person investigation. Now, we classify it as a murder enquiry.'

'Can we do that?'

'Officially, it may be difficult. Unofficially, I don't see a problem.'

'I still think we need to bring the Super in on this. Maybe grill him some more as to what he knows.' Farhan made the suggestion, realising that Isaac and their boss had an easier relationship, and Isaac would be the better of the two to do it.

'I'll phone him now,' Isaac said. Before he could call, his phone rang. He excused himself from the room. Farhan could hear a muffled conversation. Isaac returned sheepishly five minutes later.

'Important?' Farhan asked.

'Jess O'Neill.'

'Some new evidence?'

'Maybe, maybe not. It's more likely a ruse to meet up.'

'She's a good-looking woman.' Farhan had seen a photo.

'Good-looking she may be, but we've just upgraded this to a murder investigation. It wouldn't look right if I were playing around with a potential suspect, would it?'

'And if she wasn't a potential suspect?'

'You know the answer to that already.' Isaac smiled.

Isaac, no longer making excuses for a possible future romantic encounter, phoned their boss. It was nine in the evening, but Isaac knew his phone call at such an hour would not cause any problems.

'Sir, we want to upgrade this to a murder investigation.'

'Okay, stay where you are. I'll be in the office within the hour,' Goddard said.

It was closer to ninety minutes when he arrived, pizza box in hand. Isaac, who had promised to look after his diet better, could only thank him for the food.

Farhan could see that it was going to be a later finish than the previous night. *Maybe she'll be asleep when I finally make it home*, he thought, but realised it was just wishful thinking.

Isaac was the first to speak after they had finished with the pizza. 'These so-called influential persons, are they critical to the investigation?' His question was levelled at the detective superintendent.

'You're asking questions I'm not able to answer.'

'But why? If it's a murder investigation, doesn't that change the situation?'

'I don't see how.' The detective superintendent appeared to be stalling. 'There's no deceased, so how can you call it a murder investigation?'

'We're just calling it a murder enquiry. Do you want to make it official?'

Richard Goddard sat upright before he continued. 'I don't know the full story, not much more than you. Dead is okay by them. It's if she is alive that worries them,' Richard Goddard said.

'What do you mean?' Isaac could see them treading where they were not wanted, asking questions certain people did not want to be asked.

'Isaac,' his senior said, 'drop the case. Just declare that she has gone missing.'

'But why? I thought we were meant to find her. Are you suggesting we should walk away from a potential murder?' Isaac sensed the trepidation in his senior officer. It was something he had not seen before.

'We must. I'll tell my contact that we're pulling out. I'll tell him that the leads have gone cold. She's disappeared of her own free will, and will no doubt reappear when she feels inclined.'

'Do you believe what you just said?' Isaac looked the senior officer direct in the eyes.

'If her reappearance frightens some people, then what will happen if you manage to find out why she's disappeared?'

'Is that a reason to pull back?' Isaac asked. He realised what their boss was trying to say, Farhan did not.

'Some people have a reason to wish her dead. Have we considered what they might do to keep it that way?'

'Do you think it's as bad as that?' Isaac asked.

'Official Secrets Act? What do you think?'

'I believe you're probably right.'

'Then we pull out?' Richard Goddard posed a rhetorical question.

Isaac looked at Farhan. 'What do you reckon?'

'We continue.' Farhan was resolute.

'I was told by my contact that if you get close, I was to communicate with him,' Goddard said.

'We'll agree to that.' Isaac looked at Farhan, who nodded in agreement.

The detective superintendent excused himself and left the room. He returned five minutes later. 'I'm meeting with my contact tomorrow at eight in the morning. I will brief you on my return.' It was already two in the morning. Fifteen minutes later, all three left the office: Isaac to an empty bed, Farhan to a complaining wife, and Richard Goddard to a comfortable house in a pleasant suburb. Detective Superintendent Goddard was a worried man. He knew he would not sleep much that night.

***

Angus MacTavish showed none of the affability he had shown the detective superintendent on his previous visit. The man was not in good humour. 'I told you to keep your people out of this, Detective Superintendent Goddard.'

'I was under the impression that the investigation was to continue.' The detective superintendent's hackles raised by the tone of the man in front of him: the man who had deliberately failed to shake his hand.

'I thought I made it clear that they were to focus on finding the woman, not delve into speculation as to her importance.'

'It's a police investigation. How do you think it's conducted? They pry, probe, ask awkward questions, and dive into the dirty laundry that everyone carries around as baggage.'

'Don't get smart with me, Goddard. I know how the police work.'

Richard Goddard assumed the changed attitude came with being the Government Chief Whip: when all was going well – magnanimous and affable; when it wasn't – exactly what he was experiencing now. He saw no reason to let the man ride roughshod over him. He had not become the senior officer of the Homicide and Serious Crime Command at Challis Street by allowing aggressive and bombastic individuals to take control.

'Sir, your attitude is not conducive to this meeting. Last time I was here, you were more agreeable.'

'That was different.' It was clear that Angus MacTavish was used to putting other people on the spot, making them feel uncomfortable. He did not enjoy the policeman's comment.

'What was different? The fact that you fobbed me off by appealing to my good nature?'

'No, of course not; well, maybe. Apologies, this is placing me in an awkward position,' MacTavish said.

'And my people in possible danger?'

'That's possible.'

'I can call them off. Is that what you want?'

'I'm not sure. The problem is that I don't know the full story, just some parts of it.'

'Are you saying there may be some validity in them continuing?'

'We still need to find out the truth. It was one thing to be out looking for a missing woman, but if we find her murdered, then by whom? The answer may have repercussions that none of us can comprehend.'

With both men more relaxed, MacTavish called for some tea. Mrs Gregory, after a short delay, entered the room and served the tea. Both men moved from the formal seating to a couple of more comfortable chairs to continue the discussion.

Mrs Gregory, polite and agreeable, indulged in some banter with her boss. *She must have heard the raised voices*, Richard Goddard thought. *Must be used to it, I suppose.*

With the tea poured, MacTavish spoke again, this time in a more agreeable manner, 'Have your people seen any unfamiliar faces?'

'Should they have?'

'They're being watched, I'm sure of it.'

'By whom? Or is that secret?'

'I would say the security services. MI5, probably.'

'What does this woman know that's so important?'

'Detective Superintendent, I'll level with you. Initially, I thought this was about an affair she had when she was young with a senior member of the government.'

'What's so wrong about that? We live in liberated times. It's hardly a case for murder.'

'That's what I would have thought, but there was a child.'

'What about the child?'

'I don't know. It was a different time, the baby was adopted.'

'There are large swathes of the public that would see that as unacceptable.'

'Which part? Having a child out of wedlock, or the adoption?' MacTavish asked.

'Depends on which public we're talking about.'

'The voting public.'

'A child out of wedlock, thirty plus years ago, would have been seen as sinful. Necessary to cover up at all costs. Even so, would this being revealed affect the outcome of an election?'

'It could make a difference if the parties were running neck and neck, especially if the woman has been murdered.'

'That's how my detectives see it. It's the only conclusion.'

'I don't believe the government would condone murder. Silence the woman, prevent publication of her life story, but murder?'

'Are you saying that if she is found murdered, it has more sinister undertones?'

Angus MacTavish paused for a while. He seemed to the detective superintendent to be doing mental calculations, analysing the pros and cons of the situation. 'If it is found that she has been murdered, it can only mean one thing,' he said.

'Yes?'

'It's not because of an illegitimate birth and an adoption.'

'Then what is it about?'

'I don't know, and I need to know. We all need to know if we are to make rational decisions.'

'And whether it will impact the result of the forthcoming election?'

'I think an electoral result for or against the ruling party may be a minor issue if people are willing to commit murder, and on the face of it an officially condoned murder.'

'An assassination, is that what you are saying?'

'I believe that is what I am saying.' Angus MacTavish's affable manner had changed, not to anger against Richard Goddard, but to worry as to what this all meant.

'Detective Superintendent, your two men. Brief them as you see fit, and put them out in the field. Make sure they are carrying weapons. This is possibly going to be nasty.'

'Who will you inform?'

'The prime minister, in the strictest confidence,' MacTavish replied.

'Is he the father?'

'Information on a need-to-know basis. You know that.'

'On a need-to-know basis. That's correct.'

Chapter 10

Isaac and Farhan, not clear about the direction to take, and temporarily out of leads, had taken the morning in a leisurely manner. They saw no reason to continue until their senior returned from meeting with his contact. Isaac never asked the name, although he had a shrewd idea who it was.

Farhan had managed to take the children to school for the first time in a month; Isaac just lay in bed for an extra hour and thought about Jess O'Neill. He could not see her as a murderer. However, he had learnt a long time ago that the least likely person, especially in a murder case, often turns out to be the culprit. Jess O'Neill seemed to have no connection to Marjorie Frobisher, other than they were work colleagues and Jess had told Marjorie that her starring days were drawing to a close. There was still the issue of Jess and Richard Williams. *Could she have screwed Williams just because he drove a Ferrari and was rich?* He resolved to find out.

Just as Isaac intended to roll over for another five-minute nap, the phone rang. 'Two o'clock, your office. Make sure DI Ahmed is there as well.' Richard Goddard had made the call as he exited MacTavish's office.

Isaac and Farhan were in the office well in advance of the nominated time. Richard Goddard, a stickler for punctuality, arrived on the dot. He had not brought a pizza this time; Isaac was thankful.

'If she has been murdered, then the situation has changed,' the detective superintendent commenced hesitantly.

'Let's assume she has,' Isaac said.

'Her death would be advantageous.'

'Are we condoning murder here, sir?' Farhan asked.

'That's a preposterous statement.' Goddard was not amused.

'Your statement was ambiguous. Farhan was right to ask.' Isaac had almost made the same remark.

'Let me clarify.' Goddard said. 'It is evident from my contact that certain people would not be sorry to hear of her demise.'

'And why?' Isaac asked.

'She has, or had, information that would prove both embarrassing politically and personally.'

'Would they be willing to kill her to prevent that information being revealed?'

'My contact assures me they would not.'

'And others?'

'I don't believe they would have given the authority for her assassination.'

'Are you certain?' Farhan asked.

'I can't be sure of anything. I may have been fed a line. Have you seen anyone suspicious?'

Isaac answered first. 'I've not seen anyone.'

'DI Ahmed?'

'Sir, I thought it was suspicious at the time.'

'What was?'

'The time I went to the Churchill Arms with Robert Avers. There was one man. I assumed he was a local propping up the bar. Then today, when I dropped the children at school, I could swear I saw him across the road from the school.'

'Are you certain?' Isaac asked.

'I believe I am. What does this mean?'

'We're treading on toes, and they don't like it. This is where it gets complicated. We're possibly upsetting powerful and dangerous persons.'

'What kind of persons?' Isaac asked.

'The type who carry guns and MI5 identification. They may just be doing surveillance, but who knows?'

'Are you serious?' Isaac asked.

'Deadly serious. There are two options here. The first is we back off.'

'And the second?'

'If you continue, it could get nasty.'

'I'm not one for backing off,' Isaac said.

'Neither am I,' Farhan agreed.

'Very well. You will need to carry guns, just in case.'

***

Barely interrupted by the disappearance of Marjorie Frobisher, production of the soap opera watched by millions continued – skilled scriptwriting had glossed over her disappearance: nervous breakdown due to shock over her brother's death, followed by a heart attack, followed by death.

The show had even managed to ensure that the long unbroken run of record ratings continued. The storyline had gone on for six weeks, long enough according to the market researchers. In the seventh week, five weeks since Isaac and Farhan had become involved, she finally died. The hospital scene: her lying in the hospital, face mask supplying oxygen. A stand-in actress with similar features, or in this case a lie-in, as all she had to do was remain motionless.

The death spread over two weeks; the viewing audience hit over nine million. It was regarded as a great success, celebrated with gusto by those remaining in the production, production staff and actors alike.

The magazines reported her death in detail, interviewed people who Marjorie Frobisher had worked with. None wanted to be the person to spill the beans: to tell the world that she was a promiscuous bitch and good riddance. Not until a dishevelled and by now homeless Charles Sutherland, the former Billy Blythe in the soap opera, was waylaid one morning as he dragged his weary body along to the local charity soup kitchen.

He had hit rock-bottom. In less than two months he had gone from famous to forgotten to destitute. He had milked it for a few weeks after his removal from the show, but despondency had driven him to a binge of expensive alcohol and even more expensive women. The parties he had thrown, the money he had spent, the cocaine he had snorted were legendary. The so-called friends while he was throwing the money around, plentiful. The so-called friends after he was evicted from his upmarket accommodation for non-payment of rent and for trashing the place, non-existent. It was a bleary-eyed morning after his unceremonious eviction, basically a kick in the arse from some thugs employed by the landlord, closely followed by his few meagre belongings. The landlord seized anything of value and dumped the rest on the street with their owner.

Two days later and sober, Charles Sutherland acknowledged the reason for his current situation: Marjorie Frobisher. *She was the bitch*, he thought. *She put me here.* He was still an arrogant man, desperate as he blamed his life on others, not himself.

***

When the gossip magazine journalist found Charles Sutherland sitting on the pavement not far from the soup kitchen, holding a roll in one hand, coffee in a paper cup in the other, he was, at first, reluctant to talk. He thought she had come to do a story on him and his fall from grace. He was correct in his evaluation until he started to talk about why he was out on the street.

Classically trained, destined for great things, Sutherland told her. Boring and mundane, that was what Christy Nichols, a freelance contributor to the scurrilous magazine that catered to the followers of minor celebrities and nonentities, thought. She had found him, thought there may be a story in it, a story that she could get published in the magazine; but the more he talked, the more she realised he offered no great copy. He was an arrogant, overweight, and smelly man, worthy of no more than a photo and a thousand words.

She prepared to leave: her, with the picture and a signed clearance to use it; he, with two hundred pounds to use wisely or otherwise, although she knew which option Charles Sutherland would choose, as did Charles Sutherland.

'You know about Marjorie Frobisher?' he said.

'Her disappearance?' Christy Nichols sat down again on the dirty pavement, her freshly pressed, cream-coloured skirt picking up some dirt marks. She was a good-looking woman, a little overweight, which was how Sutherland liked his women. He had no time for skinny tarts with no breasts and ribs so prominent you could play a tune on them.

'Not that.'

'What then?'

'She was a bitch, you know that?' Sutherland had nothing new. Christy Nichols stood up again. There was no news here, she reasoned. She needed to change, and now there was a dry-cleaning bill to worry about. A glamorous job, others thought, writing copy for a magazine, but she was freelance, paid for the published copy, not for sitting with a man down on his luck. She had no more time, and there was a minor starlet due at the airport within a couple of hours. *Another empty-headed individual with inflated breasts, wafting into England, hoping to resurrect her career*, she thought. The celebrity was better known more for her poor choices in men and her predilection for drugs than her acting ability. She was good copy, and if Christy could score an interview and a few photos, it would pay more than a soap opera cast member, once important, now forgotten.

'There's something else.'

'What do you mean?' The disappearance of Marjorie Frobisher was still newsworthy. Her character, Edith Blythe, had been kept in the public eye for weeks due to the clever scripting on the programme. Some magazines, even the one where Christy hoped to sell the story, were running articles on what type of funeral she would have. Would it be a cremation or burial? What clothes would her friends on the programme wear? How many episodes would be consumed by the funeral and the mourning afterwards? Her death on the programme had been milked for all it was worth, and so would her funeral.

'She screwed around.'

'Hardly newsworthy, is it?'

'Maybe it is if you know who she was screwing.' Sutherland let the conversation hang.

'What do you have?' *To hell with the skirt and the dry cleaner*, the reporter thought. She was aware of the rumours, most people were, especially in the industry, but it was never regarded as good copy. Marjorie Frobisher was revered as a celebrity; her character, Edith Blythe, a pillar of society. One magazine had alluded to her unusual marriage, tested the waters, but the response had not been favourable, so they had desisted.

'I'll talk when I'm paid, only then.'

'No one's going to pay just because you make a statement that you have something of interest.'

'*Something of interest.*' Sutherland emphasised the words the reporter had just said.

'Is it that good?'

'It's dynamite.'

'I can't get anyone interested just on your word. I need facts.'

'Talk to your editor. Tell her what I've got.'

'And what have you got?'

'Unmarried pregnancy, a child adopted. Is that enough to be going on with?'

'Marjorie Frobisher. Do you mean Marjorie Frobisher?'

'Who the hell do you think I mean?' Charles Sutherland said.

***

It looked to Isaac and Farhan as if, finally, they were to get down to some real policing. Both Isaac and Farhan were armed. Isaac had one issue to clear up – Jess O'Neill and Richard Williams. Farhan felt he needed to update Robert Avers.

Robert Avers took it well. Farhan saw no reason not to tell him what they believed. Avers' reaction was of a man expecting such a statement.

Isaac's issue was complicated. His discussions with Jess O'Neill were meant to be strictly professional, yet if she had been sleeping with Richard Williams… It hardly seemed relevant to the case, although he tried to convince himself that it was. He decided to resolve the confusion in his mind once and for all.

It was a good day out at the production lot. For once, it was sunny, and Isaac had to admit the fictional town looked good. As he walked down the main street, past where the Saturday market was held, left at a grocery store on the corner, across the street and down a side alley to where Jess O'Neill's office was situated, he reflected on the task ahead. At least, that was what Isaac tried to think about. He wanted to seem professional when he encountered the woman, not a love-sick puppy, which he thought he was at the present moment.

He saw her soon enough, obviously in conference with a group of production people. She soon concluded the meeting and came over to him: too friendly, too close. He pulled back a little, she came forward. The safest approach was for him to take a seat and then her seat would, at least, maintain a professional distance. It did not as she leant forward and adjusted the position of the chair.

Isaac saw no reason to attempt to move again. He felt embarrassed, hopeful it did not show, although blushing on a black man is not the same as on a white man.

'Jess, there are just a few questions.'

'Yes, Isaac.' *Too pleasantly said*, he thought. He endeavoured to sit back on his chair. It did not help.

'We're concerned about Marjorie Frobisher's disappearance. We need to cast our net wider.'

'What does that mean?'

'I will be moving out of London, travelling for a few days.'

'Does that mean I won't be seeing you?' Too agreeable for Isaac, too tempting.

'That's correct. Before I leave, there are a couple of questions.'

'You've already said that,' she said. Isaac realised that she was on to him. She knew he was embarrassed, and she was clearly enjoying it. 'Just ask me straight. I'm certain I know the question.'

'Richard Williams…'

'You want to know whether I slept with him?'

'It's a loose bit of information that needs clarifying.'

'Not that it's relevant, but I know that Ian Stanley brings it up every chance he gets. He doesn't like it that a woman is his superior.'

'He was fine with me.'

'He's against anyone and anything that's not white and male. I'm surprised he was so pleasant to you.'

'He wasn't until he saw my badge.'

'For the record, and I do not see this as relevant, I did go out with Richard Williams a few times. He was good company and very generous, but I did not sleep with him.'

'Ian Stanley was just making mischief?'

'On one of the occasions, there was an exhibition of production equipment up north. We spent the night there, separate rooms.'

'I assume he tried it on?'

'Yes, of course, but I wasn't buying it.'

'Thank you for clarifying.'

'Now, Detective Chief Inspector Isaac Cook, was that question entirely professional?' She smiled as she made the comment.

'Purely professional.' Isaac tried to maintain a serious face, but couldn't. He smiled as well.

'For the record, I've made my choice.'

'Choice on what?'

'You did not make detective chief inspector by being naïve, did you?'

'Not at all, but we are treating this as a murder investigation.'

'And you can't be seen to be fraternising with a potential suspect?'

'That's about it.'

'I can assure you, I'm not guilty, but she could be a bitch. Not a difficult person to dislike.'

'I'll keep in touch.' He prepared to leave.

'If you want to phone and tell me you fancy me, professionally of course, then that will be okay, won't it?' She came near. She kissed him on the lips. Compromised, Isaac left soon after, but not before he had kissed her back. As he walked back down the main street on the production lot, he only hoped she was not involved.

Chapter 11

Isaac first noticed the car as he left the production lot. At any other time, he would have regarded it as inconsequential, but the situation had changed. As he weaved through the traffic, he noticed that the car kept reappearing. He wasn't sure how, as his car was a lot more powerful and he wasn't a slow driver. The car behind was pushing hard. He phoned Richard Goddard.

'Let it follow. Don't let them know you've seen them.' That was precisely what Isaac had intended in the first place. It was an unwelcome intrusion into the investigation, and a sour conclusion to an otherwise pleasant day. He failed to mention he had just kissed one of the people close to Marjorie Frobisher. He could only imagine his boss's reaction if he told him.

Isaac had planned the remainder of his day carefully. Jess was still off-limits, Sophie wasn't. He had planned to pick her up from her workplace, but decided against it with a car on his tail; better if she found her way to his apartment. She understood when he told her it was the pressure of work that prevented the pickup. As she said to him later: commitment-free and no obligation on either party to look out for the other. Pickups were not part of the deal; however, good company and good sex were.

With the car following, Isaac headed back to the office at Challis Street. Farhan was in the office. 'How's your day been?' Isaac asked.

'I told her husband that we believe his wife is dead.'

'How did he take it?'

'Better than expected. I believe he was prepared for the news.'

Farhan was not looking too well. Isaac asked the reason.

'My wife wants a separation. She believes I'm married more to this job than to her.'

'Is that possible in your religion?'

'It occurs, and besides this is England. She can do what she likes,' Farhan admitted.

'I always imagined she was a conservative woman.'

'She's certainly more pious than me. It's her mother, no doubt, who put her up to this, aiming to force me to make a choice.'

'Choice between what?' Isaac had come over to Farhan's desk, bringing a chair with him.

'Between her daughter and the police, what else?'

'But you need to make a living.'

'They believe I should be running a corner store.'

'You would be working more hours than you do now.'

'They have this idea that the shop will be downstairs and the family up.'

'What are you going to do?'

'It's the children, not my wife. They are my primary consideration.'

'Are you saying if she goes, she'll deny you visiting rights?'

'No, she can't do that. I'm worried they'll be susceptible to being radicalised.'

'Do you need time off to figure this out?' Isaac asked, although he could not see how he could accede to such a request, or how he could refuse.

'No. We've got a murder to solve, and besides, if those guys following us decide to take us out, then it's theoretical.' It was an attempt at lightening the sombre mood in the office. It did not work.

'Let's ignore those following us for the moment. We need to find a body, assuming she's dead.' Isaac was pleased that Farhan was staying on board. He was also glad that so far he had remained single. Sophie White had the right idea, he thought, but one day he could see stability and marriage and children, and in that order.

'Where's the first triangulation off her phone?' Farhan seemed to pick up in spirits after he had offloaded some of his burdens onto Isaac.

'Central Birmingham,' Isaac replied. 'Not much use to us, too many buildings, too much traffic. We need somewhere isolated.'

'We need a rural area, preferably with few buildings. A small village may be best. Even then, it will be like trying to find a needle in a haystack.'

'What else do we have?'

'Malvern, Worcestershire.'

'Too big, too many houses,' Isaac said.

'Not if there is a camera on every other lamppost.'

'That's true. What's the best way to check this out?'

'I'll go there,' Farhan offered.

'No, best if you stay here. See if you can draw a trace on any vehicle following you, and then talk to our boss. His contact may be able to help with identification.'

'You don't need to leave me here just because I've got family problems. My staying here won't change the situation, and besides, I'm not resigning from the police force. This is more than a job, it's a vocation. She doesn't understand. People sleep calmly in their beds at night because of us. What to do about my children? That's another story.'

It was later in the afternoon, after their discussion in the office, that Farhan left early to pick up his children from school. Isaac could see he was concerned, and he was making a special effort. He wondered for how long.

Police work, especially with the Murder Investigation Team, did not come with a nine to five schedule. Hours were flexible, forty a week according to the book, but most weeks more like sixty to seventy, sometimes eighty to ninety, and then there were the weekends. Saturdays, often working, Sunday, more times than he cared to remember. Sophie was flexible, Jess O'Neill may not be, but he'd take her in an instant. He put her out of his mind and left early as well.

Richard Goddard had organised a contact in Worcestershire, about three hours west, or it should be, but there was the London traffic to clear first. Isaac decided to leave early, before seven in the morning.

He wanted to call Sophie, although he didn't want her endangered. Those following him earlier in the day were unknown, possibly dangerous. Just as Isaac was leaving the car park his phone rang, hands-free.

'I'm being tailed,' Farhan said.

'Number plate?'

'I'll SMS it to you. Can you forward it to Detective Superintendent Goddard?'

'That's two to give to him.'

'You've got a tail as well?'

'Yes.'

'We'd better hope these guys are harmless. I'm heading to my home.'

'If they are who we suspect, they'll know your address already.' Isaac realised they would also know where he lived, probably knew about Sophie as well. There seemed no reason to worry. He called her. She would be over later.

***

Charles Sutherland was enjoying his redemption. The magazine had been suitably impressed, continued to be, as he revealed little snippets – enough to keep them dangling.

He was not a stupid man; he knew the value of a legally drawn up contract signed by both parties. He also knew the worth of some cash up front and the remainder when he delivered the dirt. If he gave too much, too quickly, their offer would reduce or evaporate. He was not willing to let that happen.

The mention of an open marriage titillated the magazine's editor, an attractive middle-aged woman constantly on the television offering advice on how to be successful as a female in a man's world, how to power dress, how to be like her. Sutherland found her obnoxious and overbearing, full of the smugness that comes with a portrayed persona and an inner bitchiness. He didn't trust her one bit. Sure, she was pleasant to his face, but he could see the sideways glances, the raised eyebrows when she looked over at her deputy – he had no idea what her function was in the office, didn't care either. They were paying the money and he wasn't going to upset the apple cart with a snide remark.

'You've given us very little.' The editor pressured for more.

'I've given you plenty,' Sutherland replied. The room he sat in, one of the best at one of the best hotels in the town, came with a well-stocked drinks cabinet, and the cost to him was zero. He was already halfway to drunk, and he was not going to let them get between him and the euphoria he was looking forward to. He had already phoned for a couple of high-class whores, and they were on the magazine's expense account.

Sutherland saw himself as Lazarus rising from the dead. He intended to milk it for all it was worth, and to hell with the bitch magazine editor and her girlfriend. The contract, legal and very tight, was well underway; some minor clauses to iron out, some significant money to be handed over, and then he would dish out the dirt. The magazine wanted more than salacious tittle-tattle, although it was such nonsense that drove the sales. They wanted names and events, and the more important, the more titled, and the more likely to fall from grace with a major embarrassment, the better.

'Look here,' Sutherland said. He was slurring his words, making suggestive glances at Christy Nichols, who had rescued him from obscurity. 'This will bring down the government. I guarantee you that.'

Christy Nichols, now on a suitable retainer from the magazine, had been assigned to ensure that Sutherland did not go blabbing his mouth off indiscriminately in a bar or elsewhere. She had been given a room next to his. She did not want to be there, but the retainer, the possible lift up in her career, in an industry that was full of casualties who did not make the grade, kept her firmly rooted.

She had agreed reluctantly, although she found Charles Sutherland to be a crude man with a debatable style of lovemaking. She had walked in on him when he was in full fettle with a couple of whores, all naked on the carpet in the main room. It was an innocent mistake on her part, as it was all quiet and they were hidden by the sofa. Upon seeing her, he had stood up, waved his insignificant wares at her and demanded that as he was her meal ticket, she had better strip off straight away and join in the fun.

The whores thought it was hilarious, but Christy Nichols assumed it was because they were being paid. She realised they were tolerating the nasty and unpleasant man for the same reason as her.

It was another two days before the contract was signed, and Charles Sutherland had to come forward with what he knew. He was a troubled man, not because of what he knew, but because the proof was vague. *What did he really know?* he thought. Certainly, there was plenty of innuendo, some prominent names and some – if it were true – information that would embarrass the government, especially its senior members. That's all he had, and how the editor and her lesbian friend would take it, he wasn't sure.

He decided to deal with the issue when it arose. In the meantime, he intended to enjoy the luxury on offer. He would have preferred Christy Nichols, the prudish prick-teaser as he saw her, but as she'd refused to have anything to do with him – *he should have put her availability in the contract*, he thought – then he would get her to sign for the whores. There was time to while away, and he wasn't going to sit reading a book, drinking a cup of tea, for anybody.

Chapter 12

It had been a miserable trip to Worcestershire for Isaac, rain all the way and his speed had been reduced as a result. It was close to four hours before he pulled into police headquarters in Worcester, the principal city in the county.

Inspector June Brown greeted him warmly after he had waited for ten minutes in reception at the modern, clinical looking building.

'Isaac, it's good to see you.' It was then he remembered her from his police training days. Then she had been a brunette, slim, with a figure that all the young police cadets had lusted after.

'June, long time, no see.' It was clear that he was embarrassed.

'You've forgotten me already,' she said, half-serious, half-teasing.

'No, of course not.' He had not forgotten her. The others cadets may have lusted, but it was only he who had sated the lust. She had latched onto him in the second week of training, only to let him go when the training concluded.

'Isaac, it was a good time, and you helped me through, but that's the past.'

'I never forgot you.'

'Don't talk rubbish,' she joked. 'Two weeks, and I guarantee you were shacked up with another female charmed by your obvious attributes.'

'That's not true,' he protested, not sure if she was serious or not.

'Look at me,' she said. 'I'm married with two kids, and the body not as you remember. I married an accountant, not as charming as you, but you're not the settling-down kind. You weren't then, I suppose you still aren't.'

Isaac had to admit that she had changed. Back then in training, she had a figure that could only have been described as sensational. What he saw now was a very attractive woman, but the weight had gone on, and the face had aged. He assumed he had changed as well, but he thought it could not be as much as her.

'Three,' he said.

'Three what?'

'Three weeks.'

'Okay, I was out by a week, but what woman is going to resist a man like you? You were gorgeous to women back then, still are. Am I correct?'

'I'm not sure about that, but so far I've not settled down. Tried to. A couple have moved in with me, or I've moved in with them, but it's not seemed to last for long.' He wondered if Jess O'Neill might be the one. He discounted the thought. He inwardly smiled, when he thought of the passionate embrace and the kiss when he had left her the last time.

With so much history between them, June and Isaac spent the next hour chatting about their lives. It was June who finally brought them back to the present situation.

'What's important about this woman?' she asked.

'I'm not sure I can tell you. Besides, I don't know too much myself.'

'I suppose it doesn't matter.' She resigned herself to the fact; she knew him well enough not to press for more.

'It's a directive from senior management to find this woman.'

'I know who she is, of course. The sad life of a married woman and mother, when watching the television becomes a nightly highlight.'

'It comes to us all, I suppose,' he said.

'Suburbia and raising a family has its drawbacks. I'm not complaining, though.'

Isaac felt the need to change the subject. She had become melancholy; better to focus on the missing woman. 'We know Marjorie Frobisher's phone was used there.'

'Are you certain she was though?'

'Cameras, surveillance, security may have picked her up.'

'I've already had someone looking at any there, although it's not London. There will not be so many. How long are you staying?'

'Until I get some answers on her whereabouts.'

'Good, then you can come over to the house for a meal one night.'

Isaac replied in the affirmative, but sitting down with the husband of a woman he had known intimately did not sit well with him. He would endeavour to steer away from the subject if it came up again.

The assumption that a camera would have picked up Marjorie Frobisher proved not to be so accurate. There were cameras in the banks, the hotels, even some of the shops, but relatively few of them kept the tapes for more than a couple of weeks. The stores were interested in shoplifters, and if none had been apprehended, then there was no reason to keep the record.

At the end of the first day, Isaac was anxious to get on with the task. So far, he had spent more time at the hotel than at police headquarters. It was not a case of avoidance, but the invitation to dine with the husband of a former lover continued to unsettle him.

'June, this invite to your house,' he tentatively broached the subject at the office the next day. There had been some developments in the case, but before she told him, he wanted to clear the air, state his position.'

'Tonight, at eight, come casual; my husband is looking forward to meeting you.'

'I'm not sure I can come.'

'Why?'

'It's a little embarrassing.'

'Isaac, what do you mean?'

'Our past history.'

'How quaint,' she replied, mocking him with fluttering eyelids and a coy smile.

'I'm not sure your husband would want a past lover in his house.'

'You mean the man who took my virginity.'

'Did I?'

'Of course you did, and as to being embarrassed, do you think I never slept with another man before I married my husband? I lived with his best man for six months before I started going out with him. It was even mentioned in the wedding speeches. Everyone thought it was hilarious.'

'If you're certain it's alright.'

'Of course it's alright. Anyway, you wanted an update.'

'What have you found?'

'Marjorie Frobisher stayed at one of the hotels in Malvern. She had a wig on and her face concealed. The receptionist at the hotel identified her, recognised her even, although she didn't like it and left soon after. She used a false name.'

'Any ideas after that?'

'That's all there is. As to where she went?'

'You don't know?' Isaac asked.

'All the receptionist could tell us was that she took a taxi to Worcester. The driver dropped her off at the railway station. From there she could have gone anywhere.'

Isaac's time in Worcester was at an end. It was not the function of a detective chief inspector to find out where the woman had gone. He realised they needed more help in the office.

He had only one more obligation. June Brown's husband proved to be an excellent host, the meal was perfect, and the wine that Isaac had taken, ideal. His premonition about how awkward the situation would be was ill-founded. He left for London early the next morning.

***

Isaac arrived back before eight in the morning. He had purposely left early to avoid the traffic. Not that it made any difference, as there was early morning fog on the motorway. For half the distance his speed was almost down to a crawl. It was four and a half hours of stop-start driving. Meeting up with a past lover had left him reminiscing. He felt the need of a woman. Sophie would almost certainly come over that night if he gave her a call.

He had barely walked into the office – Farhan was already there – when his phone rang. 'You've heard the news?' It was his detective superintendent on the other end.

It was evident from Richard Goddard's tone that there had been a development. 'What's happened?' Isaac could see that an early get-together with Sophie was looking unlikely.

'We've got a suspicious death.'

'Marjorie Frobisher?' Isaac asked.

'It's her brother. I heard ten seconds before you walked in,' Farhan said.

'I didn't know she had a brother,' Isaac said.

'The fictitious one.' Richard Goddard seemed excited.

'Billy Blythe?'

'That's right. The actor who played him, Charles Sutherland.'

'Do we have any details?' Isaac asked.

'Vague at the present moment. The body was found twenty minutes ago, at his hotel.'

'I need to be over there with DI Ahmed,' Isaac said.

'The local police will be taking control.'

Isaac and Farhan left the office soon after. Isaac mulled over how this impacted on the missing woman but kept it to himself. He was still tired from the drive, and not in the mood to indulge in random conversation with Farhan, who looked excited, but distant.

The trip to the Savoy Hotel took twenty minutes. It was one of the best hotels in town, and Charles Sutherland's suite was one of the best. The media was already setting up on the street outside. He intended to find out how the information regarding a minor celebrity had been leaked. It was regarded as a suspicious death, not a murder, and definitely not a free-for-all.

'Farhan, what's the matter?' Isaac realised that something was troubling his colleague.

'It's my wife. She moved out, took the children.'

'When was that?'

'This morning, when I left the house early.'

'But why?'

'The normal. How I love my job more than her. How the children never see me.'

'Doesn't she realise how important our work is?'

'She's not rational. Mind you, if I had told her who the body is, then maybe she would have changed her mind.'

'It's hardly the basis for marriage, the machinations of a soap opera.'

'Agreed, but she's like so many others.'

'What do you mean?'

'The separation of fact from fiction.'

'I need you here now.' Isaac realised that Farhan should be dealing with personal issues, but now there was a real case. He could not let him take time off.

'I know, and besides, this is where I want to be.'

How many times had he heard it? Isaac thought. *No wonder the marriage breakdown rate is so high when the spouse and the family become the lesser priority.* He knew that Sophie was just a woman to spend time with, but Jess O'Neill may want a different kind of commitment, a commitment he was unable to give.

Downstairs, the hotel looked calm. Guests were checking in, checking out. The cafes and the restaurants were open; the people appeared to be oblivious to the death upstairs. How they could avoid the melee of media outside, he was not so sure, but some were probably used to media intrusion. He recognised a few famous faces as they moved through the foyer.

His train of thought was abruptly interrupted as they exited the lift on the top floor.

Outside the lift door, a well-presented fresh-faced police constable in uniform intercepted them. 'Sirs, this area is closed off.'

'Detective Chief Inspector Cook and Detective Inspector Ahmed,' Isaac said as they both presented their identification badges.

Clearing the first obstacle, they walked to where the constable had directed them.

'Yes, what can I do for you?' A tall, red-faced man, who, at least to Farhan, looked in need of a healthy diet, stood in their way as they entered Charles Sutherland's suite.

'Homicide and Serious Crime,' Isaac said.

'Sergeant Derek Hamilton, Charing Cross Police Station.'

'Good to meet you, Sergeant. I'm DCI Cook. My colleague is DI Ahmed.'

'I'll need to see your IDs, gentlemen.'

'Fine,' the sergeant said, after checking. 'Forensics is already here.'

It was clear that guests on either side of Sutherland's suite were being moved out, their luggage visible in the corridor.

'Inspector Barry Hopkirk. Pleased to meet you.' Isaac instinctively did not like the man on introduction. He appeared to be in his fifties. He wore an ill-fitting suit, crumpled as if he had slept in it, a tie skewed to one side.

Isaac saw no reason for subtlety. 'Is moving the other guests' luggage standard procedure?'

Hopkirk, a man with a short fuse, immediately went on the offensive. 'Is that a criticism?'

'This man's death is regarded as suspicious.'

'That may be, but when we arrived, there was only a dead body.'

'You're moving guests and their luggage off the floor. Have they been interviewed, checked for a possible weapon?'

'We've got their names; they're not exiting the building, only changing rooms. Besides, there's no sign of a weapon being used,' Hopkirk said.

'That may be, but have you considered that they may be involved?' There were clearly set down procedures in the case of a suspicious death, and Hopkirk was not following them.

'There was nothing suspicious when we arrived.'

'The Savoy Hotel, a former television celebrity. You don't think that's suspicious?'

'I'm not aware of his importance.'

'Charles Sutherland. Famous actor. Are you telling me that you have never heard of him?'

'I never made the association. All I saw was a dead body.'

'What do you have here?'

'Forensics will bring you up to speed. They're inside with the body. And make sure you put on footwear protectors,' Hopkirk said.

Isaac and Farhan moved to the room where the body had been found. 'Who is the crime scene examiner in charge here?' Isaac asked.

'Who's asking?' The reply came from a small man, bent over examining the body. He wore a white coverall, his hands gloved.

'Detective Chief Inspector Isaac Cook.'

'Give me a couple of minutes, and I'll be with you.'

The dead man was naked and sprawled on the floor. It was not a pleasant sight, as the victim was clearly overweight, verging on obese. It was clear from the faeces that his bowels had relaxed.

'Nasty business,' the small man said as he came over and shook hands with Isaac and Farhan. He had removed his gloves first, thrown them into a plastic bag. He was short, ridiculously short, and Isaac had to angle his neck down to look into his face, although mainly saw the top of his head. 'Gordon Windsor,' he said.

'I don't see any sign of violence,' Farhan said.

'And you won't.' The crime scene examiner spoke with a Welsh accent. He talked slowly. Isaac thought it might be a way of controlling a stutter.

'Why not?' Farhan asked.

'Poison.'

'How did you know it was murder?'

'I didn't. Hopkirk did.'

'I just blasted him out,' Isaac said.

'That may be, but he came here due to a death at the hotel. Apparently, standard procedure at the Savoy to call the local police when there's a death.'

Isaac realised that he may have been a little harsh on Hopkirk. If that proved to be the case, he would apologise later.

'How did Hopkirk figure it was murder?' Isaac asked.

'The body lying on the floor, the drooling, the defecation. He can tell you better than me, but my understanding is that he came here for a dead body, and then he found out about the wild parties and wondered if it was drug-related, overdose or something similar.'

'What did he find?'

'Cocaine, but not much else – certainly not enough to cause death. That's when he looked around, found clear evidence of poison.'

'Careless to leave the evidence here,' Farhan said.

'Careless or disturbed? I've no idea. That's for you to find out,' Gordon Windsor said as he removed his coveralls and picked up his bag. 'For me, it's to get the body back to the morgue, deal with Forensics and then write a report. It's going to be a long night. Wedding anniversary, I was going to take my wife out for a meal at an excellent restaurant. Curiously, the restaurant downstairs, just off the foyer. Hopefully, she'll understand.'

'Will she?' Farhan asked.

'She's used to it. She'll pretend to be upset, but she'll be fine.' Farhan could only reflect on why his wife was not as sympathetic, but he assumed that Gordon Windsor did not have a mother-in-law constantly in his wife's ear.

Chapter 13

With the crime scene examiner's departure, and Inspector Barry Hopkirk a little friendlier after Isaac had apologised to him, Isaac and Farhan returned to their office. Farhan could clearly see long hours on the case. He knew it would not help with his marriage. He had a job to do, a family to provide for, whether his wife liked it or not, and being miserable and moping around was going to solve little. He decided to snap out of it and get on with the job.

'This changes the situation,' Isaac said.

'The question is whether it's related to Marjorie Frobisher,' Farhan replied as he sipped his coffee. It was a little too hot for him.

'What do we know about Charles Sutherland? Could this be unrelated?'

'Possibly.'

'If it is linked, then you know what this means.'

'What did he know?'

'Or who was he?' Farhan put forward another possibility.

'What do you mean?'

'How did he get to know of anything worth selling? It's not as if Marjorie Frobisher went around the production lot sounding off to anyone in earshot. There's also the animosity between them.'

As expected, DS Goddard was soon in their office. 'Is it clearly murder?' he asked.

'There's a strong possibility,' Isaac replied.

'Not confirmed?'

'The crime scene examiner will let us know when the autopsy has been conducted, as well as keep up updated on the toxicology analysis on the contents of the bottle.'

'The poison was in a bottle?'

'That's what we are led to believe.'

'If it's a confirmed murder, then we'll need to set up a Murder Investigation Team.'

'We've just been discussing this,' Farhan said. 'We could do with the help, sir.'

'Isaac, you'll be the senior investigating officer. Is that okay with you?' the detective superintendent asked.

'Fine, sir.'

'Now, what do I tell my contact? He's bugging me for information.'

'Downing Street?'

'Isaac, it's best if you don't pry too much into my contacts.'

'What do you know?' Isaac asked.

'Not a great deal, other than Marjorie Frobisher would be better off dead, but the murder of Sutherland? That's another situation altogether.'

'There has been no connection made between the disappearance of one and the murder of the other,' Isaac said.

'Then make the connection,' the detective superintendent replied.

'And you, sir?' Farhan asked.

'I'll see what I can find out.'

'You'll talk to your contact?' Isaac asked.

'This afternoon. He wants an update. Give me what you can before then.'

Sophie messaged soon after Goddard had left the office. Isaac replied that it was not possible. She messaged back 'understood', which with her it was.

81

Farhan had received news that his children were at school and fine.

Isaac decided to travel out to the production lot. It was a murder unless confirmed otherwise, which seemed unlikely. For whatever reason, the people he had interviewed needed to be re-interviewed, including Jess O'Neill.

Farhan headed back to the hotel.

***

If they were aware out at the production lot that one of their former stars had met an untimely death, it was not apparent. The place was a hive of activity. Every time that Isaac had been out there in the past, it had been towards the end of the day or early morning.

The end of the day, they were invariably looking through the day's filming or else finalising the script for the next day's shooting. Early morning, the production people were still in the offices, and the cast were in their dressing rooms. This time, it was just after two in the afternoon. Isaac had been on the go since three in the morning and he was starting to feel a little weary. He knew it would pass once he started interviewing the people again.

He saw Jess O'Neill from a distance. He could see her arguing with someone, but then that was her job, and apparently she was good at putting people in their place, getting what she wanted.

Richard Williams was at the production lot. It seemed unusual to Isaac. He decided to talk to him first. He waylaid him as he walked swiftly towards the central offices. Isaac was well aware that Williams had seen him and had been trying to get out of his way. To Isaac, it was a red rag to a bull. He quickened his pace and caught up with Williams just as he opened the door to the first office.

'Mr Williams.'

'Now is not an ideal time.' Richard Williams said, catching his breath. He was not as young as Isaac, not as fit, although that didn't stop him when it came to chasing the women. Sally Jenkins was nowhere to be seen, but Isaac assumed she was back in the office in the city. *No reason to bring the end of the day bit of fluff out to the production lot,* Isaac thought. Richard Williams was always on the prowl, and the production lot would be a good place to look for a new conquest. There were invariably some extras hired for the day. The pretty, young, and female would be easy prey for someone as suave as Williams. Isaac had noticed the Ferrari when he parked his car.

'It's important.' Isaac replied.

'You're here about Charles Sutherland, I assume?'

'You've heard?'

'It's all over the media. They say he's been murdered.'

'There has been no official confirmation.'

'I'll take your word on that. The media will beat anything up.'

'Officially, the death is regarded as suspicious.'

'Suspicious! That's as good as saying he's been murdered.'

'Not at all,' Isaac replied. 'A well-known person is found dead in a hotel room. There has to be an autopsy and an official investigation. That does not mean murder, or not to the police.'

'It certainly does to the media; you must know that by now.'

'In the short time that I have been involved in the Marjorie Frobisher case, I have formed a greater understanding of how the media works: hyperbole, innuendo, assumption, and clever wording.'

'Yes, you've picked it up. Marjorie Frobisher, is that murder as well? I didn't know you had found her body.'

'I need to be careful what I say. Marjorie Frobisher is still declared as missing and there is not a corpse. Is that clear enough?'

'Clear enough. Unless you have anything more to talk about, I'm busy.'

'Why are you here?' Isaac asked.

'I had to get out of the office; too busy down there with the media. The phone's ringing off the hook. I needed some space and time to work out an appropriate response to his death. Some carefully crafted words on how sorry we are to lose such a great actor in the prime of his life. Those sorts of words.'

'A truthful reflection on the passing of such a great man,' Isaac said sarcastically.

'A pain in the arse, a lousy actor, and no great loss. Is that what you expect me to say?'

'You and I need to talk.'

'Give me fifteen minutes while I draft a statement. I'll give it to the scriptwriters to tidy up the grammar.'

'Thirty minutes. Fine,' Isaac replied. He headed to the coffee machine. Seated next to a window, the sun shining in, his tiredness finally caught up with him.

'Isaac, Isaac.' He woke with a start.

'Jess,' he said, bleary-eyed.

There was no one around; she attempted to kiss him. He pulled away.

'Sorry, Jess. I don't want to be rude, but the situation has changed.'

'Charles Sutherland?'

'You've heard?'

'Who hasn't,' she said. To Isaac, she was a vision of loveliness. The sun was shining in through the window, the blouse she was wearing, delicate and almost transparent. He felt as though he wanted to grab her there and then and seduce her, but knew he could not.

'I'm here in an official capacity now.'

'He was murdered?'

'It's still listed as suspicious, but it looks that way.'

'I'm sorry that he's dead.' She seemed sincere.

'I thought you argued with him?'

'That's what happens when the pressure's on.'

'Richard Williams wasn't much concerned. Does that surprise you?'

'Not really. He's a bastard, anyway. He only cares about number one.'

'Capable of murder?'

'Richard, no way. As long as he gets plenty of frivolous women to lay, then he's harmless. Tough businessman, good at his job, but murder? I don't think so.'

'You seem to care about Sutherland's death.'

'He was actually an excellent actor.'

'That's not the impression I get around here.'

'Professional prejudice, that's all that is.'

'So why do you say he was an excellent actor?'

'Simply because he was. His problem was his attitude. Sure, he wasn't major movie star great, but in the theatre, he would have been.'

'I thought he failed in theatre, and this was his last stop before the rubbish heap.'

'It was. He did have some failings though. I'm afraid Charles Sutherland was his own worst enemy. His decline was inevitable, but…'

'Not his death.' Isaac completed the sentence.

'Why would anyone want to murder him?' she asked. Isaac had completely forgotten about his arranged meeting with Richard Williams.

'I don't know. Do you have any ideas?'

'Not really. He could be a nosey bugger, always sticking his nose in, listening at keyholes.'

'Is he likely to have heard anything?'

'It's possible.'

'That's for me to find out. Anyone else I should talk to?'

'Not really. He certainly had nothing on me.'

'Is there anything I should know?' Isaac realised he had weakened. His reply was perilously close to personal concern.

'Nothing that you need to worry about.' Sensing the moment, she moved closer to him. He failed to move away. She kissed him on the cheek.

Isaac had yet again failed in his attempt to maintain a purely professional relationship with Jess O'Neill. He left soon after.

What is it about her? he thought as he drove away from the production lot and back to the office. *Why do I keep doing this?*

***

'I've been sacked.' These were the first words to emanate from Christy Nichols on Farhan's return to the hotel. Farhan and Isaac had not spoken to her on their first visit – they had left that to Inspector Hopkirk.

'You'd better explain,' Farhan said as he sat down on the chair in her room. Not as good as Charles Sutherland's by far, he noted.

'It's for the hired help when the rich and famous come to stay.' She had observed him looking around the room.'

'And you were the hired help?'

'He thought I was more than that.'

'What do you mean?' He could see she had been crying.

'I found him out on the street. Have they told you that?'

'No one's told me anything.' Farhan had a basic understanding of the situation, in that the tab for the room was being picked up by a magazine, one of the magazines that his wife liked to read.

'I intended to write an article for the magazine. In fact, any magazine that would buy it from me.'

'What sort of article?'

'Lightweight, the type that most people want to read. Anything to do with fallen celebrities is good copy; makes us all feel a little more human, I suppose. If it can happen to them, then maybe the reader's imperfect life is not so bad after all.'

'You mean those that are no longer in the limelight?'

'That's it. Charles Sutherland was a big star, at least in the UK, and then all of a sudden he disappears from sight. After they had kicked him off the programme, he was visible on a few television chat shows, but that didn't last long.'

'What happened to him?'

'It's not what happened to him, more likely what he did to himself.'

'I'm not sure I follow.' Farhan was enjoying his time with Christy Nichols. The setting and the woman were too pleasant. He stood up, moved to the window and looked out over the panorama of London.

'He had been fired. He had plenty of money, so what does he do?'

'Saves it for a rainy day?' Farhan knew the remark was incorrect.

'Not our Charles Sutherland. He's out partying, sometimes at his place, sometimes in the various clubs around town where the drugs are available and the women are costly.'

'He blew all the money?'

'In record time, and then his landlord dumps him on the street. Throws him a couple of bags with clothes that can't be sold second-hand, and there you have it – the fallen celebrity.'

'And you were going to write a story about him?'

'Not only him. There are a few more out there.'

'Did you find the others?'

'I know where a few are supposed to be, but I found Sutherland first, and then he gives me this story about Marjorie Frobisher.'

Farhan, his interest piqued, sat down again close to her. He noticed the smell of her perfume. He got up again and sat in another seat, this time more uncomfortable. 'What story is that?'

'He knew things about her that would rock the nation, bring down the government, and so on.'

'Did you believe him?'

'I wasn't sure what to think. He seemed to know facts not commonly known. He appeared to know a lot about Marjorie Frobisher.'

'What sort of things?'

'Past lovers, some prominent. He also alluded to something more significant.'

'Her personal life is not that well hidden,' Farhan said.

'It is to her fans.'

'The magazine puts him up in the Savoy, supplies him with whatever he wants – purely on the basis that he knows a few names?'

'Yes.'

'It seems very generous. Are these names important?'

'According to him, they are.'

'You don't know the names?'

'The magazine editor may. She's the one who agreed to pay for all this. She even picked up the bills for the prostitutes.'

'Many of them?'

'A couple that I signed for. I suppose they would be called escorts, but they performed the same function as any woman off the street.'

'The women were here?'

'On a couple of occasions. The hotel complained, but I managed to smooth it over. It cost extra money, but Sutherland said for the magazine to pay or he was walking.'

'Walking where?'

'Another magazine. If what he had was dynamite, he could sell it with no trouble. He knew that.'

'Smart man?'

'Foul habits, but he knew how to negotiate. Yes, I would say he was smart.'

'You didn't like him?'

'Not at all. Not that I would kill him, though. He was my meal ticket out of freelancing into a responsible and steady position, but he could make me feel dirty.'

'You alluded to that before.'

'He thought I was paid for as well. I couldn't tell him that I found him morally reproachable and that I wished he was still in the gutter.'

'You could, and then you would be out of a job.'

'That's right.'

'Could one of the women have killed him?'

'Do you see that as likely?' she asked.

'I would have thought not. They typically perform their function, take the money, and leave.'

'I never saw anyone else in the room, but I wasn't watching all the time. It's possible, I suppose. Prostitutes murdering clients seems a little far-fetched.'

'I agree it does,' Farhan said, 'but someone was here, and subject to confirmation, someone administered the poison. We need to find these women and check out their alibis.'

Chapter 14

After leaving Christy Nichols, Farhan headed over to the company that had been supplying the women for Charles Sutherland. Located in a modern office block not far from Tower Bridge, it did not look to be the sort of place to provide prostitutes, but as Marion Robertson explained, 'We supply escorts of the very highest quality, not street-walkers. Our women are educated, beautiful, and articulate.'

'But they are available for sex?' Farhan needed to clarify.

'If that is what the client wants.' Marion Robertson was a stunner. Farhan, with an awkward wife, found solace in her presence. Christy Nichols had not been calming, quite the opposite. Marion Robertson was in her early forties, he assumed. Still slim and exceedingly attractive.

'What else would they want them for?'

'Escorts. I believe the name says it all. Some men need a date, someone to take to a function. Sometimes that is all they want.'

'It seems unusual.'

'Not at all. Rich men sometimes crave the company. They may have passed the age of wanting to screw every woman they can lay their hands on. Their wealth may have come at a cost, especially if they had started with no money.'

'What do you mean?' he asked. He noticed her mobile phone. The case appeared to be gold.

'The phone?' She had seen him glance at it.

'It looks expensive.'

'It is. A grateful client.'

'Exceedingly grateful.'

'Please, don't misunderstand,' she said. 'Not for services rendered by me. One of my girls spent a couple of weeks with him. It was just a way of showing his gratitude.'

'You mentioned before that wealth comes at a cost.' He returned to an earlier question.

'Some men, in the climb to succeed, dispense with relationships, others suffer broken marriages, others take advantage and marry a twenty-something bimbo. At a certain age, they find they need the company of a woman, but not the long-term hassles and not always the sex.'

'And the person who gave you the phone was one of them?'

'Yes. Exceedingly wealthy, obscenely, in fact. To him the cost was negligible. He was in his early seventies, and while still an attractive man, he had no need of a nymphomaniac blonde. The woman I supplied was in her late forties, highly educated, and fluent in several languages. It was her company he wanted, not a quick lay.'

'He didn't sleep with her?'

'He may have; I didn't ask.'

'Charles Sutherland. I don't think he was either rich or attractive.'

'With him, it was pure sex,' she said. 'Perverse, threesomes – that sort of thing.'

'What kind of women did he like?'

'Early to mid-thirties, stunning, not skinny and flat-chested.'

'You're able to supply that type of woman?'

'The two I sent him were exactly what he wanted. One was a housewife making some extra cash on the side. Not sure if her husband knows, probably not. The other one was single and into casual sex. She works in the city somewhere, or maybe she doesn't. I don't ask too much about their private lives. I ensure that I don't become too friendly with them.'

'More like an employment agency than a supplier of women for hire.'

'You seem not to approve of what I am doing here,' she said.

'That is not the issue here, is it? Charles Sutherland is, and the women you procured for him.'

'Procured, such an unpleasant term,' she said. 'It sounds illegal, and there is nothing illegal about what we do here. The women come of their own free will. They are not coerced in any way. The only requirements I have are that they are medically certified with a clean bill of health, and if I set up an appointment for them, they keep that appointment. Also, if they negotiate another meeting with the client, they inform me, and I receive my commission.'

'Any problems with difficult clients?'

'Rarely. On the first meeting with a new client, I have a man who takes them to the meeting and brings them back. The woman also has a panic button if there's an issue. It's happened once in the last three years.'

'Charles Sutherland, what else can you tell me about him?'

'Not a lot. I never met the man.'

'I need to contact the women.'

'I can't let you do that. They do their job, go home. Their private lives are sacrosanct.'

'At this present time, we regard Charles Sutherland's death as a possible murder. I could get a court order – even a police car to deliver it to their front door on a Saturday morning, flashing light as well.'

'I understand.' She came forward, touched him on the knee. He felt a tingling sensation go through his body. 'Is there an alternative?' she asked.

'I could meet them at a neutral location, but I'm not sure how I can keep them out of the limelight indefinitely, especially if there is a murder trial.'

'I will set it up. Give me a couple of days. One of the women has a husband and two children. She does it for them. Don't you think they will be harmed if her activities are revealed?'

'I will do all I can to keep her and the other woman out of the courts and the news,' Farhan said.

***

Isaac needed an update on how Charles Sutherland came to be sprawled naked on the floor of a hotel room. Gordon Windsor, the crime scene examiner, had alluded to a suspicious death.

Isaac knew that the suspicious death of a celebrity would require a full autopsy. He also knew that would take time, weeks possibly. An interim evaluation and the entire Murder Investigation

Team could be mobilised. Gordon Windsor was his best bet for an update. He phoned him.

'I'll be in your office in an hour,' the man replied.

In one hour, almost to the minute, he walked into the room. He was as Isaac remembered him at the crime scene, only this time he was dressed in a suit, his hair combed over to hide a bald spot.

'Gordon, give us the facts without the jargon,' Isaac said. Farhan was also in the office.

'The poison was administered in a drink,' Windsor said.

'Any sign of drugs?' Farhan asked.

'Cocaine, but it did not kill him. There was more alcohol than drugs in his system.'

'What type of poison?' Isaac asked.

'Arsenic. It's tasteless, odourless, and colourless. It was used to kill rats in the past.'

'Is it a subtle method of killing a person without it being discovered?' Farhan asked.

'Subtle, yes. The risk of it being discovered is minimal.'

'But you found it?'

'The toxicologist did. Mind you, that's only the initial analysis of the bottle found at the scene. How much was in his body, and whether it was the sole cause of death, will not be known until the autopsy report comes in.'

'Then it's a murder investigation?' Farhan asked.

'Unless advised to the contrary, that would be correct,' Gordon Windsor replied. 'They used to call it the inheritor's powder.'

'What do you mean?' Isaac asked.

'Favoured poison of women in the nineteenth century. Sprinkled in small amounts on the husband's food over a period of time and a guaranteed death, totally undetectable.'

'And today?'

'Forensics will pick it up. Only one issue, though.'

'What's that?'

'Normally a person cannot be killed with a single dose.'

'Why?'

'A sufficient dose usually causes the person to vomit.'

'But you consider it murder?'

'Vomiting is not automatic. If he had been drunk and spaced-out, he might have kept it down for long enough.'

'Are you indicating the murderer may not have known this?' Isaac asked.

'It seems possible, but they must have known that a well-known celebrity found dead in a famous hotel and in apparently good health would be subject to an autopsy.'

'Would they?' Isaac put the possibility forward.

Gordon Windsor thought for a moment. 'If it was a professional hit, they would have known.'

'Are you saying this was not a professional assassination?' Farhan asked.

'I'm purely the scientist here. You are the detectives. What I am saying is, that if they were professional, they would have known there would be an autopsy.'

'And they would not have left a bottle in the kitchen with the poison in it,' Isaac said.

'Precisely, unless they were disturbed, but even that appears unlikely. Professionals don't put bottles in kitchen sinks in the first place. Normally, it would be coat pocket to drink and then back to coat pocket.'

Gordon Windsor left the office soon after.

Both Isaac and Farhan left a little later. It was five in the afternoon. Neither would be having an early night. Isaac, so far, had not caught up with Sophie, and he was feeling in need of her. Farhan also felt the need, but he had no Sophie; in fact, no one except an empty house.

A Chinese restaurant close to the police station provided dinner. Prawn chow mein for Isaac; chicken for Farhan.

'We've assumed his death was related to Marjorie Frobisher,' Isaac said on their return to the office. 'Is that an assumption we can make?'

'What other option do we have?' Farhan replied.

'Which brings up another question. If Charles Sutherland was murdered to prevent him saying something to this magazine, then who else knows something? Is anyone else targeted for elimination?'

'How do we know?' Farhan replied. 'We only have assumptions.'

'Farhan, you're right,' Isaac said. 'I've still to meet up with Richard Williams. It is possible that he knows something.'

They were a good team, able to bounce ideas off each other, reach conclusions, formulate plans of action

'I thought you went to see him the other day.'

'He left the production lot before I had a chance to talk to him.'

'You're playing with fire,' Farhan said.

'I'm keeping my distance,' Isaac replied, a little indignant.

'No one is free of suspicion, you know that.' Farhan realised he had not been as diplomatic as he should have been, but Isaac was not only a colleague, he was a friend. As a friend, he was advising him to keep his distance from Jess O'Neill. He was sure Isaac would take his advice in the manner it was given.

***

Marion Robertson was not in a good mood when Farhan phoned the next day. 'My girls value their secrecy. I still regard this is an intrusion.'

'Marion.' Farhan knew that a degree of familiarity usually defused the tension. 'I understand your concerns, but I'm doing my job, and until told otherwise, your two women were the last persons to see Sutherland alive.'

'I understand, but they're blaming me for fixing them up with him.'

'From what you said, he paid his money, and they came to no harm.'

'That's correct, but the magazine is refusing to pay; probably afraid their reputation will be tarnished if it becomes known that they paid for prostitutes.'

'You've had non-payers before?'

'Of course, but I can hardly take them to court, can I? That will let all the cats out of the bag. Besides, I'll still pay the women.'

'Regardless of payment, I need to meet with these women. I'm trying to help you, but you will have to trust me.' Farhan said.

'I've already set up a meeting with one of the women for you. I'll send a photo. She uses the professional name of Samantha.'

'What's her non-professional name?'

'I'll let her give it to you if she wants.'

'Where will I meet her?'

'Hyde Park, close to Marble Arch. You'll find her at the entrance to the park. She'll be wearing a blue jacket. I'll send you a phone number so you can call her when you are there.'

'Time?'

'Midday, she works nearby. You can pretend to strike up a conversation with her, admire the flowers, whatever.'

'And the other woman?' Farhan asked.

'Tomorrow, but she is married and would prefer to stay that way. Her husband would probably not understand. He thinks she pays the mortgage on the money she earns working in an office somewhere.'

'You have to trust me on this. If they're not involved, then we will refer to them as X and Y,' Farhan said.

Chapter 15

The first thing Isaac noticed when he entered Richard Williams' office was that the lovely – available if you drove a Ferrari – Sally Jenkins was absent. In her seat sat another equally vivacious woman. She introduced herself as Linda. *Another rent-a-lay*, Isaac thought.

'Sally Jenkins, what happened to her?' Isaac asked as the new woman showed him into Williams' office. She hadn't been employed when Marjorie Frobisher had disappeared, and she was clearly another prick-teaser.

'I had to let her go,' Williams replied in an offhand manner. It wasn't a good enough explanation.

'It's important. Where has she gone?'

'I had to sack her.' A curt reply. Still not good enough.

'I need details. She may well be a material witness. I may need to talk to her again.'

'No doubt she will tell you the story. She started talking marriage and settling down, having a few children.'

'And you don't want that?'

'I'm still paying one silly bitch who managed to get me down the aisle. She made sure she was pregnant before we got that far. Still bleeding me for all she can. It takes my lawyers all their time to keep the situation under control. You're a tall, good-looking man, you must have similar issues?'

'True enough, but I only have a policeman's salary.'

'You're young, plenty of stamina. I need a good dose of Viagra to get going. They're with me for the money and the good life. Why can't they leave it like that?'

Isaac thought it was an honest answer. He had never regarded the women he bedded in such a manner, and he would never have spoken about them to other men. 'I need to talk to you about Charles Sutherland,' he said.

'How did he die?'

'Suspected poisoning.'

'Fine, it's a murder investigation now. I can't really avoid you anymore, or you'd have me in the back of a police car and down to the station for an all-night grilling.'

'A little melodramatic, wouldn't you say?' Isaac replied.

'A great storyline. The masses would love it, but as you say, a little melodramatic. But when has our programme been factual? Maybe once this is all over, we'll incorporate it into a storyline.'

'I would advise against it for now,' Isaac said. 'This is an official visit.'

'I know that. What happened to Marjorie? Any updates?'

'I'm not at liberty to discuss it. We are following up on various leads.' Isaac thought it a somewhat dumb response.

'You don't know where she is, correct?'

Isaac chose to ignore Williams' evaluation, unfortunately accurate. He returned to Charles Sutherland.

'Did anyone have a grudge against Charles Sutherland, a reason to want him dead?'

'A few, but murder? That's a whole different issue.'

'What do you mean?'

'A person's death may make certain people more comfortable, but killing that person…'

'Why do you say that?' Isaac realised Williams knew something.

'Murder and it's twenty-five years, hard labour, breaking rocks.'

'There are no rocks these days.'

'Yes, of course.' Williams picked up the phone to the outer office and asked the new PA to bring in some freshly brewed coffee. It gave him some time to think about what to tell the persistent policeman, and how much.

Five minutes later, and the latest plaything, who managed to give a good impression of being competent, entered and placed two mugs on the desk. She gave Isaac a pleasant smile as she left. He gave one in return. Sally Jenkins was clearly a prick-teaser, a wealthy man's entertainment. Isaac revised his earlier thoughts on the latest PA being the same, but then maybe he was biased – he fancied her for himself.

Isaac continued. 'I need you to tell who may have had an issue with Charles Sutherland.'

'I understand that. Where do you want me to start?'

'Just give me the details.' Isaac recognised procrastination. He thought it reasonable. Nobody likes dishing the dirt on someone else, and a murder enquiry always puts everyone on the defensive.

'Marjorie, obviously.'

'Why Marjorie?' Isaac knew there was mutual antagonism, but wanting someone dead indicated something more serious.

'He was always sticking his nose in, attempting to listen in on other people's conversations.'

'Is that a reason to want him dead?'

'For Marjorie, it would have been.'

'It is clear that you are not inclined to give an honest answer.'

'Confidentiality seems more important to me.'

'The seriousness of the situation demands your full compliance.'

'I know, but as the executive producer, I make it a habit to maintain the confidence of all the people that I am responsible for. As long as it's not criminal, then I don't care if they are adulterers, closet gays, incorrigible gamblers, or whether they cheat on their tax.'

'I can understand, but this is a murder enquiry. You know I could take you down the station for questioning.'

'Not without my lawyer, you couldn't. Okay, here's what I know. Sutherland had picked up some dirt on Marjorie, enough for her to be seriously worried, enough for her to come in here and demand his withdrawal from the programme.'

'You agreed?'

'I tried to reason with her, but she was adamant.'

'She threatened to walk out of the production?'

'No.'

'So why did you agree?'

'I ran it past the scriptwriters first to see how we could get rid of him.'

'Once you had a storyline, you let him go.'

'He was going anyway. Marjorie and I go back a long way.'

'I believe that has been mentioned before. Maybe you could elaborate.'

'Nothing sinister. We were both starting out. I saw myself as the great international news correspondent; Marjorie, the next great movie star.'

'Neither of you achieved your aims.'

'That may be the case, but we've both been successful.'

'It's hardly a reason to accede to her demands.'

'We lived together for nine months. The first great love for both of us, and we have helped each other over the years. Shoulder to cry on if needed. I would do anything for her.'

'You don't seem concerned that she is missing.'

'Marjorie, what could happen to her? She's a survivor, same as I am. She'll reappear when the time is right.'

'You seem remarkably confident.'

'I've known her for too long to believe that she has been murdered. And besides, what proof do you have?'

'Apart from a confirmed sighting.'

'Malvern? I knew about that.'

'Have you been withholding information?' Isaac raised his voice. *What else does Richard Williams know*? he thought.

'I'll rephrase. I assumed that was where she had gone. It was her hideout in the past. I have been there a few times in the past to meet with her.'

'Are you still maintaining a relationship with her?'

'You make it sound dirty. When she was upset, she would disappear for a few days. It didn't happen often, but she would always phone me, ask me to join her. She would do the same for me.'

'You slept with her?'

'When?'

'When you went to Malvern.'

'No, not at all. You don't understand. We have a lot of history. She knows about my skeletons, or most of them. I know about hers.'

'Is there something I should be aware of?'

'Charles Sutherland knew something. Believe me, I don't know what it was.'

'Enough to kill him?'

'I don't know. Everyone knew about Marjorie and her open marriage, and she could be a bitch, but murder!'

'Anger, dislike, and hatred gravitate to murder,' Isaac said.

'I've been too long in this business, too many scripts, not to know that administered poison is not a spur of the moment action. It's premeditated and by someone with knowledge of poisons.'

'You should have been a policeman.' Isaac had to admit the man was correct. 'Who else would *not* be sad about Sutherland's death.'

'I don't think you'll find anyone in mourning.'

'Anyone else who would have been pleased?'

'There's only one.'

'Who's that?'

'Jess O'Neill.' Isaac sat up straighter, which caused Richard Williams to offer a comment.

'I see that you know the lovely Jess.' Williams smiled. Yet again, Isaac severely embarrassed that he was allowing personal to interfere with professional.

'I've spoken to her a few times.'

'And found her delightful?'

'She is an attractive woman, I'll grant you that.'

'I tried it on when she first arrived.'

'I assumed you would have, but I'm led to believe it was not successful.'

'I even took her away to an exhibition up north. We went up in the Ferrari, best hotel, few too many drinks, but she wasn't swayed. Looking for love, I suppose.'

'Any hard feelings after that?' Isaac visibly relaxed at Williams' affirmation of what Jess had told him.

'Not at all, but be careful. You've got a murder investigation, and it's clear that you are attracted to her.'

'Why should I be careful?'

'Not in regards to Jess, but you're here on official business. It would not seem proper to show preferential treatment of one witness over another, would it?'

'I can assure you that our relationship is purely professional. Who else believes that we have a friendship?'

'Everyone out at the production lot; it's a great place for gossip.'

'Let's get back to why she would not be sad to see Charles Sutherland dead.'

'She's not told you?'

'I know she told him that his time on the programme was over, and he had responded with some choice words.'

'Stuck-up bitch, that sort of thing?' Williams said.

'That's about all I know.'

'I think you'd better talk to her again. It's more serious than that. Nobody out at the production lot knows – only me and maybe Sally Jenkins.'

'Why only you two?'

'Firstly, Jess came and told me, and secondly, Sally had a tendency to listen in to conversations.'

'What is it that Jess had against Charles Sutherland?'
'It would be best if it came from her.'
'Let me have your version first?'
'I'm afraid I cannot do that. It would not be helpful if I distorted or misinterpreted what she told me.'
'I'll grant you that. I need to see her as soon as possible.'
'Then I would suggest that you bring her in to the police station, sit her down and get her to explain. It may become an integral part of any future trial. Not against Jess, but against Sutherland.'

Chapter 16

The first of the two escorts was not difficult to spot. The entrance to Hyde Park, just across the road from Marble Arch, the designated meeting place. It had been a good choice as it was a bright and sunny day.

Farhan could not help but be struck by the woman's beauty. She was of medium height, full in the figure, not fat, dressed in what looked to him to be expensive clothes, and her shoulder length hair dark and full.

She had a pleasant smile when she came over to him and introduced herself. Farhan thought the smile was a veneer.

'I've taken time off work to come and meet you. Everyone thinks I'm at the dentist.'

'I hope I'm not as painful as all that,' he joked. He warmed to the woman, the embodiment to him of the ideal female. She appeared to have some Indian heritage, although her skin tone was light.

'It's not you. I have an image to maintain, and this man being murdered has put me in an awkward position.'

'Why?' he asked. They moved from the gate and strolled through the park. He was enjoying himself. She was nervous, but not as nervous as she had been when they first met.

'I work for Marion, but it's not the sort of thing you want your friends and family to know about, and certainly not in the office.'

'Where do you work?'

'I work with a legal firm, not five minutes' walk from here. I'm training to be a lawyer.'

'Why the escort work?'

'It pays well. Life is expensive. A junior in a legal office doesn't get paid much.'

'Is it purely money?'

'Not altogether, but it's a large part of it.'

'What's the other part?'

'I like sex.' It was an unexpected admission.

'The men can't always be pleasant,' he said.

'It's a balance. Most of the men are ageing but generous. I make sure they enjoy themselves. You don't know what kind of an aphrodisiac the money is.' It seemed to Farhan the words were spoken as a defence mechanism.

'Charles Sutherland. I am under the impression that he was not a particularly pleasant man.'

'I remember him. He was into threesomes, and he liked some lesbian play before. He liked to sit and watch.'

'You had no problem with his watching?'

'Why should I? Law school is expensive, and I intend to get through with honours at least. Then I'll find myself a good position as a lawyer, corporate law. That's where the money is.'

'And escorting?'

'I'll stop as soon as I finish law school.'

'No regrets?'

'Of course not. You sound prudish. Do you disapprove?'

'As long as no one causes anyone harm, then I maintain a neutral view.' Farhan realised he had made a similar statement to Marion Robertson, the purveyor of women such as Samantha.

'My family would disown me.'

'Then why take the risk?'

'I see nothing wrong with what I do.' She failed to answer his question.

'Can we get back to Charles Sutherland?' Farhan had deviated from his questioning. He, like Isaac, was susceptible to the charms of a woman. With Isaac, they saw him as a stud. With him, they saw someone to mother.

Isaac would take advantage; he never had, at least not yet. He had made a decision. The purity and boredom of a loveless marriage did not compensate. He would protect the children, but as for his wife, he had no further use for her.

'I wouldn't say it was an enjoyable night,' she continued, 'or two nights, as we went back again. We provided the service, spent a few hours there, and left.'

'The night he died. Were you there?'

'Yes, but when we left he had a smile on his face. He was very much alive.'

'The other lady?'

'I only know her as Olivia. We don't talk about our private lives.'

'What time did you leave Sutherland's suite at the Savoy?'

'Just after midnight. I always check the time of departing.'

'Why's that?'

'I need to ensure that my parents are asleep when I get home. I don't want any awkward questions as I walk in the door.'

'You live at home?'

'A good Muslim girl. Yes, I do. I've shocked you again.'

'Too many years as a policeman. I've seen it all. I'm not easily shocked, but a good Muslim girl, a beautiful woman, acting as an escort…'

'My name's Aisha.'

'Your real name?'

'Yes. You will keep my involvement confidential?'

'That's what I promised Marion. I will make the same promise to you, although you must realise this may soon be out of my control.'

Unaware, they had walked some distance, further than expected, and found themselves on the other side of the park. In a flurry, late for an appointment, she hailed a taxi. 'Call me once this is over,' she shouted to him from the open window. 'We can meet as friends, have a meal.'

***

'I'm sorry about this, Jess.' Isaac, acting on information supplied by Richard Williams, had no option but to call her in. If it was, as Williams had suggested, 'important', then he had to follow police procedure; no longer an informal chat and a brief kiss.

'My client will only answer questions pertaining to Charles Sutherland.' She had brought along legal representation. Isaac had phoned her before her official summons to the police station, advised her that it would be a good idea.

She had been taken aback initially but acquiesced when he had explained the situation. 'Vital evidence, evidence that may be used in court, needs to be given in the correct manner. It's best for you to come in, honestly answer the questions and clear the air.'

'I thought you were protecting me,' she had said.

'I still am. Believe me, this is the best way. We need to clear up a few accusations that have been made.'

'My dislike of Sutherland, is that it?'

'Please say no more. Come to the station in your own vehicle. Park it around the back, and no one will know you've been here.'

It was late in the afternoon when all the concerned people were present. Isaac conducted the formalities.

'This interview is being recorded and is being held in Interview Room 2 at Challis Street Police Station. I am Detective Chief Inspector Isaac Cook. Miss O'Neill, could you please introduce yourself.'

'Jessica O'Neill.'

'Detective Inspector Ahmed,' Isaac said.

'I am Detective Inspector Mohammad Farhan Ahmed.'

'Mr Wrightson.'

'I am Michael Wrightson, Solicitor, of Wrightson, Loftus and Evans.'

'The time, if we can agree, is 4.10 p.m. At the conclusion of the interview, Miss O'Neill, I will give you a notice explaining exactly what will happen to the tapes. Do you understand?'

'Yes.'

'Do you understand the reason for the interview?' Isaac asked.

'Yes,' she replied.

'Thank you. I would remind you that you're not under arrest, you need not remain here, and you are entitled to legal representation.'

Farhan sat alongside Isaac, facing Jess O'Neill's legal representative. Neither Isaac nor Farhan liked the look of him. He was a tall, slender man with pronounced features. The man spoke in a superior manner.

'Miss O'Neill, thank you for coming in.'

'I will answer all questions put forward, subject to my legal representative, Mr Wrightson, agreeing.'

'That is fine, Miss O'Neill,' Isaac responded.

'Please call me Jess.'

'Jess, it is,' Isaac replied.

She looked at Michael Wrightson. He nodded his head in affirmation and spoke to the microphone in the middle of the table. 'That is acceptable.'

'It is known that you argued with Charles Sutherland. Is that correct?' Isaac asked.

'Argued, yes, but it hardly seems relevant.'

'Why?'

She looked over at Wrightson before responding. He nodded his head. 'It's part of my job to maintain momentum, to put everyone in their place. It's a tight schedule on production days.'

'Are you saying that you only argued on production days?'

'I argue with a lot of people on production days, but nobody takes it seriously. Tensions are high, tempers are short, and some of the actors think they're major stars, worthy of preferential treatment, kid gloves.'

'Charles Sutherland. One of those?'

'Charles Sutherland and Marjorie Frobisher were the worst.'

'We will come to Marjorie Frobisher later.' Isaac realised he could not go too easy on her, and besides, Farhan was there as well. He could not be seen to be weak in front of his junior.

'My client is not sure where this is proceeding.' Wrightson felt the need to speak. 'Miss O'Neill has not been formally charged. Why is she here?'

'I am informed that Miss O'Neill had more than a dislike for Charles Sutherland. It has come to my knowledge that she had a hatred of the man.'

'That is not correct,' Jess protested.

'My client does not need to respond to that accusation,' Wrightson said. Isaac had had enough of the man; his input was obstructive.

'I am not asking Miss O'Neill to incriminate herself. I am purely giving her the opportunity to confirm her hatred for this man categorically and why. It is understood that there may have been reluctance before. The previous times that we spoke were unofficial and unrecorded. It is imperative that your client is entirely honest with us.'

Jess turned to Wrightson. 'Michael, what should I do?'

'May we halt this interview for five minutes,' Wrightson asked. 'I need to advise my client as to her legal position.'

'4.25 p.m. Interview with Miss Jessica O'Neill halted.'

'Thank you,' Wrightson said.

'I'll send in some coffee. Take as long as you like. We'll be outside.'

'Make it tea for me.' Jess managed a weak smile.

Isaac and Farhan left the room.

***

'Michael, what am I to do?' Jess turned to face Wrightson.

'You haven't done anything wrong.'

'I know, but it's a clear motive.'

'It will look worse if you don't speak now. DCI Cook, what's the situation with him?'

'I like him. He likes me. No more than that.'

'He seems to be going gentle on you. Did you sense it?'

'He seemed very rough to me.'

'I've been in these places before. He's trying to help. It would be best if you trust him with this information. I'm not only your legal representative, I'm also married to your sister. I'm family. I suggest you state clearly the full story in your own time, make a statement.'

'Why? There was no one else there.'

'It always comes out. One day, when the pressure's on the police to wrap up the case, when they have a suspect in mind, you will let it slip. I just don't think you're a good enough actor not to let it out.'

'Not good enough for the soap I produce?'

'You may be good enough for that.'

'I will follow your advice.'

'Good. If they find out later that you lied here today, they will have a clear motive.'

'It is a motive, you know that,' Jess said.

'People have murdered for less.' Michael Wrightson hoped his sister-in-law had seen sense. He was sure she had.

***

Ninety minutes after exiting the interview room, Isaac and Farhan returned.

'Interview recommenced 5. 55 p.m.' Isaac said.

'My client wishes to make a statement,' Wrightson said. Isaac hoped it was not a confession.

'Miss O'Neill, you are aware of what you are saying?'

'Yes.'

'Then please commence.'

'Charles Sutherland was a thoroughly despicable man.'

'Why do you say that?' Farhan felt the need to speak. He could see why Isaac was drawn to her. Even in a moment of sadness, which was etched on her face, she was still lovely. He wanted to put an arm around her and tell her it wasn't all that bad.

'Please allow my client to make her statement,' Wrightson said.

'Charles Sutherland,' she repeated the statement from the start, 'was a thoroughly despicable man. I can only feel intense hatred towards him. His death did not cause me any sadness. On the contrary, I was relieved and pleased to hear that he had met an unpleasant fate. The question as to why I feel relief, and why I hated him so much, is for me to explain.

'I came from a sexually abusive and violent childhood. It is something that I do not talk about. I do not want to speak about it now. On the advice of my legal representative, Michael Wrightson, who also happens to be my brother-in-law, I am making this statement. I am well aware that what I am about to tell you would form the basis for murder.

'I must state here and now, that I was not involved in the murder of this man, although the person who did kill him has my gratitude.

'As a child with a stepfather who treated the female children as his personal property for his obscene sexual gratification, I am well aware of what constitutes abuse and improper behaviour. My stepfather died when I reached the age of fourteen, early enough for me to forget the horrors of what he inflicted on me and my sister, Michael's wife. Even Michael does not know the full extent of what transpired in that evil house, and never will. My sister still suffers some lasting effects. For me, I have completely adjusted, never forgotten, but it has not caused me anguish since about my sixteenth birthday.

'Since then, there have been several men in my life, good men, who have always treated me with the greatest respect. Let me come to Charles Sutherland.

'Two weeks before his leaving the programme, I went to see him in his dressing room. It was late at night, sometime after 10 p.m. and I don't believe anyone else, apart from the two of us, were out at the production lot. I wanted to discuss his part and the script change for the next day. I would often do that with the other members of the cast, even with Charles Sutherland, so there was no reason for me not to go and see him.

'I found him in his room, drunk, from what I could see. I did not realise that he had been snorting cocaine until he became insistent that I take some with him. He was in an unusual mood, even for him.

'He became more demanding, trying to force me, attempting to grab me and to make me have a drink with him, to lighten up. I tried to leave the room, but he locked the door and put the key down the front of his trousers. He was baiting me to take the key from him. I was in a state, and at that moment, I saw my stepfather there. I kicked at him, attempted to hit him. I shouted at the top of my voice, but no one responded. The more I reacted, the more excited he became. I've seen him before in a similar situation, but now it was extreme, and I was on my own.

'He came at me, grabbed me by my shoulder and threw me on the ground. He ripped off my blouse, started fondling me, and all the time I was screaming. He tried to pull off my skirt, but I managed to take control of the situation and kneed him in the groin with all the force I could muster. He collapsed in agony. I quickly regained the key and left. That's the end of my statement.'

Nobody spoke for some time. Wrightson was the first. 'You must understand that what Miss O'Neill has told you is of great embarrassment to her. It is clear that she is distraught and should be excused from further questioning.'

'Agreed. Interview concluded at 6.20 p.m.' Isaac said.

Jess left in tears with Michael Wrightson supporting her. Isaac wanted to rush up to her, put his arms around her, and kiss her, but he did not.

'It's a good enough motive for murder,' Farhan said after she had left the building. Isaac did not answer.

Chapter 17

Angus MacTavish was not pleased when Richard Goddard phoned to make an appointment. He relented when told that confidentiality in relation to Charles Sutherland's death and Marjorie Frobisher could not be guaranteed. He was also concerned that she had been confirmed alive four weeks after her disappearance.

As usual, they met in MacTavish's office in Downing Street. 'Detective Superintendent, what have we got here?' MacTavish asked. He was not friendly.

'What do you mean?'

'This Frobisher woman still remains hidden from sight, and then we have a failed actor threatening to sound off to a magazine about something earth shattering. What's going on?'

'I think that is a question you could answer.'

'What do you mean? Are you suggesting I'm involved?'

'Not personally, but you know more than I do. You've admitted that much in the past.'

'Certainly, I know more than you. My requirement was to keep her quiet. We would never condone murder.'

'It's important that I receive more information.'

'I don't see that I am at liberty to give you much more.'

'Then I don't see how I can protect you or whoever you're trying to protect.'

Richard Goddard knew he was in treacherous waters. There was a promotion he wanted, and he was aware that getting on the wrong side of MacTavish, who answered to the prime minister, who was good friends with Commissioner Charles Shaw, the senior man in the Metropolitan Police, was not ideal.

'Detective Superintendent, of course you're right. Let's look at it from where I'm sitting. Sutherland's death may be totally unrelated. Correct?'

'Correct.'

'What sort of man was he?'

'Unpleasant, heavily into alcohol, recreational drugs and prostitutes, if he had the money.'

'Gambling?'

'Gambling as well, but that's taken us nowhere so far. We haven't found any evidence of anyone hassling him to pay up.'

'And if he's dead, he won't be paying anyway.'

'He was aiming to make a lot of money by selling his story. A gambling syndicate would wait their time before threatening him.'

'Then who killed him?'

'You mentioned the security services before.'

'I've checked with my contacts. They say it's not feasible. A kill would require paperwork. The official line is that it doesn't exist.'

'Do you trust them?'

'Not entirely.'

'The motive for killing Sutherland is still unclear.'

Angus MacTavish, at a loss on how to move it forward, excused himself from the office. A minute later, Mrs Gregory came through the door with a fresh pot of tea and some more biscuits. Richard Goddard teased her about his attempts to lose weight. She laughed, told him not to worry and left the room. It was thirty-five minutes before MacTavish returned. The detective superintendent had drunk all the tea in that time, looked out the window, and stroked the cat that had wandered in. He sensed the politician had been taking instructions.

'Sorry about that,' MacTavish apologised.

'Not a problem.'

'I told my superiors that I need to take you into our confidence.'

'They agreed?'

'Reluctantly. I've told them that you cannot find Marjorie Frobisher or solve Sutherland's murder without additional facts.'

'That's true.'

'There was a child,' MacTavish said.

'You mentioned this before.'

'The father is important, the child more so.'

'The child, does it know who its parents are?'

'Not yet, but it is trying to find out.'

'How old would this child be?'

'Late thirties, early forties.'

'Do you know who this child is?'

'No.'

'Do you know who the father is?'

'Yes.'

111

'Then where is the complication? Surely you can stop the child finding out.'

'It cannot be stopped for much longer.'

'What if the father made a public statement, acknowledged the errors of the past, embraced the child as part of his long-lost family?'

'It's more serious than that. I've told you as much as I can,' MacTavish said. 'Any more would place you and your people in a precarious position.'

'How about you?'

'I'm already compromised. I'm a marked man if this gets out.'

'And you don't really know what you are compromising?'

'I am aware that revealing the father will almost certainly bring down the government. Revealing the child is potentially catastrophic.'

'How serious?'

'My life for one, and I don't know the full details.'

'What do you want me to do?' Richard Goddard felt sympathetic towards Angus MacTavish; fear for himself and his team.

'Find out who killed Sutherland and find Marjorie Frobisher, dead or alive.'

'One more question. Does Marjorie Frobisher know who the child is?'

'It's possible.'

'Could it be why Sutherland was killed?'

'Yet again, it's unknown. My contacts think it's unlikely that he was murdered by an official assassin, but then again, who really knows?'

Detective Superintendent Goddard knew that telling Isaac and DI Ahmed was going to prove difficult. They needed to find Marjorie Frobisher, and they needed additional help.

***

Farhan had drawn the short straw. That was how he saw it when he met the editor of the magazine that had been paying Charles Sutherland's bill.

'I paid plenty out for him, including his whores. God knows why *that* Christy Nichols approved them.'

He had barely entered her office before she started with the invective, barely had a chance to introduce himself and explain the reason for his visit. A formal introduction, cut short, about how it was a murder investigation and that he would be recording the conversation.

He had set up the meeting for three in the afternoon. Her personal assistant had made it clear any earlier was not possible. He had reminded her that it was a murder investigation, and his demands had precedence over the magazine's deadline. The personal assistant made it clear that it was non-negotiable, and if he wanted to take it up with her boss, then he could. At the end of their conversation, she had quietly advised him that it was best not mentioned if he didn't want to be on the end of an ear-bashing.

As he sat there, increasingly agitated, listening to the editor, he heeded her personal assistant's words.

'What do you want to know? My time is precious.' Victoria Webster, the editor, as well-known on the television as off, was a tall woman, certainly taller than Farhan.

Close up he could see that the beautiful skin, wrinkle-free whenever she was on the television, was a result of the makeup people.

In the confines of the office, she spoke in an aggressive manner. On the television, a different persona with charm and decorum. Farhan realised that the woman that millions admired was no more than a street fighter, brought up on the street, fighting tooth and nail to be where she was, and she wasn't going back.

Her background was well-known. The illegitimate daughter of an Irish housemaid and a Roman Catholic priest. How she had risen from obscurity and despair in an austere orphanage. How she had put herself through university, worked three jobs to do it, and then at the age of twenty-two had joined the magazine. The first position, in the basement mail room, and after that, year after year, she had worked her way up the corporate ladder, until she occupied the top office, on the top floor, with the best view overlooking London, overlooking her loyal readers.

It was a good story, although not entirely accurate. Victoria Webster never intended the truth to get in the way of her ambition. Irish, she was, but it was middle-class suburbia and parents who were married. The orphanage after they had been killed in a car accident when she was eight years old, but it was not austere. University and the three jobs in part truthful, although the jobs were short-term. She was a brilliant student and many a student, and some lecturers, had succumbed to her charm and assisted in her financial viability, even sometimes with the reports and the papers she had to submit. The basement at the magazine, correct, but it was not all hard work. There was no doubt that she was brilliant at her job – the circulation attested to that fact – and her public persona was flawless, but the rise from the basement was in part due to competence and hard work, and in part due to her seducing whoever she needed to, invariably on the floor above. There were a few who, once seduced, found out that she had taken their job. She made sure that they were evicted from the building quickly, and with minimal fuss, with a generous redundancy package to ensure their silence. A few had tried to inform the owner of the magazine what she was, but he did not care as long as it was not illegal, and as long as she delivered the results.

'Miss Webster.' Farhan attempted to get a word in.

'Mrs Webster.'

'Mrs Webster, it is understood that you were willing to pay Charles Sutherland a substantial amount of money for information that he possessed, information you would print in your magazine. Is that correct?'

'That is correct.'

'I assume you are aware of the nature of this information.'

'Your assumption is incorrect.' She looked at her watch and glanced over at the man sitting next to her. She had not formally introduced him, other than to say that he was her legal adviser.

'Why is that?' Farhan asked.

'Mrs Webster is answering your questions in a spirit of goodwill,' Victoria Webster's legal adviser said.

'And you are?' Farhan had not come to Victoria Webster's office to be intimidated.

'My name is William Montgomery. I am the senior legal adviser for the magazine.'

Montgomery had been sitting on the far side of the editor's desk when Farhan had entered. Farhan thought it strange at the time that he had not risen to shake his hand. He then saw why. Montgomery was in a wheelchair.

'Mr Montgomery, Mrs Webster, I would like to remind you that this is a murder enquiry. It is fully understood that you may both be very busy, but my questions take precedence.'

'We realise that,' Montgomery said.

'Get on with it,' Victoria Webster said. 'I don't have all day for you two to have a social chat.' It was clear that Montgomery was in fear of his boss.

'This information, Mrs Webster?'

'How the hell would I know?'

'You wouldn't pay him until he had given it?'

'Do you think I'm stupid?'

Farhan found her an incredibly rude woman – nothing like her personal assistant who was sitting outside. He wondered how anyone could work for such a woman, but then with egregious abuse probably comes great reward for those who can handle the situation. Montgomery probably could, Farhan thought, even if he appeared to be a mild-mannered man, obviously under the controlling thumb of a difficult woman.

Farhan returned to the conversation. He chose to ignore the 'Do you think I'm stupid' comment. 'He may have been killed for that information. It may place you at risk. Have you considered that possibility?' It seemed to have the desired effect. Farhan hadn't considered it before, but it seemed plausible. Temporarily quietened, Victoria Webster sat down and whispered in the ear of her legal adviser.

'We would request a few minutes to discuss this, before Mrs Webster answers. Will that be acceptable?' Montgomery said in a more agreeable tone.

'Fine, I'll wait outside. Call me when you are ready.'

***

Outside the personal assistant organised coffee for Farhan and a sandwich. He reflected on his wife. *How is it that every woman I meet is exceedingly kind and generous to me, whereas she is hostile* and unpleasant; everyone that is, apart from Victoria Webster? he thought.

He decided to give the editor the benefit of the doubt. She sat supreme in the publishing industry. She had taken a lame-duck of a publication devoted to knitting patterns and handicrafts and transformed it into the premier publication in the country devoted to celebrities and movies and music. Every corner store, every newsagent, every street vendor carried the magazine, prominently displayed. He realised that she had not got to where she was without being tough when she needed to be, gentle when needed. He assumed he was not going to see that side of her today.

Twenty minutes later, his sandwich finished, his chat with the PA not ended, he was invited back into the editor's office. He noticed that this time it was an invitation, not a begrudging opening of the door.

Montgomery had moved to another part of the office, closer to some comfortable chairs.

'Detective Inspector, we will sit here if that is okay with you.' Farhan had been wrong. He was to see the gentle side of Victoria Webster.

'Fine by me,' Farhan responded. Two minutes later, the personal assistant walked in with some more coffee. He had already drunk two cups outside, but it would have seemed impolite to refuse.

Montgomery was the first to speak. 'Do you believe that Sutherland died as a result of the information he was willing to give to us?'

Farhan felt it necessary to clarify. 'It is only a supposition at this time. We have established no clear motive.'

'Are you saying there is nothing for me to worry about?' Victoria Webster asked.

'On the contrary. I will be open with you. Charles Sutherland was not the most pleasant of men. He had a tendency to argue with people and to behave in a manner outside of the acceptable norm, especially when drunk or under the influence of drugs.'

'He was a horrible toad of a man,' Victoria Webster interjected. 'I didn't like him at all.'

'Please let me finish.' Farhan needed her to be concerned, not frightened. He was choosing his words carefully. He did not want to reveal the attempted rape of Jess O'Neill as an example, but it was in the back of his mind. He also did not wish to reveal the attempt to draw Christy Nichols into Sutherland's threesome.

'Victoria, it would be best if we let DI Ahmed continue uninterrupted,' Webster said.

'You're right, William. My apologies.'

'I can understand your apprehension concerning the matter.' Farhan could see the veneer of invulnerability cracking. She appeared more than a little nervous. 'We are aware of some gambling debts, a predilection for prostitutes, usually high-class and expensive, and the occasional abuse of drugs, cocaine mainly. None of those activities as far as we can ascertain made him a candidate for murder.'

'Do you know why he was killed?' Montgomery asked.

'Am I correct that you were willing to pay him up to half a million pounds for the story?' Farhan asked.

'The final price was dependent on what he gave us,' Victoria Webster said. 'If it were only that she played around, slept with some influential men, then he would not have received the full amount, maybe one hundred thousand.'

'What were you expecting to receive?' Farhan asked.

'An illegitimate child.'

'Is that worth the full amount?'

'He said it was.'

'Did he tell you?'

'Only hints. I was going to give him another week at the Savoy, allow him to drink himself under the table, screw as many whores as he wanted, then I was going to throw him back on the street. Before throwing him out, I would have given him one more chance.'

'Do you know the name of this child?' Farhan asked.

'No idea, that's the truth. Am I at risk?'

'It is uncertain, but it would be best to take extra precautions.'

'I could make a statement in the media.'

'I would not advise that as a course of action,' Farhan said. 'Mr Montgomery can advise you. You are just focussing attention on yourself.'

'DI Ahmed's correct. It's best to keep a low profile on this.'

Farhan left soon after. Victoria Webster thanked him for his consideration. William Montgomery shook his hand.

Chapter 18

Richard Goddard was in a verbose mode when he met Isaac and Farhan. 'What do you have? he asked.

'It's not what we have, it's what you have,' Isaac said. Farhan would not have been as direct.

'I've met with my contact.'

'And?' Isaac said.

'There's a child.'

'We know that. That appears to be the clue to this whole sorry mess.'

'What do you mean?'

'Charles Sutherland was using it as a bargaining chip with Victoria Webster,' Farhan said.

'Did she know who it was?'

'No, but she's scared that she may be a marked woman.'

'Is she?'

'Potentially,' Isaac said. 'If this is dynamite, then anyone even remotely involved is at risk.'

'Including us,' Detective Superintendent Goddard said. 'We've considered it.'

'Any more tails on your cars?'

'Not recently.' Isaac said.

'Detective Superintendent, your contact. What's he got to say for himself?' Isaac asked.

'He's not willing to reveal who the child is. I believe he doesn't know.'

'Did Marjorie Frobisher, and if so, how?'

'My contact did reveal that the child is looking for the mother. They can't hold him off for much longer.'

'Are we looking for a male?' Farhan asked.

'A slip of the tongue. The assumption is male, but there's no reason to believe that it could not be female. Marjorie Frobisher would have known.'

'And the father, presumably.' Isaac said.

'Maybe, maybe not. The birth could have been hushed up, remote location, remote hospital, probably private. Even the adoption records could have been falsified.

'Let's come back to your contact, sir,' Isaac said. He was sure there was something else, something vital.

'You want more information, correct?'

'Correct.' Isaac stood up. He aimed to hover close to his senior until something more definite was revealed.

'I believe my contact is being honest when he said that the person he is reporting to would not condone murder – even if the child could be responsible for the collapse of the government.'

'Are we saying that Charles Sutherland was not a sanctioned murder?'

'Not at all. My contact stated that revealing the existence of the child would have more severe repercussions than a change of government.'

'And he doesn't know who it is?' Isaac persisted.

'I don't believe he does.'

'Someone does.'

'Who then?' Farhan asked.

'The father would be a fair assumption,' Richard Goddard admitted.

'Then why don't we talk to the father?' Isaac suggested.

'I'm not sure who he is.'

'You've a fair idea.'

'I'm pretty certain who it is.'

'Then why don't we make an appointment, and go over and meet with this person.'

'Not so easy.'

'Why not?' Isaac asked.

'He doesn't answer his phone, at least, not to us. It would need to be the Commissioner.'

'Then ask him.' Isaac saw no issue. He had met Commissioner Shaw on a couple of occasions; thought him a reasonable, approachable man.

'If we tread on too many toes, we could find ourselves back on the street directing traffic.'

'If we don't tread a little harder, we may as well let a murderer get away free and easy. Is that what you want?' Isaac asked.

'Okay, I'll talk to the commissioner, ask him to coordinate.' The detective superintendent could see his career plateauing, just as he started on the ladder to the commissioner's office. He wanted the top job in the Met, although it was still ten years away at least. He had no great wish to broach the subject with the commissioner, and he certainly did not relish confronting the father of the illegitimate child.

***

Marion Robertson had been on the phone to Farhan. The other escort was ready to meet him. He scheduled the meeting for the next day at four in the afternoon. Marion said that would be suitable, and that Olivia would meet him out in Richmond, close to the park. He allowed himself forty minutes to get there.

The next day he was late. She was angry. 'I agreed to give you ten minutes of my time, and you arrive late,' she said. Farhan remembered Samantha and how pleasant she had been. He could not say the same about Olivia. She was plainly dressed, her hair pulled back tight. She wore an old raincoat, and clothes that looked neither fashionable nor modern.

'My apologies, traffic.'

'I don't have much time,' she replied brusquely.

'This is a murder investigation. You must appreciate that I may need longer.'

'That may be, but I'm the designated mother. I'm picking up my two children as well as next door's.'

'If we can't conclude today, then maybe another time,' Farhan said.

'Secrecy is paramount. You do understand?'

'Yes,' he said. She gave a weak smile, the first sign of friendship. The smile changed her whole persona, so much so that the dowdy clothes and the severe hairstyle faded into the distance.

'You're not going to ask me why I prostitute myself, are you?'

'I'm not here to offer an opinion. I'm here because a man was murdered. A man you were intimate with.'

'I would hardly call screwing a man for money "intimate".'

'What would you call it?'

'A financial necessity.' She kept looking at her watch.

'How long have you got?'

'Twenty minutes maximum. I've been working all day, explains the clothes.'

'What type of work?'

'I work in a factory, manual work. It's dusty and not very pleasant.'

'Why do that if you can work as an escort and make decent money?'

'There you go, the same as the rest, aiming to reform me. Mind you, most want to tell me to work in an office, find a decent husband. At least you're original.'

'Believe me. I have no intention of reform. I need to find out what I can about the death of Charles Sutherland. Your background is relevant if it removes you from suspicion.'

'Or makes me more likely to be the murderer of that horrible man.'

'I suppose you're right.'

'Of course I'm right.'

'Then maybe you can answer the question why you work in a factory.'

'You'll need to know something about my life story.' They both sat on a bench by the side of the road.

'I led a troubled existence up until I was about eighteen. No abuse, good family environment, but I was wild. Something in my genetic makeup, I suppose. I moved out of the home and into a small apartment with a couple of other girls. We always had men over, more like boys on reflection. Anyway, the two girls moved in with their boyfriends, and I was left with the rent to pay. I was too proud to go home and ask for money, and jobs were hard to come by. I saw an ad in the paper, women wanted. I assumed it was prostitution.'

'Did you have a problem with that?'

'Some, but it wasn't that much of an issue. The woman I met, upmarket part of the city, took one look at me and told me I was a lot better than the usual women that came through the door. She took me under her wing and soon I was working as an escort. Great money and the men were invariably kind and gentle. A few were a little kinky, wanted me to tie them up, that sort of thing. I worked like that for about eight years.

'One day, I'm out walking through a park, idly minding my own business, when a man comes up to me. He just wanted to say hello. He meant nothing by it, and he certainly was not attempting to seduce me. We started meeting on a regular basis. He had no idea what I did to earn a living.

'Anyway, I realised that I loved him, and I wanted a life similar to my parents. We married, and all was fine, two healthy children and a mortgage. A few years ago, the economy tightened, and my husband was unable to make the payments on the house and the schooling. I said I would go out to work, so I took the job at the factory. It was purely a cover.

'Each day I would go off to the factory, bring some money in, but it wasn't much. I saw no problem with going back into escorting. Most men like an older, more experienced woman anyway, and I knew I was still attractive, even if a little rounder. I found Marion Robertson through an ad. She's been a godsend, and she always pays promptly.'

'Your husband doesn't know?'

'He must never know. I do this for him and my children. Not for any other reason.'

'I will give you the promise that I gave Samantha. I will maintain your confidentiality. I cannot guarantee that I will be able to indefinitely, but I will try. What can you tell me about Charles Sutherland?'

'There's not much I can tell you. We went there a couple of times, put on a show for him, gave him the threesome he wanted and left.'

'Your husband, wasn't he concerned that you were out at night?'

'Nightshift at the factory.'

'And he accepted it?'

'He's a trusting man, even thought I was a virgin when we first met.'

'Thank you, there's not much more I need for now. Hopefully, we will not need to meet again.'

'I hope we never do,' she said.

***

The Murder Investigation Team was now in full operation: collating, investigating, researching in the hunt for whoever had killed Charles Sutherland. The forensics report had come through: death due to a combination of alcohol, cocaine, and arsenic poisoning.

Coupled with the dead man's obesity and a heart condition, death was recorded as manslaughter, possibly murder. It was ambiguous. Isaac phoned Gordon Windsor. His statement: the arsenic may not have been of sufficient quantity to kill an average healthy male, but Charles Sutherland was obese with a heart condition. This raised the question of whether his death was the objective. Regardless of the reason, it was imperative to find the person responsible.

Before the murder, Isaac's and Farhan's activities had been kept relatively low-key, due to the sensitivity of Marjorie Frobisher's disappearance. With Isaac now juggling two jobs, one as the senior investigating officer of the MIT, the other as part of the team with Farhan looking for the missing woman, it became apparent that another person was required.

Both of them knew Constable Wendy Gladstone: Farhan in passing with a cursory 'Hello', 'How are you?', Isaac better as they had worked on a couple of cases together in the past. If you needed to find someone, then she was the best person for the job.

She came into the office early. When Farhan arrived just after seven and Isaac fifteen minutes later, she had already found herself a desk and put it close to Farhan's.

'If anyone is missing, they won't stay missing for long,' Richard Goddard had said when told that she would be joining the team.

She had given Farhan a firm handshake when he had walked into the office. Isaac received a bear hug and a kiss on both cheeks.

'Who do you want to find?' she asked. She was a smoker and the smell of stale tobacco was anathema to them. If it became a problem, Isaac resolved to talk to her about it, but not today.

'Marjorie Frobisher,' Farhan said.

'My favourite actress, my favourite programme.'

'You like the programme?' Isaac asked.

'Why not? After a day in here dealing with misery and violence, a bit of nonsense does no harm. You don't like it?'

'Neither of us likes it much,' Farhan said. He liked the woman, although he was more sensitive to the smell of tobacco than Isaac.

'Each to their own,' she said. She had brought her own coffee mug and was seated comfortably at her desk.

'Where was she last seen?' Wendy asked.

'A hotel in Malvern, Worcestershire,' Isaac replied.

'Positive identification?'

'The receptionist said it was her, and she was picked up on a street camera.'

'How long ago?'

'Three weeks, in Malvern.'

'That's seven weeks missing. Where has she been?'

'No idea' Isaac replied.

'Probably she rented a remote cottage in a nondescript village and kept a low profile,' Wendy said.

'Why would she do that?' Farhan asked.

'I don't know. Where she is now is what's important.'

'Wendy, we'll bring you up to speed,' Isaac said.

'Fine, let me get another mug of coffee. You want some?' Both Isaac and Farhan declined. Isaac knew that they would need to buy more sugar for the office.

Once she was sitting down again, Isaac commenced. 'Marjorie Frobisher's disappearance has caused some concern.'

'I know. Her fans are distraught,' Wendy said.

'It is not her fans that concern us. Marjorie Frobisher led a colourful life. In her earlier years, before she became a major star, she was involved with people who are now very influential. Those people need to know if she is dead or alive.'

'Don't worry about me. I can keep a secret.'

'We know that.'

'What's the tie-in between Sutherland and Marjorie Frobisher, then?'

'We believe he had some knowledge relating to her.'

'Enough knowledge to get him murdered?'

'It seems likely.'

'I'd better get to Malvern. Is this dangerous, by the way?'

'How are you fixed for security?'

'Pepper spray and a kick in the groin.'

Later that day, with a cash advance, a police-issue credit card, and a car, Constable Wendy Gladstone was heading to Malvern. Isaac and Farhan felt confident that she would find Marjorie Frobisher, dead or alive. Until then they had to carry on probing, asking, and hoping for a breakthrough.

Chapter 19

With Wendy in Malvern dealing with the disappearance of Marjorie Frobisher, both Isaac and Farhan were at a loose end. It had been so quiet the previous night after she had left that Isaac had left early to meet Sophie. Farhan had gone home to an empty house, although his wife was talking about coming back. He was pleased for the children, not for himself, as what she considered to be love was not how he saw it. It was a dilemma for which he had no solution.

He was a proud Muslim, and what he was contemplating was contrary to all he had been brought up to believe. His family would not understand, his children would probably not as they grew older, but he had become a contradiction, a contradiction to his faith. He knew what he must do. He was not sure how it would turn out. He needed to sow his wild oats and then maybe… Maybe then he would go back to the all-encompassing traditional family.

Isaac arrived refreshed the following morning; Farhan, the opposite, as he had not been sleeping well since his wife left. Samantha, or Aisha as she preferred him to call her, had phoned him once or twice, exceedingly friendly, but he had to remind her that as it was an ongoing murder investigation, he was not in a position to meet other than on official business. Aisha understood, or she said she did. Maybe she was like Olivia, looking for a good man. *Could he be that man?* he thought. *Could he forgive her for all the men she had slept with?* He wasn't sure, but it concerned him, kept him awake at nights thinking about her.

'Farhan, coffee?' Isaac asked, bringing him back from his daydreaming.

'Yes, please.'

Both sat at their desks.

'You're satisfied the women that Sutherland had in his room are not involved?' Isaac asked.

'I'm certain they were only there for sex.'

'Then someone must have gone in after and given him the drink.'

'A fair assumption, Isaac.'

'It doesn't help, though. Security cameras. Any at the hotel?'

'Not in the rooms and not on the floor.'

'Then someone could have entered without being spotted.'

'That's correct.'

'And it must have happened after the women left and before the maid found the body.'

'We know that he died around three to four in the morning.'

'Any record of him phoning for another woman?'

'None has been found.'

'What does that suggest?'

'That he knew the person.'

'Precisely,' Farhan agreed. 'And why didn't Christy Nichols hear the knocking and the commotion?'

'Good question, you'd better ask her.'

'What are you going to do?' Farhan asked.

'I intend to meet up with Marjorie Frobisher's children. I need to see how they feel about their mother's disappearance. Whether they are involved.'

'Why would they be involved?'

'I'm not altogether sure. If the woman is alive, then there is no involvement, but if she's dead…'

'They could have killed her.'

'If they had a motive.'

'We are assuming her death would be a sanctioned assassination?'

'It's only an assumption. We know that people in senior places in this country want her dead. That doesn't mean, however, that they committed the murder. Maybe someone else did, and it has proven advantageous to them. Charles Sutherland was a loose end; his death may have been an assassination or someone out for revenge.'

'You know what you just said. I said it on the day of the interview with Jess O'Neill. You chose to ignore me.'

'I heard what you said. I just didn't want to hear it at the time. It is a strong enough motive,' Isaac finally admitted.

Farhan changed the subject. 'I'll go and see Christy Nichols. You can go and see Marjorie Frobisher's children.'

***

Christy Nichols was not hard to find. Her experience at the Savoy had left her downtrodden and downhearted. She had temporarily given up any hope of fame and fortune in the publishing world.

'It's a cut-throat business,' she admitted when she met Farhan. They had agreed on a location in the east of the city, a small coffee shop he had visited in the past, and she knew. He had ordered cappuccino for them both, served by an Italian woman. He had made small talk, assumed she was a member of the family that owned the café, but she had told him she was just a backpacker aiming to make enough to pay her weekly costs. She said that no one in the family would work there for the hourly rate, but it was cash, so she saw no reason to complain. Besides, it was the tips that made it worthwhile. He made sure to give her a good tip.

'What are you doing at the moment?' he asked Christy.

'Licking my wounds.'

'That bad?'

'That bad. You know she refused to pay my expenses?'

'Victoria Webster?'

'You've met her?' she asked.

'On official business.'

'What did you think?'

'It would be inappropriate for me to comment.'

'I understand. Policeman's code, something like that.'

'Yes, something like that.'

'She's a bitch, isn't she? Don't answer that,' she said. Farhan smiled.

'She's right of course. It's a dog-eat-dog business. If you're soft and kind-hearted like me, it's impossible to make it.'

'Christy, did you see anything?'

'The night he was murdered?'

'Yes.'

'I saw the two women enter, but after his behaviour the previous time, I was keeping well away.'

'The women that you saw, can you describe them?' Farhan asked. He had met them both. It seemed a good idea to confirm that she was referring to the same women.

'Both were attractive, heavier build than me, but not fat. One seemed to be Indian, not very dark though, and the other one

English, in her late thirties, maybe early forties. They were both well-spoken. I had to pay someone in the hotel to let them in by the back entrance.'

'Your description sounds right.'

'You've met them?'

'They didn't want to, but it's a murder investigation. I could have forced them to come to the police station.'

'You didn't?'

'No, I met them separately in neutral locations.'

'What did you think?' She seemed curious.

'I liked them both. As you say, apart from what they do.'

'It's not for us to judge, is it?'

'Not at all,' Farhan replied. 'Life is tough. People sometimes need to make decisions to survive. Both were desperate to protect their identities.'

'Their alter egos.'

'You make them sound like superheroes or superheroines.' Farhan was not sure where the conversation was heading.

'Not really, but I can admire strong-minded, strong-willed people. I can admire Victoria Webster, not necessarily like her. I can even admire the two prostitutes, although I could never imagine myself doing something like that. What if they were seen by someone they knew? What would they do?'

'I never asked. I will the next time.'

'They won't like it,' she said. Farhan ordered two more drinks. It was evident she was in no hurry to leave, neither was he.

'It's an interesting thought. What if they had seen someone that night, someone who should not have been there? Would they have told me?' Farhan said.

'Probably not. Protecting their lives outside of prostituting themselves would be more important.'

'I suppose so.'

'You know so.'

'I agreed to keep what they told me in confidence. Christy, level with me. Why are you so interested?'

'Don't you ever feel like throwing away people's perception of respectability, just being yourself?'

'Sometimes,' he admitted. *Often*, he thought.

129

'Sorry, I'm just feeling sorry for myself. I'm not doing a lot at the present moment, just working for a local rag, gossip column.'

'How did you get into that?'

'I've been doing it for some time. I mainly work from home, make up most of the "Dear Marigold's". It pays the bills.'

'You don't look like a Marigold.'

'It's my middle name. A great aunt that my mother was fond of was named Marigold. I think my mother was having a bad day when she gave it to me.'

Farhan realised he was enjoying his time with Christy Nichols, although it was still a murder investigation, and she still remained the closest person to Charles Sutherland. He had discounted the two escorts; he couldn't call them prostitutes anymore. He didn't want to think of Samantha aka Aisha selling herself on a street corner. An escort sounded more refined. He also realised that he needed to meet her again: firstly because there was a valid reason, and secondly because he wanted to.

'Coming back to the night of the murder,' Farhan refocussed. 'The women said they left around midnight.'

'I never saw them leave.'

'Why's that?'

'No reason to. I showed them in, but I certainly did not want to see Sutherland flashing me again. I've led a sheltered life.' She seemed to be joking.

'Sheltered. What do you mean?'

'It's just a silly remark really. I had a very conservative childhood. My parents did all they could to shield me from the seedier side of life. There were no late-night parties or boys over. No alcohol in the house and certainly no bad language. I stayed there until I was in my early twenties, and then the company I worked for transferred me to London. It's left me a little prudish, not sure how to handle some situations.'

'Such as Charles Sutherland when he's high on drugs and women.'

'Yes, Charles Sutherland. I suppose another woman would have slapped his face, kicked him in the groin and screamed for help.'

'Why didn't you?'

'I think I froze.'

'Then what happened?'

'It's too shocking.'

'You need to elaborate, it's important.'

'I'm ashamed.' She was shaking visibly. Her face was red, and tears were welling up in her eyes. Farhan beckoned the Italian waitress to bring another two coffees.

'He made me do something.'

'And the other women?'

'They weren't there. They had left by then. I should have gone out with them, but I was scared.'

She sipped her cappuccino. 'He made me perform fellatio on him.'

'Why did you agree?'

'I was scared of what he would do.'

'And afterwards?'

'He laughed at me, told me I would have been a lousy screw anyway, and that I was only good for a blowjob.'

'Did you report it?'

'To who? Victoria Webster would not have been interested. Charles Sutherland was more important than me. I was only the hired help. She would have assumed I encouraged him.'

'After you left?'

'I went to my room, put my fingers down my throat – he made me swallow it all – until I vomited. I then stood in the shower for hours, so hot it almost burned, until it went cold. After that, I lay on my bed sobbing. I didn't sleep that night.'

'Thank you for telling me.'

'It makes me a murder suspect, doesn't it?'

'It's a strong enough motive. Why didn't you tell me before?'

'I was ashamed. I was concerned that it would be seen that I had encouraged him – that I was a slut.'

'You wished him dead after that?'

'Of course, any woman would, but it does not make me a murderer, does it?'

He didn't answer her question. 'Why did you tell me today?' he asked instead.

'I trust you,' she replied.

Chapter 20

Wendy Gladstone was pleased that her time in Isaac and Farhan's office had been short. She had spent thirty years in the force, pounding the beat initially in uniform with a whistle and a baton; another five, maybe six years before she retired. The concept of retirement did not excite her, but she was getting older, and arthritis was starting to set in. No one knew, not even her husband.

He had retired five years earlier. He was ten years older than her, a strapping man when she had first met him, an embittered man now. He blamed it all on the migrants coming into the country, taking everyone's job, turning the neighbourhoods into ghettoes. 'Bloody Paki,' he would say every time he saw someone Asian in the street. She had no problems with them; the family two doors down had come from India, and they were fine. She knew he would not have liked Detective Inspector Ahmed.

It was minor, and she would not make a scene about it. And the office no longer allowed smoking. In fact, she had to go out on the street, rain or shine.

She didn't hold with these modern ideas where you couldn't smoke, drink, discipline your child, or call a spade a spade in case it offended someone. Her father, a potato farmer, humble and poor, smoked all his life. He downed his five pints every night at the pub, was not averse to disciplining the children if they needed it, and he had been a good man. He had lived to his mid-eighties. Her mother, teetotal, gentle and a housewife, barely made it past sixty before she had a stroke.

Ambition had never been the driving force in Wendy Gladstone's life, although policing had, ever since childhood. Her earliest memories, apart from her doting mother and her firm but fair father, had been the local police constable: uniformed, tall helmet, riding around the area, a rugged and scenic part of the Yorkshire moors in the north of England, freezing in winter, cold in summer. She saw him as an almost saintly figure. Senior Constable Terry Clarke was a sweet-talking man who sang baritone in the local choir on a Sunday. Whenever he saw someone, he would stop and greet them. For the children – he knew them all by name – there would always be a sweet.

She soon realised, after joining the police force and being assigned to a police station in Sheffield and then London, that there were villains to be dealt with, and not all the children looked forward to an encounter with the local policeman, or in her case, the local policewoman. Some of the children were plainly disruptive, some plainly criminal, some plainly abusive.

It had been just after her fifteenth birthday that her hormones had kicked in. Brian Hardcastle, a headmaster's son and a tall, skinny rake of a boy, had not been the most suitable introduction to the joy of sex.

The barn where there consummated their lust, each taking the other's virginity, was hot and smelly. It was a five-minute affair: with him being disappointed in his performance – he had read books on the subject – and her being ecstatic. For a while, her father had tried to confine her to her room, but her mother had eventually intervened. 'It's a phase she's going through. Exploring her sexuality,' she had said. She had learnt the phrase from a book in the local library. Her father, increasingly annoyed at the ribbing he received at the pub over his wayward daughter, kept away for a few months, but in the end the ribbing ceased and he went back to his five pints a night. He was glad when Wendy joined the police force and went to Sheffield. Once out of the village, she found the need for a multitude of men had subsided.

Her husband came along when she was nineteen, an old man – at least, in her mother's eyes – of twenty-nine.

***

'One room, please,' Wendy said as she stood at the reception desk at the Abbey Hotel in Malvern. It was five-star, the sort of hotel where Marjorie Frobisher would stay. She also knew that it was beyond her salary, and if it had not been official business and a police-issue credit card, she would have found a room above a pub.

Her room, second floor with a view overlooking the Priory, was splendid. Smoke-free, which she did not like, but the window opened wide. She had a warm bath. Too many cigarettes and too many big meals had left her body worn and sagging. She had promised many times to change her ways; she always failed within a day.

Refreshed, she headed downstairs. The worst approach with the receptionist who had identified the missing woman would be to flash her badge. She knew it would put her on the defensive. It seemed best to identify her first. She was not in view, and Wendy did not want to go asking questions and raising suspicion. A good meal, a couple of glasses of wine, and an early night seemed the best approach. The next day she would find the receptionist; indulge in idle conversation about the local tourist highlights, television programmes – especially the one she was interested in.

***

Farhan met Samantha again. She was pleased when he rang. They met in the same prearranged spot as before. She brought two curries: one for him, one for her, from an Indian restaurant not far from her office. He appreciated the gesture.

'Samantha.'

'Please call me Aisha. I prefer Aisha.'

'Aisha, there was an incident the first night at the hotel. The woman you met, did you speak to her?'

'Not really. She arranged for us to come in. I think she disapproved.'

'That's probably correct.'

'Aisha, it's best if you think before you speak. I should really ask you to come down to the station and make a statement…'

'You're trying to protect me?'

'You and Olivia.'

'You've met her? What was she like?'

'I'm not sure it would be appropriate for me to tell you.'

'Did you like her? At least, you can tell me that.'

'I did not like her as much as you.'

'I would have been upset if you had,' she replied.

'She has her reasons, the same as you. Let's go back to the first night. What happened?'

'Sutherland was high on alcohol and drugs.'

'Were you?'

'Not at all. I don't even drink. I play along with the client, same as Olivia. You need to be a good actor sometimes.'

'Please continue.'

'As I told you before, we were on the floor with him.'

'And then?'

'The woman walks in unexpectedly. She must have assumed we had gone, as we were not making much noise. She was checking that all was okay, I suppose.'

'What did Sutherland do?'

'He jumped up and exposed himself to her. She looked as though she had never seen a naked man before. With her standing there and it getting late, I went into the bedroom with Olivia. We dressed in our going home clothes and left soon after.'

'Going home clothes?'

'Yes, of course. I can hardly walk in the door at my parent's house looking like a painted tart. I change into my regular work clothes, take off the perfume.'

'And the woman?'

'We were out of there in five minutes. Sutherland had sobered up by then, and she was serving him coffee. We weren't looking, but it appeared relatively calm. It wasn't for us to nursemaid them. I assumed her job was to take care of him. She may have been available as well. I don't think she was, but I never asked or cared.'

'Is there any more?'

'No, that's it. You can ask Olivia if you like, but she will confirm my statement.'

'I will take your statement, Olivia's too, if it's necessary.'

'I finish my degree in a couple of months. I'm not sure if I want to sell myself again.'

'I would have thought after one of your clients was murdered, it would not be a good option.'

'You're right of course. I've seen things, met people, been places. I'm not as naïve as you think.'

'It is the same for me,' Farhan said.

'If I stop, can we meet again?' she asked. 'Socially, that is. Or is what I have done too much for you to forget?'

'I think I can handle the situation. This is a murder investigation, and you are a material witness. It would not be advisable for us to meet socially at this time.'

'A confidential witness.'

'I don't intend to reveal your name unless it is absolutely necessary.'

'You don't want anyone to know your girlfriend is a former prostitute.' She smiled. Farhan realised she was teasing him.

'We need to keep this professional.'

'Sorry, I've embarrassed you, Detective Inspector Ahmed. We will meet again, hopefully soon. For myself, I will remain pure and chaste until you call.'

'It may be some time.'

'Time is not the issue. When is more important.'

They parted, unaware that they had yet again walked a significant distance. He knew he had made an error in letting his personal feelings interfere with his professional responsibilities. He would talk to Isaac when it was opportune, for advice.

***

Isaac instinctively did not like Fiona Avers from the first moment he met her at Robert Avers and Marjorie Frobisher's home. 'I would like to ask you about your mother.'

'Before you carry on,' she said, attempting to take control of the discussion, 'I despised my mother.'

'Why do you feel the need to tell me that before I've asked you any questions?' Isaac had seen it before. The desperate need of a witness to explain their intense dislike of a person, as if somehow it exonerated them from the crime. Often it did, but not always.

'I just want to make it clear, that's all.'

Isaac could see why Fiona Avers had never become a major star, as her mother had. He had watched her mother on the television a few times, even downloaded some episodes of her current programme off YouTube. He also found a movie she had made twenty years previously.

He did not find the characters she portrayed particularly endearing, but Marjorie Frobisher was, had been, a beautiful woman. The daughter was not. For once he felt calm. Too often a potential witness – attractive and easy to the eye – had caused him to soften his interrogational style. It was not going to happen this time.

'Are you saying that you do not miss your mother?'

'I told you in the first sentence. Don't you listen?' Fiona Avers had the manners of an alley cat.

'The disappearance of your mother and the murder of Charles Sutherland may be related. Your confrontational style is not conducive to this discussion.'

'What do I care about Charles Sutherland? The only time I met him, he wanted to put his grubby paws all over me.'

'And where was that?'

'Here, in this house. My mother was having one of her celebrity get-togethers. I didn't receive an invite – too embarrassing, having her ugly daughter around.'

'Why do you say that?'

'You've got two eyes. You tell me.'

'I'm not sure I understand.'

'I'm not beautiful, that's the problem. I may not be totally ugly, and it doesn't concern me, at least not too much, but to my precious mother, beauty and poise and grace were all-important. I'm clumsy, more likely to break the best china teapot than pour a cup of tea from it. That's how she saw it. It was always the same, even from childhood.'

'So why did you come to the party?'

'It's my home. I've a right to come, and besides my mother owed me. If she didn't make the introductions, ensured I got a part on some programme, I would have made a scene.'

Isaac saw clearly that if Fiona Avers decided to make a scene, no one would have been able to stop her.

'Did she help you?'

'She pretended to. Introduced me to a couple of producers: "drop around anytime, and we'll give you an audition".'

'Did they work out?'

'Hell, no. The first one was always too busy: come next week. The other one seemed to fancy tall, plain-looking women. He showed me the casting couch; I showed him a bunch of fives and a kick in the shin. He showed me the door.'

'What are you doing now?'

'The word got around that I'm difficult to work with. Mother probably did little to discourage that. The only decent part on offer was the casting couch producer. I should have just let him fuck me, will next time.'

'Seems a tough way to get ahead in your line of business,' Isaac said.

'Ask Mother. She's been on more casting couches than there are casting couches. She's a terrible tart. I assume you've been told.'

'I am aware that the relationship between your father and mother was unusual.'

'It was no relationship. She told him, he accepted. He loved her, still does, and he's devoted to both Sam and I. Maybe not so much to Sam, but then he's a hopeless case: drink and drugs.'

'Your relationship with your father?'

'He's a wonderful man. I've told him enough times to give her the boot and find someone else.'

Isaac wanted to get back to the issue with Charles Sutherland. First, he needed a break. Fiona went and made two coffees. She returned and placed them on the table; best china, he noticed.

'Let us get back to the incident with Charles Sutherland.'

'It was late in the evening. I was drunk, too many vodkas and whiskies, maybe a couple of beers as well. Sutherland was equally drunk. Father was upstairs asleep. He doesn't have a lot of time for entertainment people. He finds most of them vacuous and self-obsessed, which they are – my mother being the prime example.'

'Your father came to the party?'

'He played the perfect host. He ensured everyone had a drink and was fed. He spent about three hours at the party, and by then a few had left, a few were drunk and asleep in a chair, and some others were sniffing cocaine.'

'Which were you?'

'I was drunk, but not drugged. I've tried drugs, the less harmful variety, and they make me psychotic. Alcohol suffices for me.'

'Charles Sutherland.'

'I'm at the back of the house. It's a big house, as you've seen. I'm sitting there drinking steadily. He comes in on his own. He's clearly high on drugs, and I'm definitely drunk. He sees beauty in me, and I see a handsome man in him.'

'It's just the two of you?'

'The beautiful woman. The handsome man. That's what alcohol and recreational drugs do to you – make you see something that is not there.'

'I think you are playing down your appearance,' Isaac said. He had to admit that beautiful was not a description he would use, but she had some character in her face. Her manner with people was her main disadvantage.

'You don't need to be kind. Let me continue.'

'Okay.'

'We start fooling around, groping each other.'

'I thought you said his advances were unwelcome.'

'I was not entirely truthful. Anyway, soon after, I've got my skirt up around my arse, and he's on top of me going for dear life.'

'Sexual intercourse?'

'That's sounds clinical. It was just a drunken fuck.'

'So why the hatred?'

'As I'm climaxing and he's struggling to come, in walks my mother. It appears that the party has come to a conclusion and she, and one other, are the only ones left. Except for Charles Sutherland and yours truly.'

'What did you mother say?'

'Nothing. She wasn't interested in me, only the man she had brought in to fuck.'

'Sutherland's reaction?'

'He jumped up, left me dangling without concluding his part.'

'What do you mean?'

'He failed to ejaculate, shoot his load. Clear enough?'

'Clear enough.'

'And what did you think of your mother with another man?'

'Not much. She was always playing around with one man or another, but in my father's house, with him upstairs asleep… I was angry.'

'There's a scene with your mother, but what's this got to do with Sutherland.'

'He takes her side. Calls me an old tart, and said if he hadn't been drunk, he wouldn't have touched me with a barge pole. It's not the first time a man has said that to me. I was livid, making a scene, a lot of noise as well, I suppose. Anyway, my father comes down, sees what's going on, and takes me out of the room and puts me to bed with a cup of cocoa and a hot water bottle.'

'Charles Sutherland?'

'He left soon after.'

'And your mother?'

'Ten minutes later, the front door slammed shut, and she came upstairs as if nothing had happened.'

'Why ten minutes later, if Sutherland had already left?'

'She still needed fucking.'

'Who was the man?'

'Richard Williams.'

Isaac realised that here, in this one embittered woman, was the motive for two murders: the murder of Marjorie Frobisher, if she was indeed dead, and the murder of Charles Sutherland.

Chapter 21

Wendy had not announced the previous day when checking in at the hotel that she was a police officer. Experience had taught her that people become secretive and guarded once an ID badge is flashed in front of them. Even the innocent start to clam up, check what they say and how they say it. She needed the receptionist free and willing to talk. She was not a difficult woman to recognise as all the staff appeared to be young – in their twenties and thirties – except for her.

Felicity Pearson, in her late forties, maybe early fifties; her photo courtesy of a board in the hotel foyer showing 'Employee of the month'. She had already been interviewed by the police; she would not necessarily welcome a second time.

Wendy decided the best approach was to engage in idle chatter when the reception was quiet. She waited her time. It came around eleven o'clock in the morning, when those who were checking out had, and those checking in were waiting until two in the afternoon.

'I was thinking of taking a walk in the hills,' Wendy said.

'That's a good idea. It's best to take a coat. It can get cold up there at times, even snow in the winter, but not today,' the receptionist replied.

'I don't want to be gone for too long.'

'Why's that?'

'They're repeating the episode where Billy Blythe dies.' Wendy thought it a good enough way to direct the questioning towards the missing woman.

'She was in here, you know.'

'Who was?' Wendy, sounding suitably vague, replied.

'His sister.'

'You watch the programme?' Wendy said. *A fellow devotee, ideal*, she thought.

'I never miss it.'

'Nor do I. It's a shame about his sister,' Wendy said.

'I just said before. She was in here.'

'Edith Blythe?'

'Yes, his sister.'

'That must have been exciting. What was she like?'

'She didn't say much. She didn't like it when I recognised her.'

'Why's that?'

'I've no idea. She left soon after. I think it was because of me.'

Wendy noticed that Felicity Pearson was ignoring other people standing at the reception. 'You'd better deal with them first.' She did not want the receptionist getting in trouble, and then walking out of the door in a huff.

'Give me five minutes, and then we can chat some more.' Wendy could tell that the woman liked nothing more than a good conversation.

Five minutes later she returned. 'Marjorie Frobisher, that's who it was. Mind you, I wouldn't have recognised her.'

'Why do you say that?'

'Her hair was a different colour, and she wore large sunglasses.'

'How did you know it was her?'

'I only knew it was her when she came to the counter and asked for the linen on her bed to be changed. We only do it every third day, but she was adamant.'

'What did you do?'

'I phoned up housekeeping. They sorted it out.'

'You've not explained how you knew it was her.'

'You remember how she used to look when she was sad. One side of her mouth appeared to droop slightly lower than the other.'

'Yes, of course.'

'That's what she did with me. I was so excited, I asked her for her autograph.'

'Her reaction?'

'I could see she wasn't happy, but she remained polite and signed a piece of paper for me. I framed it, put it next to the television at home.'

'What happened after she had signed it?'

'She went upstairs and packed her case.'

'When she left, where did she go?'

'I organised a taxi for her.'

'Do you know the taxi she took?'

'Bert picked her up. We always try to use him for the guests. He's been driving for us for years.'

'Where can I find him?'

'Up the road, blue Toyota. You can't miss him.'

'Thanks.'

'Why are you so interested in where she's gone.'

'Her husband has asked me to find her, bring her home.'

'You've been engaging in idle conversation, making me neglect the guests, pretending to be a fan of the programme…'

'I am a fan. I also need to find her.'

'I hope nothing has happened to her.'

'We're not sure. We think she may have come to some harm.' Wendy felt she owed the woman some gossip in return.

'Is it anything to do with Billy Blythe? I never liked him. The actor who played him, his death.'

'Yes,' Wendy replied.

'Well I never,' Felicity Pearson said. The last words Wendy heard from the receptionist as she went out to find Bert, the taxi driver, was her telling some guests the latest gossip on Marjorie Frobisher. She could only smile.

***

Isaac had made two appointments that day at Marjorie Frobisher's house: the first in the morning with the daughter, Fiona Avers. The second in the afternoon with Sam Avers, the son.

Sam Avers, the elder of the two children, arrived drunk. He was unapologetic. He had a five-day beard and his breath smelt, so much so that Isaac was obliged to move chairs to one side to avoid a frontal assault of stale beer.

'Mr Avers.'

'Call me Sam, everyone does.'

'Okay, Sam. We are conducting investigations into the disappearance of your mother and the death of Charles Sutherland.'

'What's his death got to do with her?' Sam Avers responded. He coughed violently as he spoke. He lit another cigarette.

'We are not sure. I had hoped that you would have some further information that would assist us.'

'Why me? I hardly knew the man, and as for her…'

'Your relationship with your mother?'

'Hardly ever saw her, and when I did, she was off out somewhere with her rich friends.'

'Were they all rich?'

'Most were, but she hardly wanted them for their money. She had plenty, not that she gave me much.'

'I am told by your father that they give you a generous allowance and a credit card. Is that correct?'

'They only give it for me to go away. I'm an embarrassment to them. Did he tell you that?'

'I understand you live here.'

'I come and go, mostly go. I don't want to be around here any more than necessary.'

'You come here, ensure your money is available and leave.'

'That's about it,' the drunken man said. He had gone to the drinks cabinet and was pouring himself a large whisky. 'You want one?' he said. Isaac declined.

'On duty, is that it?'

'Too early for me,' Isaac replied. It wasn't true but he certainly did not want a large whisky, and he did not want to drink with the man. He did not like him; was being careful not to offend or rile.

'Suit yourself. I have to give the old man credit, he certainly keeps a good drop of whisky here, only the best.'

'Before we discuss your mother, let us consider Charles Sutherland.'

'I only met him once or twice. He could drink – more than me.'

'Where did you meet him?'

'Here once, in town another time.'

'What happened here?'

'We got drunk.'

'Nothing else?'

'Are you insinuating that I'm gay, that I fancy men?'

'Not at all. This is a murder investigation. It is important that I am thorough.'

'And besides, he liked women. The more he could get hold of, the better.'

'How do you know that?'

'I ran into him at a club in town once. He had a couple of women with him, real classy.'

'Can you please elaborate?'

'I go over to him. He's drunk. Wants to tell me what a bitch my mother is. He expects me to argue with him. I'm harmless when I've been drinking, which is most of the time, but he's angry drunk.'

'He insults your mother. What do you do?'

'I agree with him, of course.'

'And then?'

'He invites me to sit down with him. It appears he had paid plenty for these women, and he doesn't mind sharing.'

'How long did you stay in the club?'

'About two hours, and then we went to his place in Mayfair.'

'With the women?'

'Of course, what else would I go there for?'

'Continue.'

'He took one, I took the other, and then we swapped. Eventually, I fell asleep, and the next I knew it was early morning, and a bird was sitting outside on the balcony railing making a noise.'

'The women, where were they?'

'They had gone, so had Sutherland. I left soon after, nothing for me to do there.'

'Why leave? I understand from your father that you do not work.'

'Not much.'

'I spoke to your sister before. She is very fond of her father.'

'She would be. He always spoilt her, buying her presents.'

'You were not spoilt?'

'By him? No way. The most he would give me was a lecture about how to stand up straight, be a man. He was a fine one to give lectures.'

'Why do you say that?'

'He couldn't even control his wife. What sort of man allows his wife to fuck anyone she wants to, even in his house?'

'Did that happen often?'

'Not often, I suppose.'

'How often?'

'There was that time with Richard Williams. He's been screwing her for years. Did he tell you that?'

'I'm aware they were involved in the past, before your parents were married.'

'They're still involved. If you want to find out where she is, you'd better talk to him.'

'Your dislike for your mother, is it a strong enough motive to wish her harm?'

'Are you accusing me of murdering my own mother?'

'I need to ascertain the intensity of your dislike towards your mother.'

'I hated her. Not enough to kill her and she's the one with the money, not my father.'

'I thought your father was successful in his own right.'

'He made some money, but nothing like her. She was the earner in this house. No doubt why he allowed her to screw around.'

'Are you an earner?'

'I'm just a drunken layabout. My father must have told you that.'

'He mentioned you had some issues. Just one more question before we conclude.'

'Let me get a top up.' Isaac counted three whiskies consumed by Sam Avers since he arrived. It was apparent that he did not intend to stop until the bottle was drained.

'Your father. Capable of murder?'

'Him? I don't think so.'

***

Wendy Gladstone, armed with the new information, set off to find Bert, the taxi driver. He was not difficult to find. The taxi rank, a five-minute walk up the road, only had places for three vehicles. Bert's was the second. The one in front was a grey Vauxhall – looked as though it could do with a wash. Bert's blue Toyota was fresh and clean, and she could see why the hotel used his in preference to the other taxis in the small town.

'Felicity recommended me,' she said.

'From the Abbey?' he replied. She could see that he was closer to seventy years of age than sixty. He still had a luxuriant growth of hair on his head, a small bald patch just starting to show. He was dressed in a suit with a white shirt and tie. She was impressed.

'The Abbey, yes.'

'She should have phoned. I would have come down and picked you up, saved you the walk.'

'I enjoy walking,' she said, which had been true enough before arthritis set in. Now she had to take care, not walk too fast. It annoyed her that she was not as agile as she had been as a child, and then as a young woman. She complained little, and certainly to no one except her husband.

'Where can I take you?'

'I'll be honest, Bert. I've been asked to find one of your clients.'

'Are you police?'

'I was not entirely honest with Felicity down at the hotel. I told her it was her husband who had asked me. My name is Wendy Gladstone.'

'What's the truth?' the taxi driver asked. Wendy could see that he was an active man, quick of mind.

'We're treating the woman's disappearance as suspicious.'

'You're from London?'

'How did you know?'

'The accent mainly. Some others were asking about her.'

'I grew up in Yorkshire.'

'Maybe you did, but it's a London accent now. Pure cockney, although now you mention it, there's a bit of Yorkshire in there.'

'You mentioned some others looking for her?'

'You never confirmed that you were police.'

'Police Constable.'

'I didn't like them.'

'Who?'

'The two who were looking for her.'

'Did they say who they were? And I haven't mentioned who the woman is yet.'

'Felicity was desperate to tell me. My wife was excited when I told her.'

'And you?'

'I've never taken much notice of her before. I don't watch the television apart from the sport's channel.'

'Are you free to talk?' she asked.

'The taxi meter is running. I assume that's fine by you?'

'Fine, expense account. You may as well have the benefit of it as well.'

'Can it stand a decent meal?' he asked.

'Yes, why not.'

'Hop in, we'll treat ourselves to a good meal up the road.'

Bert, or Bert Collins, his full name for the report she would have to write up later, apparently enjoyed the little luxuries in life. He ordered the best, including the best wine. She knew she should not, and had been promising to go on a diet, but in the end she matched him course for course.

'She didn't say much, just mumbled a few words and paid the fare,' Bert said between gulps of wine.

'Is there anything you can tell me that will help me find her?'

'I dropped her off at the railway station in Worcester, which made little sense. We have a perfectly good railway station here which connects into Worcester.'

'Did she give you a reason?'

'I saw no reason to ask. She was paying, and Worcester is farther than the local station.'

'When you dropped her off, did she say where she was heading?'

'She saw the time and a train coming into the station. She made some comment under her breath and dashed off. I assumed she wanted to catch the train.'

'Where was it heading?'

'Paddington. Two and a half hours. I take it myself when Arsenal is playing at home.'

'She never arrived.'

'I wouldn't know about that. She paid my money, and as I said, she dashed off. There wasn't another train for some time after, so I can't see where else she could have gone.'

'The other two men. What can you tell me about them?'

'They sat in the back of the taxi and asked me to drive them around the area. They said they were up for a business conference and were taking the opportunity of a couple of hours to do some sightseeing.'

'Did you believe them?'

'No way.'

'Why do you say that?'

'It was raining heavily, could barely see where I was going, and there were no business conferences that I knew of.'

'Would you know if there was?'

'I'm confident I would.'

'As you're driving around, what did they ask?'

'They made small talk, and then they started asking about this woman.'

'Which one?'

'This Marjorie Frobisher.'

'Did that cause you some concern?'

'It did. How did they know about her? They weren't staying at the Abbey. I know that Felicity Pearson is a bit of a gossip, but why should two men, business men, be interested in the whereabouts of a woman off a programme on the television.'

'Did they say why they were interested?'

'I asked. They made up some lame reason that their wives watched the programme. Then they started offering me money, wanting to take me to the pub for a few drinks.'

'Did you tell them what you told me?'

'No. I just said that my shift was coming to a close, which wasn't true, and dropped them back at the taxi rank. That's the last I saw of them.'

'Why didn't you tell them anything?'

'You were honest. Bought me a nice meal.'

'Is that the only reason?'

'It's a good enough reason for me,' he said. There was still half a bottle of a good wine to drink. Wendy thought they might be able to drink another bottle after that. She was sure Bert would not object.

Chapter 22

Richard Williams did not appreciate the official request to present himself at the police station. He was a man used to giving orders, not receiving them. 'What right have you to demand my presence here? I'm a busy man.'

'Some new information has come to light. Information in relation to you,' Isaac said. Farhan, as usual, at his left. Richard Williams, dressed formally in a suit, sat opposite Isaac. He had brought legal representation: Quinton Scott, Queen's Counsel, of Scott, Scott and Fairlight. To Isaac, he looked landed gentry. To Farhan, he looked like a man who did not appreciate anyone who had not been born with a silver spoon in their mouth, or a white complexion with blue eyes. He had reluctantly shaken Isaac's hand, made a clear attempt to avoid repeating the same mistake with him.

Isaac commenced the interview, following the official procedure, noting the time of the interview, informing the client of his rights and asking those present to state their names and details.

'My client is here at the express request of the police. He is willing to answer any reasonable questions that are put to him,' Williams' QC said.

'Mr Williams, we are in possession of information that clearly indicates you lied to us on previous occasions,' Isaac said.

'I reject that accusation. I have upheld my responsibility and always given the truth when asked.'

'I hope that these accusations can be validated. It will be seen as police harassment if they are fabrications. The Commissioner of Police, Charles Shaw, will take a dim view of this if I am obliged to inform him,' Scott said. Isaac, a usually patient man, was enraged at the QC's attempt at intimidation.

'Let me remind you that this is a murder investigation,' Isaac said. 'I am sure that Commissioner Shaw will fully endorse my position.'

'Very well, continue.' Quinton Scott appeared subdued for the moment.

'Mr Williams, you mentioned on a previous occasion in your office that your relationship, your intimate relationship with Marjorie Frobisher, occurred many years ago, and that you have remained as friends since then.'

'That is correct.'

'Recent information indicates that your relationship has continued.'

'Our friendship has.'

'There was a party at Marjorie Frobisher's house when it became more than a friendship.'

'Who told you this?' Williams said. His legal adviser maintained a thoughtful pose, arms folded, listening to the conversation.

'Is this true?'

'No.'

'Mr Williams, I am led to believe you are lying. We are not here to pass moral judgement, we are here to ascertain the truth. Whether you are or are not sleeping with her only concerns us in relation to our enquiries.'

Quinton Scott felt the need to speak. 'My client has clearly indicated the current and past statuses. He is not required to say anymore.'

'That is his right,' Isaac continued. 'However, Mr Williams is the last person to have seen Marjorie Frobisher alive, and that is by his own admission.'

'Is that correct?' Quinton Scott turned towards his client to ask.

'I knew she was in Malvern, at least for some of the time. I went there and met her.'

Quinton Scott turned to Isaac, 'DCI Cook, I would request fifteen minutes with my client.'

'Interview halted at 11.30 a.m.'

'Thank you,' the QC said.

'I'll send in two coffees,' Farhan said.

A begrudging grunt from the QC; thanks from Williams.

***

Forty minutes later the interview recommenced. In the interval, Farhan and Isaac had managed to grab a bite to eat. Richard Williams and Quinton Scott had asked for a pizza each. A young female police officer had delivered them to the interview room.

'Interview resumed at 12.10.'

'My client would like to make a statement,' the QC said.

Richard Williams commenced. 'I have maintained a relationship with Marjorie Frobisher over the years. This has been infrequent in its nature, but as I had indicated before, we have a history of when we were both struggling to make our way in the world. There have been years when we have just been friends, others where we have been intimate.

'Marjorie phoned me from Malvern. I went there to meet her. The programme was in need of her, and I did not want her to be absent. There are a number of reasons as to why I did not tell you, not the least that I am genuinely fond of the woman. Also, the ratings and the advertising revenue were sure to be enhanced by her being on the screen, grieving elder sister, vengeful and determined slayer of those who had killed her brother.

'She was frightened. I reasoned with her, and she agreed to return to London within a few days. I offered to provide her with security, although the reason it was needed remained obscure. That is the end of my statement.'

'Do you have any knowledge of why she was frightened?' Isaac asked.

'She has skeletons in the cupboard, the same as most people.'

'Hers were substantial?'

'Yes.'

'Are you aware of a child?'

'I am.'

'Is there any more you can tell us about this child?'

'It was before we met.'

'Was the child yours?'

The QC intervened. 'My client will not answer that question.'

'It's okay, Quinton,' Williams said.

'The child was not mine.' He addressed Isaac.

'Do you know who the father is?'

'She would never tell me.'

'Did she know?'

'Are you insinuating that she may have been sleeping with more than one man?'

'Yes.'

'It's possible, of course. She was promiscuous in a casual manner. Most people were then. It was a time before HIV and Aids.'

'Does Robert Avers know about this child?'

'How would I know? You'd better ask him.'

'Do you think he knows?'

'No idea.'

Isaac could see that he had exhausted one line of questioning. He could not fault Richard Williams in his responses. 'Did you at a party at her house have sexual relations with Marjorie Frobisher?'

'Are you trying to imply that because of Charles Sutherland and his daughter, I am somehow responsible for his death?'

'I am purely attempting to ascertain whether you deny the incident.'

'I'd prefer to forget it.'

'Why is that?'

'Her daughter, plain Jane, legs up in the air with Charles Sutherland's bare arse bobbing up and down. Not one of the prettiest sights.'

'How did Marjorie Frobisher react?'

'Badly.'

'Out of shame?'

'No. She had just had the sofa reupholstered. Her daughter and Sutherland were hardly the cleanest of people. She didn't want him spraying his mongrel sperm over it.'

'She didn't care about the daughter?'

'She never had. Why should she start then?'

'Fiona Avers has a reason to dislike her mother,' Isaac commented.

'I didn't like the way Marjorie treated her children, but it wasn't for me to complain. That was Robert Avers' responsibility.'

'Is there any more?' Quinton Scott asked. 'It appears that we have lapsed into innuendo and questions on morality.'

Isaac followed official police procedures and then hit the stop button.

Williams and Scott left soon after. Isaac spoke to Farhan. 'What do you reckon?'

'He answered the questions. I can't see that he has a motive for murder.'

***

Isaac and Farhan had been tailed in their cars again. They contacted Richard Goddard. Usually, they would have just contacted the vehicle identification department, but they knew the car registrations would be classified.

Wendy, back in the office, had rearranged the furniture, to Farhan's chagrin. She reckoned the two cars tailing them might be tied in with the two men that Bert, the taxi driver, had mentioned in Malvern. Isaac was not pleased with her presence in the office, as not only did they have to contend with the smell of stale cigarette smoke, now they had the smell of wine too. Farhan was certain that she was slightly hungover.

As soon as she had debriefed them, she decided to focus her investigations at Paddington Station. On the way through Worcester, she had spoken to the ticket seller on duty at the railway station. It had been busy the day that Bert had dropped off Marjorie Frobisher, the ticket seller had said. And besides, he added, most tickets are sold from a machine. She had managed to get tapes from the security cameras at the station. They were typically kept for a period of time and then erased. One day more, he had told her, and the video would have been gone forever. The tapes she passed over to Constable Bridget Halloran, the CCTV viewing officer, on arriving at Challis Street. She would scan through using facial recognition technology and a trained eye.

Her time in the office with Isaac and Farhan was brief, and she soon left. Farhan moved his desk to where it had been at the first opportunity.

'What did the two women he paid for say? Did they see anything?' Isaac asked.

'I've already told you.'

'I know that, but we need to be sure about this. We are aware of a child. We know of Charles Sutherland, who said he knew something. We have Richard Williams, who says he doesn't know who the child is. If Williams doesn't know, how would Sutherland?'

'He must have overheard something,' Farhan said.

'If he heard Marjorie Frobisher talking on a mobile phone, that would be a one-sided conversation, and she's hardly likely to say the child's name.'

'She could have told him.'

'If she wouldn't tell Richard Williams, she's hardly likely to tell Sutherland.'

'What if she told Williams?' Farhan asked.

'If she did, then it means two things.'

'One, he lied to us, and two, he's a potential target.'

'Are we conclusively stating that Charles Sutherland was murdered because he knew something?'

'Who else could have done it?' Farhan asked.

'Christy Nichols, Jess O'Neill, Fiona Avers.'

'They each had a strong enough motive: one he had forced to indulge in oral sex, another he attempted to rape, and the other was indulging in sexual intercourse with the man until her mother walked in.'

'He was poisoned. Whoever it was needed to get hold of the poison and know the dosage.'

'Fiona Avers is callous enough. I just don't see Jess O'Neill and Christy Nichols doing that, do you?'

'Jess O'Neill could if she was vengeful enough,' Isaac replied. 'What do you reckon to Christy Nichols?'

'She seems too timid.'

'And what is it with these escorts? Why are you protecting them?'

'I gave my word that I would keep their identities confidential for as long as I can.'

'You know you will have to reveal them at some time.'

'I hope that will not be necessary.'

'You'd better hope for a confession from someone. That's their only chance. I hope you explained that you can't give a guarantee.'

'I did.'

***

With the pressure of work, Isaac just hadn't had any time to devote to Sophie. He thought she was starting to become clingy, talking about moving in with him, or him moving in with her. Neither option appealed, and besides, there was still Jess.

After the interview session at the police station, their conversations by phone had been few and far between, and whereas the attraction remained from both parties, the easy banter, the repartee, the teasing, more from her than him, were conspicuous by their absence.

He had not dwelled too much on Farhan and his desire to keep the two escorts' identities concealed, although it was out of character for his offsider. He had always been a stickler for following investigations by the book, but he assumed he had his reasons.

Isaac was aware that he was not faultless either. There were times when he had gone easy on a female witness if he thought they were not involved.

Chapter 23

'DI Larry Hill, Islington Police Station. We've got a body. Police records show that you know the name.' Isaac looked at the clock by his bedside. It said 2 a.m. Fully awake now after missing the original message, Isaac asked the caller to repeat.

'What's the name?'

'Sally Jenkins, do you know her?'

'Yes.' One of the people he had been planning to interview, but never got around to it as he was too busy elsewhere. Isaac quickly dialled in Farhan.

'It looks as if someone climbed in a window at the back of the building, forced entry, grabbed the woman and held her face down in the sink. Clear signs of a struggle,' Larry Hill said.

'What's the address?'

'14 Crane Grove.'

It took Isaac three minutes to exit his apartment, another twenty minutes to get to Islington. It was early morning; the traffic was light. The road had been blocked off – tape had been put across to keep out the neighbours, the gawkers, and the plain nosey.

Most were still in their pyjamas, even though it was a cold morning. Farhan had beaten Isaac to the murder scene. Farhan waited for him to park his car. Then they proceeded to the house, showing their identity badges to the uniformed constable standing outside. It was clear that Sally Jenkins lived well. The upstairs flat in a typical terraced house had been tastefully renovated – in the last year, Isaac thought. The decorations were fresh, the television and stereo equipment good quality. There seemed to be little in the way of food in the house, which Isaac did not see as suspicious. He rarely ate at home. The bed, queen size, showed only one occupant; one side was neat, the other ruffled. It appeared she preferred to sleep close to the open window. It was apparent on examining the body that she slept in the nude.

'Any signs of a sexual attack?' Isaac asked.

'Forensics can tell you that,' Larry Hill said. 'From what I can see, I would say not. Apart from the bruising on her legs where she kicked out, it just seems to be death by drowning.' He was a good-looking man, late forties, with the slightest sign of middle-aged spread and appeared competent. He had a healthy tan, clear skin and white teeth. Isaac had developed a knack of summing up people at the first meeting. It sometimes annoyed Sophie, the few times he had taken her out. It seemed too clinical for her.

157

'One person or two?' Farhan asked.

'I would say one,' Hill responded. 'It's not that big in here. Two, they would have held her legs firm, stop her making a noise. Professional, I'd say.'

'Why do you say that?' Isaac asked.

'Have you seen the body?'

'Yes. I met her when she was alive.'

'If Charles Sutherland was a professional assassination, and Sally Jenkins is too, then Marjorie Frobisher is almost certainly dead,' Farhan said.

'You mean the woman off the television?' Larry Hill had heard them talking.

'You weren't meant to hear that,' Isaac said.

'You think she's dead?'

'Larry, forget what you just heard. People are dying as a result of her.'

'Policemen included?'

'Nobody is safe. Certainly not Farhan and myself.'

'They said she used to play around.'

'Larry, I don't think we should discuss this anymore. We'll be taking the case over from here.'

'This is my case.' Larry Hill saw his authority being usurped.

'You're getting yourself involved in something that could get messy.'

'That sounds like a threat.'

Isaac attempted to appease the man's anger. 'This is not the first body, almost certainly not the last.'

'That's my decision. I will conduct the investigation into Sally Jenkins' death and keep you advised. The others you can deal with.'

'We'll accept your assistance. Find out what you can about suspicious people, how the window was opened.'

'DCI Cook, I've been around a while. I know how to conduct a murder investigation.'

'Apologies. We're all a bit on edge. Your assistance is appreciated.'

With no more to do, Isaac and Farhan exited the building. The weather had taken a turn for the worse. The previously eager onlookers had – bar a few – retreated inside and back to bed or to watch news reports on the television. All the major channels were in the street with their cameras focussed on the house.

'What next?' Farhan asked.

'No point going home,' Isaac said.

'I need to have a shower and change. I'll be there in an hour.'

'Give me ninety minutes.' Isaac realised he may as well return home and take a shower too. A murder scene gave him an uncomfortable feeling. A shower always seemed to help, as if he was washing the horror and the sight of the dead body away.

'Any ideas?' Farhan asked as he was getting into his car.

'We need to find this damn woman. She's the key to this.'

***

Cecil Broughton, the station manager at Paddington Station, had seen the transition of the railways for fifty years. He was still an upright man, close to retirement at sixty-five, hopeful of a reprieve due to the government considering pushing the retirement age up closer to seventy. Wendy Gladstone liked him immediately.

'Pleased to meet you,' he said as she entered his office. It had a warm feeling to it, almost a relic of an earlier age, the walls adorned with pictures of trains through the years, mainly steam. The paint on the walls was flaking in places and the carpet threadbare – how he liked it.

'Some people are taken aback when they enter.'

'Why's that?' Wendy asked.

'They expect the office to be modern and smelling of air freshener.'

'More like old leather in here.'

'27th November 1965,' Broughton proudly said.

'I was just starting school,' she replied, not fully understanding the significance of the date.

'My first week here, pushing a trolley.'

'Fifty years in the one place?'

'I moved around over the years, but I always intended to finish my time at Paddington. I remember that day well.'

'Why?'

'The last day a steam train exited this station, *Clun Castle*, heading through Slough, Swindon, Bristol, before terminating in Gloucester.'

'Do you remember them all?'

'Most, I suppose. Trains have been a passion all my life.'

What the last train had to do with the smell in the office still eluded her.

'It's the seats,' he said.

'Pardon.'

'That's the smell. I retrieved them from *Clun Castle*.'

'You sound resentful of the trains today.'

'Not at all,' he reflected. 'Brilliant technical achievements, just lacking in character. Anyway, you didn't come here to reminisce about trains from the past, did you?'

'Interesting subject, no doubt,' she said, although the modern trains suited her fine. She had been on the occasional steam train, school excursions mainly, and she only remembered them as slow and exceedingly smelly.

'You're trying to find a missing person.' Wendy could only reflect as she sat there how different he was to her husband. Broughton, alert and in his sixties; her husband, a few years younger, yet older in mind and body, and bitter about his life.

'We believe the woman boarded the Paddington train in Worcester.'

'Are you certain?' he asked.

'She probably bought the ticket from a machine at the station.'

'That makes it difficult.'

'Why's that?'

'How to identify her. Do you know what she was wearing?'

'I've already passed on details to your people. We're reviewing the tapes from Worcester Station. You have more cameras at Paddington, and people trained to watch the monitors.'

'Major issue these days. No idea where the next idiot is going to let off a bomb.'

'Any problems in the past?'

'Not since 1991.'

'February 1991. IRA, two bombs; one here and another at Victoria. No fatalities here, one dead at Victoria,' Wendy said.

'You've got a good memory.'

'Probably not as good as yours. I was assigned to Victoria to assist in the investigation.'

'It's best if I take you up to our video surveillance department. You've time for a cup of tea?' he asked. 'British Rail has an excellent reputation for making tea.'

'A tradition worth upholding,' she replied. 'I don't remember the sandwiches with the same fondness.'

'These days they come in a cellophane bag. At least they won't be stale. Not all traditions are worth preserving.'

The tea arrived, hot and milky, just the way she liked it, two spoons of sugar as well. She noticed that the station manager had Earl Grey with no sugar.

***

The walk from the office, through the heart of the station with its milling passengers, to the surveillance department took less than five minutes. Broughton's office had been nostalgic; the area she entered was not. It was modern and efficient, with numerous monitors displaying all areas of the station.

Brian Gee, a young man in his early thirties, was in charge. He introduced himself and gave the police constable a guided tour of his domain. 'State of the art, best there is,' he said.

'I'm not really into computers.' She noticed that Brian Gee was a remarkably active man, almost hyperactive. Her youngest son, Brad, had been the same as a child but had grown out of it; Brian Gee had not. He was fidgeting, moving from one foot to the other, fiddling with a pen, or picking up a piece of paper only to put it down again.

'It's not everyone's cup of tea, I suppose. I'll admit to being a computer nerd.'

'Any luck finding the missing woman?' She had supplied a description earlier before arriving at the station, although it had been necessarily vague: green dress, just below the knees, sensible black shoes, a dark overcoat, and a blue hat with a brim. She had also mentioned the sunglasses and the name of Marjorie Frobisher.

'With your description?'

'How many people were on the train that day?' she asked.

The station manager responded, 'Probably no more than one hundred and fifty.'

'Can't you isolate it to them?'

'It's not that simple,' Brian Gee replied. 'We're not looking at the trains per se. We mainly focus on the platforms, the restrooms, the main concourse. There were two trains on the platform at the time of interest. The train we are interested in, and another from the west of the country. In total that's about five hundred people. We're looking, could be a few hours yet, and then she could have changed her clothes. Even with all this technology, it's still a needle in a haystack.'

Wendy could see that it was going to take a while. She determined she would wait it out. At least at the railway station she could find somewhere outside to smoke.

***

Isaac and Farhan had not spent much time in the office since the death of Sally Jenkins. Isaac decided that his best approach was to call Richard Williams to the station. There was a great unknown to be resolved. If Sally Jenkins was killed because she knew something, then how did she get that information? And if she had that information, did that place the source in danger as well?

The situation with the media was also starting to become a nuisance. The disappearance of Marjorie Frobisher had caused speculative interest from them, with their probing cameras and microphones. The death of Charles Sutherland, now officially confirmed as murder, had taken their interest level up to serious. The death of Sally Jenkins, not a celebrity but known as the personal assistant to the executive producer, created further interest.

Isaac rethought his plan to bring Williams into Challis Street as his arrival would be seen by the media. He did not want to create added speculation on the television and in the press.

Detective Superintendent Goddard, on advice from Charles Shaw, the Met Commissioner, saw that the only option was to make a formal statement. He realised he should have done this earlier, after the death of Charles Sutherland, but he had been hesitant. Angus MacTavish had been against it, even threatened his career.

It was evident the commissioner had used his contacts and had cleared the press conference.

The press conference, hastily set up for two in the afternoon, had not allowed Isaac time to meet Williams. He had phoned him, found him to be uncommonly subdued, and sorry about the death of his former personal assistant. 'I had a lot of time for her. We had some fun together,' he said. Isaac wasn't sure if it was a genuine heartfelt emotion or whether it was for his benefit. He chose to believe the former.

He would force Williams to reveal his real emotions at a later date and to detail every bit of hidden information he possessed. Isaac and Farhan remained convinced that the deaths would continue. People were dying for a reason still unknown, and until they knew that reason, the case was going nowhere.

Charles Sutherland had known something, or had he? Sally Jenkins had died for a similar reason, but she'd had no way of finding out the information unless it was by eavesdropping, or someone had told her. If it wasn't Charles Sutherland, then who, and why?' Both Isaac and Farhan were nervous when they explained their fears to their boss, Detective Superintendent Goddard.

'We're stuck with this,' he said, 'whether we like it or not.'

Chapter 24

'Ladies and gentlemen, members of the press. Good morning.' The assembled audience for the hastily arranged press conference waited impatiently for their opportunity to put questions. They knew they would have to listen to the official police statement first: Detective Superintendent Richard Goddard to give the initial address, Detective Chief Inspector Isaac Cook to follow on. Neither man was excited at the prospect, although Isaac knew his parents would be proudly watching on the television.

Richard Goddard read from a prepared statement. 'Charles Sutherland, it is confirmed, died as the result of poisoning. We are treating his death as murder. You are now aware that a subsequent death, confirmed as the murder of a young female, is possibly related. Both were involved in a television programme, one as an actor, the other as the personal assistant to the executive producer.

'I should state that the assumption that both murders are related must remain just that, an assumption. In both cases, there appears to be no motive.

'What I can tell you is that the disappearance of Marjorie Frobisher still causes us concern. We are anxious to ascertain her whereabouts at the earliest opportunity. It is clear that when the floor is thrown open to questions, her name will be mentioned. Let me emphasise that we believe her to be missing.

'I will invite those present to ask questions. Please announce your name, the organisation you represent, and to whom you are directing the question. Please do not expect us to indulge in idle speculation.'

A quick flurry of hands in the air, a flashing of cameras as the individuals in the throng attempted to be first with their question.

'Barbara Halsall, Sky News. Detective Chief Inspector Cook, is it not a fact that you are looking for Marjorie Frobisher's body, and that the police believe her to be dead?'

Isaac's reply, predictable. 'Unless we receive information to the contrary, we continue to believe that she is alive and well.'

'Is it not clear that she is dead?' Barbara Halsall was entitled to one question; she had taken two. It was not unexpected. She had been on the television almost as long as Isaac had been alive. Few would stand in her way when she was asking questions. Richard

Goddard attempted to remind her that she was only entitled to one question. She ignored him totally.

'There is nothing to indicate that Marjorie Frobisher's disappearance is related to the current murder enquiries.' Isaac knew it was a weak response.

'Stuart Vaughan, BBC. It must be obvious to anyone, even the man in the street, that her disappearance is related.'

'It is a consideration,' Isaac conceded.

'Are you able to confirm that Sally Jenkins was naked when found?'

'Please announce your name and organisation first.' Richard Goddard attempted to wrest control of the proceedings from the media flock. He knew he would not be successful.

'Claude Dunn, News Corporation. Is it true she was found with no clothes on?' The media had become sensationalist.

'That is not the focus of this press conference,' Isaac said. He assumed Dunn must have paid someone at the crime scene for the information.

'Geoffrey Agnew, ITV. Charles Sutherland had intended to reveal details about Marjorie Frobisher. Can you let us know what those details were?'

Richard Goddard answered. 'No details were revealed.'

'A hoax on his part?' Agnew ignored the other questioners in the room, his raised voiced drowning them out.

'I did not say that.' Richard Goddard felt cornered. Angus MacTavish was watching, as was Commissioner Shaw on the television in Downing Street. The detective superintendent did not want his career to go down the drain due to an ill-chosen rebuttal. 'Both murders are ongoing investigations. All avenues of enquiry will be investigated in detail. It would be inappropriate for either myself or Detective Chief Inspector Cook to speculate.'

'And the prostitutes?' Agnew interrupted. Again, Isaac realised that someone had paid money for that information. Farhan, watching from the rear of the room, hoped it wasn't Christy Nichols or Aisha, and if it was Olivia, why? It seemed more likely to have been one of the staff in the hotel. He knew he had to find out.

'Ladies and gentlemen, I believe we have informed you as to the current situation. Regular press statements will be posted as new information becomes available. I thank you for your time.' Richard Goddard wrapped up the press conference and exited the room, followed by Isaac.

'How do you think it went, sir?' Isaac asked.

'Hopefully, well enough to save our careers.' It seemed a pessimistic reply to Isaac. He chose not to comment.

***

With the press conference concluded, Isaac was free to meet Richard Williams. It was after six in the evening when he arrived at his office in the city. Williams opened the door, the new personal assistant nowhere to be seen.

'DCI Cook, tragic business.'

'I may need to bring you into the station at some stage.'

'I thought it would have been today. Why didn't you?'

'Media scrum down there, too many people sticking their noses in. Did you have a similar problem?'

'I don't follow you,' Williams replied.

'Sally Jenkins had a tendency to listen in.'

'I believe I told you that the other week.'

'You did. Now the question is, did she hear or know of something that people would kill for?'

'Not from me.' Richard Williams seemed a little too nonchalant for Isaac.

'I'll level with you,' Isaac said. 'We have two bodies, a missing woman, and no motive, other than several women who were pleased when Sutherland was murdered. One was even delighted.'

'Sally wasn't one of them. She didn't like him and his leering remarks, but she only met him once to my knowledge.'

'And when was that?'

'Some months back. We were wrapping up production for the year. We all met at a hotel near the production lot and had a decent meal and a few too many drinks. Sutherland was drunk, making suggestive remarks, but I don't remember him going near Sally.'

'Are you sure?'

'Not totally. It was after all a party. Left the Ferrari here, took a taxi.'

'Sally left the party with you?'

'Not that she would have known about leaving.'

'Why's that?'

'Mixing her drinks, totally out of it.'

'And she said nothing?'

'About Sutherland?'

'Yes.'

'She didn't say anything that night; the next day, she could barely remember the previous evening.'

'You were with her?'

'At the place where she was found dead. I paid for it, the renovations as well.'

'The night she died?'

'I told you before that I had sacked her.'

'And you let her stay in the place?'

'Why not? I'm not a total bastard.'

'The night she died?' Isaac returned to the standard question. The question that invariably invoked a reply of 'I didn't murder her' or 'My alibi's watertight.'

'I was with my personal assistant, the new one. In her bed, if you must know.'

'She will testify to that?'

'I don't think she'll be euphoric about it, but I'm sure she will.'

'Sally Jenkins knew something. If it didn't come from Sutherland, it must have come from you.'

'I don't know of anything that would warrant murder.'

'You argued with Marjorie Frobisher before she disappeared. Was anything said in the heat of the moment, anything unexpected?'

'How many times have we discussed this?'

'How many times have you evaded the answer?' Isaac responded, his voice raised.

'Marjorie may have mentioned about the child she had when she was a lot younger, but she never mentioned the name, even if she knew it. That may be good enough for a gossip magazine, but it hardly seems sufficient to justify murder. If you wish to discuss this matter again, I will make sure my legal adviser is present.'

Isaac left soon after. The briefest of handshakes as they parted.

***

Angus MacTavish and Richard Goddard met at a pub some distance from Downing Street. The detective superintendent was anxious to be updated about the current situation, and to ascertain how his career was progressing. He was not naïve, he knew that the years of loyal service, the innumerable courses and qualifications, and unblemished service record counted for nothing if people at the top, often nameless, disapproved of the nominee. His future revolved around a missing woman, not the two murders. He also knew that he may be forced to make decisions that would affect the ongoing investigations. A major celebrity in the country was impacting his career; he did not like it.

There was no point in discussing the matter with Commissioner Shaw as he was no doubt feeling the pressure as well. His appointment was due for renewal, and questions were already being raised about his suitability. The detective superintendent, a political animal, knew why the questions were being asked. They were political in nature, lacking in substance, and were there to apply pressure on Commissioner Shaw to rein in his people. He also knew that Commissioner Shaw was not a man easily swayed. Neither was he. It was a dilemma he would face if the pressure came. It was clear that Angus MacTavish would have no trouble applying the pressure.

'Goddard, it's good to see you.' The meeting started well. The Red Lion, a short distance from MacTavish's office, hardly seemed the ideal place, as it was well frequented by politicians from both sides of the house, but MacTavish had arranged a private room on the first floor.

'Change of location?'

'Somewhere private.'

'I saw some from the other side of the house downstairs.'

'Don't worry about them. They're as thick as two short planks.'

'You saw the press conference?'

'You handled it well. You had to make a statement of some sort. Otherwise the media would have started sticking their noses in more than they already are.'

'They're a damn nuisance.' Both had ordered a pint of Fuller's London Pride, on tap, and a meat pie, a speciality of the house.

'What do you have?' MacTavish asked. He had already downed the first pint, ordered another.

'Two murders and a missing woman.'

'Apart from that.'

'There are a few suspects for the murder of Charles Sutherland; none apparent for Sally Jenkins.'

'Who would want to kill Sutherland? I'm told he was not the most pleasant person, but murder?'

'Three had a strong enough reason for Sutherland.'

'How do these people make so many enemies?'

'A male chauvinist pig is an apt description for Sutherland.'

'Not really relevant, is it?'

'It will be if one of the women killed him.'

'You know what I'm referring to.'

'Marjorie Frobisher.'

'Precisely. Where is this woman? Is she dead? Is she likely to be dead soon?'

'Are you stating that if she's not dead, she may be soon?'

'Detective Superintendent, I don't know.'

'You have some updated information?'

'I am aware that there is an assassination order out on her. Don't ask me who or where or when.'

'Why?'

'I don't know. That's the truth.'

'What do you want to do about this?'

'If you find her, protect her,' MacTavish said as he finished his third pint. Richard Goddard had just drunk one. He was prepared to order a half, but with MacTavish downing them so fast, he ordered another pint instead.

'Assuming we find her, where do we protect her? If someone's serious about killing her, are we being given the all clear to use violence?'

'Don't look for official permission from me or anyone else. If it goes wrong, everyone will deny responsibility.'

'The risk seems too high.'

'That's negative.' MacTavish slammed his beer down on the table, the froth spilling out over the rim of the glass.

'It seems realistic to me.'

'With great risk comes great reward. Do you get my drift?'

'I'm an ambitious man. I don't deny that.'

'And there's an assistant commissioner's position coming up shortly.'

'Are you saying it's mine if this is handled correctly?'

'That's up to Commissioner Shaw. He's looking for a peerage. You look after us; we look after him. You know how it works, don't you?'

'Yes, of course. We'll do what is necessary, but I'm not willing to put my men's lives at risk.'

'The black inspector looks to be a smart man. Ambitious, is he?'

'Also very competent.'

'He'll be looked after as well.'

***

The question from Agnew at the press conference had interested Farhan. How did he know about the two women Christy Nichols had signed for?

The young detective inspector knew that it wasn't necessarily the most secret piece of information. But failing a motive, it was one of their few possible lines of enquiry. Isaac was following up on Sally Jenkins' murder, with Larry Hill providing assistance where he could. Wendy was trying to find the missing woman, and Richard Goddard's last visit to the office had revealed that if Marjorie Frobisher was alive, it was up to the department to protect her at all costs.

Isaac had asked why, until their boss had taken him out of the room for a five-minute chat. On his return, Isaac ceased asking and acquiesced to his senior's request. Farhan thought he should have been more persistent.

Too many unknowns Farhan thought, but kept his own counsel. Isaac believed that following up on how Agnew knew about the prostitutes was shooting in the dark. As he had reasoned, someone let them into the hotel, Christy Nichols had shown them into Sutherland's suite, and numerous people had seen them leave.

As Farhan had explained to Isaac, they did not leave the hotel as women of the night. They would have changed, and to those moving around in the foyer of the hotel, they would have looked no different from the majority of the people there.

Farhan found himself at a variance with his DCI, who now seemed more focussed on Marjorie Frobisher than Charles Sutherland and Sally Jenkins.

Farhan was still living on his own, although the children were fine. His wife had instigated legal proceedings against him for the division of the assets – meagre as they were – and maintenance of the children.

Ironic, he had thought when he received the notification, that his wife, traditional and conservative, had no issues with embracing English law when it suited her. In her own country, she would not have found such a favourable response from the courts, where the man held predominance, but he had spent a long time in England and he saw no issues with his wife's legal demands. He just hoped that it could be dealt with without the bitterness and acrimony that so many seemed to go through when a marriage failed.

But it was not the failed marriage or the assets that concerned him the most, it was the children. Would they receive a moderate education and upbringing? Would his daughter be allowed to integrate into British society as an equal, free to choose her direction in life, free to choose who she married when the time came? He saw England for all its beauty and its benefits. It was a country he had come to love, a country that was allowing him to fast-track his career.

Chapter 25

Farhan acknowledged several minutes after leaving the office that his personal issues were just that, personal. There were two bodies, possibly more if he and Isaac did not come up with a solution soon. He laid out his plan of action. First, he first wanted to meet Aisha, although he felt sure she had not spoken to the reporter.

Christy Nichols seemed the most likely to have told the media. He realised he had not spoken to the hotel employee who had smuggled them into the hotel. He had deemed it not necessary in the initial investigations; realised now that it may have been an error of judgement on his part. Maybe that person had seen something, knew something. Christy Nichols would know who that person was.

Geoffrey Agnew proved to be of little use to Farhan. 'I only spoke to the person on the phone.'

Pressed further, Agnew claimed that the voice was muffled and that he was not sure if it was male or female. Farhan did not believe him, told him that it was a murder investigation and that withholding information was a criminal offence. Agnew, a pugnacious little man, continued to state that he was not withholding information, and any future conversations would be with his company's full legal team in attendance. Farhan knew he was wasting his time.

Christy Nichols would be easier to deal with, and she would not be threatening in her manner or evasive in her answers. At least, he hoped she would not be. He liked her. She was an ambitious woman in an industry that rewarded ambitious people, as long as that came with aggression and a complete lack of feeling or emotion. He thought that she did not have the aggression; she had even admitted it. Victoria Webster certainly did, and Christy Nichols admired her for it, but would never emulate her.

He felt fortunate that he worked within an organisation that rewarded people for their ability, not their gender or their religion or their colour, but then he was not so sure of that. The Met prided itself that it was equal opportunity, but who were the most senior people in the organisation? He knew the answer. They were male, white, Anglo-Saxon, and Christian. Sure, there were signs of change: Isaac was one example. There was every indication that he was in line to move up in the police force, but how far would he go? How far could he go? Farhan dismissed his pessimism and focussed on doing his job. He was not leaving the police force, period. It was where he belonged, he knew that.

He found Christy Nichols at the apartment where she lived on her own, a two-bedroom, first-floor conversion of a terraced house. The location, close to Hampstead Heath, was fine, the condition of the building, mediocre. She was apologetic when he knocked on the door, although she had agreed to their meeting at her apartment, instead of a local coffee shop or at the local police station as Farhan had suggested.

'Apologies for the mess.' She had made some attempt at tidying up. She was dressed in a pair of shorts and a tee-shirt.

'That's fine. You should see my place,' he replied, although he had to admit his housekeeping, woeful as it was, did not look as bad as hers. The bathroom door was ajar, and he could see the washing hanging from the shower rail.

'Take a seat, not the one in the corner though.' He could see why. It was occupied by what appeared to be an old rolled up woollen jumper, but turned out to be an old cat. 'That's Cuddles,' she said. It did not seem cuddly to Farhan. He had no great affinity for animals, no great dislike. His wife had abhorred pets in the house; he would not have been overly concerned. A family pet was good for the children, gave them a sense of responsibility.

Farhan sat on one of the two remaining chairs. Christy Nichols sat on the other, the tee-shirt tightening as she adjusted her position. He did not feel comfortable in her presence. 'Did you watch the press conference?' he asked.

'I saw some of it and then switched it off,' she replied.

'Why was that?'

'It reminded me of the events at the hotel.'

It seemed a fair response to Farhan. After all, she had been in the room next door when a murder had been committed, and Sutherland had forced her into giving him oral sex.

'One of the reporters knew about the two escorts at the hotel.'

'That seems possible,' she replied.

'Why do you say that?'

'I don't think it's the first time prostitutes have been in the hotel, do you?'

'It probably happens all the time. What interests me is who told the reporter.'

'I certainly didn't.' She went on the defensive and stood up.

'Please, the issue is not whether you did or did not. I'm not here about whether it was illegal.'

'Then why are you here?'

'Four people knew of the two women in the hotel.'

'The escorts, myself and the person who let them in.' She had resumed her seat.

'Do you know the fourth person?'

'I paid him.'

'How did you arrange it?'

'I spoke to the person who showed us to the rooms.'

'Is that the same individual you paid later?'

'No, so that makes it five, doesn't it?'

'It may be more,' Farhan said. 'I need to meet these people at the hotel.'

'It could still be the escorts. The information would have been worth several hundred pounds to someone like Geoffrey.'

'Geoffrey?'

'Geoffrey Agnew. I know him personally.'

'How?'

'Degree in Journalism. Part of the course required us to spend time as trainee journalists. I spent three weeks at the television company. Work experience, they called it; supposedly assisting in typing up the copy for that day's broadcasts.'

'And?' Farhan knew the answer.

'I learnt how to make a mean cup of coffee, and how to balance everyone's lunch order on one arm, while I struggled to press the lift button.'

'I can sympathise.'

'Similar experience for you?' she asked.

'The first couple of weeks after leaving the police college. First Pakistani, first Muslim, the first person with a university degree in the station.'

'What happened?' she asked.

'They found out soon enough that I did not bring any hang-ups with me, that I was moderate in my faith, and I was potentially a good policeman.'

'And a good person as well.'

Farhan left soon after. She had given him a name at the hotel, and an impression that she liked him not only as a policeman but as a friend. He found himself to be in a dilemma. There were Aisha and Christy and family issues to deal with. There were also two murders, possibly more. He felt that life was becoming too complicated.

***

Isaac could only reflect on the differences between Linda Harris and Sally Jenkins. One was still very much alive and sitting opposite him; the other, very much dead, and lying on a slab in a morgue. He acknowledged that Richard Williams had great taste in women.

Sally Jenkins had been young and beautiful and clearly a rich man's floozy. Linda Harris, Sally's replacement, in bed and out, according to Williams, somehow did not ring true. To Isaac, she did not seem the sort of person who would be swayed by the executive producer's charm. He thought she would have been more than capable of finding a man more her age with the wealth and the vitality she needed. He knew it was not for him to make moral judgements, only to observe and question, and to solve the murders.

A missing woman was the least of their worries, but now they were to protect her if she ever reappeared. Richard Goddard had explained the situation to him. He still didn't understand fully, although he was confident that his boss didn't either.

As the detective superintendent had said, 'It's our futures on the line here. If we get this right, influential people will look after us.'

'And if we don't?'

'We're stuffed.' Not the answer an ambitious policeman wanted to hear. Isaac saw his progression to the top as a result of competent, even exceptional policing, but he was a realist. He knew how it worked. Commissioner Charles Shaw sat in the chair that he wanted to occupy one day, although he would let his senior keep it warm in the interim. He knew that as a decent, hard-working member of the force he could climb the promotion ladder, although it was easy to slide down it if he did not play the game, flatter the inflated egos of important people, and let others take credit for results he had achieved.

Charles Shaw sat in his chair not because he had been the only contender, but because he had played the game, made the right connections. Isaac had to admit he had done a good job. His reorganisation of the bureaucratic structure of the Metropolitan Police had been good, and apart from the threat of terrorist-related activities, crime levels were down in the city. The other contenders when the previous commissioner had stepped down did not have the political savvy, had not gone to school with the prime minister, or sat on the PM's Anti-Terrorism Committee.

Isaac did not have the contacts, but he did have Richard Goddard, who had the ear of Commissioner Shaw. He was certain there was more than a mutual respect involved, although he had never asked.

***

Linda Harris had suggested the restaurant; Isaac had agreed. He hoped it would not be too expensive, as he felt obliged to pay, and getting expenses paid took forever. The mortgage on his apartment was placing him under a lot of pressure, and now he had been landed with a bill to replace the oven. He needed a promotion, not a demotion, although he realised that he was placing himself in the category of expendable, knowing too much.

Isaac ordered fish, lightly grilled, with a salad – in line with his new regime of looking after his health. He was aware that tomorrow it could be a late night and another pizza. Linda ordered a Greek salad. Both chose orange juice. The seats they occupied were close to the corner window with a limited view of the street. Camden Town, where they met, was trendy, with many of its streets of run-down terraces being renovated. Isaac appreciated the colourful atmosphere; she loved it.

'I come from Devon. Too quiet down there for me,' she said. He had dismissed her at Williams' office as another rent-a-lay.

As he spoke to her, he was not so sure. Sally Jenkins had been obvious, not especially articulate, and dressed in the office in a tarty manner. He remembered Linda in the office wearing a long-sleeved blouse, but apart from that, couldn't remember much else. At the restaurant she wore jeans with a white top.

'What brought you to London?'

'Secretarial college, and then I found work here.'

'You realise why we're meeting today?' he asked. He had finished his meal; she had barely started.

'I suppose it's to do with my predecessor's death. I'm not sure how I can help. I never met her.'

'Is there anything you can tell me about her? Any reason why someone would want her dead?'

'Apart from her lousy administration skills? I wouldn't have thought that was a reason for murder, although if she had been around, I would have felt like throttling her.'

'No good at her job?' Isaac asked. He had ordered a second glass of orange juice. He was in no hurry to leave.

'Virtually incompetent, but she wasn't employed for her office skills, was she?' Isaac thought it was a refreshingly open statement.

'What do you know of her relationship with Richard Williams?'

'Apart from him being the boss, and her the employee?'

'Yes.'

'He was sleeping with her.'

'Yes, I know.'

'He has a history of relationships with his staff,' she said.

'I am aware that Sally Jenkins enjoyed the good life he provided.' Isaac looked for a response. He could see none.

'Are you trying diplomatically to ask whether I was sleeping with him?'

'It may be relevant to the investigation.'

'The answer to your question is yes.'

'Thank you for your honesty.'

'He's used me as an alibi, hasn't he?'

'Do you corroborate his statement?'

'He was with me all night.'

Isaac felt the need to probe. 'Sally Jenkins was obviously with Williams for her own personal reasons.'

'And you want to know if my reasons are the same?'

'It may be relevant.'

'I'm not sure how. For the record, Sally Jenkins was incompetent, attractive, and easily swayed by a rich man with a fancy car.'

'Are you?'

'Not at all. For one thing, I'm competent; the car and the wealth are not important.'

'Then why?'

'He's a charming man, treats me well. Neither of us is under any illusion. It's purely fun for a while. I'll leave soon enough. Does that satisfy?'

Isaac chose not to comment. He had a casual relationship with Sophie, and it suited both of them fine. It was not for him to form an opinion on Linda Harris or Richard Williams.

The relationship between Jess O'Neill and Williams had concerned him a lot, but he had discounted it, given her the benefit of the doubt. He realised as he sat across from a beautiful woman that he had not seen Jess for a while. Their last meeting had left both of them more than a little upset.

'Sally Jenkins was murdered for a reason,' Isaac said.

'Are you concerned that I may be targeted as well?' She seemed unconcerned.

'If, as we believe, she died for something she knew or overheard, then the situation remains that you may know or have heard something.'

'I'm not sure what. You believe that Richard may know something?'

'It seems a logical conclusion. We are assuming Charles Sutherland died because he was going to talk to the magazine about what he knew.'

'And you believe Sally Jenkins knew as well.'

'It's possible.'

'Either she was involved with Sutherland or she heard something. Is that what you are saying?'

'We've discounted any involvement with Sutherland. The only information she could have would have come from Richard Williams. There seems to be no other explanation.'

'I certainly haven't heard anything in the office, although I'm not an eavesdropper. Apparently, she was.'

'If you haven't heard anything at work, maybe you have elsewhere.'

'How?'

'Does he talk in his sleep?'

'He doesn't sleep much.'

'Why do you say that?'

'Not because of me. It's the man's metabolism. He sleeps for three or four hours, and then he's prowling about, making a cup of tea, snacking from the fridge, writing emails. Mildly annoying. I need eight hours at least, or I'm cranky the next day.'

'In his limited sleep time, does he talk?' Isaac returned to the original question.

'Sometimes, but I take little notice. I'm a heavy sleeper, take a sleeping pill occasionally. Do you think Sally heard something?'

'It's a possibility.'

'If someone thinks I heard something as well?'

'You need to take care, maybe distance yourself a little from him.'

'That's not an issue. I'm not sleeping with Richard anymore. It was only a short-term fling for both of us. He likes his women a little more common than me, and I do not need a man attempting to prove his virility. I've more pride than that.'

'You'll continue to work with him?'

'I said I would until I've fixed up the administration, or until he finds a Sally Jenkins replacement.'

Isaac felt satisfied with her responses, not certain about her safety, but there was an unknown assailant, and the police could not protect everyone in potential danger. And if the murders were professional, would the police even be capable of waylaying a determined assassin?

Chapter 26

Wendy, frustrated with the slow progress on checking the security videos at Paddington Station, decided to leave early and return the next day, but not before calling in at Challis Street. She needed to check if there had been any success at finding the missing woman from the video she had obtained in Worcester.

Bridget Halloran greeted Wendy as she entered the office on the lower floor of the building. She was a good-looking woman, with a strong Irish accent. She and Wendy had hit it off when Bridget first arrived in the building a few years earlier. Both had a story to tell and an easy-going sense of humour. Wendy enjoyed being out in the field, Bridget preferred the office, even the reports that needed preparing. She had helped Wendy a few times with her spelling, which was atrocious. It can be rectified, Bridget had assured her, but Wendy never took her advice, and as long as Bridget remained in the building, she never would.

Wendy was almost fifteen years older than Bridget, yet they were firm friends, inside and outside the police force. Both were partial to a good drink, too many sometimes, and Wendy's husband had complained on more than one occasion when the taxi driver had had to assist her into the house. Bridget's long time, live-in lover had tried complaining, but as she told Wendy, 'If he starts complaining, he'll get the back of my hand and a quick push out the front door.' It was a fair statement, as a small inheritance from a favourite aunt had allowed Bridget to put the deposit down on the house, and she had no intention of allowing her lover to have any financial stake in it. Not unless he made an honest woman of her, and he didn't look like doing that anytime soon. Besides, she wasn't sure she wanted to be an honest woman. She felt the need to play up on occasions, and doing so with a ring on her finger would have offended her strict Roman Catholic upbringing. Wendy had covered for her a few times.

Bridget knew the lover would not be checking too hard on her. He was not ambitious, maintained a mundane job working for the council, but he provided company. He had his part to play in the agreement, and as long as he abided by the conditions, he was free to live with her rent-free.

'Any luck with the video?' Wendy asked after they had spent more than a few minutes nattering, making plans for another night out.

'She boarded the train. Let me show you.'

All Wendy could see was a grainy screen with what looked like a dead fly in one camera, out of focus and blurry.

'It's not very clear,' she confessed, not sure if it was her eyesight.

'They never are. No one cleans the cameras. The pollution slowly builds up. Just squint your eyes a little, may help.'

Wendy squinted; it helped a little. All she could see was a woman vaguely matching the description getting into the third carriage of the Paddington bound train. Another five people appeared to get on as well, and they were clearly not middle-aged. One was male and old, the way he walked attesting to that fact. Another two apparently newlyweds, or newly enchanted with each other. The other two, children from what she could see. It had to be Marjorie Frobisher, although the face was concealed and the resolution on the camera did not help.

By the time they had finished looking at the video, it was too late in the day to return to Paddington Station. She had phoned Brian Gee, the self-confessed computer nerd, and sent him an email attachment with the three best stills taken from the Worcester Station video. She then called the station manager, a matter of courtesy, to thank him for his help and to suggest that perhaps they could catch up for a cup of tea tomorrow, her treat, which seemed a lame remark. He was British Rail – the tea was his, and he didn't have to pay for it.

***

Christy Nichols had passed on to Farhan the details of who was involved in smuggling the two escorts into the hotel. He should have met with them first, and then Aisha.

He decided against meeting Olivia if he could. He saw her as a decent woman indulging in an unusual occupation to provide for her family, who would not have understood.

There had been pressure to reveal his contacts, a procedural requirement. He knew if there were an audit of the department, he would receive a severe reprimand. Not revealing the women's identities would hamper his promotion prospects; giving their names would cause him a moral dilemma, as they had spoken to him in confidence.

Farhan understood that Detective Superintendent Goddard was not willing to rock the boat if it affected his ambition, but would turn a blind eye if it did not. Farhan had decided come what may that Samantha's and Olivia's true identities would remain concealed, but Christy Nichols knew the agency.

Marion Robertson, the principal of the agency, may not have felt such reluctance, especially if pressure was applied: legal pressure, running a house of ill-repute, profiting from the proceeds of prostitution, employing illegal immigrants. He was certain she was not guilty of any crime, certainly none that was too serious, but if pressured, those doing the questioning would almost certainly bring up the possible avenues of enquiry, and she would have other women on her books. Farhan knew the possibility of the two women being identified was strong. He had to let them know.

He phoned Olivia. She was not pleased to hear from him. He explained the situation and asked whether she had told Agnew. She said her identity was more important than a few hundred pounds, and besides, her husband's financial situation had improved, and the need to prostitute herself was not as important, although they were looking at a bigger house to buy. Farhan saw that selling herself caused her no personal issues.

He explained the possibility of her identity being revealed. It caused her great alarm. He said that he would never reveal it, but others might. He advised her to consider her position, and if he thought her identity was soon to be revealed, he would attempt to contact her in advance. She thanked him. She sounded genuine.

Aisha was also disturbed when he phoned her, although initially she had been delighted. He had been honest with Olivia; he would be with her. Olivia meant nothing to him, Aisha did. They agreed to meet.

***

Farhan, personally involved, wishing he could be detached but knowing he could not, thought a better location than Hyde Park would be more appropriate. Aisha had taken a half-day off from work. She had something to tell him. He hoped it was not a confession.

A riverside hotel, overlooking the Thames with a clear view of Tower Bridge, was chosen by both. She arrived in her workday clothes, a smart business suit, sombre in colour, as befitted her chosen profession of lawyer. Farhan arrived, suit and tie, although he loosened his tie once they were sitting down. Both were a little excited; both showed it.

'I've got some good news,' she said. Farhan breathed a sigh of relief – it was not to be a confession. A waiter hovered, anxious to take their order. They ignored him.

'Aisha, this is official,' he said. He knew that what he needed to ask her should have been done in a more formal setting. Smiles and touching of hands across the table did not constitute official police proceedings. He knew he could not stop.

'Let me tell you my news first.' She seemed oblivious of what he wanted to ask, uninterested in her other life. She knew she was acting like a love-struck teenager out on a first date. The teenager she was not, but love-struck and the first date were certainly correct. She would not say it openly, but if asked, she would have admitted that she felt more than a fondness for Farhan Ahmed, the upright and serious detective inspector. He knew her story, her ambition, her screwing men for money. She hoped he would understand, not as a policeman but as someone she could spend the rest of her life with.

The waiter, increasingly annoyed at being ignored, eventually succeeded in taking their order. Both ordered fruit juices and salads. Business was brisk, and it was evident the establishment had the policy of quickly sit the patrons down, feed them, and get them out of the door as fast as possible, credit cards suitably debited. The punters, as the hotel landlord, a foul-mouthed Irishman, referred to the patrons. He only cared about the money in his bank account. The service the hotel provided was only there to ensure the maximum return on investment. He was not wrong about his concern for profit, for the situation in the city was challenging for any business. Rents were high, labour costs through the roof, and a riverside hotel overlooking the Thames could not easily relocate down past Canary Wharf to somewhere cheaper. The owner, a Russian businessman, based in Moscow, mansion in Kensington, knew that only too well.

Farhan also flashed his police badge and directed his glance towards a couple of young girls, obviously under age, sitting with a group of men, two tables away. The waiter understood. Farhan and Aisha would not be rushed out of the premises if the hotel did not want trouble.

'Tell me your news,' he said.

'I've passed my exams.'

'Congratulations.'

'They've offered me a more senior position. There will be some delay before I start representing clients on my own, but it's a great start.'

'Did you see the press conference with Detective Superintendent Goddard and DCI Cook?'

'I couldn't watch it. It was on the television at my home. My parents were watching it, making comments. I was too ashamed. I left the room. They wanted to speak about it later; how disgraceful it was that women behave in that manner. I changed the subject, left the house, and went for a walk. I don't want to think about that life. It's almost as if it's a dream.'

'Unfortunately, it's not a dream, and it's still a murder investigation.'

'I've not been back to Marion Robertson since. I can't imagine giving myself to another man purely for money now. I should be embarrassed to say that to you.'

'Why aren't you?' he asked.

'Maybe you can't forgive, not totally, but you are able to put it to one side, not judge me too harshly.'

'It depends on the woman.'

'Am I that woman?' she asked coyly.

'There's still the fact of two dead bodies to be dealt with.' Farhan tried to bring the conversation back to official. He knew he was losing the battle: the weather was too good, Aisha too cheerful, and her beauty distracted him totally.

'I only know about one,' she said.

'Someone told a reporter that you and Olivia were in the hotel with Sutherland.'

'It wasn't me. How can you ask? You know me well enough to know that I wouldn't do that.'

'I know. Still, I had to ask.'

'Why me? Why not Olivia? Why not the staff at the hotel? It was hardly a great secret; it's not the first time I've been there.'

'I phoned Olivia. I've yet to speak to the staff. I've also talked to Christy Nichols.'

'Why didn't you meet with Olivia?'

'I wanted to protect her identity, and besides, I don't believe she would do it. Her secret is too important.'

'And you think I might. Don't you think my secrecy is important?'

'Of course I do. That's why we haven't met recently.'

'I don't understand.' The mood had become chilly. 'You are risking my secrecy now.'

'We've met here. It would be construed by the casual observer that we are two people enjoying each other's company. Here, in this crowded place, is the most secret place. We are here because I want to protect you. Because I had a legitimate reason to meet with you.' The mood warmed.

'You've used someone at the hotel talking out of turn as an excuse to meet up with me again.'

'In part, I admit. But there still remains someone we don't know about. Someone that was able to get him naked and to take a drink voluntarily.'

'With the drugs he was on, that could be anyone.'

'Are you indicating that it could have been a man?'

'No, although it could have been his minder.'

'We've discounted her at the present time.'

'I certainly saw no one else. Olivia probably didn't either. I've stayed chaste since we last met. I said I would.'

They both ordered a glass of wine, not because they were drinkers, but because the situation required a relaxant. One hour later, they were upstairs in a room alone together. Not because of the alcohol, not because of her former profession, not because he had not been with a woman for a long time, although that had been an unsatisfactory coupling with a cold and unloving woman.

It was because they wanted to be together; because they both felt a strong emotional tie.

It was early evening when they left the hotel. He, feeling guilty that he had acted unprofessionally; she, elated in that she had experienced sex without money and had not needed to pretend. He knew his house that night was not going to feel so lonely; she, satisfied that she had found a man that she could love, a man her parents would approve of, a man who knew her secret.

Chapter 27

Early morning rush hour was not the best time to find a parking spot anywhere near Paddington Station. In the end, Wendy found a loading zone and put a police parking permit in the car window.

She knew a few delivery vehicle drivers would be cursing her – the bad language a certainty – but she had no option. Brian Gee's information seemed important. She did not like using police privilege unless necessary.

'I've found her.' She had barely entered the room when Brian Gee came up to her, shook her warmly by the hand and announced his success.

'Where?'

'The photos you sent. We were able to correlate them against the people on the station around the time the train arrived.'

'Was she wearing the same clothes?'

'That's what made it easy. We also managed to get a facial. It's not crystal clear, but it's okay. A new camera had just been installed, so it wasn't yet choked with pollution.'

Wendy phoned Isaac with the news.

After the quick phone call, she turned her attention back to Brian Gee. 'Positive ID?'

'Ninety-five percent. That's good enough for me.' He offered her a cup of coffee, tepid, out of a machine in the corner. She realised that if she wanted a British Rail cup of tea she would have to go and see the station manager, which she intended to do before she left.

'What else do you have?'

'She was met by someone.'

'Any idea who?'

'What we can see is one person, slightly taller than her and wearing a thick coat and a baseball cap.'

'Male or female?'

'Judging by the way the person walked, I'd say it was a man.'

'Any idea as to age, colour?'

'I'll give you copies of the video. Apart from male, thick coat, baseball cap, there's not a lot more I can give you. We know they exited the station and headed in an easterly direction.'

'Was she pleased to see the person?'

'Yet again, you can make your own decision. She seemed to greet the man. After that, she can be seen walking at his side with his right hand holding onto her left arm. It's difficult to tell if it was a friendly gesture. The station was very busy. Maybe he was just ensuring he did not lose her.'

She realised that she should pick up the video and head back to Challis Street at top speed and give the tape to Bridget, but she still had a cup of tea on her mind. Station Manager Broughton had the tea ready when she arrived, as well as a cheese and tomato sandwich. It was not stale. His office still had the unique smell she remembered from the previous day. It was homely and comfy, not like her home with her increasingly vague and complaining husband. She knew that one day she would need to consider placing him in a nursing home, maybe before she retired. What would she do then? Maybe travel, maybe take a course, maybe find

187

someone else to keep her company, purely platonic? She could not see herself being on her own.

By the time she arrived back at the car, it had been four hours. The delivery driver trying to park, not intimidated by the official police sign, and not showing any respect for a woman, gave her a verbal dressing down.

'You think just because you're the police, you can fuckin' park wherever you like.' He was an uncouth man, heavily tattooed, and had the appearance of someone who belonged to a motorbike gang. The tee-shirt emblazoned with Harley Davidson – a testament to the fact.

'You watch your mouth, or I'll slap a ticket on your truck for a failed brake light.'

'There ain't no problem with my lights. I checked 'em this morning.'

'There will be once I kick one of them out.'

'That's police harassment. I could have you nicked for that if I make an official complaint.'

Wendy, suitably angry, had seen it too many times. She knew that if she had been police and male, the irate truck driver would not have engaged in a slanging match, and he would have moderated his language. Female, police, middle-aged, and it was a different situation.

'Okay, I'll tell you what we do,' she said. 'I'll kick out your brake light, maybe hit it with a jack handle for good measure.'

'You do that!'

'You can call over a policeman, or I can call one for you on my police radio.'

'You do that.'

'Once he arrives, I'll show him my police ID, nice and shiny, and you can show him your truck's registration.'

'You're threatening me.' He did not seem as confident as before, and there were the parking fines to consider. He hadn't paid them, and his driving licence had expired.

'Threat? I don't think so.' She knew she had him on the defensive, realised that she should not have indulged in a verbal exchange on a busy street. After a congenial few hours at Paddington, this unpleasant foul-mouthed man had made her see red. Her temper had been a problem a couple of times over the years, even prevented her promotion.

'Okay, I'm leaving,' the driver said and drove off, cursing under his breath. Wendy left soon after, laughed to herself as she saw the driver five minutes later arguing with a policeman over an apparently bald tyre at the front of his vehicle.

***

Isaac was keeping his distance from Jess O'Neill, even though she had phoned a couple of times. He realised that if he met her, he might have weakened, and of the three women with a motive to kill Charles Sutherland, hers was very strong.

He had noticed the change in Farhan. It concerned him that he may be falling into the same trap that he had in the past. He decided to talk to him at some stage.

The information that Wendy had passed on from Paddington Station about Marjorie Frobisher, apparently still alive and now in London, concerned him. Charles Sutherland had probably died as a result of information he possessed about her. That would indicate a professional assassination, but none of the three women appeared to have any background that would suggest they were trained killers.

Could there be another woman? Isaac thought. It seemed plausible, but if it wasn't one of the three females they knew about, could it be someone else known or someone hidden in plain sight? The delays in identifying suspects and charges against persons, innocent until proven guilty, still occupied the media. His infrequent watching of television in the past had changed; TV had now become a necessity, so much so that he had installed one in his apartment, one in the office.

Sophie did not like the one at his home. Even complained when he had interrupted his undivided attention for her to watch the news. Isaac wasn't sure where the relationship was heading. Casual sex, no obligation, no guilt, sounded great to the average hot-blooded male, but he had realised in recent weeks that he was getting older, it was maybe time to settle down. He wasn't sure why he felt this. In the past, it had been a thought in passing and no more. Maybe it was Jess O'Neill. He felt the need to see her. He knew he could not unless there was some new information.

***

The next day Isaac's momentary lapse to think about Jess O'Neill was abruptly halted. A news flash on the television in the office. One of the two prostitutes known to have visited Charles Sutherland on the day of his demise had been identified. He was aware that Farhan would be upset by the news. He phoned him.

'What are they saying? Farhan asked.

'They said her name was Olivia. Is that one of the women?'

'She did it for her family. I said I would never reveal her identity.'

'You never did. It's not your problem,' Isaac said.

Farhan realised that it was his problem, and he felt the need to elaborate why. Here he was in a relationship with the other woman. If one was identified, it would not be long before the other one was found. He had to focus on protecting Aisha, helping Olivia if he could, although she would not be receptive to hearing from him. He knew he had to contact Aisha and quickly.

On ending the phone conversation with Isaac, he called Aisha – she was occupied with a client at the legal firm where she worked. He left a message, hoped she would get back to him before she heard the news from a third party. He realised he was in love. It was a complication he would not have chosen.

Still married, a divorce settlement that would almost certainly cost him the house, but that was not an issue as long as the children were fine. And then, how many police regulations had he broken? Fraternising with a witness who may be a murderer, behaviour unbecoming, concealing evidence. He could see his career dashed on the rocks of public opinion and police regulations. If it became known, would he be suspended?

Phoning Olivia was not necessary. She phoned him soon after the news broke. He reflected that she sounded calmer than he expected. 'I told my husband.'

'I maintained your confidentiality.'

'It was that Marion Robertson,' she said.

'Are you certain?'

'I phoned her. I thought she was a decent person, but prostitution always was a dirty business.'

'Why would she do that?' Farhan asked.

'There have been some reporters fishing for information, ever since that reporter on the television. If they ask enough questions, knock on enough doors…'

'Have they found out where you live?'

'Marion Robertson doesn't know my home address. Besides, she only ever contacted me on an anonymous phone number that I gave to her.'

'But she knows where we met and the school run. She set up our meeting.'

'Oh, my God, she does. They are bound to find me. I should never have met you.'

'I understand that, but it is a murder. I would have found you anyway, the same way as the reporters. I've done the best I can.'

'I know that. How am I going to protect my family?'

'It may be best to go away for a while until it blows over. Why did you tell your husband?'

'I had to. Too much guilt; he didn't deserve to find out from someone else.'

'How did he take it?'

'What do you think?'

'Badly?'

'He's in shock, not talking. I did the right thing telling him. I can only hope in time that he gets over it. Could you forgive someone you cared for?'

'In time.' He did not intend to elaborate that he already had.

The call ended; the phone rang again. 'I've just come out of a long meeting. I'm pleased to hear from you,' Aisha said.

'I don't think you'll be happy when I tell you what has happened.'

'Tell me?'

'They've found Olivia.' Farhan could hear an audible sigh on the other end of the phone. He wished he could have told her face to face, but it had not been possible.

'But how?'

'Marion Robertson. She's admitted it to Olivia.'

'Has she given my name?'

'I've no idea. I'm heading over to see her right now. Olivia obviously had a contactable phone number. How about you?'

'I changed it. You know that. I gave you the new number.'

'Marion Robertson doesn't have your contact number. How about an address?'

'No, although she knows I work in the city. I suppose they could find me.'

'Let's hope not. It's best for you not to worry. I'll see what I can do to protect the two of you.'

***

Bridget was in a talkative mood when Wendy entered her office, clutching the hard disk with the footage of Marjorie Frobisher at Paddington Station. Wendy was still a little miffed after her argument with the van-driving lout. A cup of tea, not as good as British Rail, soon calmed her down. Wendy assumed that Bridget's computer set up was not as good as Brian Gee's, but then she knew little about such matters, could barely write an email, and her typing skills were definitely one finger at a time. She had asked Bridget how she managed to type so quickly, barely looking at the keyboard, her eyes focussed on a monitor to the right of the laptop. Bridget said it was easy. Ten lessons to learn how to break the bad typing habits, and then learn the basics, centre line on the keyboard, first finger of each hand on the raised bumps on the F and the J, left hand F, right hand J.

The teacher at the local college had explained that the two letters formed the reference point. Wendy had repeatedly tried, even drove her husband crazy as she laboured away at night trying to get the hang of it, but the habit was too firmly entrenched. She gave up after six weeks and went back to banging the keyboard. Besides, if it became difficult, there was always Bridget.

'It's not very clear,' Bridget said. She had ordered in some cakes, Wendy's favourite. *There goes the diet,* Wendy thought. Not that she would ever have dieted, but it was always good to believe it was possible.

'The man she met?' Wendy asked.

'His complexion looks on the dark side, but I'm not sure if that is the camera or the lighting.'

'Can't you reference it off Marjorie Frobisher?'

'Are you certain it's her? With those sunglasses on, it's hard to tell.'

'Almost one hundred per cent.'

'It's not going to be easy to follow her down the street.'

'With all those cameras?'

'That's not the problem. It's the software and the time delays in accessing the film. There'll be a backup server somewhere; it will have been recorded. May take some time.'

'We don't have the luxury of time.'

Bridget phoned for some more food to be brought in. 'It's going to be a long day, maybe night. Are you up to it?' she asked Wendy.

'Not a problem. I'll keep you fed.'

'Slave driver,' Bridget joked. Wendy knew her husband would be complaining. *Tough*, she thought. This was more interesting.

Chapter 28

Isaac told Farhan that he was a bloody fool and should have known better. 'She is a witness, maybe more involved than we believe.'

'I met both of them, separate occasions,' Farhan said.

'I know that.'

'I kept clear of Olivia, as I knew some of her family history. I made a promise.'

'I don't think we have the luxury of giving promises.'

'I know that, but I needed her cooperation.'

'You're too kind-hearted. You know that?'

Farhan had not seen Isaac so angry before. 'What would you have done?' he asked.

'I'm not the one who has been sleeping with a witness, am I?'

'It wasn't intended, but what would you have done with the two witnesses?'

'Probably the same as you, but sleeping with one of them…'

'You make it sound sordid.'

'What was it, an easy lay? I realise that life must be difficult for you at the present moment with your wife and children not around, but sleeping with this woman. Next you'll be telling me she lives at home with her parents, contributes to the rent money.'

'She does.'

'Good God, Farhan, how do I protect you!' Isaac exclaimed. His anger was not levelled at Farhan for what he had done. Most men would have acted in the same manner, but he was a policeman, an upholder of the law, and here he was, sleeping with a prostitute who may have seen a murderer. It was indefensible. Isaac knew he should report it officially, but Farhan was too good a policeman, too good a person, to allow his career to be thrown away.

Richard Goddard had got him out of a couple of tricky situations in the past; maybe he could help. Farhan had hoped it could be kept between him and Isaac. Isaac explained it could not, and if the women were to be protected then Detective Superintendent Goddard was the best man.

Farhan relented, in part because he knew Isaac was right, but mainly because he wanted to protect the women, especially the one he loved. Her selling herself to help her get through her studies should have automatically condemned her. However, his years in the police service had made him realise that some people were good, while others were bad. Aisha, he knew, was good, as was Olivia. He hoped Detective Superintendent Goddard was good as well. He was not so sure about Marion Robertson. He would reserve judgement on her until she had been given the opportunity to mount a defence. He realised it was conditional on his being a serving policeman, and that was clearly in the balance.

***

Richard Goddard sat quietly while Farhan explained the situation about one of the escorts being identified. He explained his reason for confidentiality. Richard Goddard stated that he was not correct, but Farhan countered that, for a moderate Muslim, it was not open to discussion. He had seen the injustices against women. He was not willing to allow their lives to be prejudiced because of mistakes they may have made.

Farhan went on to explain that both women had their reasons for indulging in prostitution, and they should be protected from a scurrilous press. They were potentially material witnesses, and it was up to the police department to protect their identities. Detective Superintendent Goddard saw this as illogical.

Farhan counter-argued that legally in the United Kingdom they had not broken any law except the law of morality, and that was not a punishable offence, except by a higher power.

Isaac, amazed at the fluidity of Farhan's argument and the fluency of delivery, in the end could only sit back and declare him the winner. Goddard, suitably impressed, thanked him for his honesty and his reasons but failed to give him his unanimous support.

'Detective Inspector Ahmed, this is all very well, and given I want to give you a kick up the arse as well as a severe dressing down, which I do, how can I protect them and you?'

'Official Secrets Act?' Isaac asked.

'What has the Official Secrets Act got to do with this?'

'It's there to restrict information. Why not for these women?'

'I'll need to meet with my contact; see what we can do.'

'Angus MacTavish?' Isaac asked.

'I suppose it was pointless trying to keep that confidential,' Goddard admitted.

'What about the women?' Farhan asked.

'They need to keep a low profile. Explain that you need to know where they are.'

'Thank you, sir.'

'Don't thank me. We're not out of trouble yet, and you've still to receive my reprimand. Isaac will tell you that I don't mince words. You've been a bloody fool. Whatever you do, don't go sleeping with the witnesses until this is over. That applies to you as well, Isaac.'

***

Farhan, suitably humbled after his admission and thankful that there was a potential solution, focussed his attention on the two women. As much as he wanted to phone Aisha first, he decided that Olivia was the person most under threat. As a precaution, he had called Marion Robertson, indicated that she had committed a criminal offence by revealing the name of a witness. He was confident that she would say no more until he got to her office, which he intended to do within the hour.

Olivia was pleased to hear Farhan on the end of the phone. 'What can you tell me? What's going to happen?' she asked. Her husband was on the phone line as well. Farhan could hear him breathing.

'You're not alone?' Farhan asked.

'My husband is here with me. We're going to be alright.'

'I'd like to thank you, Detective Inspector Ahmed,' Olivia's husband said.

'This must be a difficult time for you both.'

'We love each other,' Olivia said. 'My husband will forgive me in time, I hope.'

'In time, as my wife says. I knew what she was before I married her and I know she only did it for the family. It will be hard, but we will survive.'

'Do you want to come to the house?' she asked.

'I don't think that's necessary, and besides, I already know where you live. I believe it would be best if we don't meet. Someone might be following me.'

'How do you know my address?'

'I'm a policeman. Your car registration plates. Caroline, am I correct?'

'Caroline, yes.'

'This matter is more involved than you realise. I'm not at liberty to say more. This goes beyond the death of one person.'

'What can we do?' Olivia's husband asked.

'Are you able to leave the country?'

'We've discussed it, for the sake of the children,' the husband responded.

'Any possibility?'

'My father was South African. I've citizenship there.'

'When can you go?'

'We had thought in two months. I need to give notice at work, and there's the children's schooling.'

'It would be best if you leave now.'

'I understand,' the husband said.

'Are you suggesting we hide, have fictitious names?' Olivia asked.

'Nothing so melodramatic. The press is fickle, short-term memory. You'll be forgotten in time, and there is still the other woman.'

'Is she leaving as well?' the husband asked.

'Possibly. I don't believe Marion Robertson knew how to contact her.'

'She told me she didn't, but you'd better check. She hasn't come out too well in this.'

'Maybe there are extenuating circumstances. I'll reserve my opinion until I've met with her.'

'We can leave within the week, maybe two days,' the husband said.

'Keep in contact. I'll do what I can to protect you.'

'Thank you, Farhan,' Olivia said. Her husband thanked him as well.

With one woman's situation hopefully resolved, Farhan turned to the one woman he hoped he could protect. Her phone, barely the first ring before she answered.

'Aisha, where are you?'

'Close to the office. Can we meet?' she asked.

'It's not possible. We need to maintain a distance until this blows over.'

'Why?'

'They know me. I don't want them following.'

'You would know if you were being followed, wouldn't you?'

'Most of the time, but some of them are good. The risk's too great.'

'Then it's good that we spent time together yesterday,' she said.

'I wish we could repeat it today, but your safety is more important than my lust.'

'Don't you mean love?'

'Of course, but I need to protect you now.'

'That's what people who love each other do, isn't it?'

He had to agree. 'Yes, that's what they do.'

'What do you want me to do?'

'Maintain your normal routine. Go to work, go home, act normal.'

'I'll try. It won't be easy.'

'It will not be easy for either of us, but your protection is all that matters now.'

'It will kill my father if the truth comes out. He has a weak heart.'

'Then follow my advice. Is that clear?'

'It's clear, but this is a time we should be together, not apart,' she said.

'That may be, but it's not possible. Believe me, I will be thinking of you. I can only hope that this is concluded soon.'

'Will it be?'

'I've no idea. We're floundering at the moment, not sure what the significance of the missing woman is.'

'You've never mentioned that before.'

'I'm talking out loud, that's all.'

'Are you saying Marjorie Frobisher is the key to this?'

'She worked with Sutherland, knew Sally Jenkins, and she disappeared before the murders started. It's suspicious.'

'Maybe she knew she was being targeted?' Aisha said.

'Until we speak with her, assuming she's still able to speak, we'll not know.'

'There's something about her early history,' Farhan said.

'Maybe I can help?'

'Maybe you could.'

'Give me some details,' she said. Farhan realised that he was in error, but Aisha was a smart woman, legally qualified, and she may find something the experts had missed.

'Until we know what this information is, I don't think we are any closer to solving it.'

'Send me what information you have that is relevant, some dates, and I'll scurry around. That way we can keep in touch, even if only by phone.'

***

Two minutes after ending his conversation with Aisha, Farhan arrived at Marion Robertson's office. 'I need to put my case forward before you judge me out of hand,' she said.

'I'm here with an open mind. If you help me, then maybe I am able to help you. Are we agreed?' he said.

'I had no option but to give one of the names.'

'Olivia?'

'Yes.' Farhan could see the woman was not as relaxed as at their previous meeting. She was moving around the office, unable to sit down. Farhan had chosen to sit on a chair close to her desk. He needed her to be calm.

'Please sit down.' He took the initiative and made two cups of tea using the machine in the corner. For several minutes, nothing was said.

'They threatened to expose me.'

'Who did?'

'The two men who came here.'

Farhan realised that if the woman had been threatened, then maybe she had no alternative. She certainly seemed less sure of herself, almost demure as she sat behind her desk. The assuredness, the inner calm, no longer apparent. He suggested they sat in more comfortable chairs.

'It may be best if you tell me the full story,' Farhan said calmly.

'I am ashamed of what I did.'

'You had no problem with supplying women for sex.'

'I've never had any qualms about this business. There has never been any serious trouble. I always reasoned that it was a necessary service, and no one was hurt.'

'Were you an escort once?'

'For many years. It's a long story, but I never sold myself on a street corner, and there were never drugs involved.'

'And now?'

'The mobile phone, the one with the gold case that you observed last time. That was given to me for services rendered, not some other woman. He is a wonderful man, very decent, very generous.'

'Why did you give Olivia's details?' Farhan realised that he had not been shocked by Marion Robertson's revelation.

'Is she alright?' She seemed genuinely concerned. Farhan was certain it was not a pretence. Some of her self-assuredness had returned. She sat easily in the chair. Farhan, in charge of the situation, made another cup of tea for the two of them.

'Hopefully, she will be all right.' He was unsure if he should elaborate just yet. He was aware that Olivia and her husband were buying airline tickets and were planning to leave within two days. If Marion Robertson had been pressured, then maybe she could be pressured again. What she didn't know, she couldn't tell.

'I can only hope she accepts my apologies.'

'Maybe, in time.' Farhan said. Olivia did not seem a vengeful woman; a little contrite about what she had put her husband through, but it was clear that she had no great issues with selling herself if it looked after her family. Farhan was certain she would do it again, but it was not for him to offer an opinion.

It made him reflect on Aisha. *I hope she does not think of prostitution in the same way as Olivia,* he thought. He determined to ask her the next time he saw her. He felt he could forgive her for past sins, but future sins? That seemed too much to consider.

'Will they find out where she lives?' Farhan decided not to answer the question. He had found Olivia's home address and he knew that anyone else determined would find it with little trouble.

'I said to both women that I would protect their identities to the best of my ability. I intend to do that if it is indeed possible.'

'And is it?' she asked.

'I'm not certain yet.'

'Are you able to protect me?' Marion Robertson looked unsure of herself again.

'Do you need protection?'

'The two men.'

'What can you tell me?'

'They threatened me.'

'It's best if you describe their visit here. It was here, I assume?'

'Yes, in this office.'

'I'll record this conversation. Is that okay with you?'

'Yes, that's fine.'

Farhan placed his mobile phone on the table, on record. He knew he would have to write a report afterwards – easier to record now and play back later.

'Marion, please commence. Take your time and take a break if you need.'

'I could do with a glass of water.' Farhan poured one for her.

'Last week, Thursday, mid-morning, I was in the office. I had just arranged for one of my girls to meet up with an overseas client. He's a regular when he is in the country. He always treats the girls well, so I had no problem fixing him up. It was close to eleven o'clock when two men walked into the office.'

'Just one question before you continue,' Farhan interrupted. 'Why the office? Surely you could run this business from home.'

'At home, I'm the dutiful wife; here, I'm the Madam.'

Farhan could see no reason to judge. At least the husband did not have a cold bed and a cold wife in it.

'The two men came in,' she continued. 'Normally, I keep the door locked, but for some reason I had failed to do so.'

'You assumed they were looking for you to arrange some women for them?'

'Not at all. There is no sign on the door. That's all strictly done online or by phone.'

'Understood.'

'They came in, polite and well-mannered. One sat where you are sitting now, the other one stood. It seemed as if he was there to intimidate me. He succeeded. I felt very insecure, but I maintained my composure. They said that the reason for their visit was a matter of the gravest seriousness. I was unsure what to think. There have been a few well-known clients over the years, including the son of a dictator in the Middle East, although he was a gentleman.'

'Did they introduce themselves?'

'The one sitting said his name was Howard Stone. He even showed me a business card.'

'Do you still have the card?'

'He said it was his last one and would I mind if he kept it. The other one did not offer his name, and apart from a few words, said little.'

'How long were they here?'

'About twenty minutes in total. They were both well-dressed, spoke well.'

'Not heavies, then?'

'Heavies? If by that you mean gangsters, then no.'

'So, what did they say or do that scared you?'

'The one sitting spoke calmly. He told me that they represented some clients in town, important clients, who were disturbed that a senior member of society had been potentially embarrassed, personally compromised, due to his involvement with one of my girls.'

'Did they say who this senior member of society was?'

'No, they were cagey when I asked.'

'Who do you think they were talking about?'

'I assumed it was a politician. The rich don't care unless the wife is likely to take half the assets if their dalliances became public knowledge. The politicians always worry about their reputations.'

'Has that happened in the past?' Farhan asked.

'It's happened, although I was able to keep the woman I supplied out of the newspapers. Luckily, the wife came to a confidential agreement with her husband, so no more was said, at least to us.'

'Let's assume it is a politician. What happened next?'

'The one sitting down told me that it was imperative that this person remained free of any indiscretions.'

'Did he say why?'

'He would not elaborate. I told him that my girls were specially chosen for their discretion and that they would not speak to anyone, or cause trouble.'

'And then?'

'His manner changed. He became surly, accused me of running a house of ill-repute, and that his client would ensure that firstly I would be out on the street where I belonged, letting any derelict fuck me for the price of a decent meal. My apologies for the bad language. I'm just repeating verbatim.'

'No need to apologise.'

'And secondly, he would ensure that my husband would be publicly disgraced as the consort of a whore. I could not allow that.'

'You care that much about your husband?' Farhan could not see his wife making such a statement. Marion Robertson, an escort, a supplier of women for sex, and in his society a person to be condemned, was more honourable than all those that professed piety. He admired the woman immeasurably.

'Yes. He's a good and kind man who accepts my peccadilloes with a forbearance that many would not.'

She had moved closer and touched Farhan on the knee. 'The silent one came close and leant over. He spoke quietly into my ear.'

'What did he say?'

'He told me that they had total authority, and if I did not give him some names with contacts immediately, they would personally see that I was revealed as the Madam of a brothel, and my husband would have an unfortunate accident.'

'Who did you think they were?'

'I thought they were connected with the government.'

'Why do you say that?'

'Their training. It was psychological intimidation. A gangster would have felt the need to be physical.'

'Why Olivia?'

'They were clear as to whom they wanted contact details for.'

'Samantha and Olivia?'

'They never mentioned Charles Sutherland.'

'You assume it was related?' Farhan asked.

'I don't know what I thought. I was shaking like a leaf, almost wet myself. It took me hours to calm down afterwards, and I couldn't tell my husband.'

'Why not?'

'I didn't want to upset him.'

'Why didn't you give them Samantha's phone number as well as Olivia's?'

'I wasn't sure that I had it. She tends to change the number regularly. Olivia is easier to contact. I knew her number worked.'

'How?'

'I had phoned her up earlier in the day, another client.'

'She was agreeable?'

'As always. I believe she likes the thrill of it. Is she a different person outside of the business?'

Farhan wasn't sure how much to say. What if the two men returned? Would she give up any more secrets if pressured? He assumed she would.

'A decent person.' He did not intend to elaborate.

'What if they come back?' she asked.

'Difficult question. Do you know any more about Samantha?'

'Not really.'

'Are you surprised that she changes her phone number regularly?'

'Not really. I don't know what her secret is, but she's very careful. Besides, she told me that she didn't want any more clients for a while. I sensed she had met someone and didn't want to confuse a normal relationship with selling herself on the side.'

Farhan relaxed back in his chair, almost certainly blushing.

'If they ask for Olivia again?' she asked.

'Her phone number will not work.'

'Is she safe?'

'I'm not sure. You've been threatened. Olivia is hiding, and Samantha is keeping a low profile. Our investigations have placed not only you three at risk, but indirectly brought about the deaths of two people.'

'You're a policeman; you can't stop doing your job because it may have unfortunate outcomes.'

'That is true, but it's a hornet's nest we've stirred up. We've no idea how it's going to end.'

'You said you were separated from your wife.'

'That's correct.'

'If you need company, let me know. I'll see that you are treated well. No cost, of course, but a man needs an outlet. No point bottling up the tension.'

Chapter 29

Isaac decided to visit the production lot. He wasn't sure why, apart from the fact that all three persons, two dead and one missing, had a close involvement with the place.

Until Wendy came up with some fresh information or Detective Superintendent Goddard was more forthcoming about why Marjorie Frobisher was so important, then the cast and production crew were his best bet. Maybe a snippet of information, a remark made in passing, and then a new avenue of enquiry would open up. Isaac hoped he would not make a fool of himself if he ran into Jess, but assumed he probably would.

Larry Hill had taken over the investigation into Sally Jenkins' death, at least as far as ascertaining who could have murdered her, and how that person had got into her apartment. Was the person known to her? Was Sally Jenkins relaxed when the person mysteriously appeared in her apartment after breaking in? And now Larry Hill was intimating that maybe the murderer did not come in through the window, only made it look as though he or she did. The person who had held the hapless former PA under water could have been male or female. There seemed to be no way to clarify this.

It was remarkable when Isaac arrived at the production lot how busy it was. Everywhere he looked, he saw activity.

He saw why soon enough – Ian Stanley. The series producer with the Napoleon complex was out on the war path, shouting at whoever. He saw Isaac soon enough.

'I hope you're not going to hold us up today,' Stanley said brusquely.

'Not at all. Under the circumstances, I thought it would have been quiet out here for a few weeks.'

'Are you joking? We're here to produce thirty minutes' worth of entertainment, five days a week, and then it's syndicated to two dozen television stations around the world. If we don't supply, they sue for lost advertising revenue.'

'But you've had two people murdered?'

'At the end of the day, you'll find me sympathising.' Isaac could not see Ian Stanley sympathising about anybody.

'How was the news of Sally Jenkins received out here?'

'Look, I don't wish to be impolite, but I'm busy. Can this discussion wait?'

'Sure,' Isaac replied, 'just interested to know what everyone thought.'

'A few sad faces, but everyone knew she was only working with Richard Williams because she was an easy lay for someone with money. I made an inappropriate comment once about her screwing the boss, while everyone else was being screwed by him. She was so dumb, she didn't respond, just laughed. I only hope she was better in the sack than in the office. She was damn useless, always stuffing up everyone's pay and expenses.

'That new one, Linda Harris, she's good. No idea what she sees in Richard, money or no money. I reckon she could find any guy she wanted. She seems too smart for the job, and if she's screwing Richard Williams, it must be for a reason.' Isaac noted the comment.

'Mind you,' Ian Stanley went on, his voice raised after bawling out a couple of men hastily erecting a backdrop, 'I don't know what Jess O'Neill saw in him either, and she was screwing him.'

'Is she here?' Isaac asked, upset by Ian Stanley's aspersion about Jess and Richard Williams. He hoped it did not show: it did.

'You fancy her as well?' the little man smirked. 'Can't say I blame you – if you like Richard's seconds, that is. You didn't give Sally Jenkins one as well, did you?'

It was evident to Isaac that the respect accorded him initially by Ian Stanley, due to being a ranking police officer, had dissipated. Stanley only saw him now as a black man in a suit.

Stanley's voice had carried. Soon Jess appeared. She gave Stanley a nasty look but said nothing. He only smiled and continued pushing everyone around.

'Foul-mouthed little man. I can't stand him.'

'Jess, it's good to see you. I'm sorry you heard that.'

'Give me ten minutes, and I'll be alright. He's been trying to get me off the set for a few weeks now. Any chance to make a comment or weaken my position, he takes it.'

'Will he succeed?'

'It's hard to say.'

'Why's that?

'He's good at what he does. Someone mild-mannered, politically correct, wouldn't have a chance to put this together. You don't know how much work is involved out here. Most nights I don't leave before ten at night, and he's often still working.'

'You're looking good, by the way. How are you?'

'I'm fine. It took me some time to get over that grilling you gave me down at station.'

'I was just doing my job.'

'I'm okay. My brother-in-law said you were going easy on me. It didn't feel like it at the time.'

'What about Sally Jenkins?' he asked, hopeful that it would be a more sympathetic response than Ian Stanley had offered.

'I was sad for a day or so, but she only came here a few times. Excited the men whenever she appeared, gave the women something to gossip about.'

'No other concerns about her death?'

'Of course there are! We're all worried who's next. Charles Sutherland has been murdered, so has Sally Jenkins. What about Marjorie Frobisher? Do you believe her to be dead?'

'Jess, I've no idea.' He did not elaborate that the missing woman had been seen a few days earlier.

'These deaths and Marjorie Frobisher are all related, aren't they?' she asked. Isaac noticed that as lovely as she looked she was obviously feeling the strain. *Was it Ian Stanley's innuendoes? Was it a concern that maybe she could be targeted next? Did she know something she wasn't telling him?* he asked himself. He hoped it was not the latter.

'It seems likely, but so far we've drawn a blank. We have ideas as to what the link may be, but it's vague.' Isaac felt he had spent long enough with her. Excusing himself – this time he managed to avoid the kiss – he left the production lot and headed back to his office.

***

Wendy could see that Bridget had raised more questions than answers. How would she be able to follow up on the mysterious person who had met Marjorie Frobisher at the railway station? It seemed an impossible situation. The cameras close to the station had given some clues, but cameras weren't everywhere in the city. The best she could do was to retrace the steps of the missing soap opera star as she had exited the station. Maybe someone had seen something, remembered something. She realised her chances of success were slim, but sometimes something came out of it.

She had been good at tracking missing children in her early years with the police force by trying to think as they would. Maybe it could work this time. She wasn't the sort of person to rush to Isaac Cook – understanding as he may be – and announce that she hadn't a clue. No, she was determined that she was going to find this woman, dead or alive, and at the present moment, alive seemed to be a distinct possibility. Whether safe and comfortable in a hotel or a decent house, or in a situation of despair, she had no idea.

Isaac and Farhan continued to follow up on the events that had occurred since they had been assigned the case. Then it had been a missing woman, but now! Both were struggling with how to proceed.

Also, what about the child that had been adopted? Who knew the answer? And then there was the complication of Farhan sleeping with the prostitute, still in contact with her. Isaac had noticed the secretive messages and Skype on video. He knew she was a good-looking woman, but the young detective inspector was playing a dangerous game. If their boss found out, officially he may be required to pull him off the case.

Both had come in for criticism over the handling of the case: sometimes valid, at other times racially biased. Isaac knew full well that there were people within the confines of the building who would quite happily see them fail, even at the cost of a few unsolved murders. Isaac resolved he would protect Farhan, whatever the cost. And then he had his own problems. There he was sleeping with Sophie, wishing it was Jess O'Neill. Once, in a moment of passion, he had whispered her name into Sophie's ear; not that she minded – at least, that was what she had said. Isaac hadn't been so sure, though.

Sophie had always proclaimed that it was casual sex, no strings attached, no exclusivity, but he knew enough of the world to know that women are not wired that way. They see love when there is none, reject exclusivity and profess free choice, but only say it for the man's benefit, hoping the man is wise enough to realise that what the woman really wants is exclusivity and no free choice.

The situation, both professional and personal, was becoming untenable for both men. There were just too many loose ends, and the mysterious offspring of a promiscuous woman and someone of great influence in the country seemed to be the loosest end. It was crucial to find out who the person was, but there was no obvious candidate. And Richard Goddard was keeping his distance. Isaac assumed it was to do with the upcoming promotions within senior management. He realised that his boss was desperate for an elevation, and unsolved murders didn't help.

Isaac did not like it one bit. Both he and Farhan were now carrying guns. In all his years with the Metropolitan Police, he had never once felt the need to arm himself. Of course, like all policemen he had the benefit of training and was always aware that a situation may arise when a weapon was required.

***

Isaac was sure of another long night when he met up again with Farhan in the office. Farhan had been out at the hotel checking on who had told the journalist about the prostitutes. Isaac suspected that he had also been meeting with the Indian woman; the other escort had apparently disappeared. Farhan knew where she was, he had told Isaac that much. Isaac had let the matter rest there and decided not to pursue it further. He realised that if it were important, Farhan would tell him.

The British press had finally descended on Olivia's house, to find the doors locked tight, and the neighbours bemused by the microphones thrust in their faces and the questions relating to their neighbour, Caroline Danvers. Most had said she was well-respected in the community.

Mrs Edgecombe, seventies, a little hard of hearing, and pleased at the attention, stated categorically that she had always thought something was not quite right. The press had latched on to her for a couple of days, but realised soon enough that she was an embittered lonely woman whose husband had run off with a younger woman twenty-five years previously – a woman who looked remarkably similar to Caroline Danvers/ Olivia.

The media left after a few days, finding that there was no story at Olivia's house. They turned their focus to the other woman.

It was the reason Farhan was in communication with Aisha on such a regular basis. She was worried, and there was only one person she could turn to, only one person she trusted. Farhan was not sure what he could do to help; the press was voracious, and if they wanted to find someone, they would.

'What do we do now?' Farhan asked Isaac once they were both settled back in the office after a meal at a local Asian restaurant. They had eaten there before on several occasions, and it had been fine, but tonight… Isaac wasn't so sure; his stomach was feeling queasy.

'What do you mean?' Isaac understood his colleague's concerns. It had been dragging on for too long, and there was no clarity about where they were going with the case. The leads were drying up – had dried up, if they were truthful.

'What do we have?' Farhan asked. 'We've two murders, virtually no ideas, and no clear direction as to where this is heading.'

'You're right, of course.'

'We're no nearer to finding Marjorie Frobisher, and although Wendy's done a great job, she's just coming up with blanks.'

'Wendy still seems to be our best bet.' Isaac was not too comfortable with Farhan's comment. He had known her longer than Farhan, and to his recollection, she had never failed to deliver the goods. He remained confident that she would find the woman.

'Okay, we'll give her time,' Farhan said. Isaac could tell the pressure was building up on his colleague. He felt it necessary to comment.

'You seem to be under too much pressure, becoming emotionally involved.'

'I suppose I am.'

'The woman at the hotel with Sutherland?'

'Yes,' Farhan replied emphatically.

'You're trying to protect her. An admirable sentiment, but you know it's not going to succeed. The press will find her soon enough.'

'That's the problem. It looks as if they have.'

'We'd better talk this through. You can't protect her on your own. She's a material witness, maybe not in the murder, but certainly due to her association with Sutherland. Did you expect to protect her indefinitely?' Isaac felt that a love-sick colleague was counter-productive, even though he felt empathy with him.

'I had hoped to protect her. But now it's complicated.'

'You've slept with her?' Isaac knew the answer but felt the need to ask again.

'You know I have.'

'Since you were given a warning to keep your distance?'

'Not since then, but it's been difficult. I've wanted to.'

'You know what she is, has been?'

'An escort, sure. I'm beyond making a judgement.' Farhan squirmed in his seat. He was pleased that he and Isaac were having the conversation – embarrassed that they were.

'Are you emotionally involved?' Isaac sat upright in his chair and leant across his desk for emphasis.

'I know it's illogical. I've a wife and children, and there I am falling in love with a woman who has been selling her body for money.'

'Love is blind, or so the saying goes,' Isaac said. It seemed a throw-away phrase, clichéd, but it appeared to sum up Farhan's predicament.

'As you say, love is blind. What do you reckon I should do?'

'Protect her.'

'But how?'

'What about the other woman?'

'I know where she is, but unless there's an official request, I'll keep it to myself.' Farhan did indeed know where Olivia had gone, even had a phone number. The woman was grateful and trusted him enough to tell him that the children were in school, that her husband and she were trying to work through it, and unless she received a legal request to return to the United Kingdom, they were staying in South Africa.

'You'll still have trouble keeping her out of this. If we ever find a murderer, there will no doubt be a summons issued to all witnesses to come forward, including your girlfriend. You realise that?'

'I know. What do you advise?' Farhan sat sheepishly in his chair.

'She needs to disappear.'

'But she has a career, a good career.'

'What will happen to her career when they find out?'

'It's a prestigious law firm,' Farhan said. 'I imagine that a former prostitute, high-class or otherwise, will not last long there.'

'You're right. They'll have her out of the door within five minutes. She won't have the benefit of being innocent until proven guilty. The first hint of scandal and she will be condemned.'

'She knows that. She's putting on a brave face but she's worried about the shame it will bring on her family.'

Isaac sympathised, but he could see little hope.

Questions were being asked by the media on the television and in the newspapers about what was going on. Were there going to be other murders and what were the police doing? Not very much seemed to be the consensus view.

'She can't be protected, you know that,' Isaac affirmed. 'So, what are you going to do? What are we going to do?'

'It's not your problem, Isaac. You've got your career to think about.'

'To hell with that. If we don't solve these murders, neither of us has a career. And besides, I need you with me helping, not moping around, staring at the camera on your laptop.'

'We have to get her out of the country. Is that what you think?' Farhan asked, grateful that Isaac was willing to go out on a limb for him.

'The sooner, the better. You'd better give her the facts straight, face to face.'

'I will.'

'And don't go sleeping with her.'

'I won't,' Farhan replied, although he wasn't sure that his answer had been entirely truthful.

Chapter 30

It was clear that Marjorie Frobisher had walked away from Paddington Station in the company of a man; it was not known if she had been reluctant or willingly. Wendy felt that willingly was the more likely of the two scenarios. She was applying her experience to the problem. Wayward children, when they reappeared, invariably made for someone they knew, someone they trusted.

Isaac had suggested Richard Williams as the most likely person to protect her, but he had denied seeing her when Isaac had phoned him. In fact, he had been quite annoyed over the accusation that he was possibly obstructing a murder enquiry, threatened legal action if such a statement was made again. Isaac felt convinced that he was in the clear, although angry that he could not tell the man what he thought of his pompous manner.

Besides, he had heard Linda Harris's voice in the background, and the clinking of glasses indicated they were not in the office. Isaac resented him for his good choice in women, when he was feeling the early signs of rejection from Sophie.

As much as she had alluded to not being concerned when he had inadvertently mentioned Jess O'Neill's name in a moment of passion, she had not been available to come over the last couple of times he had phoned. He couldn't feel any undue sadness, only a little frustrated that the relationship was over.

He was determined to speed up the case. After that, he would be free to call Jess. He knew she would be available.

Wendy, convinced that the only solution was to get out on the street and to commit herself to good old-fashioned legwork, was outside Paddington Station early the next morning.

The morning was bleak. Wendy had dressed accordingly, although it was not a flattering ensemble: a jacket with a scarf, trousers, and solid walking shoes. She completed it all with a red woollen hat her husband had given her.

The clearest images that Brian Gee, the nerdish computer man at Paddington Station, and Bridget Halloran had managed to come up with showed that Marjorie Frobisher and the unknown man had walked down Praed Street, in the direction of St Mary's Hospital. The rain had started; Wendy was not in a good mood. The dampness in the air was starting to play havoc with her arthritis, and she knew at the end of the day she would be in severe pain.

She soon reached St Mary's Hospital, a maroon plaque commemorating the discovery of penicillin by Sir Alexander Fleming proudly displayed underneath his laboratory window.

Marjorie Frobisher had been seen this far down the street, but after this the trail had gone cold.

The weather worsened and she decided that a warm place and a quiet coffee would be a good idea. She found a little café. It didn't look very enticing, but as she opened the door, she felt the heat. Taking a seat close to the window, she ordered a latte and a cake and pondered the situation. Was she wasting her time walking the street? What could she do? Should she go home, admit to Isaac and Farhan that she had no further ideas?

Desperate to do something, she indulged in idle conversation with the waitress, a pleasant looking woman in her late forties, the tattoos on her arm not to Wendy's taste.

'I'm looking for someone,' Wendy said after the waitress asked what she was doing out on such a miserable day.

'Anyone important?'

'Someone you'd know.'

'Not Marjorie Frobisher?' The waitress's answer surprised Wendy.

'You know her?'

'Doesn't everyone?'

'I suppose they do, but why assume it's her?'

'I told everyone in the shop that I had seen her. They all thought I was a bit crazy, and without my glasses my eyesight is a bit dodgy.'

'You didn't report seeing her.'

'I was going to, but everyone convinced me otherwise, and then it became busy. I suppose I forgot.'

'You've reported it now.'

'You're the police?'

'Yes. Is that okay by you?'

'As long as I'm not in trouble.'

'Of course you're not. We need to talk. Are you free to sit down and have a coffee with me?'

'Yes. Sure.'

Wendy noticed that the waitress, Sheila, was a nervous woman, unsure of herself. She also noticed that she took a piece of cake with her coffee. Wendy knew she would be paying for it.

'Did you speak to Marjorie Frobisher?'

'She didn't speak. The man with her did the ordering.'

'Tell me about him?'

'He spoke quietly, well-mannered. He didn't leave a tip; I remember that well enough.'

'Did he seem friendly with Marjorie Frobisher?'

'I kept staring, couldn't help myself.'

'I understand. It's not often you see celebrities walking into your café.'

'We see the occasional one when they're visiting the hospital across the road, but she was my favourite. I always watched her on the television, and here she was, sitting in my café, drinking my coffee. It'll be something to tell my family when I get home tonight.'

'This is serious. You can't tell anyone yet. Can I trust you to keep this quiet?'

'I won't say a word.' Wendy knew that as soon as the waitress got home, she would be telling everyone. There was hardly any way they could silence her, and she was the team's first concrete lead for several weeks.

'Did she look happy?'

'She seemed pleased to be with the man.'

'Is there any more you can tell me about him?'

'As I said, he was polite. In his late fifties, I suppose.'

'Fat or thin?'

'He certainly wasn't fat. He seemed a nice man.'

'How long did they stay?'

They stayed for about twenty minutes. As to where they went, I don't know. They just walked down the street. Apart from that, I've no idea.'

'Thanks, you've been a great help.'

'Is there a reward?'

'No reward. How would a fifty pound tip sound?'

'Great. They don't pay much here.'

Wendy realised on leaving the café that her pains had subsided, and there was no need to continue plodding the streets.

***

Isaac felt the need to follow up on a matter that had been giving him some concern. It had only been a casual remark by Ian Stanley, the irritating series producer and nemesis of Jess O'Neill, but it had raised some questions.

Linda Harris's earlier comment that her relationship with Richard Williams was just a bit of fun had seemed too frivolous at the time. Ian Stanley's statement about her competency had reaffirmed his suspicions. After his senior's indication that MI5 was interested in Marjorie Frobisher, Isaac's suspicions about Williams' PA seemed all the more relevant.

He bit the bullet and invited her out for dinner, socially this time. She accepted readily, too readily for Isaac, as Sophie was clearly out of the picture, not even returning his phone calls, and Jess was still off-limits.

The next day, close to seven in the evening, he met Linda Harris at a discreet restaurant close to the city centre. She ate chicken; he ordered beef. Two bottles of a particularly good wine were drunk with gusto by the two, though Isaac wasn't usually a drinker.

'Why are you working for Williams?' he asked.

'I needed a job.' She had dressed for the occasion: a short yellow skirt with a white top. Isaac had come from work and was still wearing a suit.

'You look too smart for the job.' Isaac realised he was heading into dangerous waters.

'Why do you say that?' she asked. Isaac could read the signals: the alluring smile, the closeness of her chair to his, the holding of his hand across the table.

'Sally Jenkins.'

'You're using her as the standard as to what is competent?'

'I suppose so,' Isaac replied.

'I'm competent, suitable for the job. She wasn't. But as we've agreed, she was not there for her administrative skills.'

'She was there because she was an easy lay, you said that yourself.'

'Are you insinuating that I'm an easy lay as well?'

'You told me that you were sleeping with him.'

'I told you that he was with me, in my bed.' She reminded him of their previous conversation when she had provided her boss with an alibi.

Isaac sensed some pulling back from her – she was no longer holding his hand. He excused himself to go to the toilet. He took the opportunity to splash some water on his face, hoping to revive himself a little.

Returning to his seat, he decided to stop sounding like a policeman and to enjoy the evening. The woman was attractive, too attractive, and she was great company.

Why not just enjoy the moment? he thought.

'I'm sorry. I'm acting as a policeman.'

'That's okay. I understand the pressure you're under.'

'Tell me about yourself. You said you came from Devon, but what are your plans for the future?'

'Find a better job,' She was holding his hand across the table again. Both had ordered dessert. 'I'm capable of a better job, but I'm not in a hurry.'

'Why?'

'I'd rather find myself a decent man, settle down, have a few kids.'

'Williams?'

'Not at all. I don't need a sugar daddy.'

Isaac, slightly more sober after easing up on the wine, took stock of the situation. On the one hand, he was here in the company of a beautiful, desirable woman, available if he was reading the signals right. On the other, as a policeman he knew there were questions that needed asking.

'The disappearance of Marjorie Frobisher concerns a lot of people,' he said.

'Newspapers, fans, you mean?'

'In higher quarters.' Isaac still had his suspicions about the woman sitting opposite. She seemed too smart; as if she was directing the conversation, ensuring he didn't probe too much.

'Political, is that what you mean?'

'Yes.'

'I wouldn't know,' she said. 'I'm just a humble personal assistant who's screwing the boss.' Her remark was a little too curt for Isaac.

'Linda, who are you?'

'Linda Harris, humble personal assistant. That's all.'

'We're aware that Marjorie Frobisher is somehow significant, although we don't know any details. Do you?'

'Why should I?' Her manner was frosty.

'You may have overheard something in the office.'

'You realise that you've spoilt a lovely evening by your suspicions.'

'I realise that, but it's my job.'

'I thought we were meeting outside of working hours, both off duty.'

'Off duty, that is not a term I would have expected a PA to use.'

She stood up, put on her coat, the weather outside not as frosty as the atmosphere inside the restaurant. 'DCI Cook, I'll bid you goodnight. In future, our meetings will be at your police station or my lawyer's office.'

Standing outside, as she walked briskly down the road, he could see her in an animated conversation on her phone. Whatever she was, he remained convinced she was more than Williams' bedtime companion and office administrator.

***

As Farhan was preparing for an early night, at his cold and lonely house, his phone rang. It was Olivia calling him from South Africa. She was not in a good mood; her cover had been blown.

Still thankful that he had tried to help, she had been forced to take the children out of school as the playground teasing was becoming objectionable, and it was not their problem, only hers. Also, her husband was having trouble accepting that she only sold herself for the family. Farhan was truly sorry, but Olivia still had the advantage of distance, and one or two inquisitive reporters in South Africa would soon be distracted by another, more important story.

Farhan knew he had to help Aisha. He knew he couldn't protect her if the news organisations picked up any clue as to who she was and where she was. She had told him earlier in the day about someone suspicious in her office and a couple of late-night phone calls to her house, no voice at the other end.

Farhan could only see one solution. 'You've got to leave,' he said.

She protested. 'My career, it's so important to me.'

'And your family, what about them?'

They had met at a small café in Regent Street, not far from her office. They had been pleased to see each other, although neither had made a move to embrace the other. Farhan could see she was upset.

'If they find out, it will kill them.'

'I suppose you should have thought about that before you started selling yourself.' He wasn't sure if his comment had been overcritical.

'You're right of course, but I needed to survive, ensure I passed my studies with honours. It all costs money, and my parents don't have that sort of money.'

'It's history now. Anyway, we would not have met if you had been working in a café.'

'At least there has been one good thing to come out of it.'

Farhan felt like leaning over the table and giving her a kiss. He decided that it was best if he did not. The future for them as a couple looked bleak. It was up to him to think clearly for both of them. She was obviously the better educated, but she was about to be outed as a prostitute. All that she had strived for, lost in an instance.

They had ordered coffees. Farhan drank his; Aisha barely sipped at hers. He could see in her face the sign of worry. She said it was due to the pressure of work, a particularly challenging case, involving a man accused of insider trading on the stock market.

She had tried to explain the intricacies of the case, as a diversion from the reason they were meeting. Something to do with the man's position as the financial officer for a major insurance company in the city, subject to a takeover from a larger, more aggressive company.

It was Aisha's first major case, although she was acting as a junior. It was a great compliment for her to be entrusted with the responsibility, but now it looked as if it was falling apart.

Farhan had ordered two more coffees. 'Aisha, the only chance is if you disappear. Caroline's being hassled now.'

'Is that Olivia's real name?'

'Yes, but it's best if you forget it.'

'I will.'

'We should be meeting at the police station.' Farhan had run it past Isaac first, told him the approach he was going to take. Isaac had advised him to take great care, and not to go rushing off to a hotel room with her. Farhan had said that he would be careful, but sitting with Aisha now, he wanted to forget his promise. He had to keep reminding himself that he was a serving policeman on duty, and she was a witness.

'Is there no hope?' she asked.

'If they can find Olivia, they can find you.'

'But how? You said that Marion Robertson had given Olivia's phone number to the two men who had visited her, but she didn't have mine.'

'That's true. Are you certain they are looking for you?'

'I'm pretty certain, but how?'

'Who would know where you work, where you live?'

'Only you.'

'I've kept it to myself. I received a severe dressing down from my boss for keeping you and Olivia secret.'

'If there's a court case, will I be required to be a witness?'

'You're the lawyer, what do you reckon?'

'It will depend on whether he pleads guilty or not.'

'Or she,' Farhan reminded her.

'Could it be a she?' she asked.

'Why not? The man was found naked. From what we know, he was certainly heterosexual.'

'Perversely so,' she replied. On a personal basis, Farhan did not want to know the details. On a professional basis, he had to ask.

'I must ask what you mean by that comment. Officially, unfortunately.'

'Can't you forget what I just said. I don't want to think back to that night.'

'Give me a generalisation, then.' He realised that maybe it was not relevant. If it became so, he would persevere with the question at a later time.

'He wanted us to put on a show first, toys, that sort of thing.' She kept her head low, avoided eye contact.

'We'll leave it at that.' He didn't want to hear more.
'What must I do?' she asked.
'Ideally, you should leave immediately.'
'The country?'
'Yes.'
'I can't do that.'
'You'd better let me know who's on to you. Every time you're contacted, every time there's a silent voice on the end of a phone line, let me know. We'll decide as it occurs. If I tell you the situation is impossible, then you must leave immediately. Is that clear?'

Aisha finally drank her coffee and left. She could not resist the opportunity to kiss him before she walked out the door. Farhan hoped she would be safe.

Chapter 31

Late afternoon the next day, and all three were in the office. Wendy had finally got the message not to keep moving Farhan's desk; not the other one about exhaling the smell of stale cigarettes over the other two.

She should have taken the hint with the window behind Isaac being open, even though it was cold outside. She preferred a room to be warm and cosy, just like Station Manager Broughton's office at Paddington Station.

A good-looking man, plenty of women, she thought. *Twenty years ago, I would have made a play for him myself.*

Isaac brought their meeting to order. 'Wendy, can you update us, please.'

Before she replied, Isaac leant over and closed the window.

'The person she met is almost certainly a friend.'

'You've had some luck?' Farhan said. Wendy noticed the look of the man had taken a turn for the worse since she had last seen him. He looked worried, and his clothes looked as though they could do with a good iron.

The look of a recently separated man, she thought. She thought back to ten years previously, to a rough patch in her marriage when she had moved out of the marital home. It had only been for three weeks before he apologised and she had forgiven him. She nearly left again on entering the front door of the house. The dirty dishes in the kitchen sink were disgusting, the waste paper bin was overflowing, the washing machine refused to work due to severe overloading and the place stank.

It had taken her two days to clean up the mess, two days when she could have easily have walked out of the door again. She finally calmed down, but the anger remained for months, tense months, where they barely spoke to each other.

'Luck! Good old-fashioned police work. Out on the street, talking to people.' She could sometimes be acerbic. How many times, when she had found a missing person, had she heard the word 'luck' mentioned.

It wasn't luck that had found the café; it was a case of placing herself in the right environment. The rain had helped and directed her towards the café, but if it had not, she would have kept walking the area, asking questions. Eventually, she would have stumbled upon the waitress, although it could have been days, maybe weeks. She was pleased it had been sooner rather than later, as her arthritis was giving her trouble, even though she had not walked far the previous day.

'Wendy, please continue,' Isaac said. He had worked with her before, knew she could be a bit touchy – the reason why he had not broached the subject of the stale cigarette smell.

He was aware that it would lead to a lecture about civil liberties, freedom for a person to decide whether they were damaging their health or not.

'She knew the person she met,' Wendy said. 'The waitress confirmed it was Richard Williams from a photo that I showed her the next day.'

'He knows that obstructing the course of justice, especially in a murder investigation, is a serious offence. His fancy Queen's Counsel will not be able to protect him.'

'I've not met Richard Williams. Is he the sort of person to risk imprisonment?' Wendy asked.

'Not at all,' Isaac replied. 'He's a sharp operator. If he is protecting Marjorie Frobisher, there must be a reason.'

'But meeting in London? Surely they realised the possibility of being seen. We're not the only ones looking for her,' Farhan speculated.

'Maybe they're not thinking straight. Maybe the woman is irrational. The waitress said she didn't say much. Williams may have been compromised into helping.'

'I agree with Wendy,' Isaac said. 'We're aware of the special relationship between the two of them.'

'It's up to you, Isaac,' Farhan said.

'I need to go and see him. It would help if Wendy keeps checking, tries to find out where she is.'

'I'll start on it tomorrow,' Wendy said, glad to be out of the office again. She only hoped a long soak in a warm bath and some medicine would reduce the pain in her legs.

***

Isaac felt his time the following morning would be best spent with Richard Goddard. He had set up a meeting for nine o'clock. He sensed that his superior officer was not looking forward to a visit, but it was important.

At 9 a.m. Isaac was outside his senior's office. Ten minutes later, Goddard appeared. As he was a man who was a stickler for punctuality, it seemed odd to Isaac. He chose to make no comment.

'What is it, Isaac?' There had been none of the customary 'sit down for a chat' welcome. Isaac was disturbed. He had not seen his boss like this before, and they had worked together for some years.

'Marjorie Frobisher.'

'Have you found her?'

'We think she's alive.'

'But have you found her?'

'Not yet. Soon, I imagine.'

'It would have been best if she had stayed missing. Isaac. It's become complicated.'

Isaac chose another line of questioning. 'Is there anyone else looking for her currently?'

'Why do you ask? You and DI Ahmed had people following you at one time. Is that still occurring?'

'We've not seen them for some time, but I still feel they're watching us.'

'Why do you say that?'

'I suspect someone's been planted.'

'What do you mean?'

'A woman working with Richard Williams may be more than she seems.'

'Why do you say that?'

'She's smarter than she pretends to be; definitely not the sort of woman Williams would typically employ.'

'Attractive?'

'Very.'

'There's your answer. He chooses them attractive, easy to lay. That's what your reports have indicated.'

'She doesn't seem the type that would be an easy lay, certainly not for Williams.'

'Is he sleeping with her?'

'Apparently. She gave him a cast-iron alibi when Sally Jenkins was murdered.'

'And you think she's a plant? Do you fancy her?'

'A plant, it's possible. Fancy her? I suppose I do, but I've kept my distance.'

'Are you still protecting that other woman?'

'If you mean Jess O'Neill, I've kept my distance, at least until this case is resolved.'

'Make sure it stays that way. This is becoming too complicated, and no one knows why.'

Isaac still felt that his boss knew more than he did. It seemed critical for him and Farhan to know as much, but how? If their boss did not want to tell them, there wasn't much that he could do to prise it out of him. He decided to try again.

'Sir, I need to know. We're chasing around after a woman who is directly or indirectly related to the deaths of two people. What if there is another murder? A murder we could have prevented with additional knowledge.'

'I understand what you're saying.'

'We need to meet Angus MacTavish,' Isaac said.

The detective superintendent quickly exited the office and made a phone call.

'Midday at his office,' he said on his return. 'If he tries to talk you down, stand your ground.'

'I believe I can handle him,' Isaac replied.

***

Wendy, before she continued the search for the Marjorie Frobisher in London, went into the office at Challis Street. It was empty. Isaac, she knew, was meeting Detective Superintendent Goddard. Farhan, she had no idea where he had gone. She made a strong cup of tea, extra sugar, and raided the biscuit jar. As no one was around, she opened the window and lit a cigarette, careful to ensure the smoke and ash went out of the window. She vowed to cut down.

The cigarette dispensed with, she phoned Bridget Halloran. She knew she would be able to assist. 'I need to find Marjorie Frobisher,' Wendy said.

'What did you find out?'

'She met a friend. Someone we know. We need to find out possible locations where he may have taken her.'

'Couldn't you just ask him?'

'DCI Cook will deal with that, but the situation is complicated.'

'What do you mean?' Bridget asked. It wasn't necessary for her to know, but Wendy reasoned that she had gone out of her way to assist, and besides she was a friend who she trusted.

'We need to find her before other people do.'

'What if they find her?'

'We're not sure. She could disappear again.'

'And not come back this time?'

'That's a possibility.'

'Then, for all our sakes, we'd better find her first.'

'Strictest confidence.'

'You can trust me, you know that,' Bridget replied.

'I know. I just had to say it, though.'

***

It came as a complete surprise to Isaac how agreeable Angus MacTavish was when he met him. Richard Goddard had expected him to be gruff, unpleasant, but here was the firm handshake, the pat on the shoulder, and 'pleased to meet you'.

Mrs Gregory had dealt with the tea and cakes. She took a shine to Isaac as well.

With all three men seated comfortably and Mrs Gregory in the other room, Angus MacTavish spoke. 'DCI Cook, you want to know about Marjorie Frobisher.'

'Yes, sir.'

'You realise that Detective Superintendent Goddard and I have met several times to discuss this matter.'

'Yes.'

'DCI Cook, are you aware of a child?' MacTavish asked.

'Yes.'

'And how important it is that the child does not find out who the mother is?'

'As well as the father?' Richard Goddard said.

'Detective Superintendent Goddard is right,' MacTavish said. 'In fact, the father is more important than the mother.'

'Who is the father?' Isaac asked.

'That's the problem. I just don't know.'

'You have a shrewd idea.'

'That's all I have. I know that Detective Superintendent Goddard thinks it's the prime minister.'

'Could it be someone else?'

'It's possible.'

'It may help if I have some names,' Isaac said. 'We're chasing shadows, coming up with blanks at the present moment.'

'Tell me what you've got. How about the two murders? Any leads there?' MacTavish asked.

'We know how they died, but why is unclear.'

'Tied in with this damn woman's disappearance?'

'Circumstantial,' Isaac said, 'but failing any other motives, it seems more than likely. Charles Sutherland was threatening to say something, and Sally Jenkins had a tendency to eavesdrop.'

'They may have been eliminated because someone thought they did know something,' MacTavish said.

'Someone killed them purely on the off-chance?' Richard Goddard asked, anxious to remain vital to the meeting. He had seen it before. Take DCI Isaac Cook, the tall, attractive and very black policeman along to meet someone important, and they would be immediately charmed by him, while he, the more senior of the two, a dour white man, would be left floundering. Still, he was pleased that Angus MacTavish was opening up, something he had not done with him.

'Detective Superintendent Goddard mentioned on the phone that there may be someone who is a plant,' MacTavish said.

'A woman,' Isaac said. 'She's close to the action, not involved in the murders.'

'You feel she may be keeping her ear to the ground. Can you find out if that is the case?'

'I can try. Do you want her to know we're on to her?'

'No, I don't think so. It may only precipitate another action.'

'Such as another murder?' Richard Goddard asked.

'It's possible,' Isaac said.

'Marjorie Frobisher? Dead or alive?' MacTavish asked.

Isaac wasn't sure what to say. He saw no reason to trust the man; no reason not to.

'We believe she is alive.'

'Then keep her that way. I don't believe this government or any other government deserves to be in power when they condone murder as a solution.'

'Is that what's happened?' Isaac asked.

'A can of worms. Anything's possible,' Angus MacTavish said.

'What about the plant?'

'I'll check her out for you. May take a few days.'

'Thank you,' Isaac replied.

'What do you reckon?' Detective Superintendent Goddard asked as he and Isaac drove away.

'He's a politician. How would we know if he was telling us the truth?'

'He could have just been spinning us a line.'

'Exactly. We keep the news relating to Marjorie Frobisher to ourselves. I'd say she is as good as dead if we don't find her first.'

'And if we do?'

'I've no idea. It's not our function to protect people; our function is to catch murderers, prevent further murders.'

'With Marjorie Frobisher, that amounts to the same thing.'

'You're right, but protect her from whom? Who can we trust?'

'Nobody, Isaac. Nobody.' Detective Superintendent Goddard summed up the situation succinctly.

Chapter 32

Farhan was not handling the situation well. On the one hand, he had a wife he did not love, but still the mother of his children. He realised he had not been giving them the attention that they deserved recently. Not because he didn't want to, but because of the pressure of work, and now the situation was intense. There had been two murders so far, and the number could rise. And then there was Aisha, whom he did love but could not meet, although he had made an exception when it looked as though her cover was about to be blown. He knew it was wrong, but he couldn't help himself.

He knew the right thing to do, but how? He had been married off in a loveless marriage to a cold and passionless woman. Apart from Elaine Downton, a casual fling before he had married, he had slept with no other woman. That was until he had met Aisha. One night in a hotel room with her, and he knew he wanted to spend his life with her, but was it possible?

Isaac's penchant for bedding attractive women never ceased to draw admiration from the men in the police force, but the head of such a fine Service needed to be stable, with a stable family life.

Farhan knew that in time Isaac would settle down and that he was equally at ease with the man on the street or someone in high office. Isaac had told him how the Government Chief Whip, Angus MacTavish, had acted towards him: magnanimous, friendly. Farhan had not been surprised; it happened all the time.

Farhan knew that he did not possess Isaac's innate charm. He was aware that he was not an unattractive man, but his features were not as easy on the eye. Sure, Elaine Downton had told him he had a good heart, and Aisha told him he was attractive, and that beauty is more than skin deep.

No doubt they were correct. He did have a good heart, a need to help. Isaac did as well, but he had both the exterior beauty and the inner goodness. No, Farhan admitted openly to himself, *I'll be happy to make detective superintendent.*

He also knew that while the unresolved issue of his wife remained, and his involvement with a prostitute, whether or not he married her in due course, his career was going nowhere.

He phoned Aisha. The case she had been working on had turned out successfully.

Farhan and Aisha arranged to meet later that day. Important issues to discuss, she said. They met at the same hotel down by the river, ended up in the same bed. The important matter was that she wanted to be with him. Farhan had suspected as much when he had agreed to the meeting. His protestations at the folly of it were feebly attempted.

After their lovemaking, she explained the situation. Her career was looking good, her parents were pleased, always telling their extended family back in India about how well their Aisha was doing. Also mentioning that she had a boyfriend, a senior man in the police force, a man going places.

'I'm sorry. I had to tell them something. They are still steeped in the traditions of the home country. They still believe in their making a choice as to who I'll spend my life with.'

'Have you made that choice?' he asked.

'Yes.'

'I'm not sure about the senior policeman.'

'You will be; I'm sure of it.'

'I won't be anything if this crime is not solved.'

'Maybe I can help.'

'I know we discussed this before, but how?'

'A different perspective. I'm a criminal lawyer.'

'A successful criminal lawyer now,' he joked.

'As you say, successful.'

They were glad of the opportunity to spend time together. He knew the trouble he would be in if anyone found out that he had slept with her again. Murder enquiry or no murder enquiry, he would almost certainly be suspended, pending a disciplinary hearing. The only hope of redemption would be if he came up with a new take on the murders.

'Can we come back to Sutherland?' He was aware of her wish not to discuss the matter.

'If you must.'

'Someone was able to induce him to take a drink while he was naked.'

'It can only be a woman.'

'If it wasn't either you or Olivia, then that leaves the woman who let you in.'

'Christy?'

'I wasn't aware you knew her name.'

'She introduced herself when we first met. Timid sort of woman. Just good manners, I assume.'

'I've ruled her out,' Farhan said.

'Any reason?'

'No apparent connection that would tie her in with Sally Jenkins.'

'Are the two murders related?'

'That is the assumption. The disappearance of Marjorie Frobisher seems related as well.'

'All three could be unrelated. Have you considered that?'

'Initially, but it seemed to be going nowhere.'

'And now?'

'About the same. Sally Jenkins, we're not sure. Probably someone she knew, but who? Her previous lover doesn't seem to have a reason to kill her, and his alibi is cast iron.'

'Cast iron, why do you say that?'

'He was in bed with another woman.'

'Proven?' Aisha asked.

'According to the woman.'

'Do you believe her? Maybe she's protecting him out of some misguided loyalty, maybe love. The same as you're protecting me.'

Farhan could see the reasoning. He would discuss it with Isaac, not mentioning where the discussion was held. Maybe they should just focus on one murder at a time, treat it in isolation, and not try to tie it in with the other.

It was eight in the evening when they left the hotel. Farhan back to a cold and miserable house, Aisha back to her proud parents. How she wished she had met such a good man before she had become a prostitute, but then she would not have met him. How he wished he was free to make the choice he wanted to, but there were the children to consider. He knew the road ahead was far from clear. At least, for tonight, he was pleased they had met, had made love, had discussed the case.

***

Isaac intended to meet Richard Williams at the earliest opportunity, but he did not want to barge in and then find the man's QC submitting a writ for police intimidation. It was best to wait until Wendy had found the missing woman.

Possibly then he could knock on the door. Hopefully, talk to her, calm her fears, and gain her confidence.

Bridget, as always, was pleased to see Wendy when she popped her head around the door. 'What can I do for you?' Some quick gossip and then down to work, a cup of tea in one hand, a biscuit in the other. Wendy knew the cost of assistance would be a pub lunch washed down with a couple of strong drinks.

'The woman's somewhere. We need to find her and soon.'

'She could be in a hotel. Almost impossible to find,' Bridget replied.

'Let's assume it's not a hotel. Let's work on the assumption it's a property somewhere. We know where Williams lives; it's not going to be there.'

'Why?' Bridget asked.

'Too obvious. Besides, he needs somewhere to bring his women.'

'Romancer, is he?' Bridget, always eager for some salacious gossip.

'Sugar daddy, more like.'

'Flashes his money around?'

'Ferrari. Gives them a good time. Mid-life crisis, although he should be past that by now.'

'Sounds my kind of guy,' Bridget joked.

'Unfortunately, you're not his kind of woman.' They knew each other well enough for Wendy to tease her.

'Mature and experienced?'

'Your skirt's not short enough for one thing.'

'And my breasts are not pert and upright, just dangling.'

'We both suffer from that complaint. Let's get back to Williams.'

The joking over, both women focussed on the task. Wendy felt sure the woman was ensconced in a comfortable and secure property somewhere.

'If she's not at his house, then maybe he has other properties, flats he rents out. Can you find them?' Wendy suggested.

'I can search the records.'

The results of two hours' searching and a pub lunch identified three properties: a house in Twickenham, a flat down near Canary Wharf, and another flat not far from Hackney. Wendy relayed the news to Isaac. She would check them the next day.

***

Isaac, severely angry with Farhan, did not mince his words. 'How many times have you been told to keep away from this woman? If you're seen, it's the end of your career, mine as well. And what about our boss?'

'You're not going to tell him, are you?'

'Not unless I have to,' Isaac replied. It was good that their office was insulated so his voice didn't travel. He was not a man given to anger, rarely a raised voice, but Farhan's admission that he had met with Aisha again had upset him greatly.

He had gone out on a limb to protect Farhan. Even asked their boss the last time to keep it to a severe verbal reprimand, not to put anything in writing. What if it turned out that the woman was involved in the murder? Isaac shuddered at the thought of the repercussions.

He knew that Farhan had led a sheltered life; no seducing the willing females in his later years at school and then sowing his oats after a night down the pub. Farhan, he realised, was easy prey to an experienced woman with no inhibitions about initiating sexual congress.

'How am I going to protect you?' Isaac continued. 'Look, you're a good policeman, and we work well as a team, but meeting with this woman again? I thought we agreed that you were going to talk to her, ask her to leave the country.'

'I did meet with her, but she wants to stay.'

'They'll find her eventually; you know that?'

'We both know that.'

'Both, do you mean you and her?'

'Yes.'

'This is going to end badly. She has to disappear if you want to protect her.'

'She has just been involved in a prominent legal case. Only as the junior, but the man got off. She's elated, she wants to stay.'

'She may be the most brilliant legal mind in the country, but she's also a prostitute – sold herself for sex. Do you think there is any chance for her? Her past history will surface. If not now, at some stage in the future. These things can't stay hidden forever. She must know that.'

'We both know that.'

'Have you been sleeping with her again?' Isaac asked, quickly adding, 'Don't tell me. It's better if you don't answer that question.'

'She's a smart woman; she had some ideas.'

'You've been discussing the case with her?'

'More like questioning.'

'At least that's acceptable. What did she have to say, your girlfriend?' Isaac ventured some humour. Farhan chose not to respond.

'We're assuming that the murders and the disappearance of Marjorie Frobisher are related.'

'What else do we have?' Isaac asked.

'According to Aisha, what if we are wrong? What if they are unrelated?'

'It's a possibility, but how do we ascertain that?'

'Instead of trying to make the connection, we isolate them totally from each other.'

'Sutherland's death could be unrelated, but Sally Jenkins? Why would anyone kill her?'

'Other than she knew something about the missing woman?'

'I suppose so,' Isaac replied.

'What if there is no missing woman? How would we approach the case of Sally Jenkins?' Farhan asked.

'We would look for a motive; for someone who had a reason to want her dead.'

'She wasn't raped.'

'And not a break-in that went wrong, judging by the condition of where she lived.'

'So it must have been someone she knew,' Isaac said.

'DI Hill, the crime scene officer, is intimating that someone came in the front door; the break-in may have been a subterfuge.'

'Only Richard Williams had a key.'

'But why would he want to murder her? And, anyway, he was in bed with Linda Harris.'

'She's an unknown,' Isaac admitted.

'What do you mean? I know you have your suspicions, even took her out for a meal. What was your intent there, professional or personal?'

'Both, I suppose, but she's not involved. At least, I assume she's not. She was not around when Marjorie Frobisher disappeared, nor when Sutherland was murdered.'

'So that means she's innocent of all crimes?'

'I'm not sure,' Isaac admitted.

'Why do you say that?'

'What do we know about her?'

'We are aware she's working for Williams, sleeping with him.'

'I asked MacTavish to check her out.'

'And…'

'I'm still waiting for his reply.'

'Did you fancy her?' Farhan asked.

'At first.'

'And after?'

'She became upset when I started probing. The evening ended badly.'

'What about the other woman? Are you still in contact?'

'Not for some time. It may be a good idea to maintain contact, seeing that she's a witness.'

'And potential plaything?' Farhan jested.

'So far, I've managed to keep it under control. I'm not the lothario that you are, obviously.'

'You know we'd both be in trouble if Goddard found out.'

'I've not done anything wrong yet,' Isaac announced with regret.

'Would you have slept with Linda Harris if your night had turned out differently?'

'Probably.'

'What do we really know about her?' Farhan asked.
'I think she's a fellow government employee.'
'And if she is?'
'Then she's clear of any involvement in the murders.'
'I'm not certain she is.'
'What do you mean?'
'If she's willing to indulge in sexual relations with a man purely because it's her job, what else is she capable of?'

Isaac had to agree, disturbed that a woman he almost slept with, probably would if the opportunity presented itself again, was no better than the two women who had sold themselves to Charles Sutherland.

It seemed ironic to Isaac that Farhan was getting more action than him. He knew full well that he had been sleeping with his woman again; the look on his face evidence of the fact.

Chapter 33

Wendy, pleased that the weather was more agreeable, had staked out the first place of interest, a small two-storey terrace in Twickenham. She could see that Richard Williams liked his investments well-maintained: the small garden at the front was neat and tidy, the paintwork on the exterior façade in remarkably good condition, in contrast to the other houses in the street. She assumed it had been freshly painted. Compared to her home, a dreary run-down property close to the docks, it was beautiful. Her husband had never been into home repairs, and she did not have the skills to do the work. Williams' terraced house was the sort of place she would love to own, knew she never would.

She parked her car across the street. For three, close to four hours she watched the house from inside the car. The only people she saw, a young couple pushing a child's buggy. They were clearly the tenants. Bridget had already ascertained it was rented out to a couple with one child. Wendy realised the missing woman was not at this location.

After a quick lunch she drove out to the next location, a flat close to Hackney. She would have gone to the apartment down by Canary Wharf as her second choice, more upmarket than Hackney, but it was early afternoon, and the traffic was building up. Even so, it still took her the best part of ninety minutes.

It was clear that the second property was not as salubrious as the first. It appeared to be on the third floor, in a drab, red-brick, ex-council property. There were two problems on arriving: one, she could not see the entrance to the flat, only the front window, and two, parking restrictions on account of the late afternoon rush hour were about to apply. She could only stay for thirty minutes.

She phoned Isaac. She found his manner a little distant – as if he had something on his mind. Disregarding his curtness with her, she told him about the house in Twickenham, and the flat in Hackney. She also let him know that she regarded Canary Wharf as a better possibility, and that tomorrow she would drive out there.

Farhan, meanwhile, had phoned Robert Avers to ask if he had heard from his wife.

The man's response surprised Farhan. 'I'm not going to sit at home waiting for her to knock on the door. She screwed around enough, now it's my turn.'

Farhan understood where he was coming from, careful not to let on that they believed his wife was alive and somewhere in London.

***

The next day, Wendy drove out to Canary Wharf, a massive redevelopment of the former West India Docks. Now a major financial centre, comprising major banks, financial services, and media organisations, it was also the home of some very impressive upmarket properties, primarily high-rise executive apartments.

She was convinced that it was the most likely location to find the woman: comfortable, secluded, an ideal place to hide out if you could afford it. No need to trudge down to the local supermarket to buy some food, just phone, and one of the expensive restaurants would deliver to your door, along with a good bottle of wine. And, from what Wendy had heard, Marjorie Frobisher enjoyed the good life, despised the poverty of her childhood.

It was clear that the flat, on the thirteenth floor, was too high to see anyone at ground level, unless the occupant stood right against the window.

The concierge at the front door, she felt, would not offer much help. Besides, she did not want to alert the missing woman to the fact that someone was looking for her. The easiest way was to enter the building unseen.

Observing the concierge, a smartly dressed man in his late twenties, she waited until he was distracted by a car pulling up at the front. A woman got out of the driver's seat. Wendy assumed her to be in her early fifties, obviously well-heeled judging by the shopping in the back seat of the vehicle. As the concierge went out to help, Wendy slipped past and into the building.

The lift was on the twentieth floor and descending. She hoped it would arrive at the ground floor before the concierge saw her: it did. Quickly, she pressed thirteen on the row of buttons, the speed of the lift surprising her.

Exiting the lift, she moved swiftly to flat number 1304. She pressed the bell, a woman came to the door. Wendy apologised, said she had mistaken the numbers, and it must be 1340.

The concierge barely noticed her, as she brazenly exited the lift on the ground floor and walked out of the building. He did not see the broad smile on her face.

***

Isaac knew that the situation had changed. Marjorie Frobisher was alive and well; the evidence, indisputable. Wendy had been sure, and she did not make mistakes. As she had stated, when she phoned him from Canary Wharf, 'I know that woman as well as my own mother.'

How to proceed concerned him. If he confronted her, what could he say? She had been missing for a long time, but she had not committed any crime. What would he ask her? Who was this mysterious child? Who killed Sutherland and Sally Jenkins? Why did she choose to stay missing?

If the woman decided to remain mute, there was not a lot he could do. And then, if she was scared again, she could disappear without a trace. She had done it once successfully; she could do it again.

And if he was being watched, those interested in the woman could follow him out to Canary Wharf. Could she end up dead if he acted inappropriately? Farhan, as good as he was, was not sufficiently experienced to advise on the matter. Sure, he could offer valuable advice, but what if it went wrong. Who would take the blame? He knew the answer without asking – it would be him. Richard Goddard, his detective superintendent, was the ideal choice for advice, but he was looking for a promotion, apparently very friendly with Angus MacTavish. Could either of them be trusted?

The questions outweighed the answers, and now there was the disturbing information about Linda Harris, apparently sleeping with Richard Williams for Queen and Country on official orders.

Angus MacTavish had phoned some hours earlier; said that he had been advised that Linda Harris was involved and that she was a very smart woman – devious, the word he used.

But who was MacTavish? Did he genuinely believe that no political party, even his, deserved to be elected if it sanctioned government approved murder?

Isaac felt that he had to make decisions based on his own sense of decency and to see how they turned out.

Richard Williams, the executive producer, somehow seemed integral to solving the murders. Isaac reasoned the best approach would be to meet him again. He still felt that of all the people involved, he was probably the most innocent, but then there were doubts there, Sally Jenkins being the most obvious.

What if Linda Harris was giving an alibi for Williams purely to ensure that when Marjorie Frobisher reappeared, she would be able to report to her superiors? Was she sleeping with Williams, and if she wasn't, why did she go along with his statement that she had?

Isaac could see that he had to confront Linda Harris, hope that Marjorie Frobisher was safe, at least for a couple of days. He had already asked Wendy to stake out Canary Wharf, and see if she could keep the missing, now found, woman safe.

***

Farhan and Isaac met again in the office later that day: Farhan to further discuss what Aisha had suggested; Isaac to assess how to handle the situation with Richard Williams, and whether he could be involved or not in his former PA's death.

Farhan was in a good mood; his regular conversations with Aisha continued, and his wife was no longer talking about a reconciliation. Apparently, her parents, despairing of her 'no good' husband, had suggested a divorce from Farhan and marriage to a cousin of hers, someone she genuinely liked: a devout Muslim and a good provider, as he owned a number of shops close to the family home.

He should have been distraught at his children being taken from him, but he was a practical man, moderated by his years in the police force. Life, he had come to see, was not black and white, right or wrong, good or bad. Life was about compromises, not absolutes, and his children being with a good man and a good woman, even if the man was not the biological father, was better than being in the conflict zone of a liberated man and a pious woman. He would accept the decision and wish them well.

He felt relief – as if a weight had been lifted off his shoulders. Aisha still remained a problem – an irresolvable problem.

Isaac wanted to sound out Farhan about what they had. It was evident to both of them that the situation was coming to a head. Too much was going on not to have a breakthrough in the near future. Richard Goddard had been pleased when Isaac had phoned him earlier, and let him know that he felt confident it was all coming to fruition. He failed to mention that Marjorie Frobisher had been discovered.

The detective superintendent had always been a mentor to Isaac, and it upset him that he could not be entirely honest with his boss, but there remained some uncertainties. The detective superintendent was in line for a significant promotion. Angus MacTavish could have some bearing on that promotion, and he was a definite uncertainty. Isaac could not be sure about his boss at the present moment, although nothing in his history had indicated a subversive, dishonest nature.

'Farhan, let's come back to what your friend said before.' There was to be no jesting from Isaac this time about the girlfriend.

'Sally Jenkins?'

'Richard Williams appears to be an obvious candidate, but why? Isaac asked.

'We're clutching at straws again,' Farhan said. 'It's possible if it was somehow related to Marjorie Frobisher, but murder? Would Williams be capable of committing such an act?'

'I can't see it.'

'Neither can I?'

'Who else then?'

'Linda Harris? She was around at the time.'

'She's providing an alibi for Williams. If she left him and went over to Sally Jenkins' place, would he have known?'

'Almost certainly.'

'How far from Williams' place to Sally Jenkins'?'

'Twenty minutes, no more.'

'So it's possible,' Isaac said.

'What do you intend to do? Who do you talk to first?'

'Linda Harris. If she's the murderer, she may have acted under orders.'

'And if she did?'

'Then she's a very dangerous woman. If Sally Jenkins' murder was premeditated because of what she may have known, what about Marjorie Frobisher?'

'She's dead, or soon will be, and neither you nor I will be able to protect her.'

'A disturbing reality.'

'An accurate picture, though. If her death is sanctioned officially, then she is a dead woman.'

***

Isaac phoned Linda Harris. Offered his apology, asked to see her again.

'What was the response?' Farhan asked on Isaac's return from the corridor outside their office. He had heard Isaac ingratiating himself with the woman.

'Tonight, same restaurant as before.'

'Any idea how you will bring the matter up?'

'Whether she killed Sally Jenkins or not? I don't think the evening will go too well if I do.'

'If she can sleep with Williams, and murder another woman, what chance do you have of finding out the truth?' Farhan saw a danger in Isaac's approach.

'We can't do nothing.'

'Devil or the deep blue sea. There's no other option for us, although it looks as if you, at least, will be having some fun.'

'As you did with a witness.' Isaac could not resist a little jest.

'A witness on our side. Yours could as easily kill you as make love. It's not an exciting prospect.'

'Don't worry, I'll be fine,' Isaac said.

Farhan was not so sure. His boss was possibly becoming involved with dangerous people, government-sanctioned people. He only hoped he knew what he was doing.

***

Linda Harris was undeniably friendly when she met up with Isaac. 'How are you? Good to see you,' she had gushed. Isaac, forewarned, was not convinced.

'I'm fine. Sorry about last time,' he said. He had to admit she was stunning, dressed in a floral dress, short as she preferred, and a pair of red high-heels.

'I dressed especially.'

'You look beautiful.'

'Good enough for dessert?' Her comment seemed a little too forward for Isaac, but he had to admit that she was.

'Main course, even.'

'I think we should have something to eat first, don't you?' To Isaac, it all seemed a little too orchestrated, a little too teasing. He knew some details about the woman, which caused him to be wary. Sure, he wanted her for dessert, although he would have preferred Jess O'Neill. Apart from a couple of occasions, in a pub out near where she worked, he had not seen her for some time.

He had lambasted Farhan for his indiscretions, although he had not been blameless. However, with Jess, it had remained platonic. He knew he wanted her, knew she wanted him, but so far it had not progressed beyond a passionate kiss on a couple of occasions.

Regardless of Jess, Isaac knew that Linda Harris would be dessert if the evening progressed well enough.

First, there were some questions about Richard Williams' alibi. Not answers veiled by confusion or outright denial; answers openly given, once he had broached the subject of her true employer. And even then, would she be open and truthful?

They chose a table near the back of the restaurant. Isaac ordered pork, Linda chose the veal. A good Chardonnay complemented the meal. Isaac drank sparingly; Linda with more enthusiasm.

'Linda.' Isaac knew he had to speak.

'Don't ruin the evening.' She sounded genuine.

'I hope I'm not.' He knew how he wanted the evening to end. Personal assistant or not, lover of Richard Williams or not, secretive government employee or not, he intended to bed her if the opportunity arose.

'I'm aware that you have received some information about me,' she said.

'I have.'

'And you want to know more?'

'There's been two murders, probably more if we don't find the killer, or killers?'

'Killers? Could there be more than one?'

'It's possible. We still don't have a clear motive for either murder.'

'Isaac, I honestly don't know about the murders.'

'So, why are you sleeping with Williams?'

'You sound jealous.'

'Should I be?' Isaac obliquely failed to answer her question.

'You know I work for the government, MI5.'

'That's what I've been told.'

'My superiors have given me authority to reveal certain facts if the situation came up.'

'Has it?'

'I believe it has. You are the lead policeman on the investigation into the two murders, although initially you were looking for a missing woman.'

'Marjorie Frobisher.'

'Precisely. That's who I'm looking for,' she said.

'But why? Why is she so important?'

'I'm assigned to find the woman, spy where I need to, do whatever is necessary to find her.'

'And sleep with Williams?'

'Yes, sleep with Williams if it helped with the investigation.'

'Has it?'

'Not really, but he's a decent man, a little older than normal for me. I'm still a healthy liberated female. I need to be laid on a regular basis.'

'That's a stunningly frank admission.'

'And you're a modern virile man who needs to get laid on a regular basis, as well. Am I correct?'

'That's correct.'

'And you're not getting much action lately. Jess O'Neill is definitely off the menu.'

'You know about her?'

'It's my job to know. Besides, the two of you are not the most discreet. I saw you both in a pub the other week, very cosy from what I could see.'

'Why is Marjorie Frobisher so important?' Isaac asked the most important question.

'I'm assigned to find her. As to why? I've no idea. That's the truth. Obviously, it's something important, but I don't know what.'

'I don't know either.'

You probably know more than me. Can we change the subject?'

'Are we having dessert?' Isaac asked.

'I hope so, but not here. We'll only frighten the other diners. Your place or mine?'

'My place,' Isaac replied. 'It's closer.'

Chapter 34

In the two days at Canary Wharf, conveniently based near the restaurant and a café she frequented, Wendy had seen little. She believed she had seen the woman at the window a couple of times, but it was high up, and it had been no more than a blurry silhouette. The only visitor that she recognised, almost certainly Richard Williams, judging by the way he walked. It was not possible to see the face, due to a heavy coat, a cloth cap, and a voluminous scarf. He arrived in a small car, not a Ferrari.

Isaac had phoned a couple of times, purely for an update, and Farhan had phoned once. Apart from that, she had been left alone. It suited her fine. The warmth of the sun out next to the water, or in the café, had helped her arthritis, the best it had been for some time.

She knew that her house, once her husband was established in a retirement home, would need to be sold, the rising damp too costly to repair; at least, on her meagre income and her husband's pension. The constantly moist atmosphere in the house kept chilling her bones and her body. She couldn't wait to leave.

It was on the third day when she saw the commotion. An ambulance pulled up outside the building where the missing woman was hiding. Wendy was quickly on the phone to Isaac, who was soon in his car and on the way over to meet her. Wendy, not wasting any time, was in the building, flashing her police badge at the concierge as she dashed through. Not needing to check which floor, uninterested if it was any other than the thirteenth.

Marjorie Frobisher was prostrate on the floor, the ambulance paramedic hovering over her.

'Is she dead?' Wendy shouted.

'She's still breathing.' The reply.

The paramedic was a young woman in her early thirties.

'Do you know her?' the paramedic asked. Wendy could see the name tag attached to the front of the woman's uniform: Patricia Edwards.

'It's Marjorie Frobisher.'

'The actor?'

'Yes, her.'

'I thought it was.'

'Will she live?' Wendy asked anxiously. It was her responsibility, and now the woman was dead, dying. She was not handling the situation as well as she should have.

'Touch and go, I'd say.'

'When will you know?'

'Not for me to say. I need to stabilise her, deal with the immediate situation, and get her to the hospital.'

'Any idea what happened to her?'

'Not sure. Maybe a heart attack.'

'Does it look intentional, murder?'

'I'm not the police. I'm only here to deal with the medical condition. You'll need to ask a policeman whether it's murder or not.'

'I'm a police officer, Constable Wendy Gladstone.'

'Then you can tell me.' Wendy could see the paramedic was busy. Isaac was five minutes away, and he would want answers. The key person was incapacitated, and she was responsible. Why hadn't

247

Isaac confronted Marjorie Frobisher before? Whether the woman lived or died, there was trouble coming; she could sense it.

***

Five minutes later, and Isaac entered the room. He saw the woman being taken out on a stretcher.

'DCI Isaac Cook.' He introduced himself to the paramedic.

'She's stable. It looks as though she'll live.' She had correctly anticipated what he was going to ask.

With that, the woman left with her patient. Isaac needed to spend time with Wendy and to check out the flat. He phoned Farhan and asked him to get over to the hospital.

'What's happened?' Isaac turned his attention back to Wendy.

'I don't know. She hasn't left the building in two days.'

'Anyone else been in the building?'

'Plenty in and out.'

'And did any of those contact the woman?'

'I wouldn't know. She's up on the thirteenth floor. I could hardly stand outside her door for all that time.'

'I suppose not. We should have contacted her when she first appeared.' Isaac regretted his lapse, regretted he hadn't told Richard Goddard.

And where did Linda Harris fit into the puzzle? he thought. She had confirmed she was MI5, although she had been adamant that she was only looking for the woman.

The previous night she had been anything murderous. He felt remorse afterwards, hoped that Jess would never find out, vowed not to sleep with the woman again.

Marjorie Frobisher's current condition represented trouble – trouble with a capital T.

A close investigation of the apartment revealed nothing unusual. The clothes in the wardrobe were the same as on the CCTV at Worcester and Paddington Stations. A half-eaten meal was on the dining table. Isaac noted it for checking. He phoned the medical examiner, asked him to come over. It was not a murder scene, at least, not yet, but the apartment would need to be sealed off and thoroughly checked.

It was evident that Wendy had done no wrong, but Isaac knew how the police force worked. Whenever there was a disciplinary action, there was always a scapegoat. He was the guilty party, not her, but he was young and a future detective superintendent, even head of the establishment. They would protect him, but he was not going to let a woman approaching retirement take the blame for his actions. He realised that if he took the blame then the pressure would be placed on Detective Superintendent Goddard to explain why his DCI had not followed procedure.

**

Farhan arrived at the Royal London Hospital in Whitechapel within five minutes of the ambulance transporting the unconscious woman. He left the car in a no-parking area and flashed his badge at the surprised security guard. Farhan gave him the keys and told him to move it if it was in the way. It was not his usual way of dealing with the general public, but this was an emergency. The pieces were coming together, or they would if the woman lived.

Her cover was broken; she was vulnerable. He hoped she would realise that the only protection for her was in coming clean about all she knew.

Farhan had phoned Robert Avers on the way, his number on speed dial. He sensed the man was not overly pleased. Apparently, he had been cutting quite a dashing figure around town with a woman young enough to be his daughter, although the one he had been squiring was attractive, whereas the daughter, by her own admission, was not.

Once in the hospital, Farhan flashed his badge again. Soon, he was outside the emergency room. He noticed the media starting to arrive; someone had tipped them off. He could see the hospital being deluged with cameras and microphones. Her reappearance was big news. The radio and television stations would be blasting it to the world incessantly for the next few days, until it became old news, replaced by something else.

Farhan chose to ignore the media presence. He phoned the local police station to send over some uniformed men to hold the press and any fans at bay.

Doctor Sangram Singh came out to speak to Farhan. He was a distinguished man, and as Farhan found out later on, highly respected. Due to the importance of the patient, he had been brought in to take charge. 'She'll be fine,' he said.

'What was the problem?' Farhan asked.

'Anaphylactic shock.'

He quickly phoned Isaac to update him. His reply, 'What from?' Isaac knew what it meant.

'Nuts, probably. We'll check it out.'

'Robert Avers is there?' Isaac asked.

'Along with half of the London press, or soon will be.'

'Local police?'

'They're here. I phoned them to take control.'

'Detective Superintendent Goddard wants to see all three of us.'

'We're for the high jump?' Farhan knew it meant trouble.

'Someone is, or maybe he just wants an update.'

'We can't talk to her, not for four or five hours at least. She's sedated.'

'Make sure there's a police guard on her door. It's important.' Isaac hung up. He had a defence to prepare.

***

It was unusual for Detective Superintendent Goddard to summon the team to his office. In fact, it was the first time for Farhan and Wendy.

'Isaac, what's going on here?' The detective superintendent did not seem to be in a good mood. He was not one of nature's most affable men at the best of times, but Isaac had great respect for him. Always saw him as a man he could trust, although recent events had shaken that trust.

'Marjorie Frobisher is alive,' Isaac said.

'I only have to turn the television on to know that.' It was a curt reply.

'We can question her now. Find out this great secret.'

'And when you find out, what then?'

'Hopefully, it will clarify why Sutherland and Sally Jenkins were killed.'

'Hell, Isaac, this is getting dangerous. What if certain parties don't want this solving? What if the woman's rising from the dead is putting people on edge? I've already had Angus MacTavish on the phone.'

'What does he want?' Isaac asked. He had noted that the customary cup of coffee and harmless chat had been dispensed with.

'What do you think? He wants to know what the woman is saying.'

'And you've told him what?'

'Nothing. You told me she's sedated.'

'She'll be speaking later today.'

'I hope so, for your sakes.'

'Constable Gladstone, pleased to see you,' the detective superintendent, showing a momentary friendliness, addressed her.

'Nice office you have here, sir.' Compared to Wendy's, it was palatial. Large window, panoramic view, a full bookcase and some comfortable chairs. Not for them, though. The three were sat on one side of the desk, the chairs not very comfortable. Their interrogator on the other side sat on a high-backed leather chair.

'Constable.' The previous civility gone. 'I've seen your expenses. Extravagant in Malvern, but I let it pass, as you did find some additional information about Marjorie Frobisher.'

'Sorry, sir. I'll be more careful in future.'

'Okay, but now there is an expense claim for a restaurant down at Canary Wharf, directly opposite where this woman was found.'

'I'll retract it if it's a problem, sir,' Wendy said timidly.

'That's not the problem. The problem is with DCI Cook.'

Isaac, now sitting upright and rigid in his chair, prepared himself for the worst.

'Isaac, how long have you been aware of the whereabouts of this woman?'

'Two days, going on three.'

'And you chose not to tell me.'

'We were unsure of the situation. She seemed safe enough, and we were staking out the building.'

'What did you expect me to do? Rush off to Angus MacTavish, cap in hand. Is that how you see me?'

251

'No, sir.' Isaac wasn't sure he could say much to excuse his actions.

'You don't trust MacTavish, do you?'

'I thought him a decent man, but he's a politician with a fearsome reputation for always being on the right side.'

'Isaac, you should have come to me. Now I have MacTavish baying for my blood and the head of the Metropolitan Police asking questions. What can I say? My people chose not to place their confidence in me. It hardly sounds like a ringing endorsement for a promotion.'

'Sir, do you trust MacTavish?' Isaac asked.

'Not totally, but if you had told me soon enough, we could have discussed this. I was not about to rush out the door and over to his office. Someone is after the woman, someone who would prefer her dead, instead of recovering in a hospital bed.'

'That's why we kept it secret.'

'Then who found out?'

'I've no idea,' Isaac admitted.

'DI Ahmed, Constable Gladstone, any ideas?'

'No one that I'm aware of,' Farhan said.

'Not from me,' Wendy added.

'Isaac, let's go through this in detail. Who visited her in Canary Wharf?'

'Only Richard Williams.'

'And what's he got to say?'

'I've not spoken to him yet.'

'Don't you think you should?'

'After we leave here.'

'Do it officially. He's got a lot of answering to do.'

'I will, sir.'

'DC Gladstone, DI Ahmed, you can both leave. Thanks for your time. And DI Ahmed, get to the hospital and make sure the woman is safe and still breathing. Constable Gladstone, submit your remaining claims today while I'm in a generous mood.'

'Thank you, sir.' They spoke in unison.

With the door closed and Isaac alone with his boss, the detective superintendent talked more openly.

'Isaac, I expected better from you. Why are you letting your hormones get in the way of your policing?'

'It's not that, sir.'

'Then what are you doing sleeping with Linda Harris?'

'How do you know, sir?'

'MacTavish told me.'

'How did he know?'

'What does it matter. He's somehow involved, but Linda Harris?'

'She admitted she was MI5.'

'Licensed to sleep with whoever?' Isaac thought his superior's remark inappropriate.

'With Williams, yes.'

'Did you not stop to think? She may have checked the messages on your phone while you were asleep.'

'If she found out, then she's not as innocent as she looks.'

'Isaac, why are you assuming that because she's beautiful, seductive, and available, she's not a highly-skilled operative. If she had been plain and ugly, you would have suspected her.'

'If she had been plain and ugly, she wouldn't have ended up in my bed.'

'That may be, but you can see where I'm coming from. It could have been you who gave her the lead she was trying to get from Richard Williams. Can you imagine the trouble that would cause?'

'End of my career, I would assume.'

'And mine. I'm not ready to retire yet, neither are you, but you've got to control the overriding need to bed every attractive woman that comes along. No doubt it's great fun, and obviously finding these women comes easy to you, but they're impacting on your ability.'

'There's one I would not mind making a longer-term commitment with.'

'I hope you haven't slept with her as well.'

'No, sir.'

'And what's she going to say when she finds out about Linda Harris?'

'I don't know, sir. She's been trying to contact me. Urgent, supposedly. I assume she knows by now.'

'Wrap this case up. It's been going on for too long.'

'I will, sir.'

'And don't go sleeping with Linda Harris. Or Jess O'Neill.'
'I won't, sir.'

***

Isaac, suitably chastised, returned to his office. Wendy was there filling out her expense form. Farhan was almost back at the hospital.

Isaac idly surfed the internet for a few minutes, noting that all the news websites in England were headlining the reappearance of Marjorie Frobisher and her narrow brush with death. Isaac felt he needed to act, and decisively, if he had any hope of reclaiming some credibility. Isaac knew his boss was correct, and that he shouldn't have bedded Linda Harris, but she had been available. He pondered Jess for a while, almost certain that the romance was over before it had started. He was saddened at the prospect. Maybe she would understand that it was in the line of duty, but he knew she wouldn't. She was a woman who would regard fidelity in a relationship as paramount.

He wasn't sure what he was going to say to her. He needed a few days before he contacted her. Jess O'Neill was personal; Richard Williams was not.

He phoned the man, informed him that his presence was required in the building the next morning, 9 a.m. prompt. Williams acquiesced and told Isaac that his legal representative would be present as well.

Wendy, meanwhile, had obtained a signature from Isaac and had rushed off to Richard Goddard for his counter-signature. The man had been polite to her, so she felt comfortable this one time to knock. Some medical bills were coming up for her husband, and she needed the money back as soon as possible.

Isaac mulled over the situation, realised that he wanted to speak with Jess O'Neill, clear the air if that was indeed possible. He knew it was the right action at the wrong time. He expected the worst.

'Jess, how are you?'
'Fine. What's going on?'
'What do you mean?'

'You don't phone for a few days, and then you're out with Richard Williams' latest bit of skirt.'

'Jess, that sounds like jealousy.'

'Of course it is. Do you mind explaining?'

'I needed someone to bring a new perspective to the case.'

'What a load of hogwash and you know it. You fancy her, admit it.'

Isaac, momentarily stunned, did not know how to respond. Should he tell her the truth? That the woman was MI5 and potentially very dangerous.

No, he decided. His boss had summed up the situation succinctly.

'She's a beautiful woman, Jess. I'll agree to that. This case is going nowhere, and until it does, we cannot be together.'

'You're just spinning me a line.'

'It's the truth. I had to see if she had overheard something. I'll explain later, but Williams is central to all this.'

'Because of his friendship with Marjorie Frobisher?'

'Exactly!'

'But you have her now. You can ask her.'

'Whether she will tell us anything is hard to say.'

'If I find out that you slept with Linda Harris, this romance is over before it started.' She hung up the phone. Isaac realised that he would need to address the deception another time. He knew he would need to tell her the truth. He did not look forward to that day.

Wendy, having returned with her signed expense sheet, bid farewell to Isaac and left the office early. It was the promised night out with Bridget. Next day, she would have a pounding headache and a rasping voice. A friend was coming over to her house to look after her husband that night, as she did not expect to be home until late.

Later that day, Farhan phoned to say that Marjorie Frobisher was awake and talking, but still mildly sedated. The doctor's advice, another two days before she would be fully coherent. He also said that Robert Avers was there as the dutiful husband, while his young lover had left the waiting room at the hospital in disgust. Neither of the two children had been seen, and the media was a damn nuisance and interfering with the normal business of the hospital.

Chapter 35

Quinton Scott arrived at nine in the morning as agreed. His client did not. As a Queen's Counsel, Scott was extremely expensive. He was a busy man, but as Isaac noticed, he did not seem to be in a rush to move on. Quinton Scott, if asked, would have said the meter's running, it all goes on the bill.

Farhan had made himself available, substituting another detective to keep a watch on Marjorie Frobisher. Wendy had not shown up, phoning in to say she wasn't feeling well and would be in late. Isaac knew, from the voice at the end of the phone, the nature of the illness.

It didn't matter as she had little to do – all missing persons accounted for.

Approaching 10.30 a.m. and with no sign of Williams, even his QC was starting to look agitated. Isaac felt it was time to find the missing man.

A phone call to his office, no answer. Strange, Isaac thought. The production lot yielded no results either. Williams' home phone and mobile, no answer as well.

Isaac felt there was cause for concern. Williams may have hidden a witness, may have committed an indictable offence, but he had one of the best Queen's Counsels in his corner. His unavailability made no sense.

It was clear the man was not coming; the QC left soon after. The interview was rescheduled to the next day, same time.

Wendy came into the office shortly after. She did not look well. Isaac could have expressed some sympathy, told her to take the rest of the day off, but there was a job for her. A job for both her and Farhan – find Richard Williams.

His house, a three-storey terrace in Holland Park, was the best possibility. They drove out to the house. After two minutes knocking on the door, the last twenty seconds vigorously, they realised that no one was at home, or, at least, no one who was willing to answer the door. Unable to break the door lock with a swift and hefty shove, they relocated to the back of the house, down a narrow alley to one side. The door into the kitchen at the rear was unlocked.

Entering, they moved slowly around the ground floor, up to the first floor and, finally, the second floor. There on the floor in the main bedroom lay the body of Richard Williams, a gunshot wound clearly visible. It looked like suicide, but why? Farhan phoned Isaac, who phoned Forensics and a medical team. This time, Isaac made sure to call Richard Goddard.

***

Richard Williams was dead. Whether suicide or other was immaterial at the present moment. The case into the murders had taken an unexpected turn. Isaac knew that Marjorie Frobisher was the key, but she was still not fully conscious.

If he insisted, the medical team at the hospital would have been obliged to bring her around for him to ask a few questions. What were the questions, though? Isaac wasn't sure, and Richard Goddard wasn't much help, constantly on the phone for an update: Who murdered Williams? Is it suicide or murder? What do I tell MacTavish?

Isaac had few answers, although some suppositions. He could not see Williams as the type to commit suicide, although the weapon that had delivered the fatal shot was next to the body. And if it was suicide, why? Hiding Marjorie Frobisher away at a secret location, protecting her, was at best a minor crime. There had been questions, but with a smart legal mind such as Quinton Scott's and a solid reason in that the woman's life was at risk, he would have probably got off with a suspended sentence, even credit from the admiring public for protecting the life of a much-admired celebrity. A true friend, a man worthy of admiration, would be how the public would see it; Isaac too.

If Williams had not committed suicide, then that meant murder or assassination. Was it a murder intended to look like a suicide? Was it part of a well-orchestrated plan? And where was Linda Harris? Isaac had sent someone to check out her accommodation, but it had been vacated; hurriedly, according to the landlady.

'Paid me before she left,' the landlady had said. 'No, I don't know where she's gone, but such a lovely woman. Plenty of boyfriends, no doubt, but I never saw any here.'

Isaac failed to understand why Linda Harris was taking a room in a pleasant house when she dressed as if she could afford a place of her own, but then he did not know much about her. Sure, she was good company, obviously competent and certainly agile in his bed, but who was she? A minor functionary at MI5, or was she capable of more?

He had to find her, but who knew where she would be? Angus MacTavish, but could he be trusted? Richard Goddard? Isaac ruled him out. He would know little, maybe ask MacTavish, but suspected he would not tell him. The only way he could think of making any headway was to go to the production lot. Williams' office in town was empty, maybe there was a clue there. He changed his decision about the production lot and headed to Williams' office.

***

Richard Williams' office was locked when Isaac arrived. It wasn't far from the police station, and the traffic was remarkably light for the time of day. The concierge on the ground floor let him in after he had shown his badge. Nothing seemed out of order. Williams' desk was neat and tidy, a few papers to one side. He reasoned there would be nothing of much interest there.

Linda Harris's desk seemed the most obvious. Sitting down on the chair that she and Sally Jenkins had occupied, he opened the desk drawers one by one, starting at the top left. He wore gloves, should have obtained official permission, but time was of the essence.

Richard Williams was dead, Marjorie Frobisher was under guard, but Isaac knew he was dealing with professionals. If they were determined to tie up loose ends, himself included, they would. No amount of protection would save anyone.

He thought that if Linda Harris had managed to find out the address at Canary Wharf, she hadn't used it. Or maybe she had? The doctor at the hospital had said anaphylactic shock. Something she had eaten, but Marjorie Frobisher would have been particular with what she ate, and the restaurant her meals were coming from was first-class. Surely they wouldn't have made an error.

If Linda Harris, MI5, and probably Angus MacTavish had wanted Marjorie Frobisher dead, Isaac reasoned, wouldn't it have been easier to have killed her down at Canary Wharf? Wendy had been watching, but she had been some distance away. Entry into the building was not too difficult, people were going in and out all the time, residents, tradesmen, people delivering furniture, people taking it away.

The questions continued to build, yet Isaac could not supply answers. Someone had to know, or maybe there were puzzles within puzzles, questions within questions.

The contents of the desk offered no help, but Isaac had assumed they would not. If Linda Harris, if that was her name, were a trained professional, she would hardly have left any clues behind. Everything was neat and tidy, and the computer was password locked. Isaac phoned for his people to send down a team, to secure the office and to take the computer and break its password. He thought there would be nothing on it, but it was possible – more of a long shot.

He realised that Linda Harris was long gone; vanished without a trace, probably out of the country by now.

***

Farhan stayed at Richard Williams' house until the investigations were concluded and the body removed to the morgue. The initial report from Forensics showed that the gun found at the scene, a Glock 17, did deliver the fatal shot. Farhan had noted the serial number, passed it on to the relevant people to trace the ownership – he had little hope of a result.

Farhan had been pleased when Gordon Windsor had walked into the house earlier to take charge of the examination of the body. The man had done a good job with Charles Sutherland.

'DI Ahmed,' Gordon Windsor said later, pulling down the mask covering his face and standing away from the body. He prepared to remove his coveralls, a clear sign that he had completed his work. 'Clear shot to the head, professional.'

'Murder?'

'There appears to be some attempt at making out it was suicide, but I'd say whoever shot him was disturbed.'

'The back door was open,' Farhan replied.

'Is that where he exited?'

'He?' Farhan asked.

'Could be a she, I suppose. Why do you ask? Anyone in mind?'

Farhan felt no need to elucidate.

As Williams' body left the premises in a body bag, Farhan left too. There seemed no reason to stay longer. The gun was off to ballistics to confirm that bullet and gun were related – Farhan saw it as a formality. Fingerprints looked to be unlikely. Initial investigation at the crime scene showed the signs of a professional, which raised the question why the murderer had fled if he or she had been disturbed. Why not just take out the person disturbing them, two for the price of one? More questions, few answers.

Isaac was drawing a blank as well. He saw no option but to head out to the production lot. The landlady at Linda Harris's accommodation provided little information, just said that Linda kept to herself, had no men over, and two or three nights a week she never came home at all.

First, he planned to meet up with Farhan and Wendy in the office; or was he just delaying the inevitable of meeting Jess again. He wasn't sure. He updated their boss as to what was happening.

He said he would be at the meeting as well. Isaac would have preferred that he wasn't.

***

The weather had turned miserable as Isaac drove back to the office; it matched his mood. He had committed an error of judgement in sleeping with Linda Harris, had possibly given her vital information, and he was bound to be confronted out at the production lot by the one person he wouldn't be able to lie to.

Farhan, meanwhile, was in a more upbeat mood. His wife had submitted the papers for divorce, the conditions acceptable. After dividing the assets, more to her as she would take responsibility for the children, he would still be left with enough to put a down payment on a small apartment. Maybe, with Aisha, somewhere better, but that was idle folly.

She was still a former prostitute, even though now a promising lawyer. How would he explain it to his parents, his extended family? Could it be kept a secret? And his career, so important to him – would it be jeopardised? He knew it would. Even if his family never knew, the police would, and their records were impeccable.

The police force was egalitarian, accepting of all religions, all colours, all sexual persuasions. A former prostitute married to a detective inspector should not have counted against him, officially that is; unofficially, he knew it would.

He was aware that eventually he would need to make a decision, but not yet. The inquiry into the two, now three, murders was coming to a climax, he was sure of it. Soon, he would be able to spend time with Aisha. Then he would be able to ascertain if the love between the two of them was real, or whether it was infatuation from him for a liberated, passionate woman, or from her for a reliable, decent man.

And besides, Farhan had to be honest. He was heading up to detective superintendent at most; she had the possibility of becoming a QC. Would a QC be comfortable with a mid-ranking policeman? He wasn't sure – time would tell.

Wendy, feeling better after a few hours in the office on her own, welcomed both Isaac and Farhan on their return to the office.

She had prepared some coffee for them, as well as a plate of biscuits. Chocolate, apparently her favourite, as half of them had already been consumed before Isaac and Farhan had a chance to take one.

Richard Goddard entered soon after, the frown on his forehead all too apparent – the pressure was getting to him. Wendy offered him a coffee; he accepted.

He felt no need to be discreet. Farhan and Wendy were there, and he wasn't about to send them out of the room this time. 'DCI Cook, it looks as if you've been sleeping with a murderer again.'

Wendy looked over at Farhan with raised eyebrows. Farhan just shook his head imperceptibly in return, a clear sign that he didn't know either what the detective superintendent was referring to. Farhan had known about Linda Harris, but the 'again' he did not.

'We're assuming she's the murderer,' Isaac replied. *No time for embarrassment*, he thought.

'And where is she?'

'No idea, sir.'

'What are the chances of finding her?'

'She appears to have vanished. I was about to ask Constable Gladstone if she can find her.'

'No problems, I can do that,' Wendy said.

'But where do we look?' Farhan asked.

'No idea,' Isaac replied.

'What do you mean, no idea?' Normally a man who kept his emotions in check, Richard Goddard was clearly showing the early stages of anger. His impending promotion depended on the solving of the murders, yet he didn't know which solution his superiors wanted. Did they want the culprit, any culprit? What if the killings were sanctioned assassinations? Was he expected to sweep them under the table?

'Marjorie Frobisher seems to be the key,' Farhan said.

'Farhan's right,' Isaac added.

'Then you'd better get over there and talk to her. That's if she hasn't been killed in the interim. As a team, your ability to get your key witnesses killed is outstanding. If you were as good at keeping them alive as you are at bedding them, then we would have wrapped this up weeks ago.' Isaac and Farhan sat sheepishly. Wendy enjoyed the moment. She liked to gossip, although this was not the sort of gossip she could tell Bridget after a few too many drinks.

With little more to say, Detective Superintendent Goddard left the office.

For twenty seconds, no one said anything. It was up to Wendy to break the silence.

'Do you want me to look for Linda Harris?'

'She may be difficult to find,' Isaac said.

'I'll do my best. Where do I start?'

'Her accommodation, although the landlady won't be much help.'

'Leave her to me. They always know more than they admit to; busybodies, all of them.'

As soon as Isaac had passed over the details, Wendy left the office.

Farhan and Isaac continued to discuss the case.

'What was Detective Superintendent Goddard referring to when he first came into the office?' Farhan asked, not expecting an answer.

'I made an error of judgement once before.' Isaac did not feel the need to elaborate.

'Another Linda Harris?'

'Change the subject.' An unusually curt reply from Isaac.

'Apologies. If Williams was murdered by Linda Harris, and she bolted out the back door, then who came through the front?' Farhan asked.

'Good question, and why didn't they phone the police?'

'They had something to hide?' Farhan answered rhetorically.

'The only person who would have come in the front door would be Linda Harris.'

'Or the cleaner.'

'We've discounted her,' Farhan said. 'The one day of the week she doesn't come. Besides, she would have phoned us.'

'Nobody else to our knowledge had a front door key, apart from Williams, the cleaner, and possibly Linda Harris.'

'Another woman?'

'It's possible. Williams may have had someone else.'

'Let's stand back and analyse this,' Farhan said. 'Linda Harris we know is MI5.'

'Correct.'

'Is she capable of murder?'

'Unknown, but let's assume she is.'

'Did she give any indication of that in the time you were with her?'

'No. But what does that mean? We're not even sure of her name.'

'Let's assume she is, but not the murderer of Richard Williams.'

'Then she disturbed the assassin.'

'Assassin?'

'Let's call it that. Who else would feel the need to murder him?'

'Nobody. This means he knew the identity of the mysterious child.'

'Maybe. Maybe not. We're assuming Charles Sutherland and Sally Jenkins did, but it's pure assumption.'

'But they died.'

'As did Richard Williams.'

'Can we stop this continuing if these people are determined.'

'I don't see how.'

'Marjorie Frobisher?'

'She's a dead woman. We can't protect her.'

'We need to tread carefully here. Can we trust Richard Goddard?'

'We must.'

The day had passed by the time the two men had concluded their discussion. Wendy had phoned in; the landlady was chatting happily about this and that. Wendy said she was just lonely, glad of a bit of company. And yes, she loved gossip and keeping her nose close to the front window. Wendy said she was in for a couple more hours before she had found out all she could.

Isaac told her to take her time. He, meanwhile, had to talk to his boss.

Farhan, unwisely, considering the escalating momentum in their investigation, planned to meet Aisha – he could not keep away.

Chapter 36

Richard Goddard was preparing to leave when Isaac knocked on the door to his office. The man was anxious to leave; Isaac eager to discuss Marjorie Frobisher.

'Can this wait, Isaac?'

'I'm afraid not, sir.'

'I've only got five minutes. I'm meeting with Angus MacTavish, and then I've a function to attend.'

'Five minutes it is. We believe Marjorie Frobisher is targeted for assassination.'

'Is she still safe in the hospital?'

'We're protecting her the best we can.'

'What do you want from me? We're walking into a minefield here.'

'A minefield and we don't know the way out. What do you suggest?' Isaac asked.

'We need to protect the woman.'

'Once she leaves the hospital?'

'I'll need permission.'

'From whom? And can you trust them?'

'I'm not sure who I can trust. Believe me, it would have been better for all of us if she had stayed hidden, even dead.'

'I can't believe you're saying that, sir.'

'Neither can I, but there you are. There's a mystery surrounding this woman, but nobody knows or isn't talking. Does the woman know?'

'I assume so.'

'Then get over to the hospital and stay with her. Sleep there if you must, but protect her, get her to talk. Frighten her if you have to. She'll need to be told about Richard Williams.'

'I'll deal with it.'

'The husband. Is he still there?'

'I believe so,' Isaac replied.

'Can you trust him?'

'I don't think he's involved in any of the murders.'

'He had reason to wish Williams dead. Playing around with his wife.'

'A suspect in his murder. Is that what you think?'

'It's possible.'

'Not likely. The crime scene examiner believes it's a professional hit. The shot was too precise for an amateur, and Robert Avers has no history with weapons.'

'Okay, but find out what she knows. Now is not the time for her to hold back. Whatever the truth is, it must be serious. Three murders now, maybe four if we don't act.'

'Angus MacTavish?' Isaac asked.

'What about him?'

'What are you going to tell him?'

'I'll be careful. I've no idea where he stands. He may be fine, but as you say, he's a devious politician. He'll bend with the wind, and if that means the whitewashing of a few murders, then he may turn a blind eye. I know the man is looking for a knighthood in the next New Year's Honours list.'

***

Farhan was pleased to see Aisha again. She was looking forward to him meeting her parents, but it was still premature. Until the murder of Charles Sutherland was solved, she was still a material witness.

They had chosen a secluded restaurant not far from where they had first met.

'Aisha, we need to be careful.' She was demonstrative, wanted to sit near him and give him a hug and a kiss. He was still wary of his detective superintendent's statement and the berating from Isaac.

'I've got another important case coming up. I want you to come and see me in action,' she said excitedly.

'A junior, do you get to do much?'

'Not really, but I would like you there.'

'I'll try.'

'You're busy, I know that. It's in the news. Marjorie Frobisher is in the hospital. Richard Williams dead.'

'It's coming to an end soon. I hope it is, anyway,' Farhan said. He, like Isaac, was tiring of the case. It had gone on for too long, with too many murders, and too many questions. No matter how hard they tried, they couldn't decide if it was one murderer, or two, or three.

Aisha said she couldn't stay long; she had to get home. Farhan would have preferred her to stay, maybe spend the night in a hotel. She said it wasn't possible, as she had to travel up north early the next day to meet the client.

'Will my secret be safe?' she asked.

'I'm trying. Nothing is certain. It could still come out.'

'It depends on who murdered Sutherland, I suppose.'

'If they plead guilty, then maybe there'll be no witnesses called.'

'If they don't?'

'You're the lawyer. You can answer that.'

'The defence will call every witness they can, looking for discrepancies in the evidence, contradictions in statements given.'

'That's what you would do?'

'Yes, of course. I just hope they don't find out.'

'So, do I,' Farhan said. Personally, he hoped they wouldn't. Professionally, he realised there was a strong possibility. The renewed interest in the case after the murder of Richard Williams and the reappearance of Marjorie Frobisher had caused a frenzy among the vulture press. They were still in attendance at the hospital, although their numbers were diminishing. How long before they disappeared: not known.

The plan to protect the woman that Isaac had briefly relayed earlier depended on creating a smokescreen, and then whisking the woman away unseen. It would be two days maximum before she was ready to move, and still Isaac had not interviewed her.

Farhan and Aisha parted company two blocks from her house. He had driven her home for the first time. They parted with a lingering embrace and kiss.

She would not be back for a couple of days. She promised they would find a room when she returned. Farhan knew he was breaking all the rules.

***

Wendy came into the office the next morning, updated Isaac and left. The landlady, ever-vigilant, had seen her now-departed lodger with a man outside the house on a few occasions, a big, burly man.

Not that she was nosey, the landlady had said. It was just that she liked to make sure all was in order on her street. Wendy had nodded in agreement, but quietly thought she was a busybody. She had one in her street, two doors away, who was always complaining about something or other. One day, the noise from the people who had just moved in; the next, someone's dog defecating in the street. Wendy took little notice of either, and while the noise could sometimes be irritating, it only lasted for an hour or so, and as for the dog, the owners always cleaned up.

The only good thing from the landlady was a car registration number. Wendy intended to trace it; Isaac told her not to be disappointed if it turned out to be a red herring. The security services were known for using the addresses of nondescript buildings on registrations and official forms. She said she wouldn't be, and besides, she didn't give in that easily. Isaac wished her well.

The day had started well. Marjorie Frobisher was awake and able to talk. Robert Avers was there with her, and even the two children, Sam and Fiona, had been in, although neither stayed long.

Apparently, Sam Avers had left in a huff, and the plain-looking daughter, Fiona, had walked out swearing.

Jess had phoned, wanted to meet him to discuss things. Isaac had told her he was busy, and that he would get back to her later in the day. He wasn't sure if he would, as he knew what she wanted to talk about, and he had no excuses. He thought it unusual for him to feel unfaithful to her when he had never actually been faithful to her in the first place, never slept with her, never kissed her apart from two or three times.

With Wendy out looking for Linda, and Farhan dealing with some long overdue reports, Isaac visited Marjorie Frobisher. Farhan had checked with her husband and the doctor in charge. The doctor's advice – one person, keep it low-key, friendly. Robert Avers' advice – similar. He also mentioned that he had told her of the death of Richard Williams, and she was taking it as well as could be expected.

***

As Isaac arrived at the hospital, he noticed that the media contingent had mostly moved on. The police guards outside her room were still diligent, although he knew that if a professional hit were planned, they would not be much use.

Her room had more flowers than the florist's shop he visited every Mother's Day, as well as cards from well-wishers. Her room, more like a five-star hotel suite than a private room in a hospital.

He moved to the bed, introduced himself, and put out his hand. She shook it limply. Robert Avers acknowledged him with a slight wave of his hand and a weak smile.

'Miss Frobisher.'

'Call me Marjorie.'

'Marjorie, you are aware why I am here?'

'Yes.'

'I understand that you are not fully recovered. I don't want to tax you any more than necessary.'

'That's fine.'

'Is there anything you want to tell me?'

'I'm not sure what you want from me.'

'You were missing for a long time.'
'I was frightened.'
'Are you still frightened?'
'Yes.'
'Frightened of whom?' Isaac realised that too much pressure would make her retreat into her shell.
'Important people.'
'We can protect you.'
'Not against the people who are after me.'
'And do you know why they are after you?'
'Yes. I know something.'
'Are you able to tell me?'
'I don't know who you are.'
'Detective Chief Inspector Isaac Cook. I showed you my badge.'
'That means nothing.'
'What can be done to remove your fear?'
'Nothing. These people are determined. If you are one of them, or not, makes little difference. Once I leave here, my life will be forfeit.'
'You know that sounds a little melodramatic.' Isaac realised the conversation was going nowhere as the woman was clearly frightened, and she wasn't willing to trust him.
'This is not a script from a soap opera, you know. This is real life,' she said.
Isaac found the woman to be more intelligent, more astute than he had imagined. She turned away from him and spoke to her husband. 'Do you know this man?'
'Yes, he came to the house to interview Sam and Fiona.'
'Is he from the police?'
'I'm certain he is. I've no reason to doubt him.'
Returning her gaze to Isaac. 'I need protection.'
'There's protection here.'
'How safe am I here?'
'I cannot guarantee total protection. We can find a safe house for you. Will that do?'
'If I tell you the facts?'
'We can take into custody those responsible.'

'You cannot touch them. They killed poor Richard, and all because of me.'

'I'm sorry about that,' Isaac said. 'What about Charles Sutherland?'

'He knew nothing – thought he did.'

'And Sally Jenkins?'

'Her ears were as big as her breasts. Always snooping. She may have heard too much, but Sutherland…'

'Are you saying that he was lying to the magazine?'

'Of course he was. Some innuendo, salacious gossip, nothing more. Mind you, he could make anything up and sell it to the magazine. He may have discovered the partial truth, but he didn't know the facts. Got himself killed over it, though.'

'Why do you say that?' Isaac asked.

'He had some dirt on my earlier life. I was a bit of a tart, screwing around before it became fashionable. It's hardly newsworthy, and the magazine would have kicked him out on his ear soon enough. Those who frighten me know that. I'm surprised they bothered with him.'

Isaac saw that Sutherland may be a murder, Sally Jenkins – an assassination. As for Richard Williams, it was clear that he had known what Marjorie Frobisher did.

Appearing to be tired, Isaac left her with her husband holding her hand. He did not look a happy man.

***

Richard Goddard was anxious to know what Marjorie Frobisher was saying. Isaac had promised to give him an update. He had decided that Goddard had done him right in the past, and there was no reason to believe he would do him wrong now.

'She says that Sutherland knew nothing of consequence.'

'Professional hit?'

'According to Marjorie Frobisher, he knew very little.'

'Could his death be unrelated?'

'It's possible.'

'The woman. What have you promised her?'

'Protected witness status. Can you organise a safe house for her?'

'I need something in return.'

'Name it.'

'Give me a murderer, any murderer, within the next few days.'

'Charles Sutherland's our best bet,' Isaac said.

'Any luck with Linda Harris?'

'Not yet. Constable Gladstone's following up on a lead.'

'What do you reckon?'

'If she's MI5, she won't be found.'

'I hope you weren't fond of her.'

'No fondness there,' Isaac replied.

'Let Constable Gladstone get on with it. Can you and DI Ahmed focus on who killed Charles Sutherland? What did Marjorie Frobisher say about Sally Jenkins and Richard Williams?'

'She's reluctant to say too much. I interpreted her comments to mean that Williams knew what the great secret was, and Sally Jenkins had a tendency to eavesdrop. We should regard their deaths as suspicious.'

'Professional assassinations?'

'It looks to be that way.'

'Okay. I'll organise the safe house. And I want one murderer under lock and key within two days.'

***

Farhan and Isaac met in the office two hours later. Isaac was concerned that one murder, Charles Sutherland's, was coming to a resolution but was not certain what it would be. Farhan knew Aisha wasn't involved, and if there was a murderer under lock and key, as well as a signed confession, then he may be able to protect her.

'We need to go through the possible suspects again,' Isaac said. It was just the two of them in the office. Wendy had phoned in – she was drawing a blank on the car outside Linda Harris's accommodation. She made it clear that she was not giving up.

'We can eliminate the two women,' Farhan said.

'Which two women?'

'The two escorts.'

'The two prostitutes,' Isaac reaffirmed. Farhan did not like the terminology.

'As you say,' Farhan agreed.

'Just because you're involved with one, and the other one you shipped out of the country, doesn't abrogate them from responsibility.'

'I realise that, but neither knew they were meeting with him in advance. He was just an address to them.'

'Who else then? Christy Nichols?' Isaac asked.

'You've omitted one person,' Farhan reminded Isaac.

'Jess O'Neill. I've not forgotten. Although her motive is not as strong.'

'Why do you say that?'

'Sutherland forced Christy Nichols to perform oral sex on him. With Jess O'Neill, he had attempted to force himself on her, but she managed to get away.'

'That's true, but he may have reawakened painful memories – memories that wouldn't go away.'

'We need to call them both into the station,' Isaac said. He imagined Jess's reaction would be hostile.

***

It was nine o'clock the next day when the first of the two women arrived. It had been several weeks since Farhan had seen Christy Nichols. Then, she had been a disappointed woman, consigned to being an 'agony aunt' for a local newspaper.

He remembered leaving in a hurry when it had become clear that he was welcome to stay the night. He had to admit when she walked into the police station that she looked exceedingly attractive; he wondered wistfully why he had not seized the opportunity. No longer despondent, she was full of vitality and dressed exceptionally well.

'I found a decent job. Copy editor for a quality magazine. Not that scurrilous publication that Victoria Webster puts out.'

'Good to hear,' Farhan said, but little more. She was in the police station due to a formal request, and he did not want to appear too friendly. She had brought along a lawyer, Eileen Kerr. The woman, severely dressed in a dark suit with a white shirt and thin tie; her voice, rasping and deep, the sign of a heavy smoker. Isaac had encountered her in the past, and he did not like her. He made a point of telling Farhan that the woman was aggressive, competent, and would not take any nonsense.

They used the same interview room as when Jess O'Neill and Richard Williams had come in. The formalities completed, Isaac led off. 'Miss Nichols. We have reason to believe that Charles Sutherland's death was murder.'

'I thought that was clear.' Eileen Kerr interjected.

'As you say, clear.'

'Miss Nichols, can you please recount the events of that night.'

'I'd rather not.'

'I understand your reticence, but we need to ensure that nothing was missed, no matter how minor.'

'Miss Nichols,' her legal adviser felt obliged to comment, 'has complied with the police. The matters which you are now asking her to repeat are deeply embarrassing. Is this necessary?'

'Yes, we believe it is,' Isaac replied.

'He asked me to perform an act on him. I told DI Ahmed?' Christy Nichols asked.

'Very well. I let the women in. Later I went to the apartment, and Charles Sutherland was on the ground with the women. He was offensive, naked, flashing his genitals at me.'

'And what did you do?'

'Nothing. The women left quickly, and I was there alone with him.'

'And that is when the incident occurred?' Isaac asked.

'Yes.'

'He made you perform fellatio on him.'

'Yes.'

'Is this necessary?' Christy Nichols' lawyer asked again.

'It's fine, Eileen.' Christy Nichols leant over and spoke to her lawyer.

'Was he violent with you?' Isaac asked. He needed to push some more.

'He grabbed my arm, forced me down on my knees. Threatened to harm me.' Farhan noticed the quiver in her voice as she spoke. He felt sorry for her; Isaac showed no emotion.

'I cannot allow this to continue,' Eileen Kerr said.

'I'm nearly finished,' Isaac said. 'Miss Nichols, did you at any time threaten him?'

'I may have. I was angry, frightened. I don't want to remember.'

'This must stop. This is police brutality,' the lawyer said.

'Meeting concluded at 11 a.m.' Isaac pressed the stop on the timer and switched off the recording equipment.

***

'What did you think?' Farhan asked Isaac after Christy Nichols and her lawyer, possibly lover, had left. Feeling hungry, both had walked down the street to a small Italian restaurant.

'The motive is strong enough,' Isaac replied.

'Is she capable of murder?'

'What do we know about her?'

'Not a lot. Apart from what she's told us.'

'We need to find out more,' Isaac said. 'Let's be clear here. It's either Christy Nichols or Jess O'Neill. Both had the motive. One had the opportunity. Is there anyone else we're missing?'

'If it's not a professional hit, then it's either of the two women.'

'I'd prefer it was neither, but we can't let them off. From what I can see, decent women placed in difficult circumstances with an unpleasant and odious man. He's no great loss to society, yet someone has got to pay for liquidating him.'

'Isaac, we're here to uphold the law, not discuss the relative merits of the murderer and the murdered.

'You're right. We'd better bring in Jess O'Neill.'

'We're forgetting Fiona Avers. She had a motive,' Farhan said.

'If it remains unresolved after speaking to Jess O'Neill, we'll call her in. In the meantime, how's Wendy going?'

Farhan phoned her. Apparently, the trail for Linda Harris had gone cold.

'Call her into the office. There's something more important for her to do.'

Wendy took forty minutes to arrive. 'Christy Nichols. Have you read her file?' Isaac asked.

'I've had no need to.'

'You do now. We need to know more about her,' Isaac said. 'Where she came from. What her life was like before London. Also, would she be capable of murder?'

Chapter 37

Jess O'Neill's facial expression clearly revealed her mood as she entered the interview room. Isaac had seen her walk in, but she had purposely looked the other way. He sensed it was going to be a difficult interview. Her brother-in-law, Michael Wrightson, accompanied her.

'Let it be put on record that my client is here under duress,' Wrightson said after the opening formalities had concluded. 'She answered all questions submitted last time in an open and frank manner. And, as we know, at some embarrassment. Reopening old wounds and painful memories is neither appreciated nor required. Let me further add that if as a result of today's interview it is clear there is no viable reason for her presence, it will be necessary to register a complaint.'

'Please note that certain information has come into our possession,' Isaac said after the threat from Wrightson. 'It has necessitated the presence of Miss O'Neill, as well as others, here today.' Isaac looked over at Jess. She failed to make eye contact.

'Then please submit your questions,' Wrightson responded. 'My client is a busy person.'

'Very well,' Isaac replied. 'Miss O'Neill, thank you for coming.'

'I am here under the advice of Mr Wrightson.' Still no eye contact.

'We have reason to believe that the murder of Charles Sutherland is not related to the killings of the other two people. As such, it is necessary for us to re-evaluate the evidence.'

'My client gave a full account of her relationship to Charles Sutherland, and her dislike for the man, last time. Do we need to go over that again?'

Isaac chose to ignore Wrightson's comment. 'Miss O'Neill, did you at any time threaten the man with physical harm?'

'When he was trying to rape me?'

'Yes.'

'I probably did. What woman wouldn't?'

'I am sorry. I am just trying to ascertain the facts.'

Farhan chose to remain silent. He knew the relationship between the interviewer and the interviewee. He had to admit that she was a fine-looking woman.

Wrightson continued to interject. 'This line of questioning is unacceptable.'

Isaac ignored him. He addressed Jess again. 'Can you tell me about your knowledge of poisons?'

'Is this an accusation?' Wrightson asked. 'My client does not need to answer.'

'No, you are right. She does not need to answer. I, however, need to ask.'

'Michael, it's alright,' she said to her lawyer.

Addressing Isaac, this time making eye contact. 'If you are asking whether I poisoned Charles Sutherland, the answer is no. The accusation that I would be considered is abhorrent. I did not like the man, but murder...'

'I am sorry for asking. There are others with a motive who have been asked the same question. It would be remiss if I did not ask you the question.'

He whispered in her ear, 'He's giving you a lead. Take it.'

277

Looking back at Isaac, this time a little friendlier. 'I have no knowledge of poison, other than tear gas while on assignment in the Middle East. Is that poison?'

'Thank you for your answer.' Farhan sensed the desperation of his boss to eliminate her from the inquiry, although none of her answers proved her innocent.

The interview concluded within sixty minutes. As Jess and her brother-in-law left the room, she leant over to Isaac and quietly said, 'You bastard!'

Farhan, not far away, heard what she said. He knew what it meant. He wondered how Isaac would explain away the actions that had generated such a venomous comment.

***

Wendy was delighted: the expense card reinstated, or, at least, the opportunity to use it without criticism.

Christy Nichols, the records had shown, came from a small village in the Lake District, close to the Scottish border. Wendy was heading up there, her husband in the hands of a live-in nurse for three days. Isaac had approved the cost, no option but to. He knew their boss would query it, but he wanted a result, and there were only two suspects. One he felt was innocent, not because he wanted her to be, but because her story had checked out. Jess O'Neill had grown up in in north London. She had left school with good marks and gone straight to university, majoring in English Literature. It hardly seemed to be suitable training for administering drugs, poisonous or otherwise.

The Lake District, two hundred and fifty miles to the north of London, seemed too far to drive. Wendy chose to take the train, three and a half hours to Oxenholme. She departed at eleven in the morning from Euston station, arriving just after two in the afternoon. A short taxi ride took her into Kendal, a small town of about twenty-eight thousand inhabitants. She rented a car and checked into the Castle Green Hotel. The brochures said it was the finest hotel in the town; Wendy could not disagree. The wine list looked suitably impressive. She decided to exercise the credit card that night.

The address of Christy Nichols' family was to the west. She decided the following morning would be more suitable. Light rain was falling, and she had been told that the mist could come down at any time. It appeared that the family home was isolated and down some winding roads. Wendy, although a competent driver, felt more familiar with the bumper to bumper traffic in London than an isolated country lane.

Isaac phoned as she was seated at the bar; reminded her to go easy on the credit card. *Too late,* she thought.

He updated her on his and Farhan's activities that day. And how Jess O'Neill appeared to be in the clear. Wendy thought to herself, *he needs to be careful there.* And also on how Christy Nichols seemed to be the more likely of the two, although Isaac failed to elucidate on his reasoning. She decided not to press for an answer.

Isaac was a DCI; she a lowly constable. He had the brains, the training, the instincts. He had learnt to read body language, the furtive eye movements, the change in voice tone of a defensive person, or someone just telling a plain lie. She hoped he wasn't allowing his overactive libido to get in the way.

She had known Isaac a long time. Almost from the first days when he joined the police force, then in uniform, right up until he changed over to plain clothes and his elevation up through the ranks. She had seen the women he had taken out, the women in the police force who had swooned over him. She knew he was partial to one of the women close to the murdered people, closer than she had seen him with others in the past. She reflected on Detective Superintendent Goddard's comment the other day when he had said 'Again'. She would ask her DCI when this was all over, not sure she would get an answer, maybe a knowing smile, but what use would that be? Perhaps some harmless titillating gossip for her and Bridget to speculate about, over a few drinks. She knew Bridget could keep a secret and would enjoy the story, even daydream that it was her on the receiving end of one of Isaac's amorous advances.

***

Farhan, with only loose ends to deal with, busied himself with the preparations for moving Marjorie Frobisher to the safe house. A suitable location, fifteen miles to the west, seemed ideal. Richard Goddard had approved the cost for a one-month rental on a country cottage. The woman had been precise in the quality required: no one-room apartment, no doss-house, no third-rate accommodation. Farhan had checked it out. It looked suitable for the demanding woman. To him, it looked fantastic. His wife, realising that he was close to her favourite actor, was phoning him, asking for an introduction. He felt he did not need her communication as the divorce was progressing. A solicitor from his side, another from hers, and it was proceeding amicably. He had even managed to see the children a couple of times in the last week.

Aisha was back from her trip out of the capital, hoping to catch up that night if possible, the following if not. Farhan, desperate as he was, realised there was another priority. He had to ensure Marjorie Frobisher was safe and secure. Her husband had taken a shine to him before. Apparently, she had as well. A condition of her transfer was that he was to take responsibility for her safety. He had no option but to agree.

The plan was simple; the execution, not so. The media presence had virtually evaporated, apart from a couple of junior reporters stationed out by the main entrance looking bored: armed only with a camera and a microphone, namely an iPhone. Farhan hoped they would disappear.

First, Marjorie Frobisher would put on a surgical gown. Then she would lie on a stretcher, suitably bandaged, and be taken out to a waiting ambulance. It was to look as if the patient was transferring to another hospital for specialist treatment. Once clear of the hospital and confident of no prying eyes, she would exit the ambulance and get into a car driven by a policeman, the windows tinted. The vehicle would then proceed to the cottage.

Robert Avers was aware of the plan, but he would not be going to the cottage. It was too risky.

Farhan would stay at the cottage with her until she was calm. She had agreed that she would tell Isaac all he needed to know once she was comfortable. Isaac was frustrated by her hesitancy. He could only see permanent protection for her if she revealed what she knew.

If the media was made aware of the facts, then what point would there be in liquidating her. She had told Isaac that the situation was complicated. There were other issues to consider, and Richard Williams had died because of her. She did not want others to die as well. Isaac had noted that she failed to mention Sally Jenkins.

Richard Williams, more crucial to the investigation, remained on a slab at the morgue. His body was not to be released for a few more days.

***

Wendy, a little the worse for wear, left her hotel at eight in the morning. She had slept well but woken with a throbbing headache, although not throbbing enough to deter her from a good English breakfast of two eggs, three bacon rashers and a couple of sausages, washed down with two cups of tea.

Christy Nichols' home address – Farm Cottage, Underbarrow, Cumbria. It lay five miles to the west of where she was staying. It took Wendy twenty-five minutes to drive there. A small village, it consisted of no more than fifty cottages, most of them of a stone construction. A public house stood at the main crossroads.

Wendy had to admit it was a pretty place, somewhere she could live, although she realised the climate in winter would be savage – not conducive to someone with arthritis. She had felt the pain more since venturing north, and while it was only a couple of degrees colder, it made a difference. South, a long way south where the sun shone every day, was where she was heading if the opportunity arose.

Farm Cottage, she found out from a local woman standing on a corner waiting for the bus, was up a narrow, winding lane heading away from the village. 'Don't go up there,' the woman had said.

Wendy had asked why – the answer confusing, unintelligible. She would have pursued the matter, but the bus appeared, and the woman was gone. As she climbed the slight incline towards Farm Cottage, she could see an old farm house and no perceivable activity. She did not want to go in, just to observe.

Ten minutes later, a woman with an old dog at her side appeared at the front of the house.

Wendy stayed for a few hours walking around the area. It was a walker's paradise, and she did not look out of place, apart from her stopping every few minutes for a rest. As lunchtime was approaching, she decided to return to the public house she had seen on her way up. An open fire was blazing inside, even though it was not bitterly cold outside.

'Gives it a cosy feeling,' the landlord said when she asked.

'What do you have to eat?'

'Typical pub lunches. My wife's steak and kidney, or maybe mushroom, if you prefer.'

'Steak and kidney for me. A pint of your best local bitter, as well.'

'These days, it's not local.'

'Your best, anyway.'

'Ten minutes for the pie, the beer straight away.'

Wendy noticed the pub was virtually empty, like pubs up and down the country. The local point of personal interaction supplanted by the world of instant communications and streaming movies on the internet. She missed the old days in many ways. A computer baffled her, a smartphone seemed only useful for making phone calls, the occasional SMS, and as for email, it was fine, but she could see little point in it. The police report she would usually write in long hand, and then ask Bridget to type up, the only cost a little bit of gossip. A small price to pay for such a valued service.

'What brings you up here?' the landlord asked. He was a red-faced man with an extended belly. She instinctively liked him.

'I was on business in Carlisle. I just thought I'd take the opportunity to check out the Lake District.'

'What do you reckon?' he asked. He had joined her with a pint of beer as well. Wendy could see from his appearance that he often had his beefy hand clasped around a pint of beer.

'Very pretty. The winters must be tough up here?'

'Can be. Last year was not so bad. Something to do with global warming, I assume.'

'Probably,' Wendy said.

'Are you a hiker?'

'I used to be.'

'Not now?' he asked. Wendy noticed that he had poured himself another beer, bought another for her. 'On the house,' he said as he put the two beers down on the bar.

'Thanks. Arthritis, unfortunately.'

'I've got a bit myself. It's a nuisance, but that's how it is.'

'I had a stroll up near Farm Cottage.'

'It's grim up there.'

'It seemed pretty enough.'

'Did you see anyone?'

'Just a woman and an old dog.'

'Sad story.' Wendy put her glass of beer down and took off her jacket. The fire in the corner too warm for her.

'What do you mean?'

'Bill Nichols, a strange character, used to come in here occasionally.'

'What about him.'

'Believed in corporal punishment, taking a strap to the kids if they played up.'

'Is that allowed?'

'No, of course not. But it could never be proved. His kids always supported him. Attractive children they were.'

'Where are they now?'

'I've no idea. They disappeared a few years back. The son sometimes comes back to see the mother. The daughter, not seen her since. Pretty young thing, she was.'

'What were the children's names?' Wendy asked.

'Terry, the son. The daughter, Christine, Christy. No, it was Christy. They never said much; fear of a leathering from their father, I suppose.'

'Where's the father now?'

'Dead. Accident, they said.'

'How?' She had resumed her drinking.

'He was more a subsistence farmer. Always believed the old-fashioned ways were the best. He would have used a horse and plough if he could have.'

'Did he?'

'No, but he would have. No profit margin if you don't rely on mechanised farm equipment. He had to use a tractor occasionally. Mind you, he kept a lot of cattle up there, as well.'

'So how did he die?'

'Strange story. He believed in preparing his own fertilisers, pesticides. He would come in here and complain about the prices the companies were charging when he could make them for a fraction.'

Wendy realised the landlord was talking about a subject which interested her greatly.

The first customers since she had entered the pub came in. The landlord left to speak to them, sell them some beer, and ask if they wanted to sample his wife's steak and kidney. They did. Five minutes later, he returned.

'He made a mistake, or at least, that's how it's recorded.'

'Mistake with what?'

'He used to mess around with some nasty poisons, arsenic in particular. It used to be in rat poison, not today, though. Anyway, it appears he's brewing up some rodent killer – accidentally pours some into a glass of water that was sat on his bench in the barn. Dead within minutes, they said.'

'Do you believe it?'

'No reason not to, but this is a small community – people gossip.'

'What did they say, the gossips?'

'That the wife poisoned him, or one of the children.'

'What do you believe?'

'I'm not one for gossip.'

Wendy could see no reason to stay longer in the Lake District. There would be no trouble with her expenses this time. The first thing the next day, she planned to fill out the forms and to get Detective Superintendent Goddard to sign them.

***

It was the first arrest in a case that had gone on for too long. With a clear motive and the knowledge to carry out the murder, Isaac felt he had enough for an arrest.

Farhan knew the address, so he drove. Isaac was the first to enter the small apartment. She was alarmed to see the detective chief inspector, fractionally calmer when she saw Farhan come in behind him. A uniformed policewoman accompanied them.

'Christy Marigold Nichols, I am arresting you on suspicion of the murder of Charles Sutherland.'

The woman, stunned, collapsed to the floor. Farhan lifted her up and sat her on a chair.

'I've done nothing wrong.'

'Would you please accompany us to the station,' Isaac said. It was a time for formality and following the official procedure by the book.

A police car that had followed Farhan and Isaac to Christy's apartment transported her back to the station, where she was officially charged. Her one phone call Farhan made on her behalf to Eileen Kerr, her lawyer.

She arrived soon after, fuming, desperate for reasons for the arrest.

Isaac explained the situation and informed her that a formal interview would be conducted later in the day. If she wished to have additional legal representation, then there was time to arrange it.

The lawyer, realising the situation was serious, hurried down to the holding cell to meet her client. Christy Nichols sat in a foetal position at one end of the rudimentary bed provided. She was incapable of speech. Eileen Kerr requested a doctor. One was supplied.

A strong sedative, and the accused woman subsided into a prolonged sleep.

'Tomorrow,' Eileen Kerr advised. 'I need to take advice from my client and to consider my position. This may require someone more experienced than me.'

Farhan felt a deep sadness for the woman in the cell.

Chapter 38

Isaac did not feel the sadness that Farhan felt – he felt relief. Christy Nichols who, according to Wendy, had had a turbulent childhood; mitigating circumstances would obviously be put forward in a trial. At least, the defence would put them forward, but murder was murder. The guilty had to pay for their crime, whether the murdered person was despicable or the childhood of the accused atrocious.

Wendy had been jubilant on her return from the north. Christy Nichols was in the cells before she had caught the train back to London. Now came the hard part, at least for her, the writing up of her report. She knew Bridget would not refuse to help.

According to Farhan, Christy Nichols was not handling the situation well, protesting her innocence. He had been to visit her; check she was okay. Apart from needing a shower and a change of clothes, she appeared confused. Farhan arranged for a policewoman to visit her home and obtain what she required.

Isaac felt confident that Jess O'Neill was innocent of one murder.

He had decided to tell Jess if she asked about Linda Harris, tell her if she didn't. He could always say it was in the course of duty, but he thought it a lame excuse. When would sleeping with someone be an acceptable part of a criminal investigation? He knew why he had slept with her – because he wanted to and because she was available.

As he picked up the phone to make the call, it rang. 'Isaac, MacTavish wants to see us,' Richard Goddard said.

'When?' Isaac asked.

'Now,' the reply.

Five minutes later, both were downstairs waiting for a car. Twenty minutes later, they were in Angus MacTavish's office. The man was in a jubilant mood. Isaac did not like it; he saw trouble. A possible attempt to interfere with the normal process of law.

Mrs Gregory had entered on their arrival, given Isaac a friendly smile and the choice piece of home-made cake with his cup of tea. He thanked her for her kindness.

'Great work,' MacTavish said. Richard Goddard accepted the compliment on his department's behalf.

'This wraps up the murders?' MacTavish continued.

Isaac replied, 'Only Sutherland's.'

'What about the others?'

'We do not believe they were committed by the person in custody.'

'Why not?' MacTavish asked.

'No motive.'

'But she's a murderer? Does she need any more motive?'

Isaac realised that MacTavish knew his statement was illogical; knew that MacTavish wanted the loose ends tying up, and the truth was dispensable.

'She'll never be convicted of the other two murders,' Detective Superintendent Goddard said.

'Why not?' MacTavish persisted.

'She had a clear motive for Sutherland. She never met Richard Williams and Sally Jenkins.'

Angus MacTavish stood up, turned his back on the two policemen. He faced the window. 'Officially, we need to wrap it up here.'

'The reason?' Richard Goddard asked. His promotion was due to be confirmed in a couple of days. A wrong word and he knew what would happen.

'Too many questions being asked.'

'Are you asking us to break the law? Conceal a crime?' Isaac asked.

'It's not up to me. It comes under the Official Secrets Act.'

'It's a whitewash,' Isaac said in an unchecked outburst.

'You've heard of the Civil Contingencies Act? MacTavish, now facing them, said.

'Our version of the American's Patriot Act,' Richard Goddard replied.

'We're invoking it.'

'We!' Isaac said.

'The elected government of this country. The people charged with the responsibility of knowing what's best for the people – that "WE".'

'We're condoning murder here. You realise that?' Isaac was angry and on his feet. All this time: three deaths, one solved, two to be pushed aside.

'I understand your concern, but the national interest is more important.'

Isaac resumed his seat. 'Are you confirming that two of the murders were committed by people employed in Her Majesty's service?'

'Not at all,' MacTavish replied. 'All I'm saying is that there are to be no further attempts to find a culprit for those two murders.'

'We admit we failed – case closed. Is that it?'

'Either you charge the woman you have in custody with the three murders, and make it stick, or else you state… State whatever you like: Suicide, lover's pact, whatever, but drop it.'

'This is contrary to what people expect of their government and their police.'

'For Christ's sake, Goddard.' MacTavish looked away from Isaac and directed his gaze at Isaac's boss. 'Your promotion is on the line, my career as well. Sometimes it's necessary to make decisions for the people regardless of what they expect.'

'Understood, sir,' Isaac said, although he felt uncomfortable with MacTavish's outburst.

As they drove back to Challis Street, both saying little, both still stunned by the meeting, Detective Superintendent Goddard leant in Isaac's direction. 'Are you going to follow MacTavish's directive?'

'Do you expect me to, sir?'

'I expect you to act as a policeman.'

'Your promotion?'

'Does MacTavish talk for the government or his own vested interests?'

'I don't know, sir.'

'Neither do I. I've not received any instructions from my superiors at New Scotland Yard. Until then, we continue. If my career is down the drain, so be it. We can't give up, just because a blustering Scotsman tells us to.'

'This could get dangerous.'

'I know that. What about Marjorie Frobisher?'

'We're moving her soon.'

'Make it happen today. And make sure she is safe. Her best defence, ours as well, is if she talks.'

***

Farhan, updated on the situation in a quick phone call from Isaac, moved the date for the transfer forward. The two remaining reporters stationed at the hospital had fortunately left. Robert Avers, tired of waiting for something to happen, and in need of solace, had apparently left for his young lover.

That was what he had told Farhan, although it was more likely he had tired of his wife's constant need for attention, the celebrity variety, of which she had been starved for so many weeks.

Doesn't the woman get it? Farhan had thought the last time he spoke to her. *Her life is under threat, and she still wants to act the prima donna.*

As the planned evacuation from the hospital to the cottage commenced, one of the formerly bored and uninterested reporters reappeared at the critical moment.

He saw Farhan dressed as a male nurse. Quickly, he was on the phone to his superiors.

Exiting the rear of the hospital with the woman, Farhan, oblivious to the drama at the front, continued. The vehicle left as planned, unaware that a short distance behind them followed a motorbike, its rider helmeted.

'We're being followed,' the driver of the ambulance said.

Farhan looked out of the small rear window of the ambulance – the driver was correct.

Not sure what to do, he phoned Isaac, who assigned a police car to pull over the motorcycle, minor traffic infraction if required. It was five miles before the motorcycle was stopped. Changing the original changeover location presented no problem.

Marjorie Frobisher transferred to the police car and headed out to the cottage.

'I don't like it,' she said on arrival. To Farhan, it was charming and unique – a slice of heaven. Way out of his price bracket, way in hers.

'We need to keep you safe.'

'Here! I don't see how.'

'It's isolated. We have people in the area keeping a watch.'

'What is my life worth? I hide away for weeks, and then I'm brought to this.'

'Why were you hiding?'

'My life.'

'Then why complain? We're trying to protect you.'

'I know that. Very well, I'll talk to DCI Cook.'

***

Richard Goddard had received confirmation that his promotion was proceeding. He was soon to be a detective chief superintendent, not an assistant commissioner, as MacTavish had intimated. He realised it may take him away from homicide, possibly into more of an administrative role. It did not concern him unduly, but the current case did.

The promotion was verbal, not documented, and he knew why. It was conditional on a satisfactory outcome. He sensed the hand of MacTavish, although the police were meant to be independent. He was aware that the murders of Williams and Sally Jenkins may need to be covered up – it would not be the first time that national security had overridden the normal function of the police. The concern this time: that it wasn't national security, purely an indiscretion of someone in power.

He knew he needed to let Isaac run his race, hope that he made the right decisions. If Marjorie Frobisher's information was dynamite, what to do with it? What would Isaac do? Keep it under cover, release snippets of it to the press?

Soon-to-be Detective Chief Superintendent Goddard could see that it was not over yet, not by a long shot. He needed to talk to his DCI.

He phoned Isaac, who was on his way out to the cottage. He had taken a circuitous route, hopeful that he wasn't being followed. It would not have been an issue before, but now the press, alerted after the observant reporter had seen the events at the hospital, were speculating as to what was afoot.

'Isaac, we need to talk.'

'I'm on my way to meet with Marjorie Frobisher,' Isaac responded on hands-free.

'Let me know what she says.'

'Of course.'

'We need to consider how to progress.'

'What do you mean?'

'Is it national security? Do we comply with MacTavish or not?'

'I thought we had decided to press on,' Isaac said, a little perturbed at his boss's changed attitude.

'We have. We need to know the truth, but the national interest…'

'National interest? I would have thought that was best served by the truth.'

'Ordinarily, I would agree.'

'But now?'

'Find out what she says first. We'll discuss the implications afterwards. That's all I'm saying. I'm not asking you to hold back, just exercise caution.'

Isaac did not enjoy the conversation very much. It sounded as though his boss had gone soft.

***

Isaac found Marjorie Frobisher not in a good mood when he arrived at the cottage. He decided to ignore her complaints. The information she held was what he wanted. If it was as controversial as the events of the past few months indicated, then he was not sure what to do.

He was a policeman who was possibly about to be asked to commit an illegal act; namely, the covering up of two murders, purely because they were professional assassinations. Richard Williams did not concern him as much as Sally Jenkins. He had seen her distraught parents at the funeral, especially her mother. They deserved the truth. He could envisage their reaction to a verdict of murder by an ex-lover. That was what Isaac saw as the most likely wrap up to the case. He couldn't agree, couldn't see that he could do much about it.

Christy Nichols still needed to make an official statement, and they couldn't hold her for much longer. Once finished with Marjorie Frobisher, he intended to conduct the interview with Sutherland's alleged murderer. The evidence seemed too strong to believe otherwise.

'Miss Frobisher, are you ready to tell us the truth?' Isaac asked on his arrival at her hideaway.

'Yes.'

'You are aware that your reluctance to come forward has cost the life of several people?'

'Not Charles Sutherland.'

'No, that is clear. We believe his death is not related.'

'But Richard's is.'

'Yes, that appears to be the case, as well as Sally Jenkins. We've discussed this before.'

'I'm sorry about Richard. He was a good man, a good friend.'

'He was more than that, wasn't he?'

'We lived together in the past.'

'And recently?'

'We looked out for each other. If I had not become so close to Richard, if I had not told him what I'm about to tell you, he would still be alive.'

'That's hindsight. We can only deal with the future.'

'And what will happen to you? You're a policeman. Will they force you to keep quiet? Cover it up. Allow me to be killed.'

She had hit the nail on the head. How would he react? How would anyone react in the same situation? He had no answer that would suffice.

'I'm sworn to uphold the law.' Isaac knew it was a clichéd reply. He was surprised he had uttered it.

Farhan prepared some coffee. It was clear the woman could become emotional. A policewoman stood to one side.

'When I was younger, I formed a relationship with a man.'

'How young?'

'I was sixteen. He was eighteen.'

'Where did you meet?'

'At a school dance.'

'There seems to be nothing wrong in that.'

'There wasn't, although it was before the pill and loose morals.'

'You slept with him?'

'Up against a wall. I'd hardly call that sleep. It was just too people, children really, screwing. No point pretending it was anything more.'

'Then what?' Isaac asked.

'We used to meet up every few days. Don't attempt to imagine it was a typical romance. It was sex, whether in the park, or his school dormitory, or the back of a local cinema.'

'Did you like the man?'

'Yes. And he liked me, but we were different.'

'In what way?'

'I was middle class. He was upper, a member of the aristocracy. I was Mavis Sidebottom, daughter of a successful shopkeeper.'

'No meeting of each other's parents?'

'He wanted to meet mine, but I never introduced him.'

'Any reason why?'

'I could see the reality. I was fond of him, as he was of me, but there was no future.'

'What do you mean?'

'It was a long time ago. The class structure was much stronger then. The daughter of a shopkeeper and the son of a Lord would not have been considered a suitable match. That's for the movies, not real life. Maybe today, but not then.'

'The romance ended?'

'There was a complication.'

'A child?'

'People just didn't think about the risk of pregnancy. Assumed it wouldn't happen to them.'

'What did the father do?'

'Married me quickly in Gretna Green, and then told his father, the Lord.'

'What happened?'

'Paid my father to hush it up. I spent six months hidden from the world in a convent. Once it was born, it was taken from me.'

'And what became of the child?'

'For many years, I never knew.'

'When did you find out?'

'One year ago.'

'Did you contact the child?'

'No. It was such a long time ago; I didn't feel any connection.'

'Is the child the reason these murders have occurred? The reason you are frightened?'

'When I found out who the child was.'

'Who is this child?'

'If you know, you are at risk.'

'What about the father?'

'He doesn't want it known who the child is.'

'You've spoken to him?'

'I tried, but he hung the phone up on me.'

Isaac could see it was going to be a long day. He still had Christy Nichols to deal with, as well as Jess, who was anxious to see him.

The search for Linda Harris had been abandoned. Angus MacTavish had contacted him with the news that she had been assigned overseas. Isaac accepted the truth. There still remained the issue as to who had killed Richard Williams, the assumption that Linda Harris had come in the front door, while the assassin had gone out the back. If it had not been Linda, surely they would have reported the dead body rather than leave it to Farhan and Wendy to find.

Linda Harris, now clearly identified as MI5, would not have wanted to report the murder. That may well have warranted a closer inspection into her background.

Farhan phoned for some food to be delivered from a restaurant down the road. It was only pizzas – Marjorie Frobisher complained.

The interview resumed at two in the afternoon. Farhan asked the first question. 'Does your husband know about the child?'

'No. I never told him.'

'Is he safe?' Isaac asked.

'Those who want to silence me will not harm him.'

'Are you convinced that your life is in danger?'

'They killed Richard, didn't they?'

'Why would they do that? Why not you?'

'You couldn't find me, neither could they.'

'That's true, but now you're visible.'

'I couldn't disappear forever. I'd rather be dead than continue to live as a hermit.'

'Were you?'

'Was I what?'

'Living as a hermit.'

'Almost. Before I went to Malvern, a remote place up north.'

'Yours.'

'It belonged to my father. A fishing shack, nothing else. Nobody knew about it, not even Richard Williams.'

'Why?'

'His protection, not that it did him much good. He still ended up dead.'

'You're safe here,' Isaac said.

The woman made a disparaging gesture, shrugged her shoulders. 'I'm not safe here. If they want me dead, they'll find a way.'

'The police are protecting you now.'

'And the police could be called away, told to turn a blind eye.'

'Why would we do that?' Isaac asked.

'National security.'

'Who is this child? I need to know.'

'Ask Angus MacTavish. He'll tell you.'

The statement came as a surprise. MacTavish had always been suspect, but he was now directly implicated. Isaac needed to contact his boss.

Isaac wrapped up the interview, stating that he needed to take advice. She had not been willing to make any more comments, after revealing MacTavish as a key person.

'I'll be back tomorrow,' Isaac said as he put on his coat.

295

'If I'm still here.'

'Farhan will stay.'

It had been the night that Farhan had intended to meet up with Aisha. He had no alternative, but to comply. He hoped Aisha would understand.

***

Isaac's initial reaction to Marjorie Frobisher's comment was to ask to meet his boss, but he realised this was not the most important issue.

One murder investigation had to be wrapped up. Eileen Kerr, Christy Nichol's legal representative, was in the building and acting on advice from her client, she would be the sole person with the woman at the interview.

Farhan would normally have been with Isaac in the interview room, but he was out protecting Marjorie Frobisher. Wendy was delegated in his place.

Their boss chose to observe through a one-way window into the interview room – a room that was pleasant enough under normal circumstances, dreary under any other. The accused was led in, a policewoman accompanying her. Wendy felt sorry for her but did not let it show.

Christy Nichols was very pale, her head bent, avoiding eye contact. Her legal representative, Eileen Kerr, touched her on the arm in a gesture of reassurance and friendship.

'Could you please state your name.' Isaac had started the recording, both video and audio.

'Christy Marigold Nichols.'

'You are charged with the murder of Charles Sutherland.'

'I did not kill him. I hated him, but not enough to kill him.'

'Charles Sutherland died due to ingesting a lethal dose of arsenic.'

'I did not give it to him.'

'But you knew about the effects of arsenic. Is that correct?'

'Why would I know that?'

Wendy, on a prearranged cue from Isaac, spoke. 'Your father died of arsenic poisoning.'

'Yes.'

'Then you know of the effects of arsenic?' Isaac took over again.

'He used it for rat killer.'

'You were questioned at the time of his death?'

'We all were.'

Wendy spoke again. 'I visited the village where you lived. I saw a woman at the house.'

'My mother.'

'Your relationship with your mother?'

'There is no relationship.'

'Why is that?' Isaac asked. 'Because of the death of your father?'

'No.'

'Then why?'

'She never protected me from him.'

'Him?'

'My father.'

'What did he do?'

'He beat us and...'

'Did he abuse you?'

'Sometimes. When he was drunk.'

'And that was often? Isaac asked. Eileen Kerr asked for an adjournment. Isaac refused.

'This abuse?' Wendy asked. 'We need to know.'

'He used to touch me.'

'Sexual intercourse?' Isaac had to ask.

'No. He wanted to touch me. He wanted me to touch him.'

'And you did?'

'If I didn't, he would beat me.'

'And your mother?'

'She let him.'

'She was there?'

'No, but she could have told someone, done something.'

'Why didn't you report it?'

'I was scared. If no one believed me, he would have beat me more.'

Wendy started to choke up. She had heard the story before when she had been looking for missing children. How many times, the father abusing the pretty daughter? How many times had the child been returned to the parents, their accusations dismissed? One child had been returned against her will. She had ended up dead, had hanged herself with a length of rope in her bathroom at home. Wendy, in her darkest moments, thought back to that girl.

Isaac had one question to ask, a crucial question, but it would have to wait. The accused was in no condition to continue. Her legal support argued for an adjournment. He had no option but to comply. The interview was to resume in sixty minutes.

Isaac met his boss in the adjoining room.

'What do you reckon?' Isaac asked.

'What are you trying to make her admit to? The murder of her father or Charles Sutherland?'

'Either, both.'

'Fine. Play it carefully. The father, she could get off on a technicality. It's an old case, recorded as death by misadventure. Proving that will not be so easy.'

'I realise that. I just need to break her denial.'

'Pretty woman. A shame, really.'

'Pretty, as you say, but we're here to solve a murder.'

'I understand that.'

Isaac was still anxious to discuss the other matter; his boss, not so keen.

'MacTavish?' Isaac asked.

'Wrap this up, and then we'll discuss it. Marjorie Frobisher's comment complicates the situation.'

'Why?'

'How did she know Angus MacTavish? He's not indicated this before.'

'Maybe he's not met her. Maybe someone else did.'

'Wrap Sutherland's murder up. We'll discuss MacTavish later.'

'Yes, sir.' Isaac knew it was the best he could expect.

***

Christy Nichols looked composed when she returned to the interview room. Isaac went through the formal restarting of the interview. Richard Goddard watched from outside. Wendy said little.

'It is evident,' Isaac stated calmly,' that you are aware of the effects of arsenic poisoning. Will you admit to that?'

'I knew my father used it to kill rats.'

'Did you hate your father?'

'What do you think?'

'Miss Nichols, please answer the question.'

'I hated him for what he did to me, what he made me do.'

'Enough to kill him?'

'I wished him dead.'

'You had the means and the knowledge.'

Eileen Kerr spoke, 'You are attempting to force my client to admit to a crime that the police have officially declared closed – death by misadventure.'

Isaac was careful how he proceeded. 'Charles Sutherland made Miss Nichols, by her own admission, commit an act that her father had made her do. My purpose is to establish whether the level of hate she felt for Sutherland was the same as she felt for her father.'

'I hated Sutherland. He brought back all those memories. Memories I had suppressed.'

'Memories so vivid that you saw your father standing there, not Charles Sutherland.'

'Yes. Of course I did.'

'And knowing this, you determined to kill him?'

'No.'

'I am putting it to you that you went back to his room, acted amorously, and ensured he drank the poison.'

'That's not true. You're trying to make me say it.'

Wendy felt that Isaac had overstepped the mark, but he had told her to keep quiet. Eileen Kerr wanted to speak, but could not, insistent as Isaac was on maintaining the pressure.

There was only one flaw that he could see. Where had she procured the arsenic? He decided to proceed. He was certain she was guilty. The issue of the arsenic would resolve itself later.

'Miss Nichols. You had the motive and the knowledge, and you are the only person with a sufficiently strong motive. You are guilty. Your continual denial will only worsen the case against you.'

'Are you saying I killed my father as well?'

'Did you? We can always reopen that case.'

'He was a bastard.'

'Who was?'

'My father.'

'Is that why you killed him?'

Isaac had seen it before. The moment where the accused decides to ease their conscience.

'That was an accident. I saw him do it.'

'It gave you the idea.'

'The man was obnoxious. He made me swallow it.'

'Which man?' Isaac asked.

'Sutherland.' A one-word reply.

'Is that when you decided to kill him?'

'Not then. Later.'

'Why later?'

'I had to get some arsenic.'

'You had some?'

'At my apartment.'

'Why?'

'I'm not sure. It reminded me of what killed my father,' she said. Isaac could see a plea of diminished responsibility.

'Christy Marigold Nichols. Are you admitting to the murder of Charles Sutherland?'

'I'm glad I did it. Yes, I killed him, the horrible man.'

Eileen Kerr sat back on her chair, her arms folded. Wendy held a handkerchief to her eyes to conceal the tears welling up. Isaac, who should have been feeling a degree of smugness, satisfaction on a job well done, felt neither.

Richard Goddard was delighted, congratulated Isaac on his good police work. Isaac accepted the congratulations.

Sometime after, once the written statement had been dealt with, and Christy Nichols had been returned to her cell, Isaac came back to Marjorie Frobisher's comment.

Chapter 39

'What about Marjorie Frobisher?' Isaac asked in the comfort of Richard Goddard's office.

'What about her?'

'Her relationship to Angus MacTavish.'

'She mentioned his name. What does it mean?' The detective superintendent asked.

'I don't know what it means. She has dangled the carrot in front of us. Do we take it?'

'What do you want me to do?'

'Confront MacTavish.'

'And if he denies it?'

'We'll cross that hurdle when we come to it.'

'Is there anyone we can trust?'

'Nobody.' Isaac saw the truth in his senior's question. Who could be trusted? Marjorie Frobisher? Angus MacTavish? To Isaac, there was no clear road forward, only possibilities, lies, and more lies. He knew that he would need to make decisions that could solve the case or not – his career he saw as barely viable. Whatever happened, it appeared as if he would be on the wrong side of someone or something. If Angus MacTavish was hiding something, how to get him to open up? And what about Linda Harris? He had slept with her. Did she murder Williams, and then stage the open back door at his house?

Isaac remembered that there was one other issue to consider – Sally Jenkins. She had been murdered, and on the face of it by someone she knew. Someone who had not sexually violated her. If it was someone she knew, it could only be Richard Williams. If it was female, then Linda Harris.

Isaac could not see Williams as the murdering type, but then he didn't envisage Linda Harris in that role either. All his years of policing, training, and profiling and still he got it wrong. It concerned him that he still made mistakes. Mistakes that had resulted in deaths in the past. But what of the future? Would Marjorie Frobisher be another one if he acted inappropriately?

Only one man knew the answers. Isaac decided that he needed to see MacTavish, and if his boss was unwilling, he would go on his own.

***

Marjorie Frobisher anxiously paced around the cottage. Farhan kept to one side, letting her rant and rave. The situation was tense. She couldn't stay in the cottage; she couldn't leave.

Farhan realised that she was a difficult woman. His wife idolised her, or, at least, the character she portrayed. He wondered how his wife would react if she saw the reality. Would she be able to separate the actor from the person or would she be disillusioned? It was a moot point. He knew that he had to do something to calm their key witness down. If she left, how long would she remain alive? Both he and Isaac were convinced her life was at risk. If she stayed, would she keep hitting the bottle of vodka? *Either it's death by assassin or death by alcoholic poisoning*, he thought.

There was nothing in her records that indicated abuse of alcohol, but Farhan thought that it was another fact about the woman that had been carefully concealed.

'You need to stay. It's just too dangerous out there,' Farhan had said.

Sober, she had agreed. Now, he was not so certain. She was not there charged with any crime; she was free to come and go as she pleased.

He contacted Isaac for advice. 'She's difficult.'

'She must stay.' Isaac said, not entirely focussed on his DI's concerns. He had made the decision to phone MacTavish direct.

MacTavish's first action, after agreeing to Isaac's request, was to phone Richard Goddard. He was in Isaac's office within five minutes.

'What right have you to contact MacTavish?'

'What option did I have?'

'It was my call.'

'I agree, but your position is on the line. I'm expendable; you're not,' Isaac said.

'You're no more expendable than I am, but you don't know who or what you're dealing with. 'MacTavish is the government whip. He's got the dirt on everyone.'

'Everyone?'

'Everyone of importance. He's known all along.'

'You've known this?' Isaac asked, surprised at this revelation.

'I've always suspected it. Marjorie Frobisher's statement confirms it.'

'So what do we do?' Isaac asked.

'We go and see MacTavish.'

'Someone has to tell us something. Who do you suggest?'

'MacTavish, if he'll talk. The woman, if he doesn't.'

'I don't like this. I'm meant to be a policeman. This is out of my league.'

'And mine.'

'And what about Marjorie Frobisher?' Isaac asked.

'Tell DI Ahmed to restrain her by force if he has to.'

'She won't like it.'

'What do I care. Three people are dead as a direct result of her great secret. What she wants is of little concern. I'll not have her death on my conscience,' Detective Superintendent Goddard said.

***

Life out at the production lot had returned to a semblance of normality. The soap opera was to continue, murders or no murders – the ratings and the revenues decreed it.

It had been an awkward phone call. Isaac wasn't sure how to respond when Jess O'Neill called him. 'I'm running the show now. I've assumed Richard Williams' position as executive producer,' she said. Isaac heard no malice in her voice. 'You have someone charged with Charles Sutherland's murder. It's on the internet.'

'That's true.'

'They're also saying she murdered her father as well.'

'That's pure supposition. We're not pursuing that possibility.'

303

'If I didn't kill Sutherland, am I free now? Are you?'

'Probably, but I need another few days.'

'To come up with a suitable excuse as to why you slept with Linda Harris.'

'No…' He knew he stuttered the reply.

'Maybe there was a reason. I'll forgive you this time, but next…'

Isaac sensed a woman looking for a long-term relationship, a ring on the finger. He shuddered at the thought, smiled at the possibility. He also knew that every time they argued in the future, she would bring up Linda Harris.

'I need to tie up loose ends. We're not sure how to proceed.'

'Marjorie Frobisher?' she asked.

'Yes.'

'You're hiding her?'

'Everybody seems to know that.'

'Is she being difficult?'

'We're more difficult.'

'Best of luck. This weekend, can we meet?' she asked.

'It's a date,' he said.

'Not a police interview?' she joked.

'No, it's a date.'

'At last.'

'Ian Stanley. How is he? Now that you're in charge.'

'Sycophantic.'

'That bad?' Isaac replied.

'That bad!' she acknowledged.

***

The only friendly face was Mrs Gregory. Angus MacTavish was neither welcoming nor friendly. Isaac thought he was under pressure. His boss thought he was his usual self. The atmosphere in MacTavish's office matched the weather outside – cold and dark, threatening thunder.

'Detective Superintendent Goddard, why am I receiving phone calls from your junior? Don't you have your people under control?'

'DCI Cook is frustrated with the current situation.'

'Don't you have protocols where you are? If he has an issue, he should take it up with you.'

'He did, but he decided to act against my advice.'

'That sounds like a disciplinary matter.'

'It will be addressed at a later time.'

'DCI Cook, what do you want from me?' MacTavish, in his usual manner, had stood up and leant forward over the desk. It was meant to intimidate – it succeeded, at least with Isaac's boss. With Isaac, it had little effect.

Isaac knew his career was on the line, but no amount of blustering by the senior government official was going to dissuade him. He needed to know, and it was clear that MacTavish knew.

'Marjorie Frobisher mentioned your name.'

'I've never met the woman,' MacTavish replied.

'We know that's not true, sir.'

'Maybe at some function or other.'

'Do you know her, other than that?'

'No.'

'She said that you were the person to speak to regarding this secret.'

'Which secret?' MacTavish asked. Isaac could see his face reddening with anger.

'The child.'

'I told you I knew about a child. I've never given any indication that I know who it is.' MacTavish resumed his seat and sat back in a confident manner, assured that he had allayed their concerns, hidden the truth.

Isaac knew the situation; he knew the body language. He recognised a lie. Not sure how to proceed, he fumbled forward. MacTavish was a powerful man, and powerful men had people behind them, supporting them verbally and physically. Not that he was frightened of the man, but he wanted Marjorie Frobisher to remain alive, and the truth to be revealed. A politician may regard the truth as a luxury; he, as a policeman did not.

'If the truth was known,' Isaac asked, 'would it be catastrophic?'

'Yes,' MacTavish replied.

'To certain persons?'

'To this country.'

'Is the truth better revealed?' Richard Goddard asked.

'No.' A one-word answer.

'Mr MacTavish, this cannot continue,' Isaac said. 'Respectfully, you know what is going on. We need to know.'

'Why?'

'We have three murders. One has been solved, the other two still remain unsolved.'

'They are not to be solved.' MacTavish again, on his feet. Mrs Gregory put her head around the door to offer tea or coffee. He unexpectedly snapped at her. She retreated.

'We can't cover up murders,' Richard Goddard said. 'Police procedures won't allow it.'

'Then change the procedures.'

'But why?' Isaac asked. 'And what do we call them?'

'Call them whatever you like.'

'And the truth?' Isaac asked.

'Williams was ordered. The other woman, probably.'

'This is England. We can't do that.' Isaac protested.

'Not only will you, but you will also do it today; tomorrow at the latest.'

'Marjorie Frobisher?'

'She's a marked woman.'

'Why?'

'You're both subject to the Official Secrets Act. You're both serving members of the Metropolitan Police. You will both do as you are told.'

***

Farhan, updated soon after the meeting with MacTavish, had his own problems. Marjorie Frobisher was not going to stay where she was.

'She has phoned her husband.'

'Does she know she's a dead woman?' Isaac asked.

'She knows. She regards her current life as a living death. She says she would rather be out there with her people.'

'Where is she now?'

'Still here, but Robert Avers is coming. I can't stop her, not anymore.'

'You're right. Maybe she is better off in her own home.'

'What do you mean?'

'There's no resolution to this. If she's out there, it may help.'

'She may be killed.'

'What else can we do?' Isaac said.

***

Isaac realised the weekend with Jess was unlikely, and Farhan was none too pleased either. Both knew they had no other option but to comply, but unless something changed then Marjorie Frobisher would be dead, their careers, at least Isaac's, down the drain, and two murders would remain unsolved, three if Marjorie Frobisher died as well.

Robert Avers had picked her up and taken her to their house. Farhan followed at a discreet distance.

Isaac realised that Angus MacTavish was the problem. He wondered if he was the mysterious father, but discounted it. MacTavish had grown up in Scotland, and besides, he was several years younger than the woman. They needed to check out the schools that Marjorie Frobisher had attended. It was fair to assume a school dance would focus on schools within the area. It was an angle they had not pursued before, because that piece of information had only just come from the woman herself.

It was clear that Wendy was needed again. Isaac, in the meantime, would see if Marjorie Frobisher would give him the name of the father.

The next day, Wendy, in a remarkably jubilant mood, appeared in the office.

'We need to know who this man is,' Isaac said.

'You want me to check out some schools?'

'Yes.'

'If they're still there. It's forty years.'

'The records must still exist.'

It seemed difficult for Wendy to claim for an expensive hotel this time. Mavis Sidebottom, the childhood name of Marjorie

Frobisher, had grown up in a village to the west of London, less than a forty-minute drive. The records clearly stated that she had attended St George's Boarding and Day School between the ages of 11 and 18, apart from a brief period of absence during her penultimate year. The dates aligned with her unexpected confinement.

It was also clear, as Wendy drove past Marjorie Frobisher's childhood home, that the middle-class childhood, the daughter of a humble shopkeeper, was a fabrication. The father had been a shopkeeper, but a shopkeeper of several hardware stores and the home had been a substantial two-storey house in a better part of the village. The school was for those financially able to pay. It had been a girls' school for over one hundred years, and before that a boys' school. The headmistress took delight in informing Wendy that for two years Winston Churchill had been a pupil.

The records, meticulously kept and preserved in a vault beneath the main building, were opened at Wendy's request. The vault was a treasure trove of history: full of artefacts and sporting cups, and among them, records of school dances.

Miss Home, an elderly and retiring woman, charged with recording the history of the school, opened up the relevant documents. They clearly showed that during the dates concerned, there were two school dances. Those attending from St George's and two boys' schools were recorded.

Wendy took copies of the documents to study. There seemed little purpose in visiting the other schools until the names had been checked out. She managed to treat herself to a nice lunch on expenses before she returned to London.

It was late afternoon when she walked into the office at Challis Street. Isaac was there. His day had been involved with going through all the aspects of the case, attempting to wrap it up, trying to figure out who killed who, and why?

'I need to check out these names,' Wendy said. Farhan not being there, she pushed her desk over into his area. Isaac could clearly smell stale cigarette smoke.

'Any names we know?' Isaac moved over towards her desk, sat on Farhan's chair.

'What are we looking for?'

'Member of the aristocracy; member of the government.'

'Aristocracy will have the family name, not the title,' Wendy said.

'True. I'll leave it to you.' He moved back to his chair.

***

Marjorie Frobisher, back at her home, apparently oblivious of the situation or choosing to ignore it, was making herself known to her adoring public. An impromptu interview on the steps of the house to the assembled media – according to Isaac, sheer stupidity.

Farhan had asked her to stay at home, but he had been overruled. She had breezed into her favourite restaurant as if she was the all-conquering heroine, back from doing battle, rather than the frightened woman who had run away and hidden. It seemed to be an act; an act she managed with great aplomb.

Isaac, regardless of her condition on returning from the restaurant, felt the need to confront her. Farhan had warned him that her condition was far from conducive to that. Isaac thought it might be opportune, as with a few drinks, she may be more willing to talk.

'Miss Frobisher, I need to know who the father is,' Isaac said as he sat in the front room of her house in Belgravia. She was clearly drunk, clearly in need of attention. Isaac was pleased that Farhan was with him, although judging by the lecherous look in the woman's eye, he was not sure it was safe even then.

'Forget about him.'

'Do you feel bitterness towards him?'

'Why should I?'

'You have spent a long time in hiding. Your life is at risk because of him.'

'It's not him.'

'Then who?'

'I told you before. Ask Angus MacTavish.' Isaac could see it was pointless. Robert Avers had taken himself off to the other room, apparently disgusted at her condition. It was evident she was not going to give Isaac a name. It was up to Wendy to find the father.

Once the father was identified, the son would soon be revealed. Isaac continued to deliberate as to who the son was, and why he was so important. Without a name, it was pointless speculation, and Marjorie Frobisher was of no use.

Wendy, meanwhile, excited at the prospect of success, had stayed late in the office. Normally, she would leave for home at six in the evening, but it was way past eleven, close to midnight, and still she laboured over the computer.

She admitted to no great computer skills, but she was proficient with Google. She was pleased that Isaac had agreed to come back to the office at her request.

'I've found him,' she said the moment he walked in.

'Congratulations. Who is he?'

'He's not a Lord.'

'What do you mean?'

'He inherited the title on the death of his father.'

'And?'

'The Peerage Act of 1963.'

'What does that mean?'

'Prior to it being enacted into law, no member of the House of Lords could take a seat as an elected Member of Parliament. He was able to renounce the title.'

'Marjorie Frobisher referred to him as a Lord.'

'That's what people call him. Technically, he's not.'

'Are you saying it's who I think it is?'

'Yes, there's only one person.'

Chapter 40

'I did not kill Richard.' It was not what Isaac expected to hear on picking up his phone at one o'clock in the morning.

'Where are you?' Hearing Linda Harris's voice again reminded Isaac of the guilt he felt over the night they spent together; the pleasure they had mutually enjoyed, but mainly the guilt.

'I am not in England.'

'Then why phone?'

'I just wanted you to know. Under different circumstances, we could have been something more.'

'I don't see how,' Isaac responded.

'We're very much alike.'

'Are we?'

'Yes. We are both ambitious.'

'I work for an organisation that tries to save lives,' Isaac said. 'Yours apparently condones death when it's in the national interest.'

'I was there to find out where Marjorie Frobisher was, nothing more.'

'Is her life in danger?'

'Probably.'

'Because of what she knows?' Isaac, regardless of his initial trepidation, was enjoying the conversation.

'Yes.'

'What does she know?'

'I never knew. I'm relatively junior. They never told me.'

'They?'

'My superiors.'

'Do they have a name?'

'I am not authorised to tell you.'

'Who is?'

'I don't know. I just wanted to phone and say I was sorry; to let you know that I did not kill Richard.'

'Sally Jenkins?' Isaac asked.

'She knew too much.'

'Are you saying you killed her?'

'Someone else did.'

'Who?'

'Richard.'

'Why?'

'She was blackmailing him, threatening to go to the newspapers.'

'About what?'

'Marjorie Frobisher. He did it to protect her.'

'You provided him with an alibi.'

'Yes.'

'Were you with him that night?'

'Some of it, but not in his bed.' With that, she hung up. Isaac, shocked by what he had been told, sat down for a couple of minutes to compose himself.

***

Richard Goddard, woken up from a deep slumber in the early hours of the morning, was initially angry. Upon hearing Isaac's voice, he moved to another room.

'Sally Jenkins was not assassinated,' Isaac said.

Isaac recounted the phone conversation with Linda Harris.

Goddard listened calmly. 'How do we handle this?' he asked.

'It's clear that Richard Williams knew, as did Sally Jenkins.'

'Can we prove that Sally Jenkins was murdered by Richard Williams?'

'The evidence is circumstantial. We'll never be able to prove it.'

'Are you sure?'

'Richard Williams had been in Sally Jenkins' place on many occasions. His DNA, fingerprints are everywhere. There's nothing conclusively tying him to the night of her death,' Isaac said.

'Apart from Linda Harris.' Richard Goddard realised, as did Isaac, that she was not going to come forward to point the blame at Williams. 'So how do we record it?'

'Crime unsolved, I suppose.'

'What about Richard Williams?'

'It appears to be a professional assassination. It doesn't make sense. Williams kills to keep the secret, and then he is shot because he knows it.'

'It's clear that he was not about to reveal it.'

'If Marjorie Frobisher had been liquidated, he may have.'
'Are we saying that she's safe now?'
'She still knows who this person is.'
'Will she tell?'
'Probably not.'
'She's still a target.' Richard Goddard stated the obvious.

***

An austere, wood-panelled office in the Houses of Parliament in Westminster; a meeting between two powerful men.

'Angus, have we dealt with all the loose ends?'

'Not yet. The woman remains alive.'

'And the child?'

'He continues to search for his parents.'

'What proof do we have that he does not know the truth?'

'If he knew, he would exercise his right to the peerage; his right to your title.'

'On my death?'

'He would have no issue with ensuring you had a convenient accident.'

'You know what to do.'

'I will ensure the instruction is carried out immediately.'

'She could still talk,' the father said.

'Her current behaviour indicates that possibility.'

'Angus, deal with this, and your elevation to the peerage is guaranteed.'

***

Two weeks had passed since Christy Nichols had been charged with the murder of Charles Sutherland. Sally Jenkins' death had been put on the back burner.

Richard Williams' death still occupied Farhan and Isaac's time, but only minimally. Apart from the occasional discussion, there had been no further developments.

Linda Harris's phone call, the only time she had contacted. Isaac was certain that he would not hear from her again.

Marjorie Frobisher, no longer in hiding, apparently no longer in fear of her life, was out and about, on the talk shows, in the magazines. Isaac found her a tiring woman, and he kept his conversations with her to a minimum. It was clear that the knowledge she had was not going to be revealed.

Farhan had met Aisha on several occasions, slept with her on some. The romance seemed solid, but without the constant pressure of a murder investigation that had dragged on for too long, he had begun to re-evaluate his life.

He loved her but was it a love that he could jeopardise his life and his career for? How much of it was genuine emotion? How much of it was the sexual awakening for him with a liberated woman? He realised that time would lessen the intensity for him and for her. With no further media scrutiny, her secret seemed to be safe.

Isaac had met up with Jess, although most times they planned to meet, she was too busy with her newly elevated position.

***

The accident occurred at exactly ten minutes past four in the afternoon. Widely reported, it marked another event in the turbulent life of Marjorie Frobisher.

As she left the restaurant in Sloane Street, Chelsea, apparently the worse for wear after a few too many drinks, she had inadvertently stepped in front of a taxi.

The verdict, after a short court case – the taxi driver had been charged with manslaughter – was recorded as accidental death. The defendant received a suspended sentence. It occupied the newspapers for a few weeks until the public tired of the accusation that the case was a whitewash.

Angus MacTavish duly reported to his superior. 'It has been resolved.'

Deputy Prime Minister James Alsworthy was delighted. Invariably referred to as 'His Lordship' due to his aristocratic manner, he had renounced his hereditary peerage so he could sit in the House of Commons. He would reclaim it when he tired of politics.

The former Benjamin Marshall, the adopted son of an influential family in the north of England, would never know. As Ibrahim Ali, an Islamic Jihadist convert, and the most vocal, most eloquent promoter of the movement for the introduction of Sharia in England, he had within his grasp the title of Lord Alsworthy, a seat in the House of Lords, and a fortune valued conservatively at fifty million pounds. An impassioned orator, the son of Marjorie Frobisher and James Alsworthy could not be given the prominence that the House of Lords would allow him, nor the opportunity to promote his cause.

The End

Phillip Strang

Murder House

Chapter 1

Number 54 Bellevue Street was a good address. At least, it was to Trevor and Sue Baxter. They had come down to London after a transfer from Trevor's company up north in Manchester. Trevor specialised in corporate taxation; his wife Sue, a qualified teacher, saw no problems in her finding another position in London.

They both knew it would not have been possible to purchase such a house in Manchester, but in London there was the salary and the company offer of a low-interest loan for five years while Trevor Baxter established himself. The house, three storeys, built during the reign of Queen Victoria, excited them enormously, even if it needed renovating. It had ornate ceilings, solid double brick construction, and a basement originally designed for coal which Trevor hoped to convert into a wine cellar. The burning of coal had been banned long ago, due to the pea-souper fogs that belching chimneys had caused in the city back in the fifties.

They saw it as a shame they could not use the open fireplaces in the house. At least they would be open to view once a local handyman had removed the cheap panelling that covered them.

'Always costly, home renovations,' Ted Hunter, the local handyman said. 'Everyone's the same; thinks it's easy, and it will come under budget. Mark my words, they never do.' In his fifties, Ted was as fit as any man could be after thirty-five years with the tools of his trade. He had done it all: bricklaying, painting, fitting new ceilings, patching up old ones.

'It's more than we budgeted for,' Trevor, the now more financially-encumbered mortgagor, said.

'I'm sorry, but that's how it is. You can get another quote, but they will hit you afterwards,' Ted said. He had seen it all before: enthusiastic homeowners embarking on the great challenge, assuming a couple of coats of paint, a little bit of tender love and care would transform a pig's ear into a silk purse.

Ted knew the costs would escalate once they attempted to deal with what could not be seen: dry rot, rising damp, even the foundations if the house had been built on swampy ground.

The first task in the house was to remove the encumbrance that covered the fireplace in the main room. Ted Hunter knew the house had been rented out in the past, each room converted into a depressing bedsit, with a toilet and a bathroom on the first floor, and money in a meter for hot water.

Sue Baxter had made a special effort to be present for the great unveiling of the centrepiece of the room, the fireplace. Ted had warned her that it would not be pleasant: twenty years of pigeons trapped inside the chimney as well as accumulated dust and decay. She could not be dissuaded and even wore a mask for the occasion. She was compiling a photographic history of the renovation, and she had a camera ready in her hand.

'Just ease it over to your side,' Ted said to Kyle Sanders, a thickset twenty-something of limited words and intelligence. A good worker, even if he was likely to get stroppy of a night time down the pub. He was known at the police station for putting a few smart-arses in hospital. Still, to Ted, he was trustworthy, always turned up to work on time: the ideal employee in his estimation.

'It's heavy,' Kyle said.

Jimmy Pickett stood to one side. A sullen man of forty-two, he had neither the love of work nor the strength of Kyle. Ted had only taken him on as a standby, and then only as a favour as he was married to his wife's sister. Jimmy's function, according to Sue Baxter, was to stand to one side and offer verbal encouragement liberally peppered with expletives. Not that Sue would have minded, but April, the eldest child, was upstairs after taking a day off from school, and she did not want her exposed to the foul language.

'It's coming free,' Kyle said. He was down on his knees with a lever inserted between the wall and the covering. Ted, standing up on the other side of the fireplace, was attempting a similar exercise. Both were blanketed with copious amounts of coal dust mixed with the occasional feather as they progressively freed the structure.

'Jimmy, secure the top, stop it falling over,' Ted shouted.

'I've got it,' Jimmy said. He had reluctantly been pressed into service and was coughing. Sue Baxter was unimpressed. She had spent too many years as a teacher not to know a faker when she saw one.

'It's an open fireplace,' Ted said. 'Looks to be in good condition.'

Excited, Sue pressed forward, camera in hand. Ted warned her to stand back. She could not be dissuaded.

'What's that at the bottom?' Sue asked.

'No idea,' Ted said. 'Wait till we get it free.'

Jimmy had relocated some distance away due to the coal dust exacerbating his asthma. Two minutes later, the old wooden structure was placed to one side, resting on the far wall.

April had come down to see what was happening, and Sue was taking photos. Ted had seen plenty of old fireplaces in his time, and this one, even though it was bigger than most, would need to be removed and renovated.

Down on his knees again, Kyle prodded at what appeared to be blankets in the bottom of the fireplace. There were some ropes wrapped around it.

Ted warned him to be careful on account of the dust. Jimmy had left the room. April and Sue were hovering close to Kyle.

Ted told them all to stand back. It did not look right to him. He slowly cut one of the ropes. A bone fell out.

'You'd better call the police,' he said to Sue.

Chapter 2

As the Senior Investigating Officer of the Murder Investigation Team, Isaac Cook could see that the chance of a few days off looked unlikely. There had been a couple of cases lately which had taxed his people, a well-crafted team of professionals. Everyone, not only Isaac, was looking for time off, or at least the chance to go home to the family at a reasonable hour, instead of close to midnight, as had been the case for weeks. They had just wrapped up the murder of a child, a crime that always depressed everyone in the office. It had proved hard to pinpoint the murderer until the elder brother, only eleven, admitted he was angry after the younger brother took his bike without asking. Isaac Cook knew the Youth Court would struggle with an appropriate sentence, as the child came from a good home with good parents.

The other murder, of a derelict down behind the railway station, was found to have been committed by four hooligans spaced out on crack cocaine.

'It's clearly murder,' Gordon Windsor said over the phone after a cursory inspection of the body wrapped in blankets. He and Isaac had worked together before, and if Windsor said it was murder, then it was. Isaac, as the senior officer in the department, knew it was time to bring the Murder Investigation Team back to full mobilisation, even though, after so many years, the death could be classified as a cold case.

'Your initial evaluation?' Isaac asked.

'The body's been here for thirty years, I'd say.'

'Did you say thirty years?'

'That's a guess at the present moment. We found some old newspapers under the body.' Gordon Windsor, the crime scene examiner, had been out to the scene within two hours of the body being discovered. The first person at the scene, a local detective inspector who had responded to a phone call from a distraught woman.

'What's the story?'

'Unusual. The owners are renovating the house. They removed an old wooden structure that had been built around the fireplace. That's when they found it.'

'Male or female?'

'Probably male, judging by the clothes.'

'Age?'

'Indeterminate. I'll hazard mid to late thirties.'

'Who's there at the present moment?'

'There's a uniform out the front of the house, plus a local detective inspector, Larry Hill. He says he knows you.'

'We've worked together,' Isaac replied.

'You'd better get down here before we remove the body.'

'Give me twenty minutes.'

***

'We only moved in six weeks ago, it's not what you expect to find,' Trevor Baxter, who had rushed home from work, said.

'Sorry about that, but now it's a murder investigation,' Isaac Cook said.

'Does that mean we'll have to move out?'

'For a few days.'

'I don't want to stay here,' Sue Baxter said. 'I never want to come back here again.'

'I can understand your sentiment,' Isaac Cook said. 'It's easier to deal with in time.'

'Are you sure it's murder?' Trevor Baxter asked.

'Wrapped up in a couple of blankets, tied with rope and thrust in a fireplace.'

'You're right. What else could it be?'

The husband was correct with his question, the DCI conceded. So far, there had been no cause of death, no weapon, no inspection of the body, other than of a leg bone which had fallen out when the tradesman had investigated the blankets in the fireplace. There were too many indicators to believe it could be anything but murder. Gordon Windsor would be working overtime to follow up on a definitive cause of death. If it was not murder, then the concealment of the body indicated foul play, and failing to report a death was still a crime.

The Baxter family checked into a hotel for the night, while a full investigating team went over the house with a fine-tooth comb. There was a lot of work to do before the house would be available for habitation again. The history of the house needed to be checked: who had lived there, who had owned it, and who may have had a motive for concealing a body. Bodies always give off an odour as the decaying process commences, so someone must have smelt something, or the house was empty, which seemed unlikely.

***

Forty years earlier, Bellevue Street, where the body had been found, had been no more than a seedy part of London, where the influx of immigrants from the Caribbean, Africa, and the Indian subcontinent had been deposited in slum dwellings. Isaac Cook's parents had lived in a ground floor room in a similar street when they first arrived in the country from Jamaica at that time. By the time Isaac had been born, their situation had improved, and they had secured a loan on a two-bedroom flat not far from Hyde Park. He remembered their conversations on how hard it had been on their arrival, with the aggressive landlords and their escalating rent demands. He was thankful that the protection of the tenant had improved dramatically since then, although he had had a difficult landlord before buying his flat in Willesden.

Isaac Cook had planned an early night, but that was clearly off the agenda now. He was hopeful that Jess would be sympathetic. They had met on a previous case, and she had moved in with him. He had been confident that the romance would last, but even now it was looking shaky. There had been a few arguments in the last couple of weeks, and every time, as he had expected, the name of Linda Harris had been brought up. 'You slept with her, and don't give me that nonsense that it was vital to the case. When does screwing form any part of a police investigation?'

He always knew it would cause a problem, even though they had not been an item then, merely a flirtation, but Jess never saw it as that.

***

Isaac summoned his team together. Detective Chief Superintendent Richard Goddard, their boss, attended as well. The addition of 'Chief' to his title had come about a few months previously, after a particularly trying case, where Isaac had met and bedded Linda Harris, and flirted with Jess O'Neill. Since that one night, Isaac had not heard from Linda except for a brief phone call, when she stated that she had not murdered anyone, but he was never sure as to the truth. Even though he wanted to settle down with Jess, he could see that the romance was heading to an inevitable conclusion.

Larry Hill was pleased when Isaac offered him the vacant detective inspector's position in his team. He would be transferred officially to Challis Street Police Station within the next week.

Farhan Ahmed, the previous detective inspector, had taken the opportunity of a transfer and a promotion up north. Isaac had wished him well, although the detective inspector's involvement with a former high-class escort, now a lawyer, was hampering further advancement opportunities.

Constable Wendy Gladstone was on board. He would see if she could be made up to sergeant, even though her abrasive nature had precluded this in the past, and exhaling cigarette smoke as she entered the office annoyed Isaac, and he had still not spoken to her about it. He knew that he should, but she had enough on her plate with a husband in a parlous state, even looked close to expiring due to a respiratory condition. Wendy did not speak about him much, only to say that dementia had set in, and he was too difficult for her to handle. Reluctantly, she had placed him in a nursing home, although she visited every day.

Bridget Halloran had been brought in closer to the team on Wendy's request. Previously the CCTV viewing officer, she had taken on extra responsibilities in collating all the documentation for the team. Wendy was pleased, as she was a good friend.

***

'DCI Cook, a summation please,' Detective Chief Superintendent Goddard asked, anxious to start the meeting. Isaac could do without his constant input, his need to be updated and to offer advice, but they went back a long time. Two people separated by age and rank, although each regarded the other as a friend, not just a work colleague. Richard Goddard had asked Isaac to call him Richard on social occasions, but it was too hard for him to acquiesce. It was either 'sir' or 'Detective Chief Superintendent'.

Larry Hill had arrived earlier, pleased that he was joining the team. He and Isaac had met on a previous case when the DI had been the investigating officer.

'This is the situation so far.' Isaac commenced his outline of the case. '54 Bellevue Street, Holland Park. Family of four, husband, wife, and two children, both under thirteen. They had recently moved in after the husband transferred down from Manchester. The house, judging by its condition, needs a lot of renovation. Would you agree, Larry?'

'A lot of work, a lot of money.'

Isaac continued. 'The house is over one hundred and thirty years old. It is a substantial three-storey construction that is showing the wear and tear of many years of neglect. No doubt one of the slum dwellings of the fifties and sixties, but the area is now gentrified and upmarket. However, it appears to have been rented out as single room bedsits during the nineties. After that, we believe that it has remained unoccupied up until the Baxters moved in, disputed property by all accounts. We'll need to investigate the history further.'

'Any name for the body?' Goddard asked.

'Not yet,' Larry Hill said.

'Gordon Windsor will let us know as soon as he can, but at this present time we are assuming the body to be male, aged in his thirties. No more at this time, as the body was wrapped in some blankets and tied with rope,' Isaac said.

'The cause of death?' Wendy Gladstone asked.

'We'll need to wait for confirmation.'

'It's not much to go on,' DCS Goddard said.

'Not much, sir. Bridget, can you check out the history of the house: who has lived there, who owned it? Wendy, follow up on any relevant names, go and visit.'

'Yes, sir,' they both answered.

'Larry, can you get back to the house, see how the investigating team is going? See what else they can find.'

'DCI, what about you?' Goddard asked.

'I'll stay here, put the team together, keep in contact with Gordon Windsor.'

***

Larry Hill quickly returned to the house. Trevor Baxter was there, upset that he was not allowed in until a thorough investigation was completed. The Baxters were not unreasonable people, just concerned that it was their house where the body had been found. Apparently, his wife was now talking about returning at some stage. Larry had to explain that it could be some weeks, possibly longer, before they would be given clear access. Trevor Baxter had been offered a serviced two-bedroom apartment by his company for a month, and they were moving in that day.

The crime scene investigation team did not have much to say, other than the house was in a reasonable if neglected state. Apart from the body, they did not expect to find much more of interest, and after thirty years, they were hardly likely to find any fingerprints or DNA. In fact, they assumed they would come up with nothing, other than where the wood that had concealed the body and the fireplace had come from, maybe some information on the screws used. They did not see themselves being on the premises for longer than a day.

Larry phoned Isaac with the news. It was not unexpected. With little to be achieved, he returned to Challis Street, passing by his old station to wish them well and to tidy his desk. Detective Chief Superintendent Goddard had pulled some strings, and the transfer to the Murder Investigation Team had been immediate.

Wendy and Bridget, glad to be working together, were looking into the history of the house. Bridget, a dab hand with a computer, quickly found out the salient facts regarding the house: built in 1872, and purchased by a wealthy businessman who had made his money with a few upmarket clothing stores. A local newspaper of the period attested to the fact. After that, a succession of owners: one who had committed suicide in the back bedroom in the twenties, as the economy went into a severe depression, another who had spent time in prison for living off the illegal earnings of prostitution. Even one who had run for Parliament, but failed to receive more than three hundred votes. The 1950s and 1960s showed a period as low-cost accommodation, housing immigrants flooding into the country. It was good their period of interest was later, as the records from that period were sketchy.

The key date: January 21, 1987, based on the newspaper found under the body; the assumption was that the body and the paper had been placed in the fireplace at the same time, but that was for Gordon Windsor to confirm. He had phoned Isaac five minutes earlier to say that identification should be possible. So far, he had not concluded his investigation, other than to confirm that the body was definitely male, Caucasian, and clothed. No papers had been found, but they had not checked all the pockets yet, as after so many years, with water ingression from the chimney, coupled with coal dust and pigeon feathers, every part of the body and the clothing was rotten and welded together. He indicated that it would be another twenty-four hours before an initial evaluation would be concluded, and then there would need to be a full autopsy.

Bridget, continuing her search with Wendy sitting close by, turned her attention to the relevant date. The records, easily obtained from the local council's database, showed ownership from the late 1980s up to the present time when the Baxters had bought the property. It also showed that the rates had been paid meticulously during that period, and the electricity had been connected.

Bridget gave two names on the deed of ownership: Gertrude Richardson and Mavis O'Loughlin, nee Richardson. Their addresses, or at least their last known addresses, had not been updated for twenty years. A search of births and deaths indicated that both were alive, and would be eighty-seven and eighty-five years of age respectively.

Wendy had the addresses, but after so long, they seemed to be a long shot, although both were in London and she could get out to one that day. Glad of the opportunity she informed DCI Cook on the way out. The police constable decided to visit her husband on the way, hopeful that he would be in an agreeable mood, even remember her name. She felt guilt that she was not with him more often, but life has its consequences. Her husband, a loyal local government employee, had not put his affairs in order, and she had to pay for the house and the nursing home. She had to work, and she was glad to. The arthritis that had given her trouble had subsided, although she realised it was only temporary due to the warmer weather.

Bridget, meanwhile, happy to be in the office, continued with the documentation that a murder investigation always entails. As firm a friend as she was with Wendy, as fond of a few too many drinks and idle gossip as they both were, Bridget was an office person, Wendy enjoyed being out in the field.

Bridget set to work with the filing, setting up the databases, collating what they had so far. Even at this early stage, she knew it would be another three to four hours before she could consider going home; not that it concerned her, as she was in her element.

Larry Hill had found himself a desk and was setting it up to suit him. He preferred a desk facing the window. Logging on to the department's intranet was proving difficult, but Bridget had said she would be over in five minutes to sort it out for him.

The team, supplemented by several other officers, were collecting and tagging retrieved goods from the house: precious few as it turned out. Others were preparing a case for the prosecution if a culprit was found and brought to justice. It seemed premature to Isaac Cook, in that so far there was no culprit, but procedures were procedures. Even he, a product of university and police training college, could see that the Metropolitan Police was becoming over-bureaucratised. It had been fine with the former commissioner, Charles Shaw, but he had moved on to the House of Lords.

Richard Goddard was looking for an assistant commissioner's position in a couple of years, and the new head of the London Metropolitan Police did not seem to be overly keen on him. The warm relationship with his predecessor had been good, but the new man did not have the charm or the willingness to respond to Goddard's pandering.

Even Isaac had to reflect on his future. He could see detective superintendent, possibly detective chief superintendent, but commissioner…

He needed a mentor to guide him to the top. He needed Detective Chief Superintendent Goddard, although he needed him to make commissioner first, and that was looking shaky. It was a momentary distraction to reflect on past events. It was the present that was important, and that consisted of a body slowly being unwrapped from its blankets.

Chapter 3

Wendy was clearly the most active as she had a defined task. Isaac, for once at a loose end, decided to visit Gordon Windsor.

Wendy's first address was in Richmond. The address showed it as close to the park. She arrived to find what was, on first impression, an imposing mansion. She entered through the front gate and rang the doorbell. The chimes echoed through the house.

Five minutes later, an old and wizened woman leaning on a stick came to the door. 'What do you want?'

'Constable Wendy Gladstone.'

'Are you after a donation or something?'

Wendy could see that the woman was embittered.

'I need to ask you some questions about a property in Bellevue Street, Holland Park.'

'Sold it.'

'We are aware of that, but there are still some questions we need to ask.'

'Ask then. I don't have all day to stand here talking.'

'Would it be better if I came in?'

'If you must.'

As Wendy moved through the house, the main rooms on either side appeared to be unused. The smell pervading the house was unpleasant – stale urine. Upon reaching the kitchen at the back of the house, she could see why. There were cats everywhere, and they were not fussy where they made their mess. It was clear that no attempt had been made for a very long time to keep the area clean. In the corner of the kitchen was an old camp bed.

'Do you want a cup of tea?'

Wendy could only answer in the affirmative if she wanted the woman to open up, although she couldn't see any clean cups.

The woman reluctantly moved over to the sink and pulled out a cup from the filthy water in the basin. She gave it a quick shake and a wipe with a cloth that a cat had been sitting on. Wendy shuddered at the lack of hygiene, although she knew that a cup of tea invariably loosened most tongues, and she needed this woman to talk.

'What can you tell me about Bellevue Street?'

'Not much.'

'It's part of a police investigation.'

'Nothing to do with me, is it?'

'I don't know. What can you tell me about it?'

'I sold it.'

'You've already said that.'

'What else do you want me to say?'

Wendy could see that the conversation was going nowhere. 'Why did you sell it?' she asked.

'Needed the money.'

'This must be worth more than the house you sold.'

'Can't sell this one.'

'Why's that?'

'You ask too many questions.'

'It's my job.'

'That's maybe, but I don't like people sticking their noses into my business. Every month, the council is around here complaining about the cats. Even gave me a clean-up order.'

'What did you do?'

'Same as I'm about to do with you. I told them to bugger off and leave me alone.'

'I could make it official, take you down the police station.'

'Just you try it.'

'This is going nowhere,' Wendy said.

'Then you'd better leave.'

'Before I go, let me clarify a couple of points.'

'Hurry up, I've got the cats to feed.'

'Your name is Gertrude Richardson?'

'What if it is?'

'Do you have a married name?'

'Never bothered to get married. I shacked up with a few, slept with a few more.'

'You have a sister by the name of Mavis O'Loughlin.'

'I don't have a sister.'

'The records clearly state that you do. She's two years younger than you.'

'If you mean that thieving bitch!'

'That's who I mean.'

'Haven't seen her in forty years, don't want to.'

'Any reason?'

'You're sticking your nose in where it's not wanted again.'

'We know that the two of you had joint ownership of the house in Bellevue Street.'

'Maybe we did. What's that got to do with it?'

'The sale of the house would have required both of you as signatories.'

'Not me. I gave a proxy to my lawyer.'
'Can I have his name?'
'Why?'
'We found a body at the house.'
'What's my lawyer got to do with it?'
'You don't seem very concerned about what I just told you.'
'Should I be? Seen plenty of dead people in my time. One more won't make any difference.'
'The body has been there for up to thirty years.'
'Don't look at me. I haven't set foot in *that* house for over forty years, maybe longer.'
'Any reason?'
'My business. If you're finished sticking your nose in, you'd better leave. The cats are hungry, and I'm tired. Come here talking about dead bodies, upsetting the cats. You're also upsetting me, an old woman of eighty-seven, going on eighty-eight.'

Wendy, sensing that her time had come to a conclusion, rose from the old wooden chair she had been sitting on. 'Just one question before I leave.'
'Yes, what is it?'
'Your sister?'
'Don't have a sister.'
'The one that used to share your surname.'
'I've not seen her since Bellevue Street. Dead as far as I'm concerned.'
'But she signed the sale documents for the house.'
'Somebody did. May have been her, I suppose.'

***

Isaac found Gordon Windsor down at Pathology. The body, now revealed, was clearly male. It was lying flat on a table, or at least in an approximation of flat; years of being bent over had tightened it rigid. The clothing was with Forensics who were conducting fibre analysis, attempting to find any clues that would assist. According to Windsor, a positive ID was proving difficult.

'Too many years wrapped in blankets being shat on by pigeons. Add in the water and the coal dust, and the body and the clothing have almost been mummified. That explains the unusually good condition of the skin.' Isaac, used to dead bodies – not as old as this one, though – could only agree.

'The newspaper? Placed there at the time of death?' Isaac asked.

'It looks to be that way, but why would someone bother to place a newspaper first unless they saw it as a time capsule? Instead of a few artefacts, they thought a dead body was more appropriate. Macabre, if that was the case.'

'The cause of death?'

'We'll need to wait for the autopsy. No visible signs of trauma, although that would be hard to ascertain given the condition of the body.'

'How long before they get back to us?'

'Hard to say,' Gordon Windsor said. 'No point rushing a pathologist. They take their time, afraid to get it wrong in case they have to stand up in court and defend their findings.'

'Give me a call,' Isaac said. He had seen enough, and watching the pathologist slice a body with a scalpel from up near the shoulders down to below the navel was not agreeable, even at the best of times. He had seen a pathology examination during police training; he did not want to see another.

***

Larry Hill, once he had settled in and Bridget had sorted out his IT problems, was anxious to be out on the road. He, like Wendy, did not relish extended periods in the office. He phoned her; she was glad of the call.

'I'm trying to find Mavis O'Loughlin,' she said.

'Address?'

'No one there. Looks unoccupied to me.'

'What's the plan?'

'Ask Bridget, see if she can come up with something.'

'I'll do that,' Larry said.

Bridget spent another twenty minutes before she came up with some additional leads. Larry planned to meet Wendy and to go from there.

Wendy had tried the house in Belgravia with no success. Bridget found another possibility in Primrose Hill, three miles to the north. Wendy agreed to meet Larry at the address.

The location did not look promising on their arrival. It appeared to be empty, although it was a well-maintained freestanding property. To Larry, it looked very expensive. Wendy knocked at the door, Larry walked round to the back. As he approached the back door, it opened abruptly. An elderly woman appeared; she was elegantly dressed. Larry judged her to be in her eighties.

'You can tell that bitch sister of mine that she's getting none of it.'

'Detective Inspector Larry Hill. We are looking for a Mavis O'Loughlin.'

'What's the police got to do with this?'

'We're not from your sister.'

'Why are you here?'

'We need to ask you a few questions about the property you jointly owned in Bellevue Street, Holland Park.'

'She's not getting any more money. I've given her enough already.'

'Your relationship with your sister is not our primary concern. Do you think we could come in?'

'The woman at the front banging on the door?'

'Constable Wendy Gladstone.'

'Very well. I will let her in. You can come in the back door. Remember to wipe your feet.'

Wendy could only reflect on the difference between Gertrude's mansion and Mavis's house. The property was exquisite, with everything in the right place. Wendy, who appreciated a clean house but rarely achieved it, was astonished at the cleanliness.

'Can we confirm your name as Mavis O'Loughlin?' Wendy asked.

'I reverted to my maiden name, Mavis Richardson.'

'Would it be appropriate to ask why?' Larry asked.

'Not really, but I'll tell you anyway.'

'Thank you.'

'I caught the bastard cheating on me. Both of them naked in my bed.'

'What did you do?'

'I kicked them out and then threw his clothes out of the window.'

'How long ago?' Wendy asked.

'Over forty years.'

'Have you seen your husband since then?'

'Not once. Vanished off the face of the earth.'

'Does it concern you?'

'Not really. He always had a roving eye.'

'And the woman?'

'Who do you think it was?' She looked at Wendy.

'Your sister.'

'Who else? Back then she was a terrible tart. She could not find a man for herself, so she took everyone else's.'

'That was a long time ago. Have there been other men in your life since then?' Larry asked.

'Plenty, but I've seen no need for a piece of paper and a name change. A few have moved in here, but none have stayed for long.'

'And now?' Wendy asked.

'I'm eighty-five, what use would a man be to me now?'

'Companionship.' Larry ventured a comment.

'If I were lonely, which I am not, I'd get a dog. Anyway, you did not come here to talk about my love life. What do you want?'

'A body has been discovered at Bellevue Street.'

'Number 54?'

'It was found in a boarded-up fireplace.'

'I've not seen the house for over forty years, ever since that night.'

'Which night?' Wendy asked.

'The night I caught the two of them screwing in my bed.'

'It is a long time to bear a grudge against your sister,' Wendy said.

'I forgave her within a week. It's her who can't forgive.'

'Forgive what?'

'She was in love with him, and he upped and disappeared.'

'Why did he disappear?'

'No money.'

333

'This house is yours?'

'As well as Bellevue Street and the mansion in Richmond.'

'We were led to believe that the house in Bellevue Street was jointly owned,' Wendy said.

'Legally, not financially.'

'Could you please explain?' Larry asked.

'It's simple. I was careful with my money and my men; she was not. Is this integral to your investigation, the Richardson family history?'

'The body appears to have been placed in the fireplace in early 1987.'

'I moved out in '76.'

'You owned it in 1987.'

'That's true, but it would have been empty.'

'Could you please elaborate on the financial arrangement with your sister?' Larry asked.

'The properties, all of them, were joint ownership. Given to us by our father on his deathbed. Gertrude became involved with a few unsavoury men, who fleeced her while professing love. I bailed her out; the family lawyer kept a record. In the end, she ended up with nothing but a place to live and God knows how many cats.'

'You let her stay there?' Wendy asked.

'That was the last deal. I would provide a roof over Gertrude's head in return for no more demands.'

'And she agreed?'

'She had no alternative. I believe I have given you enough of my time. I've got a social event to attend.'

Wendy and Larry realised there were more questions to ask, but they would have to wait for another time. Besides, their DCI wanted them back at the office.

Chapter 4

Isaac saw the validity of an end of day briefing and an update on activities concluded so far, activities planned for the next day. He knew that once the investigation into the body in the fireplace became more intense, it would become a luxury.

Wendy and Larry were back in the office, as was Bridget, who was enjoying her newly elevated position.

'I'll update on what we know so far,' Isaac said. Larry sat with a coffee in his hand.

'DCI, is it a confirmed murder?' Wendy asked.

'Not yet. We're still waiting for the result of the autopsy.'

'Sir, you've met Gordon Windsor?' Larry asked.

'He was over at Pathology. Forensics is inspecting the clothing.'

'Any identification?' Wendy asked.

'Not yet, and it looks as though the clothing may yield no clues, other than an approximate date when it was purchased.'

'Is 1987 a probable date?'

'It appears to be around that time. Wendy, your update.'

'Bridget found an address for Gertrude Richardson, one of the joint owners of the property before the Baxters bought it.'

'Did they own it in the 80s?' Isaac asked.

'They purchased it in 1972, sold it three months ago,' Bridget said.

'Did they live in it around the time the body was placed in the fireplace?'

'According to Mavis Richardson, she moved out in the 70s,' Wendy said. 'It's best if I conclude my report first.'

'Please do,' Isaac said.

'To reiterate, Bridget found an address for Gertrude Richardson in Richmond. It was a substantial house, mansion even, close to the park. I knocked on the front door. An old woman, later identified as Gertrude Richardson, came to the door. She was in a bad way.'

'What do you mean?'

'She was unwashed, the house showed severe neglect, and it appears that she lives in the kitchen at the back, surrounded by numerous cats that smelt awful.'

'What did she tell you?'

'It's what she didn't say that's important.'

'That's an ambiguous statement. What do you mean?'

'She's an embittered and reclusive woman who does not acknowledge that she has a sister.'

'Senile?'

'I don't think so. More likely a family feud.'

'What else did she say?'

'She stated that she had not been in the house in Bellevue Street for over forty years.'

'Did she give a reason?'

'No, but I believe I know why. Eventually the woman acknowledged, somewhat reluctantly, that she had a sister, but had not seen her for over forty years.'

'Dates coincide with Bellevue Street?' Isaac asked.

'I'll address that in a minute. She explained that she had sold the house in Bellevue Street because she had no money. I asked her why she had not sold the mansion in Richmond as it was more valuable. She said she could not. She was not willing to elaborate. Besides, she cut me short and hustled me out of the door.'

'And the sister?' Isaac asked.

'I'll let DI Hill answer that question.'

'Wendy had drawn a blank on the first address for Mavis O'Loughlin, the sister,' Larry Hill said. 'Bridget found another and I met up with Wendy at the address. A three-storey terrace opposite the park in Primrose Hill.

'Wendy knocked on the door to no avail. I went around the back. A woman opened the back door and started quizzing me, assumed I was from the sister.'

'Why would she do that? You showed her your badge?'

'Eventually, when she calmed down. After that, she let Wendy in at the front, and I entered through the back door.'

'A total opposite to the sister,' Wendy said.

'What do you mean?' Isaac asked.

'Mavis O'Loughlin, who has now reverted to her maiden name, is an elegant woman who keeps her house in pristine condition. Apart from the reason we were there, she was good company.'

'What did she have to say?'

'She has not spoken to her sister since 1976, or thereabouts, and has not seen her husband since then.'

'Related or coincidental?'

'Related. Mavis Richardson came home unexpectedly and found her husband in bed with her sister. She threw both of them out onto the street.'

'And the sisters have not spoken since?' Isaac asked.

'That's unclear. According to Mavis O'Loughlin, her sister had a tendency to become involved with the wrong type of men. Some of them had taken advantage and fleeced her for money. The debts incurred were covered by her sister, who gradually accumulated the properties under her name.'

'She allows her sister to live in squalor, while she lives in luxury?' Bridget asked.

'I don't think we can make that assumption. She forgave her sister for sleeping with her husband a week after the event, or at least, she said she did. Why the squalor, and now the animosity from both women, is unclear,' Wendy said.

'I suggest you find out as soon as possible,' Isaac said. 'Larry, can you assist?'

'No problem. Can you update us when the pathologist's report and forensics come through?'

'Will do,' Isaac said.

***

It was late at night, as Isaac drove home to the flat he shared with Jess, that he received the phone call that was to intensify the focus on the case. 'It's murder,' Gordon Windsor said.

'How?' Isaac asked.

'Signs of trauma, suffocation.'

'Where are you?'

'I've just driven over to the pathologist's. I came as soon as he phoned me up with the news.'

It was unusual for the pathologist to work so late into the night, but this body was important. The media were hovering for information; a thirty-year-old corpse had raised their interest. And now, Sue Baxter had been selling the story to a Sunday newspaper; there, emblazoned on the front page, the photos she had taken. She had dutifully handed over the camera as requested by Larry Hill, kept the memory card for herself. Isaac realised that she could be trouble if she kept talking, and now with a clear murder, the media would be pressing her for more news.

'I'll be there as soon as possible,' Isaac replied to Gordon Windsor. It was already close to ten in the evening, and Jess had made a special attempt to be at home for an intimate meal that night. Isaac phoned her to let her know that he was further delayed; she was not pleased.

Isaac had seen the signs before. How many times had someone moved in, fully understanding the challenges that a senior police officer in Homicide faced? How many times had the woman said that she understood, when clearly she did not? He had hoped that with Jess he could finally settle down. After all, she was the executive producer of a successful and long-running television drama, and as such, used to long hours and broken engagements. Sure, he had been looking forward to the evening with some good food, a few drinks, and an early and romantic night. He had to admit that the romance was withering. And then there was the issue with Linda Harris and the fact that he had slept with her, while he and Jess were only flirtatious. Her name had come up in an argument two nights previously; she was bound to be mentioned again. He had to admit that he loved, had loved Jess before she moved in, and he sensed it was the same with her, but he could see only another three to four weeks before the relationship came to a conclusion. He was sorry, but there was nothing he could do to change the situation.

'It looks like murder to me,' the pathologist, a tall, thin man, said. Isaac judged him to be in his late fifties, maybe early sixties. He had met him before and had found him to be an unusually unsociable man.

'Why do you say that?' Gordon Windsor asked. Both he and Isaac were standing close to the body: internal organs, or at least what remained of them, clearly visible. It was not a sight that

Isaac appreciated, and if he was being totally honest, he would have to admit that he could be squeamish, but this was important, and people, senior people, were looking for answers and a resolution to the case.

'Clear sign of trauma around the head, and if I'm not mistaken, evidence of suffocation.'

'Enough to stand up in a court of law?' Isaac asked.

'Not yet. I've just given you my professional opinion.'

'How long before you're sure?'

'Could be weeks. I'll need to get Forensics to run tests.'

'What can they find?'

'Why are you asking me? You are the detective chief inspector. Didn't they teach you anything at the police college?'

Isaac had seen that he was making polite conversation; the pathologist saw it as wasted time. 'Of course, DNA, fingerprints, drugs in the system,' he replied. Isaac realised it was a flippant response, but did not appreciate the pathologist's lecture. *Maybe the friction with Jess is getting to me*, he thought.

'There's trauma around the head, but not the level of bleeding that I would normally expect. Mind you, after so many years, I can't be sure.'

'You are confirming murder?' Isaac needed clarity on that one piece of information.

'Tied up, bag over head, trauma around the cranial regions. It seems conclusive.'

'Any chance of identification?' Isaac asked.

'Not from me. Forensics may have better luck.'

'What can you tell us with some degree of certainty?'

'Male, aged in his late thirties, early forties. Caucasian, height close to six feet. Apart from that, it is hard to tell any more. There is a clear sign of a broken right leg and a dislocated thumb. Apart from that, the body indicates that the man had been in good physical shape.'

'Hair colour, skin colour?' Gordon Windsor asked.

'Dark hair. Skin colour almost certainly white, but that's only because I'm classifying the body as Caucasian.'

'English?' Isaac asked.

'Hard to tell. We live in a multicultural society. Not sure that can be confirmed, although DNA analysis may help.'

'Any indication from his clothing?'

'Bought in England. We found a few labels so it may be possible to localise where it was bought. Some of the clothes looked as though they were made to measure, not out of a high-street store.'

'If it's murder, it hardly seems clever to conceal the body fully clothed,' Gordon Windsor said.

'Or hide it in a fireplace in an empty house,' Isaac said. 'But then, we don't know the state of mind of the person who placed him there, do we?'

'Must have been someone handy with wood to have built the fireplace covering.'

'If you two have finished postulating, I'm off home,' the pathologist said. 'I've spent too many hours here today for you.'

'We're finished,' Isaac replied. 'Many thanks.'

'Don't thank me. Just sign for my expenses when you receive the bill.'

***

Larry Hill and Wendy Gladstone, as agreed with their DCI, visited Gertrude Richardson. It was his first visit, her second. The welcome at the door, the same as before. 'What do you want?' the elderly woman asked.

'We have some more questions,' Wendy replied.

'I told you last time that I sold the place. Why bother me?'

'We've spoken to your sister,' Larry said.

'And who are you? I don't like men coming here.'

'Detective Inspector Larry Hill. I work with Constable Gladstone.'

'That may be, but you're not welcome here, and neither is she.'

'I could make this official,' Wendy said.

'Maybe you could, and then it will be in the newspapers. How you took a prominent member of society, eighty-five and infirm, and carted her off down to the police station.'

'Prominent?' Wendy asked.

'Once I was. Always in the society pages. Even met the King on a couple of occasions.'

'That's a long time ago to be claiming prominence, don't you think?'

'My name still counts for something.'

Both Wendy and Larry were intrigued, although neither said anything, other than to look at each other with a momentary glance and an imperceptible shake of the head.

'Can we come in?' Wendy asked.

'I don't want him near my cats. They don't like men, neither do I.'

'You did once.'

'Long time ago, maybe. Naïve then, not now.'

'Can we use another room?' Wendy asked. The old woman was correct in that they would not be taking her in handcuffs down to the police station, nor would they be forcing her to do or say anything other than voluntarily given.

'If you must. You don't want a cup of tea, do you?'

'I wouldn't mind,' Larry said. Wendy wished he had not answered in the affirmative.

'The room on the left. There are some chairs in there. I'll be back in five minutes.'

Granted entry, Larry and Wendy moved to the room on the left. It was clear that it had not been used for many years. The dust pervaded the air as they disturbed it. Larry found a chair close to the window; Wendy, another near a magnificent open fireplace. The walls were adorned with a selection of oil paintings, some old, some valuable. One of the women portrayed, dressed in the style of the seventeenth century, bore a striking resemblance to the old lady who was now making them a cup of tea. Wendy hoped the hygiene would be a little better this time; realised it probably would not.

Ten minutes later, Gertrude Richardson returned with one cat following. It made straight for Larry and jumped up on his lap.

'I've never seen that before,' the woman said.

'I have a couple of cats at home,' Larry said. 'We're very fond of them, the wife and I.'

'If my cat likes you, then so will I.'

'Do you get many people in here?' Wendy asked. She had made sure to choose what looked to be the cleanest cup.

341

'There's a woman who comes once a week to check on me and bring my shopping.'

'You don't go?' Larry asked.

'I've not been out of the front gate in five years.'

'That's a long time,' Wendy said.

'There's nothing out there that interests me.'

'Why's that?'

'As long as I've got my cats, then I want nothing else.'

'We met up with your sister,' Larry said.

'I told her.' The old woman looked in Wendy's direction. 'I don't have a sister.'

'The woman with your name,' Wendy reminded her.

'What did she have to say?'

'She told us that you fell out with her over a man.'

'What if I did?'

'It's important.'

'Not to me.'

'Is that right?'

'I suppose it is, but there's more to it than me just screwing him. And besides, she was no better.'

Larry stood up; the cat was using his new suit to sharpen its claws. His cats at home were regularly bathed, this one was not.

'Could you elaborate?' Larry asked.

'None of your business.'

'It is if it is relevant to a murder enquiry.'

'Why should it be?'

'We've yet to identify the body. Any idea who it may be?' Wendy asked.

'I haven't been in that house for a long time. How would I know?'

'We are aware the body was that of a male, aged in his late thirties to early forties, who almost certainly died at the beginning of 1987.'

'No one I know.'

'Last time I was here, you said that you had seen a lot of dead people,' Wendy reminded the old woman, who showed every sign of ejecting them from the mansion very soon.

'I was in London during the war, worked as a nurse.'

'And after the war?' Larry asked.

'We came from a privileged family, employment was for others.'

'What did you do?'

'For a couple of years, voluntary work, but mainly taking our place in society.'

'It doesn't sound much of a life,' Wendy, who had little time for the idle rich, commented.

'Endless parties and fun? It was marvellous.'

Five minutes later, Larry and Wendy found themselves outside the front door of the house. Their eviction had been executed swiftly.

'What do you reckon?' Larry asked.

'None of what she told us is relevant if the body has nothing to do with her or her sister,' Wendy replied.

'There's more she's not telling us.'

'We'll meet DCI Cook and let him know,' Wendy said.

'Until the body is identified, we'll continue probing the background of the two sisters.'

'Agreed. There still remains a strong possibility that the body is somehow tied back to them.'

Chapter 5

'What do we know about this lawyer?' Isaac asked at the late afternoon debriefing back at Challis Street Police Station.

'Only a name,' Wendy said.

'And the name?'

'Montague St John Grenfell.'

'Sounds aristocratic to me,' Isaac said. The key members of the team were assembled: Larry was standing in the corner, his back to the wall, Bridget was holding a large cup of tea and the obligatory chocolate biscuit, Wendy as well. Isaac was sipping on green tea as his weight was starting to cause him some concern.

'We checked him out in *Burke's Peerage*. He is the second son of a lord with no chance of inheriting the title and the stately home unless the incumbent dies soon,' Larry said.

'What do you mean "soon"?' Isaac asked.

'Grenfell is in his late seventies; the elder brother is two years older.'

'Someone needs to go and check him out.'

'You'd be the best person for that, sir,' Wendy said. She remembered how he had charmed Angus MacTavish, the chief government whip, on a previous case. Dealing with the elite of society seemed best suited to Isaac's disarming and pleasant manner. She knew that she was too abrasive, and her speech echoed government schooling at every utterance. Larry, although he spoke more clearly than she did, had a distinctive northern accent.

'I'll deal with Grenfell,' Isaac said. He was glad of the opportunity to get out of the office. As the senior investigating officer, the administrative side of his job was beginning to annoy him. He could see himself asking Bridget to take on a heavier workload and help him out, once she had got her primary responsibilities under control.

'And for us, sir?' Larry Hill asked.

'Keep with the sisters, see what you can find out. Bridget, can you trace this missing husband?'

'Yes, sir.'

'Good. Larry and Wendy can follow up.'

'All this may be circumstantial and irrelevant,' Larry said.

'Moving out of the house in 1986, a body placed there in 1987? It must be tied in to the women,' Isaac said.

'Agreed, sir. That is what Wendy and I thought.'

***

Bridget soon busied herself with finding out what she could about the husband. It was proving to be difficult as there were no recorded marriages in the period before 1986 for Mavis Richardson, which indicated a wedding outside the country.

However, there was a clear record of marriage in 1952 for Gertrude Richardson, which surprised Wendy. Although, Wendy realised, the woman had denied she had a sister, so why would she not deny a marriage, and now there was the question of where her husband was, although records clearly showed that he would be in his nineties now, so possibly deceased. Too many unknowns, too many instances of intrigue and subterfuge, to not believe that somehow, someway, the sisters were not involved directly or indirectly with the body.

Until the body was formally identified, Wendy and the rest of the team realised they were chasing possible red herrings. It was clear that another visit to the old woman in the mansion was required. Wendy did not relish the task.

As there was no phone at the mansion, it was a drive in heavy traffic out to Richmond. The same procedure: ring the doorbell, wait for five minutes, receive verbal abuse about her being an old woman and the cats needed feeding, and then a reluctant entry through to the kitchen.

'I contacted my lawyer about you coming here all the time. He said it was police harassment, and if it continued, then I was to register an official complaint.'

'Miss Richardson, that is your prerogative. I am only doing my job. By the way, how did you contact your lawyer? I wasn't aware you had a phone.'

'I had no intention of giving the number to you.'

'Why?'

'You're knocking on my door every five minutes. I didn't want you ringing as well.'

'There is a record of you being married back in 1952, is that correct?'

'I prefer to forget about it.'

'Why's that?'

'He was a scoundrel.'

'When did you last see him?'

'Thirty to forty years, I suppose.'

'Why did you deny that you had been married, when I asked before?' Wendy could see some softness appear in the old woman.

'It's my business, no one else's.'

'What was he like?' Wendy held a cup of tea that the old woman had given her. It was cleaner than the last time.

'A lovable rogue, charm the birds out of the trees.'

'He charmed you?'

'Yes.'

'And you've not seen him for thirty to forty years?'

'That's correct.'

'Any idea where he is now?'

'He went overseas. Apart from that, I have no idea. He could be dead.'

Although not senile, Gertrude Richardson was, nevertheless, old and frail, and excessive questioning would have achieved little more. Wendy had noticed that the woman's initial disdain at her space being invaded had subdued, and her manner, though still disarmingly blunt, was agreeable.

Realising that no more was to be gained, Wendy bid her farewell, promised to come and see her in a few days. The response was as expected, but it did not have the harsh undertone that had been present on previous visits.

***

Montague St John Grenfell did prove to be aristocratic when Isaac met him in his office. He was, Isaac knew, a man in his late seventies, but surprisingly fit and agile. He was as tall as Isaac, over six feet in height. His handshake was firm and vigorous, his manners impeccable. Isaac was impressed.

'Please take a seat,' the lawyer said. 'I only have Earl Grey. Is that fine by you?'

'Fine,' Isaac replied. As the lawyer prepared the tea, it gave Isaac the opportunity to look around his surroundings. He had to conclude that it was a good office, certainly better than his at Challis Street, but then, his was the office of a policeman, clean and functional, lacking in any charm. Grenfell's office showed the look of age, as though it had been occupied by the one person for many years. Not far from Paddington, the third-floor office was situated on Bayswater Avenue in an office building which Isaac assumed had been built over seventy years earlier. There was no lift which had given him some much-needed exercise. He wondered how Grenfell managed every day, as he noticed that the man limped.

An impressive bookcase stood to one side of the office, overflowing with legal books and assorted memorabilia. Isaac sat on a comfortable chair, Grenfell on a leather chair, a walnut desk separating them. It was clear that the man was busy as legal files littered the desk. Isaac saw no computer which seemed incongruous in the modern age. He wondered how anyone could conduct business without email and access to the internet.

Montague Grenfell returned holding two cups of tea. Isaac noticed the man's hands did not tremble as he carried them. 'You've been looking around my office,' he said.

'It's certainly more impressive than mine,' Isaac replied, aware that he had been seen.

'I've been here for over forty years. More like a home for me than an office.'

'Is it?' Isaac asked.

'Just a figure of speech, but I'd rather be here than at home.'

'May I ask why?'

'Here, I have my books and my studies. At home, there is no one.'

'Your wife?'

'I've been a widower for five years.'

'Sorry about that.'

'No need to be. People get old, people die. None of us is immortal.'

Isaac knew there were questions to be asked, and as congenial as the current setting was, he needed to redirect their conversation. 'Gertrude and Mavis Richardson, what can you tell me about them?'

'I'm not sure there is a lot. Gertrude is semi-reclusive, Mavis is more outgoing.'

'My detective inspector and constable have met them both.'

'Gertrude can be acerbic.'

'Have you known them long?'

'Since my childhood, although they are a few years older than me.'

'Where did you meet them?'

'I'm sure you're aware of my family history.'

'Second son of a lord.'

'*Burke's Peerage* could tell you that. What else?'

'That's as far as we went. So far, we have a body with no identity, and the only people with any link to that period are the two sisters. There's no reason to believe they're involved, but there is a possibility that people close to them could be.'

'My family is extremely wealthy, obscenely so. The wealth resides with my eldest brother, the lord. I'm financially secure due to a bequethment from my father in his will, but compared to my brother, it is a mere pittance.'

'Your meeting with the sisters?' Isaac repeated his earlier question.

'They were regular guests at the family's stately home.'

'Any reason?'

'They are cousins of mine, distant cousins.'

'Are they independently wealthy?'

'They both were, but now Mavis has all the money.'

'That was explained by Mavis. Gertrude denies that she has a sister.'

'Bad blood, goes back a long way.'

'Do you know the reason?' Isaac asked.

'Gertrude made some bad decisions. Mavis, always the smarter, helped her out.'

'We are aware that Gertrude signed over the properties.'

'I ensured it was legal.'

'And that's left Gertrude living in abject misery?' Isaac asked.

'Abject misery in a mansion in Richmond. I do not think so. Regardless of what Gertrude may have said, that is not the truth. There's enough money for her to live well, but she chooses the life.'

'So, why doesn't she accept the money?'

'You'd better ask her. I've offered it to her enough times, so has her sister.'

'According to both women, they have not communicated for a long time.'

'I believe I've said enough on this matter. As you have said, there is no connection between the women and the body at this time.'

'Can I clarify if the women have communicated in recent times?'

'I suggest that you talk to them further.'

Isaac prepared to leave. 'Just one more question, totally unrelated. How do you manage the stairs up to here?'

'With difficulty. It doesn't help only having one leg.'

'I didn't realise.'

'Motorcycle accident in my youth.'

As Isaac exited the building, his phone rang. 'I have some updates from Forensics,' Gordon Windsor said.

'When can we meet to discuss?'

'Your office, sixty minutes.'

***

Isaac hurried back to the office, pushed the car harder than he should have, broke the speed limit a couple of times, but the news from Gordon Windsor sounded important. Upon arrival, he found Windsor comfortably seated with a smug look on his face. Wendy was with him, having just arrived backed from Gertrude Richardson's place in Richmond. Larry was out with the other sister, Mavis.

'What do you have?' Isaac asked.

'Forensics have been able to analyse some of the clothing, even read a tag on a shirt.'

'The significance?' Isaac asked.

'Made to order.'

'Wendy, a job for you.'

'Yes, sir.'

'Anything else?' Isaac asked.

'It appears that the trousers were also made to measure, but so far they've not found a tag. They're conducting an analysis of the fabric, may come up with something.'

'How about the body?' Isaac asked.

'They're still conducting tests, but asphyxiation is looking the stronger of the two means of death, although the trauma to the skull is significant.'

'Regardless of how the man died, we still need a name.'

'I'll get on to it straight away,' Wendy said.

'Any luck with the elder sister?' Isaac asked her.

'Apart from admitting that she had been married, not a lot. She was more agreeable, seemed to appreciate the company this time. The place is a mess, should be condemned.'

'According to her lawyer, there's no reason for her to live like that,' Isaac said.

'Then why does she?'

'Senile?' Gordon Windsor asked.

'Not from what I can see,' Wendy said.

'We need to find out more about her and this mysterious husband,' Isaac said. 'How's Bridget progressing?'

'There are two husbands to find, Gertrude's and Mavis's, although both will be in their nineties now.'

'Possibly dead.'

'It's possible.'

'We need to know what happened to them anyway, but first we need to identify the body. Wendy, you and Larry better make that your priority.'

'As soon as Bridget gives us an address, we'll go and visit the tailor.'

***

'Did you know about your sister's marriage?' Larry asked Mavis Richardson. His entrance into the elegant house, this time through the front door.

'It was a long time ago. Michael Solomon has not been seen for years, same as my husband,' Mavis Richardson replied.

Larry, this time asked to sit in a more comfortable chair than on his previous visit, could only reflect that the woman still had an eye for a man, especially a younger man. The woman was older than his mother, and he was happily married, two young children, another on the way. He knew all about Isaac and his legendary reputation for seducing beautiful women. He felt no need to emulate him and especially not with someone so old, even though still remarkably attractive. Larry assumed her look came courtesy of a healthy bank balance, expensive cosmetics, and a plastic surgeon. All of which may be interesting, but there was a more important issue to consider – the unidentified body.

'Tell me about Gertrude's husband.'

'Attractive, well-spoken, lovable rogue.'

'Did you like him?'

'All the women liked him, that was the problem.'

'What do you mean?'

'He'd screw anything in a skirt.'

'And?' Larry asked, not sure of the response.

'Yes, I'm included.'

'What did your sister say?'

'She never knew. Mind you, she screwed mine, so I suppose it's all fair in love and war.'

Larry, who had been receiving SMS updates from Isaac and Wendy, continued to probe, continued to slowly move away from the woman as she edged along the sofa in his direction. 'My colleague has met your lawyer.'

'A lovely man.'

'Apparently, you have known him since you were children.'

'We're cousins, poor cousins.'

'Poor hardly seems an appropriate word.'

'Compared to his family, we were virtual paupers. Sure, we were not on our uppers, cap in hand, but their wealth was immense. One of the richest families in the country.'

'Your background?'

'Gertrude and I are the only children of Frederick Richardson, a wealthy landowner and property developer in the north of England. My father and Montague's father were half-brothers. One was conceived in the marital bed, the other was not. You must realise which of the two was illegitimate.'

'Then you and your family have no claim to the title and the wealth?'

'My father and Montague's father were brought up as brothers. Their father made no distinction, although the right of succession did. The first claim to the title belonged to the eldest son, assuming he was legitimate.'

'If either you or your sister had a son, then he is in the line of succession?'

'It's a long line, and the legitimate heirs take precedence, and besides, neither of us have had any offspring.'

***

The name on the clothing tag, although faded, had shown up under ultraviolet. Bridget had a printed scan. The name stated *'Clement Jones and Sons. Gentleman Tailors'*. It was not hard to find, located as it was on Savile Row, the address for the discerning and wealthy purchaser of men's clothing in London.

Wendy and Larry left soon after. They showed their IDs on arrival and were quickly moved into a small office at the rear. 'Not good for business, having a couple of police officers out the front asking questions,' the manager said.

'Sorry about that,' Larry said.

'What can I do for you?'

'We need to identify the purchaser of a shirt made in the 1980s. Would that be possible?'

'Difficult, but not impossible.'

As the men spoke, Wendy took the opportunity to look around the office. Everywhere there seemed to be samples of clothing, as well as numerous bookkeeping records. It smelt musty, although not unpleasant, as it was interspersed with the smell of leather and fabric. The manager, a fat, red-faced man, elegantly dressed in a suit with a waistcoat, and sporting a bowtie, seemed ideally suited to such an august establishment. Larry, who had an affinity for dressing well, could only admire what was for sale in the shop at a price he could never afford.

'How much for a suit here?' Larry asked.

'Up to four thousand pounds,' the manager said.

'A lot of money.'

'As you say, a lot of money, but the men who come in here don't look at the price, just the quality.'

'What type of men?' Wendy asked.

'City men, bankers, stockbrokers, the occasional pop star.'

'Any villains?' Larry asked.

'Confidentiality is crucial in our business.'

'Which means?' Wendy asked.

'Everyone who comes in here is treated equally. We don't ask their politics or where the money came from, only their inside leg measurement.'

'You would have records from 1986 or thereabouts?' Larry asked.

'From 1904, if you need. That's how long we've been here.'

'Mid to late eighties is all we need. What do you need from us?'

'A sample of the fabric, a photo of the garment, and a copy of the tag.'

'We can give you a copy of the label now and a picture of the garment. We will need to get a special release of a sample in a day or so.'

'What's so important?' the manager asked.

'We need to identify the owner,' Wendy said.

'Dead?'

'That's correct.'

'Not the body in the fireplace?'

'Confidentiality is crucial in our business, the same as yours,' Larry said.

'Let me have a look at the tag,' the manager said.

Wendy handed over the photocopied image.

'1985 to 1986,' the manager said.

'You can tell that from one glance?'

I remember the tag. We had taken on a new supplier of labels in 1985, but they proved unsatisfactory.'

'Any reason why?' Wendy asked.

'The labels frayed after a year or so, especially if someone had put the garment in a washing machine. We ceased using them in late 1986.'

'And the shirt?' Wendy handed over a photo.

'Long slim cotton with double cuffs, white in colour.'

'Can you give us a name?'

'It was a popular line, maybe sold three to four hundred in that colour. The best I can do is give you a list of all who purchased it. Any idea as to the age of the person?'

'Late thirties, early forties,' Larry said.

'That helps. I should be able to reduce that number to seventy or eighty.'

'When can you give us the list?'

'Ten minutes.'

'That soon?'

'Everything's computerised, and once a customer comes in, we keep him on record. No computers here in the 80s, but we've updated since then.'

'No one after about 1987,' Wendy reminded the manager.

'I figured that. It is still about seventy to eighty. Help yourself to a cup of tea while I sort it out.'

Wendy exited the shop with the list on a USB memory stick. Larry exited with a ready-to-wear shirt, which the manager had let him have for fifty per cent off the list price. Both were pleased with their visit to the shop.

Chapter 6

Forensics were taking a long time, too long for Isaac. He phoned them to see how much longer. They said another week at most. He was a man used to being proactive, and for too long he had been waiting for others to do something, rather than himself. His position within the team at Challis Street meant he had to deal with a lot of administrative tasks. Not that he minded usually, but there was just too much. The new commissioner of the Metropolitan Police had brought in additional procedures, and no excuses would be brokered for failing to comply. The previous incumbent, Charles Shaw, had been a great man, streamlining where possible, and it had helped. Now the paperwork was building up, and he was struggling to stay on top of it. Bridget had been helping as she could, but she was weighed under.

Isaac felt the need to leave the office, and besides, he had female trouble again. Jess, his live-in lover, was causing anguish. They had had another argument the night before, and it seemed inevitable that she was going to move out. It was impacting on his ability in the office, and he knew he would have to confront the issues in a few days. It upset him, as she was a woman any man would be proud to have on their arm.

He thought to visit the Richardson sisters' lawyer again, but it seemed premature, and besides what would he say to him. So far, nothing tied the sisters to the body and their association with the house in Bellevue Street could only be regarded as circumstantial. He could hardly bring the women into the police station based on nothing. He knew that identification of the body was critical, and that lay with Bridget at the present time.

'What do you have, Bridget?' Isaac drew a chair up alongside her. She looked flustered.

'Of the seventy-four on the list, I've eliminated thirty-six.'

'How?'

'They're either Arab or African. Our body is white and Caucasian.'

'That leaves thirty-eight. Can you eliminate more?'

'There'll still be seven or eight left.'

'We can get Larry and Wendy on to searching for them. Any luck with the two women's husbands?'

'Last known addresses. I've passed them on.'

'Is there a name for Gertrude Richardson's husband?'

'Michael Solomon.'

'What do we know about him?' Isaac asked.

'German, of Jewish ancestry.'

'Any ideas where he is now?'

'I gave Wendy the only address I could find, but it's old, and he would be ninety-five. Unlikely that he'll still be alive.'

***

Wendy and Larry decided to visit the last known address of Michael Solomon. The husband of Mavis Richardson, Ger O'Loughlin, was proving elusive. Bridget was struggling to find an address, other than one that was twenty years old, and Google Street View had shown that the building no longer existed.

Michael Solomon had arrived in England in 1945, the only survivor of his family from a concentration camp in Germany. Bridget had managed to find out that he had prospered over the years, and by the time of his marriage to Gertrude, he was successfully running his own jewellery business. The last piece of valid information was when he had sold the business thirty years previously. If that was correct, then the dates did not agree with what Gertrude Richardson had said. Her statement was that she had not seen him for over forty years, but there he was, running a shop not more than three miles from where she currently lived. Wendy saw another visit to the woman.

Wendy and Larry arrived at Solomon's house in Fulham at around four in the afternoon. The house was not as palatial as Gertrude's mansion, not as well maintained as her sister's house. It looked occupied. Wendy rang the doorbell. A woman in her sixties came to the door. 'What can I do for you?'

'Detective Inspector Larry Hill, Constable Wendy Gladstone,' Larry said as they both showed their ID badges.

'Is this about Daniel?' she asked. Wendy observed that she appeared to be a woman worn down by the stress of life. Her hair was showing grey roots with no attempt to conceal them. She wore a drab dress, unironed and apparently unwashed. She wore no makeup.

'Daniel?' Wendy queried.

'My eldest. A grown man and still he acts like an irresponsible child. Your people were always around here, bringing him home, or taking him down the police station. What's he done this time?'

'We're not here about Daniel.'

'Then what are you here for?'

'We're looking for Michael Solomon. This is his last known address.'

'Maybe it is, but he's not here now.'

'Any idea where?'

'Five-minute walk.'

'Can we have the address?' Larry asked.

'You can, but it won't help you much. He's been dead for eight years.'

'And you are?' Wendy asked.

'Mary Solomon. I was married to him for thirty-five years, until he died and left me with his children.'

'He was older than you when you married?'

'He was twenty-seven years older than me, but he was affluent and a good-looking man. Seemed a good catch at the time.'

'And now?'

'I miss him sometimes, but he was not a good husband.'

'Can we come in?' Wendy asked.

'If you like. Excuse the mess. I'm babysitting Daniel's son, and my daughter has dumped her two on me while she is gallivanting up in the city. No idea what she does up there, although I can imagine. They say "like father, like son", but with Michael, it's both of our children.'

Let into the house, Larry and Wendy found themselves in a small room, neat and tidy, with a television in the corner. Obviously, the one room in the house out of bounds to anyone else. Wendy could only feel sorry for her.

'What do you want to know?' the woman asked.

'What do you know of your husband before you married?' Wendy asked.

'He was married before, if that is what you are intimating?'

'Yes. Do you know any of the history relating to the woman?'

'Only that she was a bitch who kicked him out of the house after he caught her in bed with another man.'

'That we did not know,' Larry said. 'Our information is that he vanished over forty years ago, and went overseas.'

'He may have, but I met him not far from here. Fell for him straight away. Married him within six months, gave birth to Daniel three months later.'

'Tell us about him,' Wendy asked. The woman seemed relieved to have someone to talk to, although the baby crying in the other room was distracting.

'Let it cry. It will stop in a minute. Born with the mother's drug addiction. I've only got warm milk, not what it wants.'

'And your husband allowed your children to grow up like this?'

'Not much he could do, and besides, he was no better.'

'Drugs?'

'With him, it was alcohol and other women, although he always denied it. I could see the smirk on his face, the lipstick on his collar. They may have screwed him, but I was the one who had to clean up after them.'

'The children weren't disciplined?'

'By me, but then he'd come home drunk and forgive them. And then once they reached adolescence, they're out there following in his footsteps.'

'What did he die of?' Larry asked.

'I wake up at six in the morning, and he's lying next to me, dead. Gave me quite a shock. Besides, he was nearly ninety.'

'Are you saying he was still chasing women at that age?'

'He gave up on the women in his seventies.'

'Any violence?'

'Michael? Not at all, although I could have hit him sometimes for his behaviour. As I told you, he was a charmer. I always forgave him.'

It was evident to Wendy and Larry that pursuing Michael Solomon had come to a conclusion. However, they both realised that he could still be the murderer.

***

Bridget, meanwhile, had been ensconced in the office, working through the list of buyers that the manager of the tailor's in Savile Row had supplied. Of the seven that she had focussed on, two were confirmed alive and well. With five left, she started to phone around. She found two more who had answered their phones: one, a successful businessman, the other, a musician. There were three left that she had been unable to confirm; they would need to be handled by Wendy and Larry.

Isaac busied himself in the office, although he wanted to be out on the street. His senior, Detective Chief Superintendent Goddard, was keeping his distance, other than to phone at regular intervals for an update. Apparently, Trevor and Sue Baxter had been complaining about not being able to return to their house, even after the crime scene investigators had concluded their examination. It was still a crime scene, Isaac had tried to explain when they had confronted him at the police station, and as such, the crime scene tape across the front and the uniformed policeman were to stay. He thought they had understood, but there they were on the television complaining and no doubt getting paid, as Sue Baxter continued to come up with little titbits for the media.

Not true, Isaac thought every time she made an unsubstantiated complaint or comment.

Gordon Windsor had phoned to detail the pathologist's final report. It was murder, and a minor blow to the head had occurred before asphyxiation. A second more severe blow had taken place after, although the suffocation had probably killed the man, who would have almost certainly been unconscious. Also, a small tattoo in the shape of a dragon had been found on the right forearm. It appeared to have been skilfully executed.

It was clear that the body needed to be identified. Chasing after missing husbands, delving into the two sisters' relationship was fine, but if they were proven not to be involved, then it was not relevant.

Isaac called the team together for a hastily convened meeting. It was going to be a fateful evening for him, both personally and professionally. He had finally received an ultimatum from Jess O'Neill. She was to make one special effort to put on a romantic meal that night; his non-attendance would signal an end to the relationship. He would have preferred it to have ended on a pleasant note, but he was a senior police officer with a major crime. He could not just leave when it suited him.

***

It was seven in the evening before everyone was assembled back at Challis Street. Isaac had ordered pizzas for everyone. 'We need a name for this body. John Doe is no longer sufficient.'

'We found Gertrude's husband,' Larry said.

'What did you find out?' Isaac asked.

'He's been dead for eight years.'

'We'll discuss this later. For now, we need to identify this body.'

'I've given three names to Larry and Wendy,' Bridget said.

'Fine. When can you start on checking?' Isaac asked.

Wendy knew the answer required, but her husband had taken a turn for the worse. She would need to visit with him first, and then talk to the doctor about additional care, new medicine, and no doubt, an extra cost. She could not see how she could bear the cost without selling the house. 'Tomorrow morning,' she replied. 'Pressing family issue.'

There was no more for her to say, as Isaac was well aware of the situation and sympathised.

'I'll make a couple of phone calls tonight,' Larry said. 'Are we assuming the one we can't find is the body?'

'It's a fair assumption,' Isaac said. He was anxious to leave soon and to see if he could patch it up with Jess before it was too late.

'It's probably best if we call it an early night. There are only three to find, and it would be best to make personal contact rather than over a phone.'

'That sounds fine,' Wendy said. 'I'll attempt to be here early.'

'I'll stay another hour,' Bridget said. 'Tidy up some paperwork.'

'I'll stay with Bridget,' Larry said.

'I'll walk you out,' Isaac said to Wendy. 'I've got some personal business to deal with.'

***

Wendy drove straight to the nursing home. She found her husband sedated and in a confused state.

'It's only getting worse,' the doctor said.

'What can you do?'

'Keep him calm, but he's a big man. We can't have him blundering around.'

'What's your prognosis?'

'There's a heart problem. I give him three, maybe six months.'

'Can he stay here?'

'Under minor sedation, but there is the cost.'

'I'll manage.' She knew that her DCI was attempting to get her made up to sergeant. The extra money would just about cover the additional cost.

Isaac reached home just as Jess was about to give up waiting. He noticed the early signs of packing. 'It's not easy when there is a murder to deal with,' he said.

'I realise that, but sometimes we both have to make an effort. If you want to play the field again, just let me know.'

'I have responsibilities. You knew that before we got together.'

'Even before you slept with Linda Harris.'

Isaac realised the futility of the situation. If he had not slept with the woman, then maybe a longer-term relationship with Jess would have been possible, but it clearly was not. 'It was an error on my part,' he said. 'I can't undo the past, but then I don't think you can forget either.'

'Maybe it's best if we quit while we're ahead,' she said.

'Maybe it is,' he reluctantly agreed.

The meal stayed cold, the bottle of wine unopened. Jess slept on the sofa; Isaac on the bed. He could hear her sobbing, but there was nothing he could say or do. Tomorrow she would be gone. He had hoped it would end better. He was sorry it had not.

Chapter 7

Isaac woke early the next morning after a restless night. Jess had left, a note attesting to the fact on the kitchen table. She clearly stated that she would return during the day and remove her belongings. He sat down for a few minutes, shed a tear in sadness, his momentary remorse disturbed by a phone call.

'We've only got one more person to find,' Wendy said.

'Where are you?'

'In the office. Bridget and DI Hill are here as well.'

'It's only six.'

'We agreed last night to meet at five in the morning.'

'Your husband?'

'Not good.'

'I'm sorry to hear that,' he said.

'And you, sir?'

'The inevitable.'

'I thought it was that, sir. I hope it wasn't too unpleasant.'

'It was.'

'It helps to stay busy, keep the mind occupied.'

'I'll be in the office in twenty minutes.'

'DI Hill and I will be out by then. Bridget will be here.'

'Keep me posted.'

Twenty minutes later, as stated, Isaac arrived in the office. Bridget welcomed him with a cup of freshly-brewed coffee. He could see the motherly touch. Wendy had obviously told her the story.

'Two of the three were easily confirmed on Facebook,' Bridget said. 'DI Hill contacted them. There's only one left, and he seems a distinct possibility.'

'Why do you say that?' Isaac asked.

'He would have been thirty-six in 1987.'

'After 1987?'

'There is no further record of him.'

'Does this person have a name?'

'Solly Michaels. You do understand the significance.'

'Yes, it's clear.'

'Where are DI Hill and Wendy?'

'They've gone to see Gertrude Richardson. Obtain a DNA sample, if she's willing.'

'And if she's not?' Isaac asked.

'Difficult to force a woman in her late eighties, DCI.'

'Almost impossible. We'll deal with it if we come to that hurdle.'

***

Wendy thought it was too early to knock on the door in Richmond. Larry said it was too important to wait any longer. They rang the doorbell three times before the door slowly opened.

'What do you want?'

'There's been a possible development.'

'I'm feeding the cats. Come back later.'

'It would be easier to deal with it now. There are questions to be asked.'

'I sold the house. What more do you want?'

Wendy was concerned that the old woman would not hold up under questioning. She had considered bringing another policewoman skilled in dealing with a medical situation should it occur, but decided against it, as she knew the nature of the woman who confronted them at the door.

'We need to talk to you about your husband.'

'I've not seen him for a long time.'

'We found him,' Wendy said.

'Come in,' the old woman said. 'We can talk in the room we used before.' Wendy could see that the woman was disturbed by the revelation.

The same cat followed them into the room, sat on Larry Hill's lap as before. This time, he did not intend to disturb the conversation by standing up to shake it off.

'Is he dead?' Gertrude Richardson asked.

'I'm sorry, but he died of old age. You must have known.'

Wendy could see that Gertrude was close to tears. She moved over close and put her arm around the woman. Gertrude Richardson nestled her head into Wendy's shoulder, appreciative of

363

her compassion. 'He was a lovely man. I never knew why he left, although he was always playing up.'

'What did you do about it?' Wendy asked.

'Turned a blind eye. It was the way he was, but he always came back to me at night.'

'How many years were you together?'

'Eighteen years, on and off.'

'On and off?' Larry queried.

'Sometimes I'd move out, sometimes he would, but it was a good marriage. Maybe unconventional, but we lived in London during the swinging sixties. A lot of promiscuity then, and we were both guilty. When did he die?'

'Eight years ago, in Fulham.'

'Did he marry again?'

'Yes.'

'We never got divorced.'

'Bigamy?'

'It's a bit late to prosecute him now.'

'Too late,' Wendy said. 'There's another question I must ask. You will not like it.'

'What is it?'

'Did you have a child?'

'Yes,' the woman replied meekly.

'And his name?'

'Garry Solomon.'

'Where is he now?'

'I've not seen him since he turned nineteen. He was wild, always in trouble. Took after his father, I suppose.'

'Did you look for him?'

'For a long time. Even hired a private investigator, but he had disappeared. I received a postcard from India a couple of years later saying that he was fine, but since then, nothing.'

'Did it upset you?'

'For a while, but I was never overly maternal. I was not a good mother, I wanted to party too much, and Michael was not a good example. I thought India was better for him, although I would have liked to have seen him again. I suppose I never will now.'

'I need to take a sample of saliva. Would that be acceptable?'

'What for?'

'We need to collect a sample of your DNA for analysis.'

'Are you saying the body is Garry?'

'We don't know, but we must eliminate all possibilities.'

'I understand.'

After the sample had been taken, Wendy turned to the woman. 'Do you want someone to stay with you?'

'I've got my cats. Besides, I always assumed he would come to an unpleasant end. I never imagined it would be in Bellevue Street.'

'It's not been proven,' Larry said. He had purposely said little during the interview.

'It will be.'

'Why do you say that?'

'A mother knows. I can't explain it.'

***

With a clear reason, Isaac decided to confront Montague Grenfell. As the family lawyer, he should have been more forthcoming about the child of Gertrude Richardson and Michael Solomon. Isaac saw the man as being evasive in hiding information.

'I never spoke of the son because it is part of a confidentiality agreement that I have with the two sisters,' Grenfell said after Isaac had climbed the stairs to the lawyer's office.

'Why a confidentiality agreement?'

'Do you believe the body to be that of Garry Solomon?'

'It's not proven.'

'But it looks likely?'

'A strong possibility, but why Bellevue Street and why a fireplace? Too many unknowns at the present time.'

'If it is him,' Grenfell said, 'where was he for sixteen, seventeen years?'

'Unknown, although we know he was in India two years after he disappeared.'

'He was trouble.'

'We know, but since he disappeared there has been no record of him, or at least no record of a Garry Solomon. We've not checked for a Solly Michaels, and we've not checked with the fingerprint department.'

Grenfell went to make some tea. He almost spilt it on his return, due to the shaking of his hands. It concerned Isaac as on his previous visit they had been firm.

'Did you know that Michael Solomon was dead?'

'I knew.'

'And you didn't tell his wife?'

'What could I tell her? That he was living not far from her and married to another woman with a couple of children. It would only have caused more trouble.'

'But you're her lawyer?'

'I'm also her cousin and godfather to her son. What kind of bastard would I have been if I had destroyed her belief?'

'What belief is that?'

'That her son is well and happy in India, and her husband is overseas. Better to let sleeping dogs lie. And if I told her that her husband was living in a bigamous relationship, professionally I would have needed to tell the police. I couldn't do that to either Gertrude or Michael Solomon.'

'You knew Michael Solomon?'

'I did.'

'What kind of man was he?'

'He was my friend.'

'Why did he leave Gertrude?'

'That's another story.'

'I could make it official.'

'Confirm the body as Garry Solomon first. Until then it remains a secret.'

***

Larry Hill had been enjoying his time with the team at Challis Street, and he had a great deal of respect for his DCI. He knew some of the truth regarding the death of Sally Jenkins, the murdered woman whose case he had been responsible for. It irked DI Hill that the woman's death had been classified as murder by person or persons unknown. He was aware that his senior knew more, and he had quizzed him on more than one occasion, only to be told that it was classified, and the final report was confidential and came under the Official Secrets Act.

There was not much more that he could do about it, but he saw it as a blot on his career. An unsolved murder invariably reflected on the senior police officer assigned to the case. DCI Cook had told him that it did not, although in this case he even admitted that it irked him as well. Larry Hill saw an inference from Isaac that he knew who the murderer was, but he was not telling either.

Still, Larry Hill had to reflect that working with the team at Challis Street was a lot better than his previous police station. There, it had been office-bound more times than not, dealing with endless paperwork, and the senior man, a detective superintendent, had not been someone he could respect. On the couple of occasions that he had met Detective Chief Superintendent Richard Goddard, he had found him to be a decent man. A little humourless, but he left the team alone as much as possible, and he and Isaac seemed to have a good relationship.

Larry enjoyed being out with Wendy Gladstone, found her to be capable and compassionate, even if she was ageing, and did not move with the agility that he did. He reflected on how well she had handled Gertrude Richardson when she had been told about the death of her husband, and the possible death of her son.

Some secrets were clearly integral to the case. It now appeared that the time spent following up on the two elderly sisters had not been time wasted.

He did not complain about the hours he was working, although his wife, used to him being home at a reasonable time, gave the occasional gripe. He knew that she understood and was always supportive. With the newfound prestige of his position at Challis Street, the possibility of a promotion up to detective chief inspector in a couple of years seemed a distinct possibility.

His time of reflection soon came to a conclusion. 'Are you ready?' Wendy asked.

'Let's go,' he replied. Another visit out to meet the younger sister.

Larry drove. Wendy sat in the passenger's seat, telling him about her husband and his condition. It was not a subject he wanted to hear about, but she seemed to want to talk. He could at least acquiesce and offer comment when required, encouragement when needed.

'They reckon another three to six months,' she said soulfully. He had noticed that she was a cheerful woman until she spoke about her husband. He could only assume they were close.

He understood, as he and his wife were close, although sometimes they argued like cats and dogs. She put it down to her fiery Irish Roman Catholic upbringing; he, to his growing up in a rough area in a rough town in the north of England. Their arguments, he reflected, only lasted a short time, and neither dwelled for weeks on why they had argued in the first place. Money was often the main reason, and a promotion to DCI would help.

'Anyone at home for you?' Larry asked Wendy.

'My last son moved out. All I have there are a television and rising damp.'

'Not ideal.'

'Arthritis,' she said.

'What do you mean?'

'The dampness in the house is playing havoc with my aches and pains. I intend to sell it as soon as possible.'

'And your husband, are you close?'

'We were, but with dementia, it's hard to remember back to that time. Every time I go to visit, I have to take a tablet to calm myself down. Anyway, enough of my complaining. You're a good listener.'

'We're here,' he said.

Exiting the car, they both made their way to the front door of Mavis Richardson's house. The woman opened the door on Wendy's second knock.

'I've had Montague Grenfell on the phone,' Mavis said. She was obviously upset.

'What did he tell you?' Larry asked. Even though the woman was upset, she still managed to ensure they were all seated and had a cup of tea.

'He's had a visit from a Detective Chief Inspector Cook.'

'Our senior,' Wendy said.

'Michael Solomon's dead,' Mavis Richardson said.

'Had you any idea what happened to him after he left your sister?' Larry asked.

'I saw him about ten years ago, purely by chance. I was in the city, and he walked by. We recognised each other instantly.'

'What happened?' Wendy asked.

'We sat down and had a coffee.'

'Anything more?'

'Nothing more. He asked after Gertrude. He seemed to be genuinely concerned. We parted, and I never saw him again.'

'Did you tell your sister?'

'We were not talking, and besides, it would only have brought up unpleasant memories.'

'Secrets best left unspoken?' Wendy asked.

'This is a murder enquiry, you do realise this?' Larry said. He had just poured himself a second cup of tea.

'Garry?' Mavis Richardson asked.

'It's possible.'

'Not proven.'

'We're conducting DNA analysis.'

'You could be forced to give evidence, explain what all the secrets are.'

'Two old women, no more than a few years left for either of us. I don't think the fear of imprisonment would be a catalyst for us to talk. Besides, some secrets must remain hidden, regardless.'

'Are these secrets that important?' Wendy asked. She had helped herself to a small cake.

'Yes.'

Chapter 8

Forensics wasted no time once they had a sample of Gertrude Richardson's DNA. A mitochondrial DNA sequence from the mother and the body matched. Confirmation of the body as Garry Solomon accelerated the investigation. Wendy had the unpleasant task of telling Gertrude. She did not relish it, but she would do it with all haste.

Isaac made an appointment to meet Montague St John Grenfell, the sisters' lawyer. Isaac realised he knew more than he had told them so far; he needed to be pressured. It was now a full-blown murder investigation; the time for evasion belonged in the past.

Wendy, not in the best of spirits, made the trip out to Richmond. Her husband continued to wane, and now she had bad news for Gertrude Richardson, a woman with whom she felt an affinity. Sure, she did not live in a mansion surrounded by cats, but she could empathise with the loneliness of the old woman. Wendy's husband may have been difficult when he had been at home, but he had been there when she arrived. All she had now was a stone-cold house where her voice echoed. Sometimes, she felt like screaming when she got home. Challis Street was not warm and inviting, but at least there were people and noise and activity. The long hours of a murder case suited her fine; telling an old woman that her only child had died thirty years previously did not.

'It's Garry. I'm sorry.'

'I always knew it was.'

'Any more than a mother's instinct?' Wendy asked.

'Too much dirty laundry, too much history,' the woman said. Wendy could see the sadness etched on her face, regardless of the brave manner in which she laboured around the kitchen, stroking one cat and then another. She offered Wendy a cup of tea; Wendy accepted, even offered to make it for her. Gertrude Richardson declined.

'I'd like to see him.'

'It's thirty years.'

'I've seen dead bodies before, and he's still my son.'

'You said that before. What did you mean?'

'I can't talk about that now. I just want to see my son.'

'I'll arrange it for you. Do you want me to stay here with you?'

'There's a room upstairs. I would appreciate the company.'

Wendy had prepared for such an eventuality; she had brought a change of clothes and a washbag just in case. Isaac told her to stay, do what was necessary, and to keep asking questions, no matter how gentle, how innocuous.

***

Isaac realised that Montague Grenfell, even though he was in his seventies, was mentally and physically stronger. He had scheduled the appointment for two o'clock in the afternoon at the lawyer's office. As he walked briskly up the three floors to the office, he realised that an early morning jog before coming to work was doing him good.

It had been a couple of weeks since Jess had moved out, and in that time there had been no one else in his flat. He had to admit he missed her, and the only time she had contacted him was to let him know that she had paid the electricity, as they had agreed when she had moved in. An independent woman, she had intended to contribute to the upkeep of their shared accommodation.

She also let him know that she still loved him, and if…

Isaac felt sadness talking to her, but realised that the if… was not going to happen. And besides, he felt better, if sadder, being a free man. He wanted to settle down, realised he probably never would. He was not sure how it would impact on his career with the Metropolitan Police, but realised it probably would not. After all, he, the son of Jamaican immigrants, had made detective chief inspector in record time, in a society that stated equality for all, but rarely was equal. He was still after the top job at the Met, and if he was single and black and the son of immigrants, so be it. And besides, he would achieve it in record time.

'How's Gertrude?' Grenfell asked.

'You've not spoken to her?'

'I phoned. She said she was all right.'

'But you're not sure?'

'Not totally, but she was always harder to read than her sister. Mavis is an open book, what you see is what you get. With Gertrude, you could never be sure what she was thinking.'

'Constable Gladstone said she took the news as well as could be expected.'

'Ambiguous statement, don't you think?'

'My constable thought the woman looked sad. That's why she offered to stay the night with her.'

'In that awful house?'

'There's a room upstairs that's in reasonable condition.'

'Your constable can keep asking questions.'

'Her reason to stay is compassionate, no more.'

'True, true,' Grenfell said.

'Coming back to the reality,' Isaac said, 'what don't I know that I should?'

'I'm not sure where to start.'

'Let's start with the women's childhood.'

'I'll make some tea first,' the lawyer said. Five minutes later he returned. Isaac noticed that his hands were not trembling.

'They came up to our home, you would call it a stately home, every summer for two weeks. I am ten years younger than Mavis, twelve years younger than Gertrude. They treated me well, made sure I was fed and bathed as a baby. They were like sisters to me, and we were all fond of each other.'

'Gertrude and Mavis, good friends?'

'They were inseparable until their late teens.'

'What happened?'

'The inevitable. Gertrude was the more promiscuous of the two, although Mavis was far from perfect.'

'Were there many opportunities in those days for promiscuity?'

'Amongst the aristocratic and the idle rich? A different set of values for the upper classes to the proletariat. I was as much a part of it as anyone back then. I was ignored by them after they reached the age of seventeen. My chance to play up came later.'

'Did you see them much after they reached adolescence?'

'Just family occasions: weddings, deaths, the occasional baptism.'

'And then what?'

'I never saw them for many years, heard about them in the gossip columns. Both of them were regarded as beauties, and they were always popping up at Ascot for the races or at some club or another. Invariably squired by the son of a lord or a duke, sometimes in the company of a minor royal.'

'So why did Gertrude marry Michael Solomon?'

'Beauty fades, and a royal wants a virgin, and the son of a lord wants someone reasonably chaste. Gertrude did not qualify on either count. Rumours of an abortion at one stage, but I don't know if that is true or not, never asked either.'

'Was Michael Solomon wealthy?'

'Successful in trade. I suppose he was. Remember, their father was still alive then, so they only had an allowance. From what I know, Gertrude fell heavily in love with Michael, and they married within a couple of months. Her father disapproved until he met him, and then he was quickly charmed. Finally gave them his blessing and a house in Twickenham.'

'Mavis?'

'She travelled in Europe for a few years after the war.'

'And her husband?'

'I never liked him.'

'Any reason?'

'Irish.'

'Is that sufficient?'

'She met him in Italy. He wooed her, bedded her, and eventually married her once he realised that her father was on his deathbed, and she was about to get a half-share in a substantial fortune.'

'Did she?'

'It was substantial. I handled the legal paperwork, assigned each sister their proportion.'

'And the husband?'

'He lasted for a few years, until he realised that Mavis was no fool, and that his good life came with limitations, but no claim to the fortune.'

'Back then, the husband would be entitled, wouldn't he?'

'Not according to their father's last will and testament. He knew that Gertrude was susceptible to unscrupulous men, and that

373

Mavis had made an unfortunate choice in a husband. As I said, I dealt with the legal aspect to protect the women.'

'But it didn't protect Gertrude?'

'Legally and financially, it did, but there were other problems.'

'Michael Solomon?'

'Not at all. He had his problems, but he always came back to Gertrude. He would never have taken advantage of her.'

'Was there someone else?'

'Some years later there was an issue.'

'What kind of issue? Why did Solomon leave and take up with another woman in Fulham?'

'It's best if you talk to Gertrude on this one. Otherwise, I'll need her permission to tell you.'

'I could make it official.'

'It doesn't need that. Give me a day or so to clear the way. In the meantime, look after Gertrude. She has had a rough time over the years.'

***

Garry Solomon's body was still with the forensic pathologist. Apart from a desiccated shell, some hair and the tattoo, there were no other identifying marks. Isaac checked to ensure that the body would be available, to ensure there was some clothing, and that an attempt would be made to make the corpse's face acceptable to view. They stated that it would be impossible, and the best they could do would be to ensure a darkened room, and a veil covering the face. He ran it past Wendy, who spoke to the mother.

Two days after the mother's request, both Wendy and Gertrude Richardson found themselves outside the address where the body was stored. It was the first time outside the mansion in Richmond for five years for the old woman.

'Are you sure?' Wendy asked.

'I'm sure.'

They entered the building, met a well-mannered laboratory assistant who escorted them to the viewing area. The corpse rested in a coffin which the laboratory had secured for the viewing; the lid was open. The mother approached the casket timidly and looked in. She slowly pulled the veil from the face to look at her son. It was not a pleasant sight. Wendy approached and looked in as well; it upset her greatly. She saw what looked to be an Egyptian mummy. Gertrude Richardson could only see a son; her mind drifted back to him as a child, then a boy, then an adult of nineteen, which was the last time she had seen him alive. He had died at the age of thirty-six. If he had lived, he would have been in his late sixties, drawing his pension, presenting her with grandchildren. She was very sad, although she did not show it.

'Thank you,' she said to Wendy. 'I always wanted to see him again, if only for a minute. I am exhausted. Would you please take me home.'

Wendy drove her home, put her in a bed upstairs, promising to feed the cats. She then went downstairs to make the old woman a cup of tea, and prepare some food for her. When Wendy returned twenty minutes later, the old lady was lying on her back, her eyes wide open, her mouth slightly ajar. She was dead.

***

'You did well, Wendy,' Isaac said on her return to the office several hours later. As sad as it was, Gertrude Richardson had died of natural causes. There would be an autopsy, as she was an integral person in a murder investigation, but Wendy saw it as a formality. The woman, old and frail, had held on to see her son. She had died soon after as a result. Wendy had stayed at the mansion until the body had been removed. She then phoned the Battersea Dogs and Cats Home to come and take care of the cats. She counted twenty-three. Larry said he would take the one that kept sitting on his lap. Wendy decided on two that would provide company for her when she got home at night. The rest she surmised would be adopted out, more likely euthanised.

'It doesn't feel that way at the moment, sir,' she said.

'It will in time. Are you free to talk about the case?'

'It will help to take my mind off what happened. No wonder she died after what she saw in that casket.'

'You said she was used to dead bodies.'

'She never explained why. It was her son she was looking at, but she stood there showing no emotion.'

'Her lawyer said she concealed her feelings well, never knew what she was thinking. Mavis, he said, was the opposite.'

'Where's DI Hill?'

'He went out to inform Mavis Richardson. Apparently, the woman became quite emotional. Larry's still there.'

'Maybe I should go there as well, sir.'

'Not necessary. Larry took her to a formal identification of her sister. He will be here within the next hour.'

Bridget, sensing that Wendy was grieving, took her under her wing. She settled her down on a comfortable chair and gave her a strong brew of tea and a couple of chocolate biscuits, as well as some cake she had brought from home. Ten minutes later, Wendy was much better.

'She identified the body,' DI Hill said on his return to the station.

'Where is she now?'

'Back at her house. Her lawyer is with her.'

'We should go out there,' Isaac said to Larry.

'Yes, sir.'

'I'll go as well,' Wendy said.

'Go home and take it easy for the rest of the day,' Isaac said.

'She's coming home with me,' Bridget said. 'I don't think she wants to be on her own tonight.' Wendy thanked her.

It took forty-five minutes to make the trip out to Mavis Richardson's house. Larry reflected that it would only have taken twelve on the train. Isaac could only agree.

They saw Montague Grenfell's car in the driveway of the house on their arrival, a late model Mercedes. They knocked at the door.

'Come in,' Montague Grenfell said. 'Miss Richardson is composing herself. She will be down in a minute.' Isaac reflected that the man seemed at home in the house.

The woman joined them soon after. She was relaxed and agreeable, although there were signs of crying around her eyes.

'I'm sorry about your loss,' Isaac said.

'Thank you, DCI Cook. We didn't always see eye to eye, but she was still my sister.'

'There are questions to be asked, answers to be given. Is this an appropriate time?'

'There will never be an appropriate time.'

'Are you able to elaborate?' Isaac asked.

'Another time would be better,' Grenfell said.

'The truth will come out sometime. It is best to clear the air now,' Mavis Richardson said.

She went to make tea for everyone. Isaac accompanied her to assist. She appeared to appreciate the gesture.

Upon their return, Isaac placed the tray in the middle of the coffee table. Everyone helped themselves to the tea and the small cakes. 'Baked them myself,' she said.

'They're delicious,' Larry and Isaac said in unison. Everyone knew that it was small talk, the sparring before the main event. There was a secret, possibly secrets that were crucial to solving the murder of Garry Solomon aka Solly Michaels. The person most likely to know had died. Isaac was hopeful that those remaining knew as much.

'Miss Richardson, were you aware that Garry Solomon was in London during the 1980s, and possibly the years preceding?'

'I never saw him again, but he knew that he would not be welcome.'

'Did your sister know of your ambivalence?'

'Yes.'

'Can you elaborate?'

'Must I?'

'Yes. This is a murder enquiry.'

'Very well.' She sat down, perched herself on the edge of a chair. She looked unsure of herself. 'Garry had always been a disruptive child, even when he was very young. A cruel streak as well. Gertrude always made excuses; Michael always forgave. We were sharing the mansion in Richmond. It was the sixties, the swinging sixties, free love.'

'You were part of that scene?' Isaac asked.

'We were still young enough to enjoy it. We were promiscuous, always screwing around when we were in our teens, and it had carried on as we got older. It was what the elite used to get up to, although most everyone will deny it. We used to have some wild parties. Mainly alcohol, but some drugs, and often people would pair off, car keys in a bowl, that sort of thing.'

'Gertrude was married,' Isaac said.

'So was I, but it didn't seem to matter. I would pair off with her husband or someone else. She would do the same. No one appeared to be affected by it, apart from Garry. It was our mistake really, too interested in our pleasures at the expense of a minor, although he was in his early teens by then. We always ensured he was at boarding school during the week when we had the parties. Whenever he came home, it was just one happy family: picnics on the lawn, games around an open fire. Even then, he would quickly lose his temper if the game did not go his way.'

'Why your ambivalence towards him?'

'He came home early while we were having one of our parties. Supposedly, he had picked up an infection in the school swimming pool. Usually, someone would have gone and picked him up, but for some reason it had not happened this time. It was a long time ago, and I forget the details. He comes into the house; those who are not upstairs paired off are out for the count on alcohol and drugs. Not finding anyone that he knows, he climbs the stairs and enters the first room he finds.'

'What did he find?' Larry asked.

'Two naked bodies entwined.'

'Who were they?'

'His father and me, who else?'

'And then?'

'He goes crazy, starts hitting me with an iron poker used to stoke the fire. I was on top. Eventually, my husband comes in and restrains him, and I'm taken off to the hospital.'

'Serious injuries?'

'Bruising, black and blue for some weeks, but I recovered.'

'And your husband? What did he say finding you with Michael Solomon?'

'Nothing. He was off with someone else. Gertrude was with Montague.'

'So why the ambivalence? It seems he had every right to be upset.'

'Of course, but then he gets back to his school, and tells all his friends who tell their parents. It is just bad breeding. The upper classes keep their dirty laundry to themselves, but then Garry never understood that. Just common, I suppose.'

Isaac saw clearly that Mavis Richardson was a snob who saw breeding and class as paramount. He decided that he did not like her, regardless of how polite and friendly she had been towards him.

Chapter 9

Mavis Richardson's husband continued to be an enigma. The name of O'Loughlin did not automatically conjure up thoughts of aristocracy and breeding. Isaac realised that he needed to be found. He was the one person missing out of the key group.

There was also the question of what happened to Garry Solomon, or Solly Michaels as he seemed to have been known. He had come from a privileged background, but police records showed behaviour not akin to influence and importance. There were police reports available, indicating that a Solly Michaels had been picked up for drug trafficking, occasional violence, and receiving stolen goods.

Isaac felt it was necessary to find out more about him. And then the question remained, why a fireplace in a house belonging to the Richardson sisters? It was evident that the body would be found at some stage and an identification secured. Too many variables, too many unanswered questions. He needed Larry and Wendy out and about, aiming to reduce the unknowns. Wendy seemed best placed to find the missing husband, Larry better placed to find out if anyone knew the story of Garry Solomon. From all indications that would require him entering the underbelly of society, going into places where a woman might not be welcome.

'Surely Garry Solomon is more important,' Larry Hill said at the evening meeting.

'Outline your thought process,' Isaac said.

'He disappears for all those years, and then he ends up in the fireplace of the house in Bellevue Street.'

Bridget wanted to say something. Isaac waved his hand at her, a gesture to keep quiet for the moment. Wendy had questions to ask, but she knew Isaac's style. He was a team player who did not steal someone's thunder when they were on a roll.

Larry continued after taking a quick sip of his coffee. 'Garry Solomon is here in London, a petty villain. There's a fortune to be had, yet he decides not to come forward to claim any of it.'

'What about the antagonism from Mavis Richardson?' Wendy asked.

'What about it?' Larry replied. 'Garry Solomon was a villain, and by all accounts a nasty piece of work. Do you think he would care who he upset?'

'Probably not, and then there is his mother. Why didn't he contact her at least a few times over the years?'

'Maybe he did, but we'll never know now as both mother and son are dead,' Isaac said.

'I've obtained his full criminal record. It may help to fill in some of the blanks,' Bridget said.

'Great,' Larry said. 'Let me finish first.'

'It looks as if we're in for a long night. Do I need to phone for some food?' Isaac asked.

Bridget and Wendy were quick to raise their hands. Isaac knew his keep fit regime was to suffer. Jess had left a message, wanting to meet up. He quickly sent her a message stating that he was busy until ten that night. Her reply was curt.

Larry took the floor again. He stood up and leant against the wall. 'We know he's a villain, but why does he end up dead in a fireplace? The address would indicate that his murder was committed by someone he knew, someone who had access to the house.'

'But why?' Isaac asked. 'Hiding a body in a fireplace, hoping it would not be disturbed, makes no sense.'

'It must have been temporary, and for some reason the person never returned.'

'It still makes no sense,' Wendy said. 'If you intend to hide a body for a short period, there must be better places than the house.'

'Do we know where he was murdered?' Bridget asked.

'Good question,' Isaac said. 'The assumption is that it was in the house, but that's not been confirmed. After thirty years, it may be difficult to ascertain.'

'The crime scene examiner, what did he say?' Wendy asked.

'Not his call. He checked the body, and then handed it over to his crime scene investigators.'

'There are still another few variables,' Larry said. 'If Garry Solomon did not contact his mother, what about his father?'

'Another dead witness,' Isaac said.

'But his wife, or should I say his bigamous wife, is still alive,' Wendy said. 'I'll go out there tomorrow.'

'If somehow Garry Solomon had managed to avoid any contact with his parents, then why does he appear all of a sudden, only to be murdered?' Larry asked.

'Larry's right,' Isaac said. 'All those years, and not once has he contacted his parents. It seems unlikely that he had not seen his father. They both moved in the same area of London.'

'Their lawyer appears suspect,' Larry said.

'That's my thought,' Isaac replied. 'He said that there was a secret, and if the body tied in with the sisters, he would reveal it to me.'

'Now's the time, sir,' Wendy said.

The pizzas had arrived, and everyone was eating. Isaac had promised himself to keep it down to two slices, although he snuck in a third.

'Garry Solomon is murdered for a reason. Asking for money hardly seems sufficient,' Larry said.

'Montague Grenfell is the key to this,' Isaac said.

'I'll go out and see the grieving sister tomorrow,' Larry said. 'She must know something.'

'I'll meet Michael Solomon's widow.' Wendy reiterated her earlier statement.

'Bridget, can you check out Garry Solomon's movements over the missing years? See if there is anything of interest,' Isaac said.

'And you, sir?' Wendy asked.

'Montague St John Grenfell is going to give me some answers tomorrow, Earl Grey tea or no Earl Grey tea. I remain convinced that he knows something. The dead man had found out something which was dynamite. It was what got him killed. Grenfell must know something, although we must not discount Mavis Richardson.'

At eleven in the evening, the meeting concluded. Isaac sent an SMS to Jess. She sent one back to tell him it was too late, and she would talk to him another time.

Isaac went home to a cold bed and a hot drink, which was not how he liked his day to conclude.

At nine o'clock the next morning, Isaac made the climb up to Montague Grenfell's office. He had managed to have an early morning jog, and this time he ran up the stairs.

Grenfell had not been expecting a visit from the DCI. He did not seem pleased to see him.

'Sad business about Gertrude,' Grenfell said.

'Why was her son murdered?' Isaac asked. He was not in the mood for procrastination. It was clear that the shock of Gertrude Richardson seeing her son no more than a mummified shell, manifestly unrecognisable except to a mother, had been the reason for her death.

'I don't know.' Montague Grenfell, as usual, prepared tea. Isaac was aware that the man was hiding a secret. A secret that had remained hidden, unspoken, for many years. With Garry Solomon's identity confirmed and his murder proved, the secret needed to be revealed.

'We can do this down at Challis Street Police Station if that would help you to give me a straight answer.' Grenfell was perturbed by the change in the policeman's manner.

Grenfell had relaxed back in his chair, looking up into the air, resisting the need to make eye contact with Isaac. 'Neither of the two women had any other children,' he said.

'Is that a fact?' Isaac asked. 'You failed to tell me about Gertrude's son before. You could be omitting some information now.'

'I failed to mention her son before because it was not relevant.'

'You suspected it may be him in the fireplace. Am I correct in that assumption?'

'From the information you had given me about the body, it seemed likely but highly improbable.'

'Why do you say that?'

'He disappeared when he was in his teens. No one had heard from him since, except for a postcard to Gertrude to say he was in India.'

'Is it confirmed that he was in India?' Isaac asked.

'I remember seeing it. There was an Indian stamp on it. Gertrude was delighted when she received it.'

'And you felt that your suspicions about the body did not warrant informing the police?'

'There were no suspicions. He had disappeared many years before the body was placed in the fireplace. The fact that the age appeared to be about the same as Garry seemed circumstantial. I know that he was in Australia for a short period.'

'How do you know this?'

'I am the family lawyer. It's my business to know.'

'But how? And more importantly, why?'

'If both of the sisters die, then Garry Solomon would have inherited their money and assets.'

'What about their husbands?'

'Mavis was smart enough to make sure that wouldn't happen. She married for love, but she was still a realist. She knew the family wealth would make them an attractive target for smooth-talking Romeos.'

'But Gertrude lost all her money to this type of man?' Isaac said.

'She lost plenty, but not all.'

'You'd better explain that statement.'

Montague Grenfell went to make another cup of tea.

The lawyer returned and sat upright on his chair. 'I suppose I should confess something here,' he said.

'If you're about to confess to the murder, then I should caution you.'

'Nothing like that,' Grenfell replied.

'When Gertrude was in her twenties, she fell madly in love with an Italian she had met on holiday in Italy. Both Mavis and I were aware of Gertrude and her momentary fantasies, falling for the wrong kind of man only to realise very quickly that it was more lust than love. Gertrude at that time had access to half of the Richardson family fortune. In the moment of greatest love, the man could ask for anything and she would agree. This Italian gave her a story about his ailing mother back home. Gertrude, an easy target then, not the embittered woman that she became, fell for the story. He had letters and photos, even arranged for her to phone his mother. The outcome of this was that Gertrude arranged a transfer of twenty thousand pounds to his account. Remember, this is the 1950s, so in today's money that would be over two hundred thousand pounds.'

'A lot of money,' Isaac said.

'As you say, a lot of money.'

'And the Italian?'

'After it had been made clear that no more would be forthcoming, he soon disappeared.'

'And what of Gertrude?'

'Broken-hearted for a few weeks. Some years later, she found someone else.'

'Another scoundrel?'

'Not this time, but he had issues.'

'What sort of problems?'

'He couldn't keep it in his pants.'

'Unfaithful?'

'Eventually bigamy.'

'Michael Solomon?' Isaac asked.

'Yes.'

'You mentioned a confession.'

'It was clear that Gertrude, given the opportunity, would have given all of her money to one man or another.'

'You said that Michael Solomon was a friend of yours,' Isaac reminded Grenfell.

'He was, but I did not want to see Gertrude lose all her money to him.'

'But he was a good businessman?'

'Eventually, but he would take some risks, go into substantial debt. Gertrude had to be protected.'

'What did you do?'

'Mavis knew the details, and we hatched a plan. The best protection for her sister was to ensure that she had no noticeable wealth. Then any smooth-tongued man that came hunting for a wealthy woman would not find it with Gertrude.'

'I was under the assumption that she had lost all her money, and that Mavis had covered the debts.'

'Not all of it. Gertrude still had sufficient, although she was never interested in asking or checking. To her, money was there for spending. I doubt if she looked at a bank account once in her life.'

'Mavis?' Isaac asked.

'Total opposite. Mavis could tell you her bank balance down to the last pound.'

'But the hatred between the sisters?'

'There was no hatred from Mavis. She loved her sister. The problem was with Gertrude. She blamed Mavis for her life, her parlous state, even the health of her cats, the condition of the mansion. And especially for her son leaving.'

'Are you saying that her hatred was invalid?'

'If Garry had not seen his father with Mavis on the bed, then maybe he would not have disappeared, but that's past history. As I said, Michael Solomon was a friend, even if he could waste money, Gertrude's money, at times. Garry, for whatever reason, was not as the father. Mavis always saw him as common, but it was not that.'

'What was it?' Isaac asked.

385

'Being shuffled off to a boarding school at an early age may have been part of the problem. The belief that he was unloved, especially by his mother. But mainly because he was not a good person. His character, even from an early age, was disruptive, argumentative, and by the time he was nineteen, he was already getting into trouble with the police. He had been to three boarding schools, all very expensive and exclusive, and he had been expelled from the first two for stealing from the other boys. He was destined to turn out bad, and his father knew that.'

'His mother?'

'She made excuses, but she was not a good mother. Always interested in the pursuit of her own pleasures, and she was promiscuous, even more so than Mavis.'

'The parties at the mansion?'

'Harmless fun for those who partook.'

'You included?'

'Why not? I was young, and there were always plenty of women.'

'You stated before that you ensured that Gertrude had no visible wealth.' Isaac returned to Grenfell's earlier statement.

'It was clear that Gertrude would give her half of the fortune away eventually. Each time that she came to her sister for money, we would take some more and put it into a trust account.'

'And this money?'

'It's all there. The records are meticulous. Gertrude and eventually Garry were still wealthy.'

'If Garry had lived, he would have inherited money?'

'Yes.'

'Enough money to kill for?'

'I suppose so. The money was not the issue then as Gertrude still had plenty.'

'If Gertrude had so much money, then why did she live so poorly? Why did her sister allow it?'

'But she didn't. That was Gertrude's choice. She was always eccentric. The crazy old woman with the cats suited her. I had offered to fix up the mansion for her, even take the cats to the vet for check-ups, but she wouldn't have any of it.'

'Who owns the mansion?'

'Gertrude and Mavis own it jointly.'

'But Mavis said she did, and Gertrude believed it did not belong to her,' Isaac said.

'That may be, but there was an incident some years ago when Gertrude wanted her half-share to help out Michael Solomon.'

'And you didn't give him the money?'

'There was already money in the trust fund. We used that and kept the mansion. Believe me, there was never any attempt to cheat Gertrude. It was all done out of love to protect her.'

Isaac realised that Montague Grenfell had explained the situation satisfactorily. It all sounded plausible to him, but it would need to be checked out.

'Due to the seriousness of the matter, would you be willing to allow the trust fund records to be examined?' Isaac asked.

'Yes.'

Isaac intended to pass them over initially to Bridget. His instinct told him that Grenfell had acted honourably. He was still not sure about Mavis Richardson.

Chapter 10

Wendy met Mary Solomon at a restaurant close to where the woman lived.

'My daughter is looking after her children,' the woman said. Wendy noticed that she looked a lot better away from the oppressive house in Fulham.

'Mrs Solomon, I have a few questions,' Wendy said.

'Call me Mary. Besides, I am not sure if I am legally Mrs Solomon.' Wendy chose not to comment.

'Are you aware of a child from his previous marriage?' Wendy asked.

'He mentioned that there was a son.'

'Did you have any suspicions that your husband may not have been divorced?'

'None. It was never mentioned when we applied for a marriage licence. I always assumed it was legitimate.'

'And the previous wife, what did you know about her?'

'He never spoke about her. I don't even know her name.'

'She died last week,' Wendy said.

'I'm sorry to hear that.'

'Does the name Solly Michaels mean anything to you?'

The reaction on Mary Solomon's face indicated that it did.

'I met a person by that name, a long time ago. He was friendly with my husband.'

'Do you remember the year?'

'Not really. He would have been about my age.'

'What age would you have been?'

'In my early thirties.'

'Did you meet him many times?' Wendy asked.

'Only a couple of times. I assumed it was to do with my husband's business. Why did you ask about Solly Michaels?' Mary Solomon asked.

'Subject to confirmation, it was his son.'

Mary Solomon sat back on the chair, visibly shrunken. 'What else did my husband not tell me?' she asked.

'Unfortunately, we need to find out,' Wendy said.

'My eldest son is always in trouble with the police. Was Michael's first son?'

'It appears so.'

'It must be genetic. Michael's first son, and our son and daughter.'

'Your daughter?'

'A bad drug habit. She tells me she's working up in the city, but I know the truth.'

Wendy could see that the woman had been dealt a bad hand, and that life had not treated her well.

'Tell me more about your daughter,' Wendy said.

'I followed her once. She's working in a club up there, selling herself to feed her habit.'

'Does she know that you know?'

'I confronted her. She told me to mind my own business. Then she lands her mongrel spawn on me to babysit. They are only children, but I can see it already. Michael's genes have infected another generation. They'll grow up same as the mother and the grandfather.'

'What about the father of the children?' Wendy asked.

'Some mongrel or mongrels she sold herself to, no doubt. One of the children looks half-Chinese.'

'Your son's child?'

'The mother walked out on Daniel after he had hit her once too often. I am the child's mother now, although he looks fine. Maybe with this one it will be my genes and its mother.'

'Good woman, was she?'

'Lovely, but Daniel doesn't know how to treat women. His father did.'

'Solly Michaels, is there any more you can tell me about him?' Wendy asked.

So far, they had not ordered any food. Wendy rectified the situation and ordered for them both. The woman sitting opposite appeared glad to be taking a break from the drudgery of her domestic situation. Wendy was thankful that her children were fine and adult and not causing trouble. Even her husband had treated her well until his dementia kicked in.

'Michael's son by this other woman, what happened to him?' Mary Solomon asked.

'He's dead.'

'I'm sorry to hear that. He was a nice-looking man. Now I think about it, he did bear a resemblance to Michael. I must have been stupid not to notice, although he always called my husband by his first name.'

'He died in 1987.'

'How sad. Do you think Michael knew?'

'We don't know.'

389

'I'll let you know if I remember any more, but it could not have been Michael, not his own son.'

'I only hope you are right.'

After finishing their meal, Wendy walked with Mary Solomon to her house. The woman gave Wendy a hug as they parted. Wendy realised that Michael Solomon knew more than he had ever told Mary. She hoped he was not involved in Garry's death as Mary Solomon had enough to deal with. She had learnt that her husband had been a bigamist, her marriage certificate was probably not valid, and then she had two children and their offspring, and none of them looked fine. To find out that her husband was a murderer as well, a murderer of his own son, Wendy thought, would be more than Mary Solomon could be expected to bear.

***

Mavis Richardson was extremely cordial when Larry Hill knocked on her door. He had some trepidation about visiting her on his own, but everyone was busy, and besides he did not need a nursemaid to look after him.

'On your own?' she asked. Larry noticed a nice spread of food laid out on the coffee table. He had questions to ask, not the time to partake of a feast, and besides, he needed to keep his distance from the woman.

Larry seated himself in a chair close to the fireplace. Mavis Richardson sat close by in another chair. 'There are some questions,' he said.

'A lot of questions, I suppose.'

'According to Montague Grenfell, Gertrude's money was intact.'

'A lot of it was wasted, but we saved her from herself.'

'We?'

'Montague and I.'

'There was animosity between you and your sister, though.'

'Only from her side. As I told you before, I forgave her.'

'Was she aware that financially she was secure?'

'No.'

'Any reason?'

'If she had known, she would have taken action to secure her share. She was an easy touch for a charming man.'

'Michael Solomon?'

'He was exceedingly charming.'

'And he took her money?'

'He did, but he was still a good man. I'm sure he loved Gertrude, as much as she loved him.'

'Then why did he leave?'

'He loved too many women. Eventually Gertrude tired of his dalliances. And there was a scene. After that, he left.'

'They never divorced, yet he marries again?'

'What's the problem with that?' Mavis asked.

'It's illegal for one thing.'

'And the other?'

'It just seems unusual. He could have divorced Gertrude officially, and then he could have married the other woman.'

'Divorce would not have been an option for Gertrude.'

'Did he ask her?'

'Montague alluded to that fact. I never asked for the details. I had problems of my own.'

'Your husband?'

'Ger O'Loughlin.'

'And where is he now?'

'Not here.'

'Have you seen or heard from him since?' Larry asked.

'Infrequently.'

'We have no record of children. Is that correct?'

'I never had children. Never wanted them anyway. My social life was more important. A child would only have hampered my lifestyle.'

'And your husband?'

'He wanted children. My reluctance doomed the marriage.'

'And where is he now?'

'Ireland, surrounded by his brood.'

'How do you know this?'

'He occasionally contacts me. I've not seen him though.'

Larry realised that his questioning was not progressing. Ger O'Loughlin did not seem relevant, and Bridget had found proof that he and Mavis Richardson were legally divorced. The death of

Garry Solomon aka Solly Michael was the only issue. Mavis Richardson's husband was not relevant unless he could be tied in with Gertrude's family.

'Did your husband know Garry Solomon?'

'Yes. I told you that he pulled him off me.'

'We know that Garry Solomon disappeared when he was nineteen, but what about Michael Solomon?'

'He stayed around for another six months, but by then the parties at the mansion were starting to wither. Everyone was tired of the same people to swap car keys with. At first it had been fun, a titillation, but eventually it became routine.'

'Is that when you fell out with Gertrude?'

'Around that time.'

'Why?'

'She wanted money for Michael, a lot of money.'

'And you wouldn't give it to her?'

'I knew what he was up to. It wasn't financially sound, so Montague falsified the accounts to show that she didn't have that much money.'

'You effectively broke up her marriage,' Larry said.

'I couldn't let her bankrupt herself. Believe me, it was in her own best interest.'

'Did she eventually find out?'

'No.'

Larry took advantage of the spread placed in front of him, and he was only eating because he was hungry.

'A glass of wine, beer?' she asked.

'On duty. Can I come back to Garry Solomon?'

'If you must.'

'Did you ever hear from him again?'

'No, although Michael did.'

'Why do you say that?'

'Remember, I told you that I ran into him once in the street.'

'Did he mention his son?'

'He asked after Gertrude, I asked after their son.'

'His reply?'

'He said he had seen him on a couple of occasions. I asked him if the son had contacted his mother.'

'What did he say?'

'Garry could never forgive her.'

'Forgive her for what?'

'No idea. Maybe the lack of love he received from her, maybe the fact that his mother slept with other men, perhaps he was just angry, but I was the one screwing his father. He was not aware that Gertrude was off screwing someone else, although he was a smart lad. He probably assumed she was.'

'Tell me about that night,' Larry asked.

'It's old history. I am with his father, Gertrude is with Montague. Is this important?'

'I want to ascertain what happened after Garry put you in the hospital.'

'He ran out of the house. Five hours later, in the early morning, he returns.'

'And then what?'

'Nothing.'

'What did his father say to him?'

'Nothing. Garry's reaction was understandable. Michael and Gertrude took him to the Caribbean for a couple of weeks, acted the loving parents for once.'

'Did you see him again?'

'Never. Whenever he was there, I made sure to be somewhere else. That night was the last time that I saw him.'

'You never forgave him for what he did to you?'

'I've explained this before. It was his returning to school, and bragging to his friends about what he did to me that I could never forgive. As far as he was concerned, his father was welcome to screw whoever he wanted.'

'And his mother?'

'Typical male chauvinist attitude. Very prevalent in the sixties. It's alright for the man to screw around, but not the woman.'

'What did he say at school?'

'He told everyone, even the sons of friends of ours, that I was a slut. I could never forgive him for that. A sign of bad blood, Michael's blood. That's what happens when you breed outside of your class.'

'When did he finally leave home?'

'He was nineteen, hormones raging. He comes home with a female in tow and says he is off to India. He makes sure to score some money out of his parents and a bank transfer from Montague.'

'Your money?'

'Both Gertrude's and mine, although she did not know that it was.'

'Why did you agree?'

'He was still Gertrude's son.'

'And the female?'

'Supposedly he married her in India.'

'Where is she now?'

'I've no idea. Montague may know.'

Mavis Richardson excused herself and left the room for a couple of minutes. Larry took the opportunity to update Isaac regarding Garry Solomon's wife. If anyone knew what had happened in India and on their return, it would be her.

Isaac could see that information was still being withheld. It was almost as if the Richardson family and Montague Grenfell were intentionally obstructing them.

Larry continued at Mavis Richardson's house on instructions from Isaac. 'Keep probing,' Isaac said. 'What else are they withholding?'

Mavis Richardson returned with a fresh pot of tea. 'Who were you talking to?' she asked.

'My boss, DCI Cook.'

'What did he have to say?'

'He was curious as to what else we don't know.'

'I've told you everything that I know.'

'That may be, but until we started probing, we did not know that your sister had been married, or that her son had returned to England.'

'We are a private family. We don't air our dirty linen in public.'

'But this is a murder investigation into the death of your nephew.'

'That may be. My family, as with Montague's, goes back hundreds of years. There are a lot of secrets during that time, secrets best kept hidden.'

Chapter 11

'Bridget, what's your situation?' Isaac asked at the regular end of day meeting.

'Apart from collating all sundry information, I've had a cursory look at the documents the Richardson sisters' lawyer supplied,' Bridget said.

'What do you reckon?'

'I'm not an expert, but they appear to be in order.'

'Any transfer of money to Garry Solomon during the period mentioned by Mavis Richardson?'

'There were some transfers to him.'

'Can you check for a marriage certificate for Garry Solomon?' Larry asked.

'In India?' Bridget queried.

'I suppose so.'

'Almost impossible to find unless they legalised it in England. In India, it could have just been a Buddhist ceremony on a mountain top. It would not stand up in an English court of law.'

'Look anyway,' Larry said.

'What are your thoughts?' Isaac asked.

'If Garry Solomon had a child, legitimate or otherwise, then that child is due to inherit a substantial amount of money.'

'It is substantial if the records are correct,' Bridget said.

'How substantial?' Isaac asked.

'Gertrude Richardson may have regarded herself as a pauper, supported by a sister she abhorred.'

'She didn't even acknowledge that she had a sister,' Wendy said.

'According to the records, she still had a half-share in the mansion and five million pounds,' Bridget said.

'Substantial, as you say,' Isaac said.

'And it belongs to the widow is no longer alive. We need the will of Gertrude Richardson,' Larry said.

'Bridget, another job for you,' Isaac said. 'Check with the National Will Register. Otherwise, Montague Grenfell will have a copy.'

'Do you trust him, sir?' Wendy asked.

'Not particularly, that's why I'd prefer Bridget to see if she can find the will without letting him know.'

'I could do with some help. I am not an accountant. It needs a skilled person to check the documentation from Grenfell,' Bridget said.

'Wendy, your update,' Isaac said, momentarily ignoring Bridget's comment.

'Mary Solomon, the second wife of Michael Solomon, remembers meeting a Solly Michaels. She was not aware of his significance.'

'How old would he have been?' Larry asked.

'The woman can be a little vague. She has led a tough life, but from memory, she remembers him as being about the same age as she was. She thought he was in his early thirties.'

'A few years before he was murdered,' Isaac said.

'I will spend more time with her. Maybe she will be able to pinpoint the date more accurately.'

'You suspect his father?' Bridget asked.

'We're not forming an opinion on flimsy assumptions, not just yet,' Isaac said. 'We have proven that Garry Solomon was in London and that he had been in contact with his father, but not his mother.'

'She acted as though she had not seen him since he left when he was nineteen,' Wendy said.

'You were there when she formally identified the body?' Larry asked.

'She was convinced it was him, but visual identification was not possible. The body was far too decayed. It was purely DNA and dental records that proved who it was. The shock of seeing him killed her.'

'But you took her.'

'It was her son. She had a right to see him.'

'No issue from me,' Isaac said. 'What's important now is to find out more about Garry Solomon. Larry, can you focus on his criminal record, known haunts, known villains that he may have been in contact with. Wendy, it may be best if you work with Bridget and see if you can find Garry Solomon's widow.'

'And you, sir?' Wendy asked.

'Three flights of stairs and Montague Grenfell again. He knows a lot more than he's telling us.'

'Don't tell him we're looking for Gertrude Richardson's will,' Bridget reminded Isaac.

'Not at all, and find someone from Fraud to help you with the trust agreements and bank statements.'

***

Isaac saw clearly that Montague Grenfell was still withholding information. The murdered man and the lawyer shared a common ancestor with the father of one, the grandfather of the other. Montague Grenfell came from the legitimate line. Garry Richardson, however, came from the other side of the bed, in that his grandfather had not been legitimate. But as Grenfell had freely admitted, his father and the Richardson sisters' father had been brought up as brothers.

Isaac understood Grenfell's reticence, but this was a murder investigation. The time for propriety had passed, and a full and frank admission of all the skeletons in the cupboard was needed.

'I've been totally open with you, DCI Cook,' Montague Grenfell said when Isaac reminded him of the facts, and that withholding information, especially in a murder enquiry, was a criminal offence.

'You failed to mention that you had sent money to Michael Solomon and Gertrude Richardson's son, and you did not reveal that he had probably married in India. Do you deny that fact?'

'Michael told me, although I had no contact with him.'

'Garry Richardson's wife?'

'Michael assumed it was someone he had met at school, although he never met her.'

'Were there any children?'

'I have no idea.'

'Unfortunately, you have not revealed other information which we have subsequently unearthed. Is there any more that you are not telling us?'

'I have been open with you. I gave you full access to all legal and financial documents relating to Gertrude.'

'That is true. They appear to be in order.'

'You will find no errors there.'

'From what we can ascertain, Gertrude Richardson was a very wealthy woman, and subsequently her son would be. Yet you withheld that information from her.'

'As I said before, my intentions and those of her sister were totally honourable. I have no reason to reproach myself.'

'The woman lived in squalor.'

'Detective Chief Inspector, we've been over this before. Where she lived would have been restored to a liveable standard if she had wanted. I offered enough times.'

'And why did she refuse?'

'She was an old woman set in her ways. She liked the squalor and the cats defecating in the house. There was no way I, or her sister, could force her to change her ways, nor would we.'

'And what about the son? Was he entitled to any money?'

'If he had asked.'

'He didn't?'

'Never. Supposedly, he had returned from India with this woman, now his wife as a result of a wedding in a commune or on a hill top. No idea if it's legal, but it is probably not relevant under English law.'

'Children?' Isaac asked.

'I have already told you that I don't know. It is possible. If Garry was anything like his father, then she may have had a child. We looked after Gertrude even if she did not want our help. The son was young enough to look out for himself. Where he went, I never asked or cared.'

'Did Gertrude realise that her sister wanted to help her?'

'Impossible to say. Mavis, as you know, is concerned with appearances and breeding. Gertrude was not bothered by any of it. As long as she had her cats and some food, then she wanted no more. It was not Mavis and me who were the issue. It was the old woman.'

'And her money?'

'It is in trust until probate is resolved.'

***

There seemed to be two major issues confronting the investigation. Isaac summed them up at the evening's meeting. So far, they had managed to hold it every night during the investigation, even managed to take one Sunday off. Not that is helped with Jess O'Neill as she was gone and no longer answering his phone calls. He put it down to the fact that she was busy. Isaac, never a fan of television, had watched the programme she produced a couple of times in the last week, and it was clear that its standards had been maintained, although he regarded his opinion as subjective.

'We need to find out about Garry Solomon's wife,' Isaac said. Wendy, as usual, was nominated for the task.

'But why would someone murder him?' Larry asked.

'Unknown,' Isaac answered. 'How do we find out why? According to the family lawyer, there was no issue with money if he had come forward and asked.'

'Then his death is illogical,' Larry replied.

'Any ideas?' Bridget asked.

'I'm not sure about their lawyer is being totally honest,' Isaac said. It was dark outside and getting late, but he was in no hurry to get home. Larry was, as his wife was complaining about the hours he was working. Wendy's problems were more severe as her husband's hospital bills were way above her salary. She had secured an additional loan against her house, but she knew that it would not be long before she had to sell it.

Bridget revelled in the office environment with its endless challenges, and as long as Wendy was in the office, she was happy to stay. The two women's night out, invariably an excuse for too much gossip and too many drinks, had been postponed due to Wendy's visits to her husband. They were scheduling again for the weekend, but the pressure of work was now starting to eat into their socialising. Not that either woman complained too much as they both enjoyed the camaraderie of the department and the challenge of the job, even if at times it could have its sad moments.

Wendy had been with Gertrude Richardson when she had looked at the mummified, skeletal remains of her son. She had also been in her mansion preparing some food when the old woman had died, and now she had two of the woman's cats in her home, and they were still not domesticated enough to exit the house to conduct a call of nature. Bridget had her own problems at home; her layabout live-in lover, a council worker, was becoming lazier and more slovenly. She always prided herself on a tidy mind, a tidy house, and now he wasn't even washing the dishes after inviting his equally slovenly friends over. She could see that she was about to show him the door. The two women had discussed moving in together once Wendy's husband had passed away.

Larry, a happily married man, did not envy his DCI the lifestyle that he lived, although he knew of his reputation for beautiful women; who did not in the police station in Challis Street.

It was nine in the evening before the meeting concluded. Wendy had to leave to visit her husband, say goodnight to him, not sure if he would recognise her or not. Such a vibrant, active man in his younger days, then senility, then bitterness, and now a shell of a man 'waiting for the final call from his maker' as Bridget would say; not that Wendy was religious, but Bridget was. Wendy did not need the religious overtones, but it was good to have a friend who cared.

Larry took the opportunity to go home as well, promising to be in the office very early in the morning and to follow up on Garry Solomon.

Bridget, in no great hurry to go home, had another cup of coffee in her hand. 'I'll stay a couple of hours, do some preparation work for tomorrow,' she said.

'I'll keep you company,' Isaac said. He had no wish to hurry home. The only things that welcomed him there were a hot chocolate and a cold bed. *Not the ideal arrangement*, he thought.

He remembered Linda Harris's comment, the last time they had spoken, a brief phone call when she had denied responsibility for the murder of Jess O'Neill's boss: 'We could have been something more.'

Isaac wondered if that could have been possible. He had been attracted to her, even slept with her that one time, but she was MI5, a minor cog in the organisation according to her.

On reflection, he realised that she would have been an ideal woman for him, but she came with too many secrets. He thought to ask his boss if he could find out what had become of her. Richard Goddard would know who to ask, but it was just idle speculation on his part. Isaac knew there would be other women, but it was now a drought after plenty. There had been Sophie White, and then Jess O'Neill, and now, nobody.

Chapter 12

With the office empty apart from Bridget, Isaac returned to his office. He picked up the necessary paperwork, put it down again. It was not that he had an issue with it, although there was too much. It was because they had a murder and no motive.

Garry Solomon, a criminal when he had no reason to be one, had died thirty years previously and had been stuffed behind a wooden structure crudely built around the fireplace.

But why? Isaac asked himself. The body would be found one day, although thirty years seemed a long time. If it had been placed there temporarily, then why attempt to conceal it, and why had the body not been found before now. Could the house have been unoccupied, unvisited in all those years? It seemed illogical. Bridget had evidence showing that the utility bills and rates had been paid during that time.

The newspaper placed under the body at the time of incarceration had been clear enough, and the date of vacating the house and the murder were within months of each other. The house was empty when the Baxters had moved in, but what was the condition when they had first seen it? Was it full of cobwebs, creaking doors, rats?

Isaac regretted not having his previous DI, Farhan Ahmed, with him. Then it would have been the two of them late at night, putting forward the imponderables, throwing up ideas, some valid, some crazy, but somehow it worked.

Larry Hill, Farhan's replacement, was an excellent detective inspector, but he was a family man and intended to stay that way.

Farhan had been too, but his staying late in the office had cost him his marriage, an occupational hazard all too common in the police force. Even the break up of the relationship with Jess, Isaac reflected, had to a large part come about due to his job taking precedence over his emotional responsibilities.

Bridget interrupted Isaac's train of thought. 'I've found an address for Garry Solomon's wife,' she said.

'Current?'

'Twenty years old, I'm afraid.'

'At least it will give something for Wendy to work on. Do you have a name?'

'Emily Solomon.'

'Any children?'

'None that I can find.'

'The last known address of Emily Solomon is after the death of her husband, Garry?'

'By a few years,' Bridget said.

'How do you know that it is the same woman?'

'She claimed unemployment benefits. There are documents on record showing that she was the legal wife of Garry Solomon, even a marriage certificate.'

'Married in England?'

'Registry Office, but it's legitimate. There are even copies of their birth certificates.'

'In that case any children, even Emily Solomon herself, would be legally entitled as beneficiaries of Gertrude Richardson's estate.'

'That would be correct,' Bridget said.

'Did you find a copy of Gertrude Richardson's will?'

'Not yet. Her family lawyer will have a copy.'

'I would prefer to obtain a copy from an independent source,' Isaac replied.

'First thing in the morning. Is that okay?' Bridget asked. Isaac looked up at the clock. It was midnight.

'Fine,' he replied. 'Larry needs to follow up on Garry Solomon. Any luck with his criminal record?'

'Larry already has a copy,' Bridget replied. Isaac realised what a great asset she had become to the department, always one step ahead.

***

Isaac was in the office early the next day, as was the team. Wendy was first out of the door, following up on an address for Garry Solomon's widow. She took the opportunity to smoke a cigarette, once she was free of the office.

Larry was not long after, and he was heading to Garry Solomon's last known criminal haunt, although after thirty years it seemed unlikely he would find too many people who remembered him.

Isaac, at a loose end, decided that Montague Grenfell was worth another visit.

Wendy's address for Emily Solomon was close to the centre of London in an upmarket area of Mayfair, which seemed incongruous as the woman had been claiming unemployment at one stage, and Garry Solomon had never risen above being a petty criminal and small-time hooligan.

Regardless, Wendy knocked at the door of the house. It was a very elegant townhouse, even better than Mavis Richardson's.

'Emily Solomon?' Wendy asked.

'Who's asking?' The accent was working class, not upper-class Mayfair.

'Constable Wendy Gladstone, Challis Street Police Station.'

'Long way from there, aren't you?'

'That may be, but I still need to contact Emily Solomon.'

'Why?'

'Once you confirm that you are Emily Solomon, I will tell you.'

'Long time since I've heard that name mentioned,' the woman said. Wendy could see that she was an attractive woman, who prided herself on her appearance but had not dealt with her speech.

'Are you admitting that you are Emily Solomon?'

'You'd better come in.'

Wendy entered, noted the grand hallway, the staircase at the rear. She was ushered into a side room and given a chair. It was not so much a request, more of a command.

'Nice place,' Wendy said.

'It's all mine.'

'You said it was a long time since you had heard the name Emily Solomon.'

'Twenty years at least.'

'Why?'

'I'm not pleased with you being here. Nothing personal, but the past is the past.'

'Any man here?'

'What do you mean? Husband, lover, an idle screw?'

'Yes.'

'There's the occasional man when I feel the need. Other than that, I'm here on my own.'

'Where did the money come from?'

'What business is that of yours?'

Wendy noted no attempt to offer a cup of tea. It was clear that the woman had money, or at least someone did, but the room was cold and unwelcoming. None of the ornaments indicative of a family were on show: no family photos, nothing to suggest any emotional involvement of the woman with another.

'When did you last see your husband?'

'Which one?'

'Garry Solomon.'

'Sometime in the eighties, I suppose.'

'I need you to be more specific.'

'Why? It is not a period in my life that I wish to remember.'

'Let's get the date correct first and then you can tell me why. Any chance of a cup of tea?'

With the woman in the kitchen, Wendy took the opportunity to look around the room. She rustled through some photos albums but was soon interrupted. She thought she had seen a photo of a man and a woman in Indian clothes, but could not be sure. If it were important, she would claim the album as vital evidence at a later date.

'1979.'

'Are you certain?'

'The bastard left me high and dry, not a penny to my name.'

'Garry Solomon?'

'Who else?' Emily Solomon replied.

'Did you divorce him?'

'Why? We weren't married, not in this country.'

'There's a marriage certificate.'

'His idea, not mine.'

'So you were married?'

'I only went through with it because he threatened me.'

'Did he do that often?'

'Often enough, almost strangled me once.'

'But why?'

'Caught me with another man.'

'Why marry you then?'

'He said it was important for the children.'

'You have children?'

'One son, but he's just the same as his father. I haven't seen him for a few years, don't want to.'

'And your name now?'

'Emma Hampshire.'

'Married?'

'I took his name and his money.'

'This house?' Wendy asked.

'I ensured that when he died it was mine.'

'Tell me about your husband.'

'Garry? We met when we were young. We travelled over to India, sat on a mountain top, the usual hippy stuff.'

'Smoked some weed?'

'Part of the spiritual experience. All Garry could see from it was the chance to screw some of the other women. Free love, they called it.'

'And you?'

'I was guilty as well.'

'And when you returned to London?'

'Garry set himself up in business and life was good. Then our son comes along, a beautiful bouncing boy.'

'What happened?'

'Garry fell in with a bad crowd: drinking, gambling, screwing the local tarts.'

'What do you know about his family?'

'I met his father once.'

'And his mother?'

'He said she was crazy. Why are you asking these questions?'

'Mrs Solomon, I am afraid that your husband is dead.'

'As far as I'm concerned, he has been dead for over thirty years.'

'You're not upset?' Wendy asked.

'After his treatment of me? What do you think?'

'Mrs Solomon, I believe we need to discuss this. Another cup of tea?'

'Call me Emma.'

Wendy's initial impression of the woman, something of a painted tart, had dissipated. Emma Hampshire appeared to be a woman whom life had initially treated badly, but it was now treating her well.

'What can you tell me about Garry Solomon? Let's start with his family background.'

'His father I met just the once. I could see where Garry had got his manner from.'

'A charmer?'

'Father and son alike.'

'And the mother?'

'No idea about her, other than she supposedly had money. Not that I saw any of it.'

'Life was tough?' Wendy asked.

'Not really. We were happy on our return from India, and Garry soon charmed himself into a good job before he set up his own business. I found out later the first job came about after he had screwed the female owner.'

'Like the father,' Wendy commented.

'Precisely.'

'Anyway, apart from his inability to keep it in his trousers, Garry was a good provider and a good father.'

'What happened?'

'Started running with the wrong crowd. He liked to socialise, and with a few too many drinks his behaviour would become erratic. Even hit me on a couple of occasions.'

'His mother died.'

'Sorry to hear that.' Emma Hampshire appeared to be genuine in her comment. 'It can be hard to have a child and never see them.'

'Is that the same with you?' Wendy asked.

'With Garry, it was alcohol; with Kevin, it's drugs.'

'You never see him?'

'Not for a couple of years.'

'Upsets you?'

'Of course, but what can I do? It's worse when I see what he has become. He had his father's charm, and then he gets himself addicted. I caught him shooting up in here once, threw him out on the street.'

'Can we come back to Garry? He changed his name to Solly Michaels. Was there any reason?'

'With me, he was Garry. With his criminal friends, he was Solly. No idea why.'

'Tell me about the criminal activities.'

'Not a lot to tell. He was running a motor repair business, good quality cars. Business was good, and apart from the drinking and the womanising, everything was fine.'

'You accepted the womanising?'

'It used to upset me, but as I said, he was a good father and a good provider.'

'Not such a good husband.'

'Not at all. He was a good husband at first. It was later that he changed.'

'Tell me about it.'

'All of a sudden, he's flush with a lot of cash, enough to pay off our house. I asked him about it. He told me just to be thankful and not ask questions.'

'What did you think?'

'What anyone would think.'

'Drugs.'

'He said it was gambling.'

'What was your reaction?'

'I told him that dealing with drugs was unacceptable and that it was either me and his son or the money.'

'His reaction?'

'He said okay for the first couple of times, but then there's a fancy car outside, and a tart sitting in the passenger's seat. I threw a scene, and he threw me out.'

'Literally?'

'He put us into a two-bedroom flat, ensured all the bills were paid, and that I had money to spend.'

'And then?'

'He was caught, spent two years in jail, and the money dried up. I'm out on the street with nowhere to go.'

'After that?'

'I was desperate for money. I had a baby in one arm and nowhere to live.'

'Your parents?'

'I was no longer in communication with them after I took off to India with Garry. They were very religious and could never accept free love, living on a commune, and meditating on a mountain top. They had told me before I left not to come back. Both dead now, car accident some years back. They had cut me out of their will, so I never bothered to visit their grave.'

'You're out on the street, so what did you do?'

'I found a women's refuge, worked two jobs a day, slowly recovered my life, and then I met Bob.'

'Bob Hampshire? How long were you with him?'

'Twenty-five years until he died of a heart attack.'

'Tell me about him?'

'He was older than me by a few years, but we were a great couple, and he ensured that Kevin went to the best schools. Even offered to marry me, but there was still the marriage with Garry, and besides, the church's blessing meant nothing to me. And when Bob died, he left money to his previous wife and their children, this house and enough money to me.'

Chapter 13

Larry's day had been spent finding out what he could about Garry Solomon. His criminal record indicated periods of incarceration starting with a two-year stretch in 1978. The date aligned with the information that Solomon's widow had stated.

It was clear that he was then using the name of Solly Michaels, initially reported at his arrest, although shown as Garry Solomon at his court case. From there on, there had been two periods of incarceration interspersed with periods of freedom. The records indicated several addresses over the years, each one progressively less salubrious than the other. Why he had not contacted Grenfell, the family lawyer, and his ex-wife, at least, from about 1981 was still unanswered. The litany of crimes, some minor, some major, indicated an unsavoury character with few moral restraints.

The last known address, 62 Bakewell Street, Greenwich, close to the Royal Observatory and the site of the Greenwich meridian line, was not what Larry had expected. It had been thirty years since Garry Solomon's death, but the almost derelict building could not have looked much better then. It was clearly uninhabited and had been that way for some years. Larry phoned Bridget for her to do some checks.

The information that Bridget had managed to put together had shown addresses firstly in Paddington then slowly moving eastwards and downwards in quality and suburb. Judging by the condition of the house in Greenwich, this had been his last address. There seemed little possibility of finding anyone who remembered him from that time. Without much more to be achieved he visited the local pub. The Green Elephant had seen better days, but it was run down enough to offer the possibility that someone may have known the hapless Garry Solomon.

'A pint of your best,' Larry said to the man behind the bar. The man reflected the condition of the pub; he was as run down as it was.

'Comin' up,' the singularly unfriendly reply.

'One for yourself,' Larry said.

'Don't mind if I do.'

There were a few others in the pub, some slowly getting drunk, some surfing the internet on their phones, but generally it was quiet. Larry wondered how it managed to stay financially viable.

'Did you ever know a Solly Michaels?' Larry asked. He realised it was a long shot, but it had been a fruitless trip out to Greenwich, and then he had a tiresome trip back to Challis Street afterwards.

'It doesn't ring a bell.' The publican had moved closer, taken a seat on his side of the bar.

'How about Garry Solomon?'

'Are you the police?'

'Detective Inspector Hill.'

'Any problems concerning me?'

'Not at all. Bakewell Street is the last known abode of Garry Solomon, also known as Solly Michaels.'

'How long ago?'

'Thirty years.'

'I've been here for forty. If he was a drinker, then he would have been in here.'

'Why's that?' Larry ordered another two pints: one for him, the other for the publican.

'Thirty years ago, we were the busiest pub in the area. Nowadays, as you can see...'

'What changed?'

'The boutique pubs. This pub no longer suited the up and coming trendies.'

'Bitter about it?' Larry asked.

'Not really. I own the lease and the building, and as long as enough people come through the door to pay the bills, then I'm fine.'

'Garry Solomon would have probably been down on his luck, although he would have dressed well.' Larry knew that the body in the fireplace was expensively dressed, which did not tie in with the house and the area Garry Solomon had been living in.

'There was a Solly that used to come in here, but that would have been back in 1984.'

Larry checked his records. In December 1983, Garry Solomon had been released from prison after serving twelve months, with time off for good behaviour. The charge, possession of a prohibited drug.

'Looks to be the same person,' Larry said. He noticed that the advice came at the cost of two more pints of beer.

'There's not a lot to tell you. He came in here every night for a couple of months, drank his fair share of alcohol, and then he disappeared.'

'What date would that have been?'

'February 1984, give or take a few weeks.'

It would take another two pints before Larry concluded with the publican. It was clear that the time difference between Greenwich and Garry Solomon's death was relevant. The period prior to Greenwich, while it may have some bearing on his demise, did not seem as important.

Larry phoned Isaac, explained the situation, and the reason why he was not in a condition to drive back to the office.

It had happened a few times to Isaac as well, and he fully understood. He told Larry to take an early night, and he would see him in the morning. At least Larry's wife would see him at a sociable hour, but not in the best condition.

***

The following day, Larry had to find out where Garry Solomon had gone after leaving Greenwich and before his untimely death. There was a period of three years and a change in fortune to be accounted for. In Greenwich, he had been destitute, an ex-prisoner. At the time of his death, he had been affluent; at least, that was the assumption judging by the clothes that he had been wearing at the time of his death.

Bridget was checking out the ownership of the house in Greenwich, and Isaac had another planned meeting with Montague Grenfell. Isaac's suspicions, as always, came back to the family lawyer. Wendy had found Garry Solomon's wife, now she had to find his son.

Neither were regarded as primary suspects in his death, as the construction of the fireplace surround at the house in Bellevue

Street had required someone of strength, and Wendy could not envisage Emma Hampshire as being capable, and the son would have only been thirteen at the time.

As Bridget was still checking on the information Larry wanted, he decided to contact some of Garry Solomon's earlier contacts. His criminal career had not been particularly long, lasting from his first prison sentence in 1977 through to his death in 1987. There had been two terms in prison, the first lasting twenty-four months, the second, twelve months. Seven years of freedom out of ten, which to Larry seemed to be statistically correct for the average villain.

If he had become involved in drug trafficking, it could only indicate one thing, that he was short of money. But then, there was Montague Grenfell stating that money was available for the asking, but Garry Solomon had never asked, which seemed illogical.

From what the team had managed to source, neither the father nor the son was short of charm or the willingness to stick their hand out for assistance. According to Gertrude Richardson, she had not seen Michael Solomon since he left in the seventies and her son since 1970.

'There's a secret,' Isaac said to Larry on his arrival in the office.

Bridget was checking the title deeds for the house in Greenwich, and yet again it was all leading back to Montague Grenfell. The ownership was not clear, but the attempts at obscuring it were. It was obvious that it would have required a smart legal mind to put it all in place. And why was the house derelict, when it was worth a lot of money? Anyone smart enough to obscure the ownership would have been smart enough to appreciate its value.

'Are we ruling out Garry Solomon's widow?' Isaac asked.

'He treated her badly at one stage,' Larry said.

'I'm trying to find the son,' Wendy said.

'Is he important?' Isaac asked.

'Not for the murder, but he may know something.'

'But he was only thirteen when Garry Solomon died.'

'That may be, but so far we have a body, apparently affluent, but no motive, and why hide it in a fireplace?' Wendy said.

It was a question that had concerned Isaac since the case began. Why not in the basement under the floor, and then covered with concrete, or a grave in the backyard. It was almost as if the discovery was to be expected.

'Let us look at who could have placed the body in the fireplace,' Isaac said to the team.

'The body would have required one person, but sealing the fireplace? That would have probably required two people,' Larry said. He had propped the back of his chair up against the wall, the two front legs not touching the floor.

'Are we assuming one person?' Bridget asked.

'So far, we've being looking for a motive, not how many people could have been involved,' Isaac replied.

'Could be one or two,' Larry said.

'But why the fireplace?' Wendy asked.

'It seems illogical unless they intended to come back and seal the fireplace with bricks.'

'Whoever placed the wooden structure around the fireplace must have been physically strong, so that discounts any of the women that we know of. The only people capable would have been Michael Solomon and Mavis Richardson's missing husband, Ger O'Loughlin,' Isaac added.

'And Montague Grenfell,' Larry said.

'Of course, there's always the family lawyer. It always comes back to him.'

'Ger O'Loughlin is not missing,' Wendy said.

'Can he be contacted?' Isaac asked.

'Mavis Richardson will know how to contact him.'

With no more to be discussed, the team went back to their work. Wendy had spoken to Emma Hampshire, told her that it was important to contact her son. She had been reluctant to comply, but had given Wendy the address.

***

Kevin Solomon, a man of forty-three, was not difficult to find. The address, a two-bedroom flat in Hampstead, was in remarkably good condition for a man who had a history of drug abuse. Bridget had checked out his criminal record, found a history of drug possession, a few arrests for being drunk and disorderly, but no prison sentences, and no major crimes.

'The flat, is it yours?' Wendy asked. She had been invited in after showing her badge.

'Out of my price bracket,' Kevin Solomon replied. Wendy had to admit he was a good-looking man, not what she had expected.

'What is your price bracket?'

'Cheap, exceptionally cheap.'

'No money?'

'If I have some, I spend it.'

'A remarkably frank admission,' Wendy said.

'Honesty, it's part of my rehabilitation.'

'What do you mean?'

'I'm a drug addict, heroin mainly. For years, I was crazy for it. I would do anything for the next hit.'

'Crime?'

'Petty sometimes, or else I would hire out as a male escort.'

'Pay well?'

'Well enough for the next injection.'

'That doesn't explain the accommodation.'

'It's owned by the family.'

'Which family?'

'My grandmother's.'

'We were not aware that you had any contact with them.'

'My father didn't, although I knew from my mother about the family lawyer.'

'Montague Grenfell?'

'Yes, him.'

'Have you met him?'

'Once, when he came here and gave me the key to the flat.'

'Did your father have any contact with his mother or Grenfell?'

'He hated them. I doubt if he made contact.'

'And you?'

'Whatever the issue was between my father and his mother, I never knew.'

'Did you meet her?'

'I knocked on her door once. I was drugged out, attempted to explain who I was. She slammed the door in my face.'

'Why would she do that?'

'Living in a mansion fit for condemning. She must have assumed that I wanted to steal her money.'

'Did you?'

'Not really. I am not an ambitious man, lazy would be a more apt description. I knew I was in trouble with my addiction, and I was looking for somebody, anybody, to help.'

'There was your mother.'

'She wasn't much help.'

'I met her,' Wendy said. He had made them both a cup of coffee. Whereas he had given up drugs, he had not given up cigarettes. Both were sitting in the main room of the flat smoking, a luxury both obviously enjoyed.

'What did you think?' Kevin Solomon asked.

'I liked her. She seemed genuinely concerned about you.'

'Maybe she is, but I don't see her often.'

'Any reason?'

'She was quick enough to ship me off to boarding school.'

'She said your father walked out on you two.'

'After he had caught her screwing another man. Did she tell you that?'

'Tell me about your father.'

'He disappeared when I was three or four. I don't remember him.'

'You never saw him again?'

'Once, when I was about ten or eleven, but never again.'

'Did Bob Hampshire treat you well?'

'He was a good man, more like a father than my father.'

'Why the bitterness towards your mother?'

'She shipped me off to boarding school.'

'Only that?'

'It's enough.'

'I'm afraid that your father is dead.'

'I'm not surprised.'

'Why do you say that?'

'I knew about the drug trafficking and the prison sentences. From what my mother told me, he ran with the wrong crowd. He was always bound to get his wings clipped at some time.'

'Your father died in 1987 when you would have been thirteen.'

'Unpleasant death?'

'Murdered, unfortunately.'

'His death means nothing to me. I was upset when Bob Hampshire died, but my father's death leaves me cold. Does that sound callous?'

'Not at all,' Wendy replied.

With no more to be gained, Wendy left. Again, the hand of Montague Grenfell had interceded. She phoned Isaac to update him, as well as to inform Bridget. If the flat currently occupied by Kevin Solomon belonged to Gertrude Richardson, then what else belonged to her.

There was the property in Greenwich, and there was every reason to believe it belonged to Gertrude Richardson or her sister, or both. And was Gertrude as eccentric as everyone said? And what of the money and all the properties in Mavis Richardson's name? What did Grenfell know?

It was clear that Montague Grenfell needed to be brought into Challis Street Police Station, cautioned, and given a chance to explain the truth in detail.

Chapter 14

Larry followed up on Garry Solomon's earlier life. The evidence unfolding indicated that before 1976 he had been an honest man, but somehow he had become involved in selling drugs.

Larry visited Garry Solomon's business before he had turned to crime. It was located down a side street in Hammersmith. The company was still involved in servicing luxury motors, attested by the Mercedes and BMWs lined up on the forecourt.

'Garry Solomon, remember him well,' the owner, Graham Nicholson, said. A distinguished-looking man, he spoke with the accent of the well-educated.

'What can you tell me about him?' Larry asked.

'I bought this place from him back in 1976. Paid plenty for it.'

'Good buy?'

'It's kept me solvent.'

'Why did he sell it to you?'

'No idea. He said he wanted to move on, bigger fish in the sea.'

'What did you believe?'

'I wasn't concerned as to what he said, only if the business was viable. Everyone distorts the truth when they're selling or buying.'

'Can you speculate as to what was the truth?'

'He was a young man. Obviously smart and a competent businessman, but he seemed to be in a hurry to set the world on fire. He was probably a little immature to be running a business such as this.'

'Did he keep in contact?'

'Not really. He honoured the agreement we had made: introduced me to his suppliers, his customers, and then left. I never saw him again.'

'Did you ever wonder what had happened to him?'

'Why? Should I have?'

'I'm just curious. We're tracing his whereabouts from 1976 through to 1987, that's all.'

'Why 1987?'

'He died in 1987.'

'Suspicious?' Graham Nicholson asked.

'He was murdered.'

'Not a good way to end your days.'

'Apart from that, do you have any idea where he went to?'

'You're pushing the memory here. It's been many years. I vaguely remember hearing that he had fallen on hard times, but apart from that, there's not much I can tell you.'

Larry returned to Challis Street Police Station. Montague Grenfell was due within the next hour, and Isaac wanted him to be present in the interview room with him.

***

Montague Grenfell arrived at Challis Street at 3 p.m. He was not in a good mood and felt the need to verbally abuse Isaac.

In his usual manner, Isaac shrugged off the lawyer's rhetoric. As the senior policeman involved in the murder of Garry Solomon, he had a job to do, and whether Montague Grenfell was pleasant or abusive made little difference.

Isaac opened the interview with Grenfell, following all the procedures. Isaac sat on the right-hand side of the table, with Larry on his left. Grenfell sat on the other side, facing Isaac. He had not brought additional legal representation.

Detective Chief Superintendent Goddard watched from outside. He had made a special trip to come and see Isaac. The case of the body in the fireplace was not occupying the media, except on an infrequent basis. The fickle public had been diverted by world events, terrorist activity in the north of England, and the inclement and unseasonal weather in the country.

'Mr Grenfell, there are anomalies in statements that you have made to me,' Isaac said.

'I have always been truthful when asked.' Isaac realised it was Grenfell's predictable reply. A man who, by his own admission, looked out for the Richardson family's interests, even if that meant obscuring the truth from the police during a murder investigation.

'According to Gertrude Richardson's grandson, you supplied him with a flat in Hampstead.'

'That is correct.'

'When I asked you on a previous occasion, you denied any knowledge of Garry Solomon's family.'

'That is correct.'

'Why did you not tell me?'

'Firstly, you had asked me in my office, not in an interview room, duly cautioned.'

'And secondly?'

'The son has no recollection of his father, other than a fleeting childhood meeting when he was ten or eleven. He did not seem relevant to Garry's murder.'

'That is for the police to decide, not you,' Isaac said.

'I disagree. The son would have been thirteen or fourteen when his father was murdered. He cannot be implicated in the man's death,' Grenfell said. Isaac noticed that the man had tensed, almost verging on anger.

'That may be, but it is clear that you are withholding information.'

'If you ask formally, then I will answer. Apart from that, the Richardson family's personal business, and by default mine, remains sacrosanct.'

'Even when a murder has been committed?'

'Even then.'

'I don't understand.'

'My family has a history stretching back for hundreds of years. English aristocracy keep their dirty linen to themselves. It is not there to be bandied across the internet and in the media.'

'The house in Greenwich?' Larry asked.

'Bakewell Street?' Grenfell sat up at the mention of Greenwich. 'How did you find it?'

'Last known address of Garry Solomon,' Larry said.

'Who owned it, owns it?' Isaac asked.

'Gertrude.'

'And if she's dead?'

'It's a matter for probate.'

'In your legal opinion?' Isaac asked.

'I cannot answer that question.'

'Why not?'

'I represent the Richardson family. It is a matter for them.'

'You mean Mavis?'

'Yes, Mavis Richardson.'

419

It was evident to Isaac that Montague Grenfell would remain a hostile witness, only willing to give the truth when asked directly.

'Would Garry Solomon's widow be eligible to inherit Gertrude Richardson's assets?' Isaac asked.

'And her debts.'

'You are aware that his wife uses the name of Emma Hampshire?'

'Yes.'

'Which means that you are aware of the movements of Garry Solomon, the two prison terms, the convictions for drug trafficking.'

'Yes.'

'Then why are we spending the time to find out when you could have supplied us with that information?'

'If you ask, I will answer. Otherwise, what I know remains secret.'

'I don't understand,' Isaac said.

'No offence, but you are not of aristocratic birth.'

Regardless of Grenfell's statement, Isaac saw it as a slur on his good character and that of his parents.

'Let us come back to Garry Solomon.'

'What do you want to know?'

'You are aware that he and Emily Solomon were married legally in England?'

'Yes.'

'You denied any knowledge of it on a previous occasion.'

'Yes.'

'Are you aware that you may well have committed a criminal offence by your persistent lies?'

'I am well aware of the law.'

'Was Garry Solomon murdered because of something he knew?'

'Why ask me? I am the family lawyer, not his murderer.'

'Could they be one and the same?' Isaac knew he was baiting the man, attempting to get more from him than a curt reply.

'Repeat that in public and I will sue you for slander.'

'Judging by the way in which the body was concealed, there are only three people capable of committing the murder, or at least hiding the body in the fireplace: you, Michael Solomon, and Ger O'Loughlin.'

'From what I've been told, the construction around the fireplace was substantial,' Grenfell said.

'It would have required someone with the skill to build and the strength to put it in place,' Isaac said.

'That rules me out. I've only got the one leg, and as for handyman skills, I can barely change a light bulb.'

'What about Michael Solomon?'

'It's possible. He was certainly strong enough, although I never saw him do anything practical around the house.'

'Ger O'Loughlin?'

'He could have done it, but why? He had nothing to gain by Garry's death, and besides, he's long gone.'

'And you know where he is?'

'Mavis does.'

'And you?'

'Yes.'

'We need the address.'

'I'll send it to you.'

Isaac concluded the interview, knowing full well that yet again Montague Grenfell had not been forthcoming with the truth.

***

'I need you to visit Ger O'Loughlin,' Isaac said.

Normally, Wendy would have been delighted with a trip out of London, but her husband was worrying her greatly. The doctor was giving him just four to five weeks, and now she was off to Ireland. Still, she couldn't refuse as it was her job, and her promotion to sergeant was soon to be confirmed. For once, the expense account and the ability to use it did not excite her, but, as always, she would do her duty.

A flight was booked with British Airways at eight the next morning. Wendy's eldest son offered to come over to the house to feed the two cats, and to visit his father every day.

Arriving in Dublin, she picked up a hire car at the airport. The address for O'Loughlin was recent, and she had no difficulty finding him. She had even phoned in advance, and informed the

Irish police, the Garda, that she was coming. It was a formality, and as no arrests were to be made, she was free to question O'Loughlin on her own.

Any extraditions and they would be involved, but that looked unlikely, as when she had phoned the previous day, the phone had been answered by a softly-spoken woman with a distinctive Irish accent. 'My father is dying,' she had said.

Ger O'Loughlin, as explained by his youngest daughter on Wendy's arrival, was suffering from lung cancer after a lifetime of chain smoking.

Wendy found the man sitting up in bed, a ventilator forcing air into his destroyed lungs.

'How is Mavis?' Ger O'Loughlin asked, his voice rasping but weak.

'She's fine,' Wendy said.

'Still attractive?'

'Still.'

'She was a looker, couldn't keep my hands off her when I was younger.'

'She still acts younger than her age. Are you aware of her sister's death?'

'Grenfell phoned.'

'Do you hear from him often?'

'Rarely.'

'When did you last see Mavis?'

'It must be twenty-five years at least. We have spoken a few times, but both our lives have moved on. We're long-distance friends, nothing more.'

'Did he tell you about Garry Solomon?'

'Yes, and he told me that Michael Solomon had died, but I knew that already.'

'How?'

'I kept in contact with him. We used to meet from time to time over the years. When he died, his second wife phoned.'

'Did you know he was not divorced from Gertrude when he married the second wife?'

'I never asked if he had married again. I assumed they were living together and she had taken his surname.'

'Don't you go tiring my dad. He needs to rest,' O'Loughlin's daughter said after poking her head around the door.

'I won't,' Wendy said.

'Always fussing, that one,' O'Loughlin said after the young woman had retreated.

'How many children do you have?'

'Four, and a good wife as well. She'll be back in later today.'

'According to Mavis, she did not want children.'

'That's why we broke up. It was important to me, not to her.'

All Wendy could see was a tired old man close to death, but she had not travelled to talk about life now, but life back when he was younger, when he was married to Mavis Richardson.

'Sorry, but I need to ask about Garry Solomon.'

'The last time I saw him would have been around 1963, the night he walked in at the party.'

'When Michael Solomon was in bed with Mavis?'

'Wild days.' Ger O'Loughlin managed a thin smile.

'And you didn't object?'

'We were young. It was the age of free love and permissiveness. Mind you, Garry went crazy with hitting Mavis. It took all my strength to pull him off.'

'Were you a strong man?'

'I used to work out at the gym.'

'What can you tell me about the structure around the fireplace in Bellevue Street?' Wendy asked.

'Nothing. I never went around to the house after that day.'

'When she caught you in bed with Gertrude?'

'You've done your homework. Who told you?'

'Mavis. So why was she upset if you had both been indulging in wife swapping?'

'As she saw it, a wife-swapping party was by mutual consent of all parties, whereas my sleeping with her sister was a private agreement.'

'How did you see it?' Wendy asked.

'An afternoon screw, nothing more. It was not the first time that I had slept with her.'

'Mavis kicks the two of you out, subsequently forgives the sister, but not you.'

'She forgave me, but the trust that Mavis had for me was broken. We both moved on.'

At that point, the young daughter came in and asked Wendy to leave as her father needed to rest. There seemed no reason for her to stay longer in Ireland. There was a late-night flight; she intended to catch it.

Chapter 15

Larry decided to focus on Garry Solomon. His whereabouts between 1984 and 1987 were still vague, apart from the times he visited the clothing shop to buy some hand-made shirts and trousers. Solomon's last visit had been in 1986, approximately one year before his murder.

There were no criminal activities registered against either of the two names he had been using, which meant he was either honestly employed or out of the country. Or, possibly, he had managed to evade the long arm of the law. Larry saw that option as remote, as Garry Solomon had shown himself to be a small-time criminal of limited abilities. The man had received a good education, was apparently articulate and intelligent, yet he remained a petty criminal. It all seemed incongruous to Larry, who was a strong believer that a person should make the best of what was given at birth and in their life, and should always strive for more.

It was a philosophy that drove him on in his career within the London Metropolitan Police. He was aiming to make detective chief inspector within a year, superintendent in three, and chief superintendent in five. He knew that he needed one or two university degrees to achieve his final goal, but working with Homicide was demanding and he knew he was not keeping up with his studies.

The only way to achieve the degrees was to take six months off work and to study to exhaustion, sleep and study again. However, he had a family and another child on the way. It would be another five years before he could see any financial relief.

Montague Grenfell, when questioned, had offered no information as to where Solomon had gone, but Larry and Isaac had regarded that as further obstructive behaviour.

Bridget had managed to find records of a driving licence issued to Garry Solomon, the address in Knightsbridge. It seemed an upmarket location after Greenwich.

Larry saw it as a long shot, but there were no other leads. He made his way out to the property in Montpelier Square. The house was as opulent as the house in Greenwich had been rundown. He knocked on the door. A woman in her sixties answered.

'Detective Inspector Larry Hill, Challis Street Police Station.'

'What can I do for you?'

'I need to ask you some questions.' Larry showed his ID badge. The door opened fully to let him in. He observed that the house was beautifully decorated, and the woman was very attractive.

'Your name?' Larry asked once he was seated in the main room of the house.

'Barbara Ecclestone.'

'Have you lived here long?'

'It was my parents' house. I grew up here.'

'I'm looking for a Garry Solomon, or as he was also known, Solly Michaels.'

'So was I, for a long time.'

'You knew him?'

'We lived together.'

'What can you tell me about him?'

'Is he dead?'

425

'I'm sorry.'

The woman, obviously distraught, sat down to compose herself.

'I'm not surprised,' she said.

'Are you alright?' Larry asked.

'He walked out on me a long time in the past. I was upset back then. Now, it's just the shock of facing reality.'

'Did you look for him?'

'Everywhere I could think of.'

'Did he have many friends?'

'Not in the two years that he was here with me. We spent most of the time here, occasionally walking up to Harrods to buy the groceries.'

'What do you know about his past life?'

'He became involved with a criminal element, started trafficking drugs. He did time for that on a couple of occasions.'

'Were you involved with him then?'

'On and off. I went through a wild period, but, as with Garry, I settled down. Got older, I suppose.'

'What do you know about his family life?'

'He mentioned his father once or twice, although I never met him. Any mention of his mother and he would get upset. No idea why. My mother was a bitch, but I still miss her. Are they still alive?'

'The father died some years ago; the mother, recently.'

'Did she know that her son had died?'

'She did. She died soon after.'

'How sad.'

'Do you know the date when he disappeared?'

'January 21st, 1987.'

'Good memory.'

'It was my birthday. I had made a special meal, bought some champagne, but he goes out for a couple of hours and never comes back. In the end, I threw the meal in the bin and drank the champagne. Is the date significant?'

'It was the day he died.'

'And there I was getting angry, yet it was not his fault. How did he die? Car accident?'

'Unfortunately, he came to a tragic end. He was murdered.'

The woman sat down and put her face in her hands, overcome with emotion. Larry found a bottle of whisky and gave her some. Five minutes later, she revived.

'I'm sorry,' she said.

'It's an understandable reaction.'

'It's been thirty years. I've moved on since then, got married, had a couple of kids.'

'And the children?'

'They have both left home. One's married, the other one is overseas.'

'Either of them belong to Garry Solomon?'

'No.'

'Tell me about the day he disappeared,' Larry said.

'Do you want a cup of tea?'

'Yes, please.'

Five minutes later, with the tea poured, Barbara Ecclestone spoke about her time with Garry Solomon.

'I first met Garry in 1979. He was just out of prison, and I was a social worker. I was there to help him readjust to society and to ensure he went straight.'

'Did he?'

'My first ex-prisoner, my first failure.'

'What happened?'

'He called himself Solly Michaels. Soon after his release, he was back with his criminal mates. If you had met him, you would have wondered why.'

'Why?'

'A charming man, articulate, generous, great company.'

'Did you become involved then?'

'You mean lovers?'

'Yes.'

'Not at all. I was very prim and proper, still am.'

'And then what?'

'Three years later and he's back in prison. We had kept in contact over the years, and occasionally we would meet up. I think he enjoyed my attempts at reforming him.

'I started to visit him in prison, and we spoke about our lives. He was from an affluent background, shipped off to a boarding school, as was I. We were both bitter about the neglect, although, with me, it didn't affect me as badly as it did Garry.'

'Greenwich,' Larry said.

'You've been there?'

'And the local pub.'

'It was awful out there.'

'Still is.'

'Why didn't he come here instead of Greenwich?'

'My mother was still alive. And besides, Garry still had some unresolved issues to deal with.'

'Such as?'

'He was a ladies' man.'

'He was playing the field?'

'I'm sure he was. As long as I didn't know, I was fine. I loved him, foolish as it was, and I was willing to wait.'

'While he was here with you?'

'We were together virtually twenty-four hours a day.'

'Did he work during his time here?'

'He seemed to have some money coming in. I quizzed him once. He said it was from his family.'

'Did you work during that time?'

'No. We were just very happy, planning our future together.'

'Did you know about his past personal relationships?'

'His wife and son? Yes, I did. Apparently, she had upset him once, but he had forgiven her. He said that she had moved in with a good man and that his son was fine. Apart from that, he did not speak about his past.'

'Did he see them?'

'I don't think so. For some reason, past memories were always difficult for him. He dealt with the present and the future.'

'Is there any more?' Larry asked. 'The day he disappeared, what happened?'

'He went out, never returned. I've no idea where he went or who he met.'

'Thanks. I may come back to you if there is any other information that I require.'

'My husband is due back in fifteen minutes. Please stay till then. I don't want to be on my own at the present time.'

Fifteen minutes later, the husband returned. Barbara told him why a police inspector was in the house. Larry left soon after and headed back to Challis Street.

***

Detective Chief Superintendent Goddard was in Isaac's office on Larry's return to Challis Street. From Larry's side of the glass partition, it appeared to be an animated conversation.

'Isaac, how much longer is this going to take? We've other murders requiring your team's attention, and this thirty-year-old corpse is still garnering more attention than it should.'

'We're still collating the facts,' Isaac's reply.

'What have you got?'

'We now know where Garry Solomon was before his murder. His murderer is still uncertain, and why a fireplace remains a mystery.'

'Surely you must have a motive.'

'No motive is apparent.'

It was clear from DCS Goddard's visit that he was under pressure to provide a result. Isaac had ceased to relish his superior's visits. Questions as to when the case was going to be wrapped up always grated. The team were working hard, attempting to resolve it, but everyone was jaundiced by now. Their previous cases had been long and gruelling, and before Garry Solomon's body had been discovered, they had been hoping for a break from the routine. It sometimes seemed to DCI Isaac Cook that they were in a growth industry.

Wendy's promotion, due to Isaac's efforts and her good work, had come about. She was now Sergeant Wendy Gladstone, and to Isaac, a title well earned. Not that it helped with her husband who continued to wither. Under normal circumstances, she would have been entitled to compassionate leave, or at least to forbearance from the London Metropolitan Police as she juggled the emotional and financial needs of her husband and the professional needs of a policewoman involved in a murder investigation that defied logic.

Regardless, Wendy had been insistent that being at home or at the nursing home were non-constructive, and that an idle mind did no good. On several occasions, Bridget had gone home with Wendy to keep her company.

Garry Solomon's body in a house owned by his family indicated that a relative or relatives were involved, but which? Isaac had ruled out the two Richardson sisters as primary suspects: one was his mother, the other would not have had the physical strength to secure his resting place in the old house.

Ger O'Loughlin seemed a likely culprit, but why? The man had been close to death when Wendy had met him; although by his own admission he had been a strong man in his earlier years, his motive seemed weak. There appeared to be no financial gain to him. He had married Mavis Richardson, divorced her, or she had divorced him. She was a wealthy woman, but he had gained no benefit.

Isaac pondered who could have killed the man. At the time of his death, Garry Solomon was no longer involved with his criminal friends, and he was living with Barbara Ecclestone. He had money in his pocket, and besides, if he had been killed by persons other than his immediate family, they would have taken him out into the countryside, weighed him down with concrete and thrown him in the river.

Isaac realised that the motive was the key element. So far, that remained a mystery, although why Garry Solomon had remained detached from his mother was a concern. It had been his father that he had seen in bed with his aunt, yet for some reason he had maintained infrequent contact with the father, but not the mother.

It was clear that the mother, Gertrude Richardson, had been eccentric, even in her younger years. It hardly seemed a reason to maintain a hatred towards her; there had to be something more.

At the evening meeting in the office, he raised his concerns. 'I've had our boss over here grilling me,' he said.

'Not happy?' Larry asked.

'What do you think?' Wendy said. Her mood fluctuated with her husband's condition. Today she was not in a cheerful frame of mind.

'Detective Chief Superintendent Goddard is concerned that we are going nowhere with this case.'

'He's right,' Larry said.

'What do we do?' Isaac was not a man who sat in isolation issuing commands and demanding answers. He knew that a team discussion was often the best way to come up with a resolution.

'Find the motive,' Larry's reply.

'Easier said than done,' Isaac said.

'Are we certain that it's a family member?' Wendy asked.

'Who else knew about Bellevue Street, and why has the body been undisturbed for so many years?' Isaac replied.

'Records indicate occupancy of the house since 1987 when the body was incarcerated in the fireplace,' Bridget said.

'Detailed records?' Isaac asked.

'Not totally. The house had been divided up for most of the time as low-cost accommodation, each bedroom equipped with a fold-down bed and a basic kitchen.'

'What about the room where the body was found?'

'No information on that.'

'Who would know?' Isaac asked.

'The family lawyer,' Larry said.

'I don't think he will be too pleased to see me after the last time we met.'

'It doesn't concern you, does it, sir?' Wendy asked.

'Not at all. Tomorrow morning, I will go out there with Larry.'

Again, the answers gravitate towards Montague Grenfell, Isaac thought.

'Wendy, Bridget, focus on Montague Grenfell: family history, background, personal relationships, financial information. Whatever you can find.'

Both of the women nodded their affirmation.

Chapter 16

The next day at nine in the morning, Larry and Isaac drove out to Montague Grenfell's office. Isaac prepared to march briskly up the stairs to his office. He managed the first two flights before stopping abruptly. There, at the base of the third flight of stairs, a man's crumpled body, the head at an awkward angle. Larry quickly dialled 999 for an ambulance, although he could see it was a formality.

'Another body for you,' Isaac said on the phone to Gordon Windsor.

'Identity?'

'Montague Grenfell.'

'I'll be there within fifteen minutes,' Windsor said.

'This changes everything,' Larry said after Isaac had ended his phone call. Larry called the local police station. They were sending around a uniformed police officer to be stationed outside, and a local detective to secure the scene.

'It depends on if it was murder or not,' Isaac said.

'Any doubt on your part?'

'The man had one leg. It's possible he slipped.'

'Or was pushed.'

'Let's wait for Gordon Windsor. He'll be able to tell us.'

'We need to meet Bridget and Wendy to discuss this,' Larry said.

'Agreed, but first we need to meet Mavis Richardson. She needs to be told, once Gordon Windsor has brought us up to speed.'

Isaac phoned his boss. 'It's just become a lot more complicated. Garry Solomon was an old murder; this one is recent, and they are both related.'

His boss's reaction: 'Wrap this up soon. Grenfell was well connected. There are bound to be more questions, and the media will be sticking their collective noses in again.'

Fifteen minutes later, Gordon Windsor arrived. He donned his overalls, gloves, and mask before approaching the body.

'Broken neck,' he said, even before kneeling down to examine the body.

'Are you sure?' Isaac asked.

'Judging by the angle of the neck, I would say that I am correct.'

'Is it the cause of death?'

'Probably, but I will need to conduct my examination, and then the autopsy will confirm if it was or not. Whatever the cause, he died here.'

'Was he pushed?' Larry asked.

'Give my team sixty minutes, and it should become clearer.'

Isaac and Larry, realising that there was no more to be gained from their presence, left the scene.

Grenfell's family needed to be informed. Bridget would be able to supply the contact details. It was known that Montague Grenfell had no children and his wife was dead.

Mavis Richardson was excited when she first met Isaac, although deflated when told the reason for his visit.

'Were you close?' Isaac asked.

'I trusted him implicitly,' she replied. She had sat down in a corner chair, showing every year of her advanced age. It was the first time that Larry had seen her like this. He went to pour her a brandy, leaving Isaac alone with the old woman.

'I'm told that you had known him since you were children.'

'He was like a brother to me.'

'And he handled all your financial matters?'

'Totally. He had a proxy to act on my behalf.'

'Did he have many friends?'

'None that I know of. He was very close to his wife, but she has been dead for a few years.'

'Family?'

'Two brothers.'

'Do you have their contact details?'

'The elder brother, the lord, but he's senile.'

'And the younger brother?'

'I don't know where he is. I liked the elder brother, but not the younger.'

'Any reason why?'

433

'He was the black sheep of the family: always gambling, whoring, that sort of thing.'

'Do you have anyone you can call to come over and be with you?'

'I have plenty of friends. At my age, you get used to people dying. Is it murder?' Mavis asked.

'It is too early to speculate,' Isaac replied. 'Any reason to believe that it might be?'

'Not really, but Garry had been murdered. I wondered if it was related.'

'We have not made a connection between the two deaths yet.'

'But you will.'

'Why do you say that?' Larry asked.

'Montague knew everything. If you wanted to keep our family secrets, then all you had to do was rid yourself of Montague.'

'Secrets worth killing for?' Isaac asked.

'None that I know of.'

Isaac wondered if the woman knew something that she was not telling him, but realised she probably did not. She was a old woman, feeling every one of her eighty-five years, and just talking.

'Did Garry know any secrets?' Isaac asked.

'He may have found out something, but I don't know.'

'Are you hiding some information from us?'

'No.'

'Then why talk about secrets?'

'Garry died, Gertrude died, and now Montague.'

'Are you assuming they are related?'

'Not really. I'm only sorry that I never saw Gertrude before she died.'

'You cared about her?'

'Of course I did.'

'And Garry?'

'He was her son. Personally, I did not care for him, but I always made sure that he came to no harm, and that he had money and a place to live when he needed it.'

'You knew about his marriage and child?'

'Montague kept a look out for him, hired a private investigator sometimes.'

'And the rest of Garry's history?'

'The prison terms, the house in Greenwich, and Barbara Ecclestone. Yes, I knew.'

'And Kevin Solomon?'

'He's always had someone watching out for him, although he never knew it. Who do you think paid for his drug rehabilitation?'

'Very generous of you.'

'Not generous. That's what families do for each other; at least, my family.'

'What about Garry's wife?' Isaac asked.

'She's fine.'

'Any contact with her?'

'None, but she lived with Bob Hampshire for many years. He treated her well.'

'You knew him?'

'I met him once or twice, nothing more. I even met Emily, or Emma as she calls herself now. There's nothing to make of it. We moved in the same social circles, that's all.'

'Did Emma Hampshire know who you were?'

'No. I was known as Mavis O'Loughlin.'

'Constable Gladstone went to Ireland.'

'She met Ger?'

'Yes.'

'He's dying,' Mavis said.

'You know?' Isaac asked.

'His daughter phoned, asked if I wanted to visit him.'

'And what did you say?'

'I declined.'

'But you wanted to?'

'Yes, but he has his family with him. I spoke to him on the phone for five minutes. That's another one who's dying.'

Mavis Richardson then made a phone call. Five minutes later, another old woman arrived. 'Sheila will stay with me. Would you please leave.'

Larry and Isaac could see that there was another person who was going to die soon. The recent events had sapped the life out of the woman. Larry felt sad as he left the house.

***

Wendy and Bridget were in the office when Isaac and Larry arrived. Wendy was looking more cheerful, a clear indication that her husband had been more cheerful than on her previous visit to see him.

'What can you tell us, Bridget?' Isaac asked.

'Montague Grenfell was the second son of Lord Penrith. The other sons are Albert, the eldest and the current lord, and Malcolm, the younger. According to reports, the current Lord Penrith is close to death. Malcolm is the result of a second marriage of the previous lord to a younger woman.'

'The younger son's mother?'

'She's dead.'

'Someone needs to tell the Grenfell family about Montague,' Isaac said.

'A job for you, sir,' Wendy said.

'What else, Bridget?'

'All three men are childless. The title will expire on the death of Malcolm. On the passing of the eldest son, the title would have passed to Montague Grenfell. The records indicate that Lord Penrith has no money, other than a stately home and the money to maintain it. Montague Grenfell was only affluent due to his own abilities.'

'Where can we find Lord Penrith?' Isaac asked.

'Leicestershire,' Bridget answered.

'Wendy, are you up to meeting aristocracy?' Isaac asked.

'I'll need to practise my curtseying,' Wendy replied.

'Larry, can you follow up with Gordon Windsor and check out the crime scene at Bellevue Street again? See if you can figure out how a body lies undisturbed for thirty years.'

***

Sue Baxter was not pleased to see DI Larry Hill. 'I thought we were free of you,' she said.

'It is still a crime scene,' Larry said.

'One room is.'

'As you say, one room.'

Larry noted that renovations were proceeding. A body in the fireplace had given the place some notoriety and the house had been renamed 'The Mummy's Recline', a somewhat macabre reference to the body's condition and its position.

The room where the body had been discovered had been sealed off with metal bars, and police signs to the effect that it was a crime scene. Otherwise, the house had a sense of normality, a television on in another room, a dog barking, and the sound of children. He was not sure that he would want to live in a house where there had been a violent murder, but the Baxters appeared to have no issues.

'Can you tell me about the first time you wanted to enter the room?' Larry asked. He had moved with Sue Baxter to the modern kitchen at the rear of the house.

'It was sealed with a metal grille. It took us some time to get it off.'

'Was there any explanation given why?'

'None.'

'Did it concern you?'

'We thought it strange, but the house was in our price range, and the location was excellent.'

'When you first entered the room, any sense of foreboding?'

'None at all. We just thought it was a lovely room.'

'No smell?'

'It was musty. We opened the windows, and it soon freshened up. I dusted the room; ran a wet mop over the floorboards.'

'No suspicion as to why the fireplace was covered?'

'Why?'

'It seems unusual.'

'All the bedrooms had covered fireplaces. It had been sublet for years.'

'We're at a loss as to why someone would have expected the fireplace to have remained untouched for thirty years,' Larry admitted. 'It seems crucial to know. To us, it seems illogical.'

'We wondered as well,' Sue Baxter said.

'Any thoughts?'

'You're the police officer, what do you think?'

'Did you keep the grille?'

'It's down in the basement.'

'I'll get someone over to look at it. Make sure it remains untouched,' Larry said.

Chapter 17

Lord Penrith, as Wendy and Isaac found out on their arrival at his home, a decaying remnant of Georgian architecture, was beyond caring about his younger brother or anyone else.

'His mind has gone,' Katrina Smith, the pretty young nurse who had shown them into his lordship's bedroom, said. The man was propped up in bed, a television in the corner showing a melodrama.

'Anyone else in the house?' Isaac asked.

'There's a cook and a handyman. Apart from that, no one.'

'Who employed you?'

'Montague Grenfell. I met him in London, but apart from that he has not been near. I have a bank account to draw from as needed. Each month, I send him an itemised list of my costs, and he ensures to put my salary into my account. To be honest, it's a cushy number, although it will not last for much longer.'

'Why do you say that?' Wendy asked.

'His lordship is dying. He could go anytime.'

'And when he does, what do you do?'

'I'm to phone the local police and the local undertaker. After that, I am to phone the family doctor and Montague Grenfell, the new Lord Penrith.'

'Except that he won't be,' Isaac said.

'Why's that?' Katrina Smith asked.

'Unfortunately, Montague Grenfell has died.'

'He seemed a nice man.'

'What will you do now?' Wendy asked.

'Hopefully, someone will pay the bills, but anyway, I'll stay for now. I've grown fond of Lord Penrith, even if he doesn't remember me one day to the next.'

'There's another brother,' Isaac said.

'Malcolm.'

'Have you seen him?'

'The proverbial black sheep of the family. Every aristocratic family has one of them, as well as a ghost or two in the stately home,' Katrina Smith said. Isaac had to admit he liked her humour, even under trying circumstances.

'Have you seen any?' Wendy asked.

'Late at night when the wind blows it can be eerie, but no.'

'You don't believe in the possibility?'

'A healthy sceptic. If there are any here, I've not seen them.'

'What about Malcolm? Any ideas as to where he may be?'

'Montague Grenfell would have known, but I've no idea.'

'You said he was the black sheep of the family?' Wendy asked.

'Montague Grenfell mentioned him when we met in London. He asked me to phone him if Malcolm turned up. Apart from that, he told me nothing.'

It was ten in the evening when Isaac and Wendy left Lord Penrith's residence. There seemed little reason to spend the night in Leicestershire. They arrived back in London just after midnight.

Wendy had noticed Katrina Smith handling Isaac's business card, and saying she would give him a call the next time she was in London. She saw Isaac smile in return. Wendy knew Isaac would not be on his own for much longer.

***

Gordon Windsor was on the phone early the next morning. 'The door frame to Grenfell's office has scuff marks from his clothing, indicative of his being manhandled through it. And then, there are marks where he had attempted to force his shoe hard against the wall at the top of the stairs. We also found two sets of shoeprints that show a conflict situation.'

'The evidence is convincing enough to hold up in a court of law?' Isaac asked.

'The final report will state that he had been forced to the top of the stairs, and almost certainly pushed down them.'

'The broken neck killed him?'

'Yes. There was a clear break above the fifth cervical vertebra. If he had not died instantly, he would have died soon after from asphyxiation.'

Isaac phoned DCS Goddard. He was over within minutes.

'What are you going to do about this?' Goddard asked. 'The Penriths are an important family in this country. History goes back for centuries. There's bound to be media scrutiny.'

'Lord Penrith is close to death, and now his brother has been murdered' Isaac said.

'What has the media been told?'

'We have made no official statement.'

'Who could have killed Grenfell?'

'We don't know.'

'Well, you'd better find out soon.'

Goddard left soon after. The two men were firm friends, but sometimes Isaac's senior could rile him. As Isaac saw it, he had a competent team, everyone was giving one hundred per cent, but until there was a breakthrough, they were going nowhere. They knew the identity of the body, although why he died remained a mystery. Montague Grenfell had been integral to providing the reason, but now he was dead, and according to Gordon Windsor and his team, he had been pushed down the stairs outside his office.

Isaac knew full well that falling down a flight of stairs was not an automatic neck break, and there remained a possibility that his death was unintentional. However, the reason why he was at the bottom of the stairs was important, as was the identity of the person who had scuffled with him.

The main suspects were all ageing, and it was hard to believe they would have had the strength. Even with his false leg, Montague Grenfell was a fit man. He was ten years younger than Mavis Richardson, only seventy-five, and as fit as a man of sixty-five.

There was still one key person unaccounted for: Malcolm Grenfell, the soon to be Lord Penrith.

According to Katrina Smith, the bed-ridden incumbent lord was a decent man, even if he could be snobbish and she had grown fond of the man. Regardless, the next weekend she was taking time off to come and see her mother in London and to meet up with Isaac. Isaac realised that the mother might not receive many hours of her time. He smiled at the thought, which caused Bridget to look his way.

'Good thoughts?' she said.

'I suppose so.' Isaac did not intend to elaborate. 'We need to find Montague Grenfell's younger brother,' he said.

'Yes, sir.'

'Any ideas?'

'What did you find out in Leicestershire?' Bridget asked.

'Not a lot. Only that he had not been there for some time. His current whereabouts are unclear.'

'I have conducted some checks already.'

'What did you find?'

'Malcolm Grenfell is twelve years younger that Montague. That would give his age as sixty-three.'

'Anything else?'

'There appears to be no record of work, although there is a Mercedes registered in his name and a driving licence.'

'A man of independent means, is that it?' Isaac said.

'More likely a scrounging parasite, sir.'

441

'You may be right. Regardless, we need to find him. How is Wendy's situation?'

'Still with her husband.'

'A job for Larry.'

'He'll be in soon,' Bridget said.

***

'I was going to Bellevue Street this morning,' Larry said on his arrival at the office.

'The grille in the basement?' Isaac replied.

'Yes, sir.'

'What is its condition?'

'It's been damaged, but our people should be able to work with it.'

'What's your feeling?'

Both men were sitting in Isaac's office. The relationship between the two men continued to warm.

'Obviously, it was put there to deter people from entering the room.'

'The whole scenario is illogical. How does anyone expect to keep a body hidden indefinitely in a fireplace?'

'Maybe it was only meant to be there temporarily,' Larry said.

'And then it became impossible to remove, so someone puts up the grille in an attempt to conceal what was inside the room.'

'It makes some sense, but it's still bizarre. And then there is the wooden structure around the fireplace.'

'Focus on the grille for now. The reasons will become clear later.'

'Okay. I'll see you later,' Larry said. He put his empty cup on the sink in the kitchen area in the main office and left.

Isaac walked over to Bridget's desk. 'Let me have Malcolm Grenfell's address,' he said. He was glad of the opportunity to get out of the office.

***

Larry Hill arrived at the house in Bellevue Street at nine thirty in the morning. Gordon Windsor's people were already there, as was Sue Baxter, camera in hand. The woman was becoming a nuisance, and neither Larry nor Isaac had forgiven her for sounding off to the local newspaper about matters which would have been best kept confidential.

Larry reminded her again that it was a murder investigation, and what she saw and heard was not to be repeated outside the confines of the house. As usual, she said that she fully understood, and it was only for a record of the renovations on the house.

Larry had to admit that the Baxters had done a good job, and apart from a few rooms, the murder room included, the house was looking good. Larry realised that it was as well that his wife was not present, as she had been niggling him for the last few months to spend more time at home and to commit to painting the inside, at least.

He could not see the problem as their house was warm and pleasant, and the last thing he wanted at the weekend was to take hold of a paintbrush. Still, he realised on seeing what the Baxters had achieved that maybe his wife was right.

What was the more pressing problem, though? The current murder investigation was taking all his time, and the most he wanted at home was a good sleep. And judging by the way the deaths kept occurring, and the long hours that Isaac committed everyone in the department to, the time for home renovations was not possible.

His wife had made it clear that if he did not have the time, then she would get in a handyman to do it. Larry had said fine until he realised how much that would cost.

'Where's the grille?' Grant Meston asked. He was a good-looking man with flaming red hair and a ruddy complexion. Gordon Windsor had recommended him as the best crime scene investigator in his department.

'Down in the basement. They put it down there, part of Trevor Baxter's wine cellar eventually.'

The two men walked down the stairs off the hallway, followed by a camera, followed by Sue Baxter. The area downstairs was small and lit by a single light bulb hanging from the ceiling.

443

'We need extra lights down here,' Meston said. 'I've some out in the car. I'll go and fetch them.'

'Why don't you take it upstairs?' Sue Baxter asked.

'Not if we want to avoid more damage.' Grant Meston was already annoyed by the camera and the woman. Larry had forewarned him to keep his detailed findings to himself until they were clear of the house.

The crime scene investigator climbed the stairs and went to fetch the lights. Larry, eyes adjusting to the dim light, looked around the area. It was clear that Trevor Baxter's aspirations to a wine cellar were in the early realisation stage. Baxter had cleared a small corner, a mop and bucket testament to the fact. On the floor, some wine shelves, the sort they sell in the shops, were already holding several bottles of wine.

'My husband's hobby,' Sue Baxter said.

'The looking at them or the drinking?' Larry asked.

'Both.'

'Any good wines here?'

'Better than the average. Leave them for a few years, and they will be great.'

Grant Meston returned. He had run an electric cord down from a socket in the hall. Soon, two powerful fluorescent lights lit the area. No longer needing to focus to see the detail in the basement, Larry could see the grille. It had been pushed up against the far wall. Judging by the marks on the faded paintwork, it had suffered some damage when it had been removed.

'What can you find out from that?' Sue Baxter asked.

'There may be some stamps on the metalwork that will give us a year,' Meston replied, cognisant of Larry Hill's warning about Sue Baxter.

'Any chance of a cup of tea?' Larry asked.

'Sure.' Sue Baxter left for upstairs.

'Would it be easier to take it down to your office?' Larry asked.

'Normally, I would agree, but the grille's been in place for thirty years. Any fingerprints, DNA, will have long been destroyed.'

'Your initial observations?'

'Late 80s, I would say. Give me ten minutes while I check it out. Distract Mrs Baxter if you can.'

Larry left and went upstairs. He found Sue Baxter in the kitchen. 'Grant's fine. He doesn't want tea.'

'Coffee?'

'No, he's okay. He just wants to be left alone to conduct his investigation. He will be up here later.'

'My husband wanted to use the grille for his wine cellar.'

'It is part of a police investigation now, as is the basement. At least, it is for the time being.'

'When can we have the front room back?'

'It doesn't upset you as to what was found in there?' Larry asked.

'The first day it did.'

'And now?'

'Not anymore. It's as if the house had a character, almost like a haunted house.'

'It's not haunted, is it?'

'No. Not at all. 'Have you found the murderer?'

'Not yet.'

Larry sipped his tea. The woman continued to probe.

'We found some old photos,' she said.

'Of the house?'

'They were hidden at the back of an old wardrobe. Slipped down the back, I suppose.'

'Why didn't you reveal this to the police?' Larry asked, aware yet again that the woman would have sold them to the newspapers if she could.

'I never thought any more about them.'

Larry decided to ignore her blatant lie. Sue Baxter was as sharp as a tack, he knew that, and she never forgot. Regardless, he needed the photos.

'Can I see them, please?'

Sue Baxter opened a drawer in the table where she was sitting and handed them to Larry. There were four photos in total, all of them heavily marked from years of neglect.

It was clear that one showed the garden at the rear, another a picture of a child on a bicycle, and the other two a gathering of a group of adults. The adults appeared to be sitting on a sofa.

'We think that is the room where the body was found,' Sue Baxter said.

445

'What makes you think that?' Larry asked.

'The window at the rear. The curtain material seems to be the same as we found in there the day we opened the room.'

'And the people?'

'No idea.'

'You realise that these photos may become a crucial piece of evidence, yet you decided to keep them from the police.'

'I forgot, honestly.' Sue Baxter went on the defensive, regretting that she had told DI Hill about the photos.

'I need to take them for evidence.'

'Will I get them back at some stage?'

'In time.'

Grant Meston had come into the kitchen before Larry had a chance to remind Sue Baxter that withholding evidence was a criminal offence, as was talking to the media without receiving clearance. It was a moot point as her offences could not be proven to be intentional.

'Cup of tea?' Sue Baxter asked.

'Yes, please,' Meston replied.

'What did you find?' Larry asked, mindful that he had asked Grant Meston not to reveal too much in front of Sue Baxter.

'The age matches. I have taken some numbers off the hinges. It should be possible to match them to a date.'

'Anything else?'

'Nothing more. I have put crime scene tape across the grille, and across the door leading down to the basement. Mrs Baxter, please do not go down there.'

'My husband's wine?'

'He will have to leave it alone for the time being.'

Larry had to admit that although Sue Baxter could stick her nose in where it was not wanted, she was an excellent hostess. The two men stayed for another cup of tea and some sandwiches. Twenty-five minutes later, they stood outside the front gate of the house.

'What's the true story?' Larry asked.

'I found a piece of paper under one corner of the grille. It had been painted over initially, but with time, the paint has lifted.'

'Did you take a photo?'

'I sent one to your email.'

'What does it show?'

'It's a receipt for the grille, or at least, that's what I assume it is.'

'Date?'

'As best as I can tell, February 1987.'

'One month after the murder,' Larry realised. 'Could one person have installed it?'

'With some difficulty. The person would need to know how to use a drill with a masonry bit for the Ramset bolts.'

'A woman?'

'Unlikely, unless they were very practical.'

Chapter 18

By the time, Larry arrived back in the office, Wendy was there. He could see that she had been crying. Bridget was consoling her. 'It was for the best,' she was saying.

'I know, but he was a good man.'

Larry, realising what had happened, came over and put his arm on Wendy's shoulder. 'I'm sorry.'

'Thank you,' she replied meekly.

'You'd better go home,' Larry said.

'DCI Cook's already said that,' Bridget said.

'I prefer to be here. Too many memories there,' Wendy said. 'Tell me about the case.'

Larry had experienced the same feelings when his mother had died five years previously. Sitting around remembering helped little. It was best to keep the mind busy and elsewhere.

'Do you need any help with the arrangements?' Larry asked.

'Thanks for offering, but my sons will deal with it.'

'If you want to work?'

'I do. Please update me.'

'Sue Baxter, the lady of the house in Bellevue Street, has found some photos.'

'Are they relevant?' Wendy asked.

'They are old and grainy, but I think they are.'

'When did she find them?'

'Long enough ago to have informed us before.'

'Have you seen them? What do you reckon?'

'There is one with a child on a bicycle. It may be Garry Solomon. Another two photos show a gathering of adults. We need to identify them.'

'Leave it with me.'

'You will look after Wendy?' Larry said to Bridget.

'Don't worry. She'll be all right with me.'

Isaac arrived back in the office soon after, his search for Malcolm Grenfell curtailed due to the death of Wendy's husband.

'I'm so sorry, Wendy,' he said.

'Thank you, DCI. He was old and barely recognised me, but we had been together for a long time. To me, he was still the strapping young man that I met when I was nineteen. I was a bit wild then, but he soon settled me down.'

'We're here for you. Whatever you want, just let us know.' Isaac put his arms around Wendy and gave her a hug.

DCS Goddard arrived soon after to offer his condolences.

Wendy, not wishing to feel sorry for herself, an understandable reaction under the circumstances, obtained the photos from Larry. She passed them over to Bridget, who had soon found a programme on her computer to enhance them, and to remove some of the marks. Within twenty minutes, the photos were immeasurably improved.

Wendy could see the resemblance of the young boy on the bicycle to the more recent photo of Garry Solomon at nineteen.

448

Under normal circumstances, the mother would have been the ideal person for a positive identification, but Gertrude Richardson was dead. Failing that, there would have been Montague Grenfell, but he was dead as well. Mavis Richardson would have been the next logical choice, but the team had decided that the knowledge of the photos should, at least for the time being, remain concealed from the Richardsons and the Grenfells.

The team had agreed that two of the adults were Gertrude and Mavis Richardson, and Michael Solomon and Ger O'Loughlin were probably two of the men, but there were three others in the photos. Isaac thought that one bore similarities to Montague Grenfell, but he was not sure. As to the other man and woman, no one had any ideas.

Isaac, after he had updated his senior, resumed his search for Malcolm Grenfell.

Wendy thought Garry Solomon's widow, Emma Hampshire, would be a good person to talk to about the boy on the bicycle. Larry said he would go with her.

Wendy acted as though she was fine, but everyone in the office could see through the veneer. Her sons had phoned, asked how she was. The eldest had spoken to Bridget, who put Isaac on the phone.

Isaac told them not to worry as they would look after their mother and bring her home at night.

***

Emma Hampshire was preparing to go out when Wendy and Larry knocked on her door.

'Can we take a few minutes of your time?' Wendy asked. 'This is Detective Inspector Hill.' Larry briefly flashed his ID badge.

'I was just going to the gym,' Emma Hampshire said. 'Personal trainer, so he charges me if I am there or not.'

'Sorry about that,' Larry said.

'What can I do for you?'

'I want to show you a photo,' Wendy said. Larry had to admit that she was holding up well, better than he had when his mother had died.

'Fine.'

'It's old, and the condition is not great, but do you recognise the boy on the bicycle?'

Emma Hampshire studied the photo for a couple of minutes. 'It's Garry.'

'Are you certain?' Wendy asked.

'He looks just the same as Kevin at that age.'

'You took a while to answer,' Larry said.

'It just made me sad that Kevin is not here.'

'He is fine,' Wendy said.

'You've seen him?'

'Last week.'

'Drugs?'

'He was clean and living in Hampstead.'

'Can I have his address?' Emma Hampshire asked.

'He seems to blame you for boarding school, and breaking up the marriage with his father.'

'That's unfair, but he doesn't know the full story. The boarding school was strong on discipline, and Kevin needed it. He was difficult, the same as his father. It was for his own protection, not because I wanted to spend more time with Bob.'

'And the other issue?' Wendy asked.

'Garry poisoned his mind with a story about my screwing another man in his bed. I was not the guilty party, but a young child is susceptible to manipulation. Kevin believes his father's version, not mine. Besides, I would like to see my son.'

'I will talk to him and see if he agrees.'

'You couldn't just give me the phone number?'

'I'm afraid it's privileged information.'

'I understand. Please let him know that I care.'

'I will.'

Sitting outside in Larry's car, he asked Wendy what she had thought of Emma Hampshire's reply relating to the marriage break up.

'Who knows the truth. It's what the son thinks that's important, and she seems genuine in her affection towards her son.'

'Is that why you slipped her the phone number?'

'Yes.'

'What about the people in the other photos?' Larry asked.

'Mavis Richardson is the only one who would know.'

'Why?'

'If it was one of their wife-swapping parties, the other people may want to maintain their confidentiality. Mavis Richardson may not answer, or possibly give us false information.'

'We only know of two who are still alive, Mavis Richardson and Ger O'Loughlin,' Larry said.

'I'm not up to a trip to Ireland,' Wendy said.

'That's understood. We'd better go and see Mavis Richardson. If she lies or is elusive, then I will need to go to Ireland.' The idea of a trip appealed to Larry.

'You'd better make it soon.'

Mavis Richardson, as always, was accommodating and sociable. Even though their visit was arranged with at short notice, she still prepared some food and tea. Wendy nibbled at a biscuit, her eyes welling up with tears. Mavis Richardson asked if she was alright.

Wendy wiped her eyes with a handkerchief and thanked her for her concern.

'We have two photos. We would appreciate it if you will look at them carefully and tell us who you recognise,' Larry said. Wendy sat quietly, stoically putting on a brave face, not certain if she was able to talk without showing emotion.

Mavis Richardson took the photos and placed them on the table. She went to a cupboard in the corner of the room and returned with a magnifying glass. She looked at them for a few minutes.

'The woman in the floral dress is Gertrude. The other woman in the pale blue dress, that's me, although a lot younger.'

'The other woman?' Larry asked.

'The photos must be fifty years old. I can't remember.'

'1962 or 1963?'

'That sounds about right.'

'What about the men?'

'Michael Solomon and my husband, Ger, but you must have recognised them.'

'We needed you to confirm,' Wendy said. She had managed to compose herself.

'There are two other men and a woman,' Larry said.

'It's over fifty years. My memory is not as good as it used to be,' the old woman said. Larry realised that it was the first time that she had alluded to her advanced years, a clear indication that she knew exactly who the other people in the photos were.

Further encouragement from Wendy to Mavis Richardson to think hard came to no avail.

'Was it one of those parties?' Wendy asked indelicately.

'Keys in a hat?' Mavis Richardson replied.

'Yes.'

'Probably, but formal introductions were not always necessary. The people who came changed from time to time.'

Larry and Wendy stayed for another twenty minutes, but realising that the woman was not going to identify the other people, they left.

'She is probably on the phone now,' Larry said once they were clear of the house.

'And those others will be covering their tracks.'

'What about Ger O'Loughlin?'

'You'd better take a flight today,' Wendy said. 'I've got to deal with some issues.'

Larry took her home. He phoned Isaac on the way to update on Mavis Richardson and to get his approval for a flight that day. Bridget, in Isaac's office when Larry called, spoke briefly to Wendy.

'Are you sure you're okay?' Larry asked as he dropped Wendy at her front door.

'The funeral director is here. My sons are here as well. I will be okay, and besides, Bridget is coming over later. Have a safe flight.'

Larry drove to his house, picked up some clothes and an overnight bag, and made his way out to the airport. He rang the O'Loughlins' phone number. The voice on the other end, of a softly-spoken Irish woman, told him to hurry, as her father would only last a few more days.

***

Larry arrived at the O'Loughlins' house at eight in the evening. He had checked into a hotel near to the airport on his arrival. His plan was to show the photos to O'Loughlin, spend the night in Ireland, maybe have a drink or two, and then catch an early morning flight back.

'He can't talk to you tonight,' a pleasant middle-aged woman said as he entered the house.

'Tomorrow?'

'Let's see how he is. He has had a relapse. He is on some medication, but tomorrow morning around nine should be fine.'

Larry phoned Isaac to tell him about the delay. Isaac, as usual, was still in the office. Bridget had left to be with Wendy.

'We need to know the names,' Isaac said.

'Malcolm Grenfell?' Larry asked. 'Any luck finding him?'

'The first address did not check out. Bridget is trying to find somewhere else, but she's distracted with Wendy.'

'You can't blame her, sir.'

'I realise that.'

Larry took the opportunity for a few drinks that night and a good meal. The next day, he arrived back at O'Loughlin's house at 9 a.m. as agreed.

'He's better, but you can only have five minutes.'

'Thanks,' Larry said.

He was shown into Ger O'Loughlin's room. Wendy had said that the man, although incapacitated and connected to a ventilator, was coherent. The man that Larry saw seemed incapable of speech, barely raising his head to acknowledge him.

'Detective Inspector Larry Hill. I'm a colleague of Constable Wendy Gladstone.'

'Please sit down,' the man said in a whisper.

'I have two photos. We need to identify the people in the photos.'

'Show me.'

Larry gave the man's daughter the first of the photos. She placed a pair of glasses on her father and held the photo in front of him.

'Mavis, Gertrude,' the old man said.

'The other woman?'

'Albert Grenfell's wife, Elizabeth.'

453

'The men?'

'Michael, myself.'

'The other two men?'

'Albert Grenfell and a friend of his. I don't recall his name.'

'My father needs to rest.'

'I need to know who the other man is.'

'I don't know,' the man said feebly. Larry could see that he was fading fast. He now had two more names: names that would cause the investigation to look in new directions.

By 3 p.m. Larry was back in the office in Challis Street.

Isaac was back as well, after looking for the mysterious younger brother of Montague Grenfell.

'We need someone to question Lord Penrith,' Isaac said.

'You've met him,' Larry said. 'It has to be you.'

'What do we hope to gain from this?' Isaac posed a rhetorical question.

'We know he was an attendee at Bellevue Street, as was his wife.'

'What about her?' Bridget asked.

'She has been dead for ten years.'

'It is the unknown man that we need to identify. Do you think his lordship knows?' Larry asked.

'It's a reasonable assumption.'

'But he is suffering from dementia.'

'With dementia, people tend to remember events and people from years before. It's possible he may remember.'

'Is he communicative?'

Isaac made a phone call. Bridget smiled quietly to herself.

'According to his nurse, he comes and goes. A visit there is always uncertain, but regardless, I will go up in the morning,' Isaac said. 'Larry, can you look for Malcolm Grenfell?'

'Wendy will be back in the morning,' Bridget said.

'All three of you focus on this man.'

Chapter 19

Isaac phoned Katrina Smith to tell him of her plans.

'Come up tonight. There are plenty of rooms in the house.'

Isaac left the office early, ostensibly to take advantage of a few more hours of possible coherence from the lord.

He arrived at eleven in the evening. Katrina made him a light supper and showed him to his room. It was ageing, as was the rest of the house, but it had a four-poster bed and a view overlooking a lake at the rear. Katrina never made it back to her room that night.

Refreshed and feeling a lot better the next morning thanks to the nurse, Isaac made his way downstairs to the kitchen. Katrina was already there with an English breakfast for him: eggs, bacon and two sausages. A pot of coffee was brewing on the Aga cooker.

'You'll need to keep your strength up,' she said.

Isaac had to admit that he liked her.

'His lordship is not too well,' Katrina said.

'Later?' Isaac asked.

'Maybe after I have had a chance to get some food into him.'

Isaac ate his breakfast as they talked. Normally, he would have an orange juice, sometimes a bowl of cereal, but today he was going to be well-fed. After he had finished with the main course, there were two slices of toast and home-made jam.

Katrina left and went to look after her patient. Isaac sat down with his laptop and connected to the internet using his phone.

Wendy was soon on the phone.

'How are you?' he asked.

'Better for being in the office. Bridget and Larry are making a fuss of me.'

'Good. You know what is required?'

'Malcolm Grenfell.'

'Judging by the condition of the current lord, he is about to inherit Penrith House and a title. No idea if there's any money involved.'

'Old money,' Wendy said. 'They don't like to flash it around, but there will be plenty of cash somewhere.'

'Which reminds me,' Isaac said. 'Montague Grenfell's legal and financial records.'

'Bridget has someone on them. Do you want to speak to her?'

'Put her on the phone.'

'Bridget, you've been working on Grenfell's papers. Anything interesting.'

'Keith Dawson is here. He's over from Fraud.'

'Yes, I realise.'

'He's not here at the present moment, but I can give you an update.'

'Please do.'

'Grenfell's papers are meticulous. Not only does he look after the Richardsons' legal and financial matters, but he also looks after the Grenfells. All that he told us regarding Gertrude's and Mavis's relationship and financial status appears to be correct. Gertrude was wealthy, although did not know or chose to ignore it.

'Garry Solomon kept in contact with Montague Grenfell on an infrequent basis, and when requested, Grenfell would send him money. However, it was infrequent, and there is no reason to believe that they actually met. Kevin Solomon, the son of Garry Solomon, has been looked after as well. The drug rehabilitation, the flat in Hampstead, all paid for by Gertrude Richardson.'

'Did she know?' Isaac asked.

'Impossible to say. Grenfell had full authority in relation to Mavis's and Gertrude's legal and financial affairs. There is no indication that he abused that privilege. Also, the Grenfells are extremely wealthy, even if, as you say, the house where you currently are does not indicate that.'

'Is there any more?'

'Keith Dawson will update you with more detail as you require.'

'Thanks. Put Wendy on the phone again.'

'I'm here, sir,' Wendy said.

'Malcolm Grenfell, find him today. It's important.'

'How is Katrina Smith?' Wendy asked.

'Take that smile off your face, or your promotion next week to sergeant will be delayed.'

'Yes, sir.' It was the first time that anyone had seen Wendy smile in the office since her husband had passed away.

'Your husband?'

'The funeral is next week.'

'I would like to attend.'

'I would appreciate that, sir.'

Isaac put down the phone, smiled at Wendy's cheeky comment.

***

'You can try now,' Katrina said as she walked back into the kitchen at Penrith House.

Isaac could see the resemblance to the man in the photo, although the man in the bed was old and decrepit and drooling, whereas the man in the picture had been young and vibrant with a full head of jet-black hair.

'How can I help you?' the man asked, lying almost horizontal on his back in the bed. His head was propped up by two large pillows.

'I've explained to Lord Penrith as to why you are here,' Katrina said.

'We need to identify a man in an old photo,' Isaac said.

Katrina took the photo and held it in front of the old man.

'Michael Solomon.'

'We have identified Michael Solomon, Ger O'Loughlin and yourself. There is another man there.'

'George Sullivan.'

'Do you know where we can find him?'

'Haven't seen him in years.'

'Where was the last time?'

'He has a house in Berkshire.'

'Does he have a title?'

'George, no way. Good man, good in business, but no title.'

'That's all you are going to get,' Katrina said.

Lord Penrith closed his eyes and fell asleep.

'I doubt if he will last more than a few days. I'm not sure if I can make this weekend.'

'It was a good job I came up today. I'd better get back to London.'

'Do you fancy lunch before you leave?'

'What's for dessert?' Isaac asked.

'What do you want?' Isaac smiled at Katrina's suggestive response. At two in the afternoon, he left for the drive back to Challis Street. He would be in the office before 5 p.m. He needed Malcolm Grenfell, as well as George Sullivan, assuming he was still alive.

The key players were dying at an increasingly frequent rate, and the one reality of the case was that the murderer, if not dead, may soon be as a result of the ageing process.

Whatever way Isaac looked at it, he realised there was hardly likely to be a conviction, only a conclusion to the case.

Isaac walked into the office just before the end of day meeting started. Bridget was there, fussing over him as he entered. As soon as he had sat down at his desk, there was a cup of coffee in front of him.

'Grenfell's financial and legal dealings? Anything new?'

'No more than what I told you before. It appears that for the last fifteen years, his only clients have been the Grenfells and the Richardsons. What he had told you before he died seems to be correct.'

'The only problem,' Isaac said, 'is that he only gave truthful answers to questions asked. If I didn't ask, he never answered, and now he is dead.'

'There is only one anomaly,' Bridget said.

'Yes. What's that?'

'Malcolm Grenfell.'

'What about him?'

'The records show that Malcolm Grenfell was receiving a substantial payment each month for basically doing nothing.'

'How was it recorded?'

'Purely listed as expenses.'

'I don't see anything unusual,' Isaac said. 'From what we know of the Grenfells and the Richardsons, they look after their own, black sheep or no black sheep. Even Michael Solomon when he left Gertrude remained friendly with Montague Grenfell, and Garry Solomon, whether he was in trouble with the law or not, always had the possibility of help from his mother, Gertrude.'

'Even if she didn't know?' Bridget said.

'The truth as to whether she did or did not has gone to the grave with Gertrude and the family lawyer.'

'Wendy and Larry have been looking for the younger son.'

'Were you able to help them?'

'I believe they have found him, sir.'

'Good. We need to meet him soon.'

'Is he a suspect, sir?'

'Everyone is a suspect, whether they are alive or not.'

***

'Malcolm Grenfell?'

'Yes. Who are you?'

'Detective Inspector Larry Hill, Constable Wendy Gladstone,' Larry said.

'What do you want?'

'You're a hard man to find,' Wendy said.

'I value my privacy.'

To Larry and Wendy, it hardly seemed their idea of privacy. The man lived well. An attractive house in Henley to the west of London, its back garden running down to the River Thames. In the driveway, there was a Mercedes, the same registration that Bridget had found against the man's name.

'You've changed your address,' Larry said.

'I've lived here for five years.'

Wendy felt that she did not like the man, but then she had little time for the class structure that pervaded the country. If she had admitted to it, she would have stated that she was a socialist.

It was clear that there was a woman in the house, her shrill voice shouting for Grenfell to come back.

'I have a visitor. This is not a convenient time. Come back later.'

'Are you used to the police knocking on your door?' Wendy asked.

'Too often for me.'

'Why?'

'The neighbours don't agree with the parties I have here.'

'Loud, are they?' Larry asked.

'They are welcome to come, but they are all frustrated, members of the local golf club, regular churchgoers.'

'And you are not?'

'Hell, no. You only get one shot at life. I intend to enjoy myself.'

'And if that includes women and drinking and making a noise?' Wendy asked.

'Not so much for the drink, but the women, yes.'

'We are from Homicide,' Wendy said.

'Wait a minute. I'll tell her to make herself presentable before you come in.'

Two minutes later, Malcolm Grenfell returned. 'Come in.'

The woman sat on a chair in the kitchen. She was wearing an evening dress, even though it was early in the day. In her hand was a glass of champagne.

'Hi, I'm Lucy,' she said. 'Is Malcolm in trouble again?'

Wendy thought she was in her early twenties. Larry could not but look at her more than he should. Both of them would have agreed that she was vivacious, although only Larry would have appreciated the visible bare breast.

'Go upstairs,' Grenfell said. 'I'll be there shortly.'

'You'd better be hard when you get there,' Lucy said.

Wendy realised that the woman had said it to tease Larry.

'She's had a few too many drinks,' Grenfell said.

'A friend of yours?' Wendy asked.

'One of many. I make no pretence as to what I am.'

'And what is that?'

'A lecherous old man who should know better.'

The three sat down at a dining table.

'Tell me why you are here?'

'Are you aware of certain events pertaining to your family?'

'Albert is dying, and Montague will inherit the title.'

'Anything else?'

'I have no contact with Albert, and very little with Montague.'

'Why is that?' Larry asked.

'They disapprove of me.'

'Because of your lifestyle?'

'They belong to the past. They see that a title and position requires a person to devote himself to a life of sobriety and service to the community. I don't.'

'They still pay you to live the life they despise?' Larry said.

'No option. They could not have a family member of theirs demeaning himself with taking a menial job, even living with the proletariat.'

'I am sorry to tell you that Montague has died,' Wendy said.

'No, that cannot be. I spoke to him the week before last.'

'What did you talk about?'

'Albert.'

'Why?'

'Albert was the one who insisted on maintaining my lifestyle.'

'And Montague would have stopped your allowance?'

'Probably not, but I wanted to check.'

'Are you sad that Albert is dying?'

'Why? Should I be? Look at the life he led – boring and pointless. Married to the same old shrew for years.'

'She's dead.'

'A long time. The best thing she did for Albert.'

The frivolous rent-a-lay poked her head around the corner of the door. 'I need you,' she said to Grenfell.

He told her to watch the television or to have another glass of champagne. She left and went back upstairs, complaining as she went. Wendy was certain that she was snorting cocaine.

'Mind you, I did like Montague, even if he was stuffy.'

'What do you mean?' Wendy asked.

'He always had his head in a book, or was fussing over money.'

'Highly regarded by your family and the Richardsons.'

'The Richardsons,' Grenfell sighed.

'What is it about the Richardsons that causes you to sigh?' Larry asked.

'I never understood the relationship.'

'They are cousins.'

'I realise that, but we have other cousins. I never saw any of them receive the same benevolence.'

'Did you know them?'

'Twenty to twenty-five years since I've seen the two sisters.'

'The eldest one is dead.'

'Gertrude?'

'Yes.'

'I'm not surprised.'

'Why?' Wendy asked.

'Highly promiscuous.'

'She was eighty-seven when she died.'

'At least she knew how to enjoy life.'

'Not for the last few years. She had become reclusive.'

'Unhinged after her son disappeared.'

'What do you know about the son?'

'We were about the same age, shipped off to the same boarding school. He was a decent person, although he had some of Gertrude's madness.'

'What do you mean?'

'He had a wild streak. Always getting into trouble.'

'What sort of trouble?'

'At school: graffiti when he could get hold of some paint, smuggling whisky into the dormitory, even managed to seduce the headmaster's daughter. The old man caught him in bed with her, expelled him immediately. Made himself a legend amongst the pupils that day.'

'Do you know why he hated his mother?'

'Hate? He didn't hate her, quite the opposite.'

'What do you mean?'

'He loved her, but never wanted to see her.'

'Do you know why?'

'No.'

'On the death of your brother, you will become Lord Penrith,' Wendy said.

'I suppose so.'

'What are your thoughts?'

'No need to worry about the neighbours up there.'

'You would move in to the family home?'

'It will need fixing up first, but yes. Why not?'

'You intend to enjoy yourself?' Wendy asked.
'For as long as I can.'
'Garry Solomon. What do you know about him?'
'No idea what happened to him.'
'It's been on the news.'
'Too busy to watch the news.'
'Garry Solomon is dead.'
'How?'
'He was murdered.'
'Somebody's wife or daughter, I suppose.'
'We don't know why.'
'When?'
'1987.'
'That's a long time. How did Montague die?'
'He was pushed down some stairs.'
'Murdered?'
'Murdered. Or an unfortunate consequence of a fight.'
'Fight? Montague? He was a pacifist.'
'His death clears your way to the title,' Larry said.
'The title means little to me.'

The two police officers left soon after. The young woman was becoming restless again, and Malcolm Grenfell looked more in need of her services than talking to them.

Chapter 20

'George Sullivan,' Isaac said in the office on Wendy and Larry's return. 'He is the other man in the photo.'

'And you want us to find him, sir?' Larry asked.

Wendy, once back in the office, had moved over to near Bridget. Isaac could see that Wendy was in need of her friend's ministrations. For the moment, it was only Isaac and Larry.

'Any ideas about him, DCI?'

'Nothing to go on. His lordship gave the name just before he fell asleep.'

'How much longer before he dies?'

'According to Katrina?'

'Katrina?' Larry asked, knowing full well who Isaac was referring to. The office always liked a little bit of gossip, even if it was discreet.

'Katrina Smith, his private nurse.'

'How long?'

'One week, give or take a few days.'

'And then Malcolm Grenfell is the new Lord Penrith.'

'Is he excited?'

'Not sure.'

'What do you mean?'

'He professes not to care, but he's a member of the idle rich. With Albert and Montague dead, he gets the title, the stately home, and the money.'

'A good enough motive to murder Montague Grenfell.'

'As you say.'

Wendy, feeling slightly better, came over and joined the conversation. 'I didn't like him, sir,' she said.

'Malcolm Grenfell?'

'A man his age messing around with a girl in her twenties.'

'He likes young women?'

'He's a total waster, sir.'

'But is he a murderer?'

'If it affected his lifestyle, he might feel inclined.'

'Could he have killed Montague?'

'To ensure the title?' Larry asked.

'Why not?' Isaac answered.

'Montague Grenfell had control of the money, the titles to all of the properties. Did he set up a proxy in case he was indisposed?'

'It's a question that needs answering. We should ask Bridget to check.'

Wendy leant over to the door entrance and shouted for Bridget to come over.

Bridget brought a sheet of paper with her.

'Bridget, who will take control of Montague's legal and financial responsibilities?'

'I have a copy of his will, sir.'

Isaac scanned the document. 'Albert, the first executor, then Mavis Richardson. The wealth stays within the Grenfell family, so Malcolm's claim on the money and the house is secure. There is also a generous amount of money to be taken from his estate and given to Mavis Richardson.'

'What does it mean?' Larry asked.

'He trusts Mavis, but not Malcolm,' Bridget said.

'That is fine, but everyone in this will, except for Malcolm Grenfell, is over eighty years of age. Any one of them could die at any time.'

'In that case, full control would probably go to Malcolm.'

'The man has a strong motive, at least for the murder of his brother.'

'Is Mavis Richardson at risk?' Larry asked.

'DCI, you mentioned George Sullivan,' Wendy said.

'Lord Penrith identified him as the unknown man in the photos.'

'Who is he?'

'That's up to you and Larry.'

'Are we saying that Albert Grenfell and his wife attended the wife-swapping parties?'

'The photos may be unrelated. George Sullivan may know.'

'Where do we look, sir?'

'According to the elder Grenfell, he had a house in Berkshire. Not much to go on, but that is all there is. Maybe check Montague's records.'

***

Albert Grenfell died two days after Isaac had spoken to him. Wendy and Larry informed Malcolm Grenfell by phone. They could hear the sound of people and music in the background. The new Lord Penrith did not turn the music down.

The new lord was delighted and intended to enjoy his good fortune with more drink and more food. The frivolous twenty-something that Larry and Wendy met had been replaced by another.

Mavis Richardson took the news badly when Wendy told her. 'He was a good man. Old fashioned, but genuine. Who's left now?' Mavis said. Wendy thought she looked a lot older than when she had previously seen her.

'Did he attend any of your parties?'

'Yes. On a couple of occasions.'

'And his wife?'

'Once.'

'What can you tell me about George Sullivan?'

'He was a friend of Albert's.'

'He was at one of your parties?'

'We never invited him again.'

'Why?'

'He was a coarse man.'

'Would you care to elaborate?'

'We only agreed that he could come if he brought a woman with him.'

'And he did?'

'No. He came on his own.'

'But he stayed?'

'He was an attractive man. Gertrude wanted him immediately, but I could see he was trouble.'

'How?'

'He started putting his hands on me.'

'Was that a problem?'

'In front of everyone?'

'Are you saying that behind closed doors it was okay, but not in front of the guests?'

'It's basic good manners, and he had very few of them.'

'Did you sleep with him?'

'Gertrude did.'

'Why didn't you?'

'He wanted to, and if he had been more of a gentleman, I probably would have.'

'Was Montague Grenfell there?'

'No.'

'What happened after you refused?'

'He became drunk, accused me of being a prick teaser. In the end, the party ended early, and Albert led him away.'

'His wife came as well?'

'She didn't take part.'

'And Albert?'

'I slept with him the one time. Gertrude, on another.'

'Where can I find George Sullivan?' Wendy asked.

'I've no idea. He may be dead, same as all of us. I am the only one still alive. You do realise that?'

'We found Malcolm.'

'Still living it up with his young tarts?'

'You never mentioned that you knew where he was.'

'I never knew. Did Montague?'

'Montague knew everything,' Wendy said. 'And Malcolm is now the incumbent lord.'

'Does he know?'

'I told him.'

'He will destroy the good name of the Grenfells. He is the last of the line. After him, there will be no more Lord Penriths.'

'Is that a bad thing?' Wendy asked.

'I still believe breeding counts for something,' Mavis Richardson said.

Wendy realised that it was not for her to discuss Montague Grenfell's will. That was for a more formal occasion. Wendy assumed that Mavis Richardson knew its contents, but she would only live for a few more years before she died, or became too old and frail to understand what was required of her. Wendy wondered what happened in such circumstances, but assumed there was a procedure.

'Have you nominated another lawyer?' Wendy asked.

'Not yet. I'm not sure who I can trust.'

'Maybe you should.'

'Malcolm will turn the ancestral home into a bordello,' Mavis said.

'Garry Solomon had a son.'

'I am aware of that.'

Mavis Richardson appeared tired. Wendy made her excuses and left, not sure what she had achieved by visiting. The old woman had not provided any more useful information, and judging by her condition, she was not in a fit state to take on the responsibilities as the executor of Montague Grenfell's will.

Lord Penrith's wealth would be a sufficient motive for anyone, and Gertrude was independently wealthy, as was Mavis. What would happen if Mavis died? She had no living relatives, other than an ex-husband, but he was at death's door.

The only person who had anything to gain from Mavis's death would be Kevin Solomon, the son of Garry Solomon.

Wendy phoned Larry. They agreed to meet up with Kevin Solomon to see if he knew any more.

***

Isaac had received an urgent phone call from Katrina Smith, still up at Lord Penrith's house in Leicestershire. 'Malcolm Grenfell is here,' she said.

'What did he have to say for himself?'

'He was drunk; he had a woman in the car. At first, I assumed it was his daughter.'

'She's not his daughter,' Isaac said.

'He thought I was part of the deal.'

'Violent?'

'He could have been.'

'What did you do?'

'Kneed him and punched him in the face.'

'I didn't know you were so tough.'

'You've not checked out my history?'

'No.'

'Five years with the British Army, two of those in Iraq. I received training in unarmed combat and weaponry.'

'Were you on the front line?'

'Baghdad, field hospital.'

'Tell me about Lord Penrith.'

'The new one?'

'Yes.'

'He wanted to move in, spend the night. There wasn't a lot I could do to stop him. I told him his brother was still in the house.'

'They've not taken the body away yet?'

'You would think it was royalty that had died. He is lying in state, and all the staff, local dignitaries, other members of the aristocracy are filing past. It's macabre.'

'Did Malcolm Grenfell want to see his brother?'

'Hell he did. He was more interested in doing an inventory of anything valuable.'

'Is he still there?'

'Yes.'

'Can you leave?'

'Not with his brother lying dead in the other room. Can you come up?'

'It may be an excellent opportunity to meet Lord Penrith.'

Isaac arrived at the Penrith House at six in the evening. Katrina came out of the front door on seeing him arrive. She could not resist and gave him a hug and a kiss.

'He's impossible,' she said.

'What's he done?'

'He found the key to the wine cellar, and he's down there with his woman. I took a look, and it was evident she is not his daughter. Both naked and covered in wine, almost like a bacchanalian orgy.'

'I'll deal with it,' Isaac said. Katrina had phoned the local police, but they were reluctant to intervene as the man was now the lord. Isaac knew what Wendy's comment would have been.

Isaac walked down the stone steps to the basement. The two people at the bottom were unconscious drunk. Katrina came down, and they carried them both upstairs and put them to bed. Isaac assumed one bed would be sufficient for the pair.

'They won't have much to say until tomorrow,' Katrina said.

'No point going back now. Do you have a spare room?' Isaac asked.

469

'If you don't mind sharing.'

Chapter 21

Kevin Solomon was not initially pleased to see Wendy and Larry. 'What do you want?' he asked.

'A few more questions,' Wendy said.

'You'd better come in.'

'How are you?' Wendy attempted to lighten the sombre tone of the meeting.

'You gave my phone number to my mother.'

'She was concerned.'

'Not concerned enough when she put me in that boarding school.'

'What did you say to her?'

'I was polite.'

'Have you met her?'

'I said I would. She sounded lonely.'

'I think she is,' Wendy said.

'I was angry at the time, but now I'm all right,' Kevin Solomon said. 'Do you want a drink?'

'Coffee for me,' Larry said.

'Make that two,' Wendy added.

'Mavis Richardson, it is assumed, will be the executor of Montague Grenfell's will, and the proxy for his business and legal affairs.'

'What has that to do with me?'

'Your agreement with Montague. Was it watertight?'

'I signed some papers, but I've been so spaced out for the last few years, I don't know. He could have made me sign anything.'

'That's unlikely,' Wendy said.

'Why?'

'We have had qualified people checking his paperwork. The man was meticulous, and there is no trace of his cheating anyone. And besides, you're family.'

'Illegitimate family, wrong side of the bed.'

'It appears to be a minor distinction.'

'Enough to keep my father from the title.'

'Does that concern you?'

'My mother said it upset him.'

'What else did your mother say?'

'Most of the time I was either drunk or injecting myself.'

'Do you intend to stay clean?'

'I spent two years at university studying law, one of my few clean periods. I plan to make sure my mother gets her fair share after my grandmother died. I don't trust anyone.'

Wendy looked around the room. It was clear that Kevin Solomon had tidied the place, a sure sign that his mother was intending to visit. Wendy was pleased as animosity between mother and child is always unpleasant. Her sons had always been there for her except in their troublesome teens and early twenties. Then, it had been too much alcohol and wanting to bring females home. She had relaxed her strict rule on a couple of occasions, and an unknown female face at the breakfast table the next morning had given her a slight tinge of regret that she had agreed, but apart from that, it had been fine. Finally, she had drawn the line when two females and one son had presented themselves at the table one morning looking for bacon and eggs. She had made it clear that she was not a hotel nor a brothel, and if either son wanted to avail themselves of the local talent, they'd better find somewhere else.

Not that she could blame the females, as her sons took after their father with their rugged good looks, but threesomes in her house had been too much.

She had relented when her two boys had matured and settled down with steady girlfriends.

The funeral of her husband was scheduled for later in the week. She had asked Isaac to give a eulogy as he had met her husband several times over the years, and she knew he would say the right words. The sons would speak as well. Wendy knew that she would be incapable.

She had appreciated the opportunity to continue at work, and the case had focussed her mind away from her husband's death. Bridget continued to stay at Wendy's house, although one son or another was always there. Still, Bridget was female and would understand more than the sons what their mother was going through.

'Wendy, Wendy.'

'Yes, Larry. Sorry.'

Wendy, comfortable in Kevin Solomon's flat, had drifted off, probably fallen asleep for a few minutes. Her sleep pattern had been disturbed since her husband had died, and her regular eight hours had been replaced by short periods of one or two hours, sometimes three, sometimes none.

Severely embarrassed, Wendy apologised.

Kevin Solomon said not to worry.

'Do you intend to make a legal claim on the estate?' Wendy asked, pretending to be fully alert, and now sitting forward on the comfortable chair.

'If there is an issue, although, as you say, Montague Grenfell was an honourable man.'

'We believe that to be the case, but…'

'Malcolm Grenfell?' Kevin Solomon said.

'What do you know about him?' Larry asked. Wendy had moved towards the window, aiming to take in the breeze from outside, attempting to wake herself. The toll of the last few weeks was catching up with her, and once everything had settled down, she intended to take a break, sit in the sun somewhere. Hopefully, Bridget would come. If she didn't, she would go on her own.

'My mother told me what she knew once I was old enough to understand.'

'Your mother seems to have no financial problems.'

'My mother is not concerned about the money, only that she, as the widow of Gertrude Richardson's son, and I, the grandson, are treated in the correct manner.'

'And why should Malcolm Grenfell be an issue?' Wendy asked. She had resumed her seat, confident that she would not embarrass herself again. She knew the answer but wanted to hear it from Solomon.

'Somehow, the Grenfells and the Richardsons are inexorably linked.'

'Is there more to the story than we know?' Larry asked.

'From what my mother has told me, the aristocracy, or at least, the Grenfells' version, abide by a different set of values. According to my mother, I should never trust them.'

Wendy could only agree. She had only risen as far as a sergeant in the London Metropolitan Police, but she took pride in that she had benefited society, helped to reunite lost and alienated children with their parents, taken a major part in putting some villains and murderers in jail. Just because someone put 'Lord' before their name meant little to her.

'Your mother is coming?' Wendy asked.

'In about an hour.'

'Are you looking forward to see her?'

'Yes. I would appreciate some time to prepare.'

'Fine,' Wendy said.

Outside in the car, with the heater on, the two police officers evaluated what Kevin Solomon had said.

'He seems to know a lot about the Grenfells,' Larry said.

'At least, his mother does. Did she ever meet any of them?'

'She never met Gertrude Richardson, although she could have met some of the others. Did she meet Montague Grenfell personally? I suppose we will never know.'

As they sat in the car, they saw Emma Hampshire exit a black London taxi. She waved to the two of them but did not come over to speak. She appeared to be in a good mood, and her son had obviously told her about the two police officers sitting outside.

Larry suggested knocking on the door and questioning the woman. Wendy, sentimental and motherly, was firm in her response.

'No. Those two have a lot of talking to do,' she said.

***

Malcolm Grenfell, the newly incumbent Lord Penrith, was up and about by eight in the morning. The lord's young woman was still sleeping off the effects of the drunken excess from the previous night.

Isaac made sure to give the impression that he had just arrived. His lordship was not pleased to see him, although Isaac was not sure whether that was because of Grenfell's throbbing head, or whether he was just an arrogant man, or whether acquiring the title had somehow elevated him above the law and probing questions.

Regardless of what the man wanted or thought, Isaac had questions, Grenfell had the answers.

'Who is going to deal with the reading of the will and the legal and financial matters after your brothers' deaths?'

'Which brother? The former lord, or Montague?' Malcolm Grenfell made the pretence of eating his breakfast, although not in the kitchen with the staff. He was sitting at one end of a large table in a formal dining room. Isaac sat at the other end. He realised that if he had not come with the authority of the London Metropolitan Police, he would be in the kitchen, and would be expected to bow and scrape.

Katrina had forewarned Isaac that Malcolm Grenfell was taking his responsibilities as Lord Penrith very seriously, especially the part where the peasants fawned to their master. She had stated that once the previous lord was in the funeral home, then she was leaving, which was that day.

'Montague gave executor powers to that woman, Mavis Richardson. Not that she can do much, too old,' Malcolm Grenfell said.

'You know her?'

'Not intimately, as Montague obviously did.'

'What are you inferring?'

'I know about Montague and the Richardson sisters.'

'What do you know?'

'Don't be obtuse. The fact that they were screwing each other.'

'Kevin Solomon?'

'What about him?'

'Do you know him?'

'Never met him, although I went to the same school as his father.'

'Garry?'

'If he had only the one father, then Garry. Is there another one?'

The cook came in with a pot of tea. She poured a cup for Isaac, poured another for his lordship. As she left the room, and with Malcolm Grenfell's back to her, she cocked her nose in the air and held a finger underneath. Isaac smiled; he knew the universal gesture for someone with airs and graces and a snob.

'You were about the same age as Garry Solomon,' Isaac said.

'I was three years older.'

'Did you spend time with him?'

'When we were in our teens, we would go out drinking, chasing girls.'

'Later?'

'He met up with Emily. After that, we lost contact. I never saw him again.'

'You knew Emily?'

'She was a good-looking woman. Fancied her myself, but she wanted Garry.'

'Have you seen her since?'

'Around London. We moved in the same social circles. Nothing sinister.'

The young woman who had arrived with Grenfell walked into the room. Isaac thought it was more a crawl than a walk, as she was rubbing her eyes and trying to focus. Her hair was tousled, and she was wearing a dressing gown. It was tied loosely at the waist, her breasts almost exposed.

'Are you going to make me a Lady?' she asked of Grenfell after planting a semi-drunken kiss on him.

'Later maybe. I'm busy for the present.'

The woman, young enough to be Penrith's daughter, sat down on a spare chair. 'I want breakfast,' she slurred.

Judging by Grenfell's facial expression, her chances of him marrying her were slim. Isaac could see that she was going to be dumped within a short period of time. He felt sorry that such a young girl felt the need to hang around with a man in his sixties, instead of finding someone her own age. Not that it concerned him, as in his years of being an active member of the police force, he had seen many unlikely couples, some happy, others not so.

'Go down to the kitchen with the rest,' Grenfell barked, or attempted to, but his voice was still subdued and raspy after the wine of the previous night.

The woman ambled out of the door.

'What did you speak to Emily Solomon about?'

'It's been a few years, but she had moved on from Garry, or he had moved on. Regardless, she was very cosy with Bob Hampshire.'

'You knew Hampshire?'

'Good man. He worshipped Emily, although she called herself Emma with him.'

'And her?'

'She was devoted to him.'

'Tell me about Mavis Richardson. How is she going to deal with Montague's complex legal and financial matters?'

'I've no idea. What is the legal process in such issues? She is clearly not up to the task.'

'And Albert?'

'I will deal with it. There is a lawyer in the town who is reputable. I'll put the matter in his hands.'

'Trustworthy?'

'He will be with me. This is all mine now. I don't intend to let anyone cheat me out of my dues.'

'And the woman you brought up?'

'I was the brother of a lord before.'

'Better class of woman now?' Isaac said contemptuously.

'I hope so.'

Isaac left the man to his breakfast. He needed to see a friendly face; he needed to see Katrina.

Chapter 22

Larry was leaning back in his chair at Challis Street. Wendy had left early, some last-minute arrangements for the funeral. Bridget was busy, collating all the paperwork that a murder enquiry created.

She was still helping Wendy with her reports, or Sergeant Wendy Gladstone, as her promotion had come through. Bridget had managed to get Isaac's paperwork under control, and if she focussed, she could complete it within an hour.

Bridget enjoyed working in the department, even if the hours could be long, but there was not much for her at home. The former live-in lover had been unceremoniously shown the door two weeks earlier. She had come home late and he had been sitting down with a couple of friends in the kitchen, drinking beer.

'We need some food,' he had demanded.

'Get your friends out of here and clear up this mess.' Bridget saw red. The lover lived there rent free. The only requirements on him were that he kept the place clean and showed her the attention she craved.

'Woman, do what you're told or you will feel the back of my hand.'

He had tried it once before, but it had been early in their relationship, and she had forgiven him after he had sobered up, but now…

Coupled with the pressure of work and her friend Wendy's sadness, Bridget reached a decision. A well-built woman and surprisingly strong, she grabbed the man by the scruff of his neck and ejected him through the back door. The other two men sheepishly retreated.

The trio had stood outside the house for thirty minutes before she phoned Wendy, who phoned a contact down at the local police station. The trio spent the night in a prison cell. Bridget ensured that her previous companion's clothes were deposited at the police station. According to Wendy, he was warned by the local police that if he attempted to make contact with Bridget, he would be thrown in the cells for a week.

Bridget had been sad for a few days but soon got over him. Wendy offered her one of her cats for comfort, but she declined. Besides, both of the women were looking to pool their resources and move in together. Bridget's house seemed the best possibility, as Wendy's was cold and damp. They had even discussed buying a small flat somewhere warm, renting it out to holidaymakers when they did not need it.

Larry's phone rang. 'Grant Meston. We met at the Baxters.'

'How are you?'

'Fine.'

'Any update on the grille at the Baxters?'

'It was installed in February 1987.'

'You knew that already.'

'I have the name of the company that installed it.'

'And the name of who paid for it?'

'No such luck. It was a long time ago. I made a quick phone call to save you the trouble, but no one remembered.'

'Send me an email with the address, and I'll get out there,' Larry said.

Isaac arrived back in the office just after midday. Katrina Smith was still up in Leicestershire and would be down in London later that night. Isaac offered to pick her up at the station, but she had declined. Her mother was picking her up, and she should spend some time with her.

Bridget rushed into Isaac's office with a cup of coffee on his arrival. Larry came in soon after.

'Take a seat,' Isaac said. He had been a little weary after the drive down, but Bridget's caffeine-rich coffee soon revived him. Five minutes later, DCS Goddard entered the room. He was in an ebullient mood. Isaac wondered why but assumed he had been pressing the flesh with the movers and shakers again.

DCS Goddard saw a protégé in Isaac; DCI Isaac Cook saw a mentor in DCS Goddard. It did not isolate Isaac from his boss's wrath and frustration; a kick up the arse when it was needed.

Today was not one of those days.

Bridget brought another coffee for their DCS. He thanked her.

'What's the latest, Isaac?'

'Loose ends, sir.'

'DI Hill, what are you up to?' Goddard asked.

'We know where the grille that prevented entry into the murder room was constructed, sir.'

'And when are you going out there?'

'As soon as I leave this meeting.'

'Wendy?' The DCS looked at Isaac.

'The funeral is tomorrow.'

'Who will be going?'

'All of us.'

'Fine. I will be there as well,' Goddard said. 'Bridget, what have you to report?'

It was evident to Isaac that someone was asking Richard Goddard questions, or just winding him up to bring the case to a conclusion. Someone influential, but who and why? Isaac did not see it as important, and besides, it was a murder enquiry, and setting a schedule for murderer apprehended, murderer convicted, case closed did not work. As far as Isaac was concerned everyone was doing their best, even Wendy who should be on compassionate leave. But he had known the DCS longer than anyone else in the department, and when you needed support or advice, his door was always open.

'Montague Grenfell seems to have been an exceptionally precise man, very honourable and decent.'

'He still ends up murdered.'

'We're not sure about that,' Isaac said.

'There is a scuffle. He falls down the stairs, dead at the bottom. That's murder in my book.'

Isaac knew that his DCS was baiting him. 'It could have been a disagreement that unfortunately had fatal consequences.'

'Gordon Windsor's report stated clearly that the man had been manhandled through the door of his office. He then attempted to wedge his foot against the wall at the top of the stairs. It looks conclusive to me.'

'As you say, conclusive.' Isaac saw no validity in contradicting his senior's opinion.

'Were Garry Solomon and Montague Grenfell killed by the same person?' DCS Goddard asked.

'It seems unlikely,' Isaac said.

'Why?'

'There is almost thirty years between the two murders. There must be a strong possibility that the murderer of Garry Solomon is dead.'

'How much longer do you need with this case? I'm being asked to keep costs under control.'

'Not at the expense of a murder investigation,' Isaac said.

'The accountants only understand the bottom line. They are out of touch with reality, but unfortunately we all have to contend with them.'

Isaac knew that it was rhetoric and that Richard Goddard would keep the wolves at bay. And besides, the department's key performance indicators were good. The last three cases they had found the murderer and ensured a conviction within an acceptable time period.

'We are conscious of budgetary restraints,' Isaac said.

'Fine. Montague Grenfell seems the easiest case to solve,' DCS Goddard said.

'Yes.'

'I need an arrest within ten days.'

'Why ten days, sir?'

'I am to make a presentation to the prime minister on the modern police force. I intend to use your department as an example.'

'It will not be possible to present the current case, sir.'

'Understood. Unofficially, off the record, I can.'

'We will do our best.'

'Budgetary cuts?' Larry asked after DCS Goddard had left.

'Rhetoric,' Isaac replied. 'I've known the man for many years. If we keep doing our job, he will make sure we are left alone.'

'Our jobs are secure?' Bridget asked.

'Totally. Larry, you'd better chase up on that grille.'

'Five minutes, and I'm out of the door.'

'If we don't meet again, 2 p.m. tomorrow afternoon at St Agnes.'

'We'll all be there,' Larry said. Bridget nodded her head.

***

The sign over the door said 'O'Reilly's Metal Fabricators', although thirty years previously it had said Dennison. Larry was not optimistic.

'No computers back then,' Sean O'Reilly, a big blustery man with a beer belly proudly extending at his front, said. He used braces to keep his trousers up, as his waist and a belt did not provide an adequate restraint against the laws of gravity.

'I appreciate it's a long shot, but I need to try,' Larry explained. He had shown his ID badge on arrival, been afforded a friendly welcome and a quick tour of the facilities.

'Not much has changed in thirty years, apart from the computers. The majority of the work is manual labour, and it's hard to find any of the younger generation interested now.'

'Is it just you?'

'I have one man, but he's part time now. A bit long in the tooth, he's pushing seventy, and he's not much use really.'

'Why keep him on?'

'He's been here forever, even before my time, and I need the help. Once I go, the place will close down.'

'Your offsider, would he be able to remember back to 1987?' Larry asked.

'He'll be here within the hour. You can ask him then.'

Larry took the opportunity to grab a coffee and a sandwich in a small café not far from O'Reilly's.

'Tom's in the office,' Sean O'Reilly told Larry, having found him in the café.

'How did you know I was here?'

'It's the only place nearby. I always come here for my lunch,' O'Reilly said. Larry had assumed that the man always indulged in a pub lunch, but chose not to comment.

The two men walked the short distance back to O'Reilly's premises.

'This is Tom Wellings,' O'Reilly said.

'Please to meet you, Detective Inspector.'

Larry observed a small, sprightly man who had stood up rapidly on his arrival. The face etched with lines showed a healthy tan, no doubt from years of standing outside in the yard where the metal was stored, or leaning over a fabrication with a welding torch in his hand.

'How long have you been here, Tom?'

'Ever since I left school. It must be fifty years at least.'

'Don't you ever feel like retiring?' Larry asked, making general conversation before asking the important questions.

'To do what? Go fishing, play golf?'

'I suppose so.'

'Not for me. I will keep working until they take me out of here in a wooden box. Anyway, Sean pays me enough to pay for my drinks.'

'You don't look like a drinker.'

'Drink me under the table, will our Tom,' Sean O'Reilly said.

'Tom, in 1987 a metal grille was installed at an address on Bellevue Street. Do you remember that job?'

'Business was booming back then. I would not be able to remember that far back, or at least, specific jobs.'

'Is there any way to jog your memory?'

'We used to store the job cards and the accounts up in the roof when they were no longer needed. Fire hazard, I suppose, if the truth is known. They may still be there.'

'Can we look?' Larry asked.

'I suppose so,' Sean O'Reilly said. 'I've not been up there, so it won't be too pleasant.'

'Let's look anyway.'

Tom led the way. At the top of the old building, there was a small door into a roof cavity. Sean O'Reilly fetched a hacksaw to remove the lock that was secured to the door.

'What a mess,' Larry said.

All that could be seen in the light of Larry's phone was a mass of papers. The smell was overpowering. All three men retreated for fresh air.

'Are you certain it is in there?' Larry asked Tom.

'Old man Dennison was a stickler for keeping paperwork. He thought it may be needed someday for another job.'

'Old man?' Larry asked.

'Back then I was only in my twenties. Bill Dennison was in his sixties. I suppose that makes me Old Man Wellings now.'

'You? Old? Never,' Sean O'Reilly said.

'I will need to get some people from Challis Street. Is that okay by you?'

'Sure,' O'Reilly said. 'You're welcome to whatever you can find.'

Larry phoned Gordon Windsor.

Early the next morning two juniors from Gordon Windsor's department arrived at Sean O'Reilly's premises. Larry pitied them the task ahead. He stayed with them until midday and then excused himself. He had a funeral to attend.

The two juniors by that time were cursing, but as Larry had observed, they were diligent in their approach. The paperwork they retrieved was being placed carefully in containers for transportation. It would take five to six hours to complete the retrieval. From there on, it would be a case of sifting through the papers looking for 1987 and Bellevue Street and number 54.

***

The church was only two streets from Wendy's house. She arrived dressed in black, her two sons on either side of her. Bridget walked behind them.

Isaac had arrived early, as had DCS Goddard. Both men wore black suits. Larry came a little later, as he had picked up his wife. She had met Wendy once, instantly liked her, and wanted to be present.

Mavis Richardson, who had come to know Wendy during her visits to her house, sat at the rear of the church on her own. Isaac thought it a decent gesture from a woman who was in mourning herself. Firstly, for Gertrude Richardson, then Montague Grenfell, and lastly, Ger O'Loughlin, her ex-husband. News of his death had been phoned through to Larry by his daughter earlier in the morning.

Everyone was in the church when the coffin arrived. The priest, an elderly, grey-haired man, conducted the service. He was a softly-spoken man, his voice ideal for the solemnity of the occasion, although Isaac thought that at any other time his monotone would put everyone to sleep. Both sons and Bridget rose from their seats to give a bible reading.

Isaac shed a tear, as did the other members of the department. Once the coffin had left with the immediate family following the hearse in their cars, the others filed out of the church.

Isaac noticed that Mavis Richardson had left promptly, her BMW moving down the road.

483

Wendy's house had not been suitable for the wake. A hall adjoining the church had been hired. Wendy returned from the burial later in the afternoon. Isaac gave her a hug and a kiss on the cheek, as did Larry's wife. Larry gave her a hug, as did DCS Goddard.

She thanked everyone, especially their DCS.

The wake was not a time for mourning, more a time for celebration for the life of Wendy's husband.

Both sons made brief speeches.

Isaac was asked to speak on behalf of the police department, as a special request from Wendy. He was used to public speaking, having been involved in enough press conferences in his time. He had even been on television, met the prime minister on a couple of occasions.

Isaac spoke about Wendy's husband, his achievements in life, his devoted wife, his two sons. He said that her husband had supported his wife, an invaluable member of the London Metropolitan Police. It was a nice touch to the day's proceedings. Wendy thanked him later.

Eventually, the wake concluded, and Isaac left. He had wanted to meet up with Katrina, but it was too late. He would see her the following day, murder enquiry permitting.

Chapter 23

The following morning, Larry visited the two juniors who were busy sifting through the papers in a room at the back of Challis Street Police Station. Their mood was not much better than the day before.

Larry brought two coffees from a local café, hopeful that it would lighten the mood. 'What have you found?' he asked.

'Apart from a total mess?' a young woman in her twenties said. Larry thought she looked too young to be a qualified crime scene investigator, or maybe he was starting to get old. He was in his early forties, and the junior police officers straight out of police college were looking young to him. He did not like the idea of getting old, which explained why he and his wife were into a vegan diet and macrobiotics and anti-oxidants.

He thought their interest in the subject may be helping, but he and his wife were still getting older. He wondered if Tom Wellings, the seventy-year-old employee of Sean O'Reilly, had the right idea.

Here was a man who had led a good life, stress-free, and still had the ability to down the pints of a night time. Nowadays, Larry started to feel woozy after two pints, but apparently Wellings was good for six, and the next day he would be at work early, none the worse for wear.

Larry picked up some old order books, browned and covered in dust, to see if he could help.

'We have a system here,' an obviously well-fed man in his thirties said. Larry had seen him at O'Reilly's, attempting to take control of the retrieval operation. The young lady assisting him had taken little notice of him, and she had been collecting from one side of the roof cavity, he from the other. To Larry, personality counted for a lot, the ability to get on with your fellow worker was vital. It was clear that the man with the expanding waistline, even though he was still young, had very little in the way of personality and little to recommend him.

'Rose, watch what you're doing,' Duncan said, a little too loudly for Larry.

'You mind your side of the room, I'll mind mine,' Rose said. It was clear she had the measure of her colleague.

'What have you found?' Larry asked for the second time. Both Duncan and Rose had stopped work for a few minutes. Duncan took the opportunity to pop outside for a cigarette.

'Don't worry about him,' Rose said to Larry when it was just the two of them in the room.

'Fancy himself, does he?'

'And any loose piece of skirt.'

'Has he hit on you?'

'He's tried. Not a chance.'

'Apart from your colleague, what have you found?'

'There is paperwork dating back to the sixties. It had basically just been thrown in there, collecting dust and spiders' webs, and God knows how many dust mites.'

'1987 is the year we are after,' Larry reminded her.

'Not so easy. We can only sift through in a logical manner. No point diving in here and there.'

'I suppose not,' Larry said. He was enjoying his conversation with the young lady.

'We need a couple of days. Some of the paperwork, especially the work orders, are in very poor condition, eaten through by dust mites, and the rats had made a home in there at some time in the past.'

'Fine. Let me know when you find anything of interest.'

Duncan returned, bringing the smell of stale cigarettes with him. 'That's better,' he said.

Larry left the pair of them to the task, glad to be out of the room with the stuffy old smell. He took a deep breath on exiting, taking in the fresh air. The weather was getting colder, and he knew that Wendy would soon be feeling the aches and pains in her body, the signs of increasingly debilitating arthritis.

She had taken a couple of days off after her husband's funeral, but he knew she would be back in the office the next day. Larry liked the woman a lot. Sure, she smoked terrible cigarettes, her diet was certainly not vegan or macrobiotic, but she was energetic and enthusiastic and determined. He had to admire that in a person.

He was still not sure about his relationship with his DCI. He knew that Isaac was competent and loyal to his staff, Wendy's elevation to sergeant testament to that fact. He also knew that

Isaac was ambitious and determined to solve their current case as soon as possible.

***

Isaac was not in a good mood on Larry's arrival at the office. 'Mavis Richardson is dead,' he said.

'Suspicious?' Larry's reply.

'Gordon Windsor is on his way out to her house.'

'The woman was eighty-five.'

'You know what this means?' Isaac said. 'All those who could have killed Garry Solomon or knew the reason for his murder are now dead, every last one of them.'

Larry understood what his DCI was saying. Chasing Garry Solomon's murderer was of less interest than resolving who had pushed Montague Grenfell down the stairs outside his office, and if Mavis Richardson's death was suspicious, then somebody knew something about the past.

'It's all related to the death of Garry Solomon, I'm sure of it.' Isaac, like many an experienced police officer, especially in a murder investigation, had developed a sixth sense that defied logic. Larry knew he did not have it yet.

'Even Montague Grenfell's death is proving difficult,' Larry said.

'It shouldn't be,' Isaac replied. 'We know it was a man he scuffled with, the shoe size found at the top of the stairs proves that. And a woman would not have had the strength, or should I say, any of the women we know of in this case.'

'Anyone else out there that we don't know of, sir?'

'Call me Isaac. At least, when we're alone.'

'Thank you, sir, Isaac.' Larry was pleased that their relationship had developed enough to allow first names to be used.

'I still don't understand why Montague Grenfell was killed,' Isaac said. 'He was the one person who had full knowledge of the Grenfells' and Richardsons' finances and legal matters. Without him, who is going to take over? Is there anyone else capable?'

'You've always suspected that he knew more than he was telling,' Larry reminded Isaac.

'What do you mean?'

'All families have skeletons in the cupboard. Facts they would prefer not known.'

'And we can assume that the Richardsons and Grenfells had more than most.'

'And Montague Grenfell would have had the dirt on everyone, whether he chose to use it or not.'

'Don't you think we would have found out whether he had used it to his own advantage by now?' Isaac said.

'Why? Montague was careful to cover his tracks, keep all details to himself. Maybe the others didn't know they were being manipulated.'

'You believe that he could have been cheating the others, and they didn't know?'

'It's possible. What has Bridget's man come up with?'

'Nothing, other than Montague Grenfell was meticulous. He appears to have acted honourably at all times.'

'Sounds like a nomination for sainthood to me, Isaac,' Larry said. A sceptical man, he did not trust people with no vices, no apparent failings.

'You're right,' Isaac conceded. 'There has to be something about him.'

'Keith Dawson has been helping Bridget with Grenfell's records. We need him here.'

***

Gordon Windsor phoned Isaac. 'Heart attack. I will arrange for the pathologist to confirm, but she was old. I doubt if they will find anything suspicious.'

'Thanks. We are up against a brick wall with this case,' Isaac replied, venting his frustrations with the crime scene examiner.

'Everyone dying or dead?'

'That's about it.'

'Anyone still alive?'

'Only three now. Gertrude Richardson's grandson, the incumbent Lord Penrith and Garry Solomon's wife.'

'Must be one of them,' Windsor said.

'No motives, that's the problem.'

'I'm glad I'm only a crime scene examiner. I'll leave the detective work to you.' Gordon Windsor hung up and waited for an ambulance to remove the body. His team would go over the house in detail, although he was not expecting to find much.

Keith Dawson came into the office. Isaac had seen him around the office over the last few weeks. Apart from regular meetings and the daily pleasantries, they had not spoken much. Dawson, he knew by reputation and their limited communications, was a gruff man. He always wore a dark suit with a brightly coloured tie, out of sync with his less than bright manner.

'DCI, what can I do for you?' Dawson said, his body weight straining the frail chair he was sitting on.

'Montague Grenfell.'

'Excellent records.'

'No sign of fraud?'

'None that I could see. Mind you, I had been asked to check his records to see that they were in order. A man such as Grenfell could fudge the records with little trouble.'

'Is there any way to check?'

'It would help if I had something specific to go on. What are you looking for?'

Wendy came into the office with Bridget. It had only been a few days since the funeral.

'I couldn't stand it anymore,' Wendy said. 'Everyone phoning up or visiting every five minutes asking if I was fine.'

'Are you?' Isaac asked.

'As well as can be expected.'

'Ready for work?'

'Coming here is the best therapy. He is dead and buried. Moping around won't bring him back.'

Isaac was pleased to see her back in the office. Not only for her benefit, which was important to him, but there was work ahead. The case had been going on for too long, and DCS Goddard was starting to annoy him. And besides, Katrina Smith was spending time in London, and he wanted to see her more than he had.

They had managed to snatch a late-night meal together, and she had spent the previous night at his place. He liked her, maybe not as much as he had Jess O'Neill, but that relationship had been doomed due to his brief romantic encounter with Linda Harris. At least with Katrina Smith there were no incidents of misbehaviour that would damn the relationship before it had started.

Isaac still looked to settle down, find a steady woman, but each time there was something, either from the woman or from him. He knew he was a romantic looking for the ideal woman, the ideal starry night.

'You've still not said what I'm meant to be looking for,' Dawson said. Isaac's friendly banter with Wendy had not impressed him.

'*Get on with it*,' Dawson thought.

'Keith, we don't have a motive for the deaths of Garry Solomon and Montague Grenfell.'

'Do you expect me to find a motive for you?' Dawson said sneeringly.

Isaac chose to ignore the inferred criticism of his handling of the case. He knew other men within the police force, men who had been there for a long time, men who were covertly racist.

'Let's focus on Montague Grenfell,' Isaac said. 'Even if his death was unintentional, the evidence of a confrontation at his office is overwhelming.'

'So?' Dawson offered a one-word comment, as if he wanted to say 'get on with it and stop wasting my time'.

'The confrontation would indicate a recent conversation or a recent case. Now, as we know he only dealt with the Richardsons and the Grenfells, it is fair to assume it is related to them.'

'There are a lot of research notes. I haven't looked at them,' Dawson admitted.

'He told me that he spent his days in the office studying and reading. There may be something there,' Isaac said.

'I'm from Fraud.'

'So?' Isaac felt that it was his turn for a one-word comment.

'Looking at his notes is not in my area of expertise.'

'I don't understand.'

'I am an expert in legal and financial. Reading through the man's notes is not my area.'

'Do you have a problem?' Isaac looked Dawson straight in the eye. Keith Dawson, now the focus of attention, drew himself up, sucked in his stomach, although it still left his shirt hanging half out.

'I'm not the best person for the job,' he admitted.

'Bridget can work with you.'

'Okay. I can give you a day of my time. If we see anything, we'll let you know.'

'Wendy, what are your plans?' Isaac asked.

'Emma Hampshire is still around from when Garry Solomon died.'

'Fine. You concentrate on her,' Isaac said. 'Larry, we need to find who ordered the grille.'

'The record is probably there, but it's not a pleasant job sifting through thirty years' worth of papers.'

'When will we have an answer?'

'Today. I'll make myself a nuisance until they find it.'

Isaac wrapped up the meeting, giving them all a pep talk as to how this was a crucial day: a day when the pieces come together.

'How's Katrina Smith?' Wendy asked as she left the office.

'Promotion to sergeant can always be reversed,' Isaac replied with a smile.

Chapter 24

Malcolm Grenfell, the new lord, had brought up some friends from London, and they were partying around the clock. The cook who had been with the previous Lord Penrith for twenty-five years had left one day after Katrina Smith.

The young girl that Grenfell had in tow had been supplemented by another two, and according to the housekeeper, there was enough Viagra in the lord's bedroom to stock a pharmacy.

Isaac still had his reservations about the man. Of all the people in the case, he was the one with the most to gain. If Montague Grenfell had acceded to the title, he might have cut off the younger brother's allowance.

It was clear that Malcolm Grenfell was incapable of earning a salary. His forte appeared to be seducing susceptible young women, no doubt enamoured by his easy spending.

As Isaac sat back in his chair the phone rang. 'Lord Penrith,' the voice said.

The person he had been thinking about was talking to him. 'What can I do for you?'

'How long are you going to take with this bloody case?' His lordship was clearly as drunk as a lord.

'We are hoping to start arresting people in the next few days.' Isaac realised that it was not the truth, but he was looking for a reaction.

'Then bloody well hurry up.'

'Why is it so important?' He should have addressed Lord Penrith as 'My Lord', or 'Sir', but that would have been acknowledging that Malcolm Grenfell deserved respect, when he did not.

'I can't access Montague's bank accounts.'

'His death is regarded as suspicious.'

'The man had one leg. He was bound to fall down those stairs at any time.'

'Have you been to his office?'

'A few times.'

'When was the last time?'

'Two years ago, when he was not paying me regularly.'

'I was under the impression that he always paid on time.'

'Maybe he did, but not then.'

'Any reason?'

There was a pause at the other end of Isaac's phone.

'I upset Albert.'

'How?'

'I called him a miserable old man.'

'Why?'

'I was drunk. That was all.'

'If Montague had not died, you would not have become Lord Penrith.'

'Are you saying that I killed him?'

'It's a good enough motive. In fact, the only motive we have. No one else wanted him dead.'

'Montague had his secrets.'

'What do you mean?'

'I'll let you find out.' The phone line went dead. Isaac tried to ring back, but no answer.

***

Wendy, still not fully recovered from the emotions of the previous days, was glad to be back at work.

Emma Hampshire, as usual, was just about to go out when Wendy knocked on her door. Wendy was not sure if it was true or whether the woman always said it for effect. Regardless, the woman invited her in.

'I am sorry for your loss,' Emma Hampshire said. She was the same age as Wendy, but she had spent her life looking after herself: regular trips to the gym, no cigarettes, no excessive drinking.

'Thank you.'

'What can I do for you?'

'Malcolm Grenfell is now Lord Penrith.'

'Yes, I know.'

'Tell me about him,' Wendy said.

'I used to see him from time to time.'

'What was your opinion of him?'

'He was often drunk and rude.'

'Tell me about Garry?' Wendy asked.

'What's to tell? We've spoken about him before.'

'Garry was murdered for a reason, as was Montague.'

'Are you certain about Montague?' Emma Hampshire asked. She had settled back in her chair, resigned to the fact that she would have to go out later. And besides, Wendy Gladstone was good company, even if she was a policewoman.

'Mavis Richardson has died.'

'I know.'

'How?' Wendy asked.

'Malcolm Grenfell phoned me.'

'He has your number?'

'I'm in the phone book.'

'What did he say?'

'Just that Garry's aunt was dead.'

'Did you know her?'

'Not personally.'

'What else did Malcolm Grenfell say?'

'He was crude.'

'What did he say?'

'He assumed I would have screwed him for a title.'

'Your reply?'

'I was polite. I think he had a woman with him.'

'Was he serious in his offer?' Wendy asked. Everyone in the department assumed Malcolm Grenfell was only interested in women half his age.

'About screwing me or the title?'

'Either, I suppose.'

'He always tried it on when Bob wasn't looking.'

'Did you take him up on the offer?'

'No way. I was devoted to Bob, still am.'

'There are conflicting statements as to why you left Garry Solomon.'

'I realise that.'

'What is the truth?'

'It was a rough patch in our marriage. Garry's business was not going well, and he was becoming abusive.'

'How old were you?'

'I was about twenty-six, Garry was one year older.'

'And?'

'We were friendly with Malcolm Grenfell. They had been to the same school, although Malcolm was three years older.'

Wendy braced herself.

'Kevin was just three, and Garry was sleeping down at his business most nights of the week.'

'You were separated?'

'Not totally, but we were not as husband and wife.'

'Something is coming that is going to shock me, isn't it?' Wendy said.

'Malcolm came over to the house one night. He had a bottle of wine in his hand and two glasses.'

'And you let him in?'

'I wanted to say no for Garry and Kevin's sake, but I was young and lonely.'

'You slept with him?'

'The one time.'

'When he threw you out, was it because he had another woman?'

'Yes, but he treated Kevin and me well until the money ran out.'

'Have you slept with Malcolm Grenfell since?'

'No.'

'Did Bob Hampshire know?'

'No.'

'Garry?'

'I don't know. I never mentioned it, but Malcolm…'

'Indiscreet?'

'He can be after a few drinks.'

It was evident from Emma Hampshire's confession that there was another element in the death of Garry Solomon: the possibility of genuine love from Malcolm Grenfell for Emily Solomon, the possibility that Garry Solomon had found out and had been using it to his advantage.

There were still some missing elements, though. The affair between Malcolm Grenfell and Emily Solomon had occurred in or around 1977, although Garry Solomon had been alive for another ten years before his murder.

Emma Hampshire claimed to have not seen him after 1979 when he had been released from his first prison, and then it had only been a fleeting visit for him to see Kevin.

'So now we have a possible motive for Garry's death,' Wendy said. Emma Hampshire appeared to be relaxed in her chair, but Wendy could see her clutching the armrest.

'I only slept with him the once.'

'Jealousy is a strong enough reason to kill someone.'

'What jealousy? Garry was hardly a saint, and I never gave him reason to suspect me. He was a good man, always a little headstrong, given to criticising his family and the Grenfells.'

'Why the Grenfells?'

'He must have learnt some of the stories from his mother. How his grandfather was illegitimate, and the Richardsons had always been treated as the leper relations. He would surmise what his life would have been if his grandfather had not been illegitimate. If he had been born on the right side of the bed, as Malcolm.'

'Did he envy Malcolm?'

'Only the fact that he was legitimate.'

***

Larry had arrived at the room where Duncan and Rose were working. He brought them both a coffee from the café across the road. Gordon Windsor's juniors were in a more agreeable mood.

'Sorry about yesterday,' Duncan said. 'I was a bit on edge. It's a crap job, only fit for juniors.'

'Breeds character,' Larry humorously replied.

'I'll take your word for it.'

Larry noticed that the majority of the papers were stacked according to year and month. Rose had printed some labels from the printer and had stuck them to the table using tape.

'1987 is over in the far corner,' Rose said.

'You needn't have sorted the other years,' Larry said.

'What if you want another date?' Duncan said. Larry thought it was a fair comment. They had one date when the grille had been installed, but what about the bars on the inside of the windows in the house, and the person who had placed the order may have requested additional work.

It was clear that the firm back in the 80s had been exceptionally busy. There must have been over four hundred individual items: most were single sheets of paper, the rest were order books or job specifications. Larry regretted his enthusiasm. 'I'll leave it to you,' he said.

'It's a junior's job, is that it?' Rose said.

'I suppose so. I was a junior once. I know the pain you are going through. Phone me when you find something.'

'We'll send you a scanned copy,' Duncan said.

***

Isaac had spent the morning in the office dealing with paperwork. Bridget was too busy with Keith Dawson to help him out. Larry, after leaving Rose and Duncan, met Wendy for an early lunch.

'How are you?' he asked.

'That's all I've heard for the last week. Tell me about the case and where we stand,' Wendy said. She knew how she felt: she felt sad and sorry for her deceased husband. Apart from that, she was fine. Kind words and condolences did not help, solving a murder case did.

Wendy had just come from seeing Emma Hampshire. The woman's slender figure had caused some reflection on Wendy's part. She ordered a salad.

Larry, glad to be out of the home and away from the latest diet, fasting for two days a week, ordered steak and chips. He knew he would be in trouble when he got home, but for the moment he would be in heaven.

'Isaac is worried,' Larry said.

'Isaac!' Wendy exclaimed.

'Sorry, DCI.'

'That's fine. I've known him for a long time, but he will still be "sir" to me.'

'What did Emma Hampshire have to say?'

'Apart from the fact that she had an affair, or at least a one-night stand, with Malcolm Grenfell when she was married to Garry Solomon, not much.'

'Have you told DCI Cook yet?'

'Not yet. How important do you think it is?' Wendy asked.

'What do you think? Apparently, Grenfell is keen on her, but she does not reciprocate apart from sleeping with him the one time.'

'It's a motive for Garry Solomon's murder.'

Wendy phoned Isaac, or to her, DCI Cook.

Isaac's reaction was understandable. Another vital piece of information had been uncovered. Not only were the Richardson sisters screwing Montague Grenfell on a regular basis, and Albert on two known occasions, it now appeared that their behaviour had moved to the next generation, in that Gertrude Richardson's daughter-in-law had slept with a Grenfell.

Isaac wondered what sort of morality these people adhered to.

'Remember George Sullivan,' Isaac said. 'He's the one person we've not contacted yet.'

'Do you think he's important, sir?' Wendy asked.

'Maybe, maybe not, but who knows? Emma Hampshire wasn't until she gave you that little nugget.'

'I'll look for him, sir. Leave it to me,' Wendy said, her stomach rumbling. She regretted her poor choice in nourishment. *Fit for rabbits*, she thought. She called over the waitress. 'Give me what my colleague just ordered,' she said. As far as she was concerned, she would rather be overweight and happy than skinny and miserable.

As Wendy dealt with the rumbling in her stomach, Larry continued their conversation. 'George Sullivan? Any ideas?' he asked.

Wendy answered between mouthfuls of food. She was gasping for a cigarette, but that would have to wait until they were outside, and outside was cold and becoming colder due to an Artic wind from the north.

'I've not a clue,' Wendy said. 'The man must be in his eighties by now, and it's a common name.'

Chapter 25

Meanwhile, unbeknownst to them, Emma Hampshire was on the phone. 'I told Sergeant Wendy Gladstone.'

'What the hell did you do that for?'

'It would have come out one day.'

'Why? We were always discreet.'

'Someone may have seen us.'

'It's been thirty years. No one's alive now.'

'That may be true, Malcolm, but I'm tired of living with a lie.'

'You never told Bob, but you end up telling a policewoman. Do you realise where that places me?'

'No. Where does it place you?'

'Right at the top of DCI Isaac Cook's list of murder suspects.'

'And me.'

'Why?'

'If you killed Garry because of me, I may be seen as an accomplice.'

Lord Penrith realised that Emma Hampshire was talking nonsense. They had been lovers in the past, not now. Sure, he had been flirtatious on occasions since when Bob Hampshire had been looking the other way, but it had never been more than an amorous fondle from him, an indignant rebuff from her.

'I never killed him. How many times have I told you? Do you think I waited nearly ten years after our affair to kill him? I would have rid myself of him back in 1976, not waited until 1987.'

Emma Hampshire hung up, unsure whether she had been right in confronting a man who had meant something to her once. She knew him as unpredictable, his actions uncertain, and his morality of little consequence if it came between him and the life he wanted. She realised that Malcolm Grenfell and Emma Hampshire had a lot in common. He had offered her the title of Lady Penrith, half-joking, half-drunk. She had spent too much time on her own since Bob Hampshire's death, too much time pining, too much time waiting for a man to occupy her bed.

Malcolm Grenfell was a lecher, a rogue, a man who partied and whored, but she could control him. A lord needs respectability, she would give it to him.

***

Larry Hill was in the office at Challis Street when Rose phoned from the crime scene examiner's office. 'Detective Inspector, we found something.'

Larry inexplicably found himself excited at the prospect of meeting up with the woman again. 'Twenty minutes,' he replied.

'I'll supply the coffee this time,' Rose said.

'We found this,' she said later as they sat in the café.

'It's what we've been looking for.'

'There's a contact phone number.'

The photocopy that Larry had in his hand was not clear. Age and the rain seeping through the roof where it had been stored had yellowed it badly.

'We've put the original into an evidence bag and labelled it,' Rose said.

'Send it to Forensics and ask if they can pick up the details. In the meantime, can you send me a scanned copy.'

'Once I'm back in the office.'

'Thanks. We have a lady in the office who is great with computers. She may be quicker than Forensics.'

Larry realised on leaving that they had spent forty minutes chatting. It was not as if he was interested in pursuing a relationship with Rose. He was happily married and intended to stay that way. It was just that it was flattering, good for his ego, to have the company of an attractive woman for a short period.

***

'Mavis Richardson died of natural causes,' Gordon Windsor said. Isaac Cook had phoned the senior crime scene examiner for an update.

One less murder to deal with, Isaac thought.

The need to wrap up the case was long past. He had discounted the possibility of a conviction for Garry Solomon's murder. All the people who knew him had since died, except for Malcolm Grenfell and Emma Hampshire. The revelation of their affair had come as a shock.

The reason for Garry Solomon's unwillingness to contact his mother continued to baffle Isaac.

The mother had been at the party that night he had come home unexpectedly and found his aunt on top of his father. He must have known or assumed that his mother was with another man, but that should have evoked anger and hurt, hopefully followed by forgiveness.

There had been several years between that night and when he had left the house at the age of nineteen. Isaac wondered what his relationship had been with his mother in those years. Was it distant, loving, or ambivalent? The only person who may have an inkling was Malcolm Grenfell, as all the others who may have known were dead.

Isaac did not relish the trip up to Leicestershire again as the sight of the ageing Lothario cavorting with young women did not excite him. Before he met Katrina Smith, he would have been curious, as his love life had taken a definite turn from good with Jess to lukewarm, and on to non-existent.

Isaac phoned Lord Penrith, not expecting more than a few moments of his time. If the man was reluctant to speak, he would set up an interview at a police station, bring the man in, formally caution him, and then put him on the spot.

'Lord Penrith, DCI Isaac Cook.'

'Yes, DCI. What can I do for you?' Malcolm Grenfell said. Isaac noticed the man spoke with respect, and he sounded sober. *A good start*, Isaac thought.

'Answers to questions,' Isaac said.

'Let me have your questions.'

'You knew Garry Solomon when he was young.'

'I've already told you this. We were at the same school, although he was three years younger than me.'

'Did you acknowledge each other. Look out for the other?'

'Hell, no. We used to treat his year like shit.'

'What do you mean?'

'You've not been to boarding school?'

'No such luck,' Isaac replied. He had been to the local comprehensive from the age of eleven, and whereas it had served him fine, it had not had a great record of academic achievement.

'Luck! No luck if they send you to the school we went to.'

'What do you mean?' Isaac asked.

'Boarding schools for the offspring of the rich and the influential are only there to satisfy the egos of the parents, and as a dumping ground for their children.'

'Bad?'

'Sadistic teachers. They ruled with an iron rod as well as a wooden cane, split at the end to increase the pain for the unfortunate student who received ten of the best across his arse.'

'I thought that wasn't allowed.'

'Corporal punishment, the last vestige of privilege for exclusive boarding schools.'

'It sounds sadistic.'

'It was, but any student dumped there was invariably angry with their parents.'

'Did you receive any discipline?'

'More than most.'

'And Garry?'

'After he seduced the headmaster's daughter?'

'Yes.'

'They beat the shit out of him. I had left by then, but I heard about it soon after.'

'What did you think?'

'He went up in my estimation.'

'It didn't stop you sleeping with his wife.'

'Garry changed. He was treating her badly.'

'Were the two of you serious?'

'I suppose we were. She was, still is, a good-looking woman, and back then, the idea of marriage appealed.'

'And now?'

'Marriage? I don't think so. I'm still young enough, and you know what the title gets me?'

'A better class of woman.' Isaac pre-empted Malcolm Grenfell's expected crass reply.

'That's right. Is that what you phoned me for?'

'Garry Solomon never contacted his mother after the age of nineteen.'

'That's probably correct.'

'Do you know the reason why?'

'He never spoke about it. I know about the party.'

'Which party?'

'Where his aunt was screwing his father.'

'That was seven years before he walked out on his mother. And then he sends her a postcard from India two years later.'

'Montague would have known.'

Every time the answer is Montague, and he is not available, Isaac thought. Montague Grenfell's burial, after the body had been released, was due to be conducted in three days' time. Isaac planned to attend the service, the body then to be interred in the family plot in the churchyard adjoining Penrith House.

'Anyone else?'

'Emma, maybe, but no one else. It's a long time ago.'

'You mentioned that Montague had secrets. Can you elaborate?'

'Nothing concrete, but he had too many fingers in too many pies. Impossible to resist fudging the numbers.'

'Would you?'

'If I had his acumen, probably.'

Isaac terminated the phone call. In three days' time, he would be in Leicestershire. It would be a good time to conduct a formal interview. While Malcolm Grenfell had been polite on the phone, Isaac had little time for the man who, without the benefit of money and now a title, would have been out on the street scrounging for food and money.

***

Wendy was on the phone in the office following up on all the George Sullivans that Bridget had managed to identify. Bridget had used a set of criteria to narrow the field: age, wealth, reference in *Burke's Peerage*, school attended.

She had looked for a correlation between Albert Grenfell, who was known to be a snob, and George Sullivan, the criteria reflecting the fact that Albert was hardly likely to be friendly with someone who was not of an equal social standing.

Regardless, George Sullivan was a common name, and *Burke's Peerage* had not helped, as the only George Sullivan had gone to school in Scotland, whereas Albert had gone to Eton.

Wendy, as usual, was diligent in her pursuit of Sullivan. Her mood had improved after the funeral, and one night of the week she would stay with Bridget, and another night Bridget would stay with her. Bridget, she had found out, was allergic to cats, and had come up in a rash on her arms.

Larry had the paperwork with Bridget and Forensics. The phone number on the work order was indecipherable. He could see a four and an eight and a couple of other numbers, but there should be more. As for the name alongside the phone number, the rats had eaten that many years previously.

DCS Goddard was keeping his distance and had not been in the murder room for seven days. Isaac expected to hear from him at any time.

Keith Dawson continued to wade through Montague Grenfell's papers. He said little, only grumbled occasionally. Bridget ignored his protestations. He had even complained to his boss, who had complained to Isaac, who told him that there were two murders, maybe more, and if DCS Goddard needed to ensure Dawson stayed in the office with them, he would call him up.

The last comment from Dawson's boss. 'He's a miserable sod. Keep him for as long as you want.'

Isaac had met up with Katrina Smith on a couple of occasions, although not as many as he would have liked. She had found herself a job in London and was already working long hours.

She had spent a few nights at his flat, but it was early days for both of them, and no decision had been made for her to move in on a more permanent basis. Besides, her mother was prudish, and Katrina would not want to upset her without giving her fair warning.

As Albert's and his brother Montague's bodies had been released at the same time, there was to be a joint funeral. Katrina would travel up with Isaac for the funeral. They planned to spend the night in a hotel.

Wendy was going as well, mainly to take note of who attended and whether there were some unknown faces, maybe the elusive George Sullivan or maybe someone they had not taken into account.

Wendy and funerals were happening too often for her liking. There had been Gertrude Richardson's, and then her husband's. Now she had Albert and Montague Grenfell's to attend, and then two days after, Mavis Richardson. Both Larry and Wendy planned to attend her funeral, as both had come to know her well. Her death and their attendance at her funeral did not excuse her from any crime that may have been committed, but she was dead. Her guilt or otherwise would be decided at a later date.

Larry thought they were drawing blanks and there would never be a resolution for a thirty-year-old murder. Isaac, more optimistic, refused to accept his view.

Bridget's attempts to clean up the scanned copy of the work order to read the phone number for Bellevue Street had not worked. She had tried Photoshop: reduce the hue, increase the saturation, lighten, darken.

The most she had ascertained was that the number was probably in London and that it began with a five and ended with an eight. She had made a guess of what the missing numbers may have been, made a few phone calls, but only received the sound of a disconnected line.

'Phone numbers have changed since then,' Bridget had said. Regardless, she knew that a full phone number, no matter how old, could be traced, and an address and a name attached to it.

Isaac moved over to the white board in the corner. On it was listed the victims, their relationship to the suspects, possible motives, current addresses, their backgrounds and histories. He was certain that somewhere on that jumbled board was the solution to both of the murders. Instinct told him that Garry Solomon's and Montague Grenfell's murders were related; although it may not be the same murderer, the same basic motivator remained, but what?

Montague Grenfell had been pushed down a flight of stairs. Even if a culprit was found, they could easily claim self-defence, an argument, an unfortunate accident. A murder conviction seemed unlikely, more likely manslaughter unless a full confession was received. Garry Solomon was murder, no one would dispute that, but why hide his body in that fireplace? Isaac had had restless nights thinking over that.

To put the man's body in a house owned by his mother and his sister seemed callous. The condition of the body had made it impossible to ascertain whether he had been murdered in the house or elsewhere.

Michael Solomon had been friendly with his son on a casual basis but hadn't told the boy's mother, and had not attempted to look for him after his disappearance.

Isaac knew that somebody knew something, but who and what.

'Larry, let's go and see Michael Solomon's widow,' Isaac said. It was more an act of frustration on his part than a reasoned action.

'What are you thinking, Isaac?' Larry asked.

'Too many unknowns. Michael Solomon may have said something to his second wife.'

'He only had the one wife,' Wendy said.

'As you say,' Isaac acknowledged.

Chapter 26

Larry and Isaac could hear the sound of babies crying when they arrived at the house. Larry knocked on the door. A woman came to the door, her hair not brushed, her face showing anger. 'What do you want?'

'DI Larry Hill. This is Detective Chief Inspector Cook.' Both men showed their ID badges.

'Come in. Find a seat if you can.'

In the hallway of the house was a pushchair which they had to push to one side to get through. Once past, there were the remains of a child's dinner. They stepped over it and went into the only room that appeared to show any semblance of homeliness.

Five minutes later the woman came in. Isaac noticed that she had changed her dress and brushed her hair.

'Mrs Solomon,' Isaac said. 'Sorry to arrive unannounced.'

'Call me Mary.'

'Mary, you met his son.'

'Solly?'

'We refer to him as Garry Solomon.'

'Still the same man.' The voice of a crying baby echoed through the walls. Isaac found the noise irritating; Larry appeared ambivalent.

'When was the last time you saw him?'

'How would I know?' Mary said. 'Sometime in the eighties. I only knew him as my husband's friend.'

The cry of another child and Mary Solomon rushed out of the door. The sound of a smack, more crying, and Mary's harsh voice: 'Shut up, shut up. You'll be the death of me.'

Isaac could see the need for a visit from Child Welfare.

'Her children have dumped their offspring on her,' Larry said.

'No right to hit children, is it?'

'No. She needs assistance, not our criticism.'

Mary Solomon returned. 'Sorry about that. DI Hill knows the situation. If the house were not in my name, I would walk out and leave my son and daughter to it. As it is, I've taken a court order against my daughter for maintenance.'

'You don't see her?' Larry asked.

'Not often, but I'm not surprised,' the woman said. More crying from the other room. She continued speaking, determined to ignore it. 'DCI Cook, my daughter is a whore, selling herself up in the city. She is either flat on her back with her legs open, or in a ditch drugged out of her mind. My apologies for talking about my daughter like that, but that's the reality.'

'You need help,' Isaac said.

'If someone wants to help, they can take the children. My daughter's are mongrels anyway.'

Isaac could see the frustration in the woman. He could even sympathise, but a child was a child, even if it had no redeeming features and bad blood, the result of a prostitute and her client. He wanted to dislike the woman but found he could not.

'We know that Garry Solomon, Solly, disappeared in 1987. Did your husband ever mention him after that?'

'Not that I remember. Mind you, he was only my husband's friend to me, and not a good friend at that. Does it matter?'

'Probably not, but we are still not sure what happened the night Garry Solomon died.'

'Long time ago. Most are dead, I suppose.'

'Would your daughter know?'

'Unlikely. She was only nine years old back in 1987. A pretty little thing then, not the tattooed tart she is now.'

Mary Solomon rushed off back to the other room at the sound of breaking plates. Larry and Isaac excused themselves and left.

'Wasted trip, Isaac,' Larry said.

'I suppose so.'

'Must be tough when your children turn out bad.'

'Yes,' Isaac said, his mind distracted as he considered the case. 'What I don't get is why no one missed Garry Solomon. He was visible, and then he disappears.'

'And his mother Gertrude never went looking for him.'

'Precisely,' Isaac said. 'He was never more than ten to fifteen miles from her, apart from his time in India. What are the chances of not inadvertently bumping into each other?'

'It's always possible.'

'Garry Solomon was killed for a reason, yet there is no reason. His mother never finds him, and he never contacts her, apart from a postcard from India.'

'Something happened on his return to sever the relationship, and it was not when he was nineteen.'

'It's possible.'

'Who do we ask?'

'Emma Hampshire and Barbara Bishop.'

Isaac and Larry took the opportunity of an early lunch. Larry, feeling guilty and remembering the ear-bashing he had received after eating a steak on a previous occasion, kept to an orange juice and a Greek Salad. He eyed Isaac's plate, wished he had ordered pasta as well.

***

Wendy, drawing blanks on finding George Sullivan and aware of Isaac's wish to visit Emma Hampshire, suggested that she go with him instead of Larry. Isaac agreed with her recommendation.

Larry returned to the office. Wendy joined Isaac outside Emma Hampshire's house. She was pleased to see Kevin Solomon's car parked across the road.

'Emma, this is DCI Cook,' Wendy said. She had phoned ahead to tell Emma Hampshire that they were coming.

'Pleased to meet you,' Isaac said. Wendy noticed that Emma Hampshire, although thirty years older than her boss, visibly blushed as he took her hand firmly and shook it.

The Isaac Cook charm, how can any woman resist it? Wendy thought.

Kevin Solomon came to the door and introduced himself. Wendy could see that mother and son were getting along fine.

'Come in please,' Emma Hampshire said.

Wendy knew that she would have to make a point of forewarning the woman if they visited again. On the table in the dining room there were sandwiches, some cakes, and a pot of freshly-brewed coffee.

'Coffee, DCI?' Emma Hampshire asked.

'Thank you.'

It was clear that Kevin Solomon was moving back in with his mother; the suitcases in the hallway testament to the fact.

According to Keith Dawson, Emma Hampshire and her son would be well provided for once Gertrude Richardson's assets had been dealt with.

Kevin, as the only legitimate descendant of Gertrude, was to be given the responsibility of handling probate, but as he was not a qualified lawyer, he intended to re-engage with his studies.

A fellow student when he had been studying, now qualified, would deal with Gertrude. Mavis presented another problem. She had no descendants, and Kevin's father had not been on good terms with her. Kevin believed that her wealth should go to his mother as well, but Mavis's will had been ambiguous. She had placed sole responsibility in the case of her death with Montague Grenfell, and he was dead. Failing that, she had named her sister, although her sister may not have known, and she was dead too.

According to Kevin's understanding, a decision about her assets would require legal advice.

The death of Montague Grenfell was apparently causing other difficulties. The incumbent Lord Penrith may have had access to the stately home, and sufficient funds to maintain his singularly self-indulgent lifestyle, but the bulk of the wealth remained out of reach.

'What can I help you with?' Emma Hampshire asked, directing her gaze at Isaac.

'We have not been able to find out the reason for the animosity of your first husband towards his mother,' Isaac said.

'I never knew.'

'We are aware of an incident when he was twelve, although he remained in the family home until he was nineteen, barring time at boarding school, so we do not believe that the incident was the catalyst.'

'I believe it was.'

'Did he tell you the details?'

'Yes.'

'When?'

'When we were in India.'

'And then there is the postcard he sent when he was there,' Isaac said.

'We were at a retreat in the hills, puffing hash, attempting to come closer to nirvana.'

'And?'

'Have you tried it?'

'No,' Isaac replied. There had been some uppers and downers sold around the schoolyard when he was in his teens. He had tried one once, made him sick and sad. He never tried them again. Even the drunken nights with his mates, he had largely avoided; the alcohol put him to sleep and affected his ability to chat up the young women.

'Garry was melancholy, at peace with the world. He wrote the postcard, put a stamp on it, and put it in the mail. The next day he tried to get the postcard back. Even offered a bribe, but it was too late. The postcard was on its way, and there was nothing he could do about it.'

'His mother treasured it. Did you contact her?' Isaac asked.

'I phoned her once after Garry had left me.'

'Why?' Wendy asked.

'Curious, I suppose. If Garry could treat me the way he did, and he hated his mother so much, then what was she like?'

'And what was she like?'

'She knew who I was. Accused me of turning her son against her. It was not a pleasant conversation. In the end, I slammed the phone down.'

'Did Gertrude Richardson ever mention this to you?' Isaac asked Wendy.

'Never, but my time with her was limited. She was friendly that last night when she had seen Garry, but she died soon after.'

'She saw him after thirty years!' Emma Hampshire looked astonished.

'Yes,' Wendy replied.

'What did he look like?'

'Do you really want to know?'

'I suppose not.'

'Mrs Hampshire,' Isaac said.

'Please call me Emma.'

'At any time did you have reason to believe that someone would want your husband dead?'

'After he left me, he fell in with a bad crowd. They may have.'

'He was found in a house belonging to Gertrude and Mavis Richardson. Did you ever visit that house?'

'Bellevue Street? I never visited, although I knew about the mansion.'

'How?'

'Garry pointed it out once.'

'He never thought to go in?'

'He said he used to visit there as a child, nothing more.'

Isaac turned his focus to Kevin, the son. 'What do you know about your family history?'

'Mum's told me about Malcolm Grenfell. Is that what you are asking?'

'Yes.'

'People make mistakes, and I can believe what she tells me about my dad. I can remember him vaguely, but I never saw any presents or Christmas cards from him after he left. As if he didn't care.'

'Bob Hampshire did,' Isaac said.

'He was a good man.'

'Why the drugs?'

'Susceptible to them. My father's generation became alcoholic, my generation took drugs.'

Isaac felt that the interview was going nowhere. If Emma Hampshire knew anything, she was keeping it close to her chest. As for Kevin, he may have been too young.

Wendy thought that Emma Hampshire and her son were good people. Isaac tended to agree, but experience had taught him that the most unlikely people were often closer to the action than appeared at first glance. He was not ready to discount either of them yet.

***

Isaac and Wendy drove over to Barbara Bishop's house in Knightsbridge. There appeared to be no one at home on their arrival. Wendy phoned the woman's mobile. Barbara Bishop appeared five minutes later.

'Yoga class,' she said.

'This is Detective Chief Inspector Cook,' Wendy said.

The woman, wearing yoga pants and a tee shirt, looked up at Isaac. 'I need a shower. Give me five minutes. Help yourself to coffee, the cups are in the cupboard to the right of the sink,' she said.

Wendy took up the offer, found some biscuits as well. Ten minutes later the woman returned, dressed in a white blouse and a short skirt.

'Mrs Bishop, by your own admission you were the last person to see Garry Solomon alive.'

'I told Constable Gladstone this last time.'

'I am aware that you spoke to Sergeant Gladstone, and that you were very cooperative. Sometimes it pays for a different police officer to ask the same questions. Garry Solomon's death is highly suspicious, but we have no reason for it.'

'He was a good man with me,' Barbara Bishop said. 'I would have married him if he had been available.'

'What did he feel about you?' Isaac asked.

'He loved me. I'm certain of that.'

'Did he say so?'

'A woman knows, it doesn't need words.'

'What mood was he in when he left that day?'

'Cheerful.'

'And where was he heading?'

'I don't know.'

'You asked him?'

'He said he would be only forty minutes and then he was going to take me out to the movies.'

'Did you see anyone suspiciously loitering in the street?'

'No.'

Chapter 27

Forensics had come back. 'We managed to get you the phone number off the work order you sent us,' a deep woman's voice said. Larry recognised the tell-tale sign of a heavy smoker.

'Can you email it to me?' Larry asked.

'It will be in your inbox within ten seconds,' the woman replied, a rasping cough interrupting her speech.

Larry had been back in the office when the woman had phoned. He had not had much to do that morning other than to tidy his desk, always a bit of a mess due to his habit of not tidying the night before. He could not understand how Isaac managed to keep his so tidy, and then there was DCS Goddard. Their DCS's penchant for a clean desk was legendary. 'Clean desk, clean mind,' he would say if pressed.

Larry sipped his coffee, pressed the key repeatedly to refresh the inbox on his laptop. Bridget had said that it was not necessary, but he was impatient. In forty seconds, not the ten promised, he saw that he had received a new email. It was what he wanted. Bridget was working hard in her corner of the office. Larry had mentioned before to Isaac that she needed help, but Bridget, when asked, had resisted any assistance. 'It's the way I work best. If I am not under pressure, I lose focus,' she had said.

Isaac had not pursued the matter any further, and besides, he had not had a lot of time. If he was not in the office, he was worrying about the case. If he was not worrying, he was with Katrina Smith.

Once in the office, fully involved in the deliberating, the discussing, the attempts to find a solution, the time would pass unnoticed. Almost as if the hands of the clock on the wall had stopped rotating.

He knew that was why Jess O'Neill had moved out, and probably why Katrina Smith would not be in his life for too long. He sometimes wondered, not often, as he had little time for daydreaming and idle speculation, if it would be different with Katrina, although he assumed it probably wouldn't be.

He was a man who looked for a long-term companion, the patter of little feet rushing to him when he walked in the door at night after a hard day's work, the embrace of a loving woman, but he could see himself as a life-long bachelor whose life was interspersed with a succession of women. He had seen Malcolm

Grenfell in his sixties playing around with women young enough to be his daughter. Isaac did not want that for himself. He resolved to find someone to share his life with, but would it be Jess O'Neill or Katrina Smith, maybe even Linda Harris, although he did not know where she was.

'Isaac, Isaac.'

'Sorry, deep in thought,' Isaac replied, rubbing his eyes, pretending to put pen to paper.

'Fast asleep more likely,' Larry said. 'Don't worry. We're all feeling that way.' He had news, vital news, for his DCI.

'Too many hours here,' Isaac replied.

'We have a phone number for the grille.'

'And?'

'It's an old number. I tried dialling, but it came up blank. Just a hollow ring on the other end.'

'But traceable?'

'Bridget is working on it.'

'Great. Keep me posted.'

Wendy came into Isaac's office. 'Sir, I'm drawing a blank on George Sullivan.'

'How many likely candidates?'

'In Berkshire and surrounding counties, over thirty.'

'Have you contacted them all?'

'We've tried to be selective. No point phoning a George Sullivan unless he's in his late seventies to eighties, is there?'

Isaac leant back in his chair. Wendy was looking for a measured response when he could not think of one. She was the best there was at finding people, whether they wanted to be found or not. Isaac knew that she would find George Sullivan, even if he was buried in a churchyard somewhere or his remains were ash.

'You're right.' The only useful comment that Isaac could offer.

'He could have moved around the country, but collating that amount of information will take some time,' Wendy said.

'Bridget is weighed down,' Isaac replied. 'And now she is working on the phone number that Larry has found. What will this number tell us, Larry?' Isaac asked.

'Who ordered the grille to be installed.'

'So, someone gave them the key to enter the house, but not to enter the room. On the one hand, someone is trying to conceal a body, and on the other, they give a third party access to the murder scene. It all sounds bizarre to me,'

'What do you mean, sir?' Larry asked. Wendy was in the room, so the familiarity of addressing his boss by his first name was not appropriate.

'Did they install the bars on the windows.'

'It appears that way, sir.'

'If they entered the room, were they alone?'

'After thirty years? Who would know?'

'What about the old man that is still working there?'

'It's a thought. I could take him to the house. It may jog his memory.'

'You'd better do it today,' Isaac said. Larry cursed under his breath. He was an experienced police officer, and he had not thought of it. He had been slowly gaining the confidence of his DCI, and here he was, making the most basic of errors. Thirty years was a long time, but Tom Wellings came from an age before computers and smart phones.

Larry remembered that his father in his seventies could remember phone numbers and car registrations from his youth, but had no idea as to his own phone number. If anyone asked, he would open his wallet and take out a piece of paper with it typed on.

***

Bridget hurried into the office. Usually she shuffled along maintaining a predictable pace. Encountering her in the corridor was always a chore. Isaac moved fast, as did Larry, but with Bridget, it was the same lumbering forward momentum, and it was impossible to get by. But this time, she was moving fast, even knocking off some papers precariously perched on the top of Larry's filing cabinet.

'I've found an address,' she said.

'George Sullivan?' Isaac asked.

'It looks possible.'

'Wendy, fancy a trip to the country,' Isaac asked.

'Ready and willing.'

'Go easy on expenses,' Larry reminded her. He knew she would still have a slap-up meal in a quality restaurant. 'Necessary to maintain cover,' she would say afterwards.

Besides, if she came back with a result, he would sign the expense form.

Wendy took the printout from Bridget and left the office. Five minutes later, just long enough for her to collect her handbag with the police issue credit card, grab the keys to the police car, and she was gone. She always carried a small bag with her in case there was an overnight stay involved. Berkshire was not far, only thirty-five miles down the M4, no more than an hour, sometimes less if the traffic was flowing, although it could take longer at peak times. It was eleven in the morning before she turned the key in her car. She turned left as she exited the Challis Street car park. The traffic was relatively light for the time of day, apart from a truck blocking the road two miles away. She knew the area well, and she diverted down a few side streets. Soon she was heading through Chiswick and onto the M4.

The address was 81 Charter Street, Reading. Wendy found it with little difficulty. It was an attractive house, indicative of the area. A neat garden out the front, some flowers; the season was unfavourable for them to bloom, although they looked ready to once the coldness in the air had been replaced with the rays of the sun. A small dog yapped inside the house as Wendy pushed open the gate at the front. The yapping was quickly accompanied by a woman's shrill voice. 'Stop the barking, or I'll have the neighbours complaining,' it said.

Wendy noticed that the dog took no notice. She had had a dog when she first married. A spritely Yorkshire terrier who would jump up when she came in, but not for her husband, who was more disciplined with the animal. Still, her husband had shed more tears than her when it had died at the age of thirteen.

After that, both of them vowed no more dogs, although their two sons had had a collection of rabbits, guinea pigs, even salamanders, but none ever lived for long, and no one ever formed an emotional attachment. Wendy could not say that about the two cats she now owned. She realised that she had become fond of them, and she would be sad when they departed.

After two attempts at ringing the bell on the house, a two-storey terrace built in the 1950s, the door opened.

'Sergeant Wendy Gladstone, Challis Street Police Station. I'm with Homicide,' Wendy said.

'No bodies here,' the woman replied. She was attempting to hold back the dog which wanted to surge forward and welcome the visitor.

Wendy could see that making friends with the dog would gain the confidence of the woman. She bent down and patted it, even though it was old and scruffy, a mongrel of indeterminate parentage.

'He doesn't take to strangers,' the woman said.

The dog barked at Wendy's touch but stopped soon after. It was clear that the dog did not go out often, and it was in need of a good bath.

'You'd better come in. No point standing out there in the cold. Cup of tea?'

'Yes, please.'

Wendy noted that the house had seen better years; the wallpaper was fading, and the carpet was threadbare in certain areas. It was a good house in a good street, but the inside showed neglect, whereas the gardens, front and rear, showed love and affection. It seemed incongruous, but probably not related to Wendy's current line of enquiry.

The woman came back with two mugs of tea. 'Sorry, there's no sugar, although I have sweetener if you prefer.'

'Sweetener is fine,' Wendy answered. The dog had taken his place next to her. The smell of it was distracting.

'May I ask your name?'

'Victoria Sullivan.'

'And your husband is George?'

'Yes.'

'May I ask where he is?'

'He will be back soon,' the woman replied. 'Why are you interested in George?'

'You are aware of a body that was found in a fireplace?'

'It was on the news.'

'We believe that your husband visited that house at some time.'

'You don't believe he killed the man?' The woman looked alarmed at the prospect, not sure what to say, other than the inevitable defence of her husband.

'Not at all,' Wendy replied, although George Sullivan could have been as guilty as any of the others.

'Does the name Solomon mean anything to you?'

'Other than it was the name of the body.'

'And Grenfell?'

'My maiden name.' Wendy sat up, disturbing the dog, at Victoria Sullivan's reply.

'Lord Penrith?'

'He was my second cousin. We shared the same grandfather, that's all.'

As the old woman hobbled over to make them another cup, Wendy took the opportunity to SMS Isaac. 'Found him.'

Isaac's reply. 'Good.'

'What was your relationship with Albert Grenfell?'

'We exchanged Christmas cards, attended weddings, but apart from that, not a lot.'

'Any reason?'

'The title and the wealth followed Albert's line of the family. I'm from the poor side.'

'But you kept in touch.'

'Yes. He was a good man.'

The dog jumped up and ran to the front door. Its tail was wagging, but it was not yapping. 'My husband's home,' Victoria Sullivan said. A key in the lock and the door swung open.

'Down, boy, down,' the man said.

Even though he was in his eighties, George Sullivan looked to be a fit person. Wendy noticed that he stood firm, although he carried a wooden cane in one hand. He took off his coat and came into the room.

'We have a guest,' his wife said.

Wendy stood and introduced herself.

'Not often we have a visitor from the police.'

George Sullivan beckoned Wendy to sit down again. He walked over to the electric fire, the fake flames trying to create the look of a real fire but missing the effect entirely. He stood with his back to it, enjoying the heat.

'What can I do for you? I see that Victoria's provided you with a cup of tea.' He looked over at his wife. 'Any chance of one for me, love?'

Once his wife had left the room, George Sullivan whispered, 'Is this about Garry Solomon?'

'Yes.'

'I never met him, but I knew the name.'

'You're a material witness, but you never came forward?'

'I thought about it, but my wife doesn't know.'

'The parties.' Wendy ventured a guess.

'I'm embarrassed to tell you now.'

'We need to talk in detail,' Wendy said.

'Not with my wife around.' The man appeared concerned not to upset his wife. According to Mavis Richardson, he had been an obnoxious bore the night of the party.

'We either talk here or down the local police station. Which do you prefer?'

'Do you like walking?' he asked.

'Before arthritis,' Wendy replied.

'It's the same with my leg. There's a park not far from here. We could go there, grab a coffee, and you can ask me what you want.'

'And you will tell me all I need to know?'

'Yes.'

Victoria Sullivan returned and took a seat. All three drank their tea and spoke about the weather and the dog. It was evident that both were fond of the animal, even though it preferred to lie across Wendy's feet.

'We're just going out for a while,' George Sullivan said.

'Wrap up warm. You don't want to catch a cold.' The reply from the dutiful wife.

'Will you stay for tea, sergeant?' Victoria Sullivan asked.

'Thanks for the offer, but I need to get back to London.'

Chapter 28

Wendy pulled up the collar of her coat as she stepped from the heat of the Sullivans' house into the bracing wind outside.

'Global warming. Makes no sense to me,' George Sullivan said. Wendy noticed he moved with a slight limp.

The park was well looked after. Apart from the ducks in the pond, close to where they had entered, there was little movement: a few hardy souls jogging, someone doing yoga, although Wendy did not understand why or how, and a few dog owners throwing Frisbees repeatedly.

George Sullivan seemed not to concern himself with the cold. Wendy realised that she could not conduct a comprehensive interview while her feet were cold and her hands were shaking.

'There's a nice café around the corner. We'll go there,' Sullivan said.

Wendy appreciated the gesture.

The café prided itself on home-made cakes. Wendy chose two for herself. Both of them ordered lattes.

'What do you want to know?'

Wendy went through the procedure, gave him the caution about whatever you say…

'I know the rigmarole. I worked with Army Intelligence back in the 50s. During the cold war, stationed in Berlin, listening in on Russian military communications.'

'Do you understand the language?'

'I did. My mother was Russian. Nowadays, I can just about understand the Russian news on the television. Anyway, you want to know about Bellevue Street.'

'Yes. Do you mind if I record our conversation?'

'I only hope my wife never finds out what I'm going to tell you.'

'That's not a guarantee I can give,' Wendy said.

'Whatever happens, I will tell you all I know.'

'Thanks.' Wendy ordered another latte. She still had the expense account, but it appeared likely that she would not be able to give it much exercise.

'I was friends with Albert Grenfell. We had worked together in Berlin. He was a snob. I suppose you know that already.'

'It's been mentioned.'

'We started meeting on a social basis. Not often, but whenever he was in London, he would call, and we would go out to a bar or a club.'

'Disreputable?'

'Albert knew with me that I would be discreet, and I was young, not yet married, although I was courting Victoria. Sowing a few wild oats seemed fine at the time.'

'You said he was a snob.'

'What was he doing with me, is that it?'

'I suppose so.'

'Colonel in Army Intelligence counted for something. It was the cold war, spies and espionage were always in the news. My rank and my job gave me a certain allure. Today, they would say shades of James Bond, but to be honest, I spent most of my time in a room with another ten men listening to boring Russians speaking, and then writing endless reports which would have been filed within ten minutes of someone reading them.'

'Albert Grenfell liked the ideas of spies and espionage?'

'He portrayed this staid, conservative man, but underneath it, he wanted to be daring and dashing and naughty. With me, he could.'

'You started going out to bawdy clubs?'

'Not often. He was married, and his wife watched him like a hawk.'

'You met her?'

'With Victoria?'

'Yes.'

'We have been told that she was at the Richardsons' party.'

'She thought it was going to be a family gathering.'

'It must have come as a shock.'

'It came as a shock to me as well.'

'Did Albert know beforehand?'

'No, but with the Richardson sisters anything was possible.'
'Are you saying that a family gathering turned into an orgy?'
'Yes.'

Wendy, feeling hungry, ordered pasta; Sullivan ordered the same. The weather had turned bleaker outside, and it was raining heavily. George Sullivan phoned his wife to tell her he would be delayed. 'She's a terrible worrier,' he said.

'Does your wife know any of this?'
'Nothing, and that's the way I would prefer it to stay.'
'You realise the importance of what you're saying?'
'Yes.'
'And that withholding information could be seen as an offence?'
'You had difficulty finding me?' he said in reply.
'Yes.'
'Even after all these years, I am afforded some protection, some secrecy, some leniency as to my civic responsibilities.'
'What does that mean?' Wendy asked.
'Once a spy, even if not James Bond or anything glamorous, always a spy.'
'Does that mean if there was a court case, the truth could be suppressed?'
'Not in the case of Garry Solomon, but otherwise it could be.'

Wendy realised that it was not a threat, merely a statement of fact. She pressed on, only stopping to eat some more pasta.

'What changed with the family gathering?' Wendy asked.
'The younger sister.'
'Mavis?'
'Yes, that was her name. I can't remember the other sister's name.'
'Gertrude.'
'Yes, that's it. We are all sitting there. I am engaged to Victoria, but she could not come. After so many years, I can't remember why. Albert's wife is knocking back straight gin. Apparently, she became semi-alcoholic in later years. I'm drinking heavily, beer mainly, as is Albert. Gertrude is knocking back vodka and lime at a fast rate, and Mavis is drinking wine and something else.'

'Something else?'

'A drug of some sort, although I don't know what it was.'

'What happened?'

'Albert's wife becomes unconscious, and they put her in the other room. Mavis, now free of the woman, sits on Michael Solomon's lap. It doesn't seem to be the first time, either. She is kissing him full on the mouth, even though he is family. Albert sits there like a stunned mullet, unable to look, unable to look away.'

'Why?'

'I told you. Albert loved the dirty and the downright sleazy. I took him to some very discreet places where no one knew him, and he was straight into it.'

'Women?'

'Yes.'

'What happened with Mavis?'

'She moves over to Albert. Starts teasing him, tells him to loosen up. She grabs hold and kisses him. Everyone is urging him to go upstairs with her. She grabs hold of him and drags him out of the door.'

'Once they've gone?'

'Gertrude comes on to me. Back then, I was a good-looking young man, plenty of energy, always ready for a woman.'

Wendy could see that he was still good-looking, although no longer young.

'What did you do?'

'I took advantage, and took her upstairs.'

'We are aware of an incident.'

'That was me, I'm afraid.'

'Tell me about it?'

'I came back downstairs after about forty minutes. Albert reappears five minutes later, a sheepish look on his face and a big smile. His wife is still out for the count in the other room, oblivious to what has transpired.

'Gertrude moves over to Albert, Mavis makes for Michael Solomon. The younger sister was more beautiful, and I was drunk and as horny as hell. I made a scene, attempted to grab Mavis. She got angry, and I was evicted from the party. I'm ashamed of my actions, but that's the truth.'

The weather had eased outside, as had the conversation. There seemed little more to learn from George Sullivan. Wendy shook his hand and paid the bill.

As they left the café, feeling yet again the biting cold, George Sullivan turned to Wendy. 'Mavis and Gertrude Richardson?'

'Both dead, I'm afraid.'

George Sullivan shrugged his shoulders and moved on, his cane tapping the ground as he walked.

***

Isaac listened as Wendy recounted her meeting with George Sullivan. Wendy felt the man was an innocent bystander, an instinctive reaction on her part. Isaac was more sceptical: too many murders, too many innocent bystanders, but with two murders so far, and another two people dead, he hoped there would be no more.

A drunken, drug-induced impromptu orgy was hardly the reason for Garry Solomon's death, and Montague's death seemed illogical.

Larry still waited on an update from Bridget. Tracing a thirty-year-old phone number was proving time-consuming. Wendy had managed to find a phone book from the period. The only problem: it listed addresses and then phone numbers. There was no way to look for a phone number and then the address. The only advantage was that the number was in Kingston upon Thames, but even back thirty years, there had been a sizable population. It was only thirty minutes away by car, less by train, but it was a needle in a haystack without an address. Larry pestered Bridget a few too many times before she reacted: 'I'm going as fast as I can.'

Larry, realising that he had overstepped the mark, retreated and pretended to tidy his desk. He gave up after ten minutes, and went and made himself a cup of coffee.

Isaac busied himself waiting for the next development. He did not have to wait for long.

Keith Dawson, in better humour than on previous occasions, burst into his office. 'I've found something,' he said. Larry and Wendy, seeing him enter Isaac's office with Bridget in hot pursuit, moved quickly to find out what was the latest development.

All five were in Isaac's office now, a space that was full with three. Isaac suggested they move to a larger room.

'Keith, what is it?' Isaac asked.

'The man was brilliant, I'll give him that.' It was the first time that anyone had seen Dawson with anything approaching a smile on his face, but now…

'Spill it,' Larry said. 'What have you found?'

'According to Albert Grenfell, and according to the law, the wealth of the Grenfells, or at least the stately home, the real estate holdings, and the substantive majority of the money, should be inherited by the incumbent lord.'

'Seems fair enough,' Isaac said. He had resumed his seat, aware that a prolonged speech by Dawson was to ensue. Although he had to admit that Dawson's usual monotone had been replaced by an excitable speech pattern that was almost pleasant to listen to.

'Are you saying that Malcolm Grenfell is not entitled to his inheritance?'

'He's entitled if he can find it, but I've discovered what Montague did. It's brilliant.'

'Can you give it to us in language that we can understand?' Larry asked. He had little time for Dawson and his less than cheery disposition, his usually dull manner of speaking, his ability to walk by you in the office and somehow not see you.

'The wealth of the Grenfells is held in a number of trusts, offshore banks around the world.'

'Illegal?' Isaac asked.

'Dubious, more like. The wealthy are always looking for a way to hide their wealth, avoid tax, avoid death duties.'

'I thought that no longer applied,' Isaac said.

'Inheritance Tax does.'

'You'd better detail this.'

Keith Dawson stood up and positioned himself by the whiteboard. 'To most people, Inheritance Tax is purely an inconvenience. As long as your wealth is below a certain level, then it just means some additional paperwork.'

'Am I liable?' Wendy asked. She had been contemplating selling her house now that her husband had died.

'As long as it is valued lower than three hundred and twenty-five thousand and you don't have a few million pounds in an account at your local building society, then you're all right.'

'Nothing to worry about there,' Wendy said.

'Mind you, a lot of people don't realise that they could be liable. If your house is worth a million pounds, for instance, then nearly six hundred thousand pounds of it could be liable for a forty per cent tax on your death.'

'Hell,' Larry exclaimed.

'Don't worry too much. There are ways to reduce the liability, give some of your wealth to your children, your wife, and so on. And besides, it only applies at death.'

'What has Grenfell done?'

'He's taken more than fifty per cent of the Grenfells' money and put it into overseas accounts. Not strictly illegal, but I can almost certainly guarantee that he was the only person with the knowledge of how to access it.'

'And now he is dead,' Isaac said. 'What does this mean?'

'Someone knows how to access it.' Keith Dawson stood proudly as he announced the first of his great works of deduction.

'What do you mean?' Isaac asked.

'Someone has been accessing the money since his death.'

'But how?'

'Someone has found out the details and the password.'

'You have?'

'No. I have found out how to access the account and download a statement. There is another more complex password for withdrawing the money.'

'Are you inferring that Montague Grenfell gave it to someone else?' Isaac said, momentarily not annoyed with Dawson and his manner.

'Given, taken or forced!' Dawson emphasised.

'A motive,' Wendy said.

'It looks good,' Isaac said.

Keith Dawson returned to his seat. Isaac reasserted his seniority and stood where Dawson had previously. Wendy was confused about some aspects of Dawson's presentation. She would ask for his opinion on her financial status later.

527

'Let me get this right,' Isaac said. 'Without the password, it would not be possible for anyone to access the money?'

'The account is listed in Grenfell's records, although it is cryptic.'

'Cryptic?' Isaac asked.

'What was he like?' Dawson asked.

Isaac, the only person who had met him when he was alive, answered. 'Pedantic, probably obsessive. His handwriting was extremely small.'

'Some paranoias there,' Dawson replied.

'You never answered my previous question.'

'He often reversed the words and the numbers. For instance, "word" became "drow", and "12658" became "85621".'

'What the hell for?' Larry asked. His passwords were his wife's birthday.

'The hard part was knowing when he was using a cryptic variance and when he was not. And then he would vary which variation to use. Sometimes, it would be the reverse, at other times transpose one letter to the right, one to the left. It's easy once you know what to look for.'

'A nightmare,' Isaac said.

'The password to withdraw from the offshore account was not there. He must have memorised it.'

'The money would have been lost if he had not given it to someone?' Larry asked.

'Not entirely. It may have taken some time to access, years maybe, but it was not completely lost. Let me rephrase. As long as someone knew about the account.'

'His executor was Mavis Richardson,' Isaac said.

'She may know the password. You'd better ask her,' Dawson, who had taken little interest in the department, said.

'She's dead,' Wendy said.

'Murdered?' Dawson asked.

'Natural causes.'

'It's very convenient.' Dawson's usual morose style of speech had returned.

'I'll give Gordon Windsor a call,' Isaac said.

'I attended her funeral,' Wendy said. 'You know that.'

'I know,' Isaac replied, aware that the woman's body may need to come up again, a lengthy process with endless paperwork.

Chapter 29

'I don't give a damn what Dawson said. The woman died of natural causes,' Gordon Windsor said when Isaac phoned him up. Isaac had known the man for many years, and this was the first time he had known him to be angry. With the London Met, Isaac realised that Gordon Windsor had a flawless record, and Dawson's aspersions, purely based on Montague Grenfell's records, were reflecting on his professional judgement, and that of the pathologist who had conducted the autopsy of Mavis Richardson.

'It's only an idea.' Isaac tried to calm the man down.

'You'll never get the permission anyway, and if you did, what tests do you want us to conduct?' Windsor said, his previous outburst slightly mellowed.

'Toxicology?' Isaac suggested. Even he had to admit that the possibility of Mavis Richardson dying of anything other than old age seemed remote, but he had to sound out Gordon Windsor.

'The woman was eighty-five. She had led an active life and drank a little too much at times. There were signs of smoking, although minor. Clearly, her blood pressure was a little high.'

'How do you know that?'

'Tablets in her bathroom. We checked with her doctor, standard procedure, and he confirmed.'

'Until we have further reason Mavis Richardson stays where she is.'

'Messy business digging up the dead, although she's not been buried long,' Gordon Windsor said. Isaac could only agree.

Gordon Windsor hung up the phone. Isaac regretted calling him, regretted reminding him that he had made a mistake once in the past, where he had confirmed that the man had died of self-inflicted wounds but it was later found out to be murder.

Isaac was well aware that he had made mistakes over the years, pursued one person believing him to be guilty only to find that the unattractive and ill-mannered man was innocent, whereas the attractive and agreeable person turned out to have personal issues and a desire to kill.

Isaac knew that a police officer was fallible, the same as everyone else. He understood the need for procedures and paperwork as they maintained a detachment that allowed the focus to be directed to facts and evidence, not to assumptions and instincts.

It was only when he was confronted with endless paperwork that he became downhearted. DCS Richard Goddard could only sympathise, but as he had said, 'what the new commissioner wants, he gets.'

Goddard and Cook regarded each other as friends. Isaac had been over to the DCS's house on a few occasions, had even been invited to the wedding of his eldest daughter. On that occasion, he had taken Jess. That was the time when their romance was full on. She had enjoyed the ceremony and the reception immensely; even hinted to Isaac to make an honest woman of her. It was also before their first argument over Linda Harris.

Isaac realised that he kept reflecting back to Jess. Linda Harris had been attractive and briefly available, Sophie White had always been there, and Katrina Smith, his current girlfriend, was certainly attractive and he liked her a lot, but always there was Jess O'Neill in the back of his mind.

It concerned him sometimes, wondered if it was love. He just did not know. He considered whether he should phone Jess up, take her out, but he was aware that Linda Harris would reappear, not as a physical incarnation but as a mental barrier. He could forget that he had been foolish and lustful that night, but Jess never would.

He collected his thoughts and refocussed on the paperwork.

No point regretting the past, he thought.

Isaac managed another twenty-five minutes at his desk, completed a couple of reports, but it was long enough for him. Keith Dawson had caused everyone in the department to analyse the investigation.

Larry Hill, untidy desk aside, was going through his notes. A clear motive for Montague Grenfell's death had been given, and it could only mean one thing: the murderer was alive, and he had the password.

Wendy was talking to Keith Dawson, the majority of the conversation spent on the case, the rest spent on her financial status and Inheritance Tax. Dawson's constant reiteration that there was nothing to worry about was not helping.

She knew she was numerically dyslexic, and his analysis on a piece of paper showing what she owned and what she owed meant little to her. 'If I take your assets, here in the left column, and your liabilities in the right column and subtract, you are below the threshold.'

Bridget sat to one side. It seemed clear to her, but for Wendy it was not.

'Don't worry, I'll be there with you,' Bridget said.

'You understand what Keith is saying?' Wendy asked.

'It's all quite simple.'

'Not to me,' Wendy replied, feeling a little stupid that the simplest mathematics left her confused.

***

Isaac could see that he needed to give his people direction. He called them into his office. 'Gordon Windsor is adamant that Mavis Richardson died of natural causes,' he said.

Wendy was pleased to hear Windsor's comment. Bridget, who professed a belief in the Almighty and the afterlife, thanked God. Both women had not liked the idea of digging the old woman up just after she had been buried. To them it was disrespectful.

Larry, who had no such concerns, had said after Dawson's statement, 'Dig her up.'

Isaac had been brought up by Jamaican parents to believe in God and the Almighty, but also to be fearful of evil spirits. His English education had discounted the evil spirits, but he maintained an abiding respect for God, even if his visits to church were relegated to Christmas and Easter.

'I suggest we focus on Montague Grenfell's death,' Isaac said.

'I thought we were,' Larry said.

Isaac thought Larry's comment was condescending, but let it pass.

'Do we have a list of suspects, sir?' Wendy asked.

'There are two issues to consider: firstly, who would have known about the secret account, and secondly, who would have had the strength to manhandle Grenfell to the top of the stairs.'

'Malcolm Grenfell,' Larry said.

'He's the most likely suspect, but can we prove it?' Isaac asked.

'Does he have an alibi?' Wendy asked.

'We know that Grenfell died between the hours of 11 p.m. and 2 a.m. on the night of the twenty-fifth.'

'Malcolm Grenfell will not have an alibi.'

'Other than he was at home with his woman,' Isaac said.

'Judging by the condition of the girl we met, she would not be reliable,' Larry said.

'What do you mean?' Bridget asked.

'Drunk, spaced out. She was there with Malcolm Grenfell for a good time and money, nothing more. Besides, he has dumped her now. May be hard to find.'

'Who else would have known?' Wendy asked.

'Mavis Richardson, obviously. Possibly Albert.'

'They are both dead.' Larry stated the obvious.

'Agreed, but who else would have known?'

'Montague Grenfell was not the sort of man to tell anyone,' Wendy said.

'Agreed, so let's look at the more unlikely.'

'Emma Hampshire, Kevin Solomon, and the other children of Michael Solomon,' Larry said.

'What about George Sullivan?' Wendy added.

'You said he was an old man,' Isaac reminded her.

'He is, but he's still agile.'

'We are not aware of any contact between Michael Solomon's other children and Montague Grenfell. According to their mother, neither of them are of any consequence. The son follows after his half-brother Garry.'

'What do you mean?' Bridget asked.

'Petty criminal.'

'Apparently, the daughter, a heroin addict, is selling herself up in the city,' Isaac said.

'Hardly great recommendations for the offspring of Michael Solomon,' Larry said.

'As you say.'

'Should we check them out?' Wendy asked.

'We only have their mother's opinion on her children. She's probably correct, but we need to check.'

'Bridget, compile a dossier on Michael and Mary Solomon's two children. Aim to have it prepared for our 5 p.m. meeting,' Isaac said. 'In the meantime, Larry, follow up on who ordered the grille to be installed at Bellevue Street. Wendy, what are your plans?'

'I will see if I can get the contact details from Mary Solomon for her two children.'

'And you, DCI?' Larry asked.

'Gordon Windsor. I will go and visit him, have a chat. I upset him earlier, and Montague Grenfell's death is still not conclusive. It could have just been an accident.'

'There were two sets of footprints,' Larry said. 'Both men's shoes.'

'I'm aware of that, but if we are about to place pressure on our suspects, then we need our facts to be double-checked.'

'Don't forget about Emma Hampshire and Kevin Solomon,' Wendy said.

'Kevin Solomon has some legal training, and Emma Hampshire knows more than she says,' Isaac replied. 'Both of them are highly suspect.'

'I hope it's not Emma Hampshire,' Wendy said.

'Personally, I would agree, but professionally we charge the guilty person, not choose on whether we like them or not.'

'I understand,' Wendy replied.

***

Mary Solomon was not pleased to see Wendy on her doorstep again. 'What the hell do you want?' she screamed, attempting to make her voice heard over the crying of the baby that she held in one arm. Wendy could see that the woman had no idea with babies, and was holding it too tight. It was clear from the smell that it was in need of changing.

'Let me have it,' Wendy said. The baby quietened as she felt Wendy's warm body against it. Wendy, ever practical, took the baby into the bathroom up the stairs and cleaned it. Afterwards, she found a baby's bottle and filled it with milk. Soon, the baby was resting quietly.

'That's Deidre's,' Mary Solomon said. Wendy remembered that on a previous visit Mary Solomon had said that the baby had been affected by its mother's drug addiction. Wendy could see neglect by its grandmother more than the afflictions of its birth mother.

'I need to talk to your children.'

'Why do you want to speak to them?'

Wendy had noticed that the woman's hands were shaking slightly. Wendy recognised that this could be the early signs of Parkinson's, although it could just be nerves, but why? Was it because Wendy wanted to talk to her son and daughter, or because she was incapable of looking after three young children?

'Standard procedure in a murder enquiry.'

'But they don't know the people murdered.'

'I agree that is probably true, but we still need to interview them.'

'They come here to pick up the children.'

'When?'

'Deidre sometimes once a week, sometimes it's as long as three weeks.'

'It's not for you to look after them. What do you use for money?'

'She gives me the money that a drunk has given her after he has screwed her.'

'Not a very pleasant thing to say about a daughter,' Wendy said.

'Do you want me to say "for favours given". Does that sound more palatable to you? She is a prostitute who opens her legs for any man who has the price. No other way to put it.'

Wendy could see that the woman was embittered and under strain, but her estimation of her daughter seemed inappropriate.

'Your son?'

'He comes here every night, picks up his child and leaves.'

'Does he give you money?'

'Half what the child care facility up the road would charge. I'm not even on the minimum wage.'

'But they're your grandchildren.'

'Maybe they are, but they are mongrels.'

'Who?'

'My children and their children. I should never have married that lecherous bastard, and then it was not legitimate. They are all bastards, legally or otherwise.'

Wendy could see no reason to prolong the conversation. 'I need their contact details.'

'They're on my phone.'

Wendy took the details and left. She was certain the woman had serious issues, and the children should not be in her care. She had resolved once before to contact the appropriate authorities. This time, she would do so after she had contacted the woman's two children.

Chapter 30

'Nothing to do with me,' Daniel Solomon said when Wendy contacted him.

'So far, I've only given you my police rank and told you I was from Homicide.'

'Has my mother implicated me?'

'In what?'

'Montague Grenfell's death.'

'Did you know him?'

'He was friendly with my father when I was younger.'

'I can come and see you now, or you can present yourself at Challis Street Police Station.'

'It's best if you can come and see me. I will send you the details. Give me an hour.'

Wendy, with time to spare, went into a café not far from Mary Solomon's house. She was upset at the condition of the woman, and the neglect that the children in her care were showing. A latte calmed her down.

She phoned Larry. 'I'm meeting with Daniel Solomon, Garry Solomon's half-brother.'

'Do you want me there?'

'I'm not sure what to expect.'

'Give me fifteen minutes.' Larry was pleased at the opportunity to get out of the office.

Wendy had expected to find Daniel Solomon in a rundown office down a back alley, not a street-front location. The office was modern and well equipped, with three desks, a person sitting at each one.

'Daniel Solomon, pleased to meet you.' Wendy saw in front of her a relatively short man with good features and a pleasant smile. He was dressed smartly and wearing a suit jacket, but no tie. He was not what she expected.

'This is Detective Inspector Hill,' Wendy said.

'Coffee?' Solomon asked.

'Yes, please. Two sugars for me, none for DI Hill.'

'Business is good,' Solomon said once they were sitting in his office at the rear. He had closed the door securely after they entered.

'The sign outside says industrial cleaning,' Wendy said.

'I set it up five years ago,' Solomon said. 'I managed to pick up some government cleaning contracts. Never looked back.'

'We are aware that you have a record,' Larry said.

'I was wild in my youth. You won't find anything on me, apart from the occasional parking fine, maybe speeding, for the last eight years.'

'That is correct,' Larry said. He had seen Bridget's preliminary dossier on Daniel Solomon and his sister. The man had told the truth.

Wendy saw the Solomon charm in the way he spoke. He was thirty-six, the same age as his half-brother when he had died. The similarity between the two men was astonishing. Comparing them, Wendy had to wonder if breeding counted. Garry had firm features, was a rugged, handsome man, whereas Daniel was rugged but not as attractive.

'You're not what I expected,' Wendy said.

'My mother?'

'Yes.'

'Life's not been good for her.'

'She cannot handle the children.'

'Did you see mine?'

'Yes.'

'He's okay, and she looks after him well enough.'

'Your sister's children?'

'They have problems.'

'Would you care to elucidate?' Larry asked.

'Not unless it's relevant.'

Wendy noticed that they had touched a raw nerve. She changed the subject.

'When Montague Grenfell died, what did you think?'

'Nothing really. He was someone from my childhood.'

'Why is your child with your mother?'

'My wife went back home to look after her dying mother.'

'She did not take the child?'

'She knew he would be all right with me.'

Wendy thought the story strange; Bridget could check it out. The man had become edgy, irritable, as though he wanted them to go away. Neither Larry nor Wendy intended to leave until they had answers. One of the women came in from the outside office. Daniel Solomon gave her what she wanted, and she left.

'Sorry about that. Pressure of work,' Solomon said. Wendy wondered if it was pre-arranged to hurry them out. She decided to give him the benefit of the doubt.

'When was the last time you saw Montague Grenfell?' Larry asked.

Solomon looked into the air, searching for an answer. 'Over twenty years.'

'Can you be more specific?'

'I was young. People come, people go. I was not keeping a diary.' The man's reply was curt.

Larry wanted the man down the station, formally cautioned, and then he would prise the truth from him. Wendy could see Solomon's charm dissipating, a characteristic apparently all too familiar in his half-brother.

'Did you know Garry Solomon or Solly Michaels?' Wendy asked.

'My mother mentioned that you had been asking about him. I would have been six or seven when he disappeared. If I had seen him, you could not expect me to remember him.'

'Tell us about your sister?'

'Not much to tell.'

'Humour us,' Larry said. He knew when someone was avoiding direct answers to direct questions.

'She's made some bad decisions in her life.'

'Men?'

'Men, drugs, yes.'

'Have you seen her recently?'

'Once a week.'

'Why?'

'Brotherly love. It is important to some of us, you know,' Daniel Solomon said bitingly. It touched a raw nerve with Larry, who had a brother that he never saw as a result of a family dispute. It silenced him for a moment.

'I'm busy. Is there any more that you want?' Solomon asked.

'I think that's about all for now,' Wendy said.

There was one more call that day, the sister. Wendy made the phone call, a female voice answered. She noticed no great enthusiasm from the woman to meet until Wendy firmly told her that it was now, or else down at Challis Street Police Station. If she wanted, she would organise a marked police car to pick her up.

'King's Road, Chelsea. I'll meet you in front of the Saatchi Gallery.'

Wendy knew there were good restaurants in the area. Interviewing a suspect in one of them would not be inappropriate.

Larry phoned Bridget. 'Check out Daniel Solomon's business. I'll send you the details.'

***

Larry had to look twice when a woman in a smart blue dress introduced herself.

'Hi, I'm Deidre Solomon.'

Larry realised that this was no ordinary prostitute. The woman, an air of assuredness about her, oozed class and quality. He noticed other men looking her way, other women too.

'Pleased to meet you,' Wendy said.

'I can give you one hour of my time,' Deidre Solomon said.

'Lunch?' Wendy asked.

'I'm a light eater. Why not?'

The three relocated to the restaurant inside the Saatchi Gallery. Larry noted the prices were high. Wendy never looked.

'What business are you involved in?' Larry asked.

'My mother told you I'm a drug-addicted prostitute selling myself to any man with the money.'

'Something like that,' Wendy replied.

'I'm clean now.'

'And the other part?'

'I'm not ashamed. I'm still for hire at a price.'

'You are still a prostitute?' Larry asked.

'I prefer gentleman's companion, but if you want to use a cruder term, then I am.'

539

'We met your brother.'

'Good man. Did you like him?' Deidre looked over at Wendy.

Larry knew the woman was thirty-seven, though she looked younger. Her breasts were firm, the result of surgery he assumed. The colour of her skin, a light brown, was either a result of cream or a tanning salon. She wore red high-heeled shoes with a stiletto point. If he did not know her history or what she had just admitted, he would have assumed that she was one of the idle rich who strolled up and down King's Road, flaunting themselves and their credit cards. He could not tell if she had money or made the pretence to induce wealthy men to part with their cash for a few hours of her time.

'Yes,' Wendy replied, although his criminal record showed a litany of crimes when he had been younger.

Wendy scanned Bridget's updates on Deidre Solomon while Larry continued the interview: *Deidre Solomon, prostituting, shoplifting.*

Nothing major there, Wendy thought.

The brother had been in court on a charge of grievous bodily harm, but it had been dropped on a technicality, and he walked out of the court a free man. Still, to Wendy, it was interesting that the man was capable of violence.

'Do you know Montague Grenfell?' Larry asked.

'Daniel said you would ask.' Deidre Solomon ate a salad, and even then, very slowly. Wendy assumed she had a problem keeping the weight off, and semi-starvation was a necessity.

'And?'

'Yes. I knew him.'

'How?'

'With my father when I was a child.'

'And?' Larry persisted, the hesitancy in the woman's reply concerning him.

'He came to see me occasionally.'

The woman's statement caused Wendy to put down her fork. 'You knew him?' she asked.

'He was a nice old man.'

Wendy realised that they had uncovered something very relevant. She pushed her plate to one side, even though a small amount of food remained. Larry had chosen a salad, the same as Deidre Solomon, daughter of Michael Solomon, the paid lover of Montague Grenfell, if what she had told them turned out to be true. The woman had no reason to lie, and by her own admission she had placed herself and her brother at the top of the list of prime suspects.

Larry spoke to the gallery staff, showed his ID. They organised a private room. The two police officers and Deidre relocated there. One of the waitresses brought in three coffees.

Larry formally cautioned Deirdre, told her that evidence given could be used in a court of law. Neither he nor Wendy had expected any more from her other than a denial of any knowledge, and a vague recollection of Montague Grenfell.

'Could you please elaborate on your relationship with Montague Grenfell?' Larry asked. He was the more senior of the two police officers. He would take the lead role in the interview.

'He contacted my agency and arranged a booking.'

'He knew your name?'

'Not my professional name. He had chosen me from a website.'

'Did he at any time know who you were?'

'Never.'

'But you knew who he was?'

'The family history. I knew.'

'Did that concern you?'

'Why? He was not related, other than my father had been married to one of his cousins.'

'The man was in his seventies,' Wendy said.

'He was no great stud, but he was good for his age.'

'Why did you tell us?' Larry asked.

'My brother said that it's always best to be open with the police. If they find out later, it's more incriminating.'

'Wise man, your brother,' Larry admitted.

'Did Montague Grenfell tell you anything we should know about? Wendy asked.

'Such as?'

'Family secrets.'

'I was not there receiving his confession. His visits to me were not religious.'

'Carnal?' Larry asked.

'That's what I do. He was lonely; his wife had died, and he wanted company.'

'And screwing?' Wendy said.

'Say it for what it was, a fuck. And why not?'

'Are most of your clients lonely old men?' Larry asked.

'No doubt some are married, but I don't ask.'

'You asked Grenfell?'

'Never. Sometimes he talked, but then I knew who he was and some of what he was saying.'

'Did he discuss his brother?'

'No, but I know there are two. My father told me that before he died.'

'There's only one now.'

'Okay, one.'

'Are you interested as to which one?' Wendy asked.

'Why should I be?'

'We ask the questions, you answer.'

'For the record,' Deidre Solomon said, 'I knew very little about the Grenfells, other than they were upper class and I was not. Satisfied?'

'Satisfied.'

Wendy had another question. 'Your mother is looking after two children of yours. What is the situation?'

'You've seen my criminal record?'

'Yes.'

'Then you know that I sold myself on the street for years until I kicked heroin, or it kicked me.'

'What do you mean?'

'I overdosed, woke up restrained in a drug rehabilitation centre.'

'Who paid?'

'I assume it was my father.'

'Private hospital?' Wendy asked.

'Expensive. I saw a few celebrities in there. Some of them so pure, butter wouldn't melt in their mouths.'

Larry looked at Wendy. They both understood what Deidre's statement meant.

'And after you left?'

'I tried making an income standing up, but the money was lousy. In the end, I went back to what I know best.'

'Screwing for money?' Wendy asked.

'Why not? I still had the looks even after years of abuse. I sold myself from a hotel room for a few months, and when I had enough money, I fixed up the boobs, then the arse. The rest is courtesy of good makeup.'

'You've done a good job,' Wendy said.

'Thanks.'

'After you had sorted yourself out?'

'I found an agency, went on their books. They phone me and either I take the job or I don't.'

'You refuse?' Larry asked.

'I'm not into bondage.'

'Your children?'

'The unfortunate offspring of my earlier years.'

'You don't care for them?' Wendy asked.

'I try, but they bring back unpleasant memories. You've seen them?'

'Yes.'

'Reflection of the men I screwed.'

'Is that why you leave them with your mother?'

'I offered to put them up for adoption, but she wants to keep them.'

'Not what she says.'

'My mother is not well. You do realise that?'

'Yes. She needs help.'

'I've offered, but she only screams at me, calls me a dirty whore.'

'Are you?' Wendy asked.

'I was, not now.'

Chapter 31

Gordon Windsor was still a little miffed when Isaac met up with him. 'You've no right to question my competency,' he said. He had just returned from another murder. Isaac was aware of the details, and if he had been free, he would have been assigned as the senior investigating officer. As it was, he was still involved in two murders. One appeared to be reaching a resolution, although in this case, as with so many others, there was always an unforeseen piece of evidence or a statement that took them off in another direction.

Isaac had formed his opinion as to who was responsible for both murders, but the evidence, at best, was flimsy and would not hold up. A confession was necessary, and for that pressure would need to be applied.

He was not willing to apply that pressure until he was confident of a conviction.

'I apologise, but I have every right,' Isaac said.

'I'll accept your apology, but for the record: Mavis Richardson was old, her health was indicative of her age, she suffered a heart attack, and last, but by no means least, the pathologist knew of her importance. Full tests were carried out, looking for the slightest hint of an induced death. Nothing was found.'

'Exhuming her would be pointless?' Isaac asked.

'Pointless, unless you like paperwork.'

'Are you certain that Gertrude Richardson died of natural causes?'

'DCI, you're clutching at straws. Did you see her son?'

'Not closely.'

'Well, I did, as did Gertrude Richardson. It almost turned my stomach, but the woman stood there and looked. Wendy Gladstone could not take it either. What do you think a mother would feel after being confronted with the thirty-year-old corpse of her long-lost son?'

'And her dying?'

'The woman was eighty-seven and reclusive. She barely ate and was very frail. It was a good job Wendy Gladstone was with her when she died. Otherwise, she may have become a thirty-year-old corpse herself.'

'Montague Grenfell?'

'He fell down the stairs and broke his neck.'

'Is it possible to ascertain whether he slipped or was pushed?'

'You've read my report?'

'Yes.'

'I don't believe there is any ambiguity, do you?'

'Not as to the cause of death, but you did not specify that he had been pushed.'

'It's in the report. The footprints at the top indicated a scuffle. Whether he had been pushed or not is not clear. I left the report open-ended.'

***

Isaac, realising that he may have just been wasting Gordon Windsor's time, returned to the office. He knew what the issue was: it was that as the senior investigating officer he was increasingly confined to Challis Street. He enjoyed the cut and thrust out in the field, probing, asking questions when they were not welcomed, receiving answers, sometimes truthfully given, sometimes not. And in this case, a lot of the answers were just that, not truthful.

The children of Michael and Mary Solomon had brought in a hitherto unknown element. Bridget was checking out the son, while Wendy conducted some more investigations into Deidre.

Larry had enjoyed the photo gallery of Deidre on the agency's website – draped across a bed, showing what the lucky client was to receive. Wendy just saw it as lewd, but it was not for her to comment, and she was certainly not a prude. The prices for a half-hour, two hours, a full day seemed excessive to her, but the woman they had met said that she catered to the well-heeled, and in the case of Montague Grenfell, well-aged.

Wendy had submitted her expenses for the meal at the Saatchi Gallery on her return. Isaac had duly signed his approval, but he knew his DCS would hit the roof. The economy drive throughout the force was gaining momentum, and Isaac knew that once their current murder case, cases, were concluded, he would be asked to make cuts.

Isaac wanted more people for his department, not fewer. He saw it as ironic that there were financial cuts to be made, yet the consultants brought in from outside to oversee the exercise were paid excessively.

Isaac had studied economics at university, and the amount of money allocated for the purpose of saving money would have been better spent elsewhere: an extra person to ease the burden carried by Wendy and Larry, someone to deal with his paperwork.

His relationship with Katrina Smith was going well. He knew that it was a momentary passion, as did she, but neither felt any great disappointment. Both of them were still young, especially Katrina.

They met when they could, spent nights at his flat, but she was busy working in London, discussing her future, and Isaac was burning the midnight oil on the current murder investigation. He only hoped that there were to be no more deaths.

He had put forward a cogent case to his DCS for more staff, only to receive a terse reply.

'Economy drive. There's not much I can do about it. Wrap up this case, and I'll see what I can do.'

Which to Isaac meant one thing: no additional help now, and when the heat is off, then why do you want more.

Not that he could blame his DCS. He had had a rough time when Commissioner Shaw, a man who had guided his career, accepted a peerage. His replacement, a cheerless man, had not taken a shine to the DCS.

Isaac, down at New Scotland Yard the day of his first speech to the people in the building, had listened intently to the new commissioner, Alwyn Davies, had said: '…open-door policy, always open to suggestions. If you want to come and see me, be direct. I have no time for the inept and the ingratiating. Results are what I want.'

It had been meant to inspire the assembled personnel, and although they had clapped, few believed what they had heard. Clichéd comments were all very well, but that was what they were, clichéd.

In the six months since taking over, Commissioner Davies had become disliked by most in the Met. He had proven himself to be a singularly unfriendly man, and those who had taken up the offer to knock on his door had invariably been met with a rebuff. Most of them had retreated, tails between their legs.

It had been the same for DCS Goddard until he had got the measure of the man, and the former commissioner Charles Shaw had found him a place on a government committee looking into crime.

Sensing that DCS Goddard had friends in high places, as well as his known association with MacTavish, the chief government whip, had ensured that Alwyn Davies now treated Goddard with kid gloves.

***

Larry had checked with Dawson. Deidre Solomon's drug rehabilitation had been paid for by Montague Grenfell. Michael Solomon had not been a Richardson or a Grenfell, but by default he had come under their umbrella. Larry could not see how Gertrude Richardson would not have known of her husband's whereabouts, but it was a moot point, as there was no one to confirm it.

Daniel and Deidre Solomon had been seen as irrelevancies, minor players out on the periphery of the investigation, but now they were front and centre.

Deidre's acknowledgement that she had known Montague Grenfell had come as a shock. She must have known the reaction it would have caused with Larry and Wendy.

Bridget had managed to obtain her school records, and it was clear that Deidre was of moderate intelligence, whereas her brother was always top of his class, especially in mathematics.

A subsequent visit to the school, a charmless red-brick building, had been made by Wendy.

'Deidre Solomon. Yes, I remember her,' Brenda Hopwood, a dowdily dressed woman, said. Wendy imagined her shrouded in a nun's habit which would have seemed appropriate. Around her neck, she wore a large cross, which she constantly touched.

'What can you tell me about her?'

'More interested in boys than books. Always had her skirt hitched up around her waist.'

Wendy thought it a crude comment from a woman who looked as if she visited the church every day to pray for forgiveness, although Wendy could not see the prune of a woman sinning, or even breathing.

'Sexually active?' A more clinical term from Wendy.

'Yes.'

'Her brother, Daniel?' Wendy asked.

'Clever boy. I remember him well. Always with one girl or another.'

'He's a good-looking man,' Wendy said.

'I suppose he was back then.'

'You said clever?'

'He was always top of the class.'

'Anything else?'

'Not really. I caught him gambling once outside.'

'What did you do?'

'Nothing. What became of him?'

'He's doing fine now.'

'And his sister?'

'She's fine too.'

Wendy did not see the need to elaborate on the fact that Daniel Solomon had a criminal record, although no trouble for a few years, and that he was running his own business and in financial difficulty. Nor did she intend to tell the woman that Deidre had found herself a good career with what she had learnt at the school, namely the ability to hitch up her skirt and screw for money, a lot of money from what she could see.

Wendy had done the calculations. Deidre Solomon, assuming she spent twenty hours a week flat on her back, could make more money in one week than she did in three months.

***

DCS Goddard was pushing for an arrest. Isaac called in the team. Keith Dawson came, now a valued member, even if his ability to interface with the rest of the team was suspect.

Wendy had tried to relate to him, but he had been cold and dull. Larry had invited him down the pub one night after work, which Dawson had readily accepted. The man had sat at the bar, said little, nothing about his life, and had drunk his five pints and gone home. Larry realised after he had gone that Dawson had landed him with the bill.

Wendy's house sale was going ahead. There had been an offer, too low, but the estate agent was hassling her to accept. Keith Dawson had been firm when he had told her not to accept.

She was anxious to get out of the house as, due to its dampness, her arthritis was causing her lots of pain.

She could only reflect that when a case was in full swing, and when her husband had been dying, she had not had time to think about the pain. She had read a book on positive thinking, heal yourself with the power of the mind. It made some sense, but she had soon tired of it. To her, the pain was real, the house was damp, and no amount of mumbo jumbo was going to change that.

'Larry, what do we have?' Isaac asked.

'Daniel Solomon's in financial trouble. His sister is prostituting herself.'

'Apart from that.'

'That's it for the present moment. Keith is accessing Daniel Solomon's bank accounts, tax returns. Are they under suspicion?'

'We're not discounting them.'

'Wendy?' Isaac looked in her direction. She held a cup of coffee in her hand, as usual.

'I've checked Daniel and Deidre Solomon's school. Deidre has taken the only career path open to her. Her brother was a smart person then, still is by all accounts.'

'Criminal records?'

'None from either for a few years.'

'Keith, what have you found out?'

'Daniel Solomon's bank accounts appear to be in order, although I've only started checking. His tax returns have been filed on time. Nothing to report there, other than he had overpaid last year, and he received a payment back.'

'Is his company viable?'

'He has a serious cash flow problem.'

'Deidre Solomon. Have you accessed her bank accounts?'

'Not yet, although she would probably deal in cash mainly.'

'Why?' Isaac asked.

'The men who use her services don't want a credit card transaction being traced back to her, or, as is often used, a hairdressing salon. They would not want their wives to know.'

'Explanation accepted.'

'If they are implicated, it would be Daniel who would be coordinating,' Larry said.

'And Deidre who had the lever,' Wendy added.

'One screws, the other fleeces,' Larry said.

'Apart from your wording, is that what we think happened?' Isaac asked.

'No proof.'

'Keith, we need you to dig deep. Let us know when you find something,' Isaac said.

Chapter 32

'Tom will be here soon. I've got a rush job. Come in two hours, and you can borrow him for an hour,' Sean O'Reilly said.

Larry arrived at O'Reilly's on time. Tom Wellings was just finishing the rush order, although his speed was anything but a rush. The man moved calmly and with purpose. Larry noted that once he had completed one task, he would tidy before moving on to the next.

'Five minutes,' Wellings said.

'That's fine.'

Sue Baxter had been forewarned that they would be coming. She worked only five minutes from the house, and their visit would coincide with her lunch break. It had been some time since she had seen a policeman at her house, and she had hoped no more would be coming. The uniformed police outside on the street maintaining vigilance over the crime scene had long gone, as had the tape across the door into the murder room.

The Baxters had been given access to the room and had set to work to bring it up to the standard of the rest of the house.

Larry had been impressed when he walked through the front door. 'You've done a great job,' he said.

'Thank you, DI Hill,' Sue Baxter said proudly. Ted Hunter, the handyman who had made the grim discovery, had shown himself to be a competent man, although, as Sue Baxter's husband would have said, 'He still overcharged us.'

Not that the complaint would have been too forceful, as Sue Baxter, ever anxious, had phoned a local estate agent for a valuation. With booming prices in the area and the agent's determination to put it on the market, he had given them a good price, one hundred thousand pounds over what they had paid for the house and its renovation.

Sue enthusiastically had wanted to list the house immediately. It had been her husband who had said no. A renovation of a small house in Manchester, and a larger one in London, was enough for him, and besides, the house was still a crime scene.

'I doubt if we are allowed to sell it yet,' he had said. He knew it was probably not correct, but it sufficed.

'Okay,' his wife had said, and besides, she loved the house and the neighbourhood.

Larry preceded Tom into the house. 'This is Tom Wellings,' Larry said, introducing him to Sue Baxter.

'You've done a great job here, Mrs Baxter,' Wellings said.

'Thank you.'

Larry noticed the photos lining the hallway that showed the transformation from neglected and unwanted to loved and homely.

551

All three entered the murder room. The walls had been painted, the floorboards had been sanded and varnished. The centrepiece of the room, the fireplace, was resplendent in its glory.

'It gives the room character,' Sue Baxter said.

It gave Larry a chill down his back thinking about what had lain there for thirty years. Sue Baxter, despite her initial aversion when the body had been found, made no reference to the death and the mummified corpse. Larry assumed that if she could, she would have a photo of the body up on the wall in the hallway.

'Tom has worked for the company that installed the grille over the door for over thirty years,' Larry said.

'Closer to fifty,' Tom Wellings replied. He was a man with an uncluttered mind. He did not fill his mind with considering the world situation, politics, and the state of the economy. He had gone through life ensuring he had enough money in his pocket to keep a roof over his head, clothe, and feed himself, nothing more. It had given him the ability to remember trivial details that others had forgotten.

'We fitted the bars on the window,' he said.

'We took them down,' Sue Baxter said. 'Aesthetically they were not right.'

'Oversize. We used what we had in stock.'

'You remember, Tom?' Larry asked.

'Business was quiet. Old man Dennison had laid off a couple of people, so I helped out here.'

Larry had to take a seat. Here, encompassed within this man, was the first positive lead into the murder of Garry Solomon for some time.

'What do you remember?' Larry asked.

'It was a long time ago. It may need a cup of tea for me to remember.'

'I'll get you one,' Sue said. 'No more speaking until I come back.'

Larry wanted to continue with Tom, but the man was adamant. 'When she comes back,' he said.

Larry only hoped he could prevent her from talking to the media again.

'I'm all ears,' Sue Baxter said on her return. She should have been back at the school where she taught, but there was no way she was going to be prised out of the chair she was sitting in.

Tom sat, content with his cup of tea.

'Would you like to continue?' Larry asked. 'I'll record this if it's okay.'

'Fine by me,' Tom said. He appeared to appreciate the attention.

Larry placed his iPhone on the coffee table and hit record.

'We fitted the bars first. We had made a miscalculation, and I had to cut a little off one side.'

'Who let you into the house?' Larry asked.

'I'm coming to that,' Tom said.

'Please, carry on,' Sue Baxter said. She was excited, almost wetting herself from what Larry could see.

'It took us a couple of hours to install the bars. I used Ramset bolts to hold them in place.'

'We had trouble taking some out, so we just plastered over them.' Sue Baxter said.

'The grille?' Larry asked.

'It was awkward to carry, and we had trouble manhandling it into place.'

'Why were you installing the grille?' Larry asked.

'We received an order and the man paid up front.'

'It was a man?'

'I remember him. A tall man. He spoke well.'

'His name?'

'I don't remember him ever giving it to us, although he gave us all a tip at the end of the job.'

'I'll need to show you some photos later, see if you can identify him.'

'Fine by me,' Wellings said.

'What was the house like?' Sue Baxter asked.

'Not much to say. It was empty, although it appeared to be in good condition. There was a toilet down the hallway which we used, and I noticed a woman's touch.'

'What do you mean?' Larry asked.

'There were some small towels.'

'What did that mean to you?'

'I suppose it had only recently been vacated, nothing more.'

'Was an explanation given as to why you were installing a grille?'

'Never asked. It wasn't any of my business.'

Larry realised that in this one man was the possible solution to a case that had baffled them for so long.

Sue Baxter pried for more information, but there was no more available.

Wellings thanked her for her hospitality, complimented her one more time on how good the house looked.

Larry's car was outside. The two men drove a mile down the street, away from Sue Baxter's eagle eyes.

Balancing the laptop on his knees, angling the screen, Larry showed Tom Wellings the photos he had: some old, some new.

'That's him.'

'One hundred per cent?'

'I'd say ninety-nine.'

'Good enough for me,' Larry said.

Larry dropped Tom Wellings back at O'Reilly's and headed straight back to Challis Street. He was in a hurry, and the traffic was not helping. He almost ran a red light on one occasion; the fine for doing so, his responsibility.

Isaac was excited on his return. 'Well done,' he said.

***

Albert Grenfell's funeral, conducted in the church next to Penrith House, was a sombre affair. Isaac could see Malcolm Grenfell suitably dressed in a black suit leading the mourners. Wendy had come up as well. Isaac thought it may be a good idea to have two police officers present.

Isaac had brought Katrina Smith, who was in a black dress. Wendy had driven up on her own after Isaac had mentioned that he was taking someone.

Wendy, not wishing to be a wallflower, had organised a police issue car. She noticed the furtive glances from Isaac to Katrina during the ceremony.

Both the police officers noted who was present: Emma Hampshire was with Malcolm Grenfell. Also present was George

Sullivan, the previously hidden man, now very visible. His wife sat at his side.

There were some other people there, some distinguished, others dressed in plain business suits. A later investigation identified them as other aristocrats or local dignitaries from the area. They did not concern Isaac.

Ger O'Loughlin's daughter, the woman that Wendy had met in Ireland, was present. It did not seem suspicious, although Wendy would check later.

Apart from those clearly visible, there were no other family members. In light of recent developments with Montague Grenfell's murder, his body had not been released.

Malcolm Grenfell read one prayer during the service, his tone mellow and humble. Isaac thought that he handled it well, considering that he had not been fond of his brother, and he was an idle fornicating man of little worth. Perhaps the title of Lord Penrith had caused a change in him, though Isaac saw that as unlikely. Malcolm Grenfell would always be the same. There was no frivolous woman around, although Emma Hampshire looked to be very friendly with him. Maybe he preferred older women after all, or at least, Emma Hampshire.

Kevin Solomon, Emma's son, was nowhere to be seen, which was not suspicious as he had not known the Grenfells, apart from Montague briefly.

Katrina was very emotional during the service and held onto Isaac's arm. After the funeral Isaac and Wendy intended to do some probing. It would be inappropriate to conduct formal interviews, but a conversation would be fine.

Isaac thought the friendship of Lord Penrith and Emma Hampshire unusual. Their one-night stand many years ago was well known, but now they looked as if they were about to rekindle it.

Wendy needed to know why O'Loughlin's daughter had attended. There had never been any information indicating that Ger O'Loughlin and Albert Grenfell's relationship justified his daughter attending the funeral.

Intrigue within intrigue, Isaac thought. He was certain they had Montague Grenfell's murderer in the bag, apart from the proof to hammer home a confession.

555

Even Garry Solomon's case was close to conclusion, although the case against the one person now clearly identified thanks to Tom Wellings was inconclusive.

After the ceremony, the mourners moved back to Penrith House, a ten-minute walk or a five-minute drive. Isaac and Katrina chose to walk, Wendy drove. As usual, the weather was cold, and she needed to warm up with the car heater. She imagined that Penrith House would be cold and draughty; enough weekend trips when her sons had been younger to the homes of the aristocracy reminded her of that fact. She had wondered then, with all their titles and their wealth, why they didn't keep themselves warm. Lord Penrith's finances, courtesy of Keith Dawson, had shown that it was horrendously expensive, and although the Grenfells had plenty of money, it was finite.

Isaac surmised with Malcolm Grenfell as the incumbent lord, the move from finite to infinitesimal would not take long.

At the house, everyone was ushered into the main sitting room. A log fire burned at one end. Wendy made straight for it.

Malcolm Grenfell made a speech as to how his brother, a pillar of society, had served the community well and had enhanced the good name of the Penriths. He pledged that he would attempt to live up to his good name. Emma Hampshire stood close by, smiling as he spoke.

The leader of the local council spoke. He thanked the former lord for his generosity in restoring the local library, helping in the cost of repairing the clock tower at the council offices. Others, lords mainly, offered their condolences.

The speeches concluded within ten minutes, and the food and alcohol were brought out. Wendy eyed them with glee. She helped herself to a plate and a glass of wine, a good vintage according to the label.

'I'm surprised to see you here,' she said to Ger O'Loughlin's daughter.

'Why?'

'I was not aware of any contact between your father and Albert Grenfell,' Wendy said.

'You never asked.' Wendy realised that was true. Then, they had been interested in why O'Loughlin had left Mavis Richardson, not in his friendship with the Grenfells.

'They were friendly?'

'They maintained contact, conducted business together. I don't think there was any more to it than that.'

'Did you meet him when he was alive?'

'A few times. My father liked him.'

'Malcolm Grenfell?' Wendy asked.

'Today is the first time that I have met him. He's not what I expected.'

'His reputation was not good.'

'According to my father, he was idle and useless.'

'That was how we knew him, but today...'

'The woman he is with, who is she?' O'Loughlin's daughter asked. 'She's very attractive.'

'Emma Hampshire,' Wendy replied. 'Does the name mean anything to you?'

'No.'

'Emily Solomon?'

'The body in the fireplace?'

'One and the same.'

'My father told me about him just before he died. He told me a lot of things, some I would have preferred not to hear.'

'Why did he do that?'

'He didn't tell my mother, only me. A last-minute confessional, I suppose.'

'You know about the parties?'

'My father was always faithful to my mother. Always available for my sister and me. I could not believe it.'

'It was true,' Wendy said. 'Did he tell you anything else?'

'He told me that his first wife did not want children, whereas he did. It was the reason they broke up, but he was obviously still fond of her.'

'Anything else?'

'Her sister was eccentric, and her son was wild. Garry Solomon, am I correct?'

'That's right.'

'And his wife is standing over there.'

'Yes.'

'There was a reason Garry Solomon never contacted his mother. Do you know what it was?'

557

'He caught her with another man.'

'When?'

'The day he left.'

'Your father knew this?'

'He was dying. Sometimes he was coherent, at other times he was rambling.'

'This other man, did he have a name?'

'He never mentioned it, but he was talking nonsense by them. He was alert when he told me about Mavis and the parties, but a lot of what he said I couldn't understand.'

Chapter 33

Katrina had gone to talk with the staff at Penrith House. All apart from the gardener had resigned and left. All of them had come back for the funeral.

Isaac had taken the opportunity to talk to Lord Penrith. 'Good ceremony,' Isaac said. 'My condolences.'

'The old boy got a good send-off,' Malcolm Grenfell said.

'You've changed.'

'Still the same rogue underneath.'

'You're more serious. Is that permanent?' Isaac asked, although the person he really wanted to speak to was standing on the other side of the room.

'I hope not.'

'We're holding Montague's body for a few more days,' Isaac said.

'The man has left me seriously short of funds.'

'You can manage?'

'Manage yes, but until probate is dealt with, I cannot access the majority.'

'And the Richardsons?'

'Up to them.'

'Montague had their proxy.'

'Gertrude has a grandson?' Malcolm Grenfell posed a rhetorical question.

Isaac thought the man looked smug.

'You know the answer to the question,' Isaac replied.

'Emma's son. He can deal with the Richardsons' probate.'

'Your relationship with Emma Hampshire?'

'Friends, nothing more.'

'You have a history of friendship with her.'

'It's no secret that we were involved at one time.'

'While she was married to Garry Solomon.'

'He was treating her badly. I was there as a shoulder to cry on.'

'A man to bed.' Isaac waited for the reaction.

Malcolm Grenfell stood still for a moment, his face reddening in anger.

'As you say, a man to bed.' Grenfell kept his emotions in check. He knew that seducing Garry Solomon's wife was a motive. He had come so far; he was not going to destroy it by an inappropriate comment.

I will not let that working-class policeman rile me, Grenfell thought.

Isaac, a glass of wine in his hand, observed the man. It was clear he was holding something back. Before he inherited the title he had been an easy book to read, but now he had changed.

Isaac pondered whether the change was permanent, but as his mother would say, 'a leopard never changes its spots'.

Grenfell was not a changed man, only a man who pretended to change. His elevation to the title had been too swift, too suspicious, for Isaac to discount skulduggery.

In a matter of days, the previous incumbent had died, and his successor had met with an unfortunate accident. Too many coincidences for Isaac, no proof.

Isaac looked down at the floor at Lord Penrith's shoes. He judged them to be size 7. Gordon Windsor had stated that the unknown footprints at the top of Montague Grenfell's stairs had been size 10. *Scratch one murderer,* Isaac thought.

Grenfell left Isaac and started to circulate the room. Isaac had to agree that he played the part of the lord with great skill. Isaac could hear him discussing plans for a new gym at the local youth centre with a large beefy man with a flushed complexion. Isaac knew the look of a leading councillor in the area. No doubt, an estate agent or local lawyer discussing council business, seeing what was in it for him.

'It's good to see you here, Chief Inspector Cook.' Isaac was no longer alone. Emma Hampshire had come over to talk to him.

'I did not expect to see you here,' Isaac said. He had to admit that she was an attractive woman. She wore a dark dress, obviously expensive, for the occasion.

'Why?'

'Did you know Albert Grenfell?'

'I met him once.'

'When?'

'Malcolm introduced me to him in London once.'

'Yet you decided to come to his funeral.'

'He was Malcolm's brother. Besides, Malcolm asked me to come.'

'I was not aware that you were still friendly with him.'

'I told you, or Wendy Gladstone, your sergeant, that we used to see each other from time to time when I was with Bob Hampshire. We moved in the same social circle, nothing more. There is nothing sinister with my being here.'

'Malcolm Grenfell was responsible for your marriage breaking up.'

'The marriage was broken anyway.'

'Did Garry Solomon know about your affair?'

'Probably.'

'You're not sure?'

'Not totally. It was not discussed. He had found himself someone else, and that was it.'

'You were upset?'

'I had grown up to believe that marriage was forever, and my husband was dumping me for a younger version. What do you think?'

'Your plans with Malcolm?'

'I'll wait and see.'

'Does that mean more than you are saying?'

'Not really. I am an affectionate woman. Malcolm for all his faults is a good man.'

'And the other women?'

'He won't need them,' Emma Hampshire said before walking away, a smile on her face. Isaac knew what she meant. He felt the need to see Katrina; he found her with the staff.

'Hi,' he said.

'Very friendly with his lordship's friend,' she said. To Isaac, it sounded as if she was jealous.

'She's a key witness, you know that.'

'I do.'

'And now close in with the new lord,' Isaac said.

'She spent last night here.'

'With Grenfell?'

'Same bed,' Katrina said. Isaac could see no issue with that revelation, and it was clear that Malcolm Grenfell was not his brother's murderer. Salacious gossip in the kitchen did not help to solve the murders. Katrina took Isaac by the arm, first to kiss him, and then to take him back into the main room to enjoy himself.

'Stop being a policeman for once,' she said.

Isaac and Katrina had booked into a local hotel for the night. Both were anxious to be there. Isaac thought about what he and Wendy had achieved by attending the funeral. They had not come up with any new leads, other than the knowledge that Emma Hampshire and Malcolm Grenfell were continuing their affair where it had broken off thirty years previously.

Ger O'Loughlin's relationship with Albert Grenfell had no relevance. Both men had died of old age, and neither were directly implicated in the murder of Garry Solomon or indirectly in the case of Montague Grenfell.

The wake at Penrith House concluded at eight in the evening. Lord Penrith bid all the attendees farewell as they left through the front door and down the steps outside to their cars. Isaac observed Emma Hampshire at his side as if she was already the lady of the house.

Isaac had to admit that he liked her, but for a woman who had come from a lower middle-class background, she had certainly led a charmed life. There had been Garry Solomon who had turned out to be a disappointment. Then there was Bob Hampshire who had worshipped her, as she had him. And now Malcolm Grenfell who made a good pretence of being a changed man. Isaac wondered how long before Grenfell took a wife.

Back at the hotel, a timeworn building in the village, Wendy along with Isaac and Katrina had a late supper. Wendy enjoyed herself with a spread of cheese and cake. Isaac and Katrina ate sparingly.

At 11 p.m. Isaac and Katrina went upstairs together, arm in arm. Wendy smiled as they climbed the carpeted stairs. *Lucky woman*, Wendy thought.

Wendy realised that she was the same age as Emma Hampshire and that she was lonely. She felt tears in her eyes. She wiped them away with a tissue. It was her first night away from her home since her husband had died, and she did not want to be there in the hotel.

She sobered up with a strong black coffee and returned to London and the bed she had shared with her husband, the bed where her two sons had been conceived.

Isaac knew the next morning that Wendy had left: a message on his phone, a note at the reception. He could only sympathise.

***

At eight in the morning, Isaac and Katrina drove back to London. He dropped her off at the hospital where she worked. Isaac then drove to Challis Street. He was in the office by eleven.

'Sorry about last night, sir,' Wendy said as he entered.

'Nothing to be sorry about,' Isaac's reply.

Bridget came over with a cup of coffee. Isaac thanked her.

Isaac called an impromptu meeting. 'What do we have?' he asked.

'The name of who ordered the grille,' Larry said.

'It doesn't prove that he is the murderer,' Isaac said.

'An accomplice, at least.'

'Can we make it stick?'

'Unlikely,' Larry had to admit.

'We could bring him in, put him under pressure.'

'He would bring a smart lawyer with him.'

'If the person who installed the grille and the murderer are one and the same, how do we prove it?' Isaac asked.

'His motive is flimsy,' Larry said.

'Then make it stronger.'

It was evident to everyone in the room that Wendy was not in good spirits. Isaac knew that a heavy workload was the best medicine.

'Wendy,' Isaac said, 'we need to tie up Montague Grenfell's murder.'

'Do we call them in?'

'What has Keith found out?'

Bridget answered. 'He'll be here in five minutes. You can ask him then.'

Five minutes later Dawson entered Isaac's office. There was a better meeting room down the corridor, but everyone preferred Isaac's office as it was homelier. Not because of Isaac's efforts, but Bridget and Wendy, tired of their DCI's Spartan décor, had put a plant in a pot in one corner. Isaac had come to appreciate it, and each day since, he made sure to water it.

The office was full before Keith Dawson entered; it was overflowing on his entry. Larry stood up and squeezed himself into a corner.

'The money taken out of Montague Grenfell's offshore account has been transferred to an offshore bank account in Jersey.'

'Traceable?' Isaac asked.

'Subject to a warrant, yes.'

'Do you have a name for the account?'

'A company name. It doesn't help.'

'Company register?' Larry suggested.

'Offshore company, difficult to trace. Whoever took the money is smart. Not as smart as Montague Grenfell, though.'

'Why do you say that?' Isaac asked.

'The Channel Islands may be an offshore banking haven, but they still come under British law. There will be little difficulty in ascertaining who is drawing on that account.'

'How long do you need?'

'Two hours.'

'Okay,' Isaac said. 'We reconvene at three in the afternoon. Keith, you've got three.'

'Thanks.' Dawson left the office a happy man. For once he was in his element, finding a felon.

Keith worked solidly, making phone calls, sending emails, pulling in favours. Bridget brought him a sandwich for lunch, and Wendy kept him supplied with coffee.

At two in the afternoon, he moved from his seat. 'I've got it,' he said.

***

The first arrest was made at five that afternoon. Wendy and Larry accompanied by a uniform cautioned the person, applied the handcuffs.

At seven in the evening, the interview room at Challis Street was occupied. Isaac took the lead role, with Larry to his left. On the other side sat the accused and her lawyer.

Isaac dealt with the formalities as required. He gave the names of those present, and the fact that the proceedings would be videoed and a transcript would be available at completion.

All parties acknowledged, including the accused's lawyer, an imperious little man who looked as though he was going to be trouble.

'My client has committed no crime.'

'We have good reason to believe that she is an accessory to murder,' Isaac said.

'There is no evidence,' Leonard Smithers said. Larry knew him, did not like him, but he was smart. Larry had forewarned Isaac to be careful with him.

Isaac chose not to reply and turned his focus to the accused. 'Miss Solomon, you have been charged as an accessory to murder. Would you like to comment?'

Deidre Solomon sat quietly across from Isaac. Her record of prostitution was well known, and there had been a few arrests over the years. It was apparent that she had been preparing to visit a client when she had been picked up. Wendy and Larry had made a point after meeting her in Chelsea to find out where she worked, and the haunts she frequented.

'I am not guilty,' she said. Isaac had to admit she was a fine-looking woman. Her skin was clear with the slightest trace of makeup, her hair was lustrous, and the dress she was wearing looked as if it had been moulded onto her.

'You are charged with being an accessory to the murder of Montague Grenfell. We have proof.'

'What proof?' Smithers asked.

'You have been withdrawing substantial amounts of cash from a bank account in the Channel Islands.'

'What has that to do with the murder?' Deidre Solomon asked.

'That account had been dormant for some time with only a small amount of money in it.'

'I would not know that.'

'In recent weeks, you have been transferring to it from another account at least one thousand pounds a day.'

'It was my money.'

'Are you saying that you earn that every day?'

'Yes.'

'Who set up the account?'

'I asked someone to do it for me,' Deidre Solomon said. Leonard Smithers said nothing. His client was handling herself well.

'Who?'

'A friend.'

'Miss Solomon,' Isaac said. 'An offshore account is not easy to open. A friend would not have been able to open it in your name, or that of a company, without the appropriate paperwork. I am putting it to you that your brother opened the account. Is that correct?'

'Daniel is good at organising. I'm not.'

'We are arresting your brother for Montague Grenfell's murder.'

'He did not kill him.'

'Did he tell you this?'

'My client does not need to answer,' Smithers said.

'He would not harm anyone,' Deidre Solomon said, ignoring her legal advice.

'He has a history of violence,' Larry said.

'When he was younger.'

'We have documented proof that you have withdrawn substantial sums of money from this account. We also have proof that the money in that account came from an account that Montague Grenfell used. The evidence is indisputable.'

'I would not know that.'

'Who would?' Isaac asked.

'My client does not need to answer that question.'

This time, Deidre Solomon heeded his advice.

Isaac continued, aiming to break through the woman's defences, aware that as long as she kept mute, there was not a lot to hold her on.

'We have proof that the withdrawals of the money occurred after Montague Grenfell's death.'

'I don't understand.'

'Miss Solomon. Montague Grenfell was killed for a password to an account that you knew about.'

'How?'

'He visited you on a regular basis. A lonely old man in need of company, the need to talk. I am putting it to you that in a moment of weakness, he opened up about his life and ultimately the account.'

'This is pure conjecture,' Smithers said. Isaac ignored him.

'Miss Solomon, you became aware of this account, and possibly while the man was asleep, you managed to check his phone and find the account details.'

Deidre Solomon said little, other than to lower her head. 'I did not,' she whispered.

'And once you were in possession, your brother tried to withdraw money. Do you do this with other clients? Get them heady with love and sex and cheap perfume, and then fleece them.'

'This is harassment,' Smithers said.

Isaac was on a roll; he was not about to stop.

'And then when they are vulnerable or asleep, you look for bank accounts on their phones.'

'No. Sometimes,' the woman admitted, almost screaming the truth out.

Isaac moderated his tone, spoke calmly. 'Your brother found out that Montague Grenfell was smarter than most men, and that he needed another password to withdraw money. He visited Grenfell, obtained the password by force, and then hurled the man down the stairs to his death.'

'It did not happen that way.'

'How do you know?'

'Don't answer,' the lawyer said.

'It doesn't matter,' Isaac said. 'We will discuss this later.'

Chapter 34

Daniel Solomon had attempted to run when the two police cars had drawn up outside his office. He had been arrested before Deidre and was down at Challis Street in the holding cells.

Once the interview had been concluded with his sister, and careful to ensure the siblings did not see each other, he was brought up to the same interview room.

'My sister has been here.' Daniel Solomon sniffed the air, smelling her perfume.

Leonard Smithers, his lawyer as well as Deidre's, sat to his right. Isaac thought they had chosen their lawyer poorly. There had been times during the previous interview when Smithers could have advised Deidre Solomon better. Not that it concerned Isaac. He knew he had his man in the interview room and he was not going to let him get off the hook.

Isaac went through the formal procedure, advised the client of his rights and cautioned him.

'Mr Solomon, you have been charged with the murder of Montague Grenfell. Do you wish to make a written confession?' Isaac asked.

'I have killed no one,' Solomon replied. Isaac had assumed that would be the man's initial response.

'We have proof that monies belonging to Montague Grenfell were deposited in an account controlled by you.'

'What account?'

'An account at the HSBC in the Channel Islands.'

'I don't have an account there,' Solomon said.

'The bank maintains a copy of all applications. Your name and your signature will be there. Do you deny that you have an account in the Channel Islands?' Isaac's voice had risen in volume for emphasis.

'I have a lot of bank accounts.'

'Your sister had the ability to withdraw funds from one of those accounts.'

'What account?'

'The account where you deposited monies obtained fraudulently from Montague Grenfell.'

'I did not.'

'Where did your sister get the money from?'

'You'd better ask her.'

'We have.'

'My client has no more to say,' Smithers said.

'This is a murder enquiry. Mr Solomon doesn't get off that lightly.'

'Mr Solomon, your sister obtained the details of an account that Montague Grenfell had stored on his phone. She gave them to you. You attempted to withdraw money. When you realised that the account needed another password, you visited Grenfell and threatened him.'

'This is all lies.'

'We will conduct checks with other clients of your sister. This may be a scam that you have perpetrated on other men.'

'I deny all of this. This is a fabrication, attempting to make me give you a false confession.'

'Your sister screws them, and then you take their money. What do you do? Wait outside the door while she exhausts them, or do you watch? Maybe you are a pervert who enjoys watching his sister screw other men, or maybe you are jealous because it is them and not you? Have you screwed your sister, Mr Solomon?' Isaac knew he had overstepped the mark, but he wanted the man angry, as angry as hell.

Daniel Solomon was up on his feet and around to Isaac's side of the desk. Two uniforms came in and restrained him.

'After watching your sister screw Grenfell, you make a plan. You visit his office and use violence to threaten him. He resists, you grab him. You force him outside of his office. Cornered, the man gives you the password. Montague Grenfell is a smart man; he knows he can change the password once you are gone.

'You know he's correct, and if he lives you will be charged with grievous bodily harm, and you will go to prison. The money can only be yours if you avoid prison and Grenfell doesn't change the password.'

'This is harassment,' Smithers bellows.

'This is murder,' Isaac answers. 'And Daniel Solomon is guilty.'

'It was an accident. I swear it,' Solomon relaxed and started to sob. 'He fell, that's the truth.'

'Too convenient,' Isaac said. 'If he had not died, you would have killed him anyway. You had no option. It was fortunate that the fall killed him. The murder charge sticks.'

'I did not mean to kill him.'

'Okay. Montague Grenfell's death was not premeditated, but he still died. I want your confession.'

'I will not admit to murder.'

'Then admit to the rest. A judge and jury will decide at your trial as to the truth.'

'You were tough in there, Isaac,' Larry said after Solomon had been remanded pending trial.

'He'll still get off with manslaughter.'

'Deidre?'

'Accessory to manslaughter, fraud. A few years in jail, no more. Ask Wendy to visit their mother and let her know.'

***

The mood in Challis Street changed after the arrests had been made for the death of Montague Grenfell. DCS Goddard had visited the office to thank the team.

Garry Solomon's murder still remained on the books, but the team were confident they had their man, although there seemed to be no logic to it.

The man responsible for installing the grille at Bellevue Street had been identified by Tom Wellings, but there was no tie-in to the body in the fireplace. It was not believed that they had known each other, and it had been a few years since the man's last visit to Bellevue Street.

Due to the man's age, Larry phoned a friend of his at a police station closer to the man's home. A police car, no markings, transported him to the station.

Isaac and Larry followed the same procedure as they had with Daniel and Deidre Solomon.

'Mr Sullivan, we are aware that you installed a metal grille on a door at 54 Bellevue Street, Holland Park in 1987.' Isaac asked.

'After thirty years, do you expect me to remember?'

Isaac could only see a kindly old man who had shaken his hand with no sign of malice. 'What's this all about?' he had asked. 'Always happy to help the police.'

Isaac had to remind himself that thirty years previously, George Sullivan would have been a man in his early fifties, and probably fit and strong. His story and the problem with Mavis Richardson were well known, but that was some time before Garry Solomon had been murdered.

'I appreciate that it may be difficult, but it is important.'

'Assuming it is, what does it mean?'

'The grille isolated Garry Solomon's body from the rest of the house.'

'Gertrude's son,' Sullivan said.

'You were at Albert Grenfell's funeral,' Isaac said.

'As were you, Chief Inspector. And very friendly with Albert's nurse.'

Isaac could see that a forceful interview would serve no purpose. He still struggled to believe that George Sullivan had murdered Garry Solomon. No connection had been found between the two men.

'Let us assume that you installed the grille,' Isaac said. He leant back on his chair to appear less intimidating. George Sullivan had declined his right to legal representation.

'If that is what you want.'

'We are aware that you attended one of their parties.'

'I was younger. Not much use to me now.'

'Would you have installed the grille on someone else's behalf?'

'It's possible.'

'For who?'

'I am not at liberty to say. Your sergeant told you that I was with Army Intelligence?'

'Yes, and so was Albert Grenfell,' Isaac said.

'And he's dead.'

'Did he ask you?'

'It's possible, but I do not know why.'

'Were you in the habit of helping him?'

'Ex-Army Intelligence. Yes, we looked after our own. It was the time of the Cold War, still top secret. I told your sergeant that I was a pen-pusher, not a field operative. Unfortunately, it was a lie on my part. We risked our lives to help each other. Albert saved mine once. If Albert wanted something, he could rely on me.'

'And you could rely on him?' Isaac asked.

'Totally. People today do not understand the concept. They have never experienced war, being behind the enemy line, death only one bullet away.'

'Is that what you and Albert were involved with?'

'It's still classified, although I don't know why after so many years.'

***

Isaac saw no reason to hold George Sullivan any longer. The man was too old to stand trial, and there was no case against him. A metal grille on a door leading to a room with a body was not an admission of guilt, although Albert Grenfell's friendship with Sullivan might be.

Protecting the family name at all costs had been mentioned by Mavis Richardson in the past. *Would that include covering up a murder as well?* Isaac thought.

Once back at the office, he surfed the internet hoping to understand what it all meant. Five hundred years, even more recently, maintaining the family name allowed a multitude of sins, but this was the twenty-first century. Surely such behaviour would not be condoned today.

The day was drawing to a close, and he took the opportunity of an early night. He had planned to meet up with Katrina and to go out to a restaurant near Tower Bridge. There was a sense of relief in Homicide now that the Solomons were in custody.

Wendy had visited their mother. She was visibly distraught, but not surprised. She still loved them as the children she had given birth to, but according to her, they had both turned out bad, just like their father. Wendy had phoned social services to ease the burden on the woman caused by the babies. She also made an appointment to take the woman to see the doctor. She would pick her up, wait for her, and take her back. Mary Solomon appeared to have no friends, no relatives, and now no children.

Wendy knew that although life had taken a turn for the worse for her, she still had two loving sons, a friend in Bridget, and colleagues she admired and cherished. Sadness for Mary Solomon's life was temporarily replaced by contentment with hers.

Larry had an appointment with a paint brush. His wife had finally got him on home renovations, and an early break from work meant only one thing to him: purgatory.

Bridget and Keith stayed back late in the office.

***

With the most recent murder resolved, apart from the paperwork involved and the subsequent trial, the intensity of the Murder Investigation Team lessened. As DCS Goddard had said on one of his visits, 'It's a great result. Everyone should be proud of themselves.'

Wendy had taken the opportunity to have a couple of days off, as had Larry. Bridget stayed in the office as the paperwork showed no sign of abating. The prosecution case files still needed completing, and besides, the office was more agreeable than her home.

She had kicked out the malingering lover, but she missed him. He may have had his faults, but he had been there when she had arrived home at the end of the day. Now all she had was a cold house and four walls to look at, apart from the television in the corner.

Isaac continued as usual, his workload supplanted by assisting on another case. Katrina Smith was still very much in his life, but the intensity of the relationship was starting to wither, as he always knew it would. That was how his life operated, and whereas he wished Katrina well, he could see it as only a matter of time.

Keith Dawson continued to work through Montague Grenfell's records. Isaac had to admit that he had done a good job, and even though he lacked the natural camaraderie of the other people in his team, he still fitted in well. Larry's opinion of the man had changed after Dawson had even paid for a round of drinks one Friday night.

It was three weeks after the arrest of Daniel and Deidre Solomon when the department came back together. Events had moved on, and the murder of Garry Solomon had taken precedence again.

After thirty years, it would have been possible to put it to one side and declare it as unsolved. As Isaac said to the team, 'If we had arrested the murderer then, he would by now have been released from jail.'

Finding a killer after so long seemed like finding a needle in a haystack, but it had been Keith who had found it, hidden deep inside a file on Montague Grenfell's laptop. Bridget had checked, found it to be correct. It was damning evidence, and its repercussions could still be felt today after thirty years. It was a clear motive.

Katrina had told Isaac two days earlier that Malcolm Grenfell had married Emma Hampshire in a registry office in Leicestershire. Her son, Kevin, had given her away. Katrina thought that Malcolm Grenfell had changed; Isaac was not sure.

Nuptials aside, Isaac knew that he needed to question the bride and groom again. He made plans to drive up to see them, but first he needed to interview George Sullivan again.

***

It was Wendy who picked up George Sullivan from his house. It had only been three weeks since she had last seen him, but his health had deteriorated.

Not long now, Wendy thought.

George Sullivan was as always polite and amenable, although he needed Wendy's assistance into the police car.

Interview Room A at his nearest police station. Isaac was already there.

'Mr Sullivan, thank you for coming.'

'Always willing to help the police.'

Isaac went through the cautioning process, informed him of his rights. Sullivan waved them away. Isaac continued to a conclusion. It was always difficult interviewing old people, and whether Sullivan was guilty of any crime or not, it was clear that the man would not stand up in any court in front of a judge.

'We need to go over why you installed the grille on Albert Grenfell's behalf,' Isaac asked.

'It was a favour. Albert asked me.'

'He could have dealt with it.'

'Dealing with tradesmen? Not Albert's style.'

'Beneath him?' Wendy asked. She was sitting to the left of Isaac.

'If he could avoid it. I told you before that Albert was a terrible snob. Admirable in many ways, but he saw himself as above the common man. It may be an outdated attitude, but he was firm in his beliefs.'

'But you are not from his class,' Isaac said.

'The son of a butcher, and not even a gentleman's butcher.'

'Then why the friendship?' Isaac asked.

'Please. I am an old man.'

'I'm sorry, but we owe it to Garry Solomon to solve his murder.'

'I suppose so.'

Wendy organised some tea to be brought in. She also took the opportunity to ask Isaac to ease his interrogating style.

'The friendship?' Isaac asked. His manner was less forthright.

'Albert was behind enemy lines. The Stasi, the East German secret police, had captured him and were holding him on the outskirts of East Berlin. I went in and rescued him.'

'Dangerous?' Wendy asked.

'I killed two men to get him out. We were both lucky to get out alive.'

Isaac had to admire the man, even if his involvement with the death of Garry Solomon was suspected.

'You said before that you installed the grille as a favour.'

'Yes.'

'If you had known that it was being installed to cover up a criminal act?'

'If Albert Grenfell had told me, I would have still installed the grille.'

'And been an accessory to murder?'

'You both belong to a different generation,' Sullivan said. 'Albert and I had a long history. What we did all those years ago formed a bond that cannot be broken. Whether Albert knew what was in that room or not, is not important to me. I did my duty, as he would have done for me.'

'Including murder?'

'We killed in Germany, although it was called political assassination. Over there we received medals for our actions, not prison cells.'

'Let me get this clear,' Isaac said. 'You installed the grille, but you had no part in the placement of the body in the fireplace or his murder.'

'That is correct. My conscience is clear. I did my duty, and God will be my judge.'

'Thank you, Mr Sullivan. There are no more questions.'

Isaac concluded the interview. Wendy organised a policewoman to take George Sullivan home.

'What do you think?' Wendy asked Isaac outside the police station as they prepared to drive back to Challis Street.

'Albert could have killed Solomon. He had the motive.'

'How do we prove it?'

'We can't. The truth, if he knows it, lies with Sullivan.'

'Do you intend to question him again?' Wendy asked.

'No. That is the last time we will see George Sullivan,' Isaac said. 'As long as he denies any involvement in the murder, there is nothing we can do.'

Chapter 35

Isaac made the trip up to Penrith House to meet Lord and Lady Penrith. He took Wendy with him. They were met at the front entrance to the house by Lady Penrith.

'Pleased to see you,' the former Emma Hampshire said.

'It came as a surprise,' Isaac said. He had to admit she looked resplendent. Around her neck she wore an emerald necklace.

'Family heirloom,' she said, after noticing Wendy admiring it.

'I did not see his lordship as the marrying kind,' Isaac said.

'Neither did I,' Lady Penrith said.

'Then why?'

'We are both older, and neither of us wants to be on their own.'

'Malcolm Grenfell was never on his own,' Isaac said, unsure of her Ladyship's reaction.

'The women who kept him entertained were there for a good time, not him. He will never have reason to doubt my motives.'

'What are your motives?'

'To be with Malcolm, of course.'

'And the title?'

'I appreciate it, but it is not the prime motivation.'

'In the thirty years since you first slept with Malcolm Grenfell, were you ever unfaithful to Bob Hampshire?' Wendy asked.

'No. I loved Bob.'

'And Malcolm?'

'I loved him as well.'

'Complicated.'

'I don't see why. It is possible to love more than one person, difficult to live with them both. I chose Bob because he was reliable and able to provide for Kevin. Malcolm was Malcolm, and he was not reliable or the father figure that I wanted. Malcolm always knew that. We both knew that one day we would be together.'

'We need to talk to you separately,' Isaac said.

'Malcolm is waiting for you.'

***

Isaac and Wendy were ushered into a room at the back of the house.

'It used to be the smoking room. In the past, the men would retire here to smoke cigars and talk about business. The women would stay in the other room discussing needlecraft,' Lord Penrith said. He stood erect and was wearing a suit.

'Thank you for seeing us, your Lordship?' Isaac did not know why he had respected the man's title. Grenfell had self-indulgently wasted his life, yet now he looked worthy of the title; almost too good to be true.

'It's Emma. She's changed me.'

'She told us that you and she always had a belief that you would be together one day.'

'More hope, although I don't regret my past life. It was full of fun and no responsibility. Now I am involved in God knows how many charities. They even want me to judge the best vegetable of the year at the local agricultural show.'

'What do you know about vegetables?' Wendy asked.

'Not a lot. What do you want, by the way?' Lord Penrith asked. 'You've arrested the people who killed Montague.'

'We have reason to believe that Albert murdered Garry Solomon,' Isaac said.

'Preposterous. Poor old Albert wouldn't hurt a fly,' Penrith said.

'Are you aware of his time in the army?'

'Pushing a pen for Queen and country.'

'He never told you?'

'He was older than me. We had different mothers. Our conversations were few and far between.'

'Your brother was not in an office. He was undercover.'

'A spy?'

'Yes.'

'Are you saying that Albert was behind enemy lines, spying?'

'Our source is good.'

Malcolm Grenfell sat down and let out a sigh. 'Albert, a regular James Bond, licensed to kill.'

'That is correct.'

'Hard to imagine Albert with a bevy of women.'

'I don't believe that is the reality, do you?' Isaac said.

'Not really, but I have to give him credit. All those years pretending to be a stuffy aristocrat, and there he was with a story worth telling. And you believe he killed Garry?'

'Our evidence points to that conclusion.'

'Are you saying that because he killed in the army, he could have killed Garry?'

'Yes.'

'Murder! What is so significant that would justify that course of action? Unless it was maintaining the family name.'

577

***

Isaac could not fault Malcolm Grenfell. His brother Albert had been in his twenties when he had been born, so it was very possible that there was little communication between the two men.

Emma Hampshire's reason for marrying Malcolm Grenfell appeared relevant. Isaac and Wendy found her in a conservatory at the back of the house.

'We have reason to believe that your first husband was murdered by Albert Grenfell,' Isaac said. He waited to see the reaction.

'My brother-in-law, Malcolm's brother?'

'Yes.'

'Can you prove it?' Lady Penrith asked.

'The witnesses are all dead, as is the accused,' Isaac replied.

'And the motive?'

'I am not at liberty to discuss that.'

'Why not? Is it a big secret?'

'It may become relevant at a later date.'

Isaac thought that the former Emma Hampshire was on edge.

Wendy had questions of a more personal nature.

'Why did you marry so quickly?' she asked.

Lady Penrith took one step back, unsure of what to say. 'I told you before that I loved him.'

'You have been able to marry him since Bob Hampshire died,' Isaac reminded her.

'I was not ready.'

'Not ready or was it because Malcolm Grenfell had no money and no title.'

'That's an outrageous statement, Chief Inspector.' Isaac had his reaction. He had the measure of the woman.

'I put it to you that you were glad to be rid of Garry Solomon because he had no money. And then Bob Hampshire comes along.'

'You are accusing me of prostituting myself to the nearest rich man.' Lady Penrith was on her feet and shouting.

'And as long as Bob Hampshire kept you and your son in luxury, you stayed with him. Did you sleep with Malcolm Grenfell while you were with Bob Hampshire?'

'How dare you accuse me of this. I was faithful to Bob.'

'And once he died, did you resume your relationship with your current husband?'

'No, yes, sometimes.'

'What's the answer?' Isaac persisted.

Wendy looked at Isaac, uncertain where he was heading.

'We sometimes went away together for a few days.'

'While he was seducing young women?'

'Yes.'

'Did you agree with his behaviour?'

'I was not willing to marry him until he stopped.'

'Are you saying that you did not marry him for his title?'

'Yes.'

'But you were sleeping with him before. Why?'

'I'm a woman. I need a man in my bed.'

'Lady Penrith, did you know that Albert Grenfell had murdered your husband?'

'No, why would I? What was there for me to gain?'

'Protection for Malcolm Grenfell.'

'Protection from what?' Lady Penrith asked. Isaac declined to answer.

***

'You were rough on Lady Penrith,' Wendy said on the drive back to London.

'I'll apologise later,' Isaac said as he focussed on the road ahead.

'What did you hope to find out?' Wendy liked Emma Hampshire. The woman had been through a lot, and now she sat in the stately home with a title. Wendy had noticed the female touch in the house. In the hallway, there were flowers, as in the other rooms. The curtains had been flung open, the light streaming in. Upon their arrival, Wendy had noticed a van belonging to a company of professional cleaners, although not Daniel Solomon's, as the doors to his business had closed after his arrest for murder.

'I wanted her to be angry and confused. Only then would I know the truth.'

'Do you?'

'Yes.'

'What do you know?'

'Emma Hampshire is not guilty of any crime.'

Upon their return to Challis Street, Isaac called the team together, even though it was late. 'Keith, what do you have?'

'A scanned copy on Montague's Grenfell's laptop. There was a password that I had to crack first.'

'Genuine?'

'I've checked, sir,' Bridget said.

'There's only one issue,' Larry said. He was glad of the late night, a chance to get away from home renovations.

'What's that?'

'Albert Grenfell could not have murdered Garry Solomon.'

'What?' Isaac was sure they had their man, even if they could not prove it.

'He was out of the country for two months during that period.'

'Proven?'

'Conclusively.'

'George Sullivan as a favour to Albert Grenfell?' Wendy asked.

'He was not in the country either.'

'Montague?'

'It's possible,' Larry said.

Isaac, unsure how to proceed, phoned DCS Goddard. 'We are at a dead end.'

'What do you mean?'

'We can prove that Albert Grenfell did not murder Garry Solomon.'

'Other suspects?'

'Montague Grenfell, but it's not provable. And besides, he's dead.'

'What do you want to do? Shelve the investigation?'

'Not yet, sir.'

'One week maximum,' DCS Goddard said.

Isaac could see only one approach. He needed to take all those involved and push them to the limit.

Wendy would go and talk to George Sullivan, although the man was too old for intense questioning, and he would probably say very little.

Larry could talk to Kevin Solomon, now the stepson of Malcolm Grenfell, Lord Penrith.

Isaac knew that Malcolm Grenfell had been obtuse with him. This time his interview would be formal and direct. He hoped the man had good legal representation, as his legal rights were going to be severely challenged.

***

Larry found Kevin Solomon at his flat in Hampstead. The man was in a good mood and invited him in.

'Coffee?' Solomon asked.

'Yes please.'

'I assume your visit is not purely social.'

'Your mother married Lord Penrith.'

'Why not?'

'You have no problems with it?'

'Why should I? She is still young, and Malcolm is, at least, good fun. Bob Hampshire was a good man, but he was not always the most entertaining.'

'You knew Malcolm Grenfell from before?'

'He was a friend of Bob's, and my mother knew him.'

'You were aware of their past relationship?'

'I believe I told you that already.'

***

Wendy met George Sullivan. They sat in the front room of his house. His wife continued to fuss, always bringing drinks and snacks. Wendy asked if they could have fifteen minutes without interruption. Victoria Sullivan acquiesced.

'Albert Grenfell did not murder Garry Solomon,' Wendy said.

'I never thought he did,' Sullivan said.

'Why?'

'Albert was a man of honour. Killing for your country, protecting the good name of the family is honourable, but murdering a civilian for no good reason made no sense.'

'There is a motive,' Wendy said.

'Sufficient to murder?'

'Yes.'

'Even so, I cannot think badly of Albert.'

Wendy phoned Isaac. 'George Sullivan can tell us nothing more. Albert Grenfell asked him to install the grille, that is all.'

Larry updated Isaac. 'No more to tell. The trail has run cold.'

'No, it hasn't,' Isaac said. 'All three of us are going to Penrith House.'

***

Lord and Lady Penrith were not pleased to see Isaac and his team. Kevin Solomon was there, as were several prominent locals.

'This is an intrusion, Chief Inspector,' Lord Penrith said. Isaac had ensured a marked police car was outside with two uniformed officers. Isaac realised he was taking a risk here, but he could see no alternative. The only hope for a resolution to the murder of Garry Solomon lay with Lord Penrith. Lady Penrith echoed her husband's criticism.

Isaac chose to ignore them both. 'This is a murder enquiry, and I intend to resolve it today. Lord Penrith, if you will please accompany me into the other room.'

'This is my house. How dare you order me around.'

'It's either here or down the station. I have two officers outside. Any obstruction on your part and I will have you in handcuffs. Do you understand?' Isaac knew if he were wrong, his DCS would not be able to protect him.

'Emma, make my apologies to the others. Tell them we will meet again tomorrow,' Penrith said. 'Chief Inspector, I have no option.'

'Correct.'

A dining room table was in the centre of the room: Larry and Isaac on one side, Lord Penrith on the other. Isaac gave the customary caution. Penrith asked for Kevin Solomon to be present. 'He's had some legal training.'

'You murdered Garry Solomon,' Isaac directed his gaze at Malcolm Grenfell.

Emma Hampshire, who had been listening at the door, burst in. 'How dare you accuse my husband,' she said.

Wendy followed soon after. 'I couldn't stop her.'

'Very well,' Isaac said. 'Lady Penrith, you can stay, as long as I have your word that you will not interrupt. Otherwise, we will reconvene at the local police station.'

'Malcolm Grenfell, I put it to you again. You murdered Garry Solomon,' Isaac said.

Lady Penrith rose from her chair, her face ablaze with anger. Wendy took a firm hold of her and sat her down. 'You must remain calm,' she said.

'Why would I do that?' Lord Penrith replied.

'Because he came between you and the title.'

Penrith let out a nervous laugh. 'Thirty years ago, are you joking? Do you think I was interested in the title of Lord Penrith? I had two older brothers and my chance of ever claiming the title was remote. And why? What has Garry Solomon got to do with my title?'

'We have found proof that Archibald Grenfell, your grandfather, was married two times, not one as previously thought.'

'Rubbish,' Penrith said.

'He was married to your grandmother, as well as the mother of Frederick Richardson, the father of Gertrude and Mavis. Frederick Richardson was legitimate, and as such, had a claim on the title.'

'What proof?'

'I am putting it to you that you murdered Garry Solomon to hide the truth. To conceal the fact that Garry Solomon may have had a claim on this house, and possibly the title.'

'Even if that was true, he was younger than me.'

'He threatened you. Told you that he would ensure you never gained the title. Both Albert and Montague were in their fifties, so they were unlikely to have any male heirs. The title was yours if you waited long enough, and suddenly there was another person who could threaten your succession.'

'Is this true, Malcolm?' Emma Hampshire screamed.

'It's rubbish. He can't prove a word of it.'

'Garry Solomon was involved with ruthless men. He could have had you killed and then waited for Albert and Montague to die. Even assisted their deaths as well. The title may be contentious, but the Grenfell wealth never was. As the oldest surviving male relative he would have had a clear right to it.'

'He suspected the truth, but he never had any proof.'

'Suspected what? That your grandfather had married a maid, Bronwyn Richardson. That is why Frederick, Gertrude and Mavis's father, was given the surname of Richardson. To hide the truth, the shame that Archibald Grenfell had married for love, and outside of his class.'

'Albert told me.'

'Bronwyn Richardson?' Isaac asked.

'She died in childbirth. Albert knew the full story.'

'Why did Albert tell you?'

'We had an argument. I told him that I wanted to marry Emma, or Emily as she was known then. He said I could not.'

'Why?'

'Bad form taking the wife of a relative. That was Albert, always worried about the family name, even when nobody knew.'

'Is that when you decided to murder your wife's first husband?'

Kevin Solomon and Lady Penrith sat mute, unable to comprehend.

'Why would I kill Garry and then hide his body where it might be found?'

'There are two motives for the death of Garry Solomon,' Isaac continued. 'The first is so you would be able to claim Emily for yourself, but I am not sure that is the most important reason.'

'Why?' Lady Penrith asked.

'He wanted you, that is clear,' Isaac said, 'but why did he hide the body?'

'You have an answer?' Lord Penrith said, almost sneeringly.

'You killed Garry Solomon and placed him in the fireplace. You concealed the fireplace and admitted it to Albert.'

'Why would I tell Albert?'

'You needed him to protect you. If your plan went wrong and the body was found, the blame would have come back to you. Albert was crucial. You knew that Albert would not allow the good name of Grenfell and the title of Lord Penrith to be sullied by something as common as murder, especially one committed by his half-brother.'

'It's a good story, but there is no substance,' Penrith said.

'George Sullivan installed the grille at Bellevue Street, oblivious to what was inside the room. He even admitted that if he had known, he would still have installed the grille based on the bond between him and Albert.'

'You're talking in riddles, Chief Inspector.'

'You knew that in time it would be found. You planned for such an eventuality.'

'But why?'

'You did not think it would be thirty years, maybe just a few. You were aware that after Mavis Richardson found her husband in bed with Gertrude, there was a plan to sell the house. Montague Grenfell had documents attesting to the fact.'

'Why didn't they sell it?' Penrith asked.

'Montague talked them out of it.'

'Why?'

'I believe you said it yourself. Montague knew everything. He was aware of what you had done and what was in the fireplace. Albert had told him.'

'Then why after thirty years did he agree to sell it?'

'Montague had been fiddling the books. We found proof of it, and it cost him his life. The cash was running short. He must have thought that after thirty years nothing would have remained in the fireplace. He had discounted the accumulated coal dust and pigeon droppings, and they had mummified the remains.'

'If the body had been found sooner?' Penrith asked.

'There was proof of George Sullivan installing the grille, and his relationship with your brother was well known. The blame for the murder would have pointed to Albert.'

'There was no proof.'

'Montague knew that if Albert was in jail, even condemned to hang, he could still lay claim to the title and the wealth. You had confided in him, knowing full well that he would be complicit.

Documents from Garry Solomon to Albert threatening to reveal the fact that his grandfather should have been entitled to the title were with Montague. At the appropriate time, Montague would have ensured that they were found in Albert's possession. The motive was there, George Sullivan was there, and Albert's military expertise in assassination would have been revealed.'

'None of this connects back to me, it is unprovable,' Lord Penrith said.

'We have found this much. We will find more. Malcolm Grenfell, Lord Penrith, you will be going to jail for the murder of Garry Solomon. It is only a matter of time. I do not believe that you will enjoy the time until your formal arrest. You have murdered your wife's first husband and the father of your legal representative. I do not believe they will be here for very long.'

Wendy consoled Emma Hampshire who was in tears. Kevin Solomon moved away from Lord Penrith and over to his mother.

'Very clever, Chief Inspector. Garry's attempt at blackmail was amateurish. He had stumbled on the truth, and he was threatening Albert,' Penrith said.

'Are you saying Albert killed him?'

'He had no problems when Garry died.'

'You killed him?'

Malcolm Grenfell looked over at his wife. 'I did it for you, only you. Why do you think I never married?'

Lady Penrith stared at him blankly.

'Please excuse me,' Lord Penrith said. He walked over to a desk in the corner of the room and pulled open a drawer. He took out a loaded gun, Albert's old gun. He pointed it at his temple and pulled the trigger.

The End

The DCI Isaac Cook Thriller Series: Books 1 - 3

Murder is Only a Number

Chapter 1

Part 1

Stephanie Chalmers realised that her life was not as it should be. On the one hand, she had a husband who loved her; on the other, he was a lecherous bastard who would chase anyone half decent in a skirt.

It was not as though she was beaten, or impoverished, or even neglected. Gregory Chalmers, she knew, had been a good catch when she had met him ten years previously. He had only been thirty-two then, two years older than her. Already, he had his own legal practice and was doing well. He had an easy way with words and an attractive physique with a full head of black hair. Sure, she had heard about his reputation, but she was confident she could tame him, the same way she had tamed a previous boyfriend, but that damn fool went and got himself killed in a motor accident. A tragedy as she saw it, considering all the effort she had put into the relationship.

She had loved the previous boyfriend with the all-consuming passion reserved for the young and susceptible; she had no intention of repeating that mistake by falling for Gregory, her future husband, only ultimately to be disappointed. It had taken six months before he proposed to her, wed her, and then bedded her, but not necessarily in that order. She knew that he would continue to love her intensely; she knew how to do that, but she would only feel a strong affection. Still, she had reasoned, it was a good arrangement, and for nine of the ten years they had been fine.

Two children had resulted, both healthy, both obviously intelligent – a trait inherited from both parents. Stephanie had always assumed that her husband would not cheat on her, but in that she had been wrong.

Gregory Chalmers was a womaniser; he could not help himself. It had upset her the first couple of times, but then, she reasoned, he would calm down in time, and besides, the pretence of enjoying the act of procreation every other night was wearing thin; she was glad of the rest.

Regardless, Chalmers loved his wife, even if he had to sneak in late at night every few weeks, hoping that his wife was asleep – she never was.

***

It was Stephanie who first suggested they needed someone to help with the children. She was busy running her interior design business, her husband was occupied with more legal cases than he could handle.

Ingrid was the first woman to apply, a fresh-faced, clear-skinned young woman. 'I'm studying in London. My hours are flexible, so helping you out would be all right,' she had said.

Both the parents agreed that she would be good for the children, as she would pick them up from school and ensure they had their evening meal and completed their homework.

It was three months later that Stephanie first suspected something was amiss. She had come home earlier than usual one night. The children were next door with friends, although Ingrid was in the house, as was Gregory.

Upstairs, a little dismayed after the innocent looks from the two downstairs, she had seen that the marital bed was not as tidy as usual. She pulled back the cover, the evidence clearly visible. The sheets on her husband's side of the bed were creased, and they had been fresh on that morning.

Stephanie had sat down, shed a tear, drunk a glass of brandy, and then returned downstairs. By that time, Ingrid had left, and no more was said.

Two weeks passed before another occurrence with Ingrid and Gregory; two weeks where Stephanie had an opportunity to reflect on all that had transpired.

Still, she reasoned, he left her alone, and after that night the marital bed had not been used for the coupling of the man of the house and the children's helper. Stephanie Chalmers decided to let sleeping dogs lie. No point in creating unpleasantness when it was not needed. She remained civil to Ingrid; agreeable and available to Gregory, which was not too often.

***

'Ingrid, this has to stop. My wife is suspicious,' Gregory Chalmers said, four weeks into their affair. It was Thursday night, and as usual Stephanie would be home late. It was also the one night of the week when it could be guaranteed that the children were elsewhere, either next door or at a school friend's place somewhere in the area.

Chalmers had realised that the first flush of the affair with Ingrid, who was in her mid-twenties, had been incredible, but he was tired of her. She was becoming neurotic, wanting to touch him inappropriately in the house when Stephanie was there. It was fun the first couple of times but after that…

Gregory Chalmers, a philandering man who needed to chase other women, needed to feed his ego, was, he knew, at heart a one-woman man, and that woman was Stephanie.

He was aware that she knew about him and Ingrid. He had sensed it the last couple of times he and Stephanie had made love. Sure, she had been affectionate and yielding, pushing all the right buttons, but something was missing: a lack of tenderness, a tightening in her body that he had not seen or felt before.

She knew about his activities at the office with one of his clients, an attractive woman in her forties. He was almost certain that she knew about him and the wife of the local golf club captain. One of his so-called friends had called him twentieth hole Greg in front of Stephanie. Gregory knew that his wife's laugh was purely for the friend's benefit; to show him that she was naïve and silly, both of which she was not.

Only once in their years together had Stephanie referred to Gregory's wrongdoing. 'Don't bring it home,' she had said, and here he was, doing just that.

'I thought you cared,' Ingrid said in the kitchen of the house, a substantial three-storey terrace in Twickenham.

'You knew what it was,' Chalmers replied.

'Just a screw, is that it?' Ingrid said. The woman was becoming irrational, and he knew that Stephanie was due home within fifteen minutes. He now regretted that he had not resisted one last act of seduction in the elder child's bedroom.

'What did you expect? That I would leave my wife?'

'I love you, and now you are throwing me out.'

'No, I'm not. The job is still here.'

'I took the job because of you,' Ingrid said.

It had not been normal for Stephanie to phone when she left her business to drive home. It was a fifteen-minute drive when the traffic was flowing, thirty when it was not, and he knew after her phone call which of the two it would be.

Gregory Chalmers was frantic, attempting to reason with a hysterical woman and to ease her to the front door and out of the house. There was no way that either he or Ingrid could pretend to be idly conversing when Stephanie entered, and she would wonder what Ingrid was doing in the house anyway. After he had noticed that first time that Stephanie had checked the bed and seen the crumpled sheets, they had been extra careful. In fact, apart from their arranged meetings at the house, he had rarely seen Ingrid. She had wanted to meet at a local hotel, take a room, but he had declined. He had been with Stephanie a long time, and though he had seduced a few women, none had become clingy like this one.

Maybe she was too young, too immature, too unknowledgeable, he had thought, but he had discounted that very early on in their short relationship.

He knew now that Ingrid Bentham was a troubled woman, possibly delusional.

'Take your hands off of me,' Ingrid screamed as Gregory Chalmers took her firmly by the arm and marched her to the door.

'Stephanie will be back soon,' he shouted.

'Good. Then you can tell your wife that you love me, and we are to be together.'

'We cannot be together. I will stay with Stephanie, and you will leave.'

'You have never loved me,' Ingrid said. The woman had freed herself from Chalmers and was back in the kitchen, opening drawers, slamming them shut, picking up pans and hurling them to the floor. She even tipped the casserole that Gregory had prepared for Stephanie over on the floor.

She will be home in five minutes, Gregory thought. He knew there was no way he could clean up by then, and no way the woman causing mayhem would leave. He was unable to think straight, unable to even contemplate an explanation that would satisfy Stephanie when she walked in.

'Go, please go.' Gregory grabbed her again, manhandled her towards the back door. He knew that whatever happened, the evening would end badly.

Ingrid freed herself, using superhuman strength. She opened the drawer next to the sink. She took out a razor-sharp knife.

'You bastard. The same as all the other men,' she said as she drove the knife hard into Gregory Chalmers' rib cage. He fell back, stunned by what had just happened, but still alive.

'What have you done?' he gasped. He held his hand over the wound, the red blood staining his white shirt.

'I thought you were different; someone I could love, someone I could trust.'

With Chalmers leaning back against the pantry door, Ingrid came forward, her eyes ablaze, her mouth grimacing, as she thrust the knife forward, again and again. Chalmers collapsed to the ground, and died.

***

Stephanie Chalmers burst into the kitchen; she had arrived within fifteen minutes, as her now-dead husband had predicted. 'What have you done?' she screamed.

Ingrid stood at one end of the kitchen, the bloodied knife in her hand. 'He deserved to die,' she said.

Stephanie, unable to comprehend the scene, stood mute. Her husband lay on the tiled floor, covered in blood. The children's helper, a person she had trusted with the safety of her children, had murdered her husband.

Ingrid Bentham moved towards Stephanie, grabbed her by the hair and struck her across the body with the knife. Stephanie reacted, grabbed the knife, and threw it away. Ingrid, fiery mad and no longer in control, grabbed a thin knife that had been on the wooden table in the middle of the room and thrust it into Stephanie.

Stephanie Chalmers collapsed, apparently dead. Ingrid then walked over to Gregory's body and ripped open his shirt.

With the thin knife, she carefully carved the number 2 on his exposed chest. She then removed all her clothes, took a shower, helped herself to some clean clothes from Stephanie Chalmers' wardrobe, and walked out of the front door.

Chapter 2

The first notification of the events at the Chalmers' house was the blubbering voice of a child on the phone. 'Daddy and Mummy are dead.'

The operator at the emergency control centre responded at once, immediately instigating a trace on the mobile phone.

'Is there an adult there?' was her first question.

'Daddy and Mummy are dead.' This time the voice more unsettled than before.

'Can I have an address?'

'Glenloch Road.'

'Can you give me a number?'

'Daddy and Mummy are dead.'

'I need you to help me if I am to help them. What is the number in Glenloch Road?'

'64.'

Even before the name of the street had been given, the police and the ambulance services had been mobilised. Glenloch Park had been identified as Twickenham, and triangulation based on the mobile phone masts in the area had confirmed this.

It would only be seconds before the mobile number had been identified and a registered owner and address confirmed.

Local police officers were the first on the scene, only one minute before an ambulance arrived. 'It looks grim,' Police Constable O'Riordan said over the phone to his superior.

'Murder?'

'Judging by the blood, I would say so.'

'How many?'

'One, definitely; the other one looks to be in a bad way.'

'Ambulance?'

'It's here now.'

'There's a child here; he made the discovery. I would assume him to be the child of the house.'

'Okay, I'll send someone down to look after him. In the meantime, you know the procedure.'

The paramedic who had arrived with the ambulance had made a cursory check on the bloodied man lying on the floor in the kitchen.

'Careful with the evidence,' PC O'Riordan, a red-haired young man in his mid-twenties, said. Three years out of training and this was his first murder. He knew the procedure: secure the area, ensure that any evidence was left undisturbed before the crime scene examiner and his team had a chance to conduct their investigation, phone Homicide, although his superior, Sergeant Graves, back at the station, would almost certainly have dealt with that.

'The woman is still alive,' the paramedic, a middle-aged man, said.

'Serious?' O'Riordan asked, preferring not to look too closely. His first murder, his first time being confronted with so much blood. He had been trained to react calmly, although he had not yet attained the ability to detach himself from a scene of violence. He went outside and threw up, splattering some daffodils with his vomit. Taking a drink of water from a tap in the garden, he returned to the scene.

Detective Inspector Sara Stanforth was there. 'What is your preliminary report?' she asked the police constable.

'Male, clearly dead; the female is still alive, although in a bad way.'

'I can see that myself,' DI Stanforth said. O'Riordan knew her from the police station. He had only spoken to her on a couple of occasions, and both times she had been unpleasant. He assumed that their third meeting would be no different. Sean O'Riordan, ambitious and smart, but still, as yet, only a police constable, did not appreciate her style, but he knew that she was efficient.

'I arrived on the scene at 20.52 in response to a 999.'

'Yes, but what else?' Sara Stanforth said. A smartly-dressed woman, she was determined to succeed in an establishment clearly dominated by men. She knew of the glares from the men down at the station, men who should know better. Some had been friendly, especially Detective Chief Inspector Bob Marshall: so much so that they were now an item, having moved in together three months previously.

As for the others, some had been willing to treat her as an equal while the rest saw her as a bit of fluff, suitable only for making the coffee and whatever else. The whatever else she knew. Sara Stanforth knew she could be a bitch and overbearing, particularly in the station, but it came with the territory. She had to establish her credentials quickly before the typical male chauvinism took over.

'Family name, Chalmers. The dead male is probably Gregory Chalmers.'

'Probably?'

'The young boy, his name is Billy, said that it was his father, and this is the house of Gregory and Stephanie Chalmers.'

'Confirmed?' DI Stanforth asked.

'There are letters on a table in the hallway with their names on.'

Sara Stanforth had brought another woman from the station. She was with the boy, attempting to find out who he knew that could come and look after him. It was clear that he was a witness, but for now his well-being was more important.

'And the woman is Stephanie Chalmers?'

'According to Billy, it is.'

The crime scene was quickly being established, and the crime scene examiner was on his way. A neighbour, identified as a friend of Stephanie Chalmers, had come over and was tending to the young boy. His sister, known to be at a friend's house, would be staying the night there.

'Anymore you can tell us?' Sara Stanforth asked the paramedic as he removed Stephanie Chalmers from the murder scene, knowing full well that the paramedic's responsibility was to the seriously injured woman, not to the police.

'Knife wound to the lower body, loss of blood. No more than that for now.'

'We will need to interview her.'

'At the hospital, but not today.'

'When?' Sara Stanforth asked.

'Not for me to say. You'll need to check with the doctor.'

It had only been a brief conversation, but DI Stanforth knew that the paramedic had been correct. However, this was her case, her first murder as the senior police officer, and she did not intend to let anyone else take it from her.

'Constable, Sean, what else can you tell me? At least, before the crime scene examiner and his people move us out.'

'It's not a suicide pact.'

'Why do you say that?'

'If you look again, you will see some clothes stuffed in a corner and some footprints made in the blood. There was a third person.'

'The murderer?'

'That would be the assumption.'

'What else?'

'Female, judging by the discarded clothes.'

'Anything else?'

'There is a number carved into the male's chest.'

'What does that mean?' Sara Stanforth asked.

'No idea, but there it was. Number 2.'

The crime scene examiner arrived, briefly spoke to the DI and the PC, donned his overalls, put gloves on his hands, protectors over his shoes, and commenced his work.

'A full report as soon as possible,' Sara Stanforth said.

'You'll have a preliminary within two hours. The full report sometime tomorrow,' Crime Scene Examiner Crosley replied.

Stanforth phoned DCI Bob Marshall. 'I want this case,' she said.

'It's yours. Don't stuff it up.'

'I won't.'

Sara could see that PC Sean O'Riordan was a good man, and his analysis of the murder scene had been spot on. If he wanted, she would see if he could transfer over to her team.

The DI donned a similar outfit to the crime scene examiner and re-entered the murder scene. PC O'Riordan intended to remain at the scene as well. A murder investigation excited him, even if the sight of the blood had not.

***

It had been forty-eight hours since Gregory Chalmers had been murdered.

CSE Crosley had filed a preliminary report: verbally at the crime scene, in writing later that night. The full report would be coming through within a couple of days, subject to forensics.

'Gregory Chalmers died as a result of multiple knife wounds to the chest; in his case, a Mundial carving knife, with death as a result of severe blood loss. The number 2 was carved on his chest after his death,' he had said.

'How long after?' Sara Stanforth had asked.

'Difficult to be certain, but less than five minutes. And a different knife to the one that killed him. Almost certainly the knife that was used on Stephanie Chalmers. Forensics can confirm.'

'And the third person?'

'Female, mid-twenties, blonde hair.'

'Any more you can tell me about her?'

'Not really. I am only confirming the blonde hair and that it was a female. The age is assumed due to the style of the clothing found at the scene. She used a downstairs shower and helped herself to some clothes from the wardrobe upstairs. She was probably in the house for another fifteen minutes after the crime was committed. We can ascertain that she acted calmly after the earlier violence.'

'How?'

'The shower was still wet. On getting out of the shower, she dried herself and hung the towel on a hook. She also wiped the bathroom floor. Not the actions of someone frantically attempting to leave a crime scene.'

'Anything else?'

'No sign of forced entry, so we are assuming it is the woman in the photo that we found in one of the children's bedrooms.'

'Is there a name?'

'Not on the photo, although the young boy who dialled 999 mentioned an Ingrid.'

'The photo shows a woman in her twenties,' Sara Stanforth said.

'The assumption is that the murderer and the woman in the picture are one and the same,' Crosley said.

'That's it at the present moment, an assumption?' Sara asked.

'You're the lead detective on this case. It's for you to find out.'

***

'It was her,' the heavily-bandaged woman said as she sat up in the hospital bed.

'Her?' DI Stanforth asked. She had been warned that Stephanie Chalmers was still under sedation and had nearly died on the operating table. According to the doctor, she had only just made it; a miracle, he had said, which, to Sara, were not the words that she expected to hear from a doctor. Besides, she had no time for miracles. To her, there was no such thing, only hard work and sheer dogged perseverance. She realised that she was a driven woman, and the only time that she would relax her guard was in the confines of the small apartment that she shared with her DCI, and then only when the door was closed.

'Ingrid. I trusted her with my children.' It was evident to Sara that the woman's slow speech was a result of the sedation. Apart from that, she appeared coherent.

'I need to ask some questions.'

'I want that bastard woman brought to justice. She killed Gregory.'

'Yes, I know. I need your help,' Sara said. She was not an overly sentimental woman, but she could feel a profound sadness for Stephanie Chalmers.

She had noticed the two children outside and had briefly spoken to the woman who was looking after them. Stephanie Chalmers' sister had told her that the children were as well as could be expected under the circumstances. Sara Stanforth could only agree; the first time she had seen a dead body, fished out of the River Thames, bloated and naked, its hands tied behind its back, she had been upset for weeks. And the young boy, a sensitive soul according to his aunt, had seen his father covered in blood, his mother dying.

It was remarkable that he had the clarity and the intelligence to phone the emergency services and to give an address, Sara thought.

The aunt had said that she would have expected no less, but now Billy Chalmers and his sister Emma were detached from reality. They had seen their mother, asked when she was coming home, and where was Daddy.

'Ingrid?' Sara asked the woman lying in bed.

'I took her on to help with the children.'

'Did she?'

'The children loved her. She would pick them up from school. Not every day, as sometimes I would make the time for them.'

'What else did she do?'

'She would make sure they had something to eat, as well as do their homework. I trusted her until…'

'Until?'

'Do I have to tell you this?' The doctor had come in to tell Sara that she had five minutes only, no more, as Mrs Chalmers was still critically ill and in need of rest.

'If you want us to find her, bring her to justice.'

'It was Gregory.'

'Yes.'

'He couldn't help himself.'

'Take it slowly,' Sara said.

'Gregory strayed.'

'Other women?'

'Not that I gave him any reason, but that was Gregory. Any bit of skirt, and he wanted some of the action.'

'Ingrid?'

'Not for the first three months that she's with us, and then he's using our bed.'

'With Ingrid?'

'With her.'

'Did you confront him?'

'I had become used to his behaviour, but not to him using our bed to seduce the hired help.'

'You said nothing?'

'No. I know it seems silly, but he was a good man, and I did like Ingrid. After that night, I assumed they had cooled the relationship, and I had not seen any reason to doubt for some time.'

The doctor returned. 'Two minutes, no more. I must be firm.'

'What happened at the house?' Sara asked. She still needed to know, two minutes or no two minutes.

'I entered the kitchen, and Ingrid was standing over Gregory. She was holding a knife. I shouted out to her. She came over to me, grabbing me, forcing me to the ground. She was wild and out of control. I pushed her away. After that, I do not remember.'

'Why do you think she killed your husband?'

'He probably told her that the relationship was off. They only last a few weeks with him, anyway.'

'A lover's tiff?'

'I assume it was, but Ingrid was always so placid. If I had not seen her there, I would not have believed her capable.'

Sara left soon after. A nurse came into the room and administered an additional sedative to the wife of the murdered man.

Chapter 3

'This is your case. How are you going to handle it?' Bob Marshall asked. He was sucking a mint, careful not to let Sara know that he still enjoyed the occasional cigarette. There'd be hell to pay if she knew, he knew that, and for two months he had gone cold turkey, but the occasional drag, he thought, would do no harm.

In the office, Bob was always demanding of Sara. Everyone knew they were living together, and it had led him to receive a warning from Detective Superintendent Rowsome about fraternising in the office.

Not that it was any of his business, Bob had even told him, but the superintendent was a pedantic man who worried obsessively about the Key Performance Indicators in his department.

'Look here, DCI, you can sleep with whoever you like, but stuff up and you know what happens,' Rowsome had said. 'Just make sure it doesn't impact on the efficiency of your department.'

Bob Marshall, keenly aware of his senior's concerns, and also conscious of the other members of his department, kept the pressure up on Sara. Not that he had any concerns, as she had proven herself to be competent; she had even acquired begrudging respect from DI Greenstreet, a curmudgeonly old-school police officer. He did not hold with the modern ideas on policing with their emphasis on graphs and charts and performance indicators. In his day, the police dealt with the criminals using a kick up the arse and a slap around the head.

Nowadays, they had to read them their rights, accord them respect, and then lock them up in prison, three meals a day, and the luxury of a three-star hotel. He knew what Sara Stanforth represented the moment she joined the department: political correctness, policing by the book, female equality.

Still, he had to concede that she had done well dealing with a serial rapist in the area; even arrested him on her own and brought him to the police station in handcuffs.

Not many men would have stood up to him, he had thought at the time. Even Keith Greenstreet had to admit she was a good police officer, although, to him, her relationship with their DCI was something else. The sideways glances in the office, the passing too close to each other, the occasional whisper in each other's ear. Greenstreet knew what they were talking about, even if it was a long time since he had experienced any of it.

'Find Ingrid Bentham,' Sara replied to Bob's earlier question.

'Do you need any help?' Bob Marshall asked.

'DI Greenstreet, if he's willing. Also, the police constable at the Chalmers' house, Sean O'Riordan. I know he is keen to get into plain clothes. He was there at the scene; he's a smart man to have with the team.'

'Okay with you, Keith?' Bob looked over at Greenstreet.
'Fine by me.'
'Thank you, sir,' Sara said. 'Thank you, DI.'

'Don't go wasting my time,' Keith Greenstreet replied. He was approaching sixty, not in the best of health: high blood pressure, an irregular heartbeat, and carrying twenty pounds more weight than was healthy. His temperament in the office varied from morose to cheerful and back to morose; it spent more time at morose. He was not sure why Sara Stanforth had chosen him, and besides, he was the more senior of the two officers. He knew that he should be leading the investigation, but then he reasoned, DI Stanforth had something that he did not: a tight arse and the bedroom ear of Bob Marshall.

***

Police Constable O'Riordan arrived in the office at the police station later in the day. He had thanked Sara earlier when she had phoned to offer him a position in Homicide.

No longer expected to wear the regulation police uniform, he arrived in the office dressed in a dark blue suit.

Keith Greenstreet shook his hand limply. *Another young upstart,* he thought.

Sara had set up a crime board close to her desk; she was excited, and it looked like being a long night ahead. She had phoned the hospital. Stephanie Chalmers was recovering but suffering from delayed shock. Her house was still a crime scene, and on release from the hospital, she would go and stay with her sister.

'What's the plan, guv?' Sean O'Riordan asked Sara. He had found himself a desk in the far corner, as well as a police-issue laptop.

'Find Ingrid Bentham.'

'Easier said than done. She will have scarpered by now,' Greenstreet said.

Ignoring Keith Greenstreet's negativity, Sara focussed on the facts.

'We have an address for Ingrid Bentham, although she is not there.'

'What did you expect? That she would be at home waiting for you with a cup of tea.'

Sara knew why she had brought Keith Greenstreet on board. His experience would compensate for Sean O'Riordan's youthful enthusiasm, even hers. She knew that he did not respect her, other than begrudgingly, but when it was needed, it would be him who would find the woman.

'What do you want me to do?' Sean asked.

'What did you find out about Ingrid Bentham?'

'Twenty-four, blonde, spoke with a northern accent.'

'Northern is a bit vague,' Keith said.

'It's the best we've got.'

'If the woman has disappeared, she will probably head back home to the nest. You need to be more specific.'

'Do we have a recording of her voice?' Sara asked.

'Not sure,' Sean said.

'Well, then you'd better find one. Run it past someone who knows about regional accents,' Keith said.

'Keith's right. Can I trust you to deal with this?' Sara asked.

'Leave it to me,' the constable responded with his usual youthful enthusiasm.

Sara realised that this case was different. Usually, a murder would not give a definite murderer, only suspects, but in this instance there was a known killer: fingerprints and foot marks at the scene, and enough DNA to prove a case. However, the murderer had disappeared.

Stephanie Chalmers had provided an address for Ingrid Bentham. Two officers from the department had visited the address after Sara had phoned them, only to find that the woman was not there, although her flatmate was.

Sara and Sean O'Riordan visited later after their meeting at the police station had concluded.

Her flatmate confirmed that Ingrid was a quiet, pleasant young woman, friendly at the college she attended, liked by all that knew her, no boyfriends. The two women had met at college and had decided to pool their resources and to rent a small two-bedroom apartment. Apart from that, they had not socialised, other than the occasional Friday night at a local pub, where both had drunk too much on a couple of occasions.

'What else can you tell us?' Sara asked Gloria, the flatmate.

'Not much. Ingrid did not speak about her family or her childhood. I told her my life story: how I came here from Nigeria as a child, everything there was to tell. I talk too much sometimes, but with Ingrid, nothing.' Gloria spoke pure London, even though she had been born in Africa.

'Did she phone anyone?'

'Not to my knowledge. She had a mobile, but she did not use it much. She had a laptop.'

'Is it here?'

'Nothing is here; not even last week's contribution for the rent. She even took a bottle of wine that belonged to me.'

'Clothing, personal belongings?' Sara asked.

'She took all hers as well as some of mine.'

Sara had asked Crosley and his crime investigators to check the flat. The fingerprints and the DNA found at the apartment matched the crime scene at the Chalmers' house.

On leaving the flat, Sara phoned Keith Greenstreet. 'Can you follow up on Ingrid Bentham's movements after she left the flat: buses, railway stations, taxis, the normal?' Sara asked.

'Leave it with me,' he said. Even though it was late in the evening, he put on his coat as protection against the inclement weather and ambled out of the office.

'Thanks,' Sara said.

'Don't thank me now. Friday night, you owe me a pint.'

'If DI Greenstreet can work late at night, then so can I,' Sean said.

'Where are you going?'

'Back to the Chalmers' house. There may be some recordings of Ingrid Bentham's voice. It's a long shot, but it's worth a try.'

'Let me know how you go,' Sara said.

'What about you, guv?'

'Paperwork for now, and then I need to talk to Crosley.'

'The crime scene examiner?'

'Yes. See what else he can tell us,' Sara said.

***

Sara left the office late, way past midnight. Bob Marshall had waited for her.

'You're on your own on this one,' he said as they left the office. 'I'll need to ride you hard, and I can't protect you.'

'I know, Bob,' she said. It was strange: in the office, he was officious and demanding, but outside, and in the bedroom, he was caring and considerate. That was what she loved about him: his devotion to work and fair play, his ability to separate work from home. Sara knew that she had not attained that ease yet; not sure if she ever would. She would go to sleep and dream of the murder of Gregory Chalmers, the attempted murder of Stephanie. She knew that she would wake up during the night and start writing notes, surfing the internet looking for insights into the mindset of someone, in this case, female, who could murder with extreme violence, then detach herself mentally, take a shower, clean herself up, go home, pack and leave.

To her, Ingrid Bentham would need to be a callous, cruel-hearted woman, but according to Stephanie Chalmers, the children had loved her, and for a short while so had Gregory Chalmers. The children's love had been unconditional, the love of a child for an equal, whereas the husband's love had been carnal.

Sara had seen the photos of Ingrid. She was a beautiful woman, slim but not skinny. Her complexion was very pale; that may have been the photo's exposure, although more likely indicative of a woman from the north of England; her Viking heritage showing through. Sara imagined that if the woman stayed in the sun for too long, she would burn, not go brown.

Sara, objectively taking Gregory Chalmers' point of view, could see the attraction to a man in his forties, feeling for the first time the lessening of passion in his loins, the need to bed someone as fresh and sensual as Ingrid. According to her flatmate, Ingrid had been with no other man, yet she was the sort of woman that men would have lusted over.

In an age where sexual equality was taken for granted, it was strange that Ingrid Bentham remained the wallflower when all around were engaging in musical beds. That had been her life too, Sara reflected, until she had met Bob. Now, all she wanted him to do was to propose and put a ring on her finger.

Chapter 4

Sean O'Riordan arrived at the Chalmers' house at ten in the evening. A uniform stood outside. As he had driven up the road, he could see the uniform relaxing: the night was cold, and the policeman at the door was struggling to stay focussed. Crime scene tape had been placed across the front door to the house. Sean showed his badge, ensured to put on foot protectors and gloves.

The kitchen was clearly off limits, and besides, it was not the place to find a recording. The sitting room appeared to offer no possibility. There were several DVDs, but they were commercial, mainly children's cartoons and films. He was looking for something with a hand-written label. The house was still officially on lockdown as a crime scene, and Sean was aware that blundering around was not advisable. He made his way upstairs. The first bedroom was obviously the parent's room where the Chalmers had slept, and the husband had first seduced Ingrid. The next bedroom was not used, other than as a hobbies room.

The third bedroom, belonging to Billy, judging by the computer and the plane models, offered more of a prospect. It was clear that the young child was well-organised. His school books and DVDs were all lined up and in their place. Sean thought it offered the best chance of finding what he wanted.

He stood back and scanned the room, reluctant to move anything other than was necessary. He took a few photos before he touched anything. At the end of the row of DVDs, six in total, he saw one labelled 'birthday party'. The label had been printed, probably by the printer next to the computer.

He removed the DVD, placed it in a plastic bag, identified it, took a photo of where he had taken it from. The girl's room he checked on the way out of the house. He then returned to the office. He knew that his girlfriend would be fast asleep by the time he got back home in the early hours of the morning, and was aware that she would not object if he woke her up on his arrival.

Back in the office, Sean took a copy of the disk and placed it in his laptop, the screen lighting up after a few seconds with a group singing an out-of-tune rendition of 'Happy Birthday.'

There were two children and one adult; the one adult they wanted to hear.

'Billy, it's your birthday. You get to cut the cake,' Ingrid said.

Sean texted Sara, knowing that she would want to know immediately.

'Great. Six in the morning in the office. We'll need to find an expert on regional accents,' Sara replied.

She had been wide awake when the SMS had come through, going over her notes, evaluating the case, and what to do next. Bob was lying next to her; he was fast asleep. She had not heard from Keith. She called him.

'Still up,' he said.

'The same as you.'

'I've been staking out Ingrid Bentham's flat. Her flatmate has only just arrived home, drunk by the look of it. I was just about to knock on her door. Give me thirty minutes, and I'll message.'

'Thanks. Six in the morning. Okay by you?'

'I may as well not go home,' he said sarcastically, but Sara knew it was only his dry humour.

Keith gave the flatmate fifteen minutes before he knocked on the door. She had brought company home; a male voice bellowed for her not to answer the door, and to get back in the bed.

The door to the flat opened. 'Detective Inspector Greenstreet. I have a few questions.'

'It's late?' the drunk woman slurred back at him. She was naked.

'It's a murder enquiry. It's not a nine to five, sociable hours' investigation. You spoke to Detective Inspector Stanforth before.' Keith knew he was verging on harassment, but he was determined to get a result.

'I've told her all I know. Go away. I have a man here, and he's more attractive than you.'

Keith Greenstreet, not an attractive man, he knew, had been insulted enough times over the years, even shot at on a couple of occasions. The last time put him in the hospital for three weeks, while he recuperated after they had removed the bullet from his spleen.

'That may be, but he will have to wait.' Keith wedged his shoe in the door as she attempted to close it.

'If you're not going away?'

'I'm not. Tell your boyfriend to get some rest, build up his energy.'

Keith entered the apartment. It was evident that housekeeping was not Gloria's forte. The place was a mess, with clothes strewn everywhere. The kitchen sink was stacked high with dirty plates and cutlery.

'I'd better put on some clothes,' Gloria said.

'Suit yourself. I've seen enough naked women in my time.'

Gloria returned two minutes later, an oversized tee-shirt barely covering her modesty. She still wore no underwear.

'What do you want to know?'

'We need to find Ingrid Bentham.'

'Don't look at me. The bitch has left me with her share of the rent to pay, and now I need to find another flatmate.'

'How about him in the next room?'

'Him! Are you joking? He's just an idle screw. Apart from his dick, he's not much use.'

'Have you known him long?'

'Three hours. Long enough for you?'

'It's hardly the basis for a lasting relationship, is it?' Keith said.

'I don't need lasting relationships, just a man when I need one.'

'And Ingrid?'

'She never brought a man here. I asked her why not.'

'What did she say?'

'She said that she'd had enough of men, and did not need them.'

'Lesbian?'

'Not at all. I was lonely one night, made a play for her. She was angry, did not speak to me for several days.'

'Any medication?'

'Ingrid? Every day, although I don't know what it was.'

'Did you ask?'

'As long as she paid the rent, and she didn't screw the men I brought round here, what did I care?'

It was evident to Keith that Gloria, was at best an unreliable witness; at worst, a slut who screwed men as it suited her. Keith imagined that if he asked around the area, he would find out that Gloria was not as well respected as Ingrid, except in the opinions of the local studs.

The plaything for the night could be heard snoring loudly in the other room. 'It seems as if he will be no use tonight,' Keith said.

'Him? Give me five minutes, and he will be,' Gloria replied.

'What else can you tell me about Ingrid?'

'Nothing. We shared a flat, that was all.'

'Clothes, jewellery. Any that you borrowed?'

'Nothing.'

'If you lie to me, and it comes up in a court of law, you could be charged with obstructing the police.'

'Well...' There was a pause.

'Yes.'

'There was this ring.'

'And?'

'I sort of borrowed it.'

'Stole or borrowed is not my concern. Do you have it?'

'Yes.'

'Where is it?'

'In my bedroom.'

'I will need it as evidence. I'll fetch it.'

The sight in Gloria's bedroom was not pleasant. The man, a strapping tattooed individual, was lying naked on his back. The smell of stale beer was overpowering. Keith found the ring in the drawer, as Gloria had described. He placed it in a plastic bag and wrote on the outside: location, time.

He left soon after, stopping only to make a phone call on his mobile. 'I have a ring that belonged to Ingrid Bentham. It's engraved on the inside.'

'Six in the morning. Great work,' Sara replied.

***

Sara regretted that she had asked her primary team to meet at six in the morning. Not that the idea was not good, it was. It was that she was not an early morning person. Some, she knew, were at their best in the morning; others, in the afternoon and through to late at night.

It was evident the next morning as to which category her new DC belonged. There Sean O'Riordan was, bright and alert, as she staggered into the office at just after six. At least Sara had to admit that she looked better than Keith Greenstreet; the man looked as though he had slept on a bench in the park, but then, he was nearly thirty years older than her.

'Foul hour of the morning,' Keith said.

'Sleep well?' Sara asked.

'What little there was.' A singularly unexciting reply.

Sean O'Riordan, newly elevated from police constable to detective constable, was anxious and biting at the bit to get started. Sara had to concede that he suited plain clothes. His first day in the office, his suit had been brand new, off the rack, and here on the second day, there was another suit, this time a lighter shade.

Must be costing him plenty, she thought. She reflected on her early days as a detective inspector. She had served her dues, five years in uniform, initially administrative. In the past Keith Greenstreet would have said it was woman's work, but now political correctness forbade such words, and he had received a reprimand behind closed doors from his DCI on more than one occasion.

Sara was not a person to dwell on the past, and her time at her first police station north of the metropolis of London had not been the most exciting period of her life. There she was, a policewoman, a career that she had always wanted, and what did she have: a dingy bedsit; a man in the room next door who drank, and then snored, and then swore in his sleep. It had not been that many years before, and the memories were fresh. There had been a boyfriend back home in Liverpool, but she wanted a future; he wanted her at home and pregnant. Not that she did not want children, she did, but on her terms, and with Bob Marshall. It had not always been that way. Before Bob Marshall, she had been career-driven, probably a workaholic, but he had brought out maternal feelings in her.

Keith Greenstreet had been a policeman longer than Sara had drawn breath; his days with the police force were rapidly coming to an end. In the office, he would talk about how much he looked forward to the day he could hand in his badge and devote himself to personal pursuits. It was a defence mechanism on Keith's part: he had no personal pursuits, other than the occasional drink, no friends, no family other than his wife. Their marriage had been childless, not because he and his wife had not wanted children, they did, but that was how it had turned out. They had tried in the early years, but when it was clear that no children were to result, their lovemaking became infrequent; no more than the passionless coupling of two sad people, not happy with each other, unable to be apart.

Sean O'Riordan saw life differently. He was in his mid-twenties, a period in anyone's life when they are full of optimism and derring-do. To him, life offered endless opportunities, and he was a person who saw the world brightly, even at six in the morning. Apart from his police duties, he was studying for a Master's degree. He already had a Bachelor's, but it would not suffice if he wanted to become a detective superintendent.

'So, what's the plan?' Keith asked.

'The ring that you recovered. What does it tell us?' Sara asked. Keith had placed it on the table; it was still in the plastic evidence bag.

'Only that it belonged to Ingrid Bentham. As I said yesterday, there is an engraving on the inside.'

'What does it say?'

'Not much, certainly not an address as to where to send it in the case of loss.'

'Apart from that.'

'"With love, M". That's all.'

'So, unless we can tie it in, it doesn't give us very much,' Sara said.

'You know it does. What did they teach you at police training college? Every little piece of information helps, even when it seems irrelevant,' Keith said. He immediately regretted the put-down of a fellow DI. He had to admit that Sara was handling their latest case with the required professionalism. He would apologise later.

Sara chose to ignore his comment. 'What have we done to find Ingrid Bentham?'

'The usual,' Keith replied. 'Description out to all police departments, watching the airports, railway and bus stations for the woman. She'll not be easy to spot.'

'Why do you say that, DI?' Sean asked.

'You've seen her picture?'

'Yes.'

'Tell me, what did you see?' Keith asked.

'An attractive blonde woman, twenty-four to twenty-six years of age, medium height, slim.'

'No distinguishing features, tattoos, scars?'

'None,' Sean replied.

'Keith's right,' Sara said. 'Statistically, Ingrid Bentham fits the norm for at least half the white females in this country; at least in that age group.'

'Apart from the hair colour,' Sean said.

'Bottle of hair colouring will sort that out soon enough,' Keith said.

'Sean, what can you tell us about the recording you recovered?' Sara asked.

'Northern accent, nothing more, but the recording is clear enough. I'll get someone to analyse it today.'

'Fine. Keith, can you concentrate on the ring. Long shot I know, but it may help. See if you can ascertain where the ring was purchased.'

'Police databases?' Keith asked.

'It's always a possibility. This woman's deranged. We need to find her soon,' Sara said.

'Why do you think that, guv?' Sean asked.

'She murders Gregory Chalmers, almost kills his wife. Then she showers, cleans herself up, dresses in some of Stephanie Chalmers' clothes and walks out of the door.'

'And then she returns to her apartment, packs her belongings and leaves,' Keith added.

'Not the act of a normal person,' Sean conceded.

'Correct. Most people, if they kill someone in anger, will panic, rush out of the door, leave clues as to where they are, but with this woman, nothing. It's as if she knew what she was doing; as if she had killed before,' Sara said.

'The number 2,' Keith said.

'It's a possibility.'

'That's more important than the ring,' Sean said.

'The ring is still important. More pieces of the puzzle,' Sara said.

Chapter 5

Behind the scenes, a full department was focussing on the death of Gregory Chalmers. People were collating information, preparing cases for the prosecution, filing the evidence, and looking for the prime suspect.

Bob Marshall had complete faith in Sara to handle the case, although his superiors were not so sure. As usual, the media were speculating, especially the more scurrilous. Apparently, they had found out about the mysterious blonde, the 'blonde in the bed' as she was referred to. Sara realised that information could have only come from the aggrieved wife, now a widow, but why?

Nobody appreciated their dirty laundry being hung out in public, and the most scurrilous rag was emblazoned with headlines alluding to the unusual arrangement in the Chalmers' household, speculating as to whether it was a lovers' tryst, whether all three enjoyed the bed together, and if the children were safe in the house of Stephanie Chalmers.

Unfortunately, Sara realised, if you want irresponsible reporting, then the newspapers in the United Kingdom were supreme.

Stephanie Chalmers was sitting up in bed when Sara entered her room at the hospital. 'Are you better?' Sara asked, realising that it was not the most appropriate question considering that her husband had just been murdered. Still, the woman had smiled when she arrived. Around the room, there was a collection of 'get well soon' cards, and someone had sent flowers.

'Fine, although I'm probably doped up on drugs,' Stephanie said.

'I was here the other day.'

'I remember. Detective Inspector Stanforth, isn't it?'

'Sara Stanforth, as you say. Are you able to answer any more questions?'

'I don't want to remember, but I suppose I must.'

'Tell me about your relationship with your husband.'

'Gregory was a good man, a good father, but…'

'Why the hesitancy?'

'He couldn't help himself.'

'Women?'

'Not often, but every month or so there would be the signs. The late nights, the smell of perfume, the dash for a quick shower to wash off the evidence – a woman knows.'

Stephanie Chalmers held a handkerchief to her eyes and wiped away the tears. Sara could see that she had been fond of the man, even if his behaviour on occasions had been unforgivable.

'And you accepted it?'

'Reluctantly. More for the children than for me, but yes, I accepted it.'

'Ingrid Bentham?'

'That was different. I knew he had been sleeping with her, at least that one time. I had assumed that the affair was over. I thought to get rid of her, but the children adored her, and she was reliable.'

'You regret that you did not get rid of her?' Sara asked.

'What do you think?'

'There have been reports in the newspaper concerning your husband's death.'

'And on the television.'

'The newspapers are speculating that you knew of your husband and Ingrid Bentham. That you encouraged the relationship.'

'Why would they say that?'

'Is any of it true?'

'No. I had learnt to accept Gregory's behaviour outside of the house, but inside the house, never. What if the children had seen the two of them? I may have my faults, but I'm still a good mother.'

Sara sat close to the window, allowing the weak sun outside to warm her back. She had not liked hospitals ever since she had spent three days in one as a child.

'We can't find Ingrid,' Sara admitted.

'I'm not surprised.'

'What did you know about her?'

'Nothing really. Only that she came from up north, and that she was studying in London.'

'Family, friends?'

'I asked once, but she said that her parents were dead. I'm not sure if it was true.'

'You had no reason to doubt her?'

'Not until she started sleeping with Gregory.'

'Do you know why she would do that?'

'Gregory was a charming man, but he was older than her. Have you seen pictures of Ingrid?' Stephanie Chalmers asked.

'Yes.'

'She was a beautiful young woman. What would she want with an older man? We may be financially secure, but we are hardly rich, and besides, I was not going to let him go.'

'We found a ring, a gold ring. Did you ever see her wearing a ring?'

'I remember it. I asked her once about it.'

'What was her reply?'

'She said it was from her mother. It was the only time she spoke about her.'

'Her father?'

'Nothing. She would always walk away if her parents were mentioned. I don't know what the secret was, but on reflection there was always something dark about her.'

'What do you mean?'

'Hindsight. Most people are easy to read. You can tell from how they move, how they talk, whether they are educated or not, gregarious or introvert, willing to chat or more silent. With Ingrid, I was never sure. Almost as if she had an impenetrable veil in front of her.'

It became clear that Stephanie Chalmers was starting to fall asleep, and her children were waiting patiently outside with their aunt. Sara left them alone and went to see the hospital administration. In her sedated condition, the widowed woman could have mumbled something; something that one of the hospital staff could have sold to the newspapers.

***

Keith had remained in the office. His skills with a computer were limited, but he persevered. One of the things he intended to conquer once he retired. He knew that retirement meant another milestone in his life, and there was only one more after that: a quiet spot in the cemetery with a headstone, the only remembrance that he had ever existed. It was not as if anyone would be coming to place flowers on his resting place. As miserable as he appeared in the office, he knew that it was the one place where he felt at peace; the one place where he could feel content.

An engraved ring presented problems. It was not the easiest item to trace, and apart from the engraving on the inside, there was nothing more, certainly no indication as to who had manufactured it, and where it had been engraved.

The police database was comprehensive. If someone had spent time in prison, for instance, he should be able to check their personal possessions on the date of imprisonment, although there was no indication that Ingrid Bentham had spent time inside.

On the contrary, the woman gave every impression of being an average woman, friendly and attractive, except for one undeniable fact: she was a vicious murderer. But why?

Keith Greenstreet had encountered a few murderers over the years, arrested a few. With them, it had been easy. Virtually all had shown aggressive tendencies, or else they were in an abusive relationship, or they had a long history of criminal activity, but with Ingrid Bentham, nothing.

The woman did not fit the mould, yet her slaying of Gregory Chalmers and the attempted murder of Stephanie Chalmers indicated a savagery he had not seen before. And then, the woman calmly walks out of the door. It was as if she was two people. Keith could see severe psychological tendencies in Ingrid Bentham.

Keith realised that a criminal psychologist would be a good person for the team to contact. He would let Sara know on her return.

As much as he wanted to dislike his senior, at least in this case, he could not. Sure, she could be overbearing, pushy sometimes, but she was a good police officer, determined in her pursuit of justice. He would put aside his prejudices, outdated he knew, and give her all the assistance she required. He would also apologise for his earlier outburst when he inferred that she was not trained well enough to conduct the investigation.

***

Sean, eager and keen, had found a speech analyst; in fact, a person who trained actors in how to speak regional and foreign accents. The man was on the books, approved by the police for their use.

Sean made an appointment for one o'clock in the afternoon. He decided on an early lunch, and then he would take the train up to the centre of London; no point in taking a car, as the traffic was horrendous and parking was a nightmare, even with a police pass.

Anton Schmidt – an unusual name for an expert in the English language – opened the door to his office in Mayfair.

'My father was German, but I was born in England, not far from here. A true Cockney. My mother said that I was born within earshot of the bells of St Mary-le-Bow, but I'm not sure if it's true,' Schmidt said.

'I have a video recording of a birthday party. A woman is speaking. I need to know where she is from,' Sean said.

'Fine, let me see it.'

Sean put his laptop on Anton Schmidt's desk and pressed the play button once the recording was ready. Ingrid Bentham's face was clearly visible.

'That is the woman in question?' Anton Schmidt asked. 'She is very attractive.'

'And deadly.'

'The woman in the newspapers?'

'Yes.'

'Nasty business. Let me watch it for a few minutes, and then I can give you my considered opinion.'

Sean moved out of the office and left Schmidt with the recording. He took the opportunity to purchase coffee from a café below the office. He returned after ten minutes.

'Northern,' Schmidt said.

'Anything more specific?'

'Originally from the Newcastle area.'

'Age when she left?'

'Newcastle, up to her late teens.'

'And then?'

'Hard to say. There are indications of London idioms, but they are formed relatively quickly. She has probably been in London for some time, but the original accent remains noticeable. Most people's accents are formed in their youth. It's unlikely to stay hidden, no matter how hard they try to conceal it; at least, not to me.'

***

After the first couple of days, progress slowed. Sara and her team now had a clear idea as to where the woman had come from, although no firm information as to who she was. Ingrid Bentham was the name she had been using, but there were no bank accounts in that name, at least none that had any money in them, and the only address they had was the flat she had shared with Gloria. The Chalmers always paid Ingrid in cash, and there was no record with HM Revenue & Customs that any tax had ever been paid.

When questioned, Stephanie Chalmers had said that was what Ingrid wanted. It was a minor point, and the murder investigation team were interested in solving the murder of Gregory Chalmers, not indulging in a tax investigation. The ring, so far, had drawn a blank, other than the assumption that it could have been from the mother, but an uppercase 'M' did not seem conclusive.

Bob Marshall, as the DCI in charge of the team, was feeling the heat. It was on record that he and his lead detective in the murder investigation were involved in a personal relationship. Detective Superintendent Rowsome was being questioned by his superiors as to whether this would impact on the effectiveness of the investigation. He had allayed their concerns with a ringing endorsement of his DCI. He knew he had lied. As far as he was concerned, Bob Marshall was after his job, and he did not intend to let him have it. Rowsome knew that he had climbed the promotion ladder as far as he could. There were still another ten years before retirement, and he was hanging on for dear life.

'I've gone out on a limb for you,' Rowsome said in his phone call to Bob Marshall, two minutes after receiving a grilling from his seniors.

'The investigation is going well,' Bob Marshall said. It was not entirely correct, and he half-expected Rowsome to fire back at him.

'Not from where I'm sitting,' Rowsome said before hanging up his phone.

Bob Marshall knew that his decision to appoint Sara as the lead instead of Keith Greenstreet was sound, but defending that decision was not so easy. Unless there was a result within the week, he would need to consider replacing Sara. He knew what her reaction would be. He hoped it would not affect their relationship, but if he had to do it, he would.

Sara, increasingly frustrated, wondered what they could do. Each day they met and discussed what to do next. Each day they went over the evidence so far, but there was precious little.

There was no shortage of fingerprints, no question as to the murderer and no stone had been left unturned, but Ingrid Bentham had disappeared. They had traced the name back, only to find that it had come into existence four years earlier. That aligned with Anton Schmidt's analysis of the woman's accent. A check of births in the UK had revealed no Ingrid Bentham, other than a woman in her seventies.

It was clear that Ingrid Bentham was not the woman's birth name, but what was it? Keith had considered travelling up to Newcastle, utilising some of the contacts he had made over the years in other parts of the country.

Sara believed it to be a good idea, only to have it rejected due to budgetary constraints.

'Sorry, but that's how it is,' Bob Marshall had said in the office that day. Sara knew that he had refused not out of any concern over the budget, but because he thought it would be a wasted trip. He received a cold shoulder that night in the bed they shared.

Sara knew that he was under pressure to rein in costs, and under pressure to remove her from her position, but he had no right to place restrictions on her. She was angry and rightly so.

'Don't worry about it,' Keith said when told of Bob not approving his trip.

'We need a breakthrough,' Sara said, not mentioning the cold shoulder and the cold bed to Keith.

Sean had visited Gloria on Keith's suggestion. Keith had felt that a young man would have more success in finding out information than he had. Sean had knocked on the door, introduced himself, asked a few questions, and then made a quick retreat as the overly-amorous Gloria had come on to him.

Next time, the two men agreed, Sara could accompany them.

'I still reckon the number carved on Chalmers' chest is significant,' Keith said.

'We have checked,' Sara said. 'There is no record of another body with the number 1.'

'Maybe she only intended to kill one person, so there was no need for a number. With the second one, it reminded her of the first, and she decided to keep a count.'

'Keeping score?' Sean asked.

'Why not?' Keith said. 'What is the state of this woman's mind? She's clearly unhinged.'

'She's still smart enough to disappear.'

'Maybe she's done it before.'

'What do you mean?'

Keith leant back in his chair; not a pretty sight, Sara thought, but did not intend to mention it. She valued her DI's experience, even his dry humour, and the man had been big enough to apologise to her for his earlier behaviour.

'She wouldn't be the first murderer who acted and looked normal,' Keith said.

'We know that, but what are you suggesting?' Sara asked.

'She's clearly psychotic. We need an expert to analyse her behaviour.'

Sara consulted Bob; he approved the cost.

Chapter 6

Grace Nelson seemed too young to be a criminal psychologist. At least she did to Keith, although Sara had checked and found her to be in her early forties. The police database showed that she was highly qualified and able to give evidence at a trial.

Keith had to admit she had enough initials after her name. He had none, apart from two General Certificates of Education, one for geography, the other for religious studies, but as he had not travelled far, other than to France and Spain, and he professed to no strong religious views, they both seemed irrelevant. They had, however, allowed him to join the police force as a junior constable.

From there on, it had been hard work that had allowed him to rise to the rank of detective inspector.

'I've studied the case,' Grace Nelson said. Sean thought her accent was from the west of the country. He had been reading a book on the subject, but he knew he could be wrong. Regardless, she was remarkably well educated.

Sara, an ambitious woman, envied Grace her education, but the idea of sitting down to study was anathema to her. She had managed to secure a BSc in Policing and Criminal Investigation, but it had been hard-won.

So much so that she had crammed the last six months, and had completed the degree in under three years. Bob Marshall was working on a Master's, and often when she was fast asleep, or in need of attention, he would be slavishly sweating over his studies. She knew that DCI would be the limit of her career. It was not because she did not want more, but she had come to realise that a Master's degree was beyond her, and besides, she had decided that she wanted a child, Bob's child, in the next couple of years. Her biological clock was ticking, and it was winding down.

'What are your thoughts?' Sara asked Grace Nelson.

'Carving a number with a knife indicates a logical mind.'

'Sane?' Keith asked.

'Unlikely,' the psychologist replied.

'It may be best if we let Dr Nelson present first,' Sara said.

'My apologies,' Keith said.

'Paranoid schizophrenia would be my preliminary diagnosis. Ingrid Bentham displays some of the behavioural traits. Of course, my analysis is incomplete. Without seeing the woman, it is hard to be precise. Was she on medication? Have you managed to ascertain that?'

'She was on medication, but we don't know what it was.'

'It's important.'

'There's only one person who would know.' Keith looked over at Sean.

'Okay, I'll go with Sean and hold his hand,' Sara said. Her mood had improved with the psychologist in the office.

'You mentioned medication,' Sean said.

'There are some antipsychotic drugs: Chlorpromazine, Thorazine, Loxapine, Fluphenazine are just a few. There may be more than one drug, and they would need to be taken on a regular basis. The patient would need to be checked every few months, in case of issues.'

'And if the medicine is not taken on a regular basis?' Keith asked.

'Hallucinations, delusions, anxiety, anger, suicidal thoughts, obsession with death and violence, plus a few more.'

'Are you saying that Ingrid Bentham fits the profile?' Sara asked.

'I am raising the possibility. Without a close and detailed examination of the person, I can't be sure.'

'What causes paranoid schizophrenia?' Sean asked. He knew he would be reading up on the subject that night.

'Yet again,' Grace Nelson said, 'there are a number of possibilities: family history, stress, problems during the mother's pregnancy, sexual or physical abuse. There are more, but until you have the woman, my analysis remains speculative.'

***

'Come on in,' Gloria said in a friendly voice upon seeing Sean in her doorway. She was dressed provocatively, almost as if she had been expecting him. 'It's great to see you,' she said. The tone of her voice changed when Sara poked her head round the door.

'Detective Inspector Sara Stanforth. We have a few questions for you.'

Reluctantly, the door was opened, and the two police officers entered. It was clear that Gloria had been entertaining, a few empty wine bottles testament to the fact.

'What do you want? It's my weekend. Don't you ever take a rest?'

'Not when someone has been murdered,' Sara said as she looked around the room. She could not claim to be the world's greatest housekeeper, but compared to Gloria, she was fastidious.

It was evident to Sara that Gloria was high on something, and it was more than alcohol. Sara could see that the woman was a vulture when men were around. She understood why Sean had been reluctant to approach the woman again without a chaperone.

'Maybe, but what do you want from me?' Gloria said. 'I haven't seen Ingrid since she walked out. I told him that.' She looked over at Sean. He was not sure whether it was the look of anger or of disappointment. Although he knew what he felt: relief.

'Ingrid was on medication. Is that correct?' Sara asked.

'I told the old man that.'

'Detective Inspector Greenstreet,' Sara corrected her.

'Yes, him.'

'Do you have any of that medication here?'

'She took it all when she left.'

'Are you sure? You lied about the ring.'

'The ring would have covered her rent money.'

'Gloria, we need the name of the medicine.'

'Something "zine"; that's all I know.'

'And the name of the patient?'

'Ingrid Bentham, who else?'

'Did you see the name? It's important.'

'Not really. As I told the old man, sorry, Detective Inspector Greenstreet, I was not interested. Ingrid paid her rent, and we got on well enough. Apart from that, she left me alone, I left her alone. Satisfied?'

'Not yet,' Sara said. 'Do you have a man in the other room?'

'What if I do? None of your business.'

'As you say, none of my business, but if you want to get back in there with him, you'd better answer our questions, or we'll take you down to the police station.'

'You can't do that. I've committed no crime,' Gloria shrieked. A man's head appeared at the bedroom door.

Sean flashed his badge. 'Police.' The head retreated back inside the bedroom.

'Okay. The name was scratched off. I don't know where she got it from, or what it was. I never asked, and she never told me.'

'Did she take it every day?'

'How would I know? She was a good flatmate, nothing more. Some of the others have wanted to take my men, but with Ingrid I was safe. Not that she couldn't have if she wanted; she was beautiful, I'm not. Just an easy lay, that's me.'

'And the medicine's name?'

'Only what I told you.'

***

'Not so easy to obtain high-potency prescription drugs,' Keith said back in the office. He had stayed back, pleased that he had not been asked to accompany Sara to meet Ingrid Bentham's flatmate.

Not that interviewing the promiscuous Gloria was a problem, but she had reminded him of certain unassailable facts: he was getting old and he was not an attractive man. It had not worried him when he had been younger; unattractiveness had a particular lure for certain women, especially his wife. Back then, he had been young and fit, even played rugby for the local police station every weekend; just friendlies with the other stations in the area. Always good fun, always a few too many beers afterwards.

But he was no longer young or fit, and now his age had committed him to a life of celibacy; not that he minded, but… the mind was still young, even if the body was not.

The sight of the naked Gloria had caused a twitching in his loins, although he didn't fancy her. He had to admit that it was probably drunken men who found her attractive; sober, they would have looked the other way. Still, even she had tempted, and then the great put-down: old and ugly.

Sara, as always eager to push on, held court in the office. A team player, she had brought a pizza back with her. Keith was pleased at the gesture. He had worked with some miserable sods during his career, and he had to admit that working with Sara was alright.

'Where can you obtain these drugs?' Sara asked.

'Black market,' Keith's reply. 'And then some of those who obtain them legitimately sell them to make extra money.'

'Assuming that the drugs in the bathroom were antipsychotics, she may have had a prescription,' Sean said.

'If she did, then under what name, and what were the drugs?' Keith said.

'We've checked for an Ingrid Bentham. There are no prescriptions against that name,' Sara said.

'Her flatmate said that the name on the labels had been scratched off, anyway,' Keith added.

'She's hardly a reliable witness,' Sean said, ever eager to add his input. Keith Greenstreet intimidated him: the experienced DI and the wet-behind-the-ears detective constable.

'As you say, hardly reliable,' Sara conceded.

'Did she make a play for you?' Keith asked dryly. 'Was she prancing around with no underwear again?' He knew he was winding up the young constable, aware that Sara appreciated the humour.

'Apparently that is reserved for you, DI,' Sean responded. He knew he was being baited, and he had no intention of biting.

'Okay, boys. We've got a case to solve, and the DCI wants a result,' Sara said.

The drugs, assumed to be Chlorpromazine or possibly Clozapine, although not confirmed, were, according to Grace Nelson, dopamine blockers, with known side effects. Long-term use, which seemed possible with Ingrid Bentham, could cause nausea, vomiting, blurred vision and some other complaints, and Clozapine required regular blood checks.

'According to Grace Nelson,' Sara said, 'the drugs prescribed and their dosage are regularly evaluated. If Ingrid Bentham has slipped off the radar, no longer taking the right dosage, then she could be volatile, subject to change in her mental stability.'

'Likely to kill again,' Sean said.

'She's hardly likely to be taking them now,' Keith said.

'There's no way that we would know.'

'She's killed once, another murder may not concern her.'

'Twice, if the carving on Chalmers was correct.'

'As you say, Keith, her second murder. Any ideas on how to find out?' Sara asked.

'Newcastle. I have a contact there. I've already phoned him on a couple of occasions, but a personal visit always works best.'

'I'll work on the DCI,' Sara said.

Keith smiled back at her but said nothing. What he wanted to say would have broken every rule in the book of political correctness. He was certain she would get permission.

***

'If it's vital,' Bob Marshall said. As usual everyone, including Sean and Keith, was in the office late. It was past nine, and Sara needed two more hours before she had completed all the paperwork. The one unfortunate aspect of policing was the need for reporting. It wasn't that she was not good at it, as she was, but there was a murder enquiry, and sitting in the office filling in reports for senior management to survey briefly, and then file in the box of disinterest, did not excite her.

However, a deranged woman interested them more than usual. It was not the first time that a psychotic individual had been on the loose, and each time it raised interest in the media. Their interest ebbed and flowed depending on local and international events – a terrorist attack in the Middle East, an election somewhere else – but the death of Gregory Chalmers continued to appear on the internet and the television news programmes.

Bob had been asked to bring in additional help, but he was still holding firm against a recommendation from Detective Superintendent Rowsome to do it now.

'On your head,' he had said. 'I've made my recommendation. If this goes pear-shaped, then it will protect me. If you don't follow through, don't blame me if you find yourself back on the street in uniform.'

Bob Marshall recognised the threat. He had had little respect for Rowsome before; now, he had none. As far as he was concerned, Sara was doing fine, even Keith Greenstreet had admitted that to him, and he was not a man known for his benevolence to a fellow police officer.

The detective chief inspector had argued the case with his detective superintendent, put him off for the present, but he could only afford to give Sara another week at most. Then, girlfriend or not, he was going to have to pull her off the case, or at least, out of the senior officer's chair. He considered Keith Greenstreet, but he was slowing down. It would have to be someone from another station. If Sara wanted Keith up north, then she would have his permission.

'You've got your permission,' Sara said. Keith was wrapping up for the evening; more likely falling asleep in his chair.

'Don't expect me in the office tomorrow,' he said. 'Surprised he gave in so quickly.'

'DCI Marshall is under pressure for us to give him a result,' Sara said.

'Is that it?' A grin spread across Keith Greenstreet's face.

'Keith, wash your mouth out.'

'Late night bit of fun, that's all.'

'I'll forgive you if you come back with a result. What's the plan?'

'Check with a DI there, my age.'

'Retirement age, is that it?' Sara touched on a sensitive subject. He had had some humour at her expense; she was only returning it.

He did not like being reminded of the subject but accepted her comment gracefully. 'Put out to pasture, more like.'

Sean walked out with Keith. He still had another two hours' study at home, part of the requirements for his Master's degree. He was not being put out to pasture; he was only on the first rung of the promotion ladder. He had charted his course: DI in four years, DCI in six. After that, armed with a Master's degree and the experience in Homicide, he knew he could make detective chief superintendent within ten.

Ambitious he realised, but he was determined, and failure was not part of his vocabulary.

Apart from the studying at home, his girlfriend was always supportive, but becoming tired of the lack of attention she was threatening to move out. Sean thought she wouldn't, hoped she wouldn't, but sacrifices had to be made. She wanted marriage, children, and a house in the suburbs, and that needed money, especially the house, as house prices in London were going through the roof. He could barely manage the payments on a two-bedroom apartment, and it was nothing special. Even a DI could not afford the house she wanted, and he only knew one way to circumvent the slow progress to senior management, and that was hard work, lots of it.

He knew that he was up to the challenge. He only hoped his girlfriend was as well.

Sara stayed for another hour, as did Bob. With no one else in the office, their approach to each other was less formal. Once, when everyone else had gone home, they had made love in his office.

Sara was feeling the tension of the case, as was Bob, and both realised there was every possibility of a zero result.

History of previous cases had shown that paranoid schizophrenics were unpredictable, especially if they were killers. Sometimes, for no explicable reason, they would snap, commit murder, calm down, and then regain their position in society. Nor did they fit the characteristic criminal mould. They could be council workers, lawyers, professionals, even police officers, although that seemed unlikely given the rigorous scrutiny that the police went through on joining and during their career.

Chapter 7

Keith met Detective Inspector Rory Hewitt in Newcastle as planned. They had worked together on a few cases in the past, and each regarded the other as a friend.

'Good to see you, Keith. Nasty business,' Hewitt said. He was a few years younger, but closing in on retirement, the same as Keith, although he relished the prospect. An ardent golfer, he intended to try out the best courses around the world, courtesy of a substantial bequest from a favourite aunt on her passing.

'Not the first time, is it?' Keith said. It had been a hard drive, rain for most of the time, and he could feel the weariness in his bones. He knew deep down that retirement for him would not last for very long, whereas Rory Hewitt was still fit, even sported colour in his hair, although it was thinning. Keith assumed the colour came courtesy of a bottle. For Keith, what you are given is all that you get. He had no intention of dying his hair black or any other colour; there was not much left, and it was grey. And as for dieting and exercising, that was for others. Rory had tried to entice Keith to a game of golf once. Keith's comment at the end of the day was the same as Winston Churchill's, or was it Mark Twain, he was not sure which: 'A waste of a good walk.' Keith didn't have much time for walking either, but Rory had taken his comment with the humour intended.

'What do you need?' Rory asked.

'Ingrid Bentham, not her real name, carved the number 2 onto Chalmers' chest.'

'And you want the number 1? Long shot coming up here.'

'Maybe,' Keith said, 'but we've been around a long time. Our collective minds might find something not in the files.'

'No murders up here that fit the bill.'

'The best we have is that Ingrid Bentham had traces of a Newcastle accent. Apart from that, we have no idea who she is.'

'Then we need to review old cases,' Rory said. 'I'm free for a few days.'

***

Sara considered the case so far. They had a woman who had killed once, possibly twice, and there was the very real risk of a third time. Yet they had no idea who the woman was. Keith was trying to fill in some of the blanks, but Sara still had her concerns. Ingrid Bentham had arrived in London several years previously, and there were photos available to confirm that. The college she had attended had not provided much information, other than to say that she was an adequate student, hardworking, although she struggled at times.

Sara had seen reports like it before; to her, it was a euphemism for not being too bright. Sean had seen it differently, in that his research had shown that with the drugs she was almost certainly taking, she would have had difficulties in focussing.

Regardless of her educational record, she had certainly been astute enough to have gained the confidence of the

Chalmers, as well as employers in a few previous jobs, mainly shop work.

As far as Grace Nelson, the criminal psychologist was concerned, Ingrid was extreme, and she needed to be found at the earliest opportunity. Sean had taken up the search for the person who had purchased the ring that Ingrid Bentham had worn, hoping to find out where it had been engraved, but it seemed a pointless exercise. As keen as he was, he had to concede that the chances of success were slim.

It was almost certainly a wedding ring. The condition of the ring, according to a local jeweller, placed its date of manufacture as thirty years ago. Sean assumed that it had belonged to Ingrid's mother, which would indicate that the mother had given it to her. The engraving showed that to be possible.

Sara advised Sean to put the ring to one side and to focus on something else, but what? They were out of ideas on how to proceed. An all-points warning had been put out for the woman, but they had little faith in it producing a result. Ingrid Bentham had no distinguishing features, her face was symmetrical, her height and figure average for a woman of her age, or what they thought was her age. Her college records indicated twenty-four, although that was not certain.

Bob Marshall could see that Sara was floundering. The chief superintendent had already voiced his concerns over Sara's competency.

It wasn't out of any discrimination against women, Detective Superintendent Rowsome had insisted, but Bob Marshall could see the man shifting responsibility, leaving him to carry the can. As far as Rowsome was concerned, a person's ability was suspect until it was proven. This was Sara's first murder trial and it was not going well. She knew how it worked, as did Bob. Ten successes and everyone respects you enormously; one failure, even after the ten, and your reputation is shattered.

***

Keith and Rory reminisced over old cases they had worked on in the past. Keith had spent his working career in London, Rory predominantly in the north of the country, but villains are villains, and they are mobile.

They had first met twenty-six years earlier when a gang of drug pushers attempted to expand their operation throughout the country. Both of them had been detective sergeants then. Rory had dealt with the case in his part of the world, Keith in London. After that, they exchanged information about suspected criminals, or about crimes that appeared to have similarities. They had met up on a few policing courses since then, sharing a few pints of beer of a night time.

'What do you have?' Rory asked, after they had found an empty room near the back of the police station.

'What I've already told you. Female, mid-twenties, almost certainly a paranoid schizophrenic, and a murderer.'

'The photo doesn't tell us much, does it?'

'She could dye the hair, cut it, and she'd not be recognisable.'

'If she has, then it indicates that she is in control of her faculties.'

'And aware that she had committed a murder,' Keith said.

'Guilty conscience, or is she paranoid enough to believe it was the voice in her head, or Gregory Chalmers deserved to die?'

'Does it matter, at least to us? If she is as nutty as a fruit cake or as sane as you and me is not the issue.'

'Agreed. We have dealt with enough in either category over the years. Whatever she is, she's dangerous, but I don't see how I can help.'

'Rory, you keep records of people deemed dangerous. Assuming she has not committed a murder, would there be a record?'

'Mental Health Register, although I'm not sure if it would record a minor, assuming that she was in Newcastle. Any idea as to age?'

'Focus on female child offenders.'

Rory and Keith spent the day poring over old cases. Apart from the death of a youth in a school playground, there were no other incidences that looked possible, and besides, the school playground murderer had been a ten-year-old boy high on drugs.

'What about suspicious deaths?' Keith asked over a pint of beer that night.

'In the case of a minor, we may not have kept the records; always sensitive, dealing with children.'

'We're not dealing with a child now.'

'You're aware of the need to protect the rights of children.'

'Even when they grow up to be murderers?'

'Even then.'

***

The day had started with a whimper more than a bang at the police station in Twickenham. Sean, always wanting to be active, had found time on his hands. Sara was in her office drafting reports, attempting to portray the investigation into the death of Gregory Chalmers in a better light than was actually the case.

Bob Marshall had told her officially in the confines of his office the previous day that her time was running out, and unless she came up with something concrete, then he would need to take her off the case, find someone more experienced.

'You can't do that,' she had said.

'Unfortunately I must,' was Bob's reply. He had not wanted to say it, especially to Sara, but in the office, he was a policeman. At home, and out of hours, then he could be someone else. He regretted his actions after she had stormed out of the office, slamming the door hard.

Bob had slept on the sofa that night. He did not even receive the benefit of a goodnight kiss.

They had managed to eat breakfast together and to maintain a civil conversation before driving separately to the police station the next morning. Once in her office she finally forgave him, sorry that she had treated him so harshly when he had only been doing his job.

Keith was up in Newcastle, probably drinking more than he should, attempting to find out who the missing woman was. Sean, from what she could see, was at a loose end. Otherwise, the office was buzzing as usual.

***

Sara made two cups of coffee: one for her, the other for Bob, by way of a peace offering.

'Sorry,' she said when she placed it on his desk. She returned to her desk, planning to phone Keith. Apart from a brief call the day before, she had not heard from him. The key to the case seemed to lie in Newcastle, and Sara was anxious for news, any news, that would take them out of the current quandary. Until Ingrid Bentham made the next move, which could mean another murder, there was no way to move forward.

Sean busied himself looking into cases of known psychotic killers. Their ability to kill at random or in an orchestrated pattern could change due to unexpected factors. He had wandered over to Sara's office to discuss his findings when the phone call came through. Sara picked up the phone.

'Egerton Road,' she said to Sean. 'There's been a death.'

Sean grabbed his jacket; Sara picked up her handbag and phone. Within ten minutes, Sean driving, they had arrived at the address. They had not needed the number; they knew exactly where they were heading.

The road was blocked off, two uniforms on duty. Sara flashed her police badge. Sara and Sean parked twenty yards away from the apartment and walked the remaining distance.

'I found him,' Gloria said as soon as she saw them.

'Does he have a name?' Sara asked. For once, she felt pity for the woman. Gloria sat on the stairs leading up to the flat she had shared with Ingrid Bentham. It was a cold day, and she was not wearing a jacket. Sara removed hers and placed it around the shoulders of the distraught woman. Sara could see that she needed medical care, but first she and Sean had to check the murder scene.

'Hold on,' said a voice from behind. It was Stan Crosley. 'Overalls, gloves, shoe protectors,' he said.

'I have some in the car,' Sara said.

'Your car is down the road, and you were just about to check out the crime scene, so don't give me that nonsense.'

'Apologies.'

'Accepted, but I'm in charge now. What do we have here?'

Sara sat down next to the distraught woman. 'Gloria, what's his name?'

'Brad.'

'Does he have a surname?'

'Howard.'

'Have you known him long?'

'For a couple of years. We used to meet up occasionally. He fancied Ingrid, I know that, and look what she's done.'

A uniformed policewoman came and took care of Gloria, escorting her away from the building. Sara reminded her not to take her far, as she needed to question Gloria at the crime scene.

Stan Crosley led the way into the flat. 'It's a pigsty,' he said.

Sara could only agree. She could see that no attempt at housekeeping had been made since her last visit, the only difference being the increased height of the pile of unwashed dishes in the kitchen sink. 'How can anyone live like this?' she said.

Sean ignored the condition of the room.

'Get behind me,' Crosley said. 'I don't want your hobnail boots destroying the evidence.'

Sean could have said that they were not hobnailed, and his shoes had cost him plenty, but did not respond to Crosley.

In the small corridor separating the main room from the two bedrooms at the rear there were footprints. 'Probably the woman outside. I'll check later. She must have stepped in some blood,' Crosley said.

'She had blood on her dress,' Sara said.

'Find her something else to wear. I'll need forensics to check it out. Are you sure she's not responsible?'

'We are confident that she's not,' Sean said.

CSE Crosley entered the far bedroom. 'Whoever she is, she's a bloody savage,' he said. So far, Sara and Sean had not seen the body. 'Watch your step. You can see the blood on the floor. Keep to one side of it.'

Sara followed Crosley, almost felt as if she wanted to throw up, an acidic taste in her mouth. She looked away and regained her composure.

Sean came in and saw Brad Howard lying on his back in Ingrid's room. He was naked. In his chest there was a thin knife, its handle protruding.

'Straight in the heart,' Stan Crosley said. 'Mid-coitus.'

'What do you mean?' Sean asked.

'What I just said. A few more checks to confirm, but it seems conclusive. He was engaged in sexual intercourse when the knife was inserted.'

'Ingrid Bentham?' Sara asked.

'It looks as though it is. Fingerprints and DNA will confirm. She's a nasty one if it's her,' Crosley said.

'Nasty and malevolent. Evil.'

Sean shuddered at the thought of what had happened in that room; Sara remained impassive, surveying the scene.

'If you two are finished gawking, I've got a job to do,' Crosley said.

'We're finished.' Sean was feeling unwell. He had seen Gregory Chalmers, as well as his wife. On that occasion, he had vomited on some flowers in the back garden; this time, he would not vomit, but he needed a hot drink. The policewoman outside with Gloria had organised a flask of coffee from a café not far away. Sean took a plastic cup and helped himself to a drink. Gloria was sitting in the back of an ambulance; a mild sedative had been administered to her.

'He's dead, isn't he?'

'Unfortunately, he is,' Sara replied. 'Were you close?'

'Sort of, but he fancied Ingrid.'

'Had she slept with him before?'

'Saint Ingrid of the perpetual virginity?'

'Yes.'

'Never. She never had a man over, and then she kills the first one that she invites in.'

'But why?'

'It was because of me. That's why Brad is dead.'

'What are you not telling us?'

'She phoned me last night.'

'Why didn't you tell us?' Sara asked.

'She wanted the ring; the one you took. She said it was important to her, and if I had stolen it, or given it to the police, then…'

'She threatened you?'

'Yes, I was scared.'

'But you stayed here in the apartment knowing what she is capable of?'

'I've nowhere to go, and besides, this is my home, or it was.'

'Then why Brad?'

'Revenge, I suppose. I told her that the police had found the ring, and they were keeping it as evidence. I wasn't lying.'

'She didn't believe you?'

'Not at all, but then I do lie occasionally. She knew me well enough.'

'You were not here last night,' Sean asked.

'I stayed with a friend.'

'Male?'

'Female. I only came back today to pick up some clothes. That's when I found him.'

'Did you know that Brad was coming over?'

'No, but if Ingrid had phoned him, he would have come.'

Stan Crosley came out from the apartment for a break. He was carrying a change of clothes for Gloria. He saw Sean and Sara by the ambulance. 'A word, if you don't mind,' he said.

'Sure, what is it?' Sara asked.

'Did you take a look at the wall behind the door?'

'No.'

'I've got a photo here on my phone.'

Sean and Sara looked at the display as Crosley held it up to them. There was a large sheet of paper secured with tape. On it, written in blood, *Murder is only a number*. Below it was the number 3.

'She's playing with us,' Sara said. 'What kind of woman can behave like this?'

'One that is crazy; one that will kill again,' Sean said.

Chapter 8

A door-to-door investigation, conducted in the vicinity of Gloria and Ingrid's apartment, had proved negative. The night before the discovery of the body it had been raining and miserable, and very few people had been out on the street. One woman believed she had seen a man heading up to the apartment, but she had been vague in her recollection of events and certainly had not seen a woman.

Brad Howard's body, once Crosley and his team had completed their investigation at the murder scene, had been removed and taken to Pathology. An autopsy would be conducted, although the cause of death was not in any doubt. Whether he had been stabbed mid-coitus, as the crime scene examiner had said, would need to be determined.

For a woman who had been dedicated to chastity, Ingrid Bentham had indeed come a long way. The assumption with Gregory Chalmers had been that it was misguided love, coupled with paranoia, and a lack of the drugs needed to moderate her condition. But now, with Gloria and her sometime boyfriend, there seemed to be another element, even more disturbing.

Ingrid Bentham had apparently discovered the joy of killing, although it may have always been there, and now it was number 3. Sara wondered how long before number 4, and where and whom?

And what was the significance of the ring?

Sara and Sean wondered how the woman was able to appear and disappear at will. London was awash with street cameras, yet none had picked her up.

Stephanie Chalmers had left the hospital and moved in with her sister. The house where her husband had died was firmly locked up. His widow had no intention of ever entering the house again, which seemed illogical to Sara, as it was a beautiful home, but she supposed painful memories are always hard to deal with.

It had been the same with Sara when her parents had died five years before. They had been returning from a holiday when their car slid off an icy road, plunging them into a freezing river. According to the doctor, they would not have known what happened, but it gave Sara sleepless nights for months afterwards.

***

'We had better find this woman before anyone else is killed,' Rory said to Keith. Both men were nursing sore heads from the previous night.

So far, they had only drawn blanks. There were no murders attributed to minors, certainly not females, but the team back in London felt, as did Keith, that the number 1 was significant. If Ingrid Bentham had committed a murder as an adult, she would still be in prison, or at least a secure hospital for the criminally insane.

And her fingerprints would have been easily traceable, which concerned everyone. It was assumed that even if there was only a suspicion of wrongdoing as a child, her fingerprints would be on record, but in fact that was subject to the discretion of the department handling the case and the local legal jurisdiction.

Rory thought that there should always be a fingerprint record, but he was aware that there had been a period when the rights of the child, innocent or otherwise, had been paramount. Pure foolishness, he thought, but the rules were the rules.

'What do you reckon? Think carefully,' Keith said. He was getting edgy, wanting to get back to London. There was another murder. Keith assumed it was the man he had seen in Gloria's bedroom that night. He wanted to be involved, and Newcastle was even colder than London.

At least in London, he reasoned, there was always a warm fire in his favourite pub, although he wasn't much of a drinker nowadays, apart from special occasions such as the night before. He had been in his younger days, but now the bladder could not take the punishment, and the hangovers, mild and quickly dealt with in his youth, played havoc with the migraines that he had become prone to. He knew that his body had seen better days, but apart from the occasional moan, he did not complain.

'There was a case some years ago. A young boy, nine years old if my memory is correct. He died under suspicious circumstances,' Rory said.

'Suspicious, what do you mean?' Keith asked.

'There was an old quarry out near where he lived. He was found at the bottom of it. His death was recorded as death by misadventure, but…'

'What does that mean?'

'The marks at the top showed scuff marks, as if there had been a tussle of some sort.'

'Who was involved with the investigation?'

'I was, but it was some years ago.' It concerned Rory that it had slipped his mind. His mother had suffered from dementia; he hoped he was not starting to suffer the same condition.

'How many?' Keith asked.

'Thirteen, maybe fourteen.'

'It's around the right time. Do you still have your notebook?'

Rory fumbled around in a filing cabinet that was close to his desk. 'Here it is,' he said.

'12 December, 2004. Duncan Hamilton, aged nine, discovered at the bottom of Titmarsh quarry, no suspicious circumstances.'

'You said it was suspicious,' Keith reminded him.

'I've just read you the first entry. Later on, we found the scuff marks at the top of the quarry. It was a hell of a drop; the poor kid would have been dead on impact with the ground below.

'14 December, 2004. Interviewed Charles and Fiona Hamilton, parents of the deceased. One other child, Charlotte, not present.'

'Not the most enjoyable part of policing,' Keith said.

'Not at all, but it comes with the job description.'

'Do you remember what they said?'

'In my notes. "Parents distraught. Fiona Hamilton heavily sedated on doctor's advice. Broached the subject of a possible fight or altercation at the quarry. Charles Hamilton was furious and stormed out of the interview."'

'What did you expect?'

'His reaction was understandable. There they were, coming to terms with their son's death, and I'm there, casting doubt as to whether it was an accident. Even so, his storming out seemed to be an overreaction.'

'You persevered?'

'Had to. If he had been pushed, then it was murder.'

'15 December, 2004.' Rory Hewitt referred back to his notes again.

'"Charles Hamilton stated that his son, as well as the other children in the neighbourhood, often went up to the quarry, although they, or at least his son, had been warned not to."'

'Tell a child, especially a boy, and they will want to go,' Keith said. He remembered his youth. There was a fast-flowing river near his parents' house. They had warned him about the dangers, but the chance to catch a few fish always drew him there. He remembered that he had almost drowned once as he was attempting to manhandle a fish onto the bank. He didn't tell his parents, but he never went fishing there again.

'Exactly, and we were willing to accept the fact that maybe they were playing there, and he had slipped. Ready to accept that the scuff marks were as a result of Duncan attempting to hold on, or someone trying to prevent him falling.'

'It didn't end there, did it?' Keith said.

'I thought it had. Pursuing other children, possibly raising a case against them for the accidental death of a minor, would have tainted them for life. Young boys do stupid things, believing in their infallibility; most survive, although Duncan Hamilton did not. Maybe they were daring each other to look over the edge. Who knows?'

'What happened to change your mind about the case?'

'It's in my notes. "17 December, 2004. Travelled to the Hamiltons' house to interview. Charlotte Hamilton, the elder child, was in the front garden."'

'And?'

'She was singing a song.'

'And the song is significant?'

'I wrote it in my notes. "*Stupid Duncan up at the quarry, along came a sister and gave him a push.*" It was eerie.'

'Did you question her?'

'She would not speak. Psychological problems according to her parents.'

'Did you tell the parents about their daughter's singing?'

'Yes. This time Charles Hamilton sat mute; his wife spoke for both of them.'

'What did she say?'

'Fiona Hamilton stated that her daughter had an imaginative mind and to take no notice.'

'And did you?'

'What could I do? There was no proof, no witnesses, and no assistance from the Hamilton family.'

'How old was Charlotte?'

'Ten.'

'But you always suspected?'

'The song gave me the creeps. It sounded like a theme song out of a horror movie, yet it came from the mouth of a child.'

'What happened to Charlotte Hamilton after that?'

'I've no idea. The inquest was a formality. I made a statement, purely the facts, and the death was recorded as accidental. Both of the parents were present, although they did not speak, at least to me.'

'The daughter?'

'She was not there.'

***

'We need to interview the Hamiltons,' Keith said. It was a murder enquiry, and if Ingrid Bentham and Charlotte Hamilton were one and the same person, the inconvenience to the Hamiltons was of minor concern.

'Understood.'

Keith made the phone call. 'Detective Inspector Keith Greenstreet. I need to question you about your daughter, Charlotte.'

The voice at the end of the phone, female and initially friendly, went quiet. A masculine voice took over. 'She is not here.'

'Then where is she?' Keith asked.

'We have not seen our daughter for some years. We have no idea where she is.'

'Are you Charles Hamilton?'

'Yes.'

'I am requesting a formal interview. It can either be at your house or at the police station.'

'Come to the house, one hour.'

As the phone call ended, Keith could hear the faint sobbing of a woman in the background. He assumed it was Fiona Hamilton.

Rory, reluctant to venture near the Hamiltons' house again but mindful of his duty, accompanied Keith.

'It was over there,' Rory said as they entered the front garden through a small gate. 'That's where she was singing.'

The Hamiltons, on opening the door, were polite, although obviously not pleased to see DI Rory Hewitt. However, they acquiesced and invited them both in. Keith saw that the house was beautifully presented, everything in its place. Trained to be observant, he noticed the photos of a young boy lined up on the bookshelves and on the mantel over the fireplace; it could only be Duncan Hamilton. He saw no pictures of a daughter, other than of a very young child, a babe in arms almost.

Keith, realising the importance of the interview, followed procedure and notified them of their rights.

'Mr Hamilton, we are anxious to contact your daughter,' Keith said.

'We have not seen her for some years.'

'I need to ask you why not.'

'It's a family matter.'

'I'm sorry,' Rory said. 'That statement needs to be clarified.'

'DI Hewitt is correct,' Keith said. 'We believe that your daughter is a possible witness to a number of serious crimes in London. We need to find her.'

Rory handed the Hamiltons a photo taken from the Chalmer's house. Charles Hamilton took one look. His wife averted her eyes.

'After the death of our son, we decided that it was best if Charlotte received counselling,' Charles Hamilton said. He showed no emotion.

'Because of Duncan?' Rory asked. Keith realised the advantage of having someone with him who knew the family history.

'She was traumatised by his death,' Hamilton said. Keith could see Fiona Hamilton was barely able to contain her emotions. It was clear that Charles Hamilton was stoic, but his wife was of a nervous disposition.

'According to the records, Charlotte had some problems,' Keith said.

'She was always a sensitive child,' Fiona Hamilton said. Keith could only assume it was a mother's love for a child that failed to accept the reality. He wondered if they had the same suspicions about Duncan's death as did Rory.

'It was more than sensitivity, Mrs Hamilton,' Rory said.

'As you say. She had emotional problems,' Charles Hamilton conceded.

'I need to know where you sent her and the medical treatment she received,' Keith said.

'Is this necessary? Our son is dead; our daughter is missing. What more do you want from us?'

'I am truly sorry,' Keith said. 'But this is a murder investigation. It is my responsibility to bring the perpetrators to justice, to make them pay for their crimes, to prevent more deaths.'

'And you believe that Charlotte is a murderer?' Fiona Hamilton stood up, screaming. Her husband took hold of her and held her close to him. She buried her head in his shoulder.

'It may be best if you phone for the family doctor to come here, or I could arrange one for you. Mrs Hamilton could do with a sedative,' Rory said.

'That's fine. I'll make a phone call,' Charles Hamilton said. He took out his mobile and dialled. 'Five minutes, Doug. It's important.'

'Family friend, he'll come straight away,' he said to Keith and Rory on concluding the call.

It was no more than two minutes before there was a knock at the door, only ten before Fiona Hamilton was mildly sedated, allowing the interview to continue. There were questions to be answered, and the answers were needed now.

'Mr Hamilton, as you know I always had a suspicion regarding the death of your son,' Rory said. This time, Fiona Hamilton stayed calm.

'Do you have a recent photo?' Keith asked.

'It is five years old.'

'Can I see it, please?'

Charles Hamilton went over to an old writing bureau. He opened the top drawer and withdrew a photo that he handed over. Keith knew what he was looking at. Apart from the short hair and the younger face, it was Ingrid Bentham.

Keith's instinct was to phone Sara immediately, but he knew that first he had to conclude the interview.

'I need to know the name of her doctor and whether she remained in this house after the death of her brother,' Keith said.

'I will give you the contact details. After Duncan's death, her condition worsened. In the end, it became impossible for her to stay here. We found a good place for her, a well-respected mental institution, where she received the best care.

'At the age of nineteen, no longer a minor, and not subject to any restraining order, she left. After that, we have not heard from her.'

'Thank you,' Keith said.

'You believe that Charlotte killed those men in London, don't you?' Fiona Hamilton asked, her voice very quiet.

'That is not for me to comment on,' Keith said.

Charles Hamilton sat quietly for a while. He eventually spoke. 'Unfortunately, Detective Inspector Hewitt, you may have been right about Duncan's death.'

Keith could see a broken man, a broken family: one dead child, almost certainly murdered by his sister; the sister now a serial killer. He felt great sorrow on leaving the house. He knew he needed to be in London, although not before he had interviewed those in charge at the mental hospital where Charlotte Hamilton had stayed for eight of her twenty-four years.

He knew that, whatever happened, the lives of good people were forever altered due to the paranoia of one child, now an adult. He was glad that he was retiring: too much misery and despair during his time as a police officer. Informing the Hamiltons about their daughter was the last piece of bad news he intended to impart to anyone again.

Chapter 9

The mood in the office changed dramatically after Keith had phoned through from Newcastle. Finally, they had a name, even if the woman was not using the name in London.

Keith had sent a scanned photo through on his smartphone. Sara could see that it was Ingrid Bentham, as had Keith. Bob Marshall, pleased with the development, phoned through to Detective Superintendent Rowsome. The man unexpectedly showed up at the office thirty minutes later.

'Great policing,' he said. 'An arrest soon?'

'We hope so, sir,' Sara replied. Bob Marshall stood close by, absorbing the accolades, justified in his decision to keep Sara on the case, although it had been Keith Greenstreet who had provided the first significant breakthrough.

'Good woman you've got there,' Rowsome said to Bob Marshall as he left the office.

'She's a good officer.'

'That's not what I meant.'

'You're right, sir.'

'You'll not find anyone better than her.'

'I know, sir.'

The detective superintendent's comments had the tone of a command, not that Bob needed one; he knew exactly what he was going to do about Sara.

With the detective superintendent out of the office, Bob, back in DCI mode, turned to Sara. She was still glowing at the unexpected praise.

'It doesn't help much, though,' Bob said. He had found a seat close to where she was standing.

'You're right. We may have a name, even an understanding of the woman's state of mind, but no idea of her current location.'

'She's not finished her killing spree, you realise that?' Bob said. 'So far, she's killed a lover and her flatmate's boyfriend, but not the flatmate. What about her parents? Are they safe?'

'We assumed they were, but who knows?' Sara admitted.

'Then you'd better make sure they have protection.'

'Yes, DCI.'

'And tell the flatmate to make herself scarce. The woman has only killed men so far; we don't want a woman as well.'

'I will deal with that.'

'Sara, now that you're the shining star, at least in Detective Superintendent Rowsome's book, what's your plan?'

'Find Charlotte Hamilton.'

'But how? What do you have apart from a name? So far, this woman has killed two people, almost three. And one of them in her old apartment. She may be as mad as a hatter, but she is smarter than us. Why is that?'

'Luck on her part.'

'It's more than that. Ask Keith to check as to her intellectual capability. Even in her deluded state, she may be able to think rationally. She could kill again at any time.'

Sara realised that Bob, yet again, had brought her back to ground with a thud. He was right that Charlotte Hamilton could kill again, and there was nothing they could do to pre-empt her. Their only hope was to apprehend her, but if she could change her appearance as well as her identity, then the chances of picking her up on surveillance cameras or finding her at the haunts she had frequented seemed slim.

Regardless, Sara organised some uniforms to stake out the college she had attended, as well as her former flat and even the Chalmers' house.

Sara made a phone call to Charles and Fiona Hamilton. 'Charlotte had a ring; it was engraved on the inside.'

'I gave it to her the day she turned seventeen,' Fiona Hamilton said. 'It was a family heirloom. It had belonged to her grandmother.'

'How are you?' Sara asked.

'What do you think?'

'Not good, I suppose.'

The phone call ended. Sara assumed that the Hamiltons were beyond conversation.

***

The Mental Health Register showed that Charlotte Hamilton had been placed in a mental facility not far from the family home. There was no mention of Rory Hewitt's suspicion over the death of her brother, or that she was considered possibly violent.

St Nicholas Hospital, a forbidding remnant of Victoriana, the home of Charlotte Hamilton for eight years, was not a welcoming sight to Keith. The place gave him the creeps.

Rory Hewitt had accompanied him.

They negotiated reception; it was either sign in or they were not going any further, police badge or no police badge. They were ushered into a small waiting room on the first floor.

'Dr Gladys Lake, pleased to meet you.' A rotund woman came into the room and introduced herself. The top of her head did not reach Keith's shoulder. He bent his head forward and extended his hand. She shook it vigorously and with strength. He could see that she was an energetic woman; she reminded him of a teacher at the school he had attended as a child.

'We need to talk to you about a former patient,' Keith said.

'Charlotte Hamilton.'

'How did you know?'

'I've had Charles Hamilton on the phone. He's in quite a state. It seems that you have been making aspersions about Charlotte, something to do with her brother as well as the deaths of two men in London.'

'Unfortunately, they are more than aspersions. We have a warrant out for her arrest.'

'And you think that Charlotte could be responsible?'

'Is there somewhere we can talk?' Rory asked.

'My office, you'll need to excuse the mess.'

Keith could see why the woman had mentioned the mess. There were patients' files strewn across her desk, a laptop in the middle of it with a monitor to the side. Over on the far side of the office was a bookcase full of medical books.

'It's my bolthole away from all the cleanliness outside. It's the only place I can get some peace to study.'

'That's fine,' Keith said. 'What can you tell us about Charlotte Hamilton?'

'A beautiful child, no doubt a beautiful woman now.'

'She is.'

'Are you sure about this? When she left here, she had not had a relapse for a couple of years.'

'We have sufficient proof for a conviction.'

'Murder?'

'Yes, two murders now. We are worried there may be more.'

'Her brother?'

'We are not pursuing that. At least at this present time. The recent events in London concern us more.'

'Subject to patient confidentiality, I will tell you what I can. Charlotte entered here after the death of her brother; she was deeply disturbed. We evaluated her, placed her on medication, and with time and counselling, she calmed down. So much so that she attended a local school, visited her parents at the weekends.'

'Why did she not return to live with them?' Rory asked.

'It was difficult.'

'We need to know.'

'You are aware of Charlotte's medical condition?' the doctor asked.

'Not exactly. Our criminal psychologist believes that she displays the classic symptoms of paranoid schizophrenia.'

'Smart woman. With medication, Charlotte was able to lead a relatively normal life. However, …' Dr Lake paused.

'There were some issues with the Hamiltons?' Keith asked.

'Once back at the family home, even with suitable medication, she would revert to type.'

'What do you mean?'

'She would become angry, frustrated, start lashing out at the parents, harming herself.'

'Razors, that sort of thing?' Keith asked.

'Yes.'

'And back here?'

'Five minutes and she was fine, although she hated it here.'

'Are you saying she switches on and off, medication or no medication.'

'Not at all. She needs the drugs, but the dosages were too high for her to be with the Hamiltons for too long.'

'But they came every weekend?'

'Here, she was all right, and if they took her out, she gave no trouble, but near that house she had problems.'

'Do you believe it was the memory of her brother?'

'That was my assumption.'

'What do you know of the death of her brother?' Rory asked. So far, he had let Keith do the majority of the talking, but Duncan Hamilton's death was a subject that he knew more about.

'A tragic accident.'

'Nothing more?'

'Are you saying his death was suspicious?'

'Charlotte has now killed two people. It is possible that Duncan's death was not as recorded.'

'And do Charles and Fiona Hamilton know of your suspicion?'

'Yes.'

'How did they deal with it?'

'Badly from what we can see. You realise that we're only doing our duty. Charlotte Hamilton could kill again. We need to find her.'

'I have to deal with trauma every day. I understand that you must do what is right.'

'We need your help,' Keith said.

'What do you want to know?'

'Charlotte has killed one lover, as well as the lover of her flatmate. Both crimes appear to be motivated by personal anger. Is there anyone else who could be a potential victim?'

'In her state of mind? Anyone she came in contact with over the years, even me.'

'So far we have ruled out anyone female.'

'I don't see why.'

'Would she regard her parents with ambivalence?'

'Possibly.'

'We have a police guard at their house.'

'That will not stop her,' Gladys Lake said. 'Charlotte may have mental issues, but she is still a smart woman. If, as you suspect, she has reverted back to a paranoid state, then she could find a way.'

'Medication?' Keith asked. 'We are aware that she was taking some medication.'

'Chlorpromazine most likely.'

'You're not sure?'

'I've not seen her since she left here. If she is on prescription, there should be a record.'

'According to our criminal psychologist, Grace Nelson, the dosage and the medicines change over time.'

'She is right, which would mean that Charlotte is under the care of a doctor. Or should be,' Gladys Lake said.

'Black-market prescription drugs are not that easy to come by.'

'Maybe, and what I prescribed five years ago may not be relevant today, especially the dosage. And besides, a lot of patients stop taking them at times due to the side effects.'

'If she failed to take her drugs or took incorrect dosages?'

'Probably what you see now: a belief that people are out to get you, aggression, violence.'

***

With the woman clearly identified as Charlotte Hamilton, an all-points warning was issued. This time it was more accurate than the previous one for Ingrid Bentham, not that Sara Stanforth held out much hope for it. A bottle of hair dye available in any supermarket, a different hairstyle, even plain clothes, and Charlotte Hamilton could go from attractive to dull and back to attractive at will.

Sean, pleased that the case was moving forward, disappointed that his studies for a Master's degree were slipping, focussed on detailing the murderous woman's movements in the intervening five years, from when she had walked out of St Nicholas Mental Hospital until the murder of Gregory Chalmers.

Legally prescribed drugs, especially the more potent ones, would be registered and on the record. Also, they needed to know if the drugs had changed over the years, and whether she was subjecting herself to regular medical checks.

If the records were meticulous, Dr Gladys Lake should have been able to access them. After all, she had been her primary doctor for many years, and someone with a known psychotic ailment would be monitored at all times.

His father, Keith Greenstreet recollected, was susceptible to blowing his top one minute, only to be calm the next, but with

Charlotte Hamilton it was more than banging a fist on the desk in frustration. With her, it came with a knife, although no one, not even her doctor in Newcastle, had seen that possibility.

Sara, for once riding high in everyone's estimation, knew that it would not last for long.

'Five days maximum before they start questioning your ability and my judgement,' Bob Marshall had said the previous night. Detective Superintendent Rowsome was looking for an arrest; his Key Performance Indicators were slipping in a couple of key areas. With Charlotte Hamilton behind bars, he knew that his KPIs would be excellent for the next three months. The arrest of a murderer always counted for a lot, and Rowsome was looking for promotion.

Bob had an unusual way of initiating sexual congress, Sara thought. Discussing a murder was hardly the ideal conversation for a lead up to a romantic interlude, although it was not going to distract either of them. Sara knew that DCI Bob Marshall was the man for her, although he had been cagey on the subject of marriage. She knew that he had been married before, and even though there were no children, no complications, it had left him cautious.

Bob did not talk about his previous wife, which suited Sara, but sometimes the subject came up in conversation. According to Bob, she had a fiery temper coupled with a loving disposition. One wrong word on his part and she would not talk for a month, other than with monosyllabic replies.

Sara could see no problems for Bob on that account with her: she had no temper, said her mind and then forgot it. And as for not talking? She was a woman with a need. A woman in need of affection, Bob Marshall's affection, and she was not going to allow any temper tantrum to get in the way.

Next day in the office, after a successful romantic interlude the previous night, Bob Marshall was back into detective chief inspector mode.

'Sara, what are you doing about this woman, and is her flatmate safe? How about her parents?'

'We have uniforms watching out for them.'

'Not really good enough, is it?'

'What else can we do? We can hardly protect them day and night. Besides, Ingrid's, or should I say Charlotte's, flatmate is out of sight, visiting relatives in Nigeria. The woman was scared and rightly so.'

'You have an address, contact details?'

'Yes, DCI.'

'And the parents?'

'It must be tough for them,' Sara said. She remembered the brief conversation with Fiona Hamilton, the sadness in the woman's voice.

'Tough for any parent. Remember, five days and those in the office upstairs will be baying for my blood and yours. I've trusted you with this case, and so far, what do you have? Just a name. Where is this woman, what is her next move? Who is her next victim? Have you considered this?'

'Impossible to ascertain who the next victim will be.'

'Why?'

'One lover and then the lover of her flatmate.' Sara realised that her DCI was placing her under pressure for her benefit. After the praise of the detective superintendent, she had to admit that she had lost some focus. Bob was sharpening her up; she would deal with him later.

'So far, it's been people that she knows, and male.'

'Apart from Stephanie Chalmers, although we believe that was not intended. The woman walked in and found Ingrid with blood on her hands, as well as a knife. And Gregory Chalmers' death appears to be unpremeditated.'

'Brad Howard?'

'Premeditated. She calculated his death.'

'Why not kill Gloria?'

'We believe that she targets males.'

'At present. I suggest you tighten your operation. You have a full department here, and Keith will be back later in the day. I advise you to find this woman before there are any more deaths.' Bob walked away, only looking back to mouth 'Sorry.' He knew he had been a bastard, but it had only been to make her focus.

Fired up, she called in Sean. 'What do you have?'

'Not a lot. I can find clear evidence that she continued with her medication for a couple of years, but nothing after that.'

'Change of name?'

'Unlikely. No doctor would issue antipsychotic medication without a full medical history, and then he would probably check back with the primary physician.'

'Gladys Lake?'

'She told Keith that she had not seen her since the day she left the hospital.'

'It's possible.'

'Where did she get the additional medication?'

'London.'

'That gives us five years. Discounting the three years at college in London, we have two years unaccounted for. Where was she?' Sara asked.

'We'd better find out. There is an address for Charlotte Hamilton in London that Gladys Lake supplied. Supposedly, she had prescribed her medication the day she left. We should go there,' Sean said.

Chapter 10

Muswell Hill, five miles north of the centre of London, had recently been voted one of the five most desirable places to live in London. It was clear that the judging committee had not seen the address where Sara and Sean pulled up in Sean's car, a blue Ford Fiesta.

It was Charlotte Hamilton's first known address in London and not a welcoming sight. The terrace house looked to be run-down, which was incongruous given that every other house in the street was neat and tidy with fresh paint.

Sara got out of the car and knocked on the front door of the terrace house. 'What do you want?' called out a deep-voiced woman, her speech interspersed by coughing.

'Detective Inspector Sara Stanforth and Detective Constable O'Riordan. We have a few questions.'

'Very well.'

The woman, still coughing, opened the door, the security chain in place. 'We can talk here,' she said.

'Inside would be better,' Sara said.

'I don't like strangers.'

'We're here on official business. It is either in your house or down at the police station.' Sara knew what was behind the door. Sean, still naïve in many ways, did not.

'I'll get my coat.'

The door closed again. Two minutes later it reopened and the woman came out, a cigarette hanging from her mouth. 'I need to be back within the hour.'

'I can't promise you that,' Sara said.

'What's inside the house?' Sean whispered to Sara.

'This is where Charlotte Hamilton came to after leaving Newcastle. Somewhere she could earn some easy money; a place that paid in cash and did not ask too many questions.'

Sean understood.

Sara phoned a fellow police officer at the nearest police station. He agreed to them using an office there.

'Your name?' Sara asked in the quietness of the room, although it would have been better described as a broom cupboard, having just enough space for a table and chairs. All three had taken a coffee from the machine outside; the drink tasted of cardboard, the same as the cup. Sara and Sean took theirs black; the woman added milk and sugar.

'I run a clean house,' the woman said. Sara judged her to be in her fifties. Her face was blotchy from too little sun, not hard to achieve given the weather of the last few months, but this woman appeared to have had no sun for several years.

Sara went through the formalities before asking her name again.

'Mavis Williams.'

'Your age?'

'Fifty-eight. What's this all about?' The woman shifted uncomfortably in her seat, gasping for breath. Even on the trip in the back of Sean's car she had been desperate to light up, and now in the confines of the small office she was desperate to put another cigarette in her mouth. She fiddled with the packet, took out a cigarette, put it to her lips, returned it to the packet.

'We are looking for someone,' Sara said.

'Not one of my girls. They're all legal.'

'That is not our concern. If you're running a brothel, that is for the local police. We are from Homicide.'

'No one's been killed in my house.'

'Five years ago, a woman used your address. We believe she maintained that address for a further two years.'

'So?'

'We know her as Charlotte Hamilton. Does the name mean anything to you?'

'Most of my girls use fictitious names.'

'This woman was blonde. She would have been nineteen when she first used your address.'

'I don't employ anyone under twenty-one. Saves hassles with the police.'

'And your neighbours?'

'What do I care about them.'

'The woman, as I said, was blonde,' Sara continued. 'She was average height, slim and attractive. She would have spoken with a northern accent, from Newcastle.'

'Oh, her.'

'What do you remember about this woman?'

'She called herself Charlie. Unusual name, but not the silliest that I've heard. I've had my fair share of Blossom, Cherry, Honey, even had one who wanted to be called Buxom.'

'Miss Williams,' Sean said, 'what can you tell us about Charlie?'

'She was beautiful, I'll grant you that. She looked virginal the first day I saw her.'

'Was she?'

'How the hell would I know, although I charged extra on account of her supposed virginity. Men, they're all the same. Want to be the first, even in a whorehouse. At least thirty men took her virginity.'

'Did she have any inhibitions when she entered your place?' Sara asked.

'None that I could see. She took to it like a fish to water.'

'Do you know where she is now?'

'No idea, and I don't want to know.' Mavis Williams fidgeted again. 'I need a cigarette.'

'Not in here,' Sean replied.

'I'm gasping.'

'We still have further questions.'

'Not until I've had a cigarette.'

It was evident to Sara that the woman had information that could be vital. She had to give in to the woman's demand. Sean and Sara took the opportunity to have another cup of cardboard coffee.

Returning to the interview room, Mavis Williams exhaled the remains of her cigarette smoke over the two police officers. Sean stood up and moved to the window. He opened it to let out the offensive smell.

'Can't give them up,' she said. 'They'll kill me, I know that. Anyway, we've all got to die eventually.'

Sara had to agree with the 'eventually' but not due to inhaling nicotine. Bob Marshall had appreciated the occasional cigarette; she had soon put a stop to that luxury.

'How long did Charlie stay with you?' Sara asked. She had shown a picture to Mavis Williams to confirm that Charlotte Hamilton and Charlie were one and the same; they were.

'Two years, on and off.'

'On and off?' Sean asked.

'Mainly on. She rented a room from me in the back of the house. If she wasn't servicing the men at the front of the house, she was there.'

'Did she like the work?'

'Screwing drunks and foul-smelling men with hygiene issues for money? What do you think?'

'I suppose not.'

'A lot of the women are spaced out on heroin or whatever, but she wasn't.'

'So why?'

'She said she needed the money. I never asked why. It's always best to maintain a distant relationship with the women I employ.'

'Over the two years, any unusual behaviour on her part?'

'At first, she was agreeable, but with time she became irritable, sometimes irrational. The reason she left eventually.'

'We need to know the details.'

'One of her clients, a particularly unpleasant character, I think he was Polish, or maybe Hungarian. I never asked, never cared, as long as his money was good.'

'And?'

'He wanted Charlie, although I had seen her earlier on and she was in a strange mood. I knew this man was a bit kinky. He liked a bit of violence, nothing serious, just a bit of slapping.'

'You allow that?' Sara asked.

'That's between the client and the woman.'

'Charlie went with this man?'

'She was always ready for another man. Most of the women spend their money on hard drugs, but not Charlie. She saved all her money, and after two years she must have had plenty. I pay well, and the men give generous tips.'

'What happened to the client?'

'From what I can gather, he starts getting a bit violent, and then Charlie snaps. She becomes aggressive, beating the man with whatever she can find. She had a small mirror in her handbag; she breaks the glass and comes at him with the sharp fragments. The man dashes out of the room stark naked. Charlie is in hot pursuit, screaming at him. It took three of us to calm her down.'

'And afterwards?'

'We cleaned up the man and then gave him one of the other women for free. He was not that badly hurt, although he could have been.'

'Charlie?'

'I gave her one hour to pack her belongings and leave.'

'What can you tell us about her after that?'

'Nothing. I never saw her again, and that's the honest truth.'

**

'Next time, I'll take the train,' Keith said on his return to the police station in London. It was apparent to Sara that he had not been home for a shower first.

She felt that she should tell him to go home first and clean himself up, but she desisted. He was a grown man, old enough to be her father, and she had grown uncommonly fond of him: almost like a warm blanket or a child's favourite toy.

Sure, his appearance could be disarming, and his humour was questionable, acerbic at times, but within that shell of a man she recognised a decent and honest person; a person aiming to make a difference. She had little time for the lazy and inept, and with Keith Greenstreet, she recognised a kindred soul.

Life had taken its toll on him, and he looked older in the office that day than any other in the past.

'Apart from a six- to nine-month period, we have accounted for Charlotte Hamilton's movements,' Sara said.

'It's not over,' Keith said. 'This woman is lethal.'

'And we've no idea where she is.'

'And we never will. Her movements are unpredictable, and every time she moves, she changes her identity. She could be one block from here, and we would never know. We could even walk past her in the street.'

'Your thoughts, Keith. Where to from here?'

'Keep looking.'

'It's not much of a strategy,' Sara admitted.

'I agree, but what else is there. We know of all known addresses that she has used. We are aware of her ability to conceal herself and her willingness to sell herself without guilt, and then we have a woman who is intellectually bright.'

'Brighter than us, and no longer on medication.'

'That's a fair assumption,' Keith said.

'She's going to kill again,' Sara said. 'And soon.'

Chapter 11

Liam Fogarty could not believe his luck. Not only had he been rewarded with a promotion at work, but here he was with a beautiful woman.

He knew that with a bulbous forehead and a receding chin that he hid with a goatee beard he was not the most attractive of men. He realised that it was the reason he had never been successful with women. In his early teens, there had been the occasional female, equally as drunk as he had been, and each had seen beauty in the other. The inevitable result: a casual attempt at lovemaking in the back of a car, or more likely lying on the cold grass in the local park, had been the limit of his sexual experience.

It had been two years since his last woman, discounting the one he paid for every month or so.

'What are you doing here?' he asked the woman who was obviously interested in him, judging by the way she looked at him and the suggestive moves she was making.

'Looking for you.' The woman realised it was a stupid line, but then the man looked silly to her. She had not known that he was smarter than he looked, smart enough to have obtained a degree in Economics, but then that was not why she needed him.

The woman looked at the man. She was not excited at what she saw, although he looked pliable and fit for purpose.

'Do you want to dance?' Liam asked. He was well plastered, on his fifth pint, and his mates were egging him on. He was in need of a visit to the Gents, but that would have to wait. He knew his mates would have been over in an instant to grab the woman. He took another drink, Dutch courage to him. Sober, he recognised his inadequacies; drunk, his persona changed, as the balance between gregarious and fast asleep in a drunken stupor was only separated by a short time span. Even now, he wanted to sit down and sleep it off, but not with this woman closing in on him. He believed he was Adonis reincarnated; even Paris stealing Helen away from Menelaus and taking her back to Troy.

'Give her one for us,' Liam's drunken friends shouted above the noise of the club. He looked at them with a smirk. He was the lucky bastard, and they could go to Hell.

The woman grabbed him firmly and pulled him towards the dance floor. He almost tripped as she dragged him to the centre, away from his jeering mates.

'What's your name?' Liam slurred, attempting to focus. He was desperate to stagger out and to relieve his bladder, but he held on. He regretted that he had drunk so much; concerned that he would not be able to perform. The woman was giving him the right signals. He knew he was on to a sure thing.

'Does it matter?' the woman replied when he pressed yet again for her name.

'I suppose not,' Liam said. He had been deprived of a woman who had shown interest in him for too long, other than the women who feigned interest as long as he paid, but this one, she was gorgeous.

He swayed as he spoke; he wanted desperately to sober up, but the woman continued to prime him with alcohol, even taking a drink from another drunk on the dance floor who was close to collapse. The drunk had attempted to complain but the woman had just leant over towards him and given him a kiss on the cheek.

'Thanks,' she said. The drunk could see the beauty in the woman, although the woman he had been fondling on the dance floor was not too happy and stormed off. The drunk tried momentarily to cut in on Liam. The woman pushed him away, as had Liam. *No bastard is taking this woman from me,* he thought.

The woman moved in closer at his sign of bravado. She was holding him tight, her breasts pressing hard against his chest, her legs close to being entwined around his. They danced, they kissed, and all the time Liam Fogarty could feel the need of the woman. He could see the beauty in the woman, but not the venom in her eyes, the searing hatred that coursed through her veins. He could not realise that the woman was working on him, bringing him to a crescendo.

***

The club where Liam and his woman were dancing was not far from London. It was heaving that night. The music was loud and getting louder, the drinks were flowing, and the noise was overpowering. A residential estate close by had tried to have the noise moderated a few months earlier. They had formed a residents' committee to make a submission to the local council. They wanted a noise abatement order as the first step, a closure of the club to follow.

A heated meeting in the council offices had come to nothing. A formal notice had been sent to the club. Its owner, Sam Goldsmith, a shrewd businessman who had made his money to the east of London with clubs and discos, legal or otherwise, knew more about local councils than the local residents, led by a busybody by the name of Betty Arkwright, did. She had the law on her side, and a write-up in the local newspaper had garnered widespread support for her and her residents' committee.

Sam Goldsmith, impervious to the man in the street as long as he could afford his extravagant lifestyle and his two mistresses, cared little for the Arkwright woman and her sanctimonious group of narrow-minded residents. The more they complained, the more he would bribe, by way of cash and trips overseas. The local residents' committee had no chance just by waving a copy of the Environmental Protection Act 1990 at the council.

Goldsmith knew that more music, the longer trading hours, the increased patronage could only mean one thing: more money for him and the greedy councillors, their snouts in the trough.

***

It was Liam Fogarty's first time in the club: a celebration with his friends, and he was paying. Not that he minded, as they were good friends he had known since his schooldays. They were still struggling to make their mark, but there he was, regional manager for a multinational bank. It had been hard-won, a lot of sweat and tears, a lot of study and sleepless nights, a lot of time without a woman. However, tonight was his night.

In his drunken mind, the woman he was dancing with was with him because of his self-assuredness. He had noticed her pale complexion; he had certainly seen her breasts, as had his friends. 'Give them a squeeze for us,' they had hollered when they had first seen Liam and the woman together.

Liam was drunk, almost close to comatose, but his friends were worse. The club did not tolerate excessive drunkenness officially, but Liam had the money. There were over five hundred in the club that night, and four hundred would probably fail a breathalyser if they attempted to drive home.

'Do you come here often?' Liam had asked when he first saw the woman making eyes at him, swaying from side to side to show her assets. He had thought that she would disappear as he made his way towards her, but she did not. He could see a good night ahead. He realised it was a clichéd chat-up line. He had moved in close to the woman, as the noise made it impossible to hold a normal conversation.

'First time. And you?'

'Celebrating with my mates. Are you on your own?' Liam hoped that she was. A promotion and this woman in the one day was more than he could hope for. He imagined her with him, somewhere more comfortable, somewhere more intimate. He had been put down too often in the past, and usually he would have given her a wide berth. His last girlfriend, a pleasant enough woman, had not been as attractive as the one standing in front of him, but he knew that he was not an attractive man.

The last girlfriend, they used to meet on a Friday, and he would sleep over at her place on that night, but apart from that he had not felt any great emotion for her. Not that she was not affectionate, she was, but she came with a history of too many men, too much promiscuity. He had known her at school when she had been slim and cute with firm breasts and a tight arse. Then, she had not wanted to know him, but with time and a preponderance to put on weight, she had changed. When he had met her seven years after leaving school, she had gained twenty pounds and an extra chin, and her body had sagged after the birth of a child that she loved but he could only see as an encumbrance. She had professed love, but he knew the truth. She wanted a provider and a father figure for the child, the result of her promiscuity and a former student at the school they had attended.

Liam knew that when he wanted a child, he would find a good woman, maybe the woman who now had her arms around him.

'We can dance if you want,' she said as she kissed him firmly on the mouth. His mates, pretending not to notice but unable to resist, cheered.

The woman looked over at them and smiled. *You bastards*, she thought.

***

At first the music on the dance floor had been fast and frantic, with arms flying this way and that, but within ten minutes of Liam and the gorgeous black-haired woman hitting the floor, it had slowed, so much so that they had no option but to embrace and to sway with the music.

'I want you,' the woman said, her body pressing close to his.

'We need to go somewhere,' Liam said.

'Anywhere is fine by me,' she said as she pressed in close. She knew the effect she was having on the hapless individual.

'My place is nearby,' he said.

'Too far.'

The conversation continued for several minutes. Garry, one of his drunken friends, attempted to cut in. Liam pushed him away.

'Go away, find your own woman,' Liam's female said. She was almost glued to him now, and her constant gyrations up and down his body had the desired effect.

'Can I see you again after tonight?' he asked. He realised the dancing and the movement of his body were starting to reduce the effects of the alcohol. He could not believe his luck. He had looked around the club earlier before he had drunk too much. He had seen some attractive women, but sober he would not have approached them. Too many rejections by the sort of women he fancied had made him reluctant to repeat the process. Too many times had he been told that he was unattractive or fat or he smelt. It was true that his facial features were not good, nor was his body. It was not fat, more like baby fat that had not gone away. He discounted his need for greasy fish and chips and pizzas washed down with beer as the cause. The smell that they complained of he could not understand, but he thought it may be to do with the garlic which he liberally dosed on his food every day.

And now, here he was, with the most attractive woman in the club. He had not seen her on entering; assumed she had come later.

'Why worry about tomorrow?' the woman said when Liam persisted with asking her out the following day. She wore a tight blouse and a short skirt, unfashionably short. She knew she looked to be an easy lay, the effect she was trying to create. Five nights she had hidden away to the north of London in flea-bitten accommodation where only money was required and no prying questions were asked. Not that it concerned her, as she was adept at changing her appearance and her behaviour. She knew the medical diagnosis of her mental condition, but they were wrong, part of a plot to belittle her.

It was those bastards who were at fault, not her. She was the sane one, and those who conflicted with her had a limited life span. She intended to rid the world of those who caused her anguish, and as for her parents, they were the worst of them all. She tried to remember them fondly, but she could not. They could wait for another day.

Men were the problem; men who had paid for her body, men who had professed love but only wanted to screw her. Once she had dealt with this one, she would disappear for some time, but she would return.

Gregory Chalmers had treated her badly, as had his bitch wife. Brad Howard, that bitch Gloria's boyfriend, had come over quickly that night. So much for his faithfulness to her. She had seen him undressing her with his eyes before; his death had been pleasurable. She imagined that the man she was with would not be as good as Brad, but she did not intend to waiver.

As she danced close to Liam, the gormless and charmless man, she reminisced. She thought of a happy childhood, until that stupid brother of hers had teased her and then broken her collection of dolls, even pulled the leg off one. She had been ten, too old for dolls, but she had loved her collection, especially the one with the missing leg. He had deserved to die, and she was glad that she had killed him.

And then there was that bitch doctor at St Nicholas who had been pleasant to her, but she had allowed them to attach electrodes to her scalp. She remembered the trembling in her hands and feet; the restraints that held her down. She was meant to be sedated, but sometimes they made a mistake, and the pain of the electricity passing through her body had been unpleasant.

Her parents had visited her, but they never took her back home, other than for short periods. They did not want her, she could see that clearly now, and as for the medication, to hell with it. She knew what it did, how it quietened her down, but she no longer needed it. She had a purpose in life, a purpose to rid the world of all those who had caused her pain and anguish, and this foolish man who thought he could dance. He believed that he was God's gift to women, but he would not be the first or the last. He would be another marker that she was here and she was determined.

'There's a toilet out the back,' she said. 'Take me there.'

The idea excited him, although a toilet did not. He imagined a bed with silken sheets, rose petals on the pillow, a bottle of champagne with two glasses.

The club was modern and clean, but the toilet out past the kitchen belonged to another era when the club premises had been part of an industrial complex; it had not been cleaned for some time and smelt. Liam imagined rats and cockroaches, and he did not like them, but the woman was hot and whispering in his ear, then sticking her tongue in his mouth. He wanted to be somewhere else with her, and his place was only five minutes away. The woman came closer, put his hand on one of her breasts. The desire to make love to the woman was overpowering.

She pushed him down on the toilet seat, pulling his trousers down to his ankles. He was erect and ready. She straddled him with no foreplay.

'Just stay there for me,' she said.

He sat still while he maintained his erection.

'Are you ready?' she asked.

'Yes, yes,' he said gasping for breath. The woman was beautiful, even if the surroundings were not. He was aflame and unable to hold out for much longer.

'Are you ready for your surprise?'

'Yes,' he said.

The woman put one hand inside the small bag she carried. She waited for him to be at his peak, and then she thrust the thin stiletto knife into his chest. Liam, at the moment of death, clutched the knife with one hand in an attempt to remove it.

The woman removed herself from the man and put one of her fingers on the blood oozing from his body.

The toilet was concealed from general view. On leaving it she found a tap outside. She removed the clothes she was wearing, washed herself down, put on fresh clothes that had been in the small bag, and walked out of the building by way of a back gate.

She smiled as she walked away, only to break into song after a couple of minutes. *Liam thought he was a stud until I stuck a knife in his heart.*

Chapter 12

'George Street, Richmond!' Sara Stanforth said over the phone to Sean O'Riordan. She had already phoned Keith Greenstreet and given him the same directive. Crime Scene Examiner Stan Crosley had also been notified.

'What is it?' Sean asked. It was one in the morning, and he was still studying. There was an important exam the next week, and he knew he was not ready.

'Joey's.'

'I know it,' Sean said. He had been there with his friends some years before.

'There's been another murder.'

'Charlotte Hamilton?'

'It looks that way. We'll have a clearer idea out at the scene. The local police are securing the crime scene and rounding up the patrons. They are none too happy from what I've been told, but if it's her, she's been out in public and very visible.'

'Someone must have seen her,' Sean said. He was dressing as he spoke. His girlfriend woke to ask what was going on. 'The usual,' his reply. She had become used to the hours that he worked, and rolled over and went back to sleep. He thought she looked delightful lying curled up in his bed, but now was not the time for romance.

It was only three days since Keith had returned from Newcastle. Three days when the team had mostly stayed in the office analysing, debating, and trying to come up with a plan on how to find this woman.

There were extra police out on the street, and random door knocks had been conducted, but nothing. The woman baffled them with her ability to appear and disappear at will.

Keith was first at the murder scene as he only lived two miles away. Sara arrived shortly after. Sean was two minutes later. Bob Marshall came as well in Sara's car.

'What do we have?' Bob asked.

It was Keith who replied. 'Male in his thirties.'

'Fatal?'

'That's why we're here,' Keith replied.

'Then we'd better take a look,' Sara said. She went round to the back of her car and took out gloves and foot protectors. The local police had waylaid the patrons, or at least those that had not sneaked around the cordon and down a side alley.

'It will take some time to interview all of them,' Sean said.

'We have to whether they like it or not,' Sara reminded him.

Two uniforms were outside the main door, another at the back of the building.

'Who found the body?' Sara asked.

'One of the cooks. It appears he went out back for a cigarette. That's when he found it.'

The four police officers moved through the club and out to the back. The cook, a big man who looked tough but had proven himself not to be, was sitting quietly. The dead body had upset him.

Careful not to disturb the evidence, the four police officers approached by a circuitous route. Standing on the other side of the yard, with the toilet door slightly ajar, they could see the body sitting on the toilet, the head drooped forward. There appeared to be a lot of blood.

'I need to check,' Sara said. She was aware of the CSE's reaction if he saw her, but she needed to know. Close up, she could see the knife in the man's body. She looked around, a small torch in her hand, as there was no light inside, and it was still night.

'It's here,' she said.

'What's the number?' Sean asked.

'4.'

'Rowsome is going to have my guts for garters after this,' Bob said, knowing full well the man's venomous tongue, a man short on praise, long on criticism.

This was his department, and his SIO, someone he had protected from criticism, and yet again the woman had come into his patch and committed murder, and from all accounts, in sight of five hundred patrons at the busiest club in the area.

Bob Marshall knew what was coming: an immediate directive to remove Sara from the senior role.

Sara, equally aware of what was to happen, but not willing to relinquish control without a fight, focussed on the job in hand.

Stan Crosley had arrived, and he was ushering them out of the area. 'I've got work to do. The same woman?' he asked.

'It looks to be that way,' Sara replied.

'Can't you find her?' his sarcastic response.

Out front, the patrons were getting restless. Most had been drunk or close to it, and the alcohol was slowly wearing off. The local police had identified the friends of the dead man. They were off to one side.

As for the other patrons, the local police could interview them, check proof of identity and ask the mandatory questions: did you see anything suspicious, did you visit the back of the club at any time, did you see a woman with the dead man? One of the dead man's friends had supplied a picture from his smartphone.

'Liam,' one of the friends said. 'I can't believe it.'

'What can you tell me about the woman?' Sara asked. Sean was interviewing another of the friends. Keith was dealing with two others.

'We saw her, of course. Liam never had much success with women, and there he is with a looker.'

'Can you describe her?'

'It's hard. We were all drunk, celebrating Liam's promotion at work. He had just been made regional manager, and the drinks were on him. Anyway, this woman starts wrapping herself around him.'

'Can you describe her?'

'Slim, extremely attractive, especially to us drunks.'

'She's attractive, even without alcohol.'

'You know her?' the friend asked.

'Not personally, but we know what she is capable of.'

'And she killed Liam?'

'Subject to confirmation.'

Liam's friend Ken was slowly recovering from his drunkenness. Sara organised a coffee for him, one for her. One of the uniforms obliged and went and found a café still open, or it had opened once it had seen the milling throng out on the street.

'Ironic, I suppose,' Ken said.

'What do you mean?' Sara asked.

'The first time he finds an attractive woman, and she kills him. Is it the one on the news?'

'It seems possible,' Sara replied, not wanting to comment too much, knowing full well that the media would certainly grab Ken for an interview.

'Mind you, she wasn't attracted to him for his charm, was she?' Ken said.

'No.'

'I tried to move him away from her on the dance floor. The woman told me to find my own woman. If I had succeeded, it would be me dead now.'

'Probably.' A one-word reply from Sara.

'Why does she do this?'

'That's the subject of our enquiries. Anyway, what else can you tell me about the woman?'

'Dark hair, almost black, or I assume it was.'

'Why do you say that?'

'There's not much light inside the club.'

'She was previously blonde. Are you sure she had dark hair?'

'Positive.'

Sara realised that if the woman was teasing them, she could be out the front: part of her ghoulish behaviour, revelling in what she had committed.

***

'Pierced the large artery coming from the heart,' Stan Crosley said later in the morning.

'Death came quickly?' Bob Marshall asked. He had heard from Detective Superintendent Rowsome already. The death at the club had become headline news, and he would have to make a press statement.

The DCI was not sure what to say: we are following all lines of enquiry; an arrest is imminent. He knew such words would not allay the demands of an eager media desperate for any titbit of information, but what else could he offer. He could hardly say that they knew the identity of the murderer but hadn't a clue where she was.

Stan Crosley answered Bob Marshall's earlier question. 'This woman does not understand the physiology of the human body. If she had, she would have known that a knife wound to the heart does not guarantee immediate death. She did, however, luck on piercing the large artery. Anywhere else, the man could possibly have regained consciousness long enough to raise the alarm.'

'Would he have lived?'

'Unlikely, but he would have lived longer. With Gregory Chalmers, she used a large knife, but a stiletto is much smaller. With Brad Howard she was lucky as well. Is she likely to strike again?' Crosley asked.

'We can't be certain, but all indications are that she has found a taste for murder.'

'And you can't find her?'

'Unfortunately, that is the truth at the present moment.'

Sara did not speak. She had been informed by Bob that someone more experienced was to take over the case. He had not wanted to do it, but she had lost the confidence of senior management, and whereas she had done an excellent job, he had no option but to remove her. However, she would stay with the team. Keith Greenstreet had made an impassioned plea for her to remain in charge, only to be told by Bob that it was beyond his control. He knew where he would be sleeping that night.

Chapter 13

Part 2

Three years later

Detective Chief Inspector Isaac Cook knew immediately on entering the crime scene the one person who could help him. He had read the case files of Charlotte Hamilton, and it was clear who had the most knowledge about her.

The murderous woman had become notorious some years previously, even revered by deluded fools around the world. In the USA, there were plenty of women who felt that their lives had been destroyed by men. There had even been a couple of copycat killers, who after murdering their spouse or ex-boyfriend with a knife if they had one, a gun if they did not, would paint a number on the man or else on the wall.

Somehow, these people, in their anger, would justify their actions by citing Charlotte Hamilton. They were wrong, of course. The gutter press and social media had elevated Charlotte Hamilton's star way above where it should have been.

There was nothing admirable about this woman, no attempt on her part to right the wrongs wrought against women by men, no ideological stance, and no act of retribution. Charlotte Hamilton had clearly been defined by the authorities as a psychotic killer suffering from paranoid schizophrenia. However, being psychotic and paranoid had not affected her ability to evade capture.

Liam Fogarty had died a tragic and violent death due to his drunkenness and the belief that a beautiful woman desired him, not because she needed to make a sacrifice.

Sara Marshall had been right. Charlotte Hamilton had been outside the front of the club in Richmond that night while the patrons were going through the interview procedure. She had even posed with a few other people who were waiting for the police to deal with them so they could go home to sleep it off, or in the murderer's case to post pictures on Facebook. She made sure that in one of the photos she had a police officer in the background, namely Sara Stanforth, as she had been known then.

There had been a few rough months after Detective Chief Inspector Bob Marshall had removed her from the lead role in the search for Charlotte Hamilton. Forced by his superior, Detective Superintendent Martin Rowsome, he had assigned the lead role to a more experienced officer with twenty years in Homicide and a good track record.

Not that it made any difference, as he had no more success. Two months after the hapless future regional bank manager had died, and with no more deaths, no more numbers carved into men's bodies, no more numbers painted onto walls with blood, the team were reduced in number.

Keith Greenstreet had finally retired; reluctantly, he had said, but Sara Stanforth could see that he was tired, and his health was not good. He had been a good officer, someone she had grown fond of in the short time they had worked together, so much so that when she married Bob Marshall, she asked Keith to walk her down the aisle. He had even spruced himself up for the occasion, taken to exercise and a healthy diet. However, it was of little benefit, as shortly after the wedding he had succumbed and passed away. The most he had was eight months of retirement.

Sara had continued to work in Homicide, but there had been no lead roles, other than in a case of straightforward marital strife, where the husband had shot the wife, and that was only because Bob felt some guilt over her treatment regarding the Hamilton woman.

Charlotte Hamilton's parents, suffering immense guilt and sadness, had become reclusive, shunning contact with friends and neighbours. The last Sara had heard of them, they had sold up and moved to a cottage in a remote area.

Dr Gladys Lake at St Nicholas Hospital, Charlotte's home for eight years, had been assigned a police guard for a few months, after receiving a phone call one night: 'I remember,' the only words spoken.

It was Sara who had found the cheap hotel where Charlotte had been staying after she moved out of the flat she shared with Gloria, and where she had murdered Brad Howard.

Charlotte Hamilton's death count was now at four. Rory Hewitt had reopened the case into the death of Duncan Hamilton. The verdict had been changed from death by misadventure to cause of death unknown, although no one, certainly not Rory Hewitt or Duncan's parents, believed in the 'unknown'. It was clear to all three who had given that fatal push.

***

'Sara Marshall, my name is Isaac Cook,' the voice said on Sara's mobile. 'Detective Chief Inspector Isaac Cook.'

'Yes, sir. What can I do for you?'

'I need you here. Are you free?'

'I will need to pass it by my DCI.'

'I'll deal with him. It's imperative that you're here.'

'Where do you want me?' Sara Marshall asked. She knew who Detective Chief Inspector Isaac Cook was. She had seen him on a couple of occasions, even been introduced to him, although his phone call gave the impression that he had not remembered.

'35 Easton Grove, Holland Park.'

'Thirty minutes.'

'I will be there,' DCI Cook replied. 'I need you to see this.'

For once the traffic was in Sara's favour. Within twenty minutes she arrived at the house. The uniforms were visible, as was the tape surrounding the crime scene. An ambulance was parked across the street.

'Not unless you cover up,' a voice bellowed at her.

'I have gloves and foot protectors,' Sara said.

'Apologies. I'm Gordon Windsor, the CSE here. It would be best if you put overalls on as well.'

'DCI Cook?'

'He's inside.'

Sara changed quickly and proceeded inside the house. It was clear that whoever lived there lived well.

'DI, I'm Isaac Cook. I believe we've met. I wasn't sure if you would have remembered.'

To Sara, it seemed naïve to believe that any woman would not remember Isaac Cook. He was over six feet, slim, and jet black. Even she had heard of his many romances, his straightforward manner with the average person as well as the top politicians in the country. She had seen him on television on more than one occasion.

'Not sure I could forget you, sir,' Sara replied.

'I need your opinion,' Isaac Cook said.

He led the way as they moved to the first floor of the house, and into the main bedroom. It was a scene that Sara had seen before. In the centre of a queen-sized bed lay the body of a man, naked and flat on its back.

'The cleaning lady found the body,' Isaac said.

'Similar pattern.' Sara looked up at the wall. She knew why she had been asked to visit the house.

'Copycat or is it the same woman?'

'It's been three years. After so long, most people have assumed that she committed suicide.'

'Had you?'

675

'Never. She may have been mad, but she was always in control. You saw the photo on Facebook with me in the background. And Charlotte Hamilton in the foreground taking a selfie.'

'Who hasn't,' Isaac said. In fact, from what he could remember, over five million had seen that photo.

'I knew she was still alive somewhere.'

'What do you reckon? Is this Charlotte Hamilton?'

Sara moved around the room. The man appeared to be in his fifties, a little overweight, but apart from that in good physical shape. She observed the slight erection, assumed it to indicate mid-coitus, although that was for others to confirm.

The knife, with only the handle visible, was embedded in the man's throat. There was also blood congealing on his chest in the area of the heart.

'She's improved her technique,' Sara said.

'What do you mean?'

'When she killed Liam Fogarty, she only stabbed him once with a stiletto knife. Unlikely that he would have lived, but he would have lived longer had she not severed the large artery.'

'Are you certain?' Isaac asked.

'The crime scene investigators will confirm, but, yes, it's her. Did she take a shower?'

'Dried the floor, hung up the towel afterwards.'

'So much blood. Gave her plenty of writing material,' Sara said.

'The number on the wall?'

'It's the same style of writing.'

Both of them looked at the wall, an off-white colour before the blood of the victim had been used to paint the number 5.

'It's her,' Sara said. 'She's back, and she will kill again.'

'We need to work together on this.'

'The case was assigned to another officer.'

'I'll square it with your DCI.'

'Thanks. I would like to get even with this woman.'

'She's dangerous, and she knows you,' Isaac said.

'And I know her,' Sara said.

'Welcome on board.'

***

Procedurally, the responsibility for the murder investigation would lie with the Homicide team in the area where the crime had occurred.

Graham Dyer, a local businessman, had died in Holland Park, close to Challis Street Police Station, and would come under DCI Cook and his team. The other murders had occurred in the Twickenham area, Sara Marshall's area of responsibility.

Bob Marshall had no issues with his wife again taking the lead role in Twickenham, although his detective superintendent had, or at least had until Detective Chief Superintendent Goddard, Isaac's boss, had phoned Martin Rowsome and insisted.

The plan was that Sara Marshall and her team, currently only Detective Sergeant Sean O'Riordan, would stay at their office, while Isaac Cook and his team would remain in Challis Street. The stations were close enough, only thirty minutes to drive, although sometimes it could take as long as forty-five minutes.

Sara had no illusions as to what was going to happen. Isaac had been hopeful that the death of Graham Dyer was a one-off, although he had been involved in enough murder cases to know that once a murderer has acquired the taste for killing they need to feed that hunger, and Dyer had been number 5.

Isaac had read up on the previous four deaths. He had been visibly disturbed by the death of Duncan Hamilton. He had read the psychological reports from both Grace Nelson, the criminal pathologist, and Dr Gladys Lake. The behavioural patterns of Charlotte Hamilton were clearly identified; the analysis was the same from both women: highly dangerous, likely to kill again, no cognitive sense of right or wrong.

Isaac knew this time they had a problem. In the past, his murders had been centred around blackmail, revenge, anger, a need to conceal the truth, but with Charlotte Hamilton, it went deeper.

The woman was smart. IQ tests in Newcastle had shown that she was in the top ten per cent in the country, yet coupled with that was no moral restraint, no comprehension of the evil she was committing, no concern about the emotions of those who had loved her, still loved her.

The media, as ever aggressive for a good story, had soon latched on to the death of Graham Dyer. So far they did not know about the number on the wall. They had been bad enough the first time, even attempting to portray her as some kind of folk hero, at least on one internet site dedicated to the bizarre and deluded. Isaac had checked it out; it had over twenty thousand followers, although most of them were just curious and could be considered harmless. However, taking the numbers down from twenty thousand to those who read the website, maybe ten per cent, and then to those who fantasised over Charlotte Hamilton, the lone ranger, wreaking revenge on those men who had subjugated women. Even if ten per cent of ten per cent of ten per cent of twenty thousand, there was bound to be one or two crazy enough to commit murder.

Isaac hoped that the deluded would do it elsewhere; Charlotte Hamilton was enough to deal with. His team were primed and ready: DI Hill was already interfacing with his counterpart, DI Sara Marshall. Detective Sergeant Wendy Gladstone was in communication with Sean O'Riordan, and Bridget Halloran was collating the paperwork.

A joint operations room had been set up in Challis Street. Detective Chief Superintendent Goddard had attended the first meeting, given them the obligatory pep talk.

'What do we know about this woman?' Isaac asked after Richard Goddard had left.

'You've read the report?' Sara asked.

'We've all read it, but what we need is to hear it from you.'

Sara, pleased to be a rising star again, not a has-been confined to the office more often than she would have liked, stood up to speak.

'After Liam Fogarty's death, we kept the investigation open for another four months. In all that time, we found no trace of Charlotte Hamilton, other than a hotel where she had stayed after killing Brad Howard.'

'Are all the murders attributable to Charlotte Hamilton? Could any be copycats?' Larry Hill asked.

'There's no doubt. Fingerprints and DNA at all murders, apart from Duncan Hamilton.'

'She killed her own brother?' Wendy Gladstone asked.

'Psychotic. No concept of right or wrong,' Sara said.

'Medical reports aside,' Isaac said, 'what do you believe she intends to do? What are her thought patterns?'

'She killed three people in London and disappeared.'

'Any thoughts as to why?' Larry asked.

'As to why she killed three people or why she disappeared?' Sara asked.

'The latter.'

'Either she went back on medication, although we could find no prescriptions in the names that she has used and no black-market sales, or she just stopped of her own free will.'

'Is that possible?' Isaac asked.

'According to the experts it is, although the psychotic thoughts would remain.'

'The triggers being men?' Wendy asked.

'That's what we believe. So far, there have been no attacks against women, apart from Stephanie Chalmers at the first murder. We believe that only happened as a result of her walking in just after Charlotte Hamilton had killed Gregory Chalmers. Gloria, her flatmate, was not killed, although her boyfriend was.'

'Gloria, where is she?'

'I've no idea. Probably back in London, but we've had no reason to contact her for over two years.'

'We need to find Charlotte Hamilton,' Isaac said. 'Any ideas where we should look?'

'Where she's stayed hidden for three years may be a good place to look,' Sean O'Riordan said.

'But you've no idea where to look,' Larry reminded him.

'As you say, no idea, and that is the problem.'

'Job for you, Wendy,' Isaac said.

Gordon Windsor, the crime scene examiner at the murder in Holland Park, joined the meeting. 'I can confirm that samples we found at Graham Dyer's house belong to Charlotte Hamilton. As expected, he died mid-coitus, seminal fluid found on the tip of his penis. At the moment of ejaculation, she thrust the knife into his heart. This time, she missed the large artery, and he would have still been alive. He had been stabbed an additional three times in the heart and once in the throat.'

'Any clues about the woman?' Isaac asked.

'Brunette, although the roots were blonde. Also, she showered, cleaned the bathroom and left. Nothing more.'

'We conducted door-to-doors,' Larry said. 'Nobody saw anything. Graham Dyer was a local businessman, successful by all accounts. He had been married but was living on his own. One neighbour stated that he occasionally brought a woman home with him.'

'Where did he meet Charlotte Hamilton?' Bridget asked.

'Good question,' Isaac said. 'Sara, any ideas?'

'Not really. Gregory Chalmers, she met when he and his wife had advertised for someone to help with the children. Brad Howard, she knew through Gloria. Liam Fogarty, she picked up at a club in Richmond. If she wants a man, she'll find one.'

'Wendy and Larry, you'd better get down to Holland Park and see if you can trace the murdered man's movements.'

Chapter 14

Charlotte Hamilton had seen the black police officer. She imagined seducing him, and then at the right moment sticking a knife into his black heart.

She knew she had been right to stay hidden for three years; three glorious years where no questions had been asked, and everyone had been courteous and friendly, even invited her into their houses. She had not been fooled. They were no better than her parents who had deserted her, allowed her to be drugged and then electric-shocked, with the confusion and memory loss after. Sometimes she wondered about her parents: where they were, what they were doing, even wishing her stupid brother was still alive. But what if he was?

He had only been an irritant to her, teasing her, breaking her dolls, getting between the love of her parents for her. She was glad she had killed him, even though she could have saved him. She remembered him squealing as he hung on to a branch protruding at the top of the quarry. How she had enjoyed pulling the branch away from him; how she had enjoyed watching him fall and fall and fall, and then hitting the ground with a thud. The sound had been music to her ears, and if she closed her eyes, the scene was still so clear.

She had seen the sorrow in her parents' eyes, especially her mother's, that he was dead and she was still alive. They should have embraced her with the love they had shown to him, but what did they do? They threw her into that place full of crazies. Sure, she had to admit that it had not all been bad, but it was a home for the insane, and she was sane. The man who had tested her before admission had said she was exceptionally bright, yet she was locked up behind bars with people who drooled and talked nonsense and threw their food on the floor.

She remembered the woman doctor, that Lake woman. She had told them to attach the electrodes to her scalp, and then told them to crank up the electricity. They had told her that it was good for her; something to do with dopamines and incorrect electrical paths in the brain. But she knew what it was; it was to punish her for being smarter than they were, for finding out how to beat the security and to climb over the fence. They had caught her once or twice, but she had done it many times.

She wanted to leave there at eighteen, but she had stayed a year longer. She had used their hospital because she had nowhere to go, but once she figured it out, she had left. They had tried to stop her, to reason with her, but she had a woman in London who was going to look after her. All she had to do was to offer her body to any man that was willing to pay, and where was the problem in that? Hadn't she given herself enough times to the local men in Newcastle, and what did they give her? Nothing, apart from a nasty rash. At least the hospital's medicine chest had dealt with that.

And then the men in that house in London with their breath smelling of beer, their bodies of sweat and lack of hygiene. They wanted to love her, to make love to her, but what did they really want? Just a quick screw, the opportunity to prod and poke her body, and once they were satisfied, they would leave her to clean up the mess. They were the same as all the other men. Gregory Chalmers had treated her well; she had loved him, but in the end he was only a bastard as well. And then there was Gloria's boyfriend, tattooed and well-built. He thought he was something special until she had stuck the knife in him. The feel of his body beneath her as she rammed the knife in. The spurting blood covering her body. The look on his face as he realised that he was not there for love, only for death, his death. He had died for all men, although he was only one. Many men were deserving of death; she would ensure them that right.

The club had been fun, although the man had not been. He had told her his name was Liam, and he had been ugly and small and unable to satisfy her; not that it mattered, as she had been pleased with the knife in his heart. She had read in the newspaper afterwards that he could have lived if she had not happened to put her knife in the right place. One day she would thank whoever had advised her on that. Graham Dyer had been her first after three years, and his death had been assured as she knifed him repeatedly; no point in a shoddy job. He had tried to paw her in the pub, and back in his house he had tried to love her. She had no need for love; no need for a man, other than to be the receiver of a violent death.

She could see another murder, maybe the black police officer, but he would be smarter than her previous victims. And then there was that female detective inspector. She realised that women were not to blame for the troubles in the world, but for that woman, Sara Stanforth, she would make an exception. And what did a man have that a woman did not? She knew the answer to that question: the power to subjugate women, the power to put her into a lunatic asylum, the right to hit her, just because they had paid for her. And with Gregory Chalmers, the authority to profess love and then cast her off, no more than an old shoe, not even worthy of contempt.

She had not wanted to harm Stephanie Chalmers. She had been a good woman with a bad husband: a husband that cheated on her, who did not love her, only himself. Charlotte wished it could have been different, that he could have loved her and she could have been with his children, but he had been no different. She had enjoyed carving a number onto his chest, although she had not carved another since.

She knew that her mind played havoc with her thoughts, and that medication would make her see everything the same way as other people, but who was sane? Her or them?

They were the mad people, not her. She knew that given the right environment, she could act as they did. It had been easy outside that club to masquerade as an innocent bystander. The photo she had taken had been shown around the world; she was famous, and she enjoyed the feeling. She would take another to show that woman police officer and that black man that she, Charlotte Hamilton, moved the streets of London with impunity. They would never find her, and she would remove more men from society. She needed to pass the message on for other women to join her cause.

***

Isaac Cook's parents maintained an album of their son. They had photos of him as a child, as a youth, his graduation from university, and especially his time as a police officer.

They had recorded every press conference where he had spoken. They even had one of him with the prime minister, although Isaac was not sure that they would want a copy of the short video that had just appeared on Facebook. So far, Isaac could see that it had had over three thousand views, and that number was certain to rise.

Charlotte Hamilton had a Facebook account, and although it had been blocked a couple of times, it resurfaced soon enough with a different name. Those interested in her career always seemed to find it.

The video of Isaac leaving Graham Dyer's house with Sara Marshall had been clear enough, even if the camera, a smartphone, had been located on the other side of the road. It had been a cold

683

day, and most people on the street had a hat on or a hooded jacket, which would have been the ideal disguise for Charlotte Hamilton.

Isaac checked the woman's Facebook account. Now she had fifteen thousand two hundred followers. Isaac knew that the world was full of idiots, but liking the Facebook page of a serial killer seemed macabre. He assumed that all mass murderers enjoyed their infamy, and it no doubt encouraged them to cause more misery. Next time a video of a slaying would be hard to stop. Facebook may put a block on a video portraying graphic violence, but there were other websites, and they would not be so scrupulous.

'How are you going to handle this case, Isaac?' DCS Goddard had asked on his arrival at the Homicide office.

'We need to find the woman.'

'Why do you think you will succeed? The other police station had three years, and they couldn't find her.'

'We're better, sir.'

'You may well be, but this woman is smart; smart enough to video you.'

'Unfortunate, sir.'

'Downright embarrassing. My best police officer videoed by a serial killer, and you never spotted her.'

'I was with DI Sara Marshall, and she never spotted her either.'

'That's the second time on film for her. Any more and she'll need to join the actors' union, Equity.'

'I don't think she would appreciate that, sir.'

'You must have a plan.'

'Not a lot to go with. We are checking on Graham Dyer's movements, attempting to find out when and where he met Charlotte Hamilton. Apart from that, we are at a loose end. The woman disappears, reappears and disappears again.

'Then find out where.'

'Not so easy. She blends in seamlessly into the city. Apart from her predilection to murder, she's just an average citizen.'

'That may be, but I don't want any more deaths. Understood!'

'Understood, sir.'

DCS Goddard left, and Bridget came into the office. 'Bit hard on you, sir,' she said.

'He's right.'

Isaac was the best police officer in the department, but even he could not see the way forward. A murderer invariably gives themselves away eventually, but Charlotte Hamilton did not see herself as a murderer.

Back in Twickenham Sara was going over old notes. She had phoned Charlotte's father's mobile, told them to watch out for their daughter, although they had seen the news and assumed it was her. She also called Dr Gladys Lake to let her know that Charlotte had resurfaced.

Rory Hewitt, still working, although looking forward to his retirement, stationed some uniforms to watch the hospital.

Bob Marshall, Sara's husband and DCI, was concerned for his wife. She was now the mother of a one-year-old, and she should be spending time with him. Murder always burned the hours, and a child needs more than a couple of hours of exhausted attention from its mother each day.

Sara, eager to prove her mettle after her unceremonious dumping by her husband on the orders of Detective Superintendent Rowsome, intended to make amends, to show both of them that she was as good as any man, and certainly better than the man who had replaced her.

He had had less success than her, and he had left soon enough: tail between his legs, but his reputation not tinged by failure.

Hers had been, she knew that, and while she still held the rank of detective inspector, the two words had not been split by 'chief'. She knew that may not be possible without a Master's degree, and in the past the department would have paid for her studies, but for two years they had been refusing. Budgetary constraints, the official explanation; unofficially, a black mark against the candidate.

***

DS Wendy Gladstone and DI Larry Hill visited Holland Park, positioning themselves where the video of their DCI and DI Sara

Marshall had been taken. They knocked on a few doors close by; nobody remembered anyone specifically, although more than one person had been videoing the scene.

Graham Dyer owned an antique shop not far away. It was closed when they arrived, not unexpected considering that the owner was now in Pathology, and would be undergoing a detailed autopsy. He had been in his fifties, well liked locally, and led an active social life. Wendy and Larry visited some local establishments – clubs, pubs, cafés.

It appeared that he had visited most of them at one time or another, had been married and would take the occasional woman home with him. So far, nobody remembered the woman from the night of the murder, although he had been in one of the pubs earlier in the day.

An attractive female would not be noticeable, both Wendy and Larry agreed, in an area that boasted more than its fair share of beautiful women.

'The perfect disguise,' Wendy said, although, as she freely admitted, she would not have gone unnoticed. It had been some months since her husband had passed away, but she still missed him. She had joined a gym, taken up yoga, even quit smoking for a couple of weeks, but she was back on them again, although not as heavily as before.

Isaac Cook, their DCI, continued to have female trouble. Sue Smith, the latest in a long line of suitable women, had gone overseas, and he was alone again; not that he liked it, but there was not much he could do about it.

Wendy knew he could always find someone for a casual fling, but he had admitted to her on a couple of occasions that he wanted to settle down.

***

Isaac was pleased to be busy again, although troubled that a known murderer was walking the streets. The woman could be anywhere, he realised. With his other murder cases, it had been a case of sifting through the clues, interviewing people, aiming to solve the crime and to pinpoint the murderer, but with Charlotte Hamilton, none of this was needed.

The woman had been identified, the prosecution case was ready, and there was no question of her guilt. To Isaac, what he could see was a missing person's investigation, and the person in question was calculating and able to strike at will. She was a phantom whose appearances signalled another death, but where would she next appear?

Not only had she videoed him leaving Graham Dyer's house with Sara Marshall, but she was also videoing locations around London, including a distant view of the apartment block where Isaac lived. Her notoriety continued to gain momentum as she placed them on social media.

It was a world obsessed with celebrity, whether it was vacuous and worthless, talented or talentless, and it cared little that the person they sought out, even worshipped, was a psychotic murderer.

Some websites had been set up around the world by admirers, their hosting servers located in countries that did not enforce censorship, other than on their own people.

The copycat killings continued to occur: an unfaithful husband in North Carolina, a drunk homeless man in Alaska, even a male immigrant from Africa in Birmingham. And always a number had been painted on the man or on a wall, either in his own blood or with a felt pen.

None of the women involved in the copycats was as smart as Charlotte Hamilton, as they had all been caught and charged.

Isaac Cook, tall, black and intelligent, pondered the way forward. He had met Sara Marshall on a couple of occasions to discuss tactics, and to see if they could pre-empt the next murder, but both knew that Charlotte Hamilton did not commit murder by the book.

So far, she had killed five: the first, her brother, then a lover, followed by a flatmate's boyfriend. Her last murder, three years previously, had been chosen for no other reason than he had been male, and he had been willing to accompany her out to a toilet at the back of a club.

Then three years of nothing, only to return and kill Graham Dyer.

Sara Marshall thought that she could disappear again, but Isaac's instincts were more attuned. He knew she would strike again and soon.

Even he could see that the woman had a fixation on him, but why? He had seen her picture, even the video of the children's party at the Chalmers' house, and he had to admit she was beautiful. She had been twenty-four then; she would be twenty-seven now, and if she did not kill men, would be the sort of woman that he liked, her pale skin offsetting his shiny black.

'Larry, what's the plan?' Isaac asked. Both men were sitting in Isaac's office. There seemed little point in being out on the street looking for the woman.

'We can just follow up on leads.'

'Do we have any?'

'According to Sara Marshall, the woman stays within certain areas. The three murders, three years ago, were centred around Richmond and Twickenham. Now, she is close to us, here in Challis Street. There is every reason to believe that her next murder will be within four to five miles of this location.'

'Do you realise how many clubs, pubs, places of entertainment there are?'

'More than we can hope to cover.'

'Precisely,' Isaac said. 'We're being forced to wait for her to make the next move. Her increasing baiting of us indicates a change in her modus operandi. In the past, she has been a silent killer, driven by her neuroses, her belief that she was providing a service, but now she appears to want the adulation as well.'

'Plenty of sick people out there,' Larry said.

Wendy Gladstone had come into the office, bringing a cup of coffee with her. 'What do you reckon?' she asked Isaac.

'The best we can do is to issue a warning to the general public.'

'The male public according to profiling,' Wendy corrected Isaac.

'As you say, the male public.'

'Vague,' Larry said.

'Any better ideas?' Isaac asked.

'Not really, but what are they looking out for? A woman of twenty-seven, hair colour unknown, clothing unknown.'

'Miss Average,' Wendy said.

Chapter 15

A woman walked along Oxford Street, one of the busiest shopping locations in Europe. She drew no glances from the other people on the street. It was a warmer day than the previous four, but it was still cool. She wore a dark coat and jeans.

The day was drawing to a close, and it was becoming dark. She realised that she had been walking for hours, and had been deep in thought. She knew that life had given her a purpose, and she felt a degree of contentment.

For some years, she had been lost, unsure how to proceed. Integrating into a small country town had been easy. She had arrived there three years before. All that she owned or needed she carried in one suitcase and a backpack.

The old lady who opened the door at her accommodation had been pleasant and had welcomed her in with a cup of tea. Charlotte Hamilton knew that it was old-fashioned hospitality and that the woman meant well.

Dr Gladys Lake had meant well, but then she allowed them to torture her; Mavis Williams had meant well, but she expected her to let men use her body; Stephanie Chalmers had meant well, but her husband had used her.

She hoped that Beatrice Castle meant well, or…

'Call me Beaty, everyone else does,' the old lady said.

'Call me Cathy.'

A cat had climbed up on to Charlotte Hamilton's lap. It purred. Charlotte felt calm. She had had a cat as a child, but her brother had teased it, and then one day it had been run over by a car. She remembered her mother picking it up and placing it in a hole in the ground, next to the roses. 'It's the best place for him,' she had said.

Charlotte remembered that day well enough. She had made a cross out of two small branches that had fallen from a tree in the garden. Each day for a week, she visited the grave and placed a few flowers on it. Her brother had said she was crazy, and it was only a dumb animal and it had deserved to die. She knew from that day that she hated him.

It had been easy to hate him, to hate a lot of people, but she could not hate Beaty or her cat. She did not know why, but it was a good feeling; the best for a long time.

Charlotte could see that she had been running forever. First from her parents, and then from her doctor, and then from Mavis Williams and all those men. Gregory Chalmers had shown her love, real love, not just a drunken screw, but he had disappointed her. With Beaty and her cat, she could forgive him. She thought he had died, something to do with her, but her mind seemed unable to focus on negativity.

'How long are you staying?' Beaty asked. Charlotte had found the small cottage online.

'As long as I can.'

'Then I will make sure you have a special rate.'

Beaty showed Charlotte to her room. It was delightful, with a view overlooking the back garden. There was a small stream at the far end, and the sound of it lulled her to sleep at night. Occasionally Felix, the cat, would come in and curl up on the bottom of the bed.

The room, with its floral wallpaper, the morning sun streaming in through the bay window, the homely touches, reminded Charlotte of her childhood. She realised that for the first time in many years she was happy, and the negative thoughts that had plagued her had vanished.

She reflected on her life, and she could only remember the good; the bad, whatever it was, had recessed back into her subconscious.

Three years passed in an instant. A job in the local library, even a boyfriend, but it had not lasted long. For whatever reason, an over-amorous man only complicated her life, and all she wanted was simplicity. She had remembered her parents soon after arriving in the small town, and on Beaty's insistence, she had phoned them.

It had been a short conversation, but Charlotte had been pleased to hear their voices, aware that she could not return to the family home. She did not know why, but it was something serious; she was sure of that. Her parents had been pleasant, but distant; not once offering to come down and visit her, not that she wanted to see them, but it would have shown the love of parents for their child. Their child who had been lost for so many years, but had returned.

It had been Beaty who helped her integrate into the town, and Charlotte grew to love her.

She realised that the medication she carried with her was not needed, and she rarely took it. She threw it in a dustbin.

It had been good with Beaty and the cat but it had ended, badly as always. The cat had strolled out into the lane at the front of the house. Charlotte had warned Beaty how dangerous it was.

'Don't worry, there's no traffic. Felix will be alright.'

The cat did not see the delivery van, or if he did, he was too slow. The driver had not seen the cat, not that he was looking, as he was running late.

'You killed him,' Charlotte shouted.

'Not my fault,' the driver bellowed back from the safety of the vehicle. Charlotte moved her hand to the bag she carried, realised it only contained the day's groceries.

The vehicle hurtled off and was out of sight within twenty seconds.

Charlotte picked up the dead animal and carried it back to the house.

'Felix, Felix, what's happened?' Beaty screamed.

'A van hit him.'

Beaty clutched her chest and fell forward. Charlotte phoned for an ambulance. It arrived too late.

Charlotte buried the cat in the garden, put some flowers on the grave, made a small cross and left for the railway station. Her memories had come flooding back.

She knew what she had to do.

***

The Duke of York in Dering Street looked suitable. Charlotte took a seat close to the bar. A man soon joined her. He was a banker, or at least he said he was. Not that it concerned Charlotte as she had no need of his financial advice, no need of a mortgage, and besides, if she wanted a house, there was one up in Newcastle. At least, once she had removed its two inhabitants.

'Can I buy you a drink?' the banker asked. Charlotte had to admit that he was not a bad-looking man.

'Vodka and Lime.'

Charlotte knew that he was checking the goods on display. She had worn a thick coat and jeans to the pub but changed into a V-necked top and a short skirt on arrival. She knew that she looked cheap.

Let him think I'm an easy lay, she thought.

Dennis Goldman knew a sure bet when he saw one, and this woman was money in the bank. He could see that she wore no bra under the top. It had been a hard week in the city, what with the declining pound and the rise in interest rates. He had made the right call on shorting the pound earlier in the day; he knew that he was making the right call with the woman, especially as she was progressively moving closer to him.

'Are you busy tonight?' he asked the red-haired woman with the winning smile and the beautiful body.

'I'm free. Do you have anything in mind?'

'A meal and then my place,' he said.

If this one doesn't come across, it's still early enough in the evening to find another, he thought.

'How about your place first?'

Excellent, he thought.

'Is it far?' Charlotte asked.

'Five minutes in a taxi, ten if you walk.'

'Then we walk,' she said.

Charlotte drank her vodka and lime; Dennis finished his beer. They left the pub holding hands. Dennis believed himself to be a lucky man, although attracting females came easily to him. He had the talk down to a fine art. Run through the first few sentences, ensure a result. No result, move on to the next.

London was awash with beautiful women, and he was having the time of his life. He was making plenty of money, sleeping with more than his fair share of women.

This one would be another to add to the tally, he thought.

Dennis's place reflected the man: confident, brash, and modern. It was on the second floor of a converted terrace house, and it commanded a good view over London. Charlotte had to admit that she liked the apartment, even liked the man, but Gregory Chalmers had been a smooth talker, and he had turned out bad.

Besides, he brings me back here, no doubt to screw me and then dump me. I'm not the first one he's brought up here, she thought.

Dennis prepared some snacks, and brought a bottle of wine to the table in the sitting room; Charlotte continued to give the right signals.

The bottle of wine consumed, they moved towards each other. Soon, they were naked and writhing on the carpet. Charlotte was on top, the ideal position for the finale.

'You're beautiful,' Dennis gasped.

'You are suitable,' Charlotte replied.

'I'm ready.'

'Are you sure?'

'Yes.'

Charlotte leant over to her bag. She put her hand in and withdrew the knife.

'What's that for?' he asked.

'You bastard. You think women are just here to satisfy your carnal lusts.'

'What…'

The knife entered his body easily, driven by the force of the palms of both hands pushing down. The man's erection subsided as the blood drained out of his body.

Charlotte, familiar with the act of death, removed the knife; she then drove it back down again, this time harder than before. The man beneath her did not move. She took another knife from her bag, a larger knife, razor-sharp, and slit his throat. The blood spurted out. She rubbed it over her bare breasts and placed her bloodied fingers to her mouth.

'You taste great,' she said.

She then removed herself from the dead man's body and walked slowly to his shower. She washed all the blood off and shampooed her hair, careful to remove all traces of the red dye she had applied earlier in the day. She then dried herself, put on the top and jeans she had worn earlier. Before she left, she helped herself to some food from the refrigerator. She made a sandwich and walked towards the front door.

She looked back at the man lying dead on the carpet as she passed. She admired the skill with which she had carved the number 6 on his chest.

Bastard, she thought as she closed the front door behind her.

***

In one part of London, a woman bathed in the glory of her fame; in another, a police officer was coming to terms with not being in control of the situation.

Detective Chief Inspector Isaac Cook, the star of Homicide, a man slated for senior management, the protégé of Detective Chief Superintendent Richard Goddard, was floundering. He had met senior politicians, charmed them with his good manners. He had met and seduced many women, but now there was one woman who was oblivious to him. The one woman who could undermine his career if she was not stopped, and soon.

She had murdered five, and according to her website, she had killed again. So far, the department had not received any information about another murder, but the website had shown a view from the apartment, and it was clearly London. The photo of a naked man covered in blood was too disturbing for most to see. The London Metropolitan Police had attempted to block the website; it had not been successful. Charlotte Hamilton was fast attaining cult status, with a loyal band of followers: deviants, sadists, and miscreants, not to mention the extreme feminists who saw all men as superfluous.

Monday morning and it was the weekly meeting. Bridget, Wendy, and Larry were in attendance, as well as DI Sara Marshall and DS Sean O'Riordan.

There had only been one subject to discuss, and Sara was still the person with the most intimate knowledge of the woman.

Detective Chief Superintendent Goddard had joined them, at least for the first fifteen minutes. 'It's not looking good, is it?' he said.

'We are working on it, sir,' Isaac replied.

'Without any tangible results. I can find out more information about the murders and this woman on the internet than from you. Doesn't reflect well on this department, and now I have the commissioner of police on the phone asking what I'm doing, and what sort of people I have.'

'He's unreasonable,' Isaac said.

'I know that, but he's the commissioner. I can hardly tell him to go away and to let us get on with the policing, can I?'

'We're a good team, sir.'

'That may be, but this Hamilton woman is better. Mind you, she does not have a commissioner to answer to, only her admiring public. How many followers on her website now?'

'Over twenty-five thousand.'

'She's posted another death,' Goddard said.

'That is the subject of our discussion. So far, we have not received any confirmation of another murder.'

'Apart from her website,' Goddard said. This time she's posted photos.'

'She's mentally sick,' Sara said.

'That's damn obvious to anyone. Still smarter than anyone in this room.'

It was Sara who spoke first after Richard Goddard had left. 'Unfair comment.'

'We go back a long way,' Isaac said. 'His bark's worse than his bite, and besides, he is correct.'

'Have you seen the photos?' Larry asked.

'Yes.'

'Can we deduce where they were taken?' Wendy asked.

695

'It's not easy. London, and not far from here. You can see the skyline in the background.'

Chapter 16

As Sara and Sean were about to leave the office and return to Twickenham, Isaac's phone rang. He picked it up.

'Hold on,' Isaac shouted at them before returning to the phone.

'Another body?' Wendy asked.

'34 Davies Street, Mayfair. Larry, Sara, you can come with me. We cannot have everyone at the murder scene. Gordon Windsor will go spare if we all come marching in. Sean, Wendy, get ready to conduct a door-to-door. Bridget, open another file.'

Challis Street to Davies Street was no more than two miles. Traffic was heavy mid-morning. Isaac took the portable flashing light out from under his seat and secured it to the roof of his car. With the siren and the light, cars started to pull over to one side to let him through.

'Dramatic,' Gordon Windsor said on their arrival.

'What floor?' Isaac asked.

'Second. Good view, charming apartment, or at least it was.'

'What do you mean?'

'You'll see once you've kitted up.'

Two uniforms were standing outside; the crime scene tape had already been rolled out. Due to the crowd that was building up, barriers were being erected on the other side of the street. As Isaac, Larry and Sara kitted up – gloves, foot protectors, and overalls – a television crew arrived. Barry Wiltshire, their lead crime reporter, saw Isaac and made a beeline for him. Isaac told one of the uniforms to deal with it. He did not have the time to indulge in idle speculation on the street, at least not before he had seen the body and the crime scene, and even then, he did not want to speak to Wiltshire who was an obnoxious toad of a man.

Isaac and his team entered the front door of the building and climbed the two flights of stairs. Once inside the apartment, they followed the obvious route down the hallway. On the floor in the main room was the body of a man: as usual, naked and lying on his back.

'Investment banker, or at least he was. Explains how he could afford this place,' Gordon Windsor said. He had preceded them up the stairs and was standing close to the body.

The white carpet that the body lay on was covered in blood, a lot of blood. Bloodied footprints could be seen on the polished floorboards around the perimeter of the carpet. Larry felt his stomach reacting, as did Sara. Isaac appeared unmoved by the scene.

'That's where she walked after killing him.' Gordon Windsor had seen Sara looking at the footprints, trying to ascertain where they led to.

'Did she shower?' Sara asked.

'Helped herself to the food in the refrigerator too. I would estimate she spent thirty minutes here after she had killed him.'

'Identity of the deceased?' Larry asked.

'Dennis Goldman. Apparently a whiz kid with stocks and shares.'

'How do you know that?' Isaac asked.

'There's a certificate on the wall from his bank.'

Sara's phone rang, and she excused herself from the conversation. Once outside the apartment, she spoke. 'Sara Marshall.'

'Is it?' an enquiring voice asked. Sara recognised it instantly.

'Dr Lake. We are here now. It is almost certainly Charlotte.'

'She phoned me ten minutes ago,' Gladys Lake said.

'What did she say?'

'She sang a song.'

'What song? Do you remember?'

'I will never forget it as long as I live. *Oh, what fun, I slit his throat. Who will be next? Will it be you?*'

Sara felt a shiver down her spine. 'You'll need twenty-four-hour protection.'

'With Charlotte? What's the point?' Gladys Lake said.

'She has only killed men, so far. We have no reason to believe she is targeting you.'

'That may be, but I am scared.'

'Then leave. Go overseas, take an extended vacation until we apprehend her.'

'I will consider that option.'

The phone line went dead. Sara called DI Rory Hewitt in Newcastle. 'I've just had Dr Lake on the phone,' she said.

'She called me five minutes ago. We have assigned immediate protection for her.'

Sara returned to the murder scene and told Isaac about her conversation with Gladys Lake. Gordon Windsor was checking on the condition of the body. 'She did not intend him to live. Very thorough,' he said.

'Was he alive when she cut his throat?' Larry asked.

'Probably not, although his blood would still have been pumping.'

'Friday night?' Isaac asked.

'Judging by the putrefaction, the gases emitting from the body, the defecation, I would agree with that possibility. Why Friday night?'

'That was the date given by his murderer.'

'You realise she enjoys this?' Windsor said.

'She's already threatened someone else,' Isaac said. He checked Charlotte Hamilton's website. It kept being blocked, only to reappear on another server. She now had eighty-four thousand followers.

***

Wendy and Sean were outside when the other members of the team left the murder scene. They were busy organising a door-to-door. Each person assigned to the task had been given a list of questions to ask: did you see anything suspicious, did you know Dennis Goldman, did you see him with a female on Friday night between the hours of 8 p.m. and midnight, and so on.

Wendy and Sean had been given a phone number and address of Dennis Goldman's place of work; they were heading over there.

Sara called Charlotte Hamilton's parents. 'Have you heard from your daughter?'

Charles Hamilton answered the phone. 'My wife is not well enough to talk to you.'

'I'm sorry to hear that,' Sara said. She felt for Charlotte Hamilton's parents. According to Keith Greenstreet, who had met them some years previously, they were decent people who, because of their daughter, the most savage serial killer in England for many years, were now pariahs in society. They were unable to go out of their house, and if they did, then it was to a distant location, hoping they would not be recognised, to purchase the household provisions and then return as quickly as possible to the sanctity of their remote location.

'Is it her?'

'I'm sorry.'

'My wife has suffered a breakdown; attempted suicide.'

'Will she recover?' Sara asked.

'Her body may. We are broken people,' Charles Hamilton said.

'Is there anything I can do?'

'Find our daughter before she kills again.'

***

In an internet café on the northern outskirts of London sat a woman. It was the evening of the previous day, way past 9 p.m. and the café was due to close in fifteen minutes.

Long enough, the woman thought. She had become used to run-down internet facilities with their dodgy screens, keyboards with keys that stuck, especially the most used ones, and cursors that jerked their way across the screen.

A permanent connection was not possible at the bedsit she rented, and a mobile modem would not have had the capacity for the photos she was loading. She was a lonely figure in that café, but she was happy.

She was famous all over the world, her followers a testament to that fact. Each day, in all the newspapers in London, there would be an article on her latest murder, and always a photo of the black police officer.

Her intellect told her that she was taking risks. An internet connection could be checked, even the café where she was now, but she did not care.

She knew that one day all those mad people who saw her as crazy would put her in prison, but it was them, not her, who deserved to be in prison. If they were going to catch her, and she knew they would, then she would lead them on a merry chase first.

She would make the black police officer pay. They said his name was Isaac Cook: she would remember that name. And there, yet again, was that woman, that Sara Stanforth, although now they were reporting her as Sara Marshall. The woman had a husband; what joy to put a knife into him, to watch her suffer.

Maybe she would kill them both. The thought made her smile and then to laugh. The owner of the internet café, a small man with a strong accent, looked at her as she laughed. His interest waned after ten seconds, and he went back to the comic that he had been reading.

He had a motley collection of patrons coming into his café, paying five pounds for a coffee and thirty minutes' free internet, even though the connection was slow. Not that it seemed to concern the woman, a short-haired brunette, her face partially concealed by a large scarf.

If he had looked, he would have noticed that she was attractive, but he was not a man who cared about anything very much. As long as they paid, what did he care? They could be talking to a girlfriend, even indulging in phone sex, learning how to make a bomb, booking accommodation. He only wanted their money, and at five pounds for each patron, he would have enough to make a trip back to India that year.

'Five minutes,' he said.

'Fine,' the reply.

Charlotte Hamilton loaded up some more photos, checked her emails, and pressed enter. The pictures loaded slowly. She wondered what would happen when they went live around the world. Would her parents be shocked? Would Dr Lake? And what about Detective Chief Inspector Isaac Cook? Would he be shocked as well, or would he take them in his stride? She thought he would, but she needed to know. She knew that she needed to meet him.

***

Wendy Gladstone knocked on the door of the house next to Dennis Goldman's apartment. A young woman in her twenties answered the door.

'Are you aware of what has happened next door?' Wendy asked.

'I've just woken up; must have slept for two days.'

'Why?' Wendy asked.

'Just lazy, I suppose.' It did not seem a good enough answer to Wendy.

The woman moved uneasily on her feet. As she lurched forward, Wendy grabbed hold of her and eased her into the house. Dennis Goldman's apartment had been an upmarket conversion of an impressive terrace house. The young woman's house was in its original state.

'Your house?' Wendy asked as the woman revived.

'My parents. They're loaded.'

'And you?'

'I'm just the spoilt kid of the house.'

'Are you proud of that?' Wendy asked.

'I'm not bothered either way. I have a good time, plenty of friends, plenty of money. Why work?'

Wendy could have given the woman a lecture about her responsibilities, but she knew it would be wasted, and besides, she was investigating the death of Dennis Goldman.

'Do you know Dennis Goldman?' Wendy asked.

'He's a friend. We go out drinking together sometimes.'

'I am sorry to inform you that he has been killed.'

The young woman, attractive if she made an effort, put her face in her hands and cried. 'How?' she asked.

'He has been murdered.'

'I saw him on Friday. He asked me out for a drink at the Duke of York on Dering Street.'

The woman said her name was Amanda Brocklehurst. To Wendy, who had grown up in Yorkshire on a farm and who had worked hard all her life, Miss Brocklehurst represented the very worst of people. She was, Wendy thought, one of the Sloane Rangers, if that term was used still, who milled around Sloane Square in Chelsea flaunting their wealth, their titles, their wealthy parents, and their willingness not to work. Still, Wendy assumed they kept the local shopkeepers happy with their gold and platinum credit cards.

'Did he go there often?'

'All the time. So did I, especially if Dennis was there.'

'You fancied him?' Wendy asked. Sara Marshall had told her that he had been a good-looking man.

'Are you sure he's dead?' Amanda Brocklehurst was wilting again. With no one else in the house to look after her, Wendy opened a drinks cabinet in the main room, took a bottle of soda water, poured its contents into a glass and gave it to the young woman. She gulped it down in one go. Wendy had seen a bottle of brandy, the traditional pick-me-up, but did not give it to the woman. It was clear that she was suffering the effects of too much alcohol the previous night.

'I've got a thumping head,' Amanda said.

'Your fault.'

'You're not my mother.'

For that Wendy was thankful. Her sons had come home drunk on a few too many occasions. Her solution with them was a berating at the door on entry, not that it did much good, although the cold shoulder for a few days, and her unwillingness to provide them with three meals a day, did.

'Last night Dennis Goldman brought a woman back with him.'

'That's Dennis.'

'Ladies' man?' Wendy asked.

'He always had someone over for the night.'

'Even you?'

'We had an arrangement.'

'Tell me.'

'If he was lonely, or I was, then we would get together.'

'Sleep together?'

'Just friends, but yes, we would have sex. Not a crime. People do it all the time.'

Wendy could see that the rich and spoilt Amanda Brocklehurst did it all the time and that she had little worth, other than that she was young and attractive. 'Duke of York. Would he have picked the woman up there?'

'Dennis's favourite place for pickups,' Amanda replied.

Chapter 17

'Dering Street,' Wendy said to Larry as they stood in the street outside Goldman's apartment. The team of door-to-doors were slowly working their way up and down the street.

'Good looker,' Larry said. He had seen the young woman from a distance.

'Waste of space,' was Wendy's reply.

The Duke of York had been rebuilt in the nineteenth century, and apparently named after the Grand Old Duke of York who had marched his troops up a hill in France. Wendy remembered the nursery rhyme from childhood; Larry did not.

It was located in St George Hanover Square and was one of the trendy pubs in a trendy part of London.

'Do you know a Dennis Goldman?' Larry asked the woman serving behind the bar. It was still early and the end-of-day crowd had not arrived.

'I'm only new,' the woman replied with an Australian accent.

Another backpacker working for cash and less than the minimum wage, Wendy thought.

'Is the manager here?'

The cash-in-hand wandered off. Two minutes later, a middle-aged man, red in the face, appeared.

'Can I help you?' he asked.

'Detective Inspector Hill, Detective Sergeant Wendy Gladstone. We have a few questions.'

'Fancy a drink? On the house.'

Larry was tempted to ask for a beer but did not. 'Orange juice for me,' he said.

'The same for me,' Wendy replied.

The landlord pulled himself a beer. 'I need to check it anyway. Just changed the barrel.'

'Dennis Goldman.'

'Comes in here several times a week.'

'Friday night,' Larry asked.

'He walked out of here with a woman.'

'Tell us about the woman,' Wendy asked.

'Attractive, red hair, short skirt, tight top. Not much else to tell.'

'Why do you say that?'

'She was giving him the right signals. Coming in close, draping her arm around him. We could see that he was on to a sure thing.'

'We?'

'Those behind the bar.'

'Had you seen the woman before?'

'Never. Anyway, what's this all about?'

'Dennis Goldman was killed between the hours of 10 p.m. on Friday night and 2 a.m. on Saturday morning.'

'Sorry to hear that.'

'Upsets you?'

'It's not something you expect to hear. How did he die?'

'We're from Homicide,' Larry said.
'Do you mean he was murdered?'
'Yes.'
'And the woman?'
'She's our prime suspect.'
'We've got cameras in here,' the landlord said.

***

On the northern outskirts of the city, the woman slept peacefully, or at least as peacefully as could be expected with the heavy traffic outside her window. She dreamt of happy times and happy thoughts interspersed with dark places and dark thoughts. She rolled in her bed, one arm hanging down. The bed, she had known when she agreed to take the room, was old and flea-bitten. She imagined how many sweaty bodies had lain on it, how many fornicating couples had tested its springs, how many murderers had used it.

Charlotte knew the answer to the last question: one.

She moved between rational and despair, anger and melancholy, sweet dreams and nightmares, although the nightmares were becoming more frequent. She wanted to be like everyone else, but they were mad, she was not.

She woke up, the banging at the door disturbing her. 'You owe me for the next month,' the voice said. She had heard the voice before, but she was not sure where.

The door opened, and an old man in his eighties and wearing an old crumpled shirt and a pair of shorts entered. On his feet he wore a pair of slippers.

'The rent,' he said.

She would have paid him, but she had no money. The money she had saved over the years, including some that she had stolen from the men she had killed, was not sufficient. If the man had been younger, she would have given herself to him; it would not be the first time that she had exchanged sexual favours for financial independence.

'No rent, no stay. You know the rules.'

She knew the rules, although he did not. Upset her and her vengeance was absolute, no exceptions.

'I don't have any money.'

'Not my problem.' The man spoke poor English, in spite of having arrived in the country from Eastern Europe thirteen years previously. His country of birth had joined the European Community, and he left it for England and its welfare system. The house he rented, and then sublet, was his only means of income once he had exhausted his adopted country's generosity. When he had arrived in the country, he had had a wife and a family, but they were gone. To him, they were worthless. The accommodation he provided was not legal and did not satisfy any government regulations. There were no insurance policies, no fire prevention systems, no regular pest inspections. Just a bed and a wash basin; the bathroom was at the end of the hall.

'We could exchange,' she said.

'What with?'

'What do you think?'

The old man looked at the woman. He could see that she was young and nubile, not old and haggard as his wife had been. 'Ten years ago, we could have made a deal.'

'You're not too old,' she said. There had been some who had visited her when she was with Mavis Williams who must have been older than the man standing in front of her. Some were able to maintain an erection long enough, most weren't, and the man demanding money appeared to be one of the latter. She could not think of a more disagreeable prospect than seducing this man, but if it was necessary…

She had been there for three months, in that horrible room in that horrible house, and no one had suspected who she was. It was the safest place in London, and she wanted to stay.

'Thirty minutes and you're out of here,' he said. 'Tight arse or no tight arse.'

She knew that she could leave, but he stood in her way. 'We can at least part as friends,' she said.

'It's purely business.'

'I understand.'

The rent collector came and sat on the edge of her bed. She gave him a beer to drink. He opened it and gulped it down. He smelt of rotting fish and sweat. He did not see the knife in her hand, although he felt it enter his chest. He collapsed on the bed.

The woman then moved his legs parallel with the length of the bed. Thorough, as always, she slit his throat, careful to stand clear. The shower at the end of the hall was dirty and cold; this time she would forsake the cleanliness. Not wishing to bloody her hands, she took a toothbrush and rubbed it in the blood coming from his throat. One wall in that dingy bedroom was not as dirty as the others. She wrote a number with the toothbrush. It took her five minutes to complete to her satisfaction. Packing her case, she left the room and the house. On the way, she checked the landlord's room. She found nearly ten thousand pounds in cash hidden under his mattress. Now Charlotte had the rent money, but no one to pay it to.

She headed to the railway station: unfinished business.

***

Sara Marshall and Sean O'Riordan headed back to Twickenham to review the events three years before. Isaac headed back to Challis Street from Dennis Goldman's apartment; he knew what was coming.

Not only was he a reluctant celebrity courtesy of Charlotte Hamilton, but he was also a detective chief inspector who had let two murders occur. Graham Dyer was unforeseen, but Dennis Goldman was not. The celebrity of the woman was well known and would have formed the basis of many pub conversations, especially that she would thrust the knife in mid-coitus. The thought of it made Isaac squirm.

Yet an attractive female and Dennis Goldman had been swayed, and almost certainly never gave any thought to the possibility that the woman coming on too easily to him was anything other than a woman with easy virtues. The landlord at the Duke of York had sensed something was amiss, Wendy said, but Isaac did not believe his statement.

Isaac knew that hindsight was all very well, but the landlord, the same as every other man, even he, would have taken Charlotte Hamilton. Isaac knew that he had made mistakes in the past: bedding Linda Harris while pursuing a relationship with Jess O'Neill was the biggest mistake so far, but then Sue Smith had made a dent in his heart, and now she was overseas. He was soon to be forty, and he knew that a man needs someone in his life. He could see himself as a lifelong bachelor; the idea did not appeal.

Wendy disturbed Isaac's thoughts. 'Sir, we still need to find this woman.'

'How can she disappear so easily.'

'She's a Barbie Doll.'

'What do you mean?'

'The woman has no distinctive features, no moles on her face, no rear end that's too large or breasts that protrude. She's the generic young English Rose. Careful makeup, change of clothes, change of hair colour, and she is transformed.'

'You're right, of course. What about the Duke of York? How did you and Larry go?'

'The pub had cameras. Bridget's had a look at the videos.'

'Charlotte Hamilton?'

'Unless you know it's her, you'd not pick her. How about Gordon Windsor? Is he confirming that it was Charlotte Hamilton?' Wendy asked.

'It's her. How many is that now?'

'According to her count, it's six.'

'Isaac, what the hell is going on?' a voice bellowed. Wendy made herself scarce and went to talk to Larry.

'She's killed again.'

'I know that,' DCS Goddard said. 'Not only does she broadcast it in advance, as well as some pictures of you, we now have another body.'

'He should have checked before taking her to his house,' Isaac said by way of a lame excuse.

'Would you?' The DCS knew his DCI well enough to know the answer to that question. 'And now there is a damn press conference. I expect you to put up a good defence. The department's looking very shabby at the present moment, and the commissioner is breathing down my neck. I've spent enough time sweet talking that man; I don't want to blow it with your incompetence.'

'That's not fair,' Isaac said.

'I know it's not fair, but you need reminding. Whatever happens, you're carrying the can for this.'

'I won't let you down, sir.'

'Isaac, you're the best I've got. I cannot afford to lose you, but how many more deaths? The woman's identity is known. Her fingerprints, her DNA are on record. We have photos of her, and then we have her website. I'm trying to get it blocked, but it's not so easy.'

'She will only change the server again. Over one hundred thousand followers now, and they can all find her website easily enough.'

'Misguided fools?' Goddard asked.

'Only a few would be as mental as Charlotte Hamilton.'

'Only!'

'So far, there has been one copycat killer in the UK, two or three in the USA.'

'That's just what we need. Random lunatics aiming to emulate her.'

'That's what being a celebrity does to people.'

'I don't get it,' Goddard said. He left soon after. He had not seen the man so angry before.

Isaac called in Wendy and Larry. 'One week maximum or else.'

'Else what?' Larry asked.

'One week, and I'm off the case.'

'And us?'

'What do you think?'

***

Jason Martin had fancied her from the day she moved in. A casual labourer, he could not afford more than a single room in the converted house. The landlord was a pig of a man, but he minded his business and did not complain about the smell of marijuana in his room.

Martin made little in the way of money, and what he did make he spent on drugs and the occasional woman. He was an unattractive man approaching his forty-fifth year. Each and every day of the year, he wore the same clothes: a tee-shirt, a worn pair of jeans, trainers with holes in the soles, and an anorak. He moved slowly, although he had no impediment. He was a lazy man who would come home after work to smoke and to watch the television, but only the commercial channels. The national broadcaster, devoid of adverts, was not to his taste. 'Intellectual crap,' he would say each time his remote flicked through the channels, briefly pausing to look at a debate or a documentary before flicking on.

He had not had a steady girlfriend in ten years, a fact he put down to their poor taste and his irregular working hours. The new woman, young and just his type, had taken the room next to him. She was polite to him in the corridor and when they queued for the bathroom, he always let her go first as she would clean up, and there was always the smell of her perfume that lingered in the air; also, the meter on the hot water cistern would often have some remaining credit.

He had asked her out once, but she had not accepted. He had decided that she was not good enough for him, although it did not stop him from looking through the crack in the door of the bathroom as she removed her clothes and bathed herself. It also did not stop him widening the crack in the dividing wall between his room and hers, to see her naked. The wall, constructed of cheap panelling, divided a larger room. He thought his half was better than hers.

At night, when it was quiet, he could hear her talking to herself. He imagined that she could hear him. The thought of it excited him.

He had not expected the door to her room to be open when he returned at five in the morning. The urge to look in was irresistible.

He had expected to see an empty room, possibly the woman asleep. He entered, after whispering 'Hello' first.

The bed was initially hidden by the door. He looked through the crack near to the handle; a crack he had used before. He saw a man he recognised. He was not moving.

Slowly Jason, the Peeping Tom, moved forward. He recognised the landlord on the bed, his hands folded over his chest. Not sure of what he saw, Jason Martin touched the red on the man's shirt. He put his finger to his mouth; he knew the taste.

Five minutes later, he phoned for an ambulance.

Chapter 18

At King's Cross Station, the woman carried her worldly belongings. She reflected that it was not much to show for five years. In one hand, she carried a voluminous handbag. On her back, a backpack for her laptop and the photos she cherished. She also dragged a small suitcase.

There had not been time to upload the latest photos; that would be her first task on arriving at her destination. It would only be three hours, and she hoped that the body of the landlord would not be discovered before then, but she knew of the nosey man in the room next door.

As the train pulled out of King's Cross, she broke into song. *Stupid Duncan up at the quarry, along came a sister and gave him a push.*

An elderly couple looked her way, unable to hear the full words due to the noise of the train.

Charlotte smiled back at them.

She remembered little of the trip, other than the train stopping two, maybe three, times to let people off, others on. The elderly couple had left at one of the stops, only to be replaced by a family of four. Charlotte took little notice, although the little boy had tripped over her foot one time. *If he was here on his own*, she thought. She realised her destiny, her purpose with more clarity. The time for subtlety had passed.

From now on, she would intensify her efforts. The elderly couple had seen a bookish woman on the train, not the frivolous tart that had killed the banker. What would she be in Newcastle? Her bag contained all she needed by way of makeup. In her suitcase were clothes suitable for any occasion, any look, any age. So far, she had kept her age close to her own, but she could be young if she wanted, old if needed.

It was five years since she had last been in Newcastle, but it had changed little. She found an internet café close to the railway station. She had covered her face with a scarf, a perfect disguise considering the biting wind.

Four pounds, cheaper than London for forty-five minutes' internet use, a complimentary cup of coffee which was surprisingly good. *Not like the muck they serve down in London*, she thought.

She took out her laptop; the battery still had charge. She removed the connector from the old computer on the table and inserted it into her laptop. She checked the speed; it was adequate.

Ten minutes later, Isaac Cook saw the update on his smartphone. He pulled over to the side of the road and scrolled through the photos.

***

High Barnet, the furthermost station on the Northern Line of the London Underground, was only fifteen miles from the centre of London. Another murder that appeared to be the handiwork of Charlotte Hamilton. The full team had mobilised on hearing of the number on the wall, the knife in the chest, the slit throat.

Jason Martin had been surprisingly articulate once he had calmed himself. He had phoned up emergency services, given a clear description of the man's condition as well as the address.

'54 Normanton Avenue. Send an ambulance, not that it will be much use,' he had said.

The woman on the other end of the phone pressed a computer key to mobilise the police and the ambulance. She maintained the conversation to allow the software on her computer to check the phone number, its approximate location, and the owner's address. They all tallied.

The local DI, Jim Davies, had phoned Isaac on visiting the murder scene. They had met some years previously, and the modus operandi of Charlotte Hamilton was well known.

'It's one of yours,' Davies had said on the phone.

Within five minutes of the phone call, Sara Marshall and Sean O'Riordan were heading north. Wendy Gladstone and Larry Hill were in another car and moving in the same direction. Isaac had decided to take his own.

He phoned Sara after looking at the photos on his phone. 'It's not a pleasant sight,' Isaac said.

'We'll see soon enough.'

Wendy and Larry arrived first. The standard procedure: crime scene tape, barricades to keep the onlookers at a distance, a uniform at the front door of the house, which was a sad example of pre-war architecture.

The crime scene investigators from the local area were taking control. Gordon Windsor was coming up in an advisory capacity, as he had the most recent knowledge of the woman's style of dispatching men.

Wendy took the opportunity to kit up: gloves, foot protectors, overalls. She showed her badge to the uniforms and proceeded to the first floor of the house. She was stopped by Jim Davies before she entered the room.

'I work with DCI Cook,' she explained.

'Fine. Just be careful where you walk.'

Wendy saw the body on the bed; felt as though she wanted to throw up. It had been clear on entering that somebody already had. From what she could see the man was fully clothed, which was in stark contrast to Charlotte Hamilton's usual approach to dispatching her victims.

'Not much to see here, and besides, you're in my way,' the CSE said.

Wendy left the room and went downstairs. Sara and Sean had arrived.

'He's prickly,' Wendy said as Sara kitted up.

'Don't worry. I can deal with him.' Wendy thought she probably could. She would only have to smile at him.

Isaac arrived ten minutes later. He kitted up and went upstairs, which left Wendy and Larry with Jason Martin. The man was calm, and a cigarette hung from his mouth – it was tobacco, although the lingering smell of marijuana remained. Not that Wendy and Larry were concerned with his possible illegal activities. He appeared to be a sensible man and a reliable witness.

'You found the body?' Wendy asked.

'And phoned the police.'

'Can you tell us about the murderer?'

'A good-looking sort. Fancied her myself.'

'Did she respond to your advances? I'm assuming you made some,' Larry asked.

'I tried it on once. Shot down in flames.'

'Did she have a name?'

'Ingrid.'

'Tell us about Ingrid,' Wendy said.

'She arrived some time ago. She lived in the room next to me. Always civil to me when I saw her, but she kept to herself. Apart from that, there's not a lot I can tell you.'

Jason Martin forgot to mention that she had a birthmark just below her left breast, and one breast was larger than the other.

'The landlord. What can you tell us about him?'

'Not a lot. He was an unpleasant man, but he left me alone. She certainly dealt with him.'

'As you say,' Larry agreed.

'Is there any reason why Ingrid would kill him?' Wendy asked.

'He was always looking at her, and then she was struggling to pay the rent. Apart from that, I can't think of a reason.'

Isaac returned with Sara. Sean had been talking to some of the onlookers, to see if anybody knew anything.

'It's Charlotte Hamilton,' Isaac said.

'Where is she, sir?' Wendy asked.

'This time she did not clean up. She panicked, and when a person panics, they make mistakes. Find out where she went after here. This time, it should not be difficult.'

Isaac returned to the office, the others stayed at the murder scene. Isaac knew why he was being summoned back to meet Goddard. His career had been on the line more than once over the years, but this time it looked serious.

Isaac realised he had no defence. The woman moved wherever she wanted, killed whomever she wanted. Unless the team had a break, he was off the case.

It had almost cost the career of Sara Marshall, although she had survived due in part to her being an excellent police officer, in part because she had married her boss.

Isaac, apart from his mentor Richard Goddard, had no one, and this time it looked as though he was about to issue a warning to him, or at least a reprimand.

***

Charlotte walked around the centre of Newcastle looking for accommodation. Nowhere was safe, and for once she was getting desperate.

Even now, the police in Newcastle would be on the lookout for her, although she had walked past two police constables at the station and they had taken no notice. They would have if she had been wearing the same outfit as when she had killed Dennis Goldman, not only because it had been provocative, but also because Newcastle was unusually cold. Before she had gone to London, she had not thought of the climate as so bitter.

She entered a pub, pulling her suitcase.

'Bit heavy for you, luv,' the man behind the bar said.

'I'm looking for accommodation.'

'Room upstairs if you want.'

'How much?'

'We can discuss it afterwards,' the man, who looked to be the worse side of fifty, said. Charlotte noticed the tattoos on his arm and the muscular physique.

She took her luggage upstairs and had a shower. She then dressed inconspicuously and made her way out to St Nicholas Hospital. She stopped on the way to look at her old house. A young couple with a baby were there. A large dog was fetching the ball that the man threw. She had no idea where her parents were, but she would find out. She took some photos.

Charlotte walked around the boundary of St Nicholas Mental Hospital. It had not changed since she had left at the age of nineteen. It was the same foreboding edifice that represented pain and imprisonment and rejection by her parents. She checked out the back fence that she had climbed over in her early teens to meet the local boys. She wondered what had happened to them, although she assumed they were now older and wiser, not foolish and full of bravado as when they had made love to her. To them, she had been a plaything, purely for their own amusement. One of the young men had been friendly to her; Charlotte remembered him with some fondness, but, yet again, he had been deceitful, the same as Gregory Chalmers, professing love, only feeling lust.

Wrapped in a coat with a hood, and wearing warm, sensible clothing, she waited, knowing full well the routine of the one person she wanted to see. She hated the woman for taking her away from her parents, for subjecting her to pain, for giving her medicines that left her depressed or comatose, unable to react.

It was late afternoon when Gladys Lake emerged from the building and walked through a churchyard on the way to her cottage on the far side. Charlotte had been there a few times, part of her therapy and her integration into society. She remembered the lace curtains, the bay window, the old cat. It was evident now that with the Lake woman it had not been therapy, only a way for her to ease her guilty conscience after all that she had subjected her to.

'Another six months and you will be all right,' she had said. Charlotte realised that it had all been lies, and the six months had stretched to one year, then two, and then up to the age of eighteen, when she was free to leave as an adult.

***

Gladys Lake moved slowly across the churchyard, casually glancing at the gravestones as she walked. Under one arm she had some files, across her shoulder the strap of a large bag. She was wrapped up against the weather, and the rain had started again; not that it ever stopped for very long, but now it was turning to sleet.

'You never expected to see me again, did you?' the woman who had emerged from her left said.

'I'm sorry,' Gladys Lake replied.

'Have you forgotten me already?'

The doctor thought the voice was familiar, yet she could not identify the woman, which was not surprising as she had a scarf wrapped around her lower face, and a hood pulled over her forehead. All that she could see were the blue eyes.

'I have never forgiven you,' Charlotte said.

Gladys Lake quickened her pace and attempted to flee. She dropped the files that had been under one arm; she did not stop to pick them up. The woman behind her, younger and fitter, began to close in on her.

'Leave me alone, please.'

'You remember.'

A couple walking their dog entered through the far gate of the graveyard. The dog stopped to sniff the gate post, lifting its leg to make its mark.

'Dr Lake, how are you?' the man said.

'Please, I need your help.'

'Of course.'

'A woman is following me. She is dangerous. I need the police.'

The man looked over the area while the dog continued to sniff. 'I can't see anyone.'

'Please call Detective Inspector Hewitt for me,' Gladys Lake said. She handed the man her phone. He checked the contacts and speed dialled. The doctor had been unable to hold her hands steady enough to press the buttons.

Rory Hewitt found Gladys Lake at her cottage. The couple and the dog who had helped her in the cemetery were there also.

'It was Charlotte Hamilton,' she said.

'Positive?'

Rory phoned Sara who phoned Isaac. The situation had changed. The woman was on the move, and she was making mistakes. She had left a USB memory stick behind after killing the landlord where she had been staying; it only contained photos, and apart from their subject matter, it had revealed nothing more.

The killing of the landlord had been messy; her previous murders had shown a degree of calmness as she had showered, cleaned up, and left. Grace Nelson, the criminal psychologist, said it was to be expected. The shield of invulnerability made Charlotte Hamilton impervious to the possibility of capture.

Isaac set up a meeting at Challis Street. Sara Marshall and Sean O'Riordan came over; Rory Hewitt dialled in.

'Rory, is it confirmed?' Isaac asked.

'Gladys Lake is sure.'

'Is she alright?' Sara asked.

'She's fine,' Rory said, which was not altogether true. Gladys Lake had been scared witless and was under sedation.

'All-points out for her?'

'We have issued a general alert. The woman is dangerous, and she is to be approached with care.'

'Another mistake,' Wendy said.

'If she had killed Gladys Lake, then it would not have been,' Rory said.

'Do you believe she would have?' Isaac asked.

'What else? She kills people, not frightens them. Gladys Lake would have died in that graveyard if a couple walking their dog had not come in. I'm certain of that. So is Dr Lake.'

'Charlotte Hamilton's parents?'

'We're checking on them now, as well as visiting her old house. The Hamiltons' new address is not well known.'

'Do you know it?'

'Yes. We have police cars out there patrolling the area. I intend to visit after I conclude this call.'

'Then you'd better go. She has failed to kill this time. Who are her next targets?'

Chapter 19

DCS Goddard had not lost faith in his DCI, but others had. As far as the Commissioner of the London Metropolitan Police, who sat up high in his ivory tower at Scotland Yard, was concerned it was a fiasco. People were dying, and the murderer was known.

'Look here, Goddard,' the commissioner, a plain-talking man, said. 'I've not seen much to recommend this DCI Isaac Cook. Everyone tells me he is a man on the rise, destined to take my chair one day.'

Not before me, Richard Goddard thought.

'He's a good officer.' Goddard leapt to Isaac's defence.

'Good or bad makes no difference. Sure, he has a few runs on the board: dealt with that Marjorie Frobisher case, found out who had killed a man thirty years ago, and wrapped up the death of the future Lord Penrith, but apart from that… What is it with this Charlotte Hamilton? Does he fancy her?'

The DCS knew that if Isaac survived, he would have to settle down. Aspersions about his performance based on his fraternising with members of the opposite sex were counterproductive.

'That's a scurrilous remark, sir.'

'Don't get smart with me. You're only here because you were friendly with the previous commissioner and because you suck up to the politicians. The prime minister may see something special in you. I don't.'

Goddard knew that his defence of his DCI had placed him in a tenuous position. The previous commissioner had mentored him, but he was now sitting in the House of Lords and unable to protect him.

He had spent years focussing on the chance to become the commissioner of police, but the DCS realised that his efforts were yet again being thwarted, and this time by a man of little charm and no humour. Goddard knew that Isaac needed to get results, but so far he had achieved none.

Charlotte Hamilton was thumbing her nose at whoever she wanted. Her identity was well known. Her full medical history was available and had been carefully analysed, looking for patterns that would indicate where she would strike next. And now she was in Newcastle, although so far no one had been killed.

Goddard left the commissioner's office in a worse mood than when he had arrived. As much as he disliked the commissioner, and thought him to be a pompous bore, he was right in one aspect: Isaac was not providing results.

***

The Hamiltons were not pleased when Rory Hewitt arrived. He parked his car to one side of the entrance and knocked on the door.

Charles Hamilton opened it. Rory looked in, saw that their previous well-presented house had been replaced by a run-down farm cottage.

It was evident to Rory that the Hamiltons had let themselves go. Charles Hamilton wore an old pair of jeans, dirty from what Rory could see, and a shirt that was fraying at the collar.

'My wife's in bed,' he said.

'Ill?'

'Severe depression. It's as if she has given up.'

'I'm sorry to hear that,' Rory said. He could only imagine the anguish they were going through. He had heard about Fiona Hamilton's attempted suicide, but nothing more since then.

'You'd better come in.'

Rory moved down the hallway to the kitchen. In the sink, there were dirty dishes.

'Sorry about the mess. We don't do much these days.'

'That's fine.'

'You're not here for a social visit, are you?'

'No.'

'We heard about the last murder. It was her, wasn't it?'

'In the north of London?'

'High Barnet.'

'Yes, it was her.'

'Is that why you're here?' Charles Hamilton asked. Rory could see the lines on his face, the downcast eyes. His wife may have been suffering from depression, but it was evident that Charles Hamilton was not well either.

'Charlotte has been seen in Newcastle.'

'My God. Has she killed anyone?'

'Not yet.'

'You suspect she will come here?'

'It's possible.'

'If she comes, we will not stop her.'

'That bad?'

'Our deaths would be no worse than what we are suffering now.'

Rory understood Charles Hamilton's sentiment.

***

Charlotte did not know why she had spoken to Gladys Lake. She had not intended to confront the woman in the graveyard, but she had been there, and it had seemed ideal. No need for a ritual, she had thought, only a knife to the heart and then to the throat. It appeared to be a perfect opportunity: an isolated graveyard, drizzling rain. If she had only killed her, she would not have had to run away. There was a freshly-dug grave; she had wanted to throw the woman in there, but then that couple with that stupid dog peeing everywhere had interrupted her. How she hated them. How she hated that dog.

Dr Lake had deserved to die; it was her duty to rid the world of a woman who took pleasure in the torture of those that she professed to care for.

Charlotte remembered running away from the graveyard, her panic overwhelming her. Now was not the time to get caught. She still had to see her parents one more time; she was sure of that, but she had no address. The Lake woman would have known; maybe that was why she had not killed her. She would have told her as the knife slid into her.

Yes, that was it, she thought.

She knew that her mind was not as sharp as it had been. Why, when she had killed those men, had she felt nothing, yet with failure she felt guilt? She did not know, and it worried her. Her thoughts were muddled, as were her plans.

She had to leave her accommodation over the pub in the centre of town; find somewhere remote, lie low. She needed her parents. They would look after her, and if they did not, then she knew what to do.

And what of the publican? He had agreed to her price, even though she had plenty of money. That miserable penny-pinching man in High Barnet had had over ten thousand pounds hidden under his bed yet he wanted her to pay on time, and then he had rejected her body.

She would have paid him with that, but he was too stupid to appreciate the offer. Many men had used her; most had paid, some had not, some had died, yet he rejected her, even after she had shown him some of the wares. He had been interested, she knew it. The publican in Newcastle had had no such problems. He had appreciated her ten minutes after showing her the room, even neglecting the patrons downstairs waiting for their pints.

***

Isaac avoided the confrontation with Richard Goddard; he and Sara Marshall were on the train to Newcastle. It was only three hours from King's Cross; they would arrive by late afternoon.

With Charlotte Hamilton in Newcastle, and the train and bus stations being monitored, they thought there was a good chance of apprehending her. The woman was making mistakes, too many mistakes, and Isaac knew it was only a matter of time. Whether it would be soon enough to maintain his credibility, even his position on the promotion ladder, was too early to know.

Rory Hewitt met them on arrival. Sara had spoken to him before, but this was the first time meeting him in person.

'Good to see you, Sara.'

'And you,' Sara replied.

'I've booked you into the Marriott,' Rory said. Isaac thought it was outside the department's budget, but accepted graciously.

'I've scheduled an appointment with Gladys Lake.'

'Then let's go. We can check in later,' Isaac said. He was anxious to get on and to try and apprehend Charlotte Hamilton. He knew how it worked. If he came back with the woman in custody, then his career was back on track, as was Sara's. If he did not, then he knew the consequence of that as well. However their visit to Newcastle turned out, it was a crucial turning point in the investigation.

A twenty-minute drive and they arrived at Dr Lake's cottage. A uniform stood outside. Inside, Gladys Lake was relaxed. She was sitting in a chair by the window, a cat on her lap. A policewoman, assigned to stay at the cottage for the next few days, opened the door on their arrival.

'I'm fine now,' Gladys Lake said in answer to Isaac's question. She turned to Sara. 'Good to meet you after so many years,' she said.

'And you, although it's not the best way to meet.'

'Do you believe that she intended to kill me?' Dr Lake asked.

'You're an educated woman. It would be wrong to lie to you,' Isaac said. He had taken a seat on the other side of the small room. An imitation log fire burned in the corner. The cat had left its owner and moved over to him. Isaac was not a great lover of cats, having had asthma as a child that was in part exacerbated by cat fur. This time, he did not push the cat away.

'If those people had not come into the graveyard, she would have killed me.'

'It's probable,' Isaac said. 'You will need to be careful for a few days.'

'I have my patients.'

'We have assigned a policewoman to you. She will accompany you at all times. Also, another officer will be outside this house.'

Isaac asked the standard questions: mental state, what is she likely to do next, where will she be?

Dr Lake concurred with Grace Nelson's conclusions. If Charlotte Hamilton was in Newcastle, she probably had unfinished business. She had failed to kill her, but there were others that she bore a grudge against.

The three police officers left the cottage, the cat clawing Isaac's trousers as he stood up. Sara gave Dr Lake a hug.

Rory started his car and headed out of the city. The night was drawing in, and all three would have preferred to be warm and snug, a view that was echoed by a large number of the Newcastle police who were on high alert. A known serial killer was in the city and roaming free.

Teams of police officers were checking all the hotels, guest houses, and pubs throughout the city, and showing the photo of a woman with blonde hair and then dark hair. For every ten people they asked, one would say that they had seen her. Closer questioning revealed yet again that Charlotte Hamilton's features suited the generic norm, and they were false sightings.

The publican at the Bridge Hotel sat down on learning that the woman who had slept upstairs was a serial killer. He did not admit that he was one of her followers on her website.

'She was here. Not that she looked anything like your photos.'

'Why do you recognise her, then?' the young police sergeant asked.

'There is a small scar just above her left eyebrow.'

The policeman studied the photo. He could see the publican was correct. 'Good eyesight,' he said.

The publican failed to reveal that he had seen it the first night he had slept with the woman.

Chapter 20

Wendy and Larry, still back in London, traced Charlotte Hamilton's former flatmate. Gloria was in Hammersmith, happily married and with a child.

'You are aware of your former flatmate's reappearance,' Wendy said.

'Will she find me?' The child bounced up and down on the woman's lap.

'After three years?'

'She's mad, isn't she?'

'Psychotic, paranoid schizophrenic,' Larry said. Sara Marshall's files had shown that Gloria had been promiscuous. From what he could see, the woman in front of him was subdued, caring and devoted to her husband, Asuko, whom she had met in Lagos.

'She was always strange,' Gloria said.

'Our records indicate that you said she was normal.'

'Three years ago, I may have said that, but now…'

'What do you mean?'

'Her goddamn virginity.'

'You are aware of her history?'

'Who isn't. I sometimes check out her website.'

'Why?'

'Ghoulish, I suppose. She killed Brad Howard, and then put the photos on the internet. What sort of person does that? She's certifiable.'

'She probably is,' Wendy said.

'Is there anything else that may help us in our enquiries?' Larry asked.

'I told DI Stanforth all I knew. Will she find me?'

'At present, she's not in London. That is of two hours ago, but she could return at any time.'

Gloria shifted uncomfortably in her seat. Asuko, her husband, took the baby and left the room.

'Once, when she was not in the flat, I looked in her room.'

'To see what you could steal?' Wendy said. She had read Gloria's file before knocking on her door.

'I was mixed up then.'

'What did you find?'

'A drawing. There were three people. A child and two adults. There was a big cross through the child. What does it mean?'

'You are aware of her brother?'

'No.'

'She killed him when she was ten,' Wendy said.

'And she was my flatmate?'

'Yes. What do you intend to do?'

'I've already spoken to Asuko. We're going back to Nigeria. Until she is in jail or dead, we'll stay there.'

'Have a good trip,' Larry said.

***

By the time Isaac, Sara, and Rory reached the farm cottage it was dark. The only light inside the cottage came from the front room.

Rory knocked on the door; the first time, a gentle tap of the metal door knocker; the second time more vigorously. The sound of footsteps could be heard.

'Who is it?'

'Detective Inspector Hewitt. I'm here with two other police officers.'

The door opened to reveal Charles Hamilton holding a shotgun.

'You'd better give me that, Mr Hamilton,' Rory said.

'It's licensed; it's staying with me.'

'Where is your wife?'

'She's upstairs. We are taking turns to guard the cottage.'

'You would shoot your own daughter?' Sara asked.

'We have heard about Gladys Lake.'

'Dr Lake has suffered no injuries,' Rory said. 'Can we come in?'

'If you must,' Charles Hamilton said, dropping the shotgun to his side. He shouted upstairs. 'It's the police. You can come down.'

A few minutes later, Fiona Hamilton descended the stairs wearing an old dressing gown. She had red slippers on her feet, and her hair was bedraggled. She did not speak on entering the room and took a seat in the corner. The expression on her face was vacant.

'My wife is not well,' Charles Hamilton said. 'It's all been too much for her.'

Sara looked at the woman; she could only feel pity.

'Mr Hamilton, we are concerned that your daughter will come here,' Isaac said. He had found a wooden chair and was sitting on it.

'Our daughter died many years ago,' Hamilton said. His wife sat motionless, only moving to wipe her eyes with a handkerchief. Sara moved over near and put her arm around the woman. It was evident that she had not been eating properly as she was skin and bones underneath the dressing gown.

'Mr Hamilton, are you seriously willing to shoot your daughter?' Rory asked.

'She would have killed Dr Lake. Why would she not kill us, although we have no life now.'

Isaac found it difficult to concentrate: the chair was uncomfortable and the room was cold. 'Has she contacted you?' he asked.

'Not for many years.'

'Does she know where you live?'

'I don't know. It's unlikely.'

'The local police are keeping a watch on the cottage,' Rory said.

'Then tell them to leave. She will follow them,' Hamilton said.

'I'm taking Mrs Hamilton upstairs,' Sara said.

Sara left, leaving the three men together. 'My wife refuses to eat. She just drinks tea and nibbles the occasional biscuit.'

'How about you?' Rory asked.

'I do what I can, nothing more.'

Sara returned five minutes later. 'She's asleep.'

'What is the problem with your wife?' Isaac asked.

'Broken heart, although they call it depression. I suffer the same condition, but I remain resilient for my wife.'

***

Although it was late, the three police officers managed to organise some food at the Marriott. They had checked in: Isaac was on the first floor, Sara on the third.

Sara spent thirty minutes talking to her husband, checking on their son, before joining the two men. A party was in full swing in the bar next door.

Unable to talk about anything else, the three of them went over the case so far. Sara expressed her sorrow for the Hamiltons. Isaac asked about Charlotte, as Rory had seen the woman when she had been ten. He sang the song he had heard her singing, or at least a rendition of it, as he was tone-deaf.

Isaac phoned Wendy and Larry. Wendy was still in the office with Bridget; Larry had left for the day.

'I've upgraded the security for Dr Lake and the Hamiltons,' Rory said.

'Can she find the Hamiltons?' Isaac asked.

'Unlikely.'

The three, exhausted after a strenuous day, then said little more other than pleasantries unrelated to the case. Sara drank a glass of the house white, Rory a beer, and Isaac kept to orange juice.

The party next door was starting to get louder, not that the three minded. The day had been depressing, as had the last few weeks. It was good to see people enjoying themselves. Isaac rose to pay a visit to the toilet. As he moved through the throng at the party, a woman came up to him. 'Take a group photo for us, please.' Isaac obliged the group, young females out celebrating.

'And one with you.'

Isaac stood in the middle, his arm around two of the women. It was not possible to see very clearly as the light in the bar was subdued. The flash of the camera lit up the room briefly.

After the photos had been taken, Isaac received an obligatory kiss on the cheek and continued to the toilet.

'Who were they?' Sara asked on his return.

'No idea. Just some women out having fun. My God, it was her!'

Isaac rushed back to the party. He looked for the two women; he found one easily.

'Your friend?'

'Her?'

'Yes, the other woman in the photo,' Isaac asked. Rory phoned for backup.

'No idea. She just made herself welcome. Started paying for the drinks, as well.'

Two police cars arrived, road blocks were set up, people in the street waylaid. It was to no avail. The woman had disappeared.

***

Two hours later at a run-down internet café on the outskirts of Newcastle a woman took out her laptop. The man that she had paid did not look up as she placed the money on the counter. She had given him five pounds and told him to keep the change. He went back to watching porn on the screen below the counter.

The woman plugged her smartphone into her laptop. She downloaded the images, and then uploaded them to her website.

My favourite police officer, the caption. She then tagged the photo: Detective Chief Inspector Isaac Cook.

She closed the laptop, packed it into her case and left the café. Her accommodation was thirty minutes away. She would sleep well that night.

***

Isaac had tried to sleep, but it had not been possible. He had watched the television for some time, but apart from that he went over how he could have allowed a photo to be taken of him. He had not seen her clearly, and even if the light had been good, her ability at concealing herself was remarkable. He dozed after three hours, only to be woken by his phone ringing.

'You'd better check her website,' Larry said.

Isaac checked. He realised the repercussions.

He phoned Richard Goddard. It was better for him to find out from him than from someone else.

'What the hell is going on here?' Goddard exploded over the phone. 'You can't find her, but she can find you. Maybe I should employ her. The commissioner is going to go ballistic over this. Get yourself down here immediately.'

Isaac packed his case and headed to the railway station. A train left every thirty to forty minutes. He could buy a ticket at the station.

***

By the time Isaac arrived at King's Cross, the newspapers had picked up the photos. Larry met Isaac at the station and drove him to Challis Street Police Station.

Isaac walked up the stairs to Richard Goddard's office.

'I can't protect you on this one,' he said. 'Every time there is an attractive woman, you're there with your tongue hanging out. What is it? Are you lonely, not getting enough?'

'That's unfair, sir. I took a photo at the Marriott. How was I to know that Charlotte Hamilton would be there?'

'That's as may be, but I can't do anything about this. If the commissioner wants your head, he gets it.'

Isaac was aware that this time he was not going to survive. He was an ambitious police officer, yet on more than one occasion his friendly nature had got him into trouble. It had been a late night in Newcastle, and if he had been more alert, he might have studied the features of the woman who coerced him into a photo with her. His willingness to put his arm around her and her newly-acquired friend came naturally. He was a tactile man who was at ease with women as well as with men.

'Sometimes I wonder if you're worth the bother,' the DCS said.

Isaac sat upright on a chair on one side of Goddard's desk; his senior sat on the other. The leather chair he sat on looked precarious as he perched on its front edge. The man was angry, Isaac could see that, and if he had been in his position, he would have been as well.

'What about the commissioner, sir?' Isaac asked.

'I don't know. I've spent enough time with that man to know he does not suffer fools gladly, and that is what you are, a fool.'

'Yes.'

Goddard looked out of the window, unable to look his DCI in the face. He knew what he should do, was reluctant to do it.

'Make yourself scarce, at least for a few days, and just hope you have a breakthrough.'

'I will, sir.'

'Which one do you mean? Making yourself scarce or you'll have a breakthrough.'

'Both.'

'The damage is done. Let's hope we both survive.'

'You, sir?'

'I went out on a limb for you. I told the commissioner you were my best officer and that I had total confidence in you. And yet again you let me down. How many times is this now?'

'A few.'

'Damn right. So far, you've been involved with an operative from MI5 who probably murdered one of the victims in one of your cases.'

'Unproven, sir.'

'And what about Jess O'Neill?'

'Platonic, until Sutherland's murderer was arrested.'

'Charlotte Hamilton's a good-looking woman. Don't go sleeping with her.'

'I'm not a total fool.'

'Find this female, and fast. I can't hold off the commissioner for much longer.'

'The previous commissioner?'

'Shaw? He's now in the House of Lords, clothed in ermine. I doubt if there's much he can do.'

Chapter 21

Isaac's office felt cold when he returned to it after his dressing down by his boss. Some of the other people in the building had been polite as he descended the two flights of stairs. Others had smiled and then sneered when he was not looking, but he had expected that.

There he was, one of the stars of the Met, the man most likely to make it up to commissioner, the first black man to lead the most respected police force in the world. Those who sneered – he knew their names – were those who resented the idea that someone other than a pure-bred Anglo-Saxon could be allowed to hold the top job.

It had upset Farhan Ahmed, his Pakistan-born former DI. Isaac had told him to develop a thick skin and to brush it off, and now his skin was not as thick as it had been.

Charlotte Hamilton obviously had a fixation on him, as had others, and now he was on her website and the front page of at least two of the major newspapers in the country.

There was to be a press conference that afternoon. For once, Isaac's parents would not be tuning in to watch him. His attendance was not required, although his name would be on everyone's lips.

'*My date with a serial killer*,' was the headline in one of the newspapers. The other said, '*The long arm of the law*,' referring to his arm around Charlotte Hamilton.

Isaac entered his office and closed the door. He sat down, his hands behind his head, his eyes closed.

It was Larry, his DI, who knocked on the door. 'No point in dwelling on it. We still have a murderer to catch.'

'What do we know?' Isaac asked.

'They could not find the woman after…'

'After I had been photographed.'

Larry did not answer.

'We know she moved out of the pub in town,' Isaac said. 'Any idea where she went after that?'

'Not yet. I could go up to Newcastle,' Larry said.

'Best if you stay here. Rory Hewitt is a good man, and it's his part of the world.'

'Is she returning to London?'

'It's impossible to know. There's unfinished business for her up north. She failed in her bid to kill Gladys Lake, and her parents are targets.'

'Do they have protection?'

'Protection, yes. I'm not confident that it is sufficient,' Isaac said.

'With Charlotte Hamilton, it's probably not,' Larry agreed.

***

Psychotic, crazy thoughts swirled in Charlotte's mind; thoughts she knew were right, yet were wrong. An intelligent woman, she saw it all so clearly now.

The black police officer had been attractive, and she realised that she liked him, but he wanted her in jail. Her parents wanted her there as well, as did the Lake woman. She had failed there; she had to rectify her mistake, but how?

The authorities were crushing her, as they had when she was a child. Her parents had questioned her over the death of her brother. She had seen the police officer who had taken so much interest in her song that morning in the garden. She had seen the notebook and his writing down of every word. He was older now, and his hair was thinning, but it was the same man. She remembered the song: *Stupid Duncan up at the quarry, along came a sister and gave him a push.*

She had wanted to sing it for her parents, knowing they would not have liked it, but she did not. They knew of her hatred for her brother, or they should have. It was always him; he was always the favourite.

At Christmas, she had wanted another doll, but they had given her a book. They said she was too old, but what did they know. They had given Duncan what he wanted, not her. She was only a female, and they had wanted sons, not daughters. She knew that she hated them. They deserved to die, the same as the others.

***

Gladys Lake was not an easy person to protect. She was impetuous, rushing here and there. The instructions from DI Hewitt had been precise. 'Don't move without one police constable, don't allow him or her out of your sight, and lock all your doors.'

Initially, mindful to follow instructions, she had been diligent, but those who had been assigned to keep a watch on her were complaining.

Rory had been warned by the head administrator at St Nicholas that Dr Lake could be a nightmare. 'Brilliant doctor, but a scatterbrain.'

The man had been right, Rory concluded. He had seen her office with Keith Greenstreet, and it was a mess. Her cottage was better, but not much. In the kitchen, cups and saucers were not in the right place. In the main room, files were on the floor, on the table, even where the cat sat.

Gladys Lake had been asked to speak at a conference in London, and she was going. Rory had advised against it, but she had been adamant.

He knew that down there he could not protect her, and there was no reason to believe that Charlotte Hamilton intended to let her live.

Charlotte Hamilton's attention to detail and to cleanliness was well documented. It took a logical mind to kill someone and then shower, even hanging the towel up and drying the floor.

If Gladys Lake was still on Charlotte's hit list, London would represent the best opportunity.

***

Sara Marshall had been forewarned. If Isaac Cook was removed from the case, she was to take over. Her fortunes had been resurrected, and once again she was in her detective superintendent's good books.

Not that she wanted to take the lead position. She had a young child, and he was at an awkward age. He needed her to be around, but she had a career and a murder case.

Charlotte Hamilton frightened her. It was clear that she was devoid of emotion, and she would have no problems with harming anyone close to those who hurt her.

The team believed the woman to still be in Newcastle, but that was unproven, purely a supposition.

Sara and Sean O'Riordan were back in Twickenham, communicating with the team at Challis Street on a constant basis.

After the attack on Gladys Lake, it had gone quiet. It had only been six days, but it felt like an eternity.

Sara knew that Charlotte was still around somewhere. Instinct told her that, and that she would strike again very soon. Anyone as brazen as she had been in having her photo taken with Isaac Cook does not disappear for long.

The question remained as to where. Was it to be London or Newcastle? Nobody could be sure. Sara believed she would strike again in Newcastle.

***

An isolated farm cottage was not the most secure of locations, and it was fine as long as its occupants stayed there, but occasionally they needed to go out.

Charles and Fiona Hamilton made the trip to the supermarket. They had, at least for the last seven weeks, driven forty miles away to avoid confronting the locals.

This one time, they followed the police advice and drove to the town only two miles away. Charles went to get money out of the cash machine; his wife took a trolley and was filling it up with provisions for four weeks. The two police officers waited in their car, the heater on full blast. The season was changing from cold to even colder. They wondered how Charles Hamilton could walk around in just a shirt. Too many events had clouded his ability to think, to even register the climate.

His wife, Fiona, was slowly withering away; another three months and she would be dead. Charles Hamilton considered his position as he waited for his wife. He was sixty-five and still fit, but without his wife he could not continue, would not want to, and he knew their lives were forfeit.

He returned to the present and entered the supermarket. He found his wife in the second aisle loading up with cereal. She was moving slowly, not looking at what she was buying. He returned some items to where she had found them, and then took another trolley.

'Cash or credit?' the lady at the checkout counter asked.

'Cash,' Charles Hamilton's reply.

Together, Charles and Fiona Hamilton wheeled the trolleys out to their car. Charles pressed the key on his remote. The lid of the boot opened. After putting the provisions in the car, they drove out of the car park.

Neither they nor the police had noticed the woman on the other side of the road.

***

Detective Chief Superintendent Richard Goddard did not like press conferences. There were always some attending who felt the need to monopolise proceedings. The investigation was not going well, and it was hard to defend their lack of progress. Against his better judgement, he had been instructed to bring his DCI with him.

The commissioner had been adamant. 'You're a wet fish once they stick a camera in your face. Cook may be a bloody idiot, but he handles himself well. He can deal with the flak when they start asking their stupid questions.'

As usual, Goddard made the official presentation: long on content, short on fact.

At the end of his statement, the hands went up.

'DCI Cook, what is the situation with you and Charlotte Hamilton. Are you protecting her?' It was not unexpected. Liz Devon, who typically did not attend police press conferences, was a columnist for one of the gutter press publications. She did not care about the murders, only salacious gossip.

'Miss Devon, you are aware of the circumstances surrounding that photo,' Isaac said.

'You had your arm around her.'

'I was asked by a group of women partying in the hotel; it was late at night. I believe that I acted correctly when approached to take a photo of them.'

'Brent MacDonald, BBC. It is apparent that this woman is making a mockery of the police.'

'That is not the case,' Richard Goddard replied.

'The question was directed at DCI Cook,' MacDonald said.

The conference was not going well.

'I believe that she made a mockery of me, not the police force,' Isaac replied, aware that the best defence was to divert the blame, confuse the audience.

'Are you saying you are incompetent?'

'Not at all. Let me ask you, Mr MacDonald. What would you have done if you had been asked to take some photos?'

'I would have refused.' Isaac knew the man was a miserable sod and he had given a truthful answer.

'Detective Chief Superintendent, do you have confidence in DCI Cook's ability to bring this woman to justice?'

'I have total confidence,' Goddard replied.

'After six murders?' Brent McDonald persisted, aiming to evoke a response from Richard Goddard. The murder of Duncan Hamilton was generally not known about, and the official count stood at six, not seven.

'Detective Chief Inspector Cook has an impeccable record. He will apprehend this woman soon.'

'And where is she now?'

'She was last seen in Newcastle.'

'With your inspector's arm around her. It's a shame it wasn't handcuffs. Although with the incompetence of the police, DCI Cook would have been cuffed to a radiator.'

The room burst into laughter. Only two faces remained impassive.

'That is an ill-founded assertion,' Goddard said.

'You're wasting your time with this lot,' Isaac whispered to him. 'It would be better to wrap it up.'

Richard Goddard took his DCI's advice. 'Ladies and gentlemen, let me assure you that we are working hard to find this woman and detain her. You will need to excuse us.'

Both of the police officers beat a hasty retreat.

'Disaster, sir,' Isaac said.

'Unmitigated.' Goddard's monosyllabic response.

Chapter 22

Charlotte Hamilton had remembered the area that her parents had liked. It was pure chance that she had seen them that day. She could see that her mother was looking older, although her father, always the fitter of the two, had not changed.

She felt some compassion on seeing them; almost had wanted to rush up and throw her hands around them. Her love for them had been unconditional, but it was never returned, only given to her brother, her dead brother, squashed like a melon at the bottom of a quarry. She smiled at the thought of it.

It had not been difficult to find out where they lived from the overly talkative woman at the supermarket. 'We never see them here,' the lady had said. 'It's a sad story.'

'Where do they live?'

'Up the road, about five miles. There's a road off to the left, go up there until you see a small cottage. You can't miss it.'

Charlotte left the supermarket and found a car that had been left with its engine running. She got in and drove off.

The road was easy to find. As she drove along it, she saw a police car off to one side. The officer was talking on his mobile.

It was clear that reaching the cottage unseen was not possible by road, as her car would be visible from where the police car was parked. Two miles further on, she pulled the car off to one side. It was higher up the side of the hill, and the road had snaked back on itself. Down below, not more than five hundred yards away, she could see the cottage, with smoke billowing out of the chimney. It looked picture perfect to her.

There was a gate to a field. She opened it and drove the car through, parking so that it was hidden from the road. The wind was bitterly cold, but she had brought warm clothes. Satisfied that no one would see her, she walked down through the fields to the house. As she got nearer, she saw the car that she had seen at the supermarket. It was the right place.

Through the small window at the rear of the cottage she could see her father. Her mother was not visible.

Crouching down, she edged along the wall outside. The weather was getting colder, and she could feel herself shaking. She ignored her discomfort and continued to edge forward.

The door, she could see, was secured by a latch. She lifted it gently. It opened, and she entered the cottage. Her father was in the other room. It was warmer inside than out, and she removed her coat.

'Father,' she murmured.

'Charlotte!' her father exclaimed. He put down the cup that he was holding. 'What are you doing here?' He wanted to call the police but knew he could not. His mobile phone was on the table behind his daughter, a person who he had not seen for five years. A person that he loved, hated, loved. A person who had come to kill him and her mother.

'How's mother?' Charlotte asked.

'She's not well.'

'I want to see her.'

'Why are you here?'

'I needed to see you one more time before…'

'Before what?' Her father cut her conversation short. He had to admit she had changed. She had been blonde with a beautiful face the last time he had seen her. From what he could see, she had dark, shoulder-length hair, and the complexion that had been perfect was now blotchy. He could see the anger in her eyes, and hear the venom in her speech. She knew why she was there; he knew what he had to do. But could he? Could he kill his own daughter in cold blood to protect the mother? Was that possible?

He was a man who had cherished life, and now faced the ultimate dilemma: the death of his child or that of his wife. It was not a decision he could make, a decision that anyone should be forced to make, and the situation was irresolvable. His daughter was psychotic, mad, and she had killed seven times already. In her twisted mind, the killing of her parents would just be another notch in the belt, he realised.

'Are you here to kill us?'

At that moment, Charlotte realised the anger in her had subsided. It was if she was back in the village where she had spent three years with Beaty and her cat. She relaxed her guard and embraced her father.

'Why, Charlotte?' he asked as he hugged her in return. Tears were streaming down his face. At that moment, he held the loving daughter that they had known before that day: that day when Duncan had died. He pulled back from her, the daughter he loved, the murderer of his son.

'You don't love me, you never did,' she said.

'We always loved you, but you killed Duncan.'

'He deserved to die.'

'But why?'

'He broke my doll,' she said. The anger in her eyes had returned. Charles Hamilton was afraid again; afraid for his wife.

'You cannot stay here,' he said.

'This is my home.'

'The police will return. They will see you.'

'I can hide.'

'We still have your doll,' Charlotte's father said. If she stayed, he would have to call the authorities; he knew that.

'I want it.'

'Wait here, and I'll get it for you.'

Charles Hamilton went to the other room and picked up his wife's phone. He pressed speed dial to a prearranged number. The alarm flashed in the police car down the road.

'You've called the police,' Charlotte screamed. Her mother appeared at the top of the stairs.

'Go back, Fiona. Lock yourself in your room.'

Charlotte came forward, a knife in her hand. She was ready to kill her father.

'You bastard. I killed Duncan, the irritating little fool. Now I will kill you.'

The father, desperate to protect his wife, unable to kill his daughter, grabbed a vase holding some flowers and hit her across the head. Charlotte, momentarily stunned, fell back against the door separating the main room from the kitchen. Her father rushed forward to restrain her, receiving a slash across the face from a stiletto knife. He pulled back; the police car drew closer.

Regaining her senses, Charlotte retreated out through the back door and into the cold weather. She had not picked up her coat. Charles Hamilton could see her running up the hill, her warm breath visible in the almost freezing air.

The police car arrived. 'Backups are coming,' the police officer behind the wheel said.

'Anyone injured?' he asked.

'We are fine.'

'Your daughter?'

'Yes.'

'Where is she?'

'Unconscious in the kitchen.' Charles Hamilton lied. He could not kill his daughter, nor could he allow her to be caught. He knew he was wrong, and that it was a decision he would have to live with for the rest of his life.

***

Charlotte Hamilton reached the car; she was out of breath. She started the car and drove off at speed. The car had a full tank of fuel, sufficient for where she was going.

Rory Hewitt arrived at the cottage within forty minutes. 'Where is she?' he asked Charles Hamilton.

'She must have regained consciousness and left.'

Rory Hewitt knew that he had lied, but then what would he have done in a similar situation?

'Your wife?'

'I gave her a sedative. In her condition, she may not survive.'

'What do you mean? Has she been harmed?'

'No. She's let herself go, and now with Charlotte having been here, the stress may be too much.'

'She should be in the hospital.'

'An ambulance is coming.'

The team in London were notified of developments. Isaac had been trying to deal with paperwork but failing miserably as the situation with the photo in Newcastle continued to bother him.

Wendy had tried to buck him up, but with little success.

Sara Marshall was in the car and heading over to Challis Street as soon as Rory Hewitt had phoned her. She arrived in the office puffing, as she had run up the stairs. 'She's making mistakes. We'll have her soon.'

'Where is she now?' Larry asked.

'They're looking for her. She cannot have got far. It's remote up there.'

'Never assume anything with this woman,' Isaac said. 'The moment you believe she's cornered, she disappears, and the next time we find her, there's a dead body.'

'She just missed out on 8 and 9,' Sara said.

'Dr Lake. Is she safe?' Isaac asked.

'DI Hewitt has removed her to a safe location, regardless of the woman's protestations.'

'Charlotte Hamilton's coming back here,' Larry said.

'That may be, but where and when and who will she target this time?' Isaac asked.

'You may need protection, sir,' Wendy said.

'I will, as well,' Sara said.

***

Charlotte drove ten miles before realising the stolen car had probably been reported to the police. She had to dump it. All she had now was her backpack; it still contained her laptop and a change of clothes. It was clear she could not return to Newcastle. Instead, she drove to a small town in County Durham; she remembered she had an aunt there, although she would not be visiting.

From there she was sure she could take local buses and trains until she reached her destination. Her episodes of paranoia were increasing in their frequency and their intensity, but in her lucid moments she could feel tenderness for her parents, sorrow that her father had rejected her.

She knew that her time was drawing to a close, yet there was unfinished business. The Lake woman had deserved to die, but somehow she had survived. Her father, she had wanted to love, but he had rejected her. And, as for her mother, she could go to Hell.

There were others that had made her life miserable. She remembered them well. She ticked them off in her mind: 8, 9, 10.

It was a good number, but first she had to get back down south. She felt in the front pocket of her backpack; the ten thousand pounds in cash was still there. She could always buy new clothes, new disguises, and this time they would be quality.

Chapter 23

Fiona Hamilton died twenty-four hours after her daughter had visited the cottage. Her husband said it was a blessing.

Once they had been well liked and respected, but they had become outcasts. Rory Hewitt could only feel sadness for the man.

'Broken heart,' Hamilton said.

The doctor's official statement was heart failure exacerbated by a weakened physical condition due to poor nutrition.

Rory phoned the team in London. Wendy, although she had not met the woman, cried on hearing the news, as did Sara Marshall. It brought a lump to Isaac's throat as well.

Rory left the hospital at the same time as Charles Hamilton. He intended to return to the cottage on his own.

Back in London, Isaac called the team together. 'The car she stole has been found.'

'Where?' Larry asked.

'Consett, County Durham.'

'Was she seen?'

'We're checking, but the local police believe she would have taken a bus and left the town.'

'Direction?'

'She can't go to Newcastle unless it's to deal with unfinished business.'

'Gladys Lake,' Larry said.

'She will not find her.'

'Safe location?'

'Very safe. There's no way Charlotte Hamilton can find her.'

'That's what you said about her parents, sir,' Wendy reminded him. Isaac chose not to answer.

Sara Marshall and Sean O'Riordan joined the team at Challis Street.

'Why can't we find this woman?' Sara asked. She looked nervous.

'What's the problem?' Isaac asked.

'We're targets. You realise that?'

'It had crossed my mind.'

'I have a child. This woman is willing to kill her own parents. She would not have any issues with an infant.'

'You'd better find somewhere for your son,' Isaac said.

'She can't do that,' Wendy said. 'No mother would part with their child indefinitely.'

'Not even when their child may be at risk?'

'Isaac's right,' Sara said. 'If I stay with my son, she will find us eventually, and besides, I can't disappear. I know her from three years ago, and so far, Isaac and myself are the only ones who have been close to her.'

Larry felt inclined to make a comment. Isaac was still smarting over the rollicking that he had received from Richard Goddard, and was not in the mood to be reminded of the scurrilous reports in the newspapers and on the internet, not to mention the remarks in the police station.

Sara left the office. If Charlotte Hamilton were on her way, it would only be hours before she arrived. Sara had a place to take her son; she only hoped he would be safe there.

Isaac, aware that he was also in danger, organised a gun for himself. He offered to arrange one for Sara, but she declined.

Wendy and Larry went out to the Chalmers' home. Eventually, after the kitchen had been cleaned and repainted, Stephanie Chalmers had moved back in. The area where her husband had died had been bricked off. It reduced the size of the kitchen, and Stephanie did not like to spend time in there. She had organised a cook to prepare all the meals.

Charlotte Hamilton was coming back, and it was important to visit all the places, all the people that she had been involved with, to reanalyse any item of interest that could possibly help them to find her. The police had been given a directive to approach the woman with care, as she was extremely dangerous. If she did not accede to an order, they were licensed to use a Taser. If there was further resistance, they had the authority to shoot.

Charlotte's website had been updated. Her ramblings were more incoherent, although that did not seem to concern her followers, whose numbers continued to increase.

***

Stephanie Chalmers had not been able to help much. Her life appeared to have returned to pre-Ingrid Bentham. Wendy and Larry saw little to be gained by interviewing her more. Gloria was out of the country and safe, and there could only be three obvious targets: Isaac Cook, Sara Marshall, and Gladys Lake.

The movements of all three were being monitored, although Gladys Lake was the most difficult to protect. She had an agenda, and a presentation at a conference on mental health in London was more important to her than her personal safety. She had been warned not to go out on her own enough times, but she continued to ignore the advice.

There had been a couple of times at St Nicholas Hospital when she had absent-mindedly wandered off on her own. The assumption that she was safe within the confines of the building were incorrect. It was not a prison, purely a secure location.

After the death of Fiona Hamilton, Rory had kept in contact with Charles Hamilton. His wife was buried in a moving ceremony attended by Hamilton's immediate family, a few morbid onlookers, Rory, and three members of the press. Apart from that, there was no one else.

The priest had followed the traditional service, omitting any mention of the Hamilton's children. Charles Hamilton read a eulogy. He mentioned the son, but not the daughter. Rory thought the man looked old, even though he was only two years older than him. He had been a university lecturer, but at the lectern in the small church he had mumbled, sometimes incoherently, as though his mind was going. Rory put it down to grief. He wondered what would happen to the man now that he had no one to look after.

After the events at the Hamiltons' cottage, the local police had searched for Charlotte Hamilton. The car found further south indicated that she had returned to London, although that had not been confirmed.

A local bus driver in Consett thought he remembered a woman matching the description, but he had not been sure. After that, no further sightings.

***

An unpleasant, dishevelled man with bad breath and body odour was not what Charlotte Hamilton wanted to see on her return to London, but he offered anonymity, no questions asked. 'It's not much, but you can have it for twenty pounds a night,' he said.

She had not wanted to enter the building located to the east of the city of London, but her options were few. She knew that she could afford the best hotel in the city, but the police would be everywhere.

'It's fine. It's been a long trip.' The room was worth no more than ten, but Charlotte realised that the chances of being discovered were slim. It was clear that the local prostitutes brought men there, took their money, and then kicked them out of the door. The room still had the smell of cheap perfume and sweating men, even without the man who had shown her in. He had looked her up and down, imagined her naked. She knew what he deserved but lucidity had kicked in again, and she realised the cards were stacked against her. She knew she had to complete her task, yet she had not decided how.

The events in the north of the country had shaken her. No longer the success she'd had before, and the way forward was unclear. Random killings seemed to offer no satisfaction, although targeted ones still did, but when, and how?

And now she was back in London and time was running out.

Not sure where to go, Charlotte wandered the streets without purpose. Her hair was now red, her skin complexion two shades darker due to tanning cream. No longer wearing the mini skirt and the tight top that had so enticed Dennis Goldman, she was now dressed dowdily, courtesy of a shop selling old clothes for some charity or other. Conditioned as she was to disguise herself, she slouched and ambled, indicative of an older woman; she was pleased with the result.

With no purpose and no direction, subconsciously she revisited old haunts. She saw where she had killed Gregory Chalmers, even the window of the bedroom where he had first seduced her. She thought back to that night when he had taken delight in making love to her on the marital bed. In the small garden at the front, she could see the two children playing; children that she had loved as if they were her own. Stephanie Chalmers had come to the downstairs window to call them in for a meal. Charlotte could only reflect that they had been happy times, and if it had been her at the window instead of Stephanie, she could have been happy. She knew she would have been a better mother than Stephanie: always worrying about her business and whether it was a good week or bad, instead of focussing on little Billy and his sister.

She could see that the children were grown, almost at her height, especially Billy. She had been sorry that she had attacked their mother that night, but now she was sorry that she had not completed the job. Charlotte's mind was whirring, aiming to make sense of all that had transpired, seeing it all clearly, confused at the same time.

She thought about knocking on the door and pretending to be an old woman down on her luck, but she decided against it.

She had ambled past the police station in Twickenham, and seen the policewoman, Detective Inspector Sara Stanforth, now Sara Marshall. A woman who had hunted her, now married, maybe with a child, and yet she, Charlotte Hamilton, was alone and unloved and childless.

She had seen the man in Challis Street who had put his strong arm around her in Newcastle. She knew she wanted him. She wondered if it was still possible; were her disguises good enough to fool him. A dowdy old woman wearing clothes that smelt of moth balls would not succeed, although if she dressed young and seductively, then maybe she would.

Chapter 24

Newcastle Station was a foreboding sight as Gladys Lake walked through the concourse. Time had moved on since her encounter with Charlotte in the graveyard, although she took the advice of Detective Inspector Rory Hewitt and shortened her stay in London from three nights to two, which explained why she was taking the early train.

Rory Hewitt's argument had been cogent, in that Charlotte had been identified at King's Cross Station. Not that it helped as it had taken a check of two days' worth of security videos before she had been found and by then the woman had vanished. But she was in London, no one was in any doubt of that one fact, and now Gladys Lake was entering the lair of a desperate woman. A woman who had failed in her first attempt to kill her. Gladys Lake did not need Rory Hewitt or a criminal psychologist to tell her that. She knew full well what Charlotte Hamilton was capable of. After all, she had seen her in the graveyard.

The train pulled out of Newcastle Station at six in the morning for the three-hour trip to London.

With Gladys Lake leaving Newcastle, Police Sergeant Liz Castle had been relieved of guard duty. A policeman would take over in London.

'Look out for Police Constable Rob Grantham on your arrival. You have his phone number, and please, whatever you do, don't leave King's Cross Station without him,' Liz Castle said, glad of the chance to get back to some real policing. She knew she was new at the station, only three months, but so far she had been assigned the menial tasks reserved for juniors. Still, she reasoned, it would only be a matter of time before she was given a real job to do.

Three hours later the train drew into King's Cross. Gladys Lake failed to follow instructions and did not contact PC Grantham, and he was late anyway due to an accident near King's Cross. The speech she was due to give was not until two in the afternoon, and it was still only nine o'clock. She had the chance of a few hours' rest. She hailed a taxi. 'St Pancras Renaissance Hotel, please.'

Unbeknown to her, she had been seen. Charlotte Hamilton was a smart woman, everyone agreed on that, even if she was mad. She had phoned the hospital in Newcastle and had found out Dr

Lake's plans. It was pure luck for her that Dr Lake was attending the conference in London.

It had not been difficult to wait at the railway station, knowing full well that Gladys Lake had a fear of flying and did not drive, so it had to be the train. It was quicker anyway. For two days, Charlotte had waited in the station, watching Platform 2 from the comfort of a café for some of the time, or else wandering around the concourse. No one would have noticed her. She had to admit that her ability to disguise herself was good. One day old and dowdy, another young and tarty, as her facial features were still young and her body had not turned to flab, unlike her mother, although the last time at the farmhouse she had looked almost anorexic.

***

The taxi driver at King's Cross Station had complained when presented with a fifty-pound note for a fare that was only fifteen, but Charlotte had no time to wait. 'Keep the change,' she said. Another time, she would have argued with the man, but Gladys Lake had left her taxi that they had been following and was heading into the hotel.

'An old friend, I've just missed her at the station. She'll be surprised when she sees me,' Charlotte said when the driver queried why they were following another taxi.

Dressed in disguise, Charlotte was able to approach the reception and hear the woman check in.

'Room 232, ma'am,' a small, bespectacled man behind the reception said. Charlotte thought he looked like a gnome, but she managed to repress a smirk. She realised her mood was whimsical, whereas her intent was malevolent. She stood back when Gladys Lake turned around briefly. To Charlotte, it appeared to be a sign of nervousness on the woman's part; she hoped it was. She wanted the woman to suffer, as she had suffered for all those years.

Gladys Lake picked up her bag and moved towards the lift. A smartly-dressed porter took the bag from her and pressed the button inside the lift. Charlotte stood back, pretending not to look in their direction but watching intently out of the corner of one eye. The conference was scheduled for two days; no need to hurry this time.

And besides, there was still the unresolved matter of Detective Chief Inspector Cook. She was not sure what to do about him. Somehow, vengeance for those who had troubled her seemed the most suitable way forward.

Charlotte returned to her accommodation, grabbing a bite to eat at a local fish and chip shop. Always aware of her figure before, she no longer felt the need to worry. She knew her time was not long, and she had no need to be attractive and fashionable. Her wardrobe, no more than what she could carry in a suitcase, was looking the worse for wear. The ten thousand pounds she had taken from the dead landlord was still intact, apart from several hundred pounds that she had laid out on the trip to Newcastle and the incidentals necessary to maintain a low profile: wigs, dowdy clothes, shoddy accommodation.

She knew that in the past she would have cared, but now she did not.

The man who had first shown her the room at her hotel was behind the reception counter when she got back. He offered an inappropriate comment; she chose to ignore him. He was a poor quality of man, not even worthy of contempt. Charlotte took the key for her room from him with a disparaging shrug of her shoulders, and climbed the two flights of stairs. Her room smelt of damp and decay, as did the rest of the hotel. A quick shower and she lay down on the bed. Her mind was full of the days ahead, knowing full well that she was to become more visible than ever before. She realised that the police would be looking for her, and they would not be far from Gladys Lake, her primary target.

There were two days for her to deal with Gladys Lake, and, if possible, Detective Chief Inspector Isaac Cook. She counted those that she had dispatched, starting with her brother. It pleased her enough to bring a smile to her face.

***

Even with the full force of the Met behind him, Isaac did not know where Charlotte Hamilton was hiding out. Apart from being certain that she had arrived in London, no more had been seen of the woman. Gladys Lake was being subjected to continued surveillance by the police, hopeful that she was safe. Rory Hewitt had received a few choice words from Isaac because he had allowed Gladys Lake to travel unaccompanied from Newcastle to London, an ideal opportunity for a devious woman to commit murder. Police Constable Grantham, who should have been at King's Cross Station on Gladys Lake's arrival, was also given an official reprimand.

'What's the latest?' Isaac asked in his office. He had called the full team together. Police Constable Grantham was permanently assigned to Gladys Lake, as were two other junior police officers. The doctor's protection was paramount, although it was believed that close proximity to her would also present the best opportunity to catch Charlotte. Isaac was still smarting from the photo that she had taken with him in Newcastle.

Isaac knew that his career could not suffer another embarrassing incident. Even now, he was confining his movements to the office, his policing duties and his empty flat. Socialising, even if there was time, was strictly off the agenda. Charlotte Hamilton could appear at any time; an inappropriate approach engineered by her with a photo posted on the internet, and he would be suspended. His career could not take the ignominy, he knew that. He had to catch her and ensure she was put behind bars; no doubt hospital bars as it was clear that she was criminally insane.

Regardless of the lax security, Dr Lake was in London. Protection had been assigned to her day and night, although Isaac and his team felt that, going on previous form, Charlotte Hamilton would not be easily deterred.

Wendy was the first to speak that morning in the office. As usual, she was upbeat and optimistic, in sharp contrast to Isaac.

Wendy, perceptive and having known him longer than anyone else in the office, sympathised. She was used to seeing a fit, upright black police inspector, not the man in front of her now with a worried look on his face. 'Don't worry, sir. We'll find her soon enough.'

She realised it was probably a futile statement of encouragement. Apart from knowing Charlotte Hamilton was in London, they knew little more. Gladys Lake was still safe, although she was a woman not used to restrictions, and despite the best efforts of the police, all in the office knew that she still represented an easy target.

'Don't relax your guard for a minute,' Isaac had warned her when they met at her hotel for a coffee. 'Charlotte Hamilton is not far away, and she's not used to failure.'

Gladys Lake, appreciative of Isaac's visit to warn her, could only agree. 'I understand, but I can hardly hide away until you find her. Besides, I don't believe she wanted to harm her parents. All she wanted from them was unconditional love and a respite from her killing spree.'

'Can you empathise with Charlotte?' Isaac asked, not sure that the doctor was correct.

'Empathise, certainly. I need to do that with all my patients, try to understand the world from their point of view, aim to bring them back to reality.'

'And did Charlotte understand the reality? Do you believe she is aware that what she is doing is wrong?'

'I believe I've had this discussion with your people before.'

'Maybe, but I would appreciate your informing me.'

'Depends on her medication, her current state of mind, but she probably does not believe she is at fault. However, like everyone she needs love, unconditional love. Her parents would be the obvious choice to give her that, and they attempted to in the past.'

'That's before they realised that Charlotte had killed her brother, their son,' Isaac reminded Gladys Lake.

'As you say, before they realised. And it's clear they could not give her the love she wants now, and when she confronted them in their house the other week, it was always going to end badly.'

'So she could have gone to their house hopeful of a warm welcome.'

'Probably, but that's not what happened, is it?'

'No, her parents reacted badly. And your reaction if you're cornered by her? Will you be able to empathise, to show her the love and trust she craves?' Isaac asked.

'Outwardly, I probably will, but I will be shaking like a leaf. Charlotte scares me, and I know she blames me for what has gone wrong in her life.'

'Yet you do not take the appropriate precautions. You should have stayed in Newcastle,' Isaac reminded her.

'The conference I am attending is important. I needed to come.'

'Important enough to risk your life?'

'Not that important, I suppose, but I'll be careful.'

Isaac realised that his discussion with Dr Lake, pleasurable as it had been, had achieved little. Even if there were someone with her at all times, it would not be difficult in a crowded conference room to get in close and to stab her. Still, Isaac realised that he had done his best, and her fate, as well as his future, were in the hands of a delusional woman who continued to evade justice.

***

Sara Marshall, fearful for her safety but mainly for her child, had asked her mother to look after the infant for a few days. Sara instinctively knew that the current case was coming to a conclusion; she didn't know why, other than she could feel all the intricacies, all the components, of the case coming together. She had been involved with Charlotte Hamilton for too many years to believe that she would not go after Gladys Lake, and she intended to stay close to her, even if there was other protection close by. An assigned police constable, even with a photo and a description of Charlotte, would not recognise her easily, especially if she was disguised, and she was clearly proficient in that.

Sara knew more about the woman than anyone else, and she would be looking for mannerisms, the way she walked, the look in her eyes, similarities to her parents. No one else was more capable of recognising the woman, she was sure of that; no one else could save Gladys Lake.

Sean O'Riordan, Sara's constable during Charlotte Hamilton's first murdering rampage three years earlier, and now an integral member of Isaac's team at Homicide, continued to look for the woman. His girlfriend, although used to his extended working hours and his time labouring over the books at home to obtain the qualifications to raise himself from constable to inspector and hopefully as high as commander, continued to complain, although her complaints were muted in comparison to the past. Sean and Sara had agreed to work together on Gladys Lake's protection. They had run it past Isaac; he had been in agreement. If Sara was not with Dr Lake, then Sean would substitute.

Wendy Gladstone, always the best person to track someone down, and Larry Hill were involved with trying to find Charlotte Hamilton, although it was proving difficult. Her presence had not been confirmed in London, although the police officer's sixth sense told them she was there, but it was a huge city: needle in a haystack, according to Wendy, but she didn't give in easily.

And besides, if she wasn't in London, where else could she be? The people who concerned her the most – Sara Marshall, Isaac Cook and now Gladys Lake – were all in the city.

Chapter 25

A lone woman sitting in an internet café in north London raised no interest. The others sitting at their terminals were all focussed on the screens in front of them, tapping away at the keyboards. Some were surfing the web, some talking to loved ones overseas, others looking for employment; only one was planning violence.

Charlotte's mood was calm. Even though the weather was mild, she wore a thick coat, its collar turned up. Dark sunglasses, incongruous when looking at a computer screen, were not ideal, but they helped to conceal her identity. On her head, she wore a baseball cap.

It was necessary to be careful now, as her face was well known throughout the country. Even the newspaper that the man behind the desk was reading when she had paid for thirty minutes on the internet had her face on the front of it, with her history, and a warning to be on the lookout for her. She had to admit she liked the notoriety, even if it impinged on her movements, but regardless, she was hardly recognisable as she sat there in front of the well-used computer.

Her accommodation did not have Wi-Fi, in fact, it didn't have much of anything, and she was not inclined to purchase a USB modem for her laptop in case the authorities could monitor it. Once they knew her laptop's IP (internet protocol), then each time she logged on, they would be able to record all that she wrote, as well as find out where she was. No, she realised, it was better to use internet cafés, a different one each time.

As she tapped away at the computer, her mind focussed on the plan ahead. She knew where all those who were the bane of her life were. Sara Marshall was in Twickenham, Isaac Cook at Challis Street, and Gladys Lake at her hotel or the conference centre. She toyed with the idea of a romantic encounter with the black policeman before she stuck a knife into his heart, but rejected the idea, even if it brought a smile to her face. She knew that in an intimate encounter she would not be able to conceal her identity. If she wanted DCI Cook dead, then that was what would happen. Sara Marshall was another target, but not the prime one. She was a police officer, and apart from wanting to arrest her, she had done no wrong, although she still hated the woman. Gladys Lake, however, was a different matter.

Still, the need to be close to Detective Chief Inspector Isaac Cook ran strong in her veins. She knew she could not be closer, but another photo for the website, and the embarrassment it would cause him, seemed possible.

***

Wendy Gladstone and Larry Hill were out on the street; they had organised a team of one hundred constables to question people on the street at locations that seemed possible as the hiding place of Charlotte Hamilton. Without more accurate information, they had focussed close to the scenes of the past murders: Twickenham, Holland Park and Mayfair, as well as where she had killed the landlord at the cheap accommodation with the Peeping Tom, Jason Martin. That was discounted as the least likely area although it was still a good place to hide. They even ventured out to Joey's in Kingston where Liam Fogarty had been stabbed in the heart, but no one had seen the woman there, although the club was still annoying the neighbours with the noise from the rowdy drunks into the early hours of the morning. Yet Charlotte Hamilton remained elusive, so much so that Isaac felt increasingly frustrated. It wasn't helped by the ambivalence of DCS Goddard, his friend and mentor, towards him, and Isaac was no longer sure about the former of the two descriptors, as his DCS had been less than friendly since the unfortunate incident of the photogenic Isaac and the equally photogenic Charlotte appearing across the social media and on every newspaper front page, not to mention the hilarity on the early morning breakfast shows on television.

It was Wendy, his ever-loyal sergeant, who snapped him out of his inertia after she had returned from pounding the streets. She had seen him in his chair looking despondent.

'It's not that bad, sir. It'll blow over,' she said.

Isaac, forced to focus, could only agree. 'I suppose you're right,' he said. Regardless, he was the SIO on the case, and it was for him to get his backside out of his chair and to do his job. A meeting that afternoon seemed the best approach to breathe life into the search for Charlotte Hamilton.

At the nominated time, Isaac's team assembled. He had to acknowledge that they were a finely-honed team and he had been primarily responsible for bringing them together.

Larry Hill reappeared in the office five minutes before the meeting started. 'Bugger of a day. No sign of the woman,' he said. It was clear that he was not in a good mood; Isaac put it down to his wife's latest macrobiotic diet, which he was obliged to share or else feel her wrath and get the cold shoulder from her.

Larry confirmed Isaac's suspicions. 'I could do with a good plate of steak and chips.'

'Why don't you?' Isaac asked.

'My wife's right, of course,' Larry admitted, 'although it doesn't help with the hours we work.' Isaac said no more; he understood. Jess O'Neill, before she moved out of his place, had been keen on eating properly, so much so that he had tried to modify his eating habits of grabbing a bite here and there, and to wait until he was home with her. On some occasions that was very late at night, as both were busy people with demanding jobs.

Sara Marshall and Sean O'Riordan were both present, as was Bridget, who continued to do a sterling job dealing with the paperwork, assisting Isaac with his when she could.

'Any luck?' Isaac asked, looking over in the direction of Sara and Sean. Sara was looking worried.

'Not really,' Sara said. 'We know she's in London somewhere.'

'Apart from picking her up on camera at King's Cross, she's not been seen since,' Isaac said.

'She could hardly go back to Newcastle,' Sean said. 'Rory Hewitt and his team would have apprehended her if she had.'

'Are you joking?' Larry said. 'Why should they have any more luck than us? Besides, she updated on social media that she was coming to London.'

'And we trust her to be truthful?' Isaac interjected.

'She has unfinished business,' Sara reminded the team.

'Gladys Lake?'

'Yes.'

'And you, sir,' Wendy reminded Isaac.

Isaac, usually a mild-mannered man, was becoming frustrated. Apart from Larry consuming the biscuits, he couldn't see what they were achieving. Charlotte Hamilton continued to intrigue the media, although she had not killed for some time, and each time police ineptitude was implied, and on more than one occasion referred to overtly. His name had been mentioned more times than he appreciated, and whereas he had achieved some degree of celebrity, and someone had once said that any publicity was good, it didn't ring true in his case. He had become accustomed to reading accolades about himself, receiving phone calls from Richard Goddard congratulating him on excellent policing, even from the commissioner, the head of the Met, on one occasion. But now every phone call from a superior asked the same questions: when will there be an arrest, what are you doing to find this woman? Isaac realised there was one question being asked amongst his superiors: Is DCI Cook up to the task or should he be relieved of command?

He felt sure that Goddard would protect him; after all, he had ensured that Isaac was on the promotion ladder, and he had protected him well enough in the past. However, his DCS was a political animal, and he was not going to allow his career to be hindered by defending the indefensible.

***

Charlotte Hamilton, safely ensconced in her room at the flea-bitten accommodation she had found, sat on her bed. Her mood was ebullient, even if her life was in tatters.

She quietly sang a song: *stupid Duncan up at the quarry, along came a sister and gave him a push.* Although now she had another verse: *the black policeman thought he was smart until I stuck a knife in his heart.*

The melodious singing was interrupted by the sound of a jackhammer on the road outside. She looked around the room. It wasn't much for someone who had close to ten thousand pounds in her backpack.

A night in a good hotel will do me good, she thought. *Maybe the hotel where the Lake bitch is staying. So much easier to deal with her if I am close.*

She opened her bag and took out the clothes she needed: an old woollen skirt she had purchased in a charity shop, a blue jumper, some sensible black shoes, a brunette wig. She changed, applied makeup to age her face, and walked out of the door.

'The bastard can wait for his money,' she said under her breath. She still owed for two nights' accommodation, but she had no intention of coming back to pay. It was a five-minute walk to the train, although she made it in four. As the train rattled towards its final destination, she looked round the carriage. *If only they knew who was on the train,* she thought.

Virtually everyone was looking at their smartphones; some had iPads, but only one person had a newspaper. Even from where she was sitting, she could see a reference to her on the front page, as well as a picture of two men at a press conference. She recognised one, his black complexion unmistakable. A woman to one side of her looked at her for a while and looked away. Maybe the woman recognised her, she thought, but discounted it. Charlotte knew her ability to disguise herself was excellent, and that she would have no problems checking into Gladys Lake's hotel.

Thirty minutes later, Charlotte left the train at King's Cross and walked down Euston Road, heading for the hotel, and the woman who remained her main focus. An attentive receptionist at the St Pancras Renaissance Hotel signed her in, although she had used a false name and address. She paid in advance with cash and asked for the minibar to be emptied. Even so, she had taken a step back when she saw Inspector Sara Marshall sitting in the foyer drinking coffee. Charlotte felt for the knife in her pocket, resisting the urge to move closer and to insert it into the police officer's chest, as she realised that her carefully constructed plan would then be in shreds. She had already decided: first Gladys Lake, followed by Isaac Cook, followed by Sara Marshall. To Charlotte, in need of a friend, a shoulder to cry on, someone to love, Sara Marshall would have been ideal, but she was the enemy. She was someone who should understand her desire for vengeance on men, but probably would not.

Charlotte's mind swirled with impossible thoughts: a happy family, Isaac Cook, even Gloria, her former flatmate, and even Gregory Chalmers whom she had killed so long ago. If only he had loved her, she would have looked after him and his children, but knew it could not have been. She recognised that her earlier ebullience had been tinged with sadness and regret.

'Room 334,' a voice snapped her back to reality. She realised that she had been daydreaming. She hoped it wasn't noticeable, as the receptionist said nothing, and she could see that Sara Marshall was still sipping her coffee, talking to someone on her phone. Otherwise, the foyer of the hotel was quiet. Dispensing with anyone to show her to the room, Charlotte pressed the button of the lift. The room she had booked was as elegant as her previous accommodation had been flea-bitten. Appreciating the luxury, she took a lingering bath. Her mood tempered in the warm water, and for a moment, sanity reigned; the anger that she had felt had abated. Realising that her life had come full course and that there was no going back, she drew herself out of the bath, dried herself on the towel hanging behind the door and lay down on the bed.

When she awoke it was dark outside; she had been asleep for at least eight hours. Charlotte looked at the clock; it was 9 p.m. She dressed, careful to maintain her disguise, and left the room, unsure as to where she was going, although a good meal was first on her list of things to do.

As she left the hotel, she noticed her nemesis talking to someone she recognised: the police officer who worked with Sara Marshall, although she could not remember his name. Careful to give them only a sideways glance, she walked out of the front door and down the street. Feeling better after a pizza, she strolled around the area for some time, looking in shop windows, idly speculating on what could be. She saw couples walking arm in arm, elderly people hobbling down the street, even a baby in a pram being pushed by its mother. Charlotte daydreamed yet again about what her life could have been without her stupid brother, her uncaring parents, men who had wronged her, men who had used her body.

A car beeping its horn soon brought her back to reality as she walked out in the middle of the traffic, not looking where she was going. She knew that her mind was playing tricks when it was a time to be rational. There was a plan to execute, and she needed maximum focus, she knew that.

Charlotte returned to the hotel, noticing that Gladys Lake was not to be seen. She thought that it would be easy to knock on her door and to kill her there and then, but she needed to deal with others first. If she could not kill Isaac Cook, she could at least humiliate him again; that sounded fun to her. In her bag, she carried tablets that would calm her down, allow her to think clearly, but she knew that they would take away the anger, bring the regret for what she had done. She flushed them down the toilet.

***

Detective Chief Superintendent Richard Goddard was feeling the heat. A summons to the office of the Commissioner of the London Metropolitan Police was not what he wanted, especially as his relationship with the current commissioner was less than ideal.

A plain-talking man who Goddard kept his distance from if he could, the commissioner was in no mood to mince words. 'What the hell are you doing, DCS?'

Goddard had no defence, although he needed to put on a good show. The previous commissioner, a friend as well as his boss, would have been sympathetic, offering to give assistance and advice, but the new commissioner was a blunt man who spoke his mind, sometimes too freely. He was in no mood to accord the DCS standing in front of him any words of encouragement.

'We believe she's in London.'

'For Christ's sake, there's how many people in London? Eight, ten million? What chance do you have?'

'We're following up on all leads, conducting door-to-door, checking surveillance cameras.'

'That's just verbiage, and you know it. Admit it, you haven't a clue where the mad woman is.'

'Her ability to vanish is remarkable.'

'And you and your team's ability to display extreme incompetence is outstanding. Maybe I should bring in some people from my previous command to show you how to run an investigation.'

'That's not necessary, sir. My people are all competent and working hard to bring this case to a conclusion.'

'How many people dead now, eight or nine?'

'Six officially, sir.'

'What do you mean by officially?'

'Her brother's death is still recorded as accidental, and besides, she would have been a minor then.'

'Cook. What are you doing with him?'

'He's still the senior investigating officer.'

'Any more photos of him wrapped around the main suspect?'

'None.'

'You're a bloody fool to keep him in that position. I've been looking through his records: excellent policeman, but he has a habit of making a fool of himself,' the commissioner said.

'As you say, an excellent policeman who occasionally makes an error of judgement.'

'Occasionally! You should have put him on restricted duties after that photo, brought someone else in.'

'I realise that, sir.'

The DCS sensed a lessening in the commissioner's venom, although he was premature in his assessment.

'If there'is no breakthrough, then you and your team will be out. I need not add that your career and that of your star DCI will be down the drain.'

'Yes, sir.'

'Don't underestimate my resolve. The previous commissioner and your political friends will not be able to save you if I decide to act. Is that clear?'

'Clear, sir.'

'Good. Now leave and get on with it.'

Richard Goddard, with the exalted title of detective chief superintendent, left the room like an errant schoolboy summoned to the teacher's office for a dressing down. He was not in the best temper when he left. He needed someone on whom to take out his frustration; Isaac seemed the best person for that.

Chapter 26

'Isaac, I've received a right bollocking from the commissioner.' It was unusual for the DCS to use bad language, a clear indication that his visit was not social. Isaac braced himself for what was to come.

'It's to be expected, sir,' Isaac replied to Goddard's opening comment, after the DCS had firmly closed Isaac's office door behind him.

'Just because you're stuffing around, I'm forced to allow the commissioner to take it out on me. I may resent the man, but he's still our boss.'

'Under the circumstances, the team is working well,' Isaac said.

'What is it with this woman? It's not as if you don't know who the guilty person is.'

'Agreed, sir, but she blends in easily.'

'We know that already, but what are you doing to find her?'

'Sergeant Gladstone and Larry Hill are out in the field looking for her, conducting door-to-doors. Inspector Marshall and Sergeant O'Riordan are checking out old haunts, previous murder locations.'

'The woman is hardly likely to do that; but then again, she and the commissioner may be right, this department under your tutelage is incompetent.'

'I resent that, sir.'

'Maybe you do, but I'm tired of taking flak from his holiness in his ivory tower at Scotland Yard. He instructed me once before to put you on restricted duties, even to suspend you, but I didn't. And now it's on my record that I acted against advice. If she kills again, the commissioner will have me on restricted duties along with you, and I do not intend to allow that to happen. He wants to bring in someone else to run this investigation; someone from his previous command, although what good that will do, coming in cold to the case, is unclear.'

'Understood.'

Goddard, after venting his spleen on Isaac, felt his frustration at the meeting with the commissioner subside. He took a seat. Bridget, outside, noticing the mellowing atmosphere in Isaac's office and regarding it as safe to enter, came in with a cup of tea for each of the two men.

'Isaac, what can be done?' Goddard said calmly after Bridget had left.

'You're right, DCS. It should be easy. All we have to do now is to protect the living and to find one woman.'

'So why can't you find her?'

'She just has an uncanny ability. She always disguises herself, and she's not using bank or credit cards.'

'She must have money then.'

'The last man she killed had money hidden under his bed.'

'She stole it?'

'It's the only explanation. The man's ex-wife turned up at the crime scene soon after the body had been discovered. We used her for a positive ID later. Anyway, she was convinced that he had stashed his money somewhere. Called him a miserable old skinflint.'

'You checked?'

'Of course, sir. Found some money, but not much.'

'The commissioner's receiving flak over this woman.'

'You don't care much for him, sir?'

'Not the issue, is it?'

***

Since the incident with the photo in Newcastle the investigation had been progressing satisfactorily, and thankfully there had been no further deaths. Standard policing was being followed, and the paperwork, always too much, was up to date and in line with regulations. The new commissioner regarded the process as important, and while Isaac did not enjoy that side of his job, he had to reluctantly admit that it was necessary. Get a smart lawyer for the defence and any shoddy paperwork would soon be relegated to the rubbish bin as inadmissible evidence.

It had happened a few times in the past, even to Isaac, and nothing irked more than to see a guilty person walk free, thumbing their nose at the police. Isaac did not intend for that to happen this time. He was still smarting from the embarrassing photo, and the woman was already thumbing her nose, and she was not even in custody.

Admittedly, she was not doing it as much as in the past, as the woman's attempts to use social media had mostly been curtailed. Each time she posted, it was from another location. It had been possible to trace the locations, and they were always internet cafés, spread throughout the country. Her last post had been close in to London.

Wendy and Larry, hot on the trail, had missed Charlotte by no more than two hours at the last internet café. The man behind the counter had been surly when questioned, claiming that he had seen no one suspicious. Questioned further, he admitted he had seen a woman matching the woman in the photo that Larry showed him. The café, no more than twenty miles from London, had provided further proof that Charlotte was close by, although the only witness was vague and could hardly be regarded as reliable.

***

Charlotte reclined on her bed at the hotel. She was not sure what to do next. The key players were all in position, but how to execute her plan concerned her. She knew that when she made her first move, she would become more visible.

There she was in plain view, and no one had seen her, not Gladys Lake nor Sara Marshall. She had not seen DCI Cook yet, but she was determined to obtain one more photo.

The first time in Newcastle, with a frivolous group of women, the DCI had been easy to corner. She could see even then that he was attracted to women, even to her, judging by the way he gripped her around the waist when the photo had been taken. She fantasised over him, yet knew it was not possible. Tired of staring at the television and daydreaming, she left the hotel; it was the end-of-day rush hour, and the city was milling with people.

She thought about leaving the city, to get maybe twenty to thirty miles out from the centre and find somewhere to use the internet. She walked up Euston Road as far as the entrance to the London Underground. Flashing her Oyster Card at the ticket barrier she looked for the next train.

As she descended on the escalator, safely ensconced in the melee of people, she looked to the right. Ascending on the other side was Sara Marshall. Unable to resist, Charlotte looked across at her. Even as well disguised as she was, there was no way the police inspector would not recognise her. Immediately Sara started pushing her way up past the people, attempting to flash her badge and to shout 'Police'.

Equally alarmed, Charlotte pushed her way down and jumped into a train that was about to pull out, its destination unknown and unimportant.

Sara was now at the top of the escalator and on speed dial to Isaac and the team. Not waiting for a reply, she hurtled down the escalator in an attempt to catch up with Charlotte, her pulse racing at the realisation of who she had just seen. Isaac, on the other line, was unable to speak to Sara, but was able to register the noise and the activity on her end of the phone.

He quickly fired up the team, using another phone on a group call. 'Sara's in trouble.'

Sean O'Riordan answered first. 'She was heading over to meet me at Gladys Lake's hotel.'

'Wendy, Larry, get over there now,' Isaac said.

'We're on our way,' Larry's reply.

Thirty seconds later, Sara's voice was heard. 'Charlotte Hamilton, I've just seen her. St Pancras Underground.'

'Where is she now?' Isaac asked.

'No idea. By the time I could get down the escalator, she had jumped on a train and left. Probably the Victoria line, heading south.'

Isaac phoned for support. An APW was instigated: focus on all stations downline from St Pancras. Soon, every station on the line was being converged on by police cars and police officers on foot; the woman's importance ensured a maximum response from all police authorities.

Forty minutes later came the inevitable negative response from all stations. Isaac, annoyed that yet again she had eluded them, phoned his boss.

'DCS, Charlotte Hamilton confirmed in London.'

'You've caught her?'

'Not yet, but she's running scared now.'

'I'll phone the commissioner. May help to give you some time, but don't count on it.'

Sara, deducing that St Pancras Underground and Gladys Lake's hotel were too close to be a coincidence, rushed to the hotel after ensuring the police who were pouring into the station were updated. She found Gladys Lake in her room with Sean O'Riordan, two uniforms on the door outside.

'Was she coming for me?' Gladys Lake asked.

'I don't think so. She was heading in the wrong direction,' Sara replied.

'Staking out the area?' Sean asked.

'It's possible. You'd better get Wendy and Larry to check.'

***

A desperate woman took stock of the situation. Charlotte had not expected to see Sara Marshall in the underground station; she chastised herself for looking her way.

If it had not been for the eye contact, there was no way that anyone, even a police officer, would have recognised her. If the train had not been there when she ran off the escalator, she knew she could have been caught. And now there was the problem of money. Checking her bag, she still had two thousand pounds; the rest was in her room back at the hotel, along with her disguises.

If I hadn't got off one station down, she thought, having realised that the police would soon be mobilised to look for her. Her estimation was correct, and as soon as she left the station at Euston, she moved quickly away on foot. Hailing a taxi, she took it to Windsor, a small town to the west of London. Unable to think straight, too many issues to consider, she checked into a budget hotel using the name of Ingrid Bentham.

Once in the room, Charlotte took stock of the situation. 'Two thousand pounds, the clothes I'm wearing,' she said out loud to herself. She took a shower and then slept for two hours. Later, she went to a local supermarket and bought herself a few essentials: toothbrush, toothpaste, change of underwear. Apart from that, she decided to leave the rest of what she required for the next day.

She realised that the net was closing in on her. She saw clearly that the next few days would be crucial and she could not evade the police for much longer.

Wendy and Larry focussed on St Pancras; Bridget was looking at the CCTV. If Charlotte had been there, then it was clear that she knew where Gladys Lake was; it was too much of a coincidence to be discounted. Sara had been able to give a good description: red hair (obviously a wig), dark blue skirt, knee-length, blue top, possibly wool, as well as a calf-length coat, dark brown. From where she had been on the other side of the escalator, Sara had not been able to see what shoes Charlotte Hamilton was wearing.

'If she hadn't looked at me,' Sara had said, 'I wouldn't have known it was her.'

'Just hope she didn't get a photo of you,' Isaac's reply. He had been close to Charlotte Hamilton, admittedly in the dark, but he had failed to recognise her too, so he was in no position to offer any further comment.

Gladys Lake was adamant that she would continue with her presentation, regardless of the protestations from Isaac, who had come to the hotel to meet her personally. 'We can give you protective custody for the next few days,' he said. 'Charlotte's rattled now. It won't be long before we catch her.'

'That may be, but I've been preparing for this conference for the last three months. I don't intend to miss it, Charlotte Hamilton or no Charlotte Hamilton.'

'Sara, Sean, stay with Dr Lake. Day and night if you have to,' Isaac said realising the futility of further debate.

'Will do, sir,' Sean replied. Sara, concerned that her child had a nasty cough and she should be with him, nodded her head weakly.

Chapter 27

Charlotte was disturbed after the incident at St Pancras Underground Station; her manner in the train as it pulled out of the station had caused others to look at her. She had sworn out loud in anguish. She had nearly been caught and all because of a stupid error; if she hadn't looked, the woman police officer would never have recognised her. She realised she had become too nonchalant about her ability to move freely, thumbing her nose at the incompetent police officers, which was how she saw them.

She had seen Sara Marshall on more than one occasion, even walked past her in the street close to the hotel one day, almost felt like sitting close to her in the foyer of the hotel. It was arrogance on her part; she knew it now. She determined to lift her game, although events were moving quickly.

A visit to a shop selling wigs in Windsor, not far from the castle, and she was a brunette; a charity shop provided the clothes she required. The subject matter of the conference where the evil doctor would speak was academic. Charlotte had read it carefully: Human Rights and Mental Health. She knew what it meant: how to make people's lives miserable. Charlotte, knowing full well how Gladys Lake dressed, decided to dress in the same style, which made for sensible clothes and sensible shoes; not the style of clothes which she had affected when she had seduced and killed four of her previous victims.

Back at her hotel, she changed into the clothes she had bought, putting her money securely in the small bag she carried. She left her remaining meagre belongings in her hotel room and walked out of the door. She was not sure if she would be returning, but it did not matter. Her life had come full circle now, and if she could strike a blow on behalf of all those who had suffered at the hands of malevolent doctors, in buildings called hospitals but were no more than prisons, then all was fine. Whatever the day brought, she would accept it with grace.

***

Isaac, early in the office after a sleepless night, sat at his desk pondering Richard Goddard's visit the previous day.

He had left the office the previous night close to midnight, and he had returned at five in the morning. The situation weighed heavily on his mind.

Bridget and Wendy had been working together to ascertain Charlotte Hamilton's movements after the incident with Sara Marshall; not so easy considering that it had been rush hour, and the clothing described by Sara could have matched at least five per cent of all the women travelling at that time. Facial recognition, especially a retinal scan, was the best way to confirm one hundred per cent that it was the right person, but that was deemed not possible in this case. For one thing, the camera lenses at most underground stations were dirty, and secondly, their resolution was not ideal. The most that could be hoped for was a close match on the clothing.

The previous night Bridget had stayed in the office with Wendy, who kept up the supply of coffee until two in the morning. They had phoned Isaac on leaving to let him know they had a possible lead, and they would update him in the morning.

Wendy walked into the office at six in the morning, an hour after Isaac. 'The alarm didn't go off,' she said.

'That's fine,' Isaac said. 'Grab yourself a tea, and we can talk.'

'Bridget's on the way, so is Larry.'

'Fine, we'll wait for them.'

'It's going to be alright, sir.'

Isaac realised that Bridget had been talking to Wendy about the DCS's visit to his office.

Ten minutes later, all four sat down in Isaac's office.

'What do you have?' Isaac asked.

'We believe we've identified Charlotte Hamilton at Euston Underground,' Bridget said.

'Confirmed?'

'The clothing matches, as does the time.'

'Assuming it's her, what then?'

'We sent a photo to DI Marshall. She's certain it's her, as well.'

We're closing in on her.' Isaac visibly relaxed at the news, so much so that Wendy felt obliged to comment.

'We still need her under lock and key, sir.'

'Understood. Any further sightings?' Isaac asked.

'We think we picked her up outside on the street hailing a cab,' Wendy said.

'Details?'

'Not possible to identify the cab. We'll be dealing with that today; it shouldn't be too much of a problem.'

'Maybe an address?'

'Always possible. The woman's making mistakes; we should catch her soon.'

'Hopefully before she kills again.'

'And Gladys Lake?' Larry asked.

'Inspector Marshall and Sergeant O'Riordan are sticking close to her. Once she's out of London, the better it is for us.'

'And when will that be?' Wendy asked.

'Tomorrow, hopefully. So that's the agenda for today: protect Dr Lake, find and arrest Charlotte Hamilton.'

'You make it sound easy, sir.'

'It has to be, or else they'll bring in another team.' Isaac realised that he should have berated them in the same way that he had been by Richard Goddard, but he saw that as unnecessary; they wouldn't let him down.'

'We'll succeed,' Wendy said. The others acknowledged with nods of their heads.

***

Gladys Lake woke early. Today was a big day for her, and she was excited. Her approach to the welfare of the mentally ill was to be commended for its record of success. She had been allocated forty minutes for the presentation; she could have done with sixty, but there were other speakers, and the organising committee had been adamant about her allocated time.

A shower, then breakfast in her room, a concession she had been forced to make after Charlotte Hamilton had been seen close by. She would have preferred the restaurant downstairs with its greater choice of food, but even she could see that it was possibly dangerous to be so exposed, especially after it had been discovered that Charlotte had spent two nights in the same hotel as her. After she had been spotted nearby, Sean and Sara had conducted a check of the hotel's records and discovered the room that Charlotte had been using, along with eight thousand pounds and some clothes.

After breakfast, Dr Lake checked her presentation and went through it one more time. Satisfied that it was in order, she lay down on her bed again. She fell asleep until the phone rang. *Oh, what fun, I slit his throat. Who will be next? Will it be you?'*

Gladys Lake slammed down the phone and screamed for help. The two police officers stationed outside her door came rushing in.

'What is it?' the more senior of the two asked.

'She's been on the phone.'

Sean O'Riordan arrived first. He had been at the hotel since early morning and was just eating breakfast when the phone call came through from Sara Marshall. She was on her way, due in twenty minutes.

She phoned Isaac. 'Charlotte's called Dr Lake.'

'Trace on the phone?'

'Not sure yet. It looks like she used a public phone.'

'Anyway, we need it located.'

Sara arrived at the hotel to find Gladys Lake calm but still upset.

'You need to cancel your presentation,' Sara said.

'I'll be okay. I intend to honour my obligation.'

Aware, after so many times of trying, that she would not be able to dissuade the woman, Sara acquiesced. The plan she outlined to those charged with protecting the doctor was that they would take her to the event at 11 a.m. for the pre-conference get-together.

At all times, one police officer was to be at her side, which would be, unless advised otherwise, either Sara Marshall or Sean O'Riordan. Two police officers would be stationed at the main entrances to the venue, and police would be interspersed throughout the building. All persons entering would be checked and their credentials established.

As it was a two-day event, it was clear that Charlotte Hamilton's window of opportunity was limited, at least in London.

At the conclusion of the day's activities, Dr Lake was to be taken back to the hotel and protected at all times. On the third morning after arriving, she would travel to the railway station to catch an early train back to Newcastle. A discreet police escort consisting of six officers, including Sara and Sean, would accompany her to Newcastle where she would be placed under the protection of Rory Hewitt and his team. At no time, and Sara was adamant about this, was Gladys Lake allowed to be out of sight of the police.

As Sara explained, it was not only about protecting Dr Lake. It was also about capturing Charlotte Hamilton who was preparing to take some action, although where and when was not known.

***

Wendy and Larry were at Euston Underground. The security videos had identified Charlotte Hamilton but not where she had gone after leaving the station.

The taxi rank offered the best opportunity, and six officers, as well as Wendy, were working the taxis one by one, although the drivers were not pleased to be delayed. However, they could not avoid the police, and it was always best to keep on the right side of the law; they knew that.

Larry was the first to make a breakthrough. 'That's her. She was a nervous woman, kept asking me to drive faster,' an Indian Sikh driver said.

'What can you tell me about her?' Larry asked.

'Can't it wait? It's the best time of the day to make money.'

'Official police enquiry.'

'Then be quick.'

'Where did you take the woman?'

'Windsor, an excellent fare at that time of night. There's a train out there, but for some reason she preferred to come with me.'

'Address?'

'Just in front of the castle, that's all. Can I go now?'

'Subject to giving your details. We'll need a statement later from you.'

'That's fine. I'm a good citizen. Always willing to help.'

The Sikh driver gave his details. Larry could see no reason to detain him further. However, he had not been able to provide a precise address.

'Important, is she?'

'Very.'

'Okay. You have my phone number, but as I said, I dropped her in front of the castle. No more than that.'

Isaac, now aware of where Charlotte had gone, was soon on the phone to the police station in Windsor. Larry and Wendy left Euston soon after Larry's success, and with their team headed towards the small town, twenty miles to the west, that was invariably swamped by tourists hoping for a glimpse of royalty. It was still early; there was a chance they could stop Charlotte before she left there.

Sergeant Bevin Downton met them on arrival at the police station in Alma Road, no more than a mile from Windsor Castle, and the last known location of Charlotte Hamilton.

'What can I do for you?' Downton, a tall man with dark wavy hair, asked.

'Your team is ready?' Larry asked.

'One step ahead. Once you phoned and explained the situation, we had people out on the street asking passers-by. Also, we're checking the hotels now. If, as you say, she's running scared, she may have stayed close to the city centre, or moved on somewhere else.'

'Not likely that she's moved,' Wendy said. 'Time's against her now, and she knows it. We believe that she will strike today in London. She's already phoned the target; scared the living daylights out of her.'

'Give us three hours, and we should have checked the main possibilities,' Downton said.

***

Charlotte wandered down by the river, throwing some bread for the ducks to eat. It was still early, too early to complete what remained unfinished from Newcastle. Usually, she would skip breakfast, but today, for no apparent reason, she decided that a full stomach was needed.

'Full English breakfast, dear?' the waitress at the small café asked.

'Yes, please,' Charlotte replied. She checked inside her bag; all that she needed was there.

Ten minutes later, her breakfast arrived: tomatoes, eggs, bacon and sausages. Charlotte gulped down the meal, paid the bill and left the café. She walked to the railway station in Windsor and took the 7.55 a.m. to Waterloo. From there it was a one-mile walk across Waterloo Bridge to Chancery Lane, and the London International Medical Centre where the conference was to be held, although she intended to leave the train at Vauxhall, two miles further away from the venue.

She realised that there would be police at Waterloo looking for her; her phone call to Gladys Lake would have alerted them to her primary target. A rational person would not have made such an error, but she was no longer rational, only focussed. If she was to die in the attempt, so be it, but Gladys Lake had to die first.

The train moved rapidly to its destination, Charlotte barely registering the movement. It was only when she heard the driver announce 'Vauxhall next stop' that she raised herself from her seat.

As she had predicted, there was no police presence at the station, only railway security, and they weren't looking for her. She left the station on the side closest to the river and walked up the Albert Embankment; it was only 9.30 a.m., and time was on her side. A police car came hurtling by, its siren blaring. For a moment, Charlotte moved over to one side, closer to the river, but the car did not stop. She resumed her steady pace up the road, passing Lambeth Bridge, Westminster Bridge and the Houses of Parliament; at any other time scenically impressive, but not for Charlotte. She came to Waterloo Bridge and looked around for a heightened police presence; she could see none. The crowds had started to form on the bridge: locals going about their usual business, tourists with iPhones taking photos, mainly selfies to post on social media. None of them interested her as she maintained her pace over the bridge, looking left and right, straight ahead, not noticing the River Thames flowing beneath her. Leaving the river, she reached the Strand and turned right, eventually reaching Chancery Lane and her destination. The police car outside was the first sign of trouble; the second, the two police officers checking everyone entering the building.

Anxious to ensure that her plan was not thwarted, she walked around the edifice looking for another way in. She found Clifford's Inn Passage, a lane to one side of the building. History would have told her that the name referred to an Inn of Chancery, one of the country's legal institutions that had been founded in 1344, but she was not interested in that, only in whether the passage would afford her entrance into where she wanted to go. Moving up the lane, she found a small door; it was unlocked. She turned the handle and entered the basement of the conference centre. She ascended a flight of stairs: yet again, police. A cupboard solved the problem; it contained cleaning utensils and a cleaner's uniform. She put it on and moved around the building, pretending to clean. Soon she reached the room where Gladys Lake was to present her paper; it was empty. Easing herself into a space beneath the elevated stage, she waited.

It had been luck that the room was empty when she had entered. Within a few minutes, people started to file in, ready for the opening speech at midday. Gladys Lake entered the room just before it started, in the company of Sara Marshall. Charlotte watched them come down the stairs through a crack in the raised-floor's plinth. Up on the stage, the microphones were being given a final test: 'One, two, three. Can you hear me at the back?' They could.

Charlotte listened to the boring speeches about subjects that she had knowledge of after years in a hospital. Gladys Lake was due to speak at 2 p.m.

Charlotte, unsure how to proceed, waited patiently, although it was dusty where she was, and there was evidence of vermin. Regardless, she kept still, hoping that an opportunity would present itself. She saw the doctor fiddling with her notes, talking to Sara Marshall, looking around the room nervously. At ten minutes before her nominated time, Gladys Lake rose and left the room in the company of the police officer. Charlotte cursed, unable to follow them. She moved back, finding an exit. Quickly, unseen, she moved around behind some partitions to the rear of the room and through a side door into the corridor outside. At the other end, she could see the Ladies toilet; her assumption was that was where the two women had gone. She gingerly approached the door, listening for voices, hearing muffled sounds from the other side. Charlotte checked her bag and withdrew the knife she carried.

Carefully she pushed opened the door; it squeaked. Once through it, she concealed herself behind a pillar. Certain of her target, she moved forward.

'What the –' Sara Marshall shouted in surprise, instinctively shielding her body from the knife that Charlotte held.

'Where is she?' Charlotte demanded. Her face was red with anger.

Sara realised that Dr Lake was safe as long as she stayed in the cubicle. She shouted to her, 'Don't move.'

'In there, is she?'

'There's no way out,' Sara, her pulse racing, said. She knew that if she could reach her phone, there would be police officers nearby to take down the woman confronting her.

'There was no way in, but here I am. I intend to finish what I started. To show those doctors in the other room what happens when you torture innocent people.'

Sara used all her training in negotiation to attempt to calm the woman. She was a strong woman, and in her state, unpredictable. Sara moved away from protecting Dr Lake's cubicle, aiming to distance herself from the knife. She hoped the doctor would have the good sense to remain where she was.

Charlotte moved forward, matching the distance between her knife and Sara Marshall. Sara could feel her panic increasing and attempted to calm her nerves. She was a seasoned police officer, similar scenarios had been practised in training, but here was the real thing, and it was nothing like she had been taught. Then, there had been an element of make-believe, and there was no way that any harm would befall those who failed the test, but now: one mistake, one wrong word, one action, and there would be death.

'Two for one,' Charlotte said, grimacing. Sara could see that the situation was precarious. She thought of her child without a mother, all because of her chosen career and a mad woman.

'It's over, Charlotte. You cannot escape,' Sara said.

'With Dr Lake dead, what do I care?'

'You need help, Charlotte,' Sara said, hoping to delay the woman's next action. Sara pressed her hand against her left pocket; her phone was there, but there was no way to use it, not while the woman was watching her intently. One wrong move and the knife would be propelled forward.

'I'm coming for you,' Charlotte taunted the woman in the cubicle.

'Please, Charlotte, dear Charlotte. I always cared for you, did what I thought was right.' The sound of Gladys Lake's voice indicated the fear she was feeling.

'Electric shocks and cold baths, is that how you care? Nobody cared for me, not my father, not my mother, and not that brother of mine.'

'You killed your brother?' Sara asked.

'He deserved to die.'

'Nobody deserves to die,' Gladys Lake said.

'Those men who treated me badly did.'

Sara could see that the conversation was weakening the resolve of the woman in front of her; the knife was not held as erect as before. She kept talking.

'What did you plan to do after here?' Sara asked.

'I have no plans. I've already told you.'

'There is help available for you, you know that.'

'Help! Drugged out of my mind until I'm no more than a vegetable. No thanks.' The knife grip firmed.

Sara moved further back, unable to avoid the direct impact of the blade. At the crucial moment, she managed to step sideways to avoid the full length of the blade entering her body. Charlotte came in again, Sara feebly trying to push her away. Gladys Lake, aware of what was happening, opened the cubicle door. It was the wrong move.

At that moment the door from the corridor opened and two women entered.

'Help,' one of them screamed. Charlotte, taking advantage of the situation, bolted for the door, pushing the two women to one side. She ran along the corridor, somehow avoiding the other police officers in the building and found the stairs to the basement. She hurtled down them and out of the door and back into Clifford's Inn Passage. She could hear police sirens in the distance, coming closer. She removed the uniform she had been wearing, as well as the brunette wig, and walked, almost ran, down the street, aiming to distance herself from the police.

Chapter 28

Five minutes after the events at the conference centre, Isaac was in his car and on the way, the blue flashing light and the siren easing him through the traffic. A police officer down, the most serious offence in an officer's book.

What concerned him was that one of his team had been stabbed. Details were sketchy. Her husband, Bob Marshall, had been notified.

Arriving at the conference centre, Isaac parked his car, taking no notice of whether he was interfering with the usual flow of traffic, and headed into the building. He rushed up the stairs, a policeman on the door showing him the way. Thankfully, the constable had recognised him and waved him through. An ambulance had arrived just before him; a medic bent over Sara's still body. Gladys Lake was also administering assistance, holding Sara's head in her lap, although it was evident to Isaac that the doctor was in need of aid too.

The doctor looked up at Isaac as he entered. 'She's going to be alright,' she said. 'The knife did not go too deep.'

Bob Marshall arrived ten minutes later. Sara, by that time conscious, although sedated and bandaged, meekly acknowledged his presence.

After the initial concern about Sara, Isaac took stock of the situation. He noticed the delegates at the conference filing out, their names and a brief statement obtained, although there was no need to detain them for long. Once again, Isaac realised, Charlotte Hamilton had made fools of them; he knew what was coming next.

Wendy phoned Isaac from Windsor. Bridget had phoned her. 'DI Marshall?'

'She'll survive. Luckily, she managed to avoid the full force of the knife. She'll be sore for a while and out of action for a few weeks, but she'll live.'

'We found where she was staying. She registered as Ingrid Bentham.'

'She's not thinking straight,' Isaac said.

'Not much else to tell you. We found a bag and some clothing. Apart from that, nothing.'

'It's probably not relevant now. She's here in London, and not far away.'

'What about the police at the conference centre? How did they let her get in?' Wendy asked.

'Good question,' Isaac said. 'Someone will need to do some serious explaining later, but for now we need to find this woman. If there's no more where you are, then you and Larry had better get back to Challis Street as soon as possible.'

'We'll leave in five minutes.'

***

DCS Goddard phoned, as expected. 'Sara Marshall?'

'Her condition is stable,' Isaac replied.

'And Dr Lake?'

'Shaken, but otherwise unharmed.'

'Good. Now tell me what happened.'

'Charlotte Hamilton attacked DI Marshall in the Ladies toilet. Gladys Lake was in one of the cubicles and protected.'

'How did Charlotte Hamilton get in there? I thought the place was secured.'

'I had asked the local police station to provide security.'

'And they failed?'

'Correct.'

'I'll need a full report on my desk by tomorrow morning.'

'Yes, sir.'

'I've already had the commissioner on the phone. He wants a full internal enquiry as to how a known murderer can walk into a secured location and then attempt to kill a police officer.'

'She wasn't after Sara Marshall.'

'That's as may be, but she's been attacked, and the commissioner intends that heads will roll; yours and mine, if he can arrange it.'

'Understood, but our primary concern is finding Charlotte Hamilton.'

'You'd better find her within twenty-four hours, or you're off the case.'

'Harsh, sir.'

'Not harsh. It's a directive from the commissioner. Your replacement is due in London within a day. I can't stop this, and with a police officer almost fatally wounded, I'm not in a position to put forward a case for your retention.'

Isaac sat down on a nearby chair. He had had some tight scrapes in his career, but this was the most severe. He wasn't usually a drinker, but if he had been at home, he would have opened the bottle of brandy that he kept for such occasions.

***

Charlotte walked and ran down Fleet Street, the former home of the major newspapers in the country. She could not think, only run, and remove herself from the area of the conference centre. As she hurtled down the street, she glanced in the occasional shop window. Without the wig, she could see Charlotte Hamilton staring back at her, not an old lady or a tarty female, but the Charlotte Hamilton that she knew, as did the police.

What a mess, she thought.

She turned right down Salisbury Court and Dorset Rise, joining Tudor Street. Once out of the immediate area, she slowed her pace to a brisk walk. Her breathing was still heavy, and she was perspiring. With no feelings of guilt about what had occurred, she found a café.

'Cappuccino and a slice of cheesecake, please,' she said, when asked by the waitress.

A police car drove past; it took no notice of where she was sitting close to the front window. Charlotte discounted it.

The waitress brought her the coffee and the cake. Charlotte took her time to drink and eat. She thought through what had just occurred, and what to do next. Outwardly, she resembled an average person just going about their daily business: worrying about their job, their children, how to pay next month's mortgage.

She left the café and walked down the street, turning right on Farringdon Street. She crossed Blackfriars Bridge, keeping her head low. Where to head for was uncertain, but she knew it had to be out of London.

***

'Your career's finished. You know that,' Detective Chief Superintendent Goddard said.

'Yes, sir,' DCI Cook said. For once, the friendly handshake with his superior and mentor was dispensed with. Isaac was standing upright in the DCS's office; Goddard was sitting down, although he looked ready to burst.

'I've had the commissioner on the phone three times today already. If Marshall had died, can you imagine the problems that would have caused?'

'Full inquiry.'

'And the rest. They would have my head on a plate for letting you continue with this case. All that nonsense about you being the future commissioner of the Met down the drain.'

'I never held much store to it,' Isaac said, which was not altogether true. He had been working his way up to the top by exceptional policing, obtaining the right qualifications, and, if needed, charming those who could help.

Richard Goddard had guided his career from the start, from when he had been a junior constable and Goddard an inspector. The previous commissioner had seen something in him, but the new commissioner did not like Isaac, any more than he liked the DCS, and Isaac was clearly Goddard's man.

Isaac's good relationship with the former government whip Angus McTavish would not help as he was now sitting in the House of Lords. He was unlikely to want to sully himself with a DCI whose latest case had resulted in six murders, almost a seventh.

'You'd better sit down, Isaac,' Goddard said. 'Let's see if we can salvage anything out of this sorry mess.'

'Sara Marshall is going to be fine,' Isaac said, attempting to alleviate the tension in Goddard's office.

'I know that, and from all accounts, she handled herself well. No doubt she'll receive an award for exceptional courage, probably the Queen's Police Medal. At least, she'll have my recommendation and the commissioner's, that's if I'm still around.'

'That bad, sir?'

'What do you think?' Goddard's mood changed again. 'You were given this case when the death count stood at four. Or was it five?'

'Four. Graham Dyer was the first, in Holland Park.'

'And the count now?'

'Six.'

'How can I defend you? It's not as if you didn't know who the murderer was. This Charlotte Hamilton has made us laughing stocks.'

'Three were murdered some years previously when DI Marshall was running the investigation of the crimes down in Twickenham.'

'Hardly a defence for your ineptitude, and besides, she was relatively inexperienced, her first murder case. You're a DCI with an exceptional track record; plenty of convictions under your belt. What can I say? What can I do?'

'Have you explained this to the commissioner?'

'The man's an arrogant fool,' Goddard said.

'First time you've said that.'

'First time I've not cared if he hears or not. Isaac, I can't defend you on this one.'

'I know that. Protect yourself if you can.'

'It doesn't work like that, and you know it. If one goes, we both go. Anyway, enough complaining and criticising. What do we have? And make us both a cup of tea.'

For a few minutes, the conversation turned away from Charlotte Hamilton, and the two men spoke as friends and colleagues. The commissioner phoned Goddard, who answered in an obsequious manner.

'Your replacement will be here within the hour,' Goddard said.

'What do you want me to do?' Isaac asked.

'Play it by the book. Give him all the assistance he needs, although he may bring his own people, start from scratch.'

'That would be sheer madness. Charlotte Hamilton's out there, probably not far from here, and she failed with Gladys Lake. There's no way of knowing when she'll strike next.'

'Agreed. Your team is still with you, although the new SIO may purloin them.'

'They'll be reluctant to afford him the support they gave me.'

'That's understood, but they're professionals. They'll do their duty. You'd better tell them that. Now, what can you tell me about Charlotte Hamilton?'

'Since the attack on Sara Marshall, nothing.'

'What do you mean?'

'She vanished.'

'But how did she get out? You had the venue surrounded.'

'We did, but she slipped through a door at the rear of the building.'

'She's not Harry Houdini. Didn't your people cover all possible points of entry?'

'They missed that one. We've put out an APW on her; she can't have gone far. All the bus and train stations are being monitored.'

'In the rush hour!'

'She blends in well.'

'Okay. What's the situation with Gladys Lake?'

'She's returning to Newcastle earlier than planned.'

'Is she safe there?'

'She intends to secure herself at her hospital. It's safer than here, and we believe Charlotte Hamilton to be close to London.'

'But she could return to Newcastle.'

'We realise that possibility, but regardless, the mental hospital she works at does have good security. Also, DI Rory Hewitt, up in Newcastle, knows Charlotte Hamilton by sight.'

'Very well. Outline the plan.'

'Gladys Lake will be taken to King's Cross by a police car at two in the afternoon. That's the earliest we could arrange adequate protection. She will board the train. There will be six police officers in plain clothes on the train, as well.'

'Are you expecting the Hamilton woman to reappear?'

'It's a possibility.'

'And where will you be?'

'I'll be travelling with Dr Lake, as will some of my team. Assuming that my team is not occupied with the new SIO.'

'If they are, make sure they are out of the office in time. Make up a ruse if you must.'

'That's what I planned.'

'Is Gladys Lake the bait?'

'Not really, but if Charlotte Hamilton makes an appearance, we'll be there to nab her.'

'Good plan, as long as no one else is killed. And if the new SIO starts causing trouble, act professionally. If you catch this woman, the accolades go to you.'

'And you, sir.'

'Correct. But if she's caught on the new SIO's watch...'

'He's the hero of the hour, and you and I are dead meat,' Isaac said as he left his DCS's office.

Goddard shrugged his shoulders in agreement.

***

Charlotte continued to move away from where she would be recognised. She had considered her life expendable, if only it would ensure the death of her torturer, but now...

If only that woman had not got in my way, she thought.

She reflected on the events at the conference centre: the Ladies toilet, the knife in her hand, Sara Marshall separating her from her target, the knife entering her body, Dr Lake in the cubicle, inches from her. If only those two women had not come in, she would have completed her task. Now the plan was in shreds again, and she had nowhere to hide. She knew that she needed sanctuary. She needed her friend, where she had spent three years; she needed Beaty. But Beaty was dead; dead as a result of the shock of seeing her dead cat.

Charlotte realised that she had been the only person who had really cared for her, and if she wasn't there, at least the area would be.

She walked towards Southwark, careful to avoid being too visible. A discount clothing store on the way gave her the opportunity to buy a thick coat; she had dispensed with the previous one in Windsor. Although it was not the coldest day of the year, it did not look out of place to the people scurrying along the street.

Taking stock of her appearance, she realised that she was still too recognisable. She bought a hat, which under normal circumstances she would not be seen dead in.

She chuckled at her appearance, but she knew she would not be recognised, at least by a patrolling police car; not even by a police officer on the street.

Slowing her pace, Charlotte reviewed the situation. She knew she still had a task to complete, but when and how? Gladys Lake, she knew, would be protected. As for Sara Marshall, she did not care whether she lived or died. The knife which she had used was at the conference centre, discarded as she left the building. She needed another.

Once at Southwark, realising that there was no transport available to her destination, she continued to head south, joining up with Old Kent Road. Another two miles, and she boarded a bus. She smiled to herself as she sat in its warmth and the comfort, thinking how easy it was for her to fool the police.

Chapter 29

Nothing had changed from what Charlotte could see, apart from Beaty, her friend, the only person who had cared for her, being dead and buried in the local churchyard. Although not religious, Charlotte visited the grave, placing on it some flowers which she had purchased from a florist.

'Cathy,' a voice startled Charlotte. It was a name she had not used since she had lived with Beaty.

'Mrs Jenkins, how are you?'

'Fine. We haven't seen you for a long time.' The woman had been a friend of Beaty and Charlotte, or Cathy as she was known then. Charlotte remembered that she had bad eyesight, surprised that she had recognised her, and that she never watched television or read a newspaper, which was as well.

'I couldn't stay after what happened.'

'I know. We were all fond of Beaty, although she preferred you to all of us,' Mrs Jenkins said.

'I was so upset I had to leave that day. Not only Beaty but Felix.'

'His grave's still in the garden. Do you want to visit?'

'Yes, please,' Charlotte replied. 'I hope Beaty won't mind, but I'll take one of her flowers for Felix.'

'I'm sure she won't.'

Mrs Jenkins, a similar age to Beaty, chatted away as they walked the short distance to Beaty's cottage. She gave Charlotte all the gossip: who had married whom, who had left whom, even who was having an affair. She even updated Charlotte on the boyfriend she'd had in the town, and that he had married and was now the father of twins. Charlotte felt as though she had come home.

Beaty's cottage was now occupied by a couple from London who had relocated to avoid the hustle and bustle of the big city. They invited the two women in for tea. Charlotte put on some sunglasses and darkened her face with tanning cream, remembered it from when she had left some years ago, although the furniture had changed, and Felix the cat had been replaced by

Ben, the Jack Russell Terrier, who instinctively liked her and came and sat beside her. Charlotte patted the dog and remembered Felix the cat and Beaty; a tear came to her eye. 'Pleasant memories,' she said, which was true.

She gave a thought to her past and could feel no anger, only regret about what she had done. She wanted to stay in that chair with that dog and that open fire forever.

'Stay the night,' the couple said.

'Thank you. Too many memories here for me, but thanks all the same.'

Charlotte went out to Felix's grave. Even though there were new owners, the small cross she had put there was still in place. She tidied the area surrounding it and laid the single flower on the grave.

She said a little prayer and silently mouthed a few words. 'Forgive me Beaty and Felix for what I have done. You were the only two that loved me, I know that now.'

***

Isaac returned from Richard Goddard's office to find the new man in place – Detective Chief Inspector Seth Caddick. He had arrived early.

'Pleased to meet you, DCI Caddick,' Isaac said as he shook the man's hand firmly.

'Fine mess you've got yourself into here,' was the reply from the man, a Welsh accent unmistakable. 'You'd better bring me up to speed if I'm to catch this woman. How many have died now?'

'Six, possibly seven.'

'It's not going to look good on your record, is it?' Caddick's reply.

Isaac, a man not willing to judge people too harshly on first meeting, could only come up with one conclusion: he didn't like him. To Isaac, who was willing to encourage and only criticise when necessary, his replacement was the complete opposite. Isaac studied the man more carefully than when he had first walked in the door. Caddick was as tall as he was; although he carried at least another twenty pounds, it was muscle, not flab. He had a full head of hair, although it was greying at the sides. Isaac judged his age to be about forty-five.

'Where's your team, apart from the one who was stabbed?'

'Out looking for Charlotte Hamilton.'

'Do they have a plan or are they just aimlessly wandering around?'

'They're professionals. They don't just wander around,' Isaac's curt reply.

'Maybe, but I'll be bringing in some of my people in the next couple of days, to deal with this Charlotte Hamilton woman.'

'Your prerogative, DCI,' Isaac said.

'I'll need your office.'

'I'll move out for you.'

Isaac found a desk close to Larry's and settled himself there. He could see Caddick making himself at home. He was on the phone, not attempting to lower his voice. 'No worries, commissioner. I'll soon lick this team into shape.'

Isaac had judged the man correctly; he was a sycophant who ingratiated himself with his superiors at every opportunity.

Larry entered the office, a look of surprise on his face at seeing his DCI sitting at the desk next to his. He looked over at Isaac's old office, saw the new man in place. He rolled his eyes at Isaac; Isaac nodded.

'Detective Inspector Larry Hill, sir.' Larry introduced himself to the new man.

'Caddick, DCI Caddick,' the man replied. He shook Larry's hand with a bear-like grip.

'Pleased to meet you.'

'Where have you been?' It seemed to Larry a criticism, not a question.

'I've been with our people trying to find out where Charlotte Hamilton has disappeared to.'

'From what I know of her and Challis Street, she's probably outside here having a coffee.'

'Unlikely,' Larry said, not sure how to handle the man's surly attitude.

'That may be, but I need to be updated by the team if we are to prevent any more murders.'

'She seems to be focussed on Dr Lake at the present moment. CI Cook has ensured that she is well protected.'

'She was meant to be well protected at the damn conference, but the woman got through, almost killed DI Marshall,' Caddick said.

'That's true.'

Larry, summarily dismissed, sat down at his desk.

'You've met our new SIO,' Isaac said.

'Gruff sort of man.'

'DCI,' a voice shouted from the other side of the room.

'Our master beckons,' Larry murmured.

Isaac re-entered his former office.

'Yes, DCI,' Isaac said.

'I need to meet the team as soon as possible.'

'They're busy at the present moment.'

'Where?'

'Apart from DI Marshall, who you know about, Sergeant O'Riordan is staying close to Dr Lake in case Charlotte Hamilton reappears.'

'Unfinished business?'

'That's what we believe.'

'Who else?'

'You've just met DI Hill, and Sergeant Wendy Gladstone is looking for the woman.'

'I was told that she was excellent at finding missing people.'

'She is.'

'But not this woman.'

'Not entirely true, but with this woman we've always been one step behind. DI Hill and Sergeant Gladstone found where she stayed in Windsor, but she had left by then.'

'Not much use then, is it?'

'I can't agree with you on that. Any evidence or information assists.'

'Agreed, but policing by the book isn't working. What's the latest on this woman?'

'After the conference centre, we traced her movements down as far as Blackfriars Bridge.'

'How?'

'CCTV monitoring the traffic picked her up. That's why Bridget Halloran, our CCTV viewing officer, is not here.'

'She's out checking the videos?'

'We're looking south of the Thames.'

'And then?'

'Hopefully, we'll find out where she's gone.'

'What's the psychologist's analysis of the woman.'

'Dr Lake believes she's fixated on her. There have been two attempts on her life, so far. Charlotte Hamilton has succeeded with every previous victim.

'Is Dr Lake, the best person to give an analysis?'

'You've brought yourself up to speed on this case?'

'Not totally.' It was a frank admission from the new SIO. Isaac knew that this was not about a new broom to resolve the case; this was the commissioner looking after his people. Ousting him, and no doubt Richard Goddard, his DCS.

It was evident to Isaac that Detective Chief Inspector Seth Caddick would not be up to speed for some time, and if there was to be a resolution to the case, it was up to him.

***

Charlotte woke up the next morning when a cup of tea was brought to her. She had slept well. As it had been with Beaty, so it was with Mrs Jenkins. A cat which had climbed up on her bed during the night slept peacefully.

'That's Brutus. He's been out ratting all night. If you don't mind, I'll leave him there.'

'I don't mind,' Charlotte said.

'Bacon and eggs?'

'It sounds lovely.'

'Twenty minutes. You can have a shower; I've put a towel there for you. Also, I washed and ironed the clothes that you wore yesterday. I hope you don't mind.'

'You're too kind.'

'Not at all. I know how much Beaty and Felix loved you. It's the least I can do.'

Charlotte remembered back to her time in the town before; how much she had loved it there and how much she had loved

Beaty, more than her own parents. She determined to stay in Sevenoaks and to forget about her past, even though she could not resist the need to phone the St Pancras Renaissance Hotel and to ask about Gladys Lake.

As she sat down to breakfast, Mrs Jenkins spoke. 'You can stay here as long as you like. At least until you are settled.'

'I would like that very much,' Charlotte said as she ate her breakfast.

She had spent three years with Beaty, the best years of her life, when there had been no medication, no doctors, no anguish on her part, and no recriminations for the murders she had committed. She wondered if they had only been imaginings on her part, a result of her schizophrenia.

'More toast?'

'Yes, please, and some of your jam.'

'Made it myself.'

'I remember your jam from before.'

'Where did you go?' Mrs Jenkins asked.

'After Beaty and Felix?'

'Yes.'

'I was so upset. They meant everything to me.'

'But you had friends here; friends who would have cared for you.'

'It's complicated.'

'Let's talk no more about it. You're here now. That's all that matters.'

'I'm here now, and this time I'll stay.'

It was eight in the morning as Charlotte wandered around the town, that she saw him. It was the driver of the truck that had killed Felix. Her anger flared, and she reached into her bag for a knife. It was not there, and he was gone.

She left the town by the next train. Her peace was gone, only to be replaced by an uncontrollable rage and a desire to inflict a fatal wound on the woman who had destroyed her life – Dr Gladys Lake.

***

'She took a bus to Sevenoaks, thirty miles south from here,' Wendy said on the phone to Isaac.

'Our new SIO is here.'

'What's he like? As charming as you, sir?'

'Charming is not a word I would use.'

'Don't worry. We'll soon have this woman. We'll make sure you get the credit for her capture.'

'Thanks. What can you tell us about Charlotte?'

Larry sat alongside Isaac, the phone on speaker. Caddick sat in his office, looking through the reports.

'How did you find her?' Larry asked.

'Bridget found her on Old Kent Road, CCTV cameras. After that, good old-fashioned legwork. A couple of local constables with me, and we started showing Charlotte's most recent photo. That's how we found her.'

'Are you going to Sevenoaks.'

'I'm on the road now. I've got the two locals from Southwark with me. I'll be there in forty minutes. Also, I've phoned the local station there.'

'Do you need Larry?'

'It would help.'

'I'm on my way,' Larry said. 'Give me one hour.'

'How about you, sir?' Wendy asked.

'I'm travelling to Newcastle with Dr Lake. Sean O'Riordan is coming with me.'

'She should be safe.'

'With Charlotte Hamilton?'

'You're right. If she's in Sevenoaks, we'll find her.'

'And if you don't, she's still coming after Dr Lake.'

'She's tenacious.'

'And deadly.'

'Don't get too close. She'll either take your photo or stick a knife in you.'

'She'll probably do both if she gets the chance,' Isaac said.

***

Careful not to be seen, Charlotte left the train two stations before its final destination at Charing Cross. She realised that London

Bridge Station was not the ideal location, but she could not delay. It was already mid-morning, and Gladys Lake was due to check out around two in the afternoon. That could only mean that she intended to catch the 4.15 p.m. train from King's Cross.

Charlotte checked her bag; she still had fifteen hundred pounds. A local shop provided a change of clothes and a cheap wig. She also purchased a kitchen knife in a discount store.

She walked across London Bridge and up Princes Street, before turning into Cheapside Street, eventually connecting with Farrington Road which took her close to King's Cross Station. She found a small restaurant and ate a good meal.

She knew she was early, but she needed to check out the area: entry and exit points, roads and side streets to vanish down if the police were there.

Charlotte sang her song quietly, repeating all the verses as she waited for the woman.

Stupid Duncan up at the quarry, along came a sister and gave him a push.
Liam thought he was a stud until I stuck a knife in his heart.
Oh, what fun, I slit his throat. Who will be next? Will it be you?
The black policeman thought he was smart, but I killed him anyway.

Charlotte knew that Dr Lake would be accompanied by the police, and it would not be possible to board the train at King's Cross, as they were bound to be on the lookout for her. She had attempted to kill the woman twice now, once in Newcastle, the other time in London, and they knew that she was determined and unlikely to desist.

Once the knife had entered the doctor's body, she knew she would have no further use for life. Until she had that blood-soaked knife, there was no freedom from the torment that cursed her: fluctuating between sanity and malevolence, the loving environment of Beaty and Felix, the torture in Newcastle at the mental hospital, the love of her parents for her brother Duncan and their disinterest in her.

The weather had turned colder, and a biting wind blew. Charlotte knew that if Dr Lake was coming, it would be soon.

As expected, ten minutes later, a police car drew up at the station. Gladys Lake emerged, clearly visible. Charlotte felt a nervous tingle knowing that her prey was so close, yet so far. Also visible was the black policeman, DCI Cook, and another police officer that she recognised. The man she had seen with Inspector Marshall at Joey's, the night she had killed Liam Fogarty, the least satisfying of her murders.

She wanted to rush across the road and to deal with the doctor there and then, but it had an element of risk. Besides, she wanted to savour the moment, not just a quick thrust in and out. She wanted to enjoy the doctor's death, to hear her plead for mercy.

Realising that killing the doctor was not possible at King's Cross, Charlotte put her backup plan into action. She walked around the immediate area. A woman struggling with the key to the door of her house, her arms laden with shopping, her car on the street with its engine running. Charlotte jumped into the driver's seat and took off. In the rear-view mirror, she could see the woman running down the street. The time was 2.20 p.m.

***

Larry Hill, in Sevenoaks, phoned Isaac as he was boarding the train at King's Cross Station. 'The local police in Sevenoaks identified her. Apparently, she was seen at the railway station earlier in the day. Also, she went by the name of Cathy Agnew here, and she was well known in the town.'

'Which train did she catch?' Isaac asked.

'Early, 8.45 a.m.'

'London?' Isaac asked a rhetorical question.

'Charing Cross. Unfortunately, she's back up there with you.'

'Don't worry. This time we're armed, and we're sticking close to Dr Lake.'

'She's going to try again, you know that.'

'We know it. I've stationed plain clothes in every carriage, and I'll be with Sean O'Riordan and Dr Lake from here to Newcastle. After that, she's Rory Hewitt's responsibility.'

'There's not much Wendy and I can do to help,' Larry said.

'Agreed. It's probably best if you both get back to Challis Street and update DCI Caddick.'

'I can't say I like him much.'

'That's as may be, but he's got the ear of the commissioner. If he's to take over on a permanent basis, then you'd better stay on his side.'

'What about DCS Goddard? Can he do something?'

'If we catch Charlotte Hamilton, then anything is possible. Without a result, both the DCS and I are out and back on traffic duty.'

'A bit dramatic.'

'At the least demoted or transferred out to the suburbs.'

An announcement sounded in the station. *The 4.15 p.m. to Newcastle is leaving in ten minutes from Platform 4. First stop Peterborough.*

***

Charlotte, using the GPS installed in the BMW, made good time; twenty minutes after stealing the car she was on the A1 and heading to Peterborough. She had travelled on the train from Newcastle many times, and she knew it would arrive in Peterborough at 5 p.m. She had a greater distance to travel, and the train was quicker. The drive should take two hours; she had one hour and fifty minutes.

Exceeding the speed limit on more than one occasion, she made the trip in one hour and forty-two minutes. She left the car and rushed into the railway station. Quickly purchasing a ticket, she waited for the train from London to pull in. It arrived on time. Charlotte looked for familiar faces; she saw none.

As the train stopped, she climbed into the second carriage. She knew she would need to search the train. Her disguise was good, she knew that, but there was no way to fool the DCI again, as she had that night in Newcastle.

Charlotte sat patiently in her seat waiting for the train to leave. It was still some distance to Newcastle; she had time. Carefully she looked around the carriage; no one she knew. She felt safe.

In the fourth carriage, Isaac stood. He looked around, phoned his men up and down the train: nothing.

'Looks like we're okay,' he said.

'What happened to her?' Sean asked. Both he and Isaac were sitting close to Gladys Lake on the trip from London: one on either side of her.

'I won't feel safe until I'm back in Newcastle,' Dr Lake said.

'We'll be there soon enough,' Isaac replied.

The train pulled out five minutes after it had arrived in Peterborough; its next destination, Doncaster.

Charlotte felt the knife in her bag. It would be dark outside before the train arrived in Newcastle; she decided to wait for another ninety minutes.

Sean went and purchased some food and drinks for his party of three; Charlotte ate nothing, not moving from her seat. She didn't even complain when the child in the seat behind kept prodding the back of hers with his feet. She felt as if it was the end of a long journey.

The light outside the train started to dull, a sign of the impending night. Unwilling to wait any longer, she pulled up the collar of her coat, ensured the hat she wore concealed her face, and moved forward in the train. She walked through the first carriage, scanning left and right; attempting to move her eyes, not her face. There was no sign of her prey and her bodyguard.

She retraced her steps, back through the second carriage where she had been sitting; the third carriage was the same as the first. She took a seat.

A suspicious woman, at least to Charlotte stood at one end of the third carriage. Charlotte arose from her seat and moved into the fourth carriage. Immediately a message on Isaac's phone: 'She's heading your way from the front of the train.'

Charlotte saw the woman on the phone, realised that she had been spotted. She lunged at the woman, caught her a glancing blow with her fist, causing the woman police officer to fall back and onto the floor. Charlotte moved forward, oblivious to the danger and the outcome. Sean was first to spot her. 'Stop,' he yelled.

Charlotte took no notice and kept moving forward. Sean went to draw his gun from its holster, but the train was full. A child was running up and down the corridor between him and the woman. Charlotte pushed the child to one side with her foot and continued forward, reaching Sean. He attempted to grab her. She pulled her knife out from her bag and slashed him badly across the face; he fell to one side, holding his face and attempting to control the bleeding.

Isaac was right behind Sean. He pulled his gun. 'Stop, or I'll shoot.'

'Shoot then. I only want that bastard woman.'

The passengers on the train, confused about what was happening, craned their necks; one man stood up.

'Sit down!' Isaac shouted. 'Police. This woman is extremely dangerous.'

In the confusion, Charlotte moved forward again. Gladys Lake stood up. 'Charlotte, please stop, you need help.'

'Not your help,' Charlotte replied.

Isaac stood between Charlotte and her target. Some of the passengers were screaming in fear; some had hidden in their seats. A child cried.

'Charlotte, stop,' Isaac warned her again.

She ignored him. The distance between the two of them was no more than six feet. Isaac realised that he had no option but to pull the trigger. The bullet hit her in the left leg, causing her to falter. His police training had taught him to aim for the torso, but the risk of hitting people in the carriage was too high.

Undeterred and apparently impervious to the injury, she continued. Isaac pulled the trigger again, this time hitting the other leg. Charlotte, unable to continue, fell forward. 'You bastard,' she mumbled weakly, blood trickling down her legs.

As she fell, she raised the knife in front of her. She collapsed into Isaac's arms, the knife piercing his shoulder. By this time, Sean, temporarily recovered, had taken control of the situation. One of the plain clothes had phoned for an ambulance to be at the next station, five miles away.

Charlotte, wounded but not fatally, was treated by Gladys Lake on the train as it headed to the station. Isaac, not so badly injured, although in a lot of pain, held a towel that he had been given by one of the passengers to his wound, the blood soaking it.

'Don't worry, Charlotte. I'll look after you,' Dr Lake said.

Charlotte, unable to speak, looked horrified.

Sean O'Riordan phoned DCS Goddard to update him, then DCI Caddick. After the situation had stabilised, he phoned Wendy and Larry. Sara Marshall, on hearing the news, phoned Charlotte's father.

'I'll make sure she is treated well,' the sad man replied.

Charlotte had killed seven people, including her own brother, yet her father still loved her.

The End

Printed in Poland
by Amazon Fulfillment
Poland Sp. z o.o., Wrocław